SO-AXB-445

PROUD
DESTINY

★　❀　★　❀　★　❀　★　❀　★

Also by Lion Feuchtwanger

FICTION

STORIES FROM FAR AND NEAR

SIMONE

DOUBLE, DOUBLE TOIL AND TROUBLE

JOSEPHUS AND THE EMPEROR

PARIS GAZETTE

THE PRETENDER

THE JEW OF ROME

MARIANNE IN INDIA

THE OPPERMANNS

JOSEPHUS

SUCCESS

THE UGLY DUCHESS

POWER

GENERAL

THE DEVIL IN FRANCE

MOSCOW, 1937

THREE PLAYS

PEP

TWO ANGLO-SAXON PLAYS

★　❀　★　❀　★　❀　★　❀　★

Lion Feuchtwanger

PROUD DESTINY

A Novel

THE VIKING PRESS

New York · *1947*

Translated by Moray Firth from the German manuscript
entitled *Waffen für Amerika*

COPYRIGHT 1947 BY THE VIKING PRESS, INC.

PUBLISHED ON THE SAME DAY IN THE DOMINION OF CANADA
BY THE MACMILLAN COMPANY OF CANADA LIMITED

The author wishes to express his gratitude to
Robert O. Ballou and Hilde Waldo for their assistance to him in the final revision of the English text.

PRINTED IN U.S.A.
BY COUNTRY LIFE PRESS

TO MARTA

Contents

✤ ★ ✤

*H*ERE *begins the novel* Proud Destiny, *also called* Arms for America.

It is the story of the wit and folly, the crafty stupidity, *and the overconventionalized corruption of a decaying society.*

You will find in it charming ladies and brilliant, vain men, intellect combined with an empty heart and full hearts combined with a maladroit hand,

A great man amid a world of fops,

The theatre and politics, enmity and friendship, lasciviousness and coquetry, love and business.

And the eternal sameness in eternal flux.

You will also find in this book men who believe in the possibility of continually learning more about the laws of human evolution,

And in the possibility of adapting ourselves to these laws so that we may establish a world that shall be more and more enlightened by the spirit.

The story tells further of the struggle of men, of words, and of ideas revolving around an economic upheaval.

Nor does it forget to tell of the blindness of men when faced with the march of history,

Or of the indissoluble association in which all are linked, yet which few are prepared to recognize,

Or of faith in the slow, the very slow, yet certain, growth of human reason between the ice age that has passed and the one that is to come.

★ ❁ ★ ❁ ★ ❁ ★ ❁ ★

PART ONE

ARMS FOR AMERICA

★ ❁ ★ ❁ ★ ❁ ★ ❁ ★

The artistic representation of history is a more
scientific and serious pursuit than the exact
writing of history. For the art of letters goes to
the heart of things, whereas the factual report
merely collocates details.

—ARISTOTLE

He alone reads history right who, observing how
powerfully circumstances influence the feelings
and opinions of men, how often vices pass into
virtues and paradoxes into axioms, learns to
distinguish what is accidental and transitory in
human nature from what is essential and im-
mutable.

—MACAULAY

★ ❧ ★ ❧ ★ ❧ ★ ❧ ★

Chapter One

BEAUMARCHAIS

❧   ★   ❧

T HE road from Versailles to Paris led through a green and
pleasant countryside. It had been raining during the morning,
but now the clouds had scattered, the sun was shining through,
and Pierre enjoyed the damp freshness of a beautiful afternoon in
May.

Only twenty-four hours before, on his return from London, he
had been beset by doubts lest the recent changes in the Cabinet should
have wrecked for good the ingenious enterprise to which he had devoted so much thought and effort. It would have been by no means
the first time that fate had played him a scurvy trick. Things, however, had taken an auspicious turn. In a frank and lengthy interview
with the Minister it had become evident that Versailles was more
than nibbling at his proposals. Count Vergennes had displayed a far
deeper interest in his project than his cautious letter had given reason
to suppose, and the pledges offered today by the Government surpassed any hopes he had dared to entertain. The great scheme was as
good as launched.

Pierre's carriage had reached the fork where the road turned off
towards Clamart, and he told the coachman to slacken his pace. Leaning back on the cushions, with a slight smile on his lips, he mentally
reviewed the steps by which his success hitherto had been achieved.

Pierre Caron de Beaumarchais had been living in London during
the past few months as a secret agent of the French Government. The
tasks on which his adroit, quick-witted talents had been employed were
hidden from the public eye, not over-nice, and of no great importance.
They had occupied but little of his time and afforded him leisure for
the working out of weightier plans.

Since the outbreak of the great struggle between King George III
of England and his American colonies, Pierre Caron de Beaumarchais
had ardently espoused the cause of the insurgent Americans. Like
many other intellectuals in Paris, and even in London, he had greeted
the men of Boston, the "rebels," as allies fighting to put into practice
the tremendous ideas of the French and English philosophers. These

men were resolved to lead a simple, natural life, not an existence crippled by convention, prejudice, and arbitrary despotism as was the case in London and Paris. The men of the New World wanted to found their order on liberty, reason, and nature. And it was these men whom the King of England wished to constrain, with fire and sword, to desist from their noble intention.

Pierre was supporting the Americans not merely with his heart and his lips. He was promoting their cause by active deeds. Welcomed in every circle of London society, and on friendly terms with leading figures among both Whigs and Tories, he had ample opportunity to gain an insight into numerous details of the struggle with the colonies. He accumulated an abundance of information, sifted it, drew his conclusions, and without having received any authorization to do so submitted reports to Louis XVI and his Ministers which were distinguished by their clarity and a far-sighted understanding based on familiarity with the facts.

As Pierre reviewed in his mind's eye the reports and memoranda to which he had appended his signature, he could justly pride himself on having, as a self-appointed secret agent, acquired a more comprehensive grasp of the ramifications of the Anglo-American conflict from the very outset than had the French Ambassador himself. His predictions had been confirmed by events.

All his communications to Versailles had concluded with the urgent recommendation to help in the weakening of England by supporting the insurgents. The conflict between England and her colonies afforded France a unique opportunity to wipe out the wretched peace treaty that had been imposed on her by the English twelve years before.

Pierre was well aware that the French Government could not openly espouse the cause of the American rebels. War with England would have been the inevitable consequence, and neither the French fleet nor the French Army was strong enough to face such a contingency, quite apart from the precarious state of the national finances. But there was a way out of this difficulty, and Pierre had already hit upon it.

He smiled with satisfaction. His reports had been written and his advice tendered with the honest design of aiding the Americans to further the cause of liberty and reason. But idealistic efforts were occasionally known to yield material rewards. Only fools thought it disreputable to do business in a good cause, and Pierre was no fool. With the keen intuition of a shrewd business man, and of a political agent accustomed to intrigue, he had perceived from the start that a careful fanning of the flames would enable the struggle for freedom to be waged not only in the interests of idealism, but also to the advantage of his own pocket.

Bearing in mind, therefore, the fact that France could not yet afford to provoke a war with England, he had proposed to the French Government that the Americans should be given secret help while avoiding any danger of the Government itself being compromised. The rebels would be supplied with arms and other necessities by private merchants, apparently working on their own account and at their own risk, but in reality subsidized and assisted in every possible way by the Government of France.

After much pulling this way and that, when Pierre had almost given up hope of ever being able to win over the Foreign Minister, Count Vergennes, to the acceptance of his project, things had eventually turned out in accordance with his calculations. That very day he had succeeded in nailing down the Minister to a definite promise, and Vergennes had authorized him to launch the undertaking he had so boldly planned. From now on he could offer munitions of war to the American insurgents as the accredited plenipotentiary of the King of France.

Pierre was pleased with himself. The insurgents' requirements were numerous and varied. Their equipment was miserably deficient, the output of their few factories was meagre, and there were thirty thousand men to be fitted out from top to toe and supplied with all the necessities of war. Vergennes had asked him whether he and his business associates were really in a position to procure such an abundance of material and arrange for its transport overseas. "Certainly!" he had replied, boldly and without hesitation—adding, however: "On condition, of course, that the Royal Arsenals are prepared to sell us arms on favourable terms and that we are not kept too short of funds." After promising to get into touch with the Minister for War, Vergennes had broached the most ticklish question of all. He inquired what Pierre had in mind as the maximum subvention to be expected from the Government.

Pierre had decided beforehand that he could risk putting his plans into motion if the Government offered a subsidy of at least a million livres. Now, however, he realized that he had hitherto been merely toying with the project. A million livres! What a ridiculously exiguous capital with which to establish an organization that was to supply the complete equipment for thirty thousand troops! Yet if he asked for more, if he stretched the bow too far, the whole scheme might be wrecked.

Behind the apparent calm with which he faced the smiling and expectant Minister, his brain was racing furiously as he reconsidered the position and tried to make up his mind how much he dared to ask for. "I think," he said, "that three million should suffice." There was a short silence, during which the two men gazed at one another. "This is going to settle the fate of America—and my own as well," thought Pierre to himself.

"We can promise you two million," the Minister said at last. "The first million will be provided by the French Government. The rest we shall obtain from the Spaniards."

As Pierre drove back to Paris that lovely afternoon in May he was almost dazed by his success.

The carriage which was conveying him through the green and pleasant countryside was a little too sumptuous. On the box sat the coachman in his rich livery, with a little Negro attendant at his side. An even more ornately attired lackey sat behind and stared vacantly into the distance. Pierre himself looked a little dandified in his ultra-fashionable clothes and with the unusually large diamond that sparkled on his finger.

He could not have been blamed for feeling tired after these last strenuous days, what with the settling of his affairs in London, his rapid journey, and his interview with Count Vergennes, but he was not the man to take things easy. Though he was already forty-four, and inclined to put on flesh, he looked younger and could have been taken for thirty-five. His face was plump and fresh-complexioned, his slightly receding brow was unfurrowed, the shrewd brown eyes were alive with expression, and a full-lipped, handsomely curved mouth smiled beneath a straight, pointed nose. An air of good nature was lent to the astute countenance by the cleft, weakish chin and the suspicion of a double chin that emerged from the collar of his expensive coat.

They had reached Issy, and the nearer they approached to Paris the more actively did his mind become engaged in speculations on the future. The firm he intended to found must be housed in a manner worthy of the purpose it was destined to fulfil. His present business premises would have to be entirely reconstructed and refurnished. A name for the new firm flashed through his mind—a Spanish name. He had a warm corner in his heart for Spain, which had always brought him luck. He would call the firm Roderigue Hortalez. He smiled. From now on he would be Señor Roderigue Hortalez.

Two million livres! It sounded a large sum! But there were thirty thousand men to be equipped, and ships to be fitted out for the transport of vast supplies across the Atlantic Ocean. It was lucky for him that his timber business had brought him useful contacts with the big shipping firms, though even so he would have to stretch his credit to the limit. From five to six millions would be needed as a preliminary investment. And when would the Americans pay? *How* would they pay? For a moment a cold chill ran down his spine. But he shook off his fears at once. Whatever the issue might be, trading in world history held a fascination that was lacking in the timber trade.

It was a pity that everything had to be done under the cover of secrecy! He wanted to talk about it. He wanted to proclaim to the world the tremendous mission with which he had been entrusted. Vergennes had impressed on him, however, the importance of keeping his lips sealed. The fiction of a private undertaking, carrying on an innocent business with its own capital, had to be maintained at all costs. Even so, the English would make every effort to throw difficulties in their way and flood the Foreign Minister with diplomatic protests. If Pierre allowed himself to indulge in indiscretions he would under no circumstances be able to count on the protection of the French Government. On the contrary, he would be disowned without scruple. That had been made clear to him with discourteous bluntness by the usually so-courteous Vergennes. There was nobody with whom Pierre would be able to discuss the enterprise that was to change the history of the world, except a few business associates and his principal employees. He would appear to outward eyes merely as Monsieur de Beaumarchais, the target of many men's ridicule and hostility, forbidden to lay his trumps on the table for the confounding of his adversaries and those who jeered at him.

This uncomfortable reflection that flitted through his mind was soon erased by the cheering thought of the tremendous role for which he had been cast. It was a foregone conclusion that the American rebels were lost without French aid, and he alone, Pierre de Beaumarchais, by his zeal and fiery eloquence, his knowledge of men and adroit handling of the situation, had persuaded the weakling King Louis and his vain Ministers to agree in principle that this aid should be accorded them. Whether it would reach the Americans, and to what extent it would meet their needs, depended now solely on him. The fate of the New World beyond the seas, the future progress of humanity, depended on his skill and cunning.

His swift imagination painted a picture of the course events would take. He saw muskets and uniforms piling up in the storehouses at the French ports, and the piles grew higher and higher. He saw the broad-beamed ships of the firm of Hortalez and Company putting out to sea, loaded with cannon for the insurgents, and returning laden with indigo and tobacco for him, for Pierre. He savoured in anticipation the success of his plans. Yes, this was the supreme enterprise for which he had always longed, an enterprise worthy of a Beaumarchais.

He had no doubt of his capacity for the task. Success had come to him in matters which, though of less importance, had involved the surmounting of perhaps even more formidable obstacles. With every turn of the wheels bringing him nearer and nearer to his own city of Paris and to a fresh field of exciting activity, there passed before his mind's eye in a rapid series of dissolving views the whole multicoloured kaleidoscope of his past fortunes and disasters.

An abundance of almost incredible catastrophes was offset by an even richer abundance of successful ventures. As the son of a clock-maker and an apprentice to the trade, he had been employed at the royal court winding the timepieces of His late Majesty, Louis XV. After he had attracted the attention of the old King by his alert and agreeable manner, the King's elderly daughters had taken a fancy to him and he was engaged to teach them the harp. The shrewd but crotchety financier Duverny noticed him, initiated him into the devious byways of high finance, and finally made him his partner. Pierre was an apt pupil. With his social talents and gift for intrigue he furthered the interests of the firm of Duverny and at the same time lined his own pockets. He bought titles and court offices and flourished exceedingly, enjoyed the friendship of many men and the love of many women, but his nimble wit and inability to control his tongue also earned him many enemies.

Then came his first two plays, written in the intervals of a crowded existence absorbed in business affairs on the one hand and love affairs on the other. They were intended as a diversion, but in the process of composition he began to take his diversion seriously. His two marriages followed. Both his marriages were happy, both his wives had been rich and handsome, but each of them died soon afterwards and nothing remained to him but the forest of Chinon, a large timber business in which he had invested part of their fortunes, and a flood of calumniation.

When Duverny, the great financier and Pierre's venerated teacher, also died, Pierre plunged still more deeply into the eddying whirlpool. Ugly lawsuits, followed by a spate of unjust legal decisions, swept him into financial ruin. He was flung into gaol, stripped of his dearly purchased offices and titles, and deprived of his civil rights.

Yet the harshness of the law turned out to be a blessing in disguise, for it led to the writing of his brilliant political pamphlets, and it was these witty pamphlets, even more than his comedy of Figaro, the barber of Seville, which spread his fame throughout the world. They procured him the favour of men of influence, one of whom, since the deprivation of his civil rights debarred him from holding public office, secured for him a post as one of the King's secret agents. This had been the first step in his climb to further heights, until at last he reached the peak on which he stood today.

Today he had reached a turning-point. Here was his opportunity to make a clean sweep of the ghosts that loomed out of the past and encroached upon the present. The brazen injustice of his condemnation by the courts could now be rendered null and void. For the stupid judgment pronounced on him by the Supreme Court of Paris was still in force. There was a charge against his name, a "stain" upon his character. It was time to change all that, he decided. He would force the Cabinet to grant him the right of appeal and to reinstate him among his fellow citizens. If the Government rejected his demand they could look round for somebody else to do their involved and ticklish jobs for them. None but Beaumarchais could bring to completion the scheme that Beaumarchais had thought out.

The carriage was rolling over the cobblestones of Paris. With darting glance he observed the passers-by and took in the various objects by the wayside. Whenever he returned to Paris he felt a renewed pride at being a son of the greatest and loveliest city in the world, but scarcely ever had his heart swelled with such unrestrained joy as it did today. Pierre Caron de Beaumarchais, the famous politician, business man, and playwright, was good-natured and on occasion even nobly magnanimous; however, there was a streak of theatricality in his make-up, and he was filled with a boundless craving for self-assertion that bordered on the ridiculous. Swift and sure in his judgment of men, yet he never looked below the surface. A brilliant writer and amusing companion, he could carry his hearers away by a display of emotional rhetoric or devastate his adversaries by the keenness of his corrosive wit. He was very astute, but lacking in wisdom. He possessed a lust for enjoyment, but could bear misfortune and deprivation with fortitude. He was accessible to all the great ideas of the age, even when they contradicted one another. Many called him famous, but some dubbed him notorious. Wherever he went he was followed by the envy and spite of those upon whose interests he infringed, and the weapons with which he was attacked were often tipped with venom; but there were many, both men and women, and not the worst of their kind, who were well-disposed towards him, and some there were who loved him and would have been ready to sacrifice everything on his behalf.

He had seen and done much, he was stuffed full of past experience, yet he had not become blasé. At the age of forty-four he regarded the future with the same curious, expectant eyes as when, at the age of sixteen, he had run away from his father's shop to knock about the streets of Paris. He still threw himself whole-heartedly into every experience that came his way. Economy was alien to his nature. He was lavish with his time, his money, his talents, and his life.

His carriage had reached the teeming streets of the inner city. He sat a little more upright and tried to look his best. His face was familiar to half Paris, and he was greeted by one passer-by in ten. He was conscious of the fact that innumerable people were turning round to look at him and were saying to one another, "That's Monsieur de Beaumarchais, the great financier and author! He has a finger in every Government pie." Yet they had not even the vaguest suspicion of the tremendous mission with which he had just been entrusted for the better ordering of the world. What a pity, what a frightful pity, that he could not tell his fellow Parisians about it! Even his sister had to be kept in ignorance, to say nothing of his father. They were devoted to him and he to them, but they were too temperamental to keep such a secret.

He would soon be home, and they would be curious and expectant as they besieged him with their tender solicitude. His smile grew broader, lighting up his handsome fresh-coloured features, as the carriage drove into the bustling rue de Condé and pulled up in front of his house.

☆   ☆   ☆

It was a cheerful supper-party. Word had gone round that Pierre was back from London and, apart from members of the household, a number of relatives and intimate friends had turned up. It was all free and easy and intimate for the Caron family were a noisy, inquisitive crew and Pierre's happy mood infected them all. They had a feeling of deep admiration for their Pierre, whose name was more frequently on people's lips than that of anybody except the Queen. Immediately on his return from London he had been received at Versailles, so there was evidently something pretty important brewing. All their questions, however, were parried with a complacent smile, and the most he would say was, "Well, Julie, if you would like to get another carriage or hire a few more servants, I've no objection."

That was all he would reveal. On the other hand, he talked a great deal about his sojourn in London. The climate was abominable, but seemed to agree with the women, to judge from their clear delicate complexions. There were redheads there who . . . and with complete lack of inhibition, he recounted sundry amorous affairs.

Julie hung on her brother's words. She was a lively, agreeable person of forty, strongly resembling Pierre, with the same fresh colouring, large, straight nose, and shrewd brown eyes. He was her idol, and in order to be with him she had refused a number of offers of marriage. She tried to have a word in all his affairs, and they often quarrelled furiously, though there was always a passionate reconciliation the same day. They seemed to enjoy both the quarrel and the reconciliation.

Pierre's secretary, Maigron, reported in his matter-of-fact way that over a hundred visitors had called during the day to pay their respects to Monsieur de Beaumarchais on his return. "Yes," said Pierre's old father in his high-pitched voice, which showed no signs of advanced age, however, for he still had all his teeth. "Paris has noticed that our Pierre is back again." His son clapped him on the shoulder, smiling a bit ironically and much pleased. The whisper had soon gone round that Beaumarchais was in high favour, and they all came wagging their tails. Yet he would not be unjust. They had come even when things went ill with him; whether or not fortune smiled, there were many whose admiration did not waver.

He turned his eyes away and looked towards the side of the table where Paul Theveneau was sitting. He smiled at him and received a happy smile in return. They had first met when a dispute with Paul's brother had brought Pierre the enmity of Paul too, but hostility had soon changed to admiration, and Pierre was proud to have won the younger man's friendship. Paul's loyalty and devoted attachment to Pierre were unquestioned; he was thoroughly conversant with all the ins and outs of his master's complicated and devious financial transactions, he was extremely efficient, he had come through with flying colours in one responsible job after another, and he could create order out of chaos when even Pierre himself had lost his way.

Outwardly there was nothing about Paul that was at all impressive. He looked, in fact, rather an object for pity. His clothes hung on him, and his small, emaciated hands twitched as he carried the food to his mouth. Above the sloping shoulders, however, a pair of large brown eyes shone with the vitality of youth from a round, handsome face, and he had a devilishly clever brain that made him an indispensable member of Pierre's staff. He was only twenty-six, but he suffered from a throat malady and the doctors gave him but a few more years to live.

A recently published book on the West Indies became the topic of conversation, and the omniscient Philippe Gudin launched into a learned discourse on the important role played by the islands in the national budget of France. Philippe Gudin, the scholar, was the most loyal of all Pierre's loyal friends. He had a deliberate manner of speaking and was fond of long, weighty sentences. Of comfortable build and capacious appetite, he had unbuckled his breeches under his long, wide coat and tucked up the lace frills of his cuffs so that they should not get in the way as he ate. Leaning back in his armchair, which he completely filled, he quoted from memory imposing statistics on the imports of sugar, tobacco, indigo, cotton, cocoa, coffee, and pepper.

"If they had listened to me," broke in Pierre, "we could have derived far greater profits from these possessions of ours. I once worked out a scheme for securing a monopoly of the trade in Negro slaves which would have supplied enough money for the King to carry out the progressive reforms of Turgot. We should then have more liberty and justice in this country." To himself he added, "And more money for America.

"When the new commercial treaty with Spain has been signed," he concluded, "they will perhaps take my scheme out of its pigeon-hole."

This turned the conversation to the subject of Spain, where Pierre had spent the best, and certainly the wildest, months of his life. Perhaps the most dramatic episode of his whole career, which had been characterized by dramatic incidents, was when he forced Clavigo, the

cowardly deceiver who had seduced his sister Lisette, to make amends
for the wrong he had done. Yes, his life in Madrid had been an amazingly intricate and fascinating spectacle, compounded of passion, wit,
and music, of financial coups, high politics, the writing of verses, the
world of the theatre, and pretty, compliant women. Yet, attached to
his family as he was, he had found time amid all the hubbub and
turmoil to send his father and sisters long, exciting letters in which
he described his experiences with such a wealth of visual detail that
nothing was left to their imagination. Now that he had again returned
from a long and successful journey they quoted these earlier records
and found much amusement in reminding one another of individual
incidents.

Julie asked him to sing some Spanish songs, *seguidillas* and *sainetes,*
and the others too added their pleas. The guitar was brought in, but
before he had finished tuning the instrument another visitor was announced, Monsieur Lenormant d'Etioles. Richly but inconspicuously
dressed, in a neat and somewhat old-fashioned style, he did not seem
to mind the fact that his costume emphasized his sixty years.

Monsieur Lenormant was inclined to corpulence. His small, deep-
set eyes lent a melancholy air to his fleshy visage, and deep furrows
stretched from his nose to the corners of his full-lipped mouth. It was
the face of an epicure who had gone through disillusioning experiences
and learned to distrust his fellow men, but had no intention of abandoning the enjoyment which life had to offer.

Pierre had written to Monsieur Lenormant from London that he
was returning to Paris on very important business and looked forward
cordially to seeing him at the earliest possible moment. Though he had
hoped in his heart that Lenormant would call on him that very evening, it was a hope that he had hardly dared to admit to himself.
Lenormant sometimes kept even the First Minister waiting for days
at a time, and his visit to Pierre was the crowning happiness of that
auspicious day.

Charles-Guillaume Lenormant d'Etioles was a member of the old
nobility. Any post at court would have been open to him and he could
have had any title he wanted, but he liked to keep in the background
and was content to be called simply *"secrétaire du roi,"* a modest distinction which even Pierre had been able to procure for himself in the
days before he was condemned to lose his civil rights. He farmed the
taxes of two provinces and had a finger in numerous enterprises. His
prudence and luck were proverbial, and he was a man of business to
the finger-tips, but since as an aristocrat he could not openly engage
in mercantile or industrial occupations he employed others to act
for him.

Pierre had first met this influential gentleman at the house of
Désirée Mesnard, the actress, and he was quite well aware that Lenor-

mant had sought his friendship originally only because he was in love with Désirée and apprehensive lest Pierre should damage his chances in that direction. Gradually, however, the two men had taken a liking to one another, and this developed into a sincere friendship. Beaumarchais admired Lenormant's keen business instinct and frequently asked his advice, while Lenormant was glad to find such an apt pupil and helped him when things went badly. It was he who had used his influence in high quarters to secure Pierre the appointment as secret agent in London, and they called one another "Charlot" and "Pierrot."

Julie pressed Monsieur Lenormant to join the other guests at table and busied herself with placing wine and dessert in front of him. While he nibbled politely at a piece of candied ginger the conversation turned once more to Spain, and Philippe Gudin, thinking he was doing Pierre a favour, reminded him of his promise to sing some Spanish songs.

With the entry of Lenormant, however, Pierre had forgotten all about Spain and was thinking only of America. He had counted on Charlot's becoming a partner in the firm of Hortalez and Company, for he needed from five to six million livres and a sum of that order was beyond his normal resources. Lenormant's participation would bring in other investors automatically. In any case, Pierre was on tenterhooks to know what his friend would say to the scheme, and he could hardly wait to break the news; so, firmly but gracefully, he consoled the company with a promise to sing to them another time, indicated to Julie that she should give the sign for the guests to rise from table, and withdrew to his study with Lenormant, Paul Theveneau, and his secretary, Maigron.

When the candles in the study had been lit, the spacious, ornately furnished room slowly emerged from the darkness. In the four corners stood busts of Aristophanes, Molière, Voltaire, and Beaumarchais himself. In addition there was a magnificent round mirror, set in an elaborate and costly frame, which reflected the great show of the working Pierre. The walls were covered with pictures and decoration of various kinds, with the exception of the central space on one of the longer walls, which was kept bare. This empty space was reserved for a portrait of the late Monsieur Duverny by the most esteemed portrait-painter of the time, Duplessis. It had been bequeathed to Pierre by Duverny, but during the proceedings concerned with his unfortunate lawsuit the will had been contested and the picture had been adjudged the property of the other heirs. He had set his mind on getting it back, and the bare space on the wall served as a constant admonition.

At Pierre's invitation Charlot took a seat at the writing-table, a massive piece of furniture that was particularly striking on account of the artistic skill with which it had been fabricated. Many rare woods from overseas had been used in its making by the master craftsman

Pluvinet, the carvings were by Dupin, and if it was not the most hand-some writing-table in France it was certainly the costliest.

The four men were now in private conference. Charlot sat and gazed in front of him with half-closed eyes. Maigron selected a sheet of paper and picked up one of those new-fangled writing utensils that Lenormant detested, since they were regarded as vulgar, namely, a lead pencil. Maigron, who had been Pierre's confidential secretary for years, was a silent man, rarely offering an opinion. Even now his face betrayed no sign of expectancy. Paul Theveneau, on the other hand, was able to conceal his excitement. He sat perched on the edge of his chair with his large, feverish eyes fixed on Pierre's lips.

Pierre stood as he talked, or paced to and fro. With fluent ease, and artfully building up the effect, he told of the memoranda he had addressed to the King and his Ministers and of the culminating interview with Vergennes. He explained how he had asked for three million livres, though he had calculated that one million would be enough at a pinch, and then with a casual air of modesty concluded by revealing that the Government had given him a binding promise of two million.

Even the normally undemonstrative Maigron looked up at the mention of this figure. Paul Theveneau made no attempt to hide his enthusiasm, but with flushed face and shining eyes jumped up from his chair, seized Pierre by the hand, and said, in a voice that showed how deeply he was stirred, "At last there is somebody to give us more than words. At last there is someone who is prepared to act."

Young as he was in years, Paul was a long-headed man of business, and Pierre was pleased at his excitement. The important thing, however, was what effect his statement had had on Monsieur Lenormant.

Lenormant said nothing. His round, melancholy face remained impassive, and the veiled eyes beneath the large, convex forehead concealed his thoughts. There was a lengthy pause until Pierre could no longer contain himself and blurted out, "What do you think, Charlot?"

They all looked at Lenormant as, in his low, oily voice, he asked in a thoughtful, matter-of-fact way, "And who is going to pay if the Americans are beaten?"

"They won't be beaten," declared Pierre resolutely.

"One thing seems certain," Lenormant continued. "The insurgents have no funds."

"But they've got goods," Pierre retorted eagerly. "They've got indigo, tobacco, and cotton."

"How do you know," asked Charlot, "that they will let *you* have these goods?"

"They are fighting for their liberty," replied Pierre ardently. "They are inspired by the ideals of Montesquieu and of Rousseau. Men like that pay their debts."

Charlot again lapsed into silence. He merely gazed at Pierre, and the curve at the corners of his mouth deepened slightly. This smile of his was perhaps imperceptible to the others, but Pierre knew it of old and it filled him with dread. The smile came from deep down, from a wealth of experience that had led to the learning of many lessons, and it had more than once caused Pierre's faith to droop and his confidence to melt away. Now, for a moment, he glimpsed with blinding clarity the risk to which his American enterprise was exposed, but he recovered in an instant his feeling of self-reliance and muttered inwardly, "So what? It's America. I'll take my chance."

Lenormant still said nothing. "On the other hand," he murmured at last, "a Government subsidy of two millions is not bad."

"No, a subsidy of two millions is not bad," intervened Paul Theveneau, moved by an almost malicious feeling of triumph. He usually kept discreetly in the background in the presence of the *fermier général,* but he was carried away by the magnitude of the scheme. "Not at all bad," he repeated, and strode swiftly up and down the room, unable to control his emotion. He cut a slightly grotesque figure as he shambled to and fro, with his coat hanging on his thin frame and his close-fitting stockings emphasizing the meagreness of his calves, but both Pierre and Charlot watched his excited behaviour with indulgent sympathy, and not even Maigron disapproved of his exuberance.

From his early youth Paul Theveneau had longed to find a man whom he could honour and a cause in which he could believe. Then he had met Pierre and was fired with enthusiasm for the latter's bold ideas, for the way in which he conjured breath-taking projects out of the air. He was convinced that Pierre was destined to play a major role in history once opportunity knocked at his door, and now the moment had come. It was symbolized in the word *America.*

"I had hoped, Charlot," said Pierre, again addressing himself courteously to Lenormant, "that you might perhaps find an offer of participation in this venture not unwelcome."

"I do not exclude such a possibility," replied Lenormant, his deep-set, melancholy eyes gazing straight in front of him. "Will you give me the pleasure of dining with me tomorrow evening, my dear Pierrot? That will give me time to think the matter over."

Though Pierre was familiar with Lenormant's ways, and that he did not embark lightly on hazardous schemes, he was disappointed at having to wait yet another night and another day before knowing whether he could count on his support.

Meanwhile it had grown late, and Charlot took his leave. A footman preceded him with a lighted candelabrum as he descended the broad staircase, and Pierre insisted on accompanying him to the front door.

Julie was waiting at the head of the stairs when Pierre returned, and she threw herself on his neck, half laughing, half in tears.

"So you have been eavesdropping?" he asked.

"Of course I have," she replied. Next door to Pierre's study was a small private cabinet in which he sometimes received ladies who came to see him on business matters, and Julie was in the habit of concealing herself there when conferences were taking place in the larger room. "It is mean of you," she reproached him affectionately, "to tell your Charlot about your successes and not me. I am very angry with you, but I am so happy," and she embraced him again.

"Calm yourself, Julie!" he exhorted, and led her back gently to the little cabinet.

The room contained nothing but two chairs, a large sofa, and a chest, in which Pierre kept his most precious mementoes. Among these was the plan of a contrivance he had invented many years ago and which was now being used by clockmakers all over Europe. The manuscripts of the brochures which had made him world-famous lay side by side with the original manuscript of *The Barber of Seville,* the receipts for the payments he had made to acquire his title of nobility and the offices he had held at court, and a selection of the love letters he had received from various women. He would soon be in a position to add a further document, one of historical importance.

In this room that contained his most treasured relics Pierre unburdened himself of his secret to his sister. He had not intended to tell her anything, and he should have taken precautions against her eavesdropping ; nor was it wise of him to let her know more than she had already learned ; but he had had to control his enthusiasm when communicating his scheme to Charlot and he could no longer keep his exuberance in check. He painted the future in glowing colours, and they looked at one another with shining eyes as they erected together their edifice of dreams. Then, however, he conjured her not to mention the matter to a living soul, not even to their father, since old men were loquacious and secrecy was essential to success. They said good night and kissed before they parted.

Emile, Pierre's valet, was waiting up to help his master to bed, and as he lent an adroit hand in the removal of the stiff, heavy coat and other garments he inquired respectfully whether Monsieur had had a good day. "A very good day," replied Pierre. "I wish all good Frenchman days like this." Emile drew back the brocaded hangings behind which an ornate bed stood upon its dais. Pierre accepted a candied fruit, sipped slowly at a nightcap, and allowed himself to sink back on the pillows. Emile tucked the bed-clothes around him and drew the curtains again so that the rays from the night-light shone only faintly within the alcove. With a loud, happy yawn Pierre turned over on his side, curled up, and closed his eyes.

Before he had time to drop off to sleep, however, the light grew stronger as the curtains were once more pulled back. "What is it now, Emile?" he asked without opening his eyes.

But it was not Emile; it was Pierre's father. The old man looked very frail in his dressing-gown and slippers as he sat down on the edge of the broad, low bed. "Tell me, my son," he began, "what has really been happening. I can quite understand that you did not want to say anything in front of the girls. Women talk too much. But now we are alone."

Pierre blinked sleepily. The thin, hairy legs that emerged beneath the hem of the dressing-gown were those of an old man, but the eyes were alert and youthful as they rested with tender curiosity on the face of his son. Pierre's relations with his father were of a dual nature. Old Caron came from a family of Huguenots, but after being forcibly enlisted in the Army as a Protestant he had abjured his faith, accepted an appointment as clockmaker to the royal household, and become an ardent Catholic. Pierre's way of life had brought them into conflict, and the boy ran away after being apprenticed to his father's trade, but he eventually returned to the fleshpots of his parents' house. Before the prodigal was taken into favour again his father made him sign an agreement in which both his rights and duties as a son were laid down with a wealth of precise detail. It was not the last occasion on which the old man predicted that his offspring would come to a bad end, but the prediction proved false as Pierre climbed to dizzy heights. In order to confirm his patent of nobility Pierre urged his father to give up his bourgeois calling, a demand which was indignantly rejected. Pierre then reminded him that when, some years previously, he had taken the drastic step of abandoning his Protestant faith, neither the material nor the spiritual consequences had been unfavourable. The old man had at last succumbed to persuasion, but he retained his sense of pride.

Pierre was fond of his father. He attributed his success both in the construction of stage-plays and in the devious intrigues of politics and business, which demanded the skilful dovetailing of a hundred tiny wheels and cogs, to the old man's teaching and the experience he had acquired during his period of apprenticeship. That was something he never forgot. He showed his gratitude to the old man by taking him into his house and setting aside an annuity for him. The annuity was accepted, then refused, and finally accepted once more. He moved into Pierre's house, moved out again, then moved back. When Pierre lost his lawsuit and the privileges that wealth had brought him, the old man asked mockingly whether he did not regret having forced him to give up his honourable trade, but in recent years the two had lived together on the best of terms and enjoyed many a hearty laugh both at themselves and at the stupidity of the rest of the world. Though they would still occasionally indulge in mutual pin-pricks, and even say malicious things that hurt, each was confident of the other's love and devotion. When Pierre took his father walking in the park at Versailles, and presented him to his aristocratic friends, he would introduce him affectionately as "My good old father," and the old man, standing very upright in his bourgeois coat, would bow courteously, but not too deeply.

Now old Caron was sitting on the edge of the bed in which was ensconced the son he idolized, the son of whom he had prophesied that no good would come of him, and he could not conceal the glad curiosity with which he waited to hear of the latest stroke of good fortune.

Pierre had felt a deep satisfaction in telling his friend Charlot about his success. A tide of renewed happiness had come over him as he discussed it with Julie. To talk about it with his father was the height of bliss.

The old man leapt up from where he was sitting and ran gesticulating up and down the room with the skirts of his dressing-gown flapping about his legs. He muttered to himself, ran back to the bed, and stroked his son's face. Pierre forgot how tired he was, sat bolt upright, and allowed his enthusiasm even freer rein than when he had disclosed the great secret to his sister. Staring into the dim glow of the night-lamp, with an almost stupidly ecstatic smile on his features, he voiced to himself and to his father the visions that floated through his brain. The fleet of ships belonging to the firm of Hortalez and Company, the ships belonging to Pierrot, to Pierre-Augustin de Beaumarchais, would put to sea laden with cannon, muskets, and powder, and these munitions of war—his, Pierre's, munitions of war—would smash the tyranny of England and spread freedom throughout the world. To say nothing of the vast treasure, the rich cargoes of indigo, cotton, and tobacco, that this same fleet would carry back to the family of Caron de Beaumarchais.

The old man had enjoyed a good education, he had read a great deal, and he was Frenchman enough to be proud of the share France had taken in the opening up and colonizing of the New World. He resented the fact that England had deprived France of her American possessions and compelled Christian Frenchmen to resort to such abominable methods as allying themselves with redskins and scalping white men. Now his son was helping the colonists, those men of reason, the sturdy rebels of Boston; those children of nature, the Quakers, to pay the English back in their own coin.

Deep down in his heart old Caron had never quite succeeded in freeing himself from the notion that his defection from the Huguenot faith had been a sin and that God would exact retribution from his children unto the third and fourth generation. Whenever anything had gone wrong during his life he had been stirred by a feeling of guilt on account of his apostasy. Now it became clear to him that God understood and sympathized with the unfortunate position in which a Huguenot found himself who had been pressed into military service against his will. God approved of his wishing to be a decent clock-maker, even though a Catholic, rather than a Huguenot dragoon. God was understanding, and God forgave. Otherwise He would hardly have entrusted Pierre with such a world-shaking mission.

André-Charles Caron, relieved at last of his deep-seated apprehension of guilt, stroked his son's hand. "America!" he murmured to himself. "My son is going to liberate America!"

☆   ☆   ☆

Pierre was in the habit of doing a great deal of his work in the morning before he left his bed-chamber, for it was the custom in aristocratic society, and one which coincided with his own inclinations, to receive friends and acquaintances during the toilet. It flattered him to have people crowding into his room while he was dressing, a motley throng of suppliants for his favour who came to petition his aid, to submit their grievances, or to enlist his co-operation. It was a medley of ambition and misery, respect and impertinence, greed for profit and the urge to self-assertion, which was thus spread before his eyes.

This time the rumour had circulated that he was about to launch an important new venture, of more than ordinary scope, and his visitors overflowed into the corridor.

Pierre had always found pleasure in distributing his favours, and now the opportunities for extending his patronage were unbounded. The firm of Hortalez and Company needed agents in every port, it would have to employ clerks, book-keepers, liveried servants, and messengers, and Pierre could cause manna to rain down from heaven. As he sat at his toilet-table, with Emile and the hairdresser busied about him, he waved his hand, greeted an acquaintance, exchanged a joke or a friendly word, and played the gracious gentleman. When not able to grant a request immediately, he at least offered a word of hope.

A merchant seaman named Captain Adelon had come to inquire whether Monsieur de Beaumarchais would be sending any ships across the Atlantic. He had made the crossing no less than one hundred and twenty-three times and he could give the best of references. Pierre thought it worth instructing Maigron to make a note of the Captain's name.

Madame Chaix, with whom Pierre had been somewhat more than friendly ten years or so before, ventured to remind him that she was married to a master joiner with a workshop of his own. She was still an attractive creature, and Pierre had no doubt that Madame Chaix's husband could be usefully employed in the fitting up of his new offices in the Hôtel de Hollande. Maigron noted the address.

One of his visitors was the son of a cousin of his father's second wife. Another was a nephew of his Sister Tonton's husband. Some smelt a chance of doing profitable business, others were anxious not to incur the enmity of the influential writer, and among these were men in high position. For instance, Baron de Trois-Tours, who had money invested in the Pelletier dockyards, the most important on the north coast of France, and Monsieur Gaschet of the shipping-firm of Testard and Gaschet in Bordeaux. Pierre's heart swelled within him when even the Chevalier de Clonard entered the room, the Chevalier de Clonard who represented the powerful *Compagnie des Indes.*

Monsieur Clairval of the *Comédiens Italiens* had not omitted to put in an appearance. There was a latent hostility between Pierre and the great actor which dated back to the time when the former had given a first reading of his play, *The Barber of Seville,* to the company of the *Théâtre des Italiens.* They were delighted with it, but the production came to naught. Clairval, who would have played the role of the barber, had once been a barber himself and did not want his audiences to be reminded of that fact, so the piece was given to the rival theatre, the *Théâtre français,* where it achieved a tremendous success. Clairval conveniently forgot that he had ever refused the part and he was anxious not to let the opportunity escape him of visiting his dear friend Pierre on his return from abroad.

Pierre caught sight of Métra, a journalist who had more than once singled him out for a spiteful attack. "What is your price these days, my friend?" he asked amiably.

"A colleague like you," replied Métra, "can always rely on the maximum discount."

Pierre, however, had already ceased to pay him any attention. A wave of triumph had surged through him as he saw, just behind the journalist, the dignified, striking features of Monsieur Régnier. This distinguished gentleman, a judge of the Supreme Court, had deigned to call upon a man who, in the eyes of the law, had a "stain upon his character."

One petitioner came forward after another, and Pierre had a word for them all. He knew how to deal with people, and even when he said little he did so in a way that made his visitor feel that he had been the particular object of attention. This morning audience would have continued even longer if a servant had not whispered in his ear that a lady was awaiting him in his study. The lady was Mademoiselle Mesnard.

That was just like Désirée! She came to see him in his own home and did not worry about the conventions. She was not even disturbed by the fact that the normally good-natured Julie showed her plainly on every possible occasion how much she disliked her.

Julie saw in Désirée Mesnard the main cause of all the misfortune that had ever fallen to Pierre's lot. It was on her account that he and the jealous Duc de Chaulnes had once come to blows, and de Chaulnes had been responsible for Pierre's being cast into prison. Because of this, it had been impossible for Pierre to look after his interests adequately when his lawsuit came up for trial, and therefore in Julie's opinion it was Désirée's fault, and nobody else's, that the case had been lost. She could not comprehend how Pierre could bring himself in the circumstances to have her portrait hanging in his house, and she told him on many occasions that she could not stand the sight of the woman. He only laughed, however, when she urged him to have the picture removed. It was a very fine portrait, he would say, by Quentin de Latour, and Désirée was a very fine girl.

Pierre took leave of his visitors and repaired to the study, where he saw Désirée sitting on the massive writing-table. She had swept aside the various papers and other objects to make room for her own slender form. She was of medium height, very slim, with auburn hair, rather pert and perfectly at ease. When Pierre entered she burst out laughing. "Was it a good idea of mine to come and see you?" she asked.

He smiled as he looked at her pretty, tomboyish face with its slightly retroussé nose. "It is good to see someone sensible who has not come to ask a favour," he said, and kissed her hand, her throat, and the side of her neck.

"Well, you old cheat," she retorted, "I hear you are hatching some big scheme. I can see that I shall soon have to get you out of Fort l'Evêque again." Fort l'Evêque was the name of the gaol.

Pierre and Désirée were old friends. They had both been children of the Paris streets, they both loved Paris, and they were both passionately attached to the theatre. They had gone through many sordid experiences in their climb to fame, they were worldly wise, took and enjoyed life as it came, and did not try to pretend either to themselves or to one another that things were different than they were. She had won celebrity as an actress and her house was the resort of distinguished authors, influential officers of the royal court, and business magnates. She gathered around her men who held power in their hands, because she found them useful, but she was not dazzled by great names. She knew with how little wisdom France was being governed, and with sound common sense she despised the aristocracy and the men of affairs. It was the same with Pierre. They had both wormed their way deeply into the ranks of the privileged class, yet they both regarded these privileged members of the nation with the same fathomless, slightly envious scorn. The mutual passion that had once swept them both off their feet had long since passed, but a firm and lasting friendship had remained, and though they sometimes did not see one another for weeks or months at a time, even when they were both in Paris, they knew that each could count on the other if need should arise.

Désirée jumped from the table and opened the door leading to the little cabinet to see whether Julie was eavesdropping, then she wrinkled her roguish little nose and said, "The coast is clear. You can fire away."

Pierre told her in a calm, objective way about his American venture. Bombast would have been out of place with Désirée, and she listened attentively as he spoke. Like everybody else of progressive mind in Paris she had heartily espoused the cause of the American rebels and the great experiment they had undertaken of establishing a state on the basis of freedom, nature, and reason. "I was afraid," she said, "that you might again be hatching out one of your old schemes, such as a monopoly of the slave trade or the procuring of a new mistress for the King of Spain who would act as your private spy. But America! That is a cause worth working for."

"And by an agreeable coincidence," commented Pierre slyly, "enthusiasm for the good cause will this time be combined with profit. It is going to be a very big thing, Désirée. Compared with my firm of Hortalez, the *Compagnie des Indes* will look like a minnow."

"I seem to have heard something like that before," replied Désirée.

"Ah, but today," he assured her, "I not only say so. It *is* so."

"My best wishes go with you, Monsieur de Beaumarchais," she retorted mockingly, "but I have frequently noticed that while you conceived the idea, others skimmed the cream."

"This time I will do the skimming," he insisted. "This time nobody is going to make a fool of me. There is no possible chance of that. I have never before been faced with the prospect of profits on such a scale."

"Well, at any rate, Pierre," said Désirée warmly, "I am glad that this time there can be no doubt of the worthiness of the cause."

Pierre was aware of that without being told. What he wanted to hear from her was a word of encouragement about the financial prospects. On the previous day, before mentioning the matter to Lenormant, he had asked himself whether he should not take Désirée into his confidence before doing so. Charlot was in love with her, and Pierre had never scrupled to use women in the furtherance of his purpose. Yet he had hesitated. The relations between Charlot and Désirée were rather involved, and by using her as a go-between he was just as likely to hinder his object as to further it. Now, however, that she had come to see him of her own accord and he had already told her so much, he cast doubt to the winds and confessed the hopes he entertained of enlisting Lenormant's collaboration.

At the mention of Lenormant's name she made a grimace, and a vertical line appeared between her brows as she squinted thoughtfully down her nose. Her relations with the *fermier général* were the one indeterminate feature in her life, which was otherwise cut to a clear pattern. He was different from the other men she knew, cool yet passionate, a melancholy brooder who relished the good things of life, despising romance yet longing for it, and though he sometimes subjected even her to his wounding irony she realized how deeply he loved her and how hard he struggled to keep his emotions under control. He both attracted and repelled her, she regarded him with mingled respect and contempt, but though she would have ruthlessly exploited any other man's weakness she did not do so in his case. She did not know herself what exactly she wanted from Charlot. She had never put a high price on her virtue, she had never been sparing of her love, since that was not a practical possibility in Paris for a woman who intended to get on in the world, so from time to time she admitted Charlot to her bed, but she treated him worse than she treated her other lovers, leaving no doubt in his mind that she had no affection for him. When he asked more from her, suggesting that she should give up her independence and become his acknowledged mistress, she merely shrugged her shoulders, made an impish grimace, and said nothing.

It was the contradictions in his nature that attracted her and she would watch with a curious interest as his misanthropic mood changed to one of tender sentiment. With other men she could always see clearly what course their friendship would take, but with Charlot anything was possible. He might throttle her or he might ask her to marry him.

She was aware that Charlot liked Pierre, but she was also convinced that he was jealous of him and she could not rid herself of a haunting fear that he might one day take a fearful revenge on the younger man. It would be dangerous, so she thought, for Pierre to enter into partnership with such an incalculable person. For all his intrigues, Pierre was an innocent, good-natured fellow who was never able to bear animosity for long and only wanted to get as much enjoyment as he could out of life. He would be no match for the embittered malice that sometimes surged in the heart of Charlot.

"If I were in your position I would think twice," she warned him, "before taking Charlot into partnership."

"He is my friend," said Pierre.

"That is why I am giving you this advice," she replied enigmatically. "He is so powerful," she continued. "In the end he always swallows up everything on which he lays his hand."

Pierre refused to be dismayed. "Don't worry, my dear," he laughed. "Anyone who tries to swallow this Jonah will soon find himself anxious to disgorge him again."

☆　　☆　　☆

Despite his wealth and aristocratic birth Lenormant had not found life a very easy matter. Thirty-seven years before he had married a very young, very beautiful girl, with agreeable qualities of mind, but without fortune and without influential connections. He was of slow, melancholy temperament and had hesitated for some time before deciding on his marriage with Jeanne-Antoinette Poisson, but during the early years of their union he had cause for nothing but rejoicing at the step he had taken, and his love for Jeanne only grew more passionate. Then one day, without warning, she left him to become the King's acknowledged mistress and to govern France under her new name of the Marquise de Pompadour. It was a blow from which he thought he would never recover. Later on she had offered him everything, an embassy, even her own return to his house, but he maintained his pride and dignity and rejected her as well as her offers.

He had long since emerged from the abyss of suffering into which he had been plunged, but as a changed man. He had become bitter and sarcastic, anxious to taste the sweets of life and lustful for ambiguous adventures. He flung himself with grim enjoyment into one complicated business venture after another, and soon accumulated a colossal fortune. Morose as he was, he never relaxed in his search for pleasure. Over the main gateway of his chateau at Etioles was emblazoned the motto *Vanitas, vanitatum vanitas, omnia vanitas,* but the owner of the château was always surrounded by lovely women, while his parties were renowned for their splendour and taste.

Lenormant had fallen in love with Désirée Mesnard when he first saw her picture. This was not the portrait that hung in Pierre's house, but a pastel painted by Perronneau, which showed her as a pretty, cheerful girl with an engaging freshness. When Lenormant met her in the flesh he was astounded to see how far she excelled her portrait. At moments he was assailed by a longing to escape from the plethora of art and artifice by which he was encircled into a world of elemental vigour and simplicity, and in his private theatre he was wont to produce farces that were distinguished by the most primitive type of native humour. He soon discovered how much blunt common sense lay concealed behind Désirée's air of frail charm, and this, combined with her indifference to scandalmongering gossip, as well as her pert, realistic Parisian wit, filled him with delight. There were traits in her which he had loved in his dead Jeanne. In Jeanne, too, wisdom had been compatible with high spirits, a sober outlook with a sense of romance, and she had possessed the same gift of not letting the sordid aspects of life veil for her its cheerful brilliance.

He was fifty-seven when he first met Désirée, then a girl of twenty-one, and he was gratified to observe that the young actress was attracted by the singularity of his character, the mixture of melancholy and sybaritism, his good taste, his understanding of the theatre, and his sardonic philosophy. At the same time he did not delude himself as to his ability to hold his own among her younger and more amusing friends without the support of his wealth and prestige. Nevertheless, he regarded it as a stroke of good fortune that this young woman should have come into his life, and that at an age when passion was waning it should have fallen to his lot once more to fall in love. He suffered, indeed, when he saw with what unconcern Désirée gave herself to this man or that, but he had learned his lesson and was resolved not to destroy his own happiness a second time out of a sense of injured pride. He made no attempt to encroach upon her independence.

His only serious rival was Pierre, and of this he was fully cognizant. He was perfectly well aware of the footing on which they stood with one another, and their loyal friendship, founded on a kinship of mind, seemed to him more dangerous than any romantic attachment. Désirée's devotion to Pierre inspired him with a deep envy. He, who could not take things lightly and for whom life had not always gone smoothly, was vexed at the way in which Pierre seemed to act as a magnet so that people were attracted to him and success fell into his lap almost without his having to lift a finger. Pierre always came off best in the end. He was able to shake off adversity as a dog shakes off drops of water. Much as Lenormant liked him, he would not have grieved if Pierre too had learned to know the meaning of ingratitude, treachery, and suffering.

Now Pierre had come to ask his help in supplying arms to America. They had dined together, and there Pierre was sitting and waiting anxiously for his decision.

It was a brilliant idea to establish a private company while in reality acting as an agent of the French Government, a most ingenious notion, but if it was to develop into anything more than a dazzling piece of stage-work, if the rebels were to be equipped in a way that would enable them to face seasoned English troops, then the three or four millions that Pierre had in mind were too paltry to be considered. The man who was bold enough to engage in such a scheme must have unlimited credit at his disposal, he must be able to wait for his money, he must be prepared to hold on for a long, long time. Lenormant himself possessed the strength to stretch such a colossal bow, and the prospect of fat profits was a strong temptation, but was Pierre the right man to co-operate with in the solution of the problems that would confront them? Would he be sufficiently sober and matter-of-fact? Deep within his brain there gnawed the as-yet-unformulated thought of how Pierre would brag and strut before Désirée—"Here you see the man who is fitting out the American Army, the man who is making history!" No, he wasn't going to help Pierre build up the millions that he would need for his scheme.

Lenormant broke the silence that had fallen between them. In his oily voice he explained that though the prospect of large profits was undoubtedly favourable, the risks too were enormous. Not only could it be assumed that one ship in two would fall a prize to the English fleet, but any hope that the Americans would pay their debt was a little vague. Much as he admired the rebels' enthusiasm for liberty, this praiseworthy emotion was no adequate guarantee of their eventual solvency. In the most favourable circumstances their backers would have to wait for years before they saw the colour of their money. A rough calculation had led him to conclude that an initial capital of about ten millions would be required if they were to carry the project through. As he mentioned this large sum he cast a worried look at Pierre from his sleepy, deep-set eyes.

Pierre was taken aback and answered listlessly, "I thought that the abnormally advantageous nature of this speculation, which must be even more evident to you than it is to me, would act as an inducement to your joining me in the firm of Hortalez."

"I have just been trying, my dear Pierre," said Lenormant with a skilful pretence at good-humoured tolerance, "to point out to you that the risks are greater than the prospects would warrant. I am growing old and my lust for hazardous ventures is not what it was."

"But have you not just renewed your licence to farm the taxes of your two provinces?" asked Pierre.

Lenormant replied to this question by asking another. "Is there any risk in that for a man who can afford to wait?" he inquired with provoking calm. "The King has bailiffs and, if need be, soldiers to exercise compulsion when debtors are reluctant. Will the firm of Hortalez be able to send soldiers against the rebels if they are delinquent?"

"I had expected," said Pierre, not without a certain bitterness, "that my friend Charlot would be eager to join me in this enterprise. I had expected my friend Charlot to be the first to offer his help to the Americans and to me."

"Please do not be so hasty, my dear Pierrot," replied Lenormant soothingly. "Who says that I am not prepared to offer you my help?"

The way in which Charlot was playing with him angered Pierre, yet on the other hand he knew from experience that Lenormant was generous and amiably inclined towards him. "It is only in the early stages that I shall need the money, if I need it at all," he suggested uncertainly.

This was just what Lenormant had been waiting for. He was quite prepared to assist with a loan. From his knowledge of Pierre he was convinced that the latter would soon find himself in rough waters and have to ask for a prolongation. And that was where he, Charlot, would come into his own. Even if he were to lose his money, or at any rate a part of it, the interview at which he would be able to watch Pierre writhing in embarrassment as he pleaded for consideration would be well worth the loss. "You see," he commented, "it is not so difficult for us to reach agreement! I can let you have a loan, particularly if it's to be a short one, whenever you want it. How much do you need?"

"I think," said Pierre, still hesitantly, "that I shall be able to manage with a further million."

"It is at your disposal," replied Lenormant promptly.

Pierre drew a deep breath of relief, yet at the same time he was slightly bewildered. Charlot was doing him no trifling service in advancing such a large sum, but did he really believe the risks were too great to justify his investing his money rather than lending it? "Thank you, Charlot," he said. "I thank you from the bottom of my heart." His voice was less firm than usual, a fact that betrayed his confusion.

"It is a pleasure to serve you, my friend," replied Lenormant deprecatingly. "As far as the rate of interest is concerned, your representatives will find me very accommodating." He paused for a moment and looked at Pierre with a friendly air. "But," he continued, and wagged his finger at him jestingly, "keep the money together, Pierrot!" Then in a low, gentle tone he murmured, "I lend money only on short term, and I collect the debts that are due to me, my friend. Mind you, it is well known that I never fail to collect my debts."

This was the kind of jest in which Charlot liked to indulge. A disagreeable form of humour, it was true, but Pierre shook off the feeling of disquiet before it had time to take hold of him. Charlot had consented, and that was the main thing. Had he not been resolved to see the business through even if his total funds from all sources had amounted to no more than a million? Now he was going to get two million from the Government and a further million from Charlot. "Thank you once again," he said, and his tone was as light and friendly as that of Lenormant had been. "Thank you in the name of America, of France, and of myself."

☆   ☆   ☆

A night and a day had passed, and yet another night, and Pierre had still not found time to visit Thérèse. On the previous morning he had sent her a note promising to come some time during the evening, and in the evening he had let her know that he would come today. Thank heaven, Thérèse was a girl who would understand. From their very first meeting he had known that she was the only possible wife for him, and during all the years of their association he had played continually with the resolve to marry her forthwith. But Julie had been jealous of Thérèse from the outset, and on the only occasion when Pierre had dared to hint at his intention of bringing home a wife there had been a violent scene and she had threatened to leave the house. It was true that she had immediately been overcome with remorse and had declared that Thérèse was a charming young creature, in every respect far superior to herself, with whom she would be able to get on excellently, but Pierre cherished no illusions on that score. If he married Thérèse it would not be long before the impetuous Julie withdrew in a fit of sulks, and Julie was indispensable to his well-being. Not only was she the ideal housekeeper for his expensive establishment, but she satisfied an essential need of his nature by allowing him to swagger and boast of his achievements and by putting no check whatsoever on her own lavish admiration. Thérèse would never leave him even if there was no formal bond between them.

Her house was not far away and he went on foot. He smiled as he thought how often he had made this short journey, and with what pleasure he had done so. His business interests were dispersed over the face of the globe and he had many times covered great distances in order to look after his affairs, but his real life was centred in the tiny triangle between his house, his office, and the house in which Thérèse dwelt. This impetuous adventurer was at heart a family man. After wild days and nights he sought the bourgeois comforts of his family circle, consisting of his father, his sisters, his nephews, his nieces, his uncles, his aunts, and his cousins of both sexes.

He rang the bell and a maid opened the door, but Thérèse was already waiting for him at the threshold of her room. She was wearing a negligee, as he had secretly hoped she would, and there was not the slightest cloud on her face to signify that she reproached him for his tardiness in coming. Hastening towards her and taking her head in both hands, he bent it gently backwards and a little to one side. She was tall, nearly as tall as himself, and he gazed deeply into her vivacious eyes. Slowly, and with deliberation, he kissed her forehead, followed with his lips the high arched curve of her eyebrows until the long lashes sank, kissed the bow of her mouth, and let his hands glide down along her firm, rounded chin, her throat, her breasts.

Thérèse kept her eyes closed. Three years ago, when she was only just seventeen, she had read his pamphlets, and his resounding attack on injustice and privilege had stirred her to the depths. She had not believed that anyone could be so bold and yet have so light a touch, such elegance and verve. She was carried away by his sparkling wit and, abandoning her normal reserve, found some pretext to visit him.

Thérèse was not given to precipitate action and her judgment was sound. During the past three years she had had time to discover the superficial, vain, and frivolous element in Pierre's character, but that part of him which she loved was strong enough to make her accept the rest. It was his own cause for which he had taken up his pen, but it was also the cause of all those who had suffered injustice under a brazen and arrogant system. It was his own cause for which he was fighting when he poured ridicule on the aristocracy, for they had submitted him to insults and were trying to hold him down, but he was spurred on by something more, by a deep joy in battling against the rooted prejudices of the world. Behind all his boasting and theatricality lay a profound conviction of what was true and great. When he saw injustice and abuse, whether directed against himself or against others, he did not pause to consider before starting in to attack. That was what Thérèse saw in him, and that was what she loved.

He had been long away, and he had much to tell her as she sat upon his knee and submitted to his caresses. In the past forty-eight hours he had already told the story three times, to Charlot, to Julie, and to his father, each time the same story and yet different. As he now unfolded it to Thérèse it again took on a different colouring. He explained to her its political significance, how the insurgents had everything—sufficient men, a spacious country, a just cause, their own enthusiasm, and the moral support of the whole world—except one essential that they could not do without. The one thing they lacked was arms. "And that is what we are now going to send them," he concluded.

Thérèse's grey eyes were radiant. She had hoped from the beginning that the rebels would be successful, and she kept demanding further details about their prospects. It pleased him that she should be more interested in this than in the business side of it, for he wanted his wife to see in him the author, the fighter for liberty and reason, not the speculator. He basked in the warmth of her enthusiasm, which was free from the sometimes silly exuberance in which Julie was wont to indulge. Thérèse never lost her contact with reality.

He was silent for a time, and pondered once more whether he should not take steps to hasten their marriage.

Thérèse knew quite well what was going on in his mind. It was not an agreeable position to be merely his mistress, and there was nothing she would have liked better than to have him legitimize their union, but she understood his temperament and was afraid that if he were to lose Julie on her account it might raise a barrier between them, and since she did not worry unduly about gossip and scandalmongering, and had enough money of her own to be independent, she preferred to wait.

He mused again on the face Julie would make if he suddenly said to her, "I am going to marry Thérèse next week." He made a wry face himself at the vision he had conjured up. He had only too often allowed himself to be carried away by a momentary impulse, and since he had hesitated so long there was no harm in a little further delay.

He said to Thérèse, "Since my affairs have gone so well, and I am now launching this great new venture, you must permit me to do something which I hope will give you pleasure. My little house at Meudon with the overgrown garden that you are so fond of—may I make you a present of it? I will have it thoroughly done up, of course. We could drive out together sometimes and spend a day or two by ourselves in the peace of the countryside."

☆   ☆   ☆

The following days were a wild rush for Pierre. He had interviews with shipowners, contractors, and financiers, conferences with the gentlemen of the Foreign Office, the Admiralty, and the Arsenal. He had to find cannon, muskets, munitions, uniforms, linen, boots, blankets, and tents. Ships had to be chartered for the transport of all this material, the equipment for thirty thousand men, across the Atlantic Ocean. He had promised the gentlemen at Versailles that a considerable part of the supplies would be on its way overseas possibly by the autumn, and certainly before the end of the year.

If he threw himself even more ardently than was his wont into the carrying out of his scheme, it was because he was trying to stifle a gnawing doubt that began to worry him more and more. In order to deliver his consignments by the stipulated date it was necessary for him to pay out large sums immediately. His own funds, together with the credit granted him by Lenormant, were soon exhausted, yet the first million livres promised by Vergennes had not yet materialized. When he hinted discreetly at the Foreign Office that his need was urgent, he was informed equally discreetly that the money had to be provided from secret funds and the delay was due solely to difficulties of book-keeping and the inevitable bureaucratic routine. This sounded plausible, but meanwhile he had nothing in the way of concrete proof that the money would be forthcoming, since in such a delicate situation the Government could not put its signature to a written agreement.

He was soon made to realize that the contractors and shipowners were perfectly well aware of the extent to which he was forced to depend upon their good will, for they began to raise their prices. Things would not be so bad if he could count at least on receiving the stocks of weapons from the royal arsenals which the Foreign Minister had led him to expect. That would relieve him of part of his worries, and he could show the private contractors that they were not so indispensable to him as they thought they were.

There was plenty of material available at the arsenals. Monsieur de

Saint-Germain, who had taken over the Ministry of War a year before, had set himself the task of modernizing the country's armaments. Many types of weapons had therefore become obsolete, and everything depended on whether Pierre could persuade the Minister to fall in with his plans and let him have the unwanted stocks at a cheap enough price, perhaps for the mere cost of the metal.

He called at the Royal Arsenal, where the Minister for War had his headquarters. It was nearly twelve months since he had last met Monsieur de Saint-Germain, and he had then been struck by the Minister's alert and youthful appearance despite his seventy years. Now, when he was shown into Saint-Germain's presence, he was surprised to see how greatly he had aged during the short period that he had been in office. His shortish figure in its simple uniform was still erect, but it was evident that he had been working under considerable strain and his ashen face was deeply furrowed.

The Minister had good reason to be worried. When in the previous year the young monarch had appointed him to carry out certain reforms in the Army, the whole of Paris had exulted at his choice of an upright, progressive general whose reputation as an organizer matched his record as a great soldier. Saint-Germain had set to work energetically, increasing establishments and improving the quality of equipment, yet cutting down expenditure. This had not been achieved without abolishing many lucrative sinecures which had hitherto been reserved for the court nobility, and moreover he had promoted officers of low birth to the higher commands, thereby acquiring enemies in influential quarters. It was generally assumed that the good-natured but weak-willed King would be forced before very long to drop his efficient Minister, and Pierre could well believe that Saint-Germain's care-worn look was due to the difficulties with which he was being confronted.

He had expected that the old general, after his experience of the trials of office, would scent some dubious intrigue behind the plan which was about to be laid before him, and that he would greet it with suspicion. So he did not immediately broach the subject of the guns and munitions, but laid himself out first of all to inspire confidence. What the insurgents needed most of all, he explained, was organization and training. He, Pierre, who was for the time being the only representative, so to speak, of the Americans in France, had come to seek the Minister's advice as to the best way in which succour could be sent to these children of reason and nature. Nowhere was there to be found more fruitful soil for Saint-Germain's reformatory principles than on the other side of the ocean, where there were no deep-rooted prejudices to stand in their way. In America it would be possible to organize an army strictly in accordance with the ten basic rules which the Minister had laid down in his manual on the art of war.

Saint-Germain listened with growing interest. This Monsieur de Beaumarchais did not appear to be the unscrupulous speculator and profiteer that his reputation would have led one to expect. The Minister condescended to enter into a discussion. Pierre had studied his brief and revealed a close acquaintance with the subject. He listened patiently while Saint-Germain launched into a lengthy and detailed elucidation of his reforms. The old man was enjoying the interview.

It was only when the Minister had finished that Pierre began to touch upon the question of arming the insurgents. It was not a matter, he declared, of equipping regular troops, but of arming a militia. This militia required simple weapons that could be used without the necessity for a long period of preliminary training. The new arms which the Minister was providing for the French Army would be of little use to the Americans, since it would be some time before they could learn to handle them. Here Pierre looked worried.

Saint-Germain showed particular interest at this stage and disclosed an idea which had just occurred to him—the very idea that Pierre had been trying to put into his mind. In the circumstances which Monsieur de Beaumarchais had explained to him, he said, it was in his power to offer the insurgents very considerable help. Owing to the re-equipment of the French Army numerous types of guns and other arms had been rendered obsolete so far as His Majesty's troops were concerned, but for a militia such as Monsieur de Beaumarchais had described they would be ideal. He would willingly place at the disposal of the insurgents such unusable stocks as were available at the arsenals. The details could be discussed by Monsieur de Beaumarchais with the First Secretary at the Ministry of War, Count de Montbarrey.

Pierre was relieved at the outcome of the interview. He had never felt quite comfortable when discussing business with honest, simple souls like Saint-Germain, since their reactions were so incalculable. With Count de Montbarrey, on the other hand, he would be quite at home. Montbarrey was a reckless gambler, always in debt, and with no scruples whatsoever about exploiting the openings offered him by his official position for the straightening out of his own tangled finances. For this purpose he made use of one of his mistresses, the opera singer de Violaine. Whenever an important post in the Army fell vacant, Mademoiselle de Violaine submitted to him a list of candidates who were prepared to pay for the appointment, and in most cases Montbarrey succeeded in obtaining the consent of the unsuspecting Minister.

By his skilful method of approach Pierre had ensured that the stocks available at the arsenals were ready to be handed over as soon as he could collect them, but unless Count de Montbarrey could be persuaded to show good will in the matter he might set the price too high. He might even introduce inconvenient complications with the result that endless delays would ensue. There was only one way of avoiding such a *contretemps*. The Count must be informed, delicately of course, that he would come in for a percentage on the sales. Pierre was not niggardly when an accommodation of this kind was required.

The firm of Hortalez and Company, as he explained to Montbarrey, was worried about the selection of the arms to be sent to the insurgents. The order received from the Americans was couched in too general terms; he and his associates in the firm were business men, who could make no claim to expert military knowledge. He would therefore be eternally beholden to the Count if the latter would be so very kind as to recommend an adviser with the necessary technical experience. Naturally, the firm of Hortalez would not expect such services to be given without adequate recompense.

The smiling Count darted a quick look at the smiling Pierre from his crafty black eyes. He mentioned a few names, only to reject them again immediately, and finally cried, smiting his brow, "I've got just the man for you!" As Pierre had expected, it was a gentleman of the circle frequented by the Count's mistress, Mademoiselle de Violaine.

He thanked Montbarrey, ceremoniously bade him good day, and left the Royal Arsenal in a happy frame of mind.

☆　　☆　　☆

Ever since the conflict had arisen between the English Crown and its American colonies, there had been people in Paris with ambitions to play a role as advocates of the rebel cause. When they got wind of the negotiations being conducted by Monsieur de Beaumarchais, their hearts were filled with envy and they began to be unpleasant.

There was a certain Doctor Barbeu Dubourg in particular. Apart from being a physician, a botanist, a dabbler in politics, a man of business, an author, and a philanthropist, he had translated the works of Doctor Benjamin Franklin, who of all the leading Americans enjoyed the highest reputation in Europe. Dubourg prided himself on being the first man to espouse the American cause on this side of the ocean. As soon as he heard that Monsieur de Beaumarchais was preparing to go to their aid he paid him a visit.

He sat in his chair opposite Pierre, stout and smug, and explained how it had come to his ears that Monsieur de Beaumarchais too was interested in the question of helping the Americans. It would not be unknown to Monsieur de Beaumarchais that he, Doctor Dubourg, had the honour of being able to call the great Benjamin Franklin his friend. He had therefore come to ask Monsieur de Beaumarchais whether he had perhaps any useful suggestions to offer which he, Doctor Dubourg, could pass on to Franklin and the Americans.

Pierre had conceived an immediate dislike for this fat man, with his flabby face and little eyes, his pouting lips and affable smile, his bourgeois dress, his way of playing with his stick, his pinches of snuff, and his habit of sucking his teeth. His complacent pretence of modesty, his pompous loquacity, his naïvely conspiratorial manner, were all irritating in the extreme. It was true that the fellow had access to all the salons, that he was possessed of considerable influence and it was advisable not to fall foul of him, but Pierre was accustomed to giving free play to his antipathies no less than to his sympathies, and against his wiser instincts he replied with arrogant courtesy that though he was much gratified by Doctor Dubourg's amiable offer he had his own agents and these were fully capable of transmitting any advice he had to give by swift and safe routes to Philadelphia. Doctor Dubourg, a little nonplussed, repeated his offer with an even greater display of verbosity than before, Pierre reiterated his refusal, and they took a chilly leave of one another.

Doctor Dubourg was a good-natured man, but this was the first time in his life that he had ever experienced such a rebuff. He sat down and indited a letter to Count Vergennes. Monsieur de Beaumarchais's fertility of imagination, he wrote, his honesty, his zeal for everything that was good and great, were beyond dispute. Yet there could hardly be anybody less fitted for business negotiations. Monsieur de Beaumarchais was given to ostentation. It was also rumoured that he kept women. In brief, he was regarded as a spendthrift, and no serious business man in France would have anything to do with him.

The Minister read this letter. There was nothing particularly new in the allegations put forward by Doctor Dubourg. But Doctor Dubourg had not hitherto supplied anything but useless advice, while Beaumarchais had on many occasions proved his worth. Vergennes read the letter through a second time, smiled, ordered a copy to be sent to the firm of Hortalez, and left it to Monsieur de Beaumarchais himself to compose a reply.

Pierre replied in due form. "My dear Doctor Dubourg," he wrote. "What connection has it, pray, with the affairs of the Americans that I am regarded as a spendthrift and a keeper of women? In any case I have been doing this for the last twenty years. At first I kept five of them, four sisters and a niece. Two of them, alas, have since died, so now I am only keeping three, two sisters and a niece, though even this, of course, is an extravagance for a man without rank or titles. And what would you say if you knew that my conduct is even more scandalous—in that I am keeping men as well as women, namely, a nephew, who is both young and good to look upon, and my unhappy father, who is responsible for having brought the undersigned disgraceful libertine into the world? But for heaven's sake, Monsieur, do not reveal this to the Count de Vergennes, otherwise he might lose the good opinion he has of me."

From the day when Vergennes proved his confidence in Pierre by sending him Dubourg's letter, Pierre's affairs began to prosper.

The contract he signed with the Ministry of War surpassed anything he had dared to expect. The Royal Arsenal supplied two hundred cannon for the mere cost of the metal, forty sous a pound. Cast iron was calculated on a basis of ninety francs per thousand pounds weight, and even the muskets were remarkably cheap.

And, at last, he received the subsidy for which he had been so anxiously waiting, the million promised him by the Foreign Minister, a million *livres tournois* in gold and in bills.

Pierre emptied the sacks of gold onto his massive writing-table until every inch of its surface was covered with coins. These gold coins were stamped with the images of many monarchs: they bore the features of Louis XIV, Louis XV, and Louis XVI, of Maria Theresa of Austria, Frederick of Prussia, and Charles of Spain. Pierre stared in fascination at the abundance of shining disks, at the bills signed by Count Vergennes and countersigned by his First Secretary, Conrad-Alexandre de Gérard, and he smiled a deep smile of satisfaction.

☆   ☆   ☆

Pierre's associates on the far side of the Atlantic were still unaware of the existence of the firm of Hortalez and Company and its activities on their behalf. He had been working to some extent in the dark, without having come to any fixed understanding with the Americans. When he was in London a certain Mr. Arthur Lee, a youngish gentleman who appeared to be filled both with enthusiasm for his country's cause and with admiration for his own genius, had introduced himself to Pierre as the representative of the colonies. It had been whispered to him that the real envoy of Versailles was not the French Ambassador, but Monsieur de Beaumarchais, and Pierre had made no attempt to disabuse him of this notion. Mr. Lee had been at great pains to win his confidence, and had been assured in return, though in rather enigmatical terms, that he could rely upon the unstinted aid of France. Pierre had promised to present him to the Count de Vergennes, but when on his arrival back in Paris he mentioned Mr. Lee's name to the Minister, that cautious diplomat refused to hear any more. He could not possibly receive a man who was known in London to be an agent of the rebels. The sensitive Mr. Lee, who believed that Pierre had failed to display the necessary zeal, promptly took umbrage, cancelled his projected visit to Paris, and declined to have any further relations with the firm of Hortalez.

Meanwhile, however, the Congress in Philadelphia had decided to appoint a special plenipotentiary for France, and before very long there appeared in Paris a gentleman of the name of Silas Deane.

Before Pierre had time to call upon him, Mr. Deane found his way of his own accord to the Hôtel de Hollande. He was a man of prosperous bourgeois appearance, somewhat oddly dressed, with a satin waistcoat richly embroidered in a design of flowers covering his bulging stomach. It soon became evident that he was a man of business with whom things could be discussed on a business-like basis. He knew no other language than English, possessed not the faintest conception of the ways of the French capital, and was very grateful for the services which the firm of Hortalez was able to offer him.

Doctor Dubourg made an attempt to interpose his own person in the negotiations, but at Versailles Mr. Deane received the unequivocal assurance that the only agent who enjoyed the confidence of the French Government was Monsieur de Beaumarchais. Neither he nor Pierre had any difficulty in coming to terms with one another, and a formal agreement was speedily drawn up. The firm of Hortalez and Company, represented by Monsieur de Beaumarchais, entered into an obligation to deliver to the Continental Congress, represented by Mr. Deane, the complete equipment for thirty thousand men, and included in the contract was an enumeration of the items which the firm promised to supply as a minimum. The Continental Congress, for its part, bound itself to transmit payment for the goods received at a date not later than eight months after the delivery of each consignment, not less than forty-five per cent of the amount due being in bills and the rest in commodities.

Pierre's heart leapt for joy when he held the contract, duly signed and sealed, in his hands. He went straight to Lenormant. What had Charlot to say now? Pierre strode excitedly up and down the room with an air of triumph. What had he not achieved in such a short time! The French Government had paid over the first million, the Spanish Government had formally promised to contribute the second. The Royal Arsenal was supplying the major part of the necessary equipment at the cheapest possible prices. And now there was this magnificent contract with the plenipotentiary of the Congress. Did Charlot still think the business risky?

Lenormant watched his friend with veiled eyes as he strode up and down and proudly counted his successes. Then, slowly and carefully, he read through the document. "Not longer than eight months after delivery, forty-five per cent in bills, fifty-five per cent in commodities! A very good contract," he commented. He looked up at Pierre. "Who is this Mr. Deane?"

"The representative of the Congress," replied Pierre, a little startled.

"Yes, I know," said Lenormant amiably. "He says so expressly in this agreement. But what is the Congress? Who, or what, stands behind the Congress?" And he gazed at Pierre with an air of melancholy.

"Behind the Congress," cried Pierre with increasing excitement, "there stands a hard-working nation of three million people, there stands a country with vast, unexploited treasures, there stands—"

"Yes, I know," interrupted Lenormant. "But to whom do these treasures belong? You can have the signatures of the rebels, and you can have the signatures of the loyalists." He examined the signature on the document thoughtfully. "Mr. Silas Deane," he murmured, and shrugged his shoulders.

"Listen, Charlot," said Pierre. "It is permissible to doubt the soundness of any undertaking. But you know well enough that this contract is backed by the resolute determination to stand by it. Its terms will be carried out, and by both parties. In any case you must admit that the firm of Hortalez is more firmly established today than when we first discussed it and weighed its chances. You were then generous enough to place funds at my disposal to be repaid at a moderate rate of interest. Now that the prospects are so infinitely more favourable I should reproach myself for behaving shabbily if I did not once more ask you to come in with me as a partner." There was a note of persuasive warmth in his voice as he spoke.

Lenormant kept his eyes fixed in front of him, his round head with its domed forehead slightly lowered. The contract was not so bad. In fact, it was a very good contract, provided there was a strong man behind it who possessed sufficient influence with the French Government to exercise pressure, if need be, on the Americans. A man like himself, for example. If he were to interest himself in this venture there was a great deal to be made out of it. He would come in for a share of the profits, the lion's share. Yet it would always be Pierrot who would enjoy the credit of having first conceived the scheme. Little Pierrot would reap the reward of fame.

"My dear Pierre," he said, in his deliberate, courteous way, "it is extraordinarily kind of you to suggest a change in our business arrangement. But, as you know, I am something of a pedant. I like to stick to an agreement once it is made, and I am prepared to take the risk that it will turn out to my disadvantage. I would prefer," he concluded amiably, "to leave things as they are, and shall be content with the interest and guarantees to which we have both agreed."

Pierre was deeply concerned at this reply. He had assumed that Lenormant would jump at the renewal of his offer. He found Charlot's attitude incomprehensible. Could he have made a mistake? Could he, after all, have underestimated the risks involved? Charlot had a keen nose for such matters.

Disturbed and worried, he returned to the Hôtel de Hollande. As soon as he entered his handsome suite of offices, however, his ill-humour was scattered to the winds. The insolence of Doctor Dubourg's letter to Vergennes had spurred him on to furnish the Hôtel de Hollande even more sumptuously than he had at first intended, and in his present mood he took particular pleasure in its showy splendour. He had been right to set up this proud mansion as visible evidence of his faith in the justice of his cause and the certainty of his profits.

As he read through the contract once more he shook his head and smiled. How absurd it was of Charlot to be obsessed by such doubts! They could have been due to nothing but a momentary fit of depression. He sent for Maigron and, with a light heart, dictated a letter to the Continental Congress.

"Gentlemen," he began. "I have been induced, by the high esteem in which I hold that brave nation which under your leadership is so stoutly defending its freedom, to collaborate in your noble enterprise. A great business house has been established for the purpose of supplying you with everything that you may need in the prosecution of your just war. I have entered into a formal agreement with your plenipotentiary here in Paris and propose to consign to you before the end of the present year the following items of equipment."

He had been walking up and down as he dictated, while Maigron took the letter down in shorthand with one of his new-fangled pencils. Now he stood still and read slowly from a list he held in his hand:

216 guns
290,000 issues of powder
30,000 muskets
200 gun-barrels
27 mortars
13,000 projectiles
8 transports

further: the complete equipment for 30,000 troops, consisting of

30,000 blankets
30,000 pairs of boots
30,000 pairs of shoe-buckles and garters
60,000 pairs of woollen stockings
30,000 handkerchiefs
120,000 buttons

further:

95,000 yards of cloth for tunics
42,000 yards of lining
180,000 yards of linen for military shirts
15,000 pounds of thread
1,000 pounds of silk
100,000 strong sewing needles

The list was unending and Pierre enjoyed its full savour as he read it aloud. Then he let his hand sink and said, "Well, Maigron, we did quite nicely, didn't we?"

He went on dictating:

"Your representatives, gentlemen, will find in me a reliable friend. They will always find a welcome in my house, money in my chests, and support of every kind in any activity they may undertake, whether public or clandestine. So far as lies within my power I shall sweep away all obstacles in the Cabinets of Europe that might stand in your way. In every port of France and Spain I shall maintain an agent who will call upon the captain when one of your ships arrives in order to offer him whatever assistance he may need. The King of France and his Ministers will be constrained to take official steps when protests are received from foreign countries about this infringement of commercial treaties, but you may rely upon my indefatigable zeal, gentlemen, to remove all difficulties from your path. I shall see to it that all prohibitions are either evaded or withdrawn. All operations that may be required for the transaction of our business will be put in hand.

"From now on, gentlemen, I beg you to look upon my house as the focus of all activities in Europe that may be calculated to benefit your cause, and to regard me as one of your most ardent adherents, who entertains no more heartfelt wish than that for your success. Please accept this assurance of the deep respect and esteem with which I have the honour to sign myself, your most obedient servant, etc.

"Tell me, Maigron," he asked his secretary, "don't you think that is an uncommon letter?"

"I certainly doubt whether the gentlemen in Philadelphia will ever have received one like it before," replied Maigron dryly.

When his secretary had gone, Pierre again read through his agreement with Mr. Silas Deane. Then, confirmed in his feeling that all was well, he stored it away in the chest together with the plans of his invention, the manuscript of his play, and his most treasured love letters.

Yet he could not entirely clear from his mind the vague apprehension inspired by Lenormant's scepticism, and he felt the need for a heart-to-heart talk with some sensible person who was free from irrational bias. Paul Theveneau would not do, since he shared Pierre's enthusiasm. He went to see Désirée.

"You have come just at the right moment," she greeted him. "We are starting rehearsals the day after tomorrow."

The *Théâtre français* had decided on a new production of *Georges Dandin,* Molière's comedy of the rich booby who marries the poor but aristocratic Angélique. She deceives him to the top of her bent, but though he discovers her *in flagrante delicto* he is helpless in view of her superior wits. She succeeds in putting him in the wrong and, in league with her aristocratic parents, forces him to go on his knees and crave her pardon for all the suffering she has caused him.

Désirée was to play the part of Angélique, and, her relations with Charlot being what they were, the situation was not lacking in piquancy. Pierre smiled as he thought of the wry face that Charlot would make when he heard the news. *"Tu l'as voulu, Georges Dandin."*

When Désirée was first offered the part she had thought more of what Lenormant might say than of *Georges Dandin,* but as soon as she had made up her mind to accept she concentrated on her interpretation of the role. She was obsessed by her art, an actress from the crown of her head to the soles of her feet, and she had already begun to live the part of Angélique. The *Théâtre français* maintained an inviolable tradition in the performance of Molière's plays, and she wondered whether she dared attempt to introduce any changes in the customary interpretation. During the past few days she had been racking her brains, discussing first one possibility and then another, and changing her mind half a dozen times.

Pierre was one of the very few people she knew who really understood the theatre, and when he arrived she almost fell on his neck. Without giving him time to say what he had come for, she poured into his ears the problems that were agitating her and began to demonstrate the way in which she thought the various scenes ought to be played. With his keen interest in the stage he allowed himself to be carried away by her excitement and had soon forgotten the reason for his visit. They grew heated over questions of gesture and intonation, argued, quarrelled and agreed by turns, and had neither eyes nor ears for anything except the task on which they were engaged.

Three hours passed by—he had intended to stay no more than an hour—before she said, taking a deep breath, "All right, now let us have a break."

With a sigh of satisfaction he rejoined, "I'll have supper with you, Désirée, and then we can continue rehearsing."

Stimulated as they were by their exertions, they sat down to a cheerful meal, gossiping about the *Théâtre français* and what was good or what was bad in its traditional way of acting, about the actors themselves, and about the possibility of reforms. Pierre was fond of *Georges Dandin* and appreciated its cruel, full-blooded humour. From his fund of expert knowledge he explained to her the technique by which Molière had achieved his effects, and showed her what was outmoded and what was still permissible. Désirée listened with deep interest. When Pierre spoke of the theatre he was even more clever, more brilliant than when he was enlarging upon the theme of freedom.

Gradually, however, the subject of the American negotiations recurred to him and he skilfully turned the course of the conversation in that direction. He told her what had been happening, and finally, between two glasses of wine, he read out to her his letter to the American Congress. He read it with appropriate gestures, savouring the triumph of the figures he had quoted and the ring of his sonorous phrases.

Désirée, grateful for his help with her part, repaid him for his interest in her interpretation of Angélique by giving him her undivided attention when he spoke of his own affairs. But as he read, her expression grew more and more disapproving. "Do you know the men," she asked, "who constitute this American Congress?"

"No, I don't," he replied, slightly irritated. "I know their names, but of course they are no more than names to me. I have heard about Franklin and Washington and Thomas Paine, and when I was in London I made the acquaintance of a certain Arthur Lee. Lee is not an agreeable fellow, but he is full of enthusiasm and I have no doubts about his honesty, while this Silas Deane they sent over to see me is a man for whom I would go through fire and water."

Désirée sat thinking hard. "I am trying," she said, "to imagine to myself what kind of men they are, these members of your Congress. They are probably mostly men of mature years, who have achieved a certain position in life and gained the confidence of their fellow citizens, merchants, lawyers, and people of that kind."

"Well?" inquired Pierre challengingly. "Are you suggesting that business men cannot also be idealists?"

"Not at all," she conceded. "But this much is certain. If they are business men they will be astonished at receiving a letter such as the one you have just written."

"One cannot write about the arms that are going to win them their freedom as if one were writing about a consignment of herrings," he declared in a surly tone.

"You had the Parisians in mind, the public who read your pamphlets," she retorted. "I am afraid that the worthy citizens of Philadelphia will not take you for a serious business man."

"For what else can they take me, with all these guns and uniforms?" he flared out angrily.

Désirée replied, "Perhaps for someone who is pretending to transact business while in reality he is only passing on equipment which has been supplied free of charge by the French Government."

"You mean, they won't pay?" he asked in a quieter tone, and visibly disconcerted. He was thinking of Lenormant, and of the comment made by his secretary, Maigron. Perhaps it really would have been wiser if, instead of sending a letter that had gushed straight from his heart, he had written to Philadelphia in more sober and matter-of-fact terms. Perhaps they really were men who objected to paying their debts, and if that were so, his letter might strengthen them in the belief that the consignments he was sending across the Atlantic were a gift from the King of France. He discarded the thought before it had time to take a grip on his mind. "Come, come," he said. "I have a good contract with the reliable Mr. Deane. The Congress will pay, of that I have not the slightest doubt. I am dealing with the representative of an honest nation."

"Let us hope so," replied Désirée dryly, and returned to the subject of *Georges Dandin*. They resumed the rehearsal, but Pierre's thoughts were elsewhere and he did not stay long.

☆ ☆ ☆

Though he was prepared to accept the temporary financial loss that was the only result, for the time being, of his American venture, Pierre was resolved to exploit his relations with the Government at Versailles for the purpose of obtaining the annulment of the judicial verdict which prevented him from holding any office of honour.

He had been living for three years now in a kind of civic twilight, an absurd situation for one of the most celebrated writers in Europe who, besides being favoured at court, was the darling of the female members of society, a welcome guest at the most aristocratic salons, a popular figure in the cafés of Paris, and the trusted agent of the King's Ministers. Hitherto, when reference had been made to his equivocal position, he had passed it off with a jest, but his apparent equanimity had only been a pose. He went to see Vergennes with the fixed determination not to quit the Minister's room before the latter had promised to institute proceedings with a view to revision.

With bold and fiery eloquence he declared that if the Government of His Most Christian Majesty thought fit to entrust a man with such an important and honourable commission, it could not fail to free him at once from the disability which had been inflicted on him by prejudiced judges. The Government's own prestige was at stake.

Vergennes gazed at Pierre thoughtfully. He had long since made up his mind to help the American insurgents, for he was afraid that if they should find themselves in a hopeless situation they might eventually become reconciled to the Motherland, with the result that France would have lost for ever the opportunity of revenging herself on England for the humiliation of 1763. On the other hand, he realized much better than Pierre that it would be a long time before France could risk a war. So Pierre's project of clandestine support had been very timely, and he could think of no more likely man for the purpose than Pierre himself. Vergennes was not lacking in the sentiment of gratitude, and he was prepared to do his best for the author of such an ingenious scheme.

Nevertheless, since it was his habit to move warily, he replied, "You are always in such a hurry, my dear fellow. I'm not unwilling to help you, but is speed so essential? Does it have to be done at once?"

"Yes! Yes! Yes!" cried Pierre. "It must be done at once! I am apprehensive," he continued, amiably but with veiled insolence, "lest my efforts should be less whole-hearted than would otherwise be the case. So long as I am subject to this disability there is a danger that the Americans may receive less guns and munitions than we had expected."

Count Vergennes was not the man to be intimidated by such a thinly disguised threat, but he was impressed by the resolute, even grim, expression on Pierre's face. For the first time he saw Pierre without that slight aura of absurdity which had concealed the deep wound inflicted by the wrong he had suffered, and he realized the courage that had been needed to laugh away the injustice for three years with a witty *mot*. So, without taking the remark amiss, he said, "Very well! I will have a talk with my colleague at the Ministry of Justice." And he concluded with a smile, "The Americans shall have their cannon and their muskets."

Pierre thanked him profusely, but this time he wanted to make quite sure that things would begin to move. "You have so many affairs of State to occupy your mind, Count Vergennes," he suggested, "that it would be presumptuous of me to expect that you should assume an extra burden of work on my behalf. The Government has hitherto made use of my services in a number of different capacities, and this has encouraged me to usurp on this fleeting occasion the functions of your secretary. I have been so venturesome as to draft a letter for you to the Advocate-General." With a smile at once brazen and charming he handed the document to the Minister. It ran as follows:

"The urgent requirements of the King's business necessitate the undertaking by Monsieur de Beaumarchais in the near future of a number of lengthy journeys. He is reluctant to proceed on these before a decision has been come to with regard to the reconsideration of the verdict delivered at his trial. If, therefore, you would be so good as to take the requisite steps in this matter, you would place me under a deep obligation. Believe me, etc. . . ."

"All you have to do is to append your signature, *Monsieur le Ministre*," said Pierre roguishly.

The Minister debated within himself whether he should order this insolent fellow from the room. Deciding not to do so, he replied with a laugh, "You are even more impudent than the characters in your comedies," and with that he signed his name.

"I knew that you would understand and sympathize with my position," said Pierre with sincere gratitude, and he picked up the letter to see to its immediate delivery.

He was looking forward to spreading the news of this fresh success.

Thérèse in particular, who so passionately shared his concern for the restoration of his good name, would be even more pleased than he was himself, and it was a happy coincidence that he had just received a note from her asking him to come out and see her at Meudon as soon as he could get away.

Thérèse had moved into the house that he had presented to her, and the changes she had made were different from what he had contemplated. He had left the reconstruction and furnishing to her own discretion, and to his astonishment she had planned everything as simply as possible. When he first saw the house in its refurbished condition he had had difficulty in concealing his annoyance, and for a moment the thought flashed through his mind that perhaps it was just as well they did not live together. Today, however, he was filled to bursting with the news he had to impart, and he was glad that she had asked him to come out to Meudon. He set out without delay and the horses could not carry him fast enough. When the house came in sight he found that it was really not so bad as he had thought. Simplicity was, after all, very much in the fashion nowadays, and Thérèse, with her usual good taste, had chosen for herself the proper setting.

As she came to meet him he noticed at once that there was something different about her. Though she appeared to be in good spirits, she welcomed him with an unaccustomed air of embarrassment, and scarcely had they entered the house when she said, "I have something to tell you, Pierre." Her normal self-assurance seemed to have left her and she could not find the right words. She smiled, stammered, broke off again, yet was obviously joyful.

Pierre could not grasp what it was all about, but gradually a light dawned on him and his joy too knew no bounds. Thérèse was going to have a child, his child! There had been no children of his first marriage, and those of the second had died. He probably had a son or a daughter growing up somewhere in Spain, but the mother had parted from him in anger and he had never been able to discover what had happened to them. Now he was going to have a child by Thérèse, and nothing could be more wonderful! By a happy chance she had told him about it just when he had succeeded in persuading the Minister to put through his appeal. And that reminded him. Thérèse did not yet know about his interview with Vergennes. He poured the story into her ear and her excitement was kindled by his own. A pink flush suffused her cheeks, and her lips parted slightly in a smile of happiness, as she murmured, "This is a great day for us, Pierre." Her voice was very low, but it sounded deeper and more resonant than was its wont.

Now that there was somebody who shared his pride and satisfaction, Pierre's feeling of blissful fulfilment was complete. Yes, Thérèse really understood him. She was the woman destined to stand beside him. The two of them belonged to one another, now more than ever.

"Yes," he said, repeating her words, "this is indeed a great day for us." There was a passionate warmth in his voice as he added, "And now we are going to get married, Thérèse. I won't listen to any further objection." Hardly had the words left his lips, however, when he was again beset by a feeling of uneasiness about the house. "As soon as my appeal has been heard," he concluded, "we shall get married."

Her large grey eyes beneath their arched brows grew a shade darker as she pondered on his words. "As you think best, Pierre," she said softly and a little uncertainly. "How long is it likely to be before you know the result?" she asked.

"It should not take long," he replied. "Perhaps two or three months."

That was true. But it could also take much longer if the courts wanted to drag the case out, and he felt a slight regret at having put off the date of his marriage to Thérèse. However, the thing was done and she seemed content. They did not resume the subject, but began to discuss possible names for the child. They agreed eventually that if it was a boy it should be called Alexandre, and if it was a girl they would christen it Eugénie. "The first of my ships to sail for America," declared Pierre boisterously, "shall receive the name of Alexandre. The second shall be the Eugénie. That will provide for either eventuality."

☆   ☆   ☆

At the Château d'Etioles, the estate of Monsieur Lenormant, they were celebrating his sixty-first birthday. Monsieur Lenormant's parties were famous, and nobody ever refused an invitation.

The beautiful park, laid out in the English style, formed an ideal setting for these occasions. The sky was cloudless and a slight breeze cooled the air. The ladies mostly wore gaily coloured costumes with large hats. There were marquees scattered about, and table-cloths were spread on the lawns where the guests could sit at their ease to eat, drink, or play childish games. For those who preferred more exciting entertainment than blind man's buff or *criquet,* there were card-tables both indoors and in the open air.

As the day grew cooler the great park became crowded with people, and there was much whispering and pointing out of the numerous ladies and gentlemen of the court who had accepted the host's invitation. There were the Duc d'Ayen, the Count and Countess de Noailles, the young Duc de la Rochefoucauld, and Madame de Maurepas, the wife of the First Minister. Désirée Mesnard attracted considerable attention. The rehearsals of *Georges Dandin* did not allow her much leisure for social amusements, but Monsieur Lenormant, perhaps because of the role she was playing, had begged her to make a point of coming. As she strolled across the lawns, dainty, red-haired, with a slightly impertinent air of self-assurance, she was escorted by a throng of male admirers.

Madame de Maurepas was accompanied, as she so frequently was, by her closest friend, the Countess de Montbarrey. They were both sitting on the terrace sipping iced lemonade and exchanging malicious comments about the other guests. Madame de Maurepas, glancing at Désirée, murmured, "That little caterpillar is looking very thin, in spite of the fact that she is nibbling at such a juicy leaf."

There were many young people present. Paul Theveneau strolled about, looking flushed and animated. With the realization of a mortally sick man that his time was short, he always craved company and friendship, affection and stimulus. The presence of so many pretty young women in their gay costumes enlivened him. He could not really complain about his lack of success with women, but when one of them refused to take any notice of him in spite of his efforts to make himself pleasing to her, he at once became discouraged and fell into a fit of depression. Perhaps his shyness sprang from the consciousness of his physical defects, though he was not unaware that his clever features and the passion that could light up his eyes were sufficiently attractive to make a woman forget the frailty of his body.

On a bench near by he caught sight of a tall girl sitting alone. Her eyes were vivacious, with long lashes and arched brows, her chin was firm and round, her shoulders and breasts gleamed with a faintly brownish tinge above her expensive, but very simple, mauve frock. He had often met Thérèse, but today she looked different. It seemed to him as if he were seeing her for the first time. Pierre really was a man on whom fortune smiled. His life was one unbroken stream of breathtaking adventures and the current only grew broader and louder, while he, Paul, had but a brief time left on earth, and what had life yielded him? Pierre probably did not even realize how lucky he was. He took what came his way as if it were only his due.

Thérèse smiled at Paul as he walked towards her. This boyish, eager young man, who was so obviously in love, appealed to her. She knew how ill he was and was filled with sympathy. He was always loud in praise of Pierre and she appreciated his devotion. Moving a little aside to make room for him on the bench, she invited him to sit beside her and they spoke of Pierre's great new venture. He explained to her the temptations and dangers implicit in its vast scope, and though she was not very interested in the business details it warmed her heart to recall that Pierre had always spoken to her of its political repercussions, but never of the personal risk to which he was exposed. Both she and Paul were surprised that Pierre had not yet put in an appearance. He was the life and soul of Monsieur Lenormant's famous parties, and everybody missed him when he was not there.

At last Pierre arrived. Embracing Charlot, he begged his pardon for being so late. He had been on the point of leaving his house when the courier appeared with the mail from overseas and he had not been able to resist the temptation to open it at once. It had been well worth while, went on Pierre mysteriously, his face radiant. News of the highest importance had come from America, and he asked his host's permission to communicate this news forthwith both to him and to the assembled guests.

He took his stand on a small hillock under an old maple tree, while the guests gathered round him curiously. Then, surrounded by the expectant ladies and gentlemen of Paris and Versailles in their gay costumes, and after waiting until the hubbub had died down to a murmur and the murmur had faded into a deep silence, he made the following announcement:

"Ladies and gentlemen! A document has just reached me which was approved unanimously by the Congress of the United Colonies of America, or rather the Congress of the United States of America, and promulgated at the beginning of July. I have here the English text of this declaration. Permit me to read you a translation of it." And he read the document aloud, translating as he went:

"When in the course of human events it becomes necessary for one people to dissolve the political bands which have connected them with another, and to assume among the powers of the earth the separate and equal station to which the laws of nature and of nature's God entitle them, a decent respect to the opinions of mankind requires that they should declare the causes which impel them to the separation. We hold these truths to be self-evident, that all men are created equal, that they are endowed by their Creator with certain unalienable rights, that among these are life, liberty and the pursuit of happiness. That to secure these rights, governments are instituted among men, deriving their just powers from the consent of the governed, that whenever any form of government becomes destructive of these ends, it is the right of the people to alter or to abolish it, and to institute new government, laying its foundation on such principles and organizing its powers in such form, as to them shall seem most likely to effect their safety and happiness."

Pierre was stirred to renewed enthusiasm as he read out the resounding phrases, and his emotion was transferred to his audience. As he stood there on a slight elevation under the spreading branches of the old maple, a sea of excited faces gazed up at him. One of Lenormant's dogs, a large black-and-white-flecked great Dane, had come into the park, and Pierre stroked its head with one hand while he held his manuscript in the other. He made no attempt at oratorical effect, and at times his voice grew hoarse with excitement. When he got stuck in his extempore translation he did not hestitate to break off a sentence and begin again, and this made it seem as if he were making an original speech on the spur of the moment.

"Prudence, indeed, will dictate that governments long established should not be changed for light and transient causes," he read slowly, "and accordingly all experience hath shewn that mankind are more disposed to suffer while evils are sufferable, than to right themselves by abolishing the forms to which they are accustomed. But when a long train of abuses and usurpations, pursuing invariably the same object evinces a design to reduce them under absolute despotism, it is their right, it is their duty, to throw off such government, and to provide new guards for their future security. Such has been the patient sufferance of these colonies; and such is now the necessity which constrains them to alter their former systems of government."

What Pierre was reading was not new to his hearers. The ideas were familiar to them from the writings of Montesquieu, Helvétius, Voltaire, and Rousseau; but whereas these ideas had hitherto appeared to them in the guise of a play of wit or an intellectual exercise, they had now suddenly become transformed into deeds, into a political reality. They were no longer something they had read in books or heard on the lips of philosophers, but were being proclaimed as the maxims of men who were setting out to establish a new form of state.

The deep silence remained unbroken. Even the lackeys, who had been directed to continue serving refreshments, stood stiffly on the grass verges of the park holding the full plates in their hands and listened with necks craned forward. It was so still on that crowded lawn that one could hear the twittering of the birds and the murmur of the breeze. They were all gazing up at Pierre, most of them with admiration, some wrathfully as if he himself were the author of the declaration, but all in a state of tension. Many of them were aware that he had entered into business relations with the revolting colonies, and not a few had found in this a cause for mirth. But now nobody was smiling. They all realized that this Pierre Caron de Beaumarchais was engaged in a task that might change the course of history, that he represented France's participation in the great movement that had been started by the men of the New World, and that he was reading a document that held deep meaning for him:

"The history of the present King of Great Britain is a history of repeated injuries and usurpations, all having in direct object the establishment of an absolute tyranny over these states. To prove this,

let facts be submitted to a candid world. He has refused his assent
to laws, the most wholesome and necessary for the public good."

Paul Theveneau's large shining eyes were fixed on his friend and
master. He stood in a slack attitude, his head stretched forward from
his sloping shoulders, eagerly drinking in the words as Pierre read
out the charges levelled by the Congress of the United States against
the King of England. He forgot the women round about him, he forgot the malady that was eating away his life, he heard only the sonorous ring of the proclamation, the deposition of an unworthy King and
the establishment of liberty. America, war in a just cause, arms for
America, the great mission—these thoughts filled his brain, together
with the awareness that his friend had been chosen and that he himself was called.

Even Madame de Maurepas was listening with strained attention.
When Pierre first began to speak she had whispered some joking remark to her friend, Countess de Montbarrey. The young Duc de la
Rochefoucauld hissed in her ear, "Please, Madame, do not interrupt."
This was something that had never happened to her in her life before
and, more in astonishment than annoyance, she had broken off in the
middle of a sentence.

Someone had spread a rug for Thérèse on a grassy mound and she
sat gazing up at her lover, her whole being absorbed in the words that
fell from his lips. She loved him more deeply than ever as she watched
his face glowing with excitement. He had tried to conceal from her the
danger he was running, for it was the cause which interested him
most, the noble cause of civic liberty. The declaration, and the way he
was reading it, reminded her of the brochures which had first attracted
her to him, at the time when he was fighting not only on his own
behalf, but in order to obtain justice for all, when he was defending
the commoners of the world against the privilege of aristocracy. His
voice took on an added note of solemnity as he read the enumeration
of the Americans' grievances against the British Crown:

"He has dissolved representative houses repeatedly, for opposing
with manly firmness his invasions on the rights of the people. He has
erected a multitude of new offices, and sent hither swarms of officers
to harass our people, and eat out their substance. He has kept among
us, in times of peace, standing armies without the consent of our
legislatures."

The actor Préville of the *Théâtre français* listened with his strong,
expressive face frozen into a mask. He was powerfully stirred by the
words of the declaration, yet at the same time he was furious at this
Caron de Beaumarchais who always managed to steal the best part of

someone else's thunder. Not only did people credit him with the chief
share in the success that had been achieved by *The Barber of Seville,*
though he was merely the author, while it was the actors, and in particular the player of the principal role, Figaro-Préville, who had
carried off the laurels, but here he was actually purloining the comparatively trifling kudos that was to be derived from Monsieur Lenormant's party. For weeks past the actors had been rehearsing a little
farce to be performed after supper; for years they had been studying
the arts of enunciation and rhetoric, and now there came this dilettante
who stood under a tree, scratched a dog's head, read from a sheet of
paper in an amateurish way without having made any effort at preparation and was continually getting entangled in what he was saying
—and at the end he would reap all the applause.

Old Caron stood proudly erect, gazing enraptured at his son. When
he had last attended divine service in a Huguenot church, the priest
to whose sermon he had listened had appeared to him as the supreme
symbol of a just and vengeful wrath. Here was an even more powerful
monument of righteous indignation. The memory of the priest dissolved in his mind before the picture of the man standing under an old
maple tree, launching thunderbolts against the English tyrant, and
ringing the bells of freedom. Pierre continued his reading of the inventory of the misdeeds of the King of England:

"He has combined with others to subject us to a jurisdiction foreign to our constitution, and unacknowledged by our laws; giving his
assent to their acts of pretended legislation: For quartering large
bodies of armed troops among us, for cutting off our trade with all
parts of the world, for imposing taxes on us without our consent,
for transporting us beyond seas to be tried for pretended offences,
for suspending our own legislatures, and declaring themselves invested with power to legislate for us in all cases whatsoever. He has
abdicated government here, by declaring us out of his protection and
waging war against us."

Among those who were staring up at Pierre as he read the American colonists' Declaration of Independence was a portly gentleman,
dressed in bourgeois garments of rather foreign cut, with a flowered
satin waistcoat stretched across his capacious stomach. It was Mr.
Silas Deane, the envoy of the United Colonies of America. He listened carefully, he noted the excitement of the crowd, he realized that
it had something to do with America, but he was ignorant of the
French language and he did not understand a single word. Among all
those hundreds he was the only one who did not know that he had
ceased to be the representative of the United Colonies and had become
the representative of the United States.

Some distance away, at the back of the throng, stood Doctor Dubourg, who had deliberately taken up a position where he would not be conspicuous. He had wondered what that empty-headed poseur, Pierre Caron, would have to say that could impress such an audience. When it became clear that Pierre had something of the very greatest importance to say, Doctor Dubourg was for a moment mortified that it was not he who had been the one to communicate this pregnant news to the select company of Monsieur Lenormant's guests. Pierre, of course, could afford the luxury of a special courier from Le Havre, while he would probably not hear about it from his agents for another twenty-four hours. Dubourg soon forgot his animosity against Pierre Caron, however, so deeply moved was he by the noble terms of the declaration, and in his mind's eye he conjured up a picture of his great friend, Doctor Benjamin Franklin. So Franklin had cast the die! He had taken the decisive step! Dubourg mentally translated the spirited manifesto back into the measured, impressive English of his esteemed friend:

"He has plundered our seas, ravaged our coasts, burnt our towns, and destroyed the lives of our people. He is at this time transporting large armies of foreign mercenaries to complete the works of death, desolation and tyranny, already begun with circumstances of cruelty and perfidy scarcely paralleled in the most barbarous ages. He has excited domestic insurrections amongst us, and has endeavoured to bring on the inhabitants of our frontiers, the merciless Indian savages, whose known rule of warfare, is an undistinguished destruction of all ages, sexes and conditions. In every stage of these oppressions we have petitioned for redress in the most humble terms; our repeated petitions have been answered only by repeated injury. A prince whose character is thus marked by every act which may define a tyrant, is unfit to be the ruler of a free people. Nor have we been wanting in attentions to our British brethren. We have warned them from time to time of attempts by their legislature to extend an unwarrantable jurisdiction over us. We must, therefore, acquiesce in the necessity, which denounces our separation, and hold them, as we hold the rest of mankind, enemies in war, in peace friends."

Désirée sat bent forward on a footstool, her cheek supported on her hand, her brows knitted in thought. She listened to the reading of the document as if it were the big scene from a play of a new and exciting kind. It was strange that she should first hear these simple, dignified phrases, which were no doubt destined to be repeated many times and for centuries to come, from the lips of the elegant, witty, and light-hearted Pierre. He glanced across at Lenormant. The latter had a brooding expression on his face, a slightly vacant look such as one sees in the eye of people who are listening to music. It was not possible to read his thoughts. Perhaps he was tracing in his mind the possible repercussions of this declaration of human rights on the venture which he and Pierre had in common.

Désirée turned her eyes toward Pierre. He obviously had forgotten that the great manifesto closely concerned the business on which he was engaged. She could see that he was not employing any rhetorical arts or any pose, that every word he spoke came from his very depth, as he stood erect, his voice thundering to the tense and silent crowd the resounding peroration of the great document:

"We, therefore, the representatives of the united States of America, in General Congress assembled, appealing to the Supreme Judge of the world for the rectitude of our intentions do, in the name, and by authority of the good people of these colonies, solemnly publish and declare, That these United Colonies are, and of right ought to be, free and independent states; that they are absolved from all allegiance to the British Crown, and that all political connection between them and the state of Great Britain, is and ought to be totally dissolved. And for the support of this Declaration, with a firm reliance on the protection of divine Providence, we mutually pledge to each other our lives, our fortunes and our sacred honour."

For almost a full minute after he had concluded there was not a sound to be heard from the elegantly dressed ladies and gentlemen of Paris and Versailles. Then they clapped their hands in tempestuous applause, rushed forward to embrace him, and poured out a flood of incoherent congratulation. Their enthusiasm was as spontaneous as if they had been listening to something in which they themselves were immediately concerned, instead of its having happened some weeks ago and several thousand miles away. One would have thought that they themselves were the authors of the manifesto and Pierre their spokesman.

There were, it is true, a few who felt that such excitement was hardly becoming and should not be allowed to continue too long. Madame de Maurepas, for instance, remarked to her friend, the Countess de Montbarrey, "There is nobody who has such a talent for spicing his business transactions with the flavour of adventure as our Toutou." She was in the habit of calling Pierre her "Toutou."

Nor did the host whose birthday was being celebrated, Monsieur Lenormant, share in the general joy. His face had lost its look of brooding absorption, and when he was asked whether he did not find the insurgents' declaration an admirable piece of work he courteously nodded his head in assent, but in his heart of hearts he was by no means pleased with the tone of the declaration. He was progressive;

minded, he sympathized with their cause, and was only too glad to see the English brought down a peg. Yet as a convinced adherent of the authoritarian monarchy in France he believed that an enlightened despotism was the best form of government and feared that if the rebels should win too clear-cut a victory the flames of revolt and anarchy might be kindled in France too. The happenings in Philadelphia were, of course, to be welcomed, but Monsieur Lenormant was no friend of exalted rhetoric; he thought that any display of feeling should be a purely personal matter, and that injustice could best be countered in public by a mask of irony. These worthy people of the West had their qualities, but good taste was not one of them, so much was certain, and Pierre might have found something better to do than recite this emotional declaration of theirs with such rhetorical embroidery. Monsieur Lenormant was a little upset at his birthday party's being spoilt by the introduction of a false note.

He went up to Pierre, who was still surrounded by a throng of guests. The great dog had not left his side, but continued to nestle against him to have its head scratched. Pierre was fond of dogs and knew how to get on with them. His own bitch Caprice wore a collar with the inscription, "My name is Caprice and Pierre de Beaumarchais belongs to me. We live in the rue de Condé." Lenormant smiled in the almost imperceptible way that was peculiar to him and said, "That was a vigorous pronouncement you have just read, my dear friend. The rebels certainly have put everything to the hazard, both their lives and their fortunes. That required courage. It was a brave thing to do." He pressed Pierre's hand—whether in congratulation or in sympathy was not quite clear—and moved away.

☆   ☆   ☆

During the following weeks Mr. Silas Deane maneuvered his corpulent and dignified person through the unaccustomed maze of Paris as the busy envoy of the United States of America. He was consulted by Pierre, he negotiated with shipowners, interviewed contractors, and felt that he was being helpful. Pierre introduced him to various influential gentlemen who had expressed their sympathy with his compatriots, including the Count de Broglie, a Marshal of France, who besides being a member of one of the oldest families of the French nobility was enormously rich. The Marshal, whose military exploits had carried his reputation far beyond the shores of France, made a deep impression on the merchant from Connecticut. He had been prepared, if the Americans should invite him, to accept an appointment as "Governor-General" and assume control both of the political administration and of the Army. With this in view he had sent his own emissary to America, a certain Colonel de Kalb who had

saved his life at the Battle of Rossbach and was now his friend and
confidential agent, for the purpose of entering into contact with the
insurgents. Colonel de Kalb, an efficient soldier and a man of affairs,
had brought back a mass of useful information, though he also had to
report that for the time being the Americans were reluctant to issue
the invitation which the Marshal had indicated his readiness to accept.
This, however, did not diminish the warmth of de Broglie's sympathy
for their cause.

Silas Deane had been instructed to recruit a number of capable officers, especially gunners and engineers, for the American Army, and
he told the Marshal about this. Colonel de Kalb was quite willing to
throw in his lot with the Americans. Since he was not of aristocratic
birth, even the "de" being of dubious authenticity, there could be no
question of his receiving further promotion in the French Army. He
would not even have reached the rank of colonel had it not been for
the Marshal's influence. Silas Deane was pleased and proud to offer
this seasoned soldier, in the name of the Congress, a commission as
Major-General in the American service, and de Kalb introduced him
to other officers who were prepared to follow his example. These were
mostly younger men, and the gratified envoy engaged them *en bloc* at
a rank in each case one step higher than the rank they had held in the
French Army.

When, however, it came to giving them an advance of pay and providing for their preliminary equipment and transport overseas, he
was faced with difficulties. The Congress had placed only a trifling
sum of money at his disposal, promising that he should receive further funds from the sale of prizes brought into French harbours by
American sea captains. There had been no prizes, and Silas Deane's
resources were nearly exhausted. He was unable to meet the bills that
were falling due, the shipowners, contractors, and army officers were
having to wait for their money, and he wrote letter after letter to the
Congress urging that goods and money should be dispatched forthwith in settlement of the claims of Monsieur de Beaumarchais as well
as funds to cover his own needs. The Congress remained silent or returned noncommittal replies.

Silas Deane was a patriot and devoted to the cause of liberty. To
serve this cause he had abandoned his flourishing business in Connecticut and was proud to be the representative of the United States.
He was a man of good sense and understood the ways of the world.
He knew that the Congress had to find money for its immediate and
most pressing requirements, that the money was not there, and that
the war was not going well. However embarrassing the position in
which he found himself, he realized that there was good reason why
the leaders of the nation ignored the pleas of their distant envoy in
Paris.

What he did not know, on the other hand, was that Congress was being confirmed and strengthened in its negative attitude by the advice of that Mr. Arthur Lee whose acquaintance Pierre had made in London. Already wounded in his vanity by the failure of Monsieur de Beaumarchais to procure him the promised audience at Versailles, he was doubly offended when the Congress omitted to offer him the appointment of plenipotentiary in Paris. Of naturally suspicious temperament, he persuaded himself that the firm of Hortalez was a pretence, a mere façade, and he had no scruples in communicating his opinion to his influential brothers in Philadelphia. The supplies that were being sent by the firm of Hortalez, so he wrote, were a gift from the King of France to the United States. If Monsieur de Beaumarchais and Mr. Silas Deane declared otherwise, this could be due only to their desire to extract illicit profits from the transaction. The Congress read these letters, the Congress had no money, the Congress thought itself justified in believing the reports of its London agent and in turning a deaf ear to the ever more urgent representations of its envoy in Paris.

When Silas Deane finally reached the end of his resources and was unable even to meet the cost of his lodgings at the Hôtel d'Hambourg, there was nothing left but to explain his situation to the obliging Monsieur de Beaumarchais. Sweating with embarrassment under the flowered waistcoat that covered his capacious paunch, he unfolded the story of his difficulties. Pierre was taken aback. If the gentlemen in Philadelphia could not even place at the disposal of their accredited representative the few hundred dollars he needed on which to live, what was going to happen when they were asked to pay the millions that would be owing to the firm of Hortalez? He recalled the imperceptible smile on the face of Charlot, the way in which he had said, in that oily voice of his, "The rebels certainly have put everything to the hazard, both their lives and their fortunes," but his expression revealed nothing of the worries that had again begun to assail him. With a sympathetic smile he replied that the firm of Hortalez would be glad to advance Mr. Deane whatever sum he might require.

Mr. Deane's broad features lit up. What a stroke of luck it was that he should have found a man like Monsieur de Beaumarchais in Paris, who seemed to conjure up munitions for America with a stamp of his foot, who spoke English, and who was prepared to wait patiently until such time as the Congress could pay for the goods that had been delivered! He even supplied funds for one's personal expenses in case of emergency!

For two or three weeks Silas Deane was safe. But what was going to happen after that?

The next mail from America brought comfort. The Congress, it is true, did not dispatch any further funds, but it announced the appointment of a second representative in Paris, namely, Doctor Benjamin Franklin. If this world-famous figure should take over the conduct of affairs, then Silas Deane's troubles would be over. Though it would be some months before Franklin arrived in Paris, it was some consolation to Mr. Deane to know that a time limit had been set to his difficulties.

☆   ☆   ☆

For all his vanity and tendency to light-hearted speculation Pierre was a hard worker and brilliant organizer. The storehouses of the firm of Hortalez were soon crammed to overflowing with munitions, uniforms, and equipment of all kinds; transports were waiting to be loaded at the ports of Le Havre, Cherbourg, Brest, Nantes, Bordeaux, and Marseilles; captains and crews had been hired to steer the ships across the Atlantic. The firm had its own agents in all the larger French seaport towns, the most important of these being Messrs. Emmery, Vaillant, and d'Ostalis in the north and Messrs. Chassefierre and Peyroux in the south. Some of these agents were reliable but of inferior capacity, others were efficient but not reliable, and the time had come for Pierre to see how things were getting on there.

The activities of the firm of Hortalez were being closely watched, however, by the British secret service, and Monsieur de Gérard, the First Secretary at the Foreign Office, was continually impressing on Pierre the necessity for the strictest discretion. The northern harbours in particular were swarming with spies. Pierre therefore sent Paul Theveneau to the north, while he himself, accompanied by his friend Philippe Gudin, set off incognito for the south on a "study and pleasure trip" as Monsieur Durand. He was fond of travelling, a keen observer of foreign scenes, and eager to enjoy the experience of new cities and new friends. The contemplative, easy-going, and pleasure-loving Gudin was an ideal companion for a journey of this kind. Deeply devoted to Pierre, bearing no rancour when he was kept in the dark about the latter's intricate business affairs, he was always at hand when his services were needed, and kept out of the way when he felt that his presence would only be a disturbing factor. His undisguised pleasure in food and drink helped to stimulate his friend's similar tastes, he possessed a sense of humour, and he was always ready to take part in any fun that was going. Moreover he had an unlimited fund of useful knowledge that was at Pierre's disposal whenever he should require it.

The two friends travelled up and down the southern provinces of France, enjoyed the sight of the rich countryside that was spread out before them in the fullness of late autumn, stayed comfortably at the best inns, and took their pleasure of the wine and the women. Nor did they ignore what history had to offer. Philippe Gudin was an enthusiastic antiquarian, the architecture of the past was a living thing to him, and he was able in imagination to reconstruct the ancient ruins through which they wandered and to people them with their former occupants. Pierre was receptive to these memories of a bygone age and liked to adorn Philippe's accounts with his own fanciful wit, whereupon his companion would mournfully comment, "What a pity, Pierre, that you never studied! You would have become a scholar of the first order. What a genius our French classical tragedy has lost in you!"

Pierre's invariable answer was, "Oh, leave me in peace, Philippe. I prefer things as they are." He shared his friend's view that he had it in him to become a tragic poet of the calibre of Corneille or Racine, and that had circumstances been different he might have reached such heights, whereas at the most he would now be looked upon by posterity as another Molière; yet at bottom he was grateful for the fate which had ordained for him the role he was playing in the world. It was his belief that with the privileges of birth the privileges of intellect, too, were beginning to decline before the dawn of the new privilege of wealth. He himself possessed all three. Intellect had been bestowed upon him in the cradle. Wealth and the title of nobility had been won by his own efforts.

At times he would leave his companion for hours, and even days, on end while he attended to his business affairs, and Gudin would occupy his solitude with studying and writing. Gudin compared himself to a shadow that hovered round graves and ruins, conjuring up the spirits of the dead for the instruction of future generations, while his great friend visited shipyards and docks for the benefit of his fellow men, providing work for thousands of busy hands and directing the purposeful thinking of a thousand minds. Pierre was a Viking, a monarch of the seas, setting out on the conquest of new lands for his people.

When they were in the company of their new-found acquaintances, with Pierre's wit and high spirits exercising their usual fascination, Philippe Gudin was not always able to control his wagging tongue, but hinted that Monsieur Durand was really the celebrated Monsieur de Beaumarchais. When they asked Pierre whether this was so, he always denied it vigorously—in such a way that everyone realized it must be true.

It was thus that Pierre, during a sojourn at Bordeaux, allowed himself to be inveigled into an affair that caused him much amusement at the time, but was later to give rise to vexatious repercussions. In the yards of Testard and Gaschet he was having a large ship entirely reconstructed from stem to stern and this occasioned the necessity for frequent visits to the offices of the firm, though Monsieur Gaschet himself was the only one who was aware of his identity. A new theatre had recently been erected in Bordeaux, and for the opening performance the management had selected *The Barber of Seville,* which was now in active rehearsal. Pierre passed the theatre a number of times every day, and it was almost more than he could do to resist the temptation of going inside and saying to the actors, "I'm the one. I'm Beaumarchais." However, he succeeded in controlling the impulse and even warned the loquacious Gudin that his incognito must be preserved at all costs. Philippe nodded with the air of a conspirator and replied, "You can rely on me."

One evening, when they were seated at the inn, someone at the next table declared that Pierre's face seemed familiar to him, and Gudin indulged in a broad grin that gave the game away. On the following morning the rumour was circulating everywhere that Monsieur de Beaumarchais was staying in the city for the dual purpose of helping in the liberation of America and attending the opening performance of his play. Before another day had passed Pierre was called upon by a deputation of actors with the request that he should give them the benefit of his personal advice during the rehearsals. He inquired with a polite smile what advice such experts of the stage could expect from a simple gentleman like Monsieur Durand. The actors returned his smile and replied that if Monsieur Durand insisted on remaining plain Monsieur Durand they would be the first to respect his wishes, but they would be infinitely grateful for his assistance at rehearsals. He acceded to their request, threw himself into his task, and offered useful suggestions which they were only too happy to follow. The opening night was a triumph, the actors pointed to Monsieur Durand who was sitting in a box, the audience gave him an ovation, and Pierre raised his hand in smiling protest as he exclaimed, "But, my friends, my name is Durand!"

Thoroughly pleased with himself he returned to Paris, where he was at once made to realize that the sweets of which he had drunk had bitter dregs. When he called upon the Count de Vergennes he was received not by the Minister, but by Monsieur de Gérard. Pierre did not like dealing with Monsieur de Gérard. The latter's attitude was always correct, but he displayed nothing of the humane philosophy and friendliness of Vergennes. On this occasion de Gérard's reception was particularly chilly.

"It will not be unknown to you, Monsieur," he began straightway after the preliminary greeting, "that Lord Stormont has several times called personally at the Foreign Office to protest against the dubious, or rather no longer dubious, activities of the firm of Hortalez and Company, and he has submitted documents in proof of his accusations. We pointed out to you from the outset, Monsieur, that we should be exposed to difficulties with England on your account and we impressed upon you the imperative necessity of refraining from any act of imprudence. We have now learnt that at Bordeaux, while work of a nature calculated to awaken suspicion was being carried out on two large ships, a certain Monsieur Durand was present at a performance of *The Barber of Seville* and that everyone was aware who this Monsieur Durand really was. What could have been in your mind, Monsieur, when you permitted yourself to behave with such indiscretion? Did it not occur to you that it is His Majesty's Government which has to answer for your conduct?"

Pierre, gnawing his lip with chagrin, replied that if the English had been led to take an interest in the activities of the firm of Hortalez, it could only have been because others, with less sense of responsibility, had babbled irresponsibly, and he mentioned the name of the honest and well-meaning, but pompous and loquacious, Barbeu Dubourg.

De Gérard refused to accept this excuse. "You will pardon me, Monsieur," he retorted sharply, "but I must beg you not to assume that we are more stupid than we really are. We are very well informed, both about you and about Doctor Dubourg, and we have had enough of your indiscretions. You must decide whether you are prepared in the future to consider yourself as acting on behalf of this Ministry, and to regulate your behaviour accordingly, or as a private individual who can allow himself to indulge in any caprice." It was with a feeling of impotent wrath that Pierre closed the door of de Gérard's office behind him.

There were difficulties not only in Paris, but also in the north, where Paul reported that though three ships were ready to leave, the English were employing every means at their disposal to detain them in port. They were submitting fresh protests daily to the Admiralty, and the French authorities, despite their willingness to close an eye, were forced to pretend that they were conducting a strict investigation. In these circumstances he could not risk leaving things to Emmery and Vaillant, but thought it better to remain in the north until the boats had sailed.

Pierre would have liked to go to Brest himself. He was sufficiently confident of his ingenuity and presence of mind to believe that if he were on the spot he would very soon succeed in foiling the machinations of the English and in seeing that his ships set sail, either with or without the formal permission of the port authorities. Also he was desperately anxious to watch his first transports putting out to sea. But he thought grimly of his interview with Monsieur de Gérard. It was unfortunately impossible for him to go personally to Brest.

In any case it was extraordinarily decent of Paul to stay in the north so long. Pierre well knew what a wrench it was for Paul to stay away from Paris, and that his passion for the wonderful city was enhanced by the ever-present realization that his time was short. He wanted to live his life to the full while life was still left to him.

Moreover, winter was approaching and a sojourn on the shores of the Atlantic could only endanger his health.

Pierre told Thérèse of the three ships laden with arms that were waiting to set sail from Brest and Le Havre. They were called *Alexandre, Eugénie,* and *Victoire.* More superstitious minds might have wondered whether any significance could be attached to the order in which they raised anchor. Thérèse asked about the possible effect of the sea air on Paul's weak chest.

"I am worried," replied Pierre, "and I have told him so, but he insists on staying and writes that it will not be long now."

A week later news was, in fact, received from Paul that he would be returning to Paris within a few days. The *Victoire* had already sailed, and unless unexpected contingencies should arise in the meantime the other two would also be at sea by the time the letter was in Pierre's hands.

Pierre sat at his great writing-table with this letter in front of him and smiled thoughtfully. He was gazing at the empty space on the opposite wall that was reserved for the portrait of which he had been so unjustly deprived. Yet he did not see the empty space. He saw only the ships, his ships, carrying to America the arms that he had procured, arms to be used in the fight for freedom and the establishment of a better world.

Chapter Two

FRANKLIN

❉ ★ ❉

THE OLD man stood on deck gazing at the shore. He was enveloped in a thick fur coat, for it was in the early days of December and very cold, and a fur cap was set upon his massive skull, from which sparse white locks hung down over his collar.

A strong wind was blowing, and even in the calm Bay of Quiberon the ship was dancing up and down. The old man, as he peered through his steel-rimmed spectacles, clung involuntarily to the railing with both hands.

It had not been a long voyage, the crossing to Europe having taken a bare five weeks, but it had been far from agreeable. Not that he had been troubled at all by the constant high winds, since old Benjamin Franklin never suffered from sea-sickness. The long sittings of the Congress had tired him out before he started on the voyage, he was in sad need of exercise, and the unpalatable food on board ship had still further lowered his vitality. Since the fresh poultry was too tough for his teeth he had had to live chiefly on salt beef and sea-biscuits, with the result that he was suffering from a mild attack of scurvy. He was worried by thick dandruff on his scalp and a rash on other parts of his body, but worst of all had been the continuous menace that was never far from his thoughts. In the presence of his two grandsons, the seventeen-year-old William and the six-year-old Benjamin, he had shown no trace of apprehension. Day after day he had measured the temperature of the water and the atmosphere, pursued his study of the Gulf Stream, and worked methodically with the boys in an effort to improve both his and their knowledge of the French language. Behind his pretence at equanimity, however, there always lurked the uneasy feeling that they might be overtaken by an English warship. If that should happen his life would hardly be worth a day's purchase.

Luckily everything had gone well, very well in fact, since the *Reprisal,* during the latter part of the voyage, had succeeded in capturing two small enemy merchantmen, one with a cargo of wine and timber, the other carrying linseed and alcohol. Now the coast was in sight and all danger was past. Franklin stood at the railing feeling a little weak in the legs, particularly at the knees, and there in front of him stretched the shores of France, the land he had come to win over to the American cause.

The captain of the ship, Lambert Wickes, a cheerful, boisterous fellow, stepped up to him and shouted in order to make his voice heard above the wind, "How are you today, Doctor?"

"Thank you," replied Franklin, "as well as ever."

"I fear," the captain roared back, "that we shan't be able to manage it today." They had intended to sail up the estuary of the Loire as far as Nantes.

Franklin searched up and down the coast that lay ahead. "What is the name of this place?" he inquired.

"Auray," replied the captain.

"I want you to put me ashore here, if that is possible," Franklin said with an air of decision.

"Certainly, Doctor," responded Captain Wickes. "I will get everything ready. It will take a couple of hours in this wind." And he went off to make his preparations.

Franklin stayed on deck. The sight of the heaving sea and the breath of the wind on his cheeks did him good. In a few hours he would be on firm land again, the land where he was to spend the coming years, his last years no doubt, for he had reached the biblical age and in a month or two would be seventy-one. He did not feel old. This start on a new venture, his journey into uncertainty, demanded the whole of his energies and had the effect of rejuvenating him. As a statesman and a scientist his reputation was world-wide, yet fundamentally he was more or less where he had been when, at the age of seventeen, he ran away with hardly a penny in his pocket and dependent solely on his own resources and such experience as life had brought him. When he landed in France he would be almost as poor and destitute as when he had landed in England. His wife was dead, his only son had gone over to the English, to the camp of the enemy, and had been rightly branded as a traitor in the United States. He had handed over to the Congress, as a loan, all his available capital, and his financial situation for the few years that remained to him was bleak. Thus the best, the only, thing he possessed was the task ahead— that infinitely hard, necessary, and blessed task, of conquering France for the American cause.

While he was talking to Captain Wickes and trying to make up his mind whether or not to land at that spot, the expression on his face under the fur cap had been that of a crafty old man, with eyes that peered keenly, if not suspiciously, through their steel-rimmed spectacles, and lips pursed in a sly smile. Now that he was alone again he removed his spectacles and his fur cap and stood facing the wind. Though his expression hardly changed, he seemed to be a different man. The large thoughtful eyes were youthful and alert, the broad, high forehead, from which the wind blew back the sparse locks, gave him an imperious look, and his reddened countenance generally, with the deep furrows across the brow and at the side of the nose and the heavy, powerful jaw, was impressive with strength, experience, resolution, and pugnacity.

As he gazed at the land where his future lay, the great task before him seemed almost tangible, and he was ready, even eager, to meet it.

The two boys came up on deck and laughed excitedly as they staggered towards their grandfather, clinging to one another as the tossing of the ship flung them first to one side, then to the other. The smaller lad, Benjamin Franklin Bache, his daughter's son, was fresh-faced, with delicate blond down on his cheeks; and as for William Temple Franklin, the older boy, was it not delightful to look at him, thought the old man, as he held that large, straight nose of his into the wind with such an audacious air? And what a merry, vivacious red mouth he had above that firm chin! He had inherited his chin from his grandfather. Otherwise, unfortunately, he possessed many of his father's qualities. One must not allow the young rogue's good looks to delude one.

The boys were excited because they had learned from the sailors that there was no prospect of their reaching Nantes for some time and they were anxious to know whether they were going to be taken off in boats. They jumped for joy when the Doctor told them that they were, and ordered them to start packing at once. "Have you had my bath prepared?" he asked William.

William was dismayed at this, and admitted that he had forgotten all about it. He was very forgetful, though his attractiveness in other ways made it difficult to be angry with him, and he showed his remorse with such impetuosity that his grandfather refrained from rebuke.

Bathing aboard the swaying ship demanded something of an effort, and though the Doctor had contented himself with very little luggage, he had not sacrificed the bathtub which had been constructed for his special use. He laid great store by his hot bath, in which he liked to soak. The tub was made of very tough wood with a high back curved like a shell so that he could sit in it at his ease. It could also be closed over by means of a lid, leaving only the shoulders, neck, and head jutting out. In this way the water could not splash about, and anyone with whom the Doctor wished to converse during his lengthy bath was invited to seat himself comfortably on the lid.

Today the Doctor had only the company of his thoughts. His grandsons were busy packing, and he lay in his tub stretching his tired limbs enjoyably in the warm water and cautiously scratching his scurf as he allowed his thoughts to wander.

No, young William was not a very conscientious lad! Whenever he found anything more agreeable to occupy his mind he straightway forgot what he had been told to do. That could not be said of his father, however, traitor as he was. The latter, much as he liked the good things of life, was never forgetful of his career. He was a handsome fellow, the older William. He had not the slow, ponderous air of *his* father. He cut a much more elegant figure, and had winning ways. Young William had objected strongly to being taken away from his father and carried off to France with his granddad. But he, the old man, had taken immediate action. He had not hesitated for a single moment. The boy had to accompany him to Paris, to grow up in a healthy atmosphere, far away from his renegade father who had permitted himself to be seduced by the inducements and bribes of the Government in London and was now lying in Litchfield gaol as he deserved. But a watchful eye would have to be kept on young William! Though he had not inherited his father's calculating ruthlessness, there was a thoughtless surfeit of high spirits in the little rascal and he was fully aware that he could count on his grandfather's indulgence. "Yes, we Franklins are a high-spirited lot," mused the Doctor. "My son William was not born in wedlock, his son William was not born in wedlock, and it does not look as if young William will restrict himself to the siring of legitimate children in France in his time. They have inherited their temperament from me. My son and grandson have inherited many of their qualities from me, and it is odd how different we all are, all three of us, despite the things we have in common. It takes very little to change a man's nature from top to bottom."

The Doctor rang for more hot water. "Little Benjamin's parents are not much to speak of, either," he continued musing to himself. "His mother Sally is a decent, well-meaning woman, and I am very fond of her, she has plenty of sound common sense, but she isn't much to speak of. And that husband of hers, Richard Bache, is a worthy fellow, a very worthy fellow, but nothing more, nothing more at all. Of course, they didn't like my taking little Benjamin away from them, but there can be no possible doubt that he will be better brought up in France under my supervision than he could be in Philadelphia by Mr. and Mrs. Bache." In any case, he had duly recompensed his son-in-law by making him his deputy at the Ministry of Posts. He could not do much harm there and would be able to tackle the job all right. Of course his, old Benjamin's, enemies would set up a hullabaloo about any measure Richard might take or not take, but what did that matter? The Lord knew, he had sacrificed enough for America and the American cause! Nobody had the right to grudge him the use of his influence to help his relatives on a bit.

There were plenty of people in Philadelphia who welcomed an op-

portunity to vent their spleen on him. Even when he made his proposal that special envoys should be sent to France, these suspicious
fellows had kept on inventing new objections. The old deep-seated
hostility dating back to the French and Indian War had not yet
died out. Many of them still regarded the French as their hereditary
enemies, as worshippers of idols, as the serfs of an absolute monarchy,
as frivolous fops who were not to be trusted. It had cost him many
an effort to convert his colleagues in Philadelphia, but in the long run
they had realized that France was their natural ally in the war against
the King of England, and that without France's help they could not
win. Nevertheless it was with little expectation of success that they
had delegated him to represent them on this side of the Atlantic, and
it certainly had to be admitted that the prospect of establishing a
French alliance was practically hopeless. Well, be that as it may, this
was not the first hopeless mission on which he had been engaged, and
which he had yet managed to bring off. The Doctor stretched himself
in his bath, his lips pressed firmly together so that they formed a thin
line. He would succeed this time too!

The funds with which they had provided him were pitifully inadequate. The Congress was hard up, and he would find it difficult to live
in a way at all befitting his position. Three thousand dollars! That
was all he had to establish and maintain an agency as the representative of the United States. The *Reprisal* had a cargo of indigo aboard
that could be sold, and the proceeds would come in useful, but it was
not very sumptuous provision to make for the envoy from the New
World. He would have to live from hand to mouth.

He knew the value of money, and was not above exploiting to his
own advantage such opportunities as were available. Nor was he
particularly scrupulous in his choice of means when it came to lining
his pockets. But there were limits, and he knew what they were. The
English, for instance, had offered him bribes, offices, and titles if he
would exert his influence to bring about an understanding with the
colonies. The Doctor's brow darkened. There were people in Philadelphia who would not hesitate to entertain such an offer. His own
son William had been tempted and had fallen. But he himself knew
where the limits lay, and before he would agree to try and bring
about such an "understanding" he would put a rope round his old
neck.

His colleagues in Philadelphia would display little gratitude for
anything he might be able to do in Paris. Nowhere in the whole world
was old Benjamin Franklin viewed with such critical eyes as in Philadelphia. Not only were there numerous Tories there who hated him,
loyalists like the Shippens, the Stansburys, the Kearsleys, and the rest
of them, but he had enemies among the Republicans as well. Even in
the Congress he was disliked by the "aristocrats," and the resolution to

send him to Paris as their envoy was passed only after a lengthy
debate. The Doctor smiled, a grim, discerning smile, gentle and bitter.
There were some who thought that he could not represent them wor-
thily in Paris. It was true that, apart from General Washington, there
was no other American who enjoyed a world reputation, but he was
after all the son of a tallow-chandler, one could not get over the fact
that he had once been penniless, and he was only a Doctor *honoris
causa* who had never studied at a university.

No, he would receive little recognition from Philadelphia and not
much helpful advice, but there would be frequent urgent admonitions
to extract further assistance from the French Government and plenty
of wrathful reproaches for not having extracted more. He would not
allow himself to be vexed at this, however. He had grown older and
wiser, and he knew his fellow men.

They said of him in London that he had prevented a reconciliation
between the colonies and the King merely out of a sense of injured
pride, in order to revenge himself for those humiliating proceedings in
the Privy Council.

When he thought of those proceedings the old man's blood boiled,
despite his philosophic temper. Admitted that he had not behaved quite
correctly, as an official in the King's service, in publishing those letters
from the Governor which shed such a clear light on the Government's
intrigues and lack of good will. But the situation had been such that
the publication of the letters was justified, and any of the gentlemen
who took part in that session of the Privy Council would have acted
in the same way if he had been in his position. Yet because they were
able to charge him with having committed a formal act of impropriety,
they had treated him like a common scamp. He had been forced to sit
there for a whole hour listening to the savage denunciation of the
Solicitor-General, and how they had all smiled at one another, the
Prime Minister and the noble lords, how they had nodded and put
their heads together and stared at him as if he had perpetrated some
base and monstrous crime! He had been wearing his thick blue suit of
Manchester velvet, which was new at the time, and as he was sitting
next to the fire he had perspired even more than he would have done
anyway. But he hadn't let them see what a storm was raging inside
him. He did not twitch a muscle of his face or utter a word in reply.
It was best to keep silent in the presence of those hostile lords and
let the Solicitor-General abuse him to his heart's content, absurd and
impertinent as his accusations were. How the fellow had thundered
and thumped the table in front of him! It had been a disgusting spectacle, the most disagreeable experience of his whole life. He had been
sixty-eight at the time, with a world-wide reputation as a philosopher,
one of the leading men in his own country, and he had had to submit

to a dressing down as if he were a schoolboy who had stolen money from his father's till.

He had often declared that anger was a form of temporary insanity, and he had repeated this to himself as he sat there so impassively, but inwardly he was seething with fury, and of one thing he was quite certain. As he sweated by the fireside and listened to the insults that were being hurled at him by the Solicitor-General, a deep change came over him and he realized once for all that no reconciliation was or ever could be possible with these noble lords of the English King. For seventeen years he had visited the houses of these great gentlemen as a welcome guest, he had conversed with them on the most friendly terms, they had paid tribute to his learning, his scientific spirit, and his philosophy. And now they sat and grinned while that ranting lawyer bawled like a fishmonger and showered him with calumnies. Now they were showing themselves in their true light. They were glad of the opportunity to jeer at him. They scoffed at him because he was not one of themselves, because he was not an aristocrat, but a mere bourgeois, the son of a tallow-chandler, who had dared to stand up and speak on behalf of all those who did not belong to the privileged class.

That hour was deeply graven on his memory, and though his wrath had evaporated, the realization remained. Nor had he forgotten the anger which had seized him at the subsequent behaviour of his son. He had sent William an objective account of what happened and advised him to resign his post in the Government service. "You are aware now," he had written, "of the way in which I have been treated. I leave you to think the matter over and to draw your own conclusions." William had thought the matter over and he had drawn his conclusions. He had informed his friends in England that he in no wise shared his father's political views. Now William had the opportunity of revising his opinions in Litchfield gaol.

The water in the bath was beginning to cool. Should he ring again for more hot water? It was not really worth it. He would soon have to get ready to land. Two more minutes and he would reach for the towel.

There was no point in allowing one's anger to simmer. One had to take life as it came. Life was stupid, but wonderful, it was both good and bad, it was mad, but very, very pleasant. Human weaknesses must be accepted for what they were. They must be taken into account and exploited for the good cause. That was the way he had looked at things, and that was the way he would continue to look at them. He had never given up, even when the situation was at its worst. He had faith in his country, in the power of reason, and in the reality of progress. He knew what he could do, and he knew what he could not do, and he believed that he still had a contribution to make to human progress. He was an old man, a little tottery in spite of his robust appearance, and he was hampered by gout as well as this confounded scurf. To crown it all, his son was a dubious character, a reactionary opportunist. Yet he still felt the strength in himself to carry out the task for which he had undertaken this journey to France.

Slowly and cautiously the Doctor climbed out of his bathtub, emitting an occasional slight grunt that was partly the expression of his feeling of well-being, sat down dripping wet beside the coal brazier, which was protected by an iron fire-guard, and with his stout body bent forward proceeded methodically to dry himself.

Then, still stark naked, he walked across to the chest in which he kept his most important papers, including his credentials, the written instructions given him by the Congress, and other secret documents. He took from this chest a paper headed: "Proposals for a Treaty of Peace to be concluded between England and the United States, which the Right Honourable Dr. Benjamin Franklin is authorized to submit to the Government of His Majesty the King of England." Franklin had had this document drawn up as a safeguard in case he and his ship should be captured by an English man o' war, so that he would be protected in his quality of peace envoy. Otherwise there would probably have been a rope waiting for him. Now that they were in sight of the French coast he did not need the document any longer. On the contrary, it might even be dangerous to keep it after he had landed in France. He tore the bulky package, sheet by sheet, into tiny strips, threw the pieces into the brazier, and watched them burn.

☆   ☆   ☆

The little boat, with Benjamin Franklin, William Temple Franklin, and Benjamin Franklin Bache abroad, danced across the spurting white foam of the greenish-grey waves and reached the shore with some difficulty. Astonished and suspicious Breton villagers watched them land, but after involved negotiations a shabby coach was procured, a couple of ancient nags pulled wearily at the shafts, and they set off at a moderate trot followed by a farewell salvo from the *Reprisal's* guns.

At Nantes the Doctor took up his residence at the house of the commercial agent Gruet, who had dealings with the Congress. He was very tired and would have welcomed two or three days' rest, but there was little chance of this. Though the Congress had not made any public announcement of its appointment of envoys to France, and Franklin was careful not to reveal the fact that he had come in a political capacity, he was celebrated far and wide for his learning and the detachment of the American colonies from the English Crown was put down generally to his account. A stream of visitors came to call upon him, and from the questions with which they plied him he realized how abysmally ignorant they were about his country. He listened amiably to what they had to say, answered them in as few words as possible, and begged them to excuse his taciturnity on the ground that his French was so poor.

His host, Monsieur Gruet, on the other hand, was loquacious and thought it his duty to acquaint his guest with conditions in France. To his astonishment Franklin learned that American business affairs in Paris and Versailles were being conducted not, as he had assumed, by his friend and translator, Doctor Dubourg, but by a certain Roderigue Hortalez, alias Caron de Beaumarchais.

Franklin had, of course, heard of Beaumarchais and had even read one or two pamphlets written by him in connection with some lawsuit or other. He had found these rather too effervescent, too fluent and superficial, too rhetorical and lacking in wisdom. Monsieur de Beaumarchais, so it seemed to Franklin, was nothing but a sensational journalist, and he was disquieted to discover that this man was regarded in France as the most important and energetic upholder of the American cause.

The wealthy merchants of Nantes insisted on giving a great ball for the Doctor, and this caused him some embarrassment, for though he had brought a suit with him to be worn on ceremonial occasions, the thick blue one of Manchester velvet that had added so much to his discomfort during those humiliating proceedings in London, was carefully packed away in a trunk tied round with numerous cords and he had not intended to take it out until he got to Paris. He decided to wear his simple brown bourgeois coat.

The brown coat struck the citizens of Nantes as just the right garb for a frugal sage from the primitive West, and his appearance at the ball was a great success. His deliberate and affable manner formed an effective contrast to the agile gallantry and witty scepticism which local society had copied from the Parisian salons, and the ladies in particular were ravished by the grave air and old-fashioned charm of their famous guest. He was the talk of the town. Whenever he appeared in public he was greeted with deep bows of respect, and his fur cap and steel-rimmed spectacles became a feature in the life of Nantes.

Among the numerous visitors who called to present their compliments during his stay was a boyish-looking young man, very thin, with sloping shoulders and a round, handsome face lit up by large brown eyes of unusual radiance—a certain Paul Theveneau.

Paul had remained in the north in order to pay his respects to Franklin immediately on the latter's arrival, and he stood gazing at him with shining eyes, obviously deeply affected at being in the presence of the celebrated American. Franklin was moved by such a display of naïve enthusiasm and he smiled at him amiably, but when Paul explained that he had come as the representative of the firm of Hortalez and its chief, Monsieur de Beaumarchais, both the smile and the amiability disappeared and Paul was dumbfounded to see the sudden change that came over the fleshy countenance of the kindly old sage. The Doctor stared at him severely, his eyebrows seemed to arch themselves even higher, his wide mouth was set in a grim line, and the furrows of his forehead deepened. It was a powerful, weatherbeaten, menacing face into which Paul looked. "You tell me that these transports of Monsieur de Beaumarchais are already at sea?" asked Franklin. His voice was low and courteous, with scarcely a trace of dislike or suspicion.

Hitherto Paul had been speaking in English, though with a certain difficulty, but now he had recourse to his accustomed French. Feeling himself to be on the defence, he spoke with redoubled warmth of the achievements of his friend Pierre. The three ships, *Victoire, Alexandre,* and *Eugénie* were on the high seas, he declared, loaded with munitions for America—48 guns, 6,200 muskets, 2,500 projectiles, and a very large quantity of uniforms. Furthermore, in the storehouses of Monsieur de Beaumarchais there were weapons and equipment for thirty thousand men awaiting transport. Paul enumerated the different items from memory.

Franklin listened without allowing his features to betray his thoughts. What this young man was saying signified a considerable service to the Congress and the American Army, yet he could not conquer the feeling of repugnance that had been inspired in him by the name of Beaumarchais. Nor could he help being annoyed at the apparent elimination of his friend, the worthy Doctor Dubourg. "I may no doubt assume," he said, "that the French Government has been offering Monsieur de Beaumarchais its full support."

"Yes and no, Doctor," replied Paul. "They were, of course, interested at Versailles in the supply of munitions of war to America, but they were equally anxious that the British ambassador should not be provided with grounds for complaint. Permit me to inform you of the true situation, Doctor Franklin," he added warmly. "The arms that are being consigned to your country have been procured by my friend Monsieur de Beaumarchais alone, on his own initiative and under enormous difficulties. This was rendered possible only by the exercise of all his talents and the assumption of considerable risk."

Franklin gazed tranquilly at the excited young man. "I am glad to hear," he said in measured tones, "that weapons for our soldiers are on the way. We can make good use of them. There are not many of us, and in the long run we shall find it difficult to wage the fight for humanity alone. I thank you, Monsieur, for the information you have offered me." His last words were spoken in French, which he articulated slowly and with a disjointed, stiff effect.

Paul realized with dismay that the interview was at an end. He had looked forward to this meeting with high hopes, and now Franklin was treating him as if he were a defaulting contractor. He could not conceive how a man who was prepared to sacrifice his position, his fortune, and his life for the cause he had at heart could be so cold and so aloofly sceptical, but he determined not to judge the Doctor too hastily. He withdrew, resolved to seek a second interview later.

The opportunity came when Monsieur Gruet, three days afterwards, invited a few select friends to meet Franklin at dinner. To his joyful astonishment Paul saw how different again was the Doctor's bearing on this occasion. If he had been taken aback at their first encounter by the American's frigid attitude, he was now able to understand why he had struck the imagination of so many people. Paul himself fell a willing victim to the old man's spell. It was odd how the rather ponderous little jests and homely anecdotes with which he bestrewed the conversation, how everything he said, even though it was of trifling interest, seemed in some peculiar way to be steeped in his personality.

They spoke a great deal about religious matters. The latitudinarian views of Parisian society were reflected in the opinions expressed by the guests at Monsieur Gruet's dinner-party. They commented humorously on the superstitions of the local peasantry, indulged with malicious wit in the drawing of parallels between these superstitions and the tenets of the Roman Catholic Church, and told indecent stories about the clergy.

Franklin listened with affable reserve. They had no doubt expected him to join in the discussion, but he remained silent. Finally one of them asked him straight out what his views were on the clergy. "I should prefer not to generalize," he answered in his halting French. "Among the clergy there are many men of serious mind who are trying to bring their faith into harmony with the discoveries of science. There are others who take pleasure in hurling their thunderbolts against scientific doctrines." And he launched into a discourse on his own experiences in this way when he installed his lightning-conductor. One parson, for instance, had declared that such activity was tantamount to tempting God. If one set about controlling the artillery of heaven, that was a task to which the strength of mortal man was unequal. Another had preached that lightning was one of the means by which mankind was punished for its crimes and warned against the commission of further offences. Any attempt to avert the full effect of lightning constituted an intervention in divine right, and was therefore a sin.

The free-thinkers of Nantes refused to let the matter rest there. They obviously wanted to extract from Franklin an unequivocal admission which they could turn to account in the propagation of their own ideas. "We have been informed, Doctor Franklin," suggested one of the guests, "that in a treatise entitled *On Liberty and Necessity, Pleasure and Pain,* you voiced doubts concerning the survival of the soul after death and questioned the validity of the theological distinction between man and the animals."

"Did I really do that?" asked Franklin amiably. "Well, well! In my youth I wrote many things which would have been better left unsaid, and I am only glad that these little treatises met with so little success and therefore did not reach a wide public." And he lifted to his lips a glass of the excellent Burgundy that his host had provided in honour of a guest whom he knew to be a connoisseur.

Paul thought that the others would now cease their importunate inquiries, since it must be evident to them that in the Doctor's view such problems were personal ones which each individual must settle for himself, but the free-thinkers were not to be intimidated, and their spokesman bluntly asked: "Would you be so good as to inform us, Doctor Franklin, what opinions you now hold on these matters?"

The old man fixed the speaker with a calm, unwavering eye and was silent for so long that they all began to feel uncomfortable. Then he opened his mouth and said, "My ideas have changed. There can be no doubt about that. I even ask myself at times why we should really deny the possibility of the existence of a Supreme Being and of the immortality of the soul."

The questioner gnawed his lip. "Nevertheless," he persisted, "I regard you as one of us, my dear Doctor Franklin. You have never contributed, by any utterance that might be open to misinterpretation, to the increase of superstition on this earth."

"I fear, Monsieur," replied Franklin with a smile, "that I must undeceive you. I have always been careful not to disturb others in the enjoyment of their religious emotions, even when I found their opinions difficult to tolerate or verging on the ludicrous. I went to considerable lengths in this endeavour. You must know that in Philadelphia we have sects of various kinds, and that some of these hold diametrically opposite views. I have shown favour to them all without distinction, and each of these sects has received a contribution from me towards the establishment or renovation of its place of worship. If I should die today, I can truly say that I am at peace with all of them. It seems to me, Monsieur, that if one is determined to be tolerant one should not show intolerance just towards those who are believers." These words were spoken in a friendly manner, with no trace of acidity, so that even the free-thinkers did not take offence.

Yet they still wanted to have the last word. "Can you enlighten us," asked their spokesman, "as to the reasons why you have never publicly acknowledged your belief in a Supreme Being?"

Franklin responded, half-jokingly, "I cannot imagine that a Supreme Being would lay store by a public acknowledgment of that kind. At least, I have never noticed that He makes any distinction between believers and heretics by, let us say, stigmatizing the latter with the special marks of His displeasure."

Here Paul intervened in the discussion and suggested with an air of deference, "Could you say a word or two, Doctor Franklin, about the way in which, if at all, your faith in God determines the nature of your actions?"

"I think," said Franklin, "that the best way to honour the Supreme Being is by behaving decently towards the other creatures whom He has created. It is this standard of decent conduct that I have tried all my life to achieve."

The persistent spokesman still refused to admit defeat, and he urged, "But surely you question the divinity of Jesus of Nazareth? Or don't you?"

Franklin turned his broad face thoughtfully towards his challenger. "That is a problem I have not studied," he replied, "and I hardly think it worth while racking my brains about it at this time of day. You see, young sir, I am an old man, and it seems probable that in the fairly near future I shall have the opportunity of discovering the truth without too much exertion on my part."

In this indirect and half-ironical way, Franklin answered the inquisitive free-thinkers in his halting French. Paul was amused. By his oracular replies the old man had said everything and said nothing, and Paul admired the playful skill with which he had warded off the awkward questions addressed to him.

Franklin left for Paris on the following day. Paul would have given anything to accompany him. Alternating as he did between shyness and audacity, Paul could be very obstinate once he had set his mind on a particular purpose, and to anybody else he would have persisted in offering himself as escort, but he hesitated to make such a proposal to Franklin. He did, however, appear to speed his departure. In the courtyard stood the capacious travelling coach of Monsieur Gruet, with the horses already harnessed, and the last preparations were being made.

The Doctor was upstairs in his room talking to a few of his new-found friends who had come to see him off, and servants were bringing him his cloak, his fur cap, his thick gloves, and his stick carved from the wood of an apple tree. As he was helped into his cloak he chatted in his tranquil, affable way with Paul. "I am grateful to you, my friend," he said, "for the valuable information you have brought me."

Paul flushed with pride at being addressed by the old man as his friend. He looked thin and dwarfed beside the massive figure in the fur coat, with the heavy, jutting jaw and luxuriant eyebrows.

"It will be a hard nut that I shall have to crack in Paris," said

Franklin, with a hoarse sigh from the depths of his voluminous wrappings. He spoke softly, so that only Paul could hear him, as they stood at the window gazing down into the snow-carpeted yard where strong-armed porters were stowing the last pieces of baggage into the coach. These were iron-bound boxes containing the Doctor's most important papers and his books. One of the porters heaved away, with a second man to help him, but there was a particularly heavy case that they could not lift, and a third porter hastened to their aid.

The first one waved him away. "That's all right," he cried in a panting voice that came up to the two men listening at the window. "That's all right. It's going. Ça ira." And with a deafening crash he tipped the box into the carriage.

"Ça ira, mon ami, ça ira," murmured Franklin, and an almost imperceptible smile curved the corners of his wide mouth as, leaning on Paul's shoulder, he descended the stairs rather laboriously to the courtyard where his grandsons were awaiting him.

☆   ☆   ☆

A halt was made at Versailles. They could have travelled straight through to Paris, but the Doctor was tired and he booked a room at the Hôtel de la Belle Image.

Even before supper was announced a visitor arrived from Paris, a stout, imposing gentleman with a flowered satin waistcoat covering his capacious stomach. It was Mr. Silas Deane. His face beamed with joyful excitement as he shook Franklin's hand and seemed as if he would never let it go. He at once launched into a flood of words, not knowing where to begin or where to leave off, about the complicated negotiations with Count Vergennes, the enemy spies that were swarming at the ports, the constant protests from the English Ambassador, the ships that were being prevented from leaving harbour, the officers whom he had recruited and whom he was unable either to pay or to transport overseas, the Congress which sent noncommittal replies and no money. What a relief it was that Franklin had arrived at last to take the heavy responsibility off his shoulders! The loquacious Deane poured all his worries into the ears of the silent Franklin, then, hardly pausing for breath, proceeded with a chuckle to tell him how the English Ambassador, when he heard that Franklin was due to arrive shortly, had put pressure on Count Vergennes to veto his sojourn in Paris. Vergennes had agreed to do so, but on the advice of the ingenious Monsieur de Beaumarchais he had sent the courier bearing instructions to that effect to Le Havre, where Franklin could not be reached. Once the American envoy was in Paris they could not, of course, expel him. Silas Deane wondered what they would have done without their resourceful Monsieur de Beaumarchais.

While Deane was still putting his famous colleague into the picture, a Negro boy in an elaborate livery arrived with a letter for Franklin. Monsieur Caron de Beaumarchais informed the great man from the New World in ceremonious phrases that he would esteem himself happy if he might be permitted to pay his respects that very day. Franklin stared uneasily at the beautifully written, delicately perfumed note, then replied courteously that he felt too fatigued to receive Monsieur de Beaumarchais that evening.

His long journey and the exuberant verbosity of Silas Deane really had exhausted him, and he was glad when his visitor took his leave. A further caller was announced, however, whom he could not refuse to see, Doctor Barbeu Dubourg. Dubourg embraced Franklin, thumped him on the back, and the two stout old gentlemen seemed completely to fill the little room at the Hôtel de la Belle Image. Again and again Dubourg assured his friend how young and well-preserved he looked, while Franklin congratulated Dubourg on his youthful and robust appearance. Inwardly each was saddened to see how old the other had grown, and Franklin thought to himself in an access of melancholy, "Here I am telling lies again; a dozen tombstones couldn't do it better."

Dubourg's heart was full to overflowing, and his feelings found vent in an excited spate of incoherent anecdotes and reminiscences. He talked about their mutual friends, about the Academy, recent publications concerning the principles of the physiocrats, the dismissal of the Minister of Finance, Baron Turgot, his own translations of Franklin's works, the precarious state of the national finances, the new financial controller, Jacques Necker, the attitude of the Count de Vergennes, and the intrigues at court. Half a dozen times or more he said what a blessing it was that they at last had Franklin in their midst. It was far from his intention to depreciate the efforts of the assiduous and patriotic Silas Deane, but after all the latter did not possess the calibre that was needed in an envoy sent to represent the American revolutionaries, and it was no wonder that a sensation-loving writer of comedies like Monsieur de Beaumarchais should have been able to set himself up in the eyes of the court and the city as *the* advocate of the American cause, as if the threads of all the activities being conducted in Europe on behalf of the thirteen States were gathered in his hands.

Franklin had already experienced a sense of disquiet when Silas Deane recounted to him so enthusiastically the transactions in which Beaumarchais was engaged, and he could well understand the wrath of his friend Doctor Dubourg at being shouldered to one side, but he had not forgotten, either, the hymn of praise which Paul Theveneau had sung in honour of his chief. "They tell me," he said, "that this Beaumarchais has considerable supplies upon the high seas, something like six thousand muskets—I do not remember the precise figures."

"Yes, that is true," conceded Dubourg, "but when one has the Royal Arsenals and the secret funds of the Foreign Office to draw on, there isn't much magic in it."

"Did all the money come from the French Government?" asked Franklin.

"Oh, of course a certain amount was derived from other sources," admitted Dubourg surlily, "but wherever he got it from, the fact remains that the whole of Paris looks upon him as the representative of American interests, and that is a bad thing. He is not a man of serious mind." Dubourg repeated the words in French: He is completely lacking in serious qualities. "But," he added consolingly, "that is now going to stop. With Doctor Franklin on the spot Beaumarchais has, of course, reached the end of his tether." And he thumped Franklin on the back affectionately.

During supper they discussed their mutual literary interests and the business matters arising from these. Monsieur Rouault, the publisher, was anxious to bring out a large edition of Franklin's popular little book, *The Way to Wealth,* in a translation by Dubourg under the title *La science du bonhomme Richard*. Dubourg believed this to be the best of all his translations, since he found the easy tone congenial, and as they plied away with hearty appetite at the ample viands he read out to Franklin in French the anecdotes and aphorisms of Poor Richard.

On the following day, accompanied by Deane and Dubourg, Franklin set out for Paris, where he installed himself at the Hôtel d'Hambourg. Space was very limited and William, who had been entrusted with the task of unpacking his grandfather's papers and putting them in order, soon found himself in difficulties. Everything was soon scattered about in utter confusion and the boy stood gazing at his handiwork with a charming, helpless, and utterly innocent smile.

Rumours that Franklin was on his way from Nantes to Paris had preceded him, and scarcely was his arrival known when numerous admirers of his writings and achievements called to pay their respects. Beaumarchais was an early visitor, but the Doctor did not receive him alone. There were two others present, and though Franklin was very polite and spoke with appreciation of what Beaumarchais had accomplished for America, he remained aloof and amiably ignored Pierre's suggestion that they might perhaps soon have an opportunity for private discussion. Pierre was nonplussed, but with his accustomed optimism quickly consoled himself as he recalled what Paul had told him of his first chilly interview with the Doctor and the American's subsequent change of attitude. He had no doubt that the same thing would happen in his case too.

Meanwhile further callers had put in an appearance. There seemed no end to them as they bowed, shook his hand, embraced him, and poured a flood of rapid French into his ear, while he sat there looking large and venerable, his sparse white locks falling over his shoulders, his wide mouth expanding at times in a friendly smile, listening keenly, but saying little.

At the entrance to his hotel a large crowd was waiting to catch a glimpse of the American envoy, philosopher, and advocate of liberty. When he emerged from the doorway the description of him that had been carried on the wings of rumour was confirmed. He was wearing his steel-rimmed spectacles and the famous fur cap. The enthusiasm was tremendous. He had intended to go out for a drive, and his carriage was waiting, but in spite of the slippery streets and the cold he decided to make his way on foot with a helping hand from his attractive young grandson, William. All along his route the great man was greeted with touching respect. If he could perform a service for his country in this inexpensive manner, he thought to himself with a sly smile, he was prepared to wear his fur cap until the dog days.

During the next few days the newspapers, the salons, and the cafés echoed and re-echoed with the name of Franklin. Lord Stormont was furious and called upon Vergennes. The Minister of Police thought of making any reference to Franklin in public a penal offence, but the Count de Vergennes was afraid of the ridicule to which the Government would be exposed by such a decree and the suggestion was dropped.

The excitement grew. What a man he was, this inventor of the lightning rod, founder of American independence, and author of philosophical and scientific works of the first rank! Had there ever been another who combined achievements of this order with such extreme simplicity? That was the way one expected a sage to look, patriarchal, fur-capped, and bespectacled, that was the picture they had formed in advance of the famous expounder of natural philosophy, of Poor Richard, *le bonhomme Richard,* who had fused the noblest doctrines of antiquity with the teachings of modern science. With the swiftness that was habitual in Paris the fame of the great "Franquelin" spread. Monsieur Léonard, the Queen's hairdresser, the first tonsorial artist in the world, invented a new coiffure for the ladies of the court, a tall, crinkly construction which was copied from Franklin's fur cap and given the name *coiffure à la Franquelin.* His portrait was hung over the fireplace in society drawing-rooms and on the walls of coffee-houses, painted on the lids of snuff-boxes, and printed on handkerchiefs. The lightning portrait painters had a busy time and their wares were sold at every street corner.

Doctor Dubourg brought his friend one of these pictures which he had purchased in the streets, and they both examined it with great amusement. Franklin was depicted with his fur cap, his steel-rimmed spectacles, and his stick carved from the wood of an apple tree, every inch of him a solid bourgeois, a real *bonhomme*. The portrait was encircled by a Latin motto which said: "He has torn the lightning from the sky and the sceptre from tyrants." Nearly all the pictures were framed within this resounding classical motto, the author of which was Baron Turgot, the former Minister of Finance, one of Franklin's friends and a leader of the physiocrats.

"It is a good motto," commented Franklin, still contemplating the picture.

"Yes," replied Dubourg. "If ever you had a friend and admirer, it is Turgot."

"It is a great pity that they brought about his fall," said Franklin, "but I feared from the start that he would not prove supple enough for Versailles. A statesman must not lose patience. He must be prepared to apply himself to devious courses."

"In the American affair, at any rate," retorted Dubourg, who was still smarting at the recollection of his failure, "he did not show any lack of patience. He never gave away a sou to help America while he was Minister of Finance. I talked to him like a parson offering exhortations to a dying man, but he always gave me the same answer, 'The cause of America is in accordance with the general line of progress, so it is bound to succeed even without financial help from us. We must keep our money for our own reforms.' "

"Was he not right, from his point of view?" asked Franklin.

Doctor Dubourg gazed at his friend reproachfully.

☆　　☆　　☆

Franklin's objective attitude never ceased to astonish his acquaintances. Dubourg and the other French intellectuals who sympathized with the American colonists could understand the coolness with which the court regarded their democratic ardour, but surely even Versailles must realize the unique opportunity presented by the conflict in which England was engaged to take revenge for the defeat and the peace treaty of 1763. These intellectuals raged against the delaying tactics of the faint-hearted French Ministers. Why the devil did they not recognize the United States of America and conclude a commercial agreement with them?

Franklin, on the other hand, found the attitude of the French Government quite sensible, in fact the only possible one. The condition of the French finances gave cause for serious anxiety, and war, even a successful war, would inevitably bring about a collapse. In these circumstances even a zealous supporter of American ideas like Turgot

had fought tooth and nail against the danger of launching the country
into a war with England because of aid offered to America. In any
case France could wage war only after an understanding with her
allies, Spain and Austria. Absolutist Austria had no interest in the
victory of a republican America, while Spain feared lest her own
colonies should be incited to revolt if their neighbours to the north
were successful. Franklin realized the state of affairs and did not
share the indignant impatience of Dubourg and his fellow intellectuals,
but was content to bide his time and to refrain from embarrassing
the Ministers by putting premature pressure on them.

The caution imposed upon the French Government, however, did
not apply to the populace, and Franklin felt free to canvass his cause
among the Parisians. He had learned from early experience as a
printer, publisher, author, and statesman, how to win over public
opinion. He had been born with the gift of building up ideas in men's
minds, and if the court could not officially recognize him as the
emissary of America, he would be America's emissary to the French
people. That was far from a trifling responsibility and provided an
amusing situation.

Unfortunately, Franklin was not the only representative of the
United States in Paris. When the Congress appointed him it had
not only accredited Silas Deane with the same duties and privileges,
but also Arthur Lee, the scheming gentleman who had been so touchy
in London.

Franklin did not get on at all badly with Silas Deane. Though that
good-humoured patriot hardly possessed the calibre required for dab-
bling in high politics, he was at least useful when it came to matters
of trade. He confined himself to what he understood and freely
acknowledged Franklin's superior weight of metal.

Arthur Lee, on the other hand, travelled to Paris with the fixed
intention of censuring and sabotaging everything that Franklin might
do or say.

Lee came from a well-known family in Virginia. He had been a
kind of youthful prodigy, and before completing his twentieth year
had published a number of brilliant political pamphlets. The whole
family held radical and progressive views, and it was his brother,
Richard Henry Lee, who formulated and moved the resolution in
the Congress which declared that the colonies were henceforth independent. Arthur Lee himself, now thirty-seven years of age, had been
working in Europe for years on behalf of the colonists.

When the Congress sent him to Paris he was at first delighted, but
to his bitter disappointment he soon discovered that Franklin completely overshadowed him.

It was not the first time that his path and that of Benjamin Franklin
had crossed. In London they had worked together, or rather side by

side, as agents of the colony of Massachusetts, and even then the hot-headed young man, with his taste for shrill words and gestures, had found it difficult to collaborate harmoniously with the tranquil old Doctor *honoris causa*—that was the way he always referred to him—who insisted on weighing the pros and cons before he would act. Lee had long yearned for the old man to go and leave him in command of the field—instead of which he now found himself in Paris, at a time when the fate of his country was being decided, once more being cramped and hampered by this phlegmatic, overrated old dodderer.

The lank figure of Arthur Lee wandered with gloomy disapproval through the crowded offices of the Hôtel d'Hambourg, peering about him suspiciously, offering advice, and prepared to be cantankerous. He had not forgotten the offence to his feelings inflicted on him by Beaumarchais, whom he regarded as a swindler, and was always discovering evidence which confirmed his suspicion that the funds provided by Versailles were being embezzled. He warned Silas Deane against the Frenchman, and when Deane took up the cudgels on the latter's behalf his suspicion of Deane too hardened into certainty. So he warned Franklin against both Beaumarchais and Deane, and when Franklin declared that he had not yet made up his mind about Beaumarchais, this only served to convince Lee that the Doctor *honoris causa* was in league with the other two for the purpose of lining their several pockets.

His grudge against Franklin deepened as the days went by. What did this so-called Doctor's achievements amount to, anyway? He had made a few scientific discoveries that might, perhaps, be of some practical use, and Arthur Lee would not venture to express an opinion so far as they were concerned; but what Lee did understand was that the old man was letting things drift, and what else was to be expected from one who had always been a shuffler and whose son, moreover, was a Tory? This Benjamin Franklin was a hypocrite. It was a cheap trick always to wear his brown coat and fur cap, so that he could play at being the frugal philosopher and impress the simple Frenchmen. Yet Lee had seen with his own eyes how the cunning old man was prepared to dress as elegantly as anyone else when he appeared in the smart drawing-rooms of London or Philadelphia, and it was not exactly a frugal existence he was leading here in Paris with his sumptuous cuisine, with old wines and young women, with his carriage and his servants. Benjamin Franklin was certainly no Diogenes.

That Franklin's two colleagues were more of a hindrance than a help became clearly evident when they were received by the Foreign Minister. Franklin had doubted whether they would be received at Versailles, and he breathed a sigh of relief when a polite Secretary from the Foreign Office called at the Hôtel d'Hambourg with a message to the effect that Count Vergennes would feel honoured if the three American gentlemen would deign to pay him a visit. It must be understood of course, added the Secretary, that Count Vergennes was unaware, and had no wish to be aware, that the gentlemen had come on behalf of the Congress in Philadelphia. He was receiving them solely in their private capacity.

Arthur Lee nearly foamed at the mouth. This was a monstrous affront, and they must refuse categorically to call upon the Minister. His two colleagues had the greatest difficulty in converting him to a more reasonable frame of mind. Franklin knew that Vergennes had had no easy task in persuading the reluctant monarch to sanction the secret aid that was being given to America, and he regarded the Foreign Minister's readiness to receive the three commissioners as a token of courage and good will.

Vergennes was just as Franklin had pictured him, with an air of courteous and benevolent charm, adroit, with a frequent touch of irony, and never off his guard. These were qualities which the American knew how to appreciate. With evident sincerity Vergennes expressed his pleasure at meeting the great philosopher with whose writings he was already well acquainted. This was no empty compliment, for he read English fluently and did not have to rely upon Dubourg's translations.

For all his good breeding, the Minister practically ignored the other two. Silas Deane took this as a matter of course and was content to sit in silence, happy that his celebrated colleague had made such a good impression, but Lee was furious at what he regarded as a slight. When he attempted to intervene in the discussion with some witty comment, Vergennes would listen politely and then turn back at once to Franklin.

One of the questions asked by the Minister concerned the powers invested in the Congress. Before Franklin could reply, however, he added that he was of course inquiring merely as a private individual who was interested in political philosophy. In his quality as Minister to His Most Christian Majesty he could not take cognizance of the existence of the thirteen United States. So far as he was concerned these were still colonies belonging to the English Crown which had become involved in a regrettable conflict with their sovereign. "But though the Foreign Minister," he continued, "deeply deplores the attitude of the colonies, Monsieur de Vergennes sympathizes thoroughly with the position taken up by the Congress. As Monsieur de Vergennes I believed from the very beginning that a peaceful solution of the conflict was out of the question. I know the English Government. I am aware of their stubborn egotism, and I am filled with anger when I think of the humiliating treaty which was forced upon us by the English in the year '63. Every Frenchman clenches his fist when the name of Dunkerque is mentioned, and the Control Commissioner whom England has placed there to deride our country." It was strange to mark the contrast between the vehemence of these words and the Minister's outward composure. He spoke in a low conversational tone as he played with his quill.

While he listened to Count Vergennes, Franklin could not help thinking that without the successes achieved by the Americans, England would scarcely have been in a position to exact such harsh terms at the peace settlement and to send a Control Commissioner to set up his headquarters in the devastated city of Dunkerque. Franklin himself had supplied arms in that war against France, and General Washington, to whom Paris was now paying homage, had acquired his practical knowledge of warfare and won his spurs on the same occasion. During the further course of the conversation the Minister observed that, if he might be permitted to offer a word of advice, he would recommend them for the time being to refrain from any conspicuous demonstrations. There were in any case a number of people in Paris who made it their business to promote the American cause in words that lacked nothing of inflammatory zeal. He had little doubt that the mere presence of a man like Franklin would be far more effective than the most vigorous speeches.

Arthur Lee was fuming inwardly. Franklin, however, to Lee's angered astonishment, sat amiably in his chair and said in his slow, halting French, "There is certainly nobody in a better position than yourself, Count Vergennes, to understand the circumstances in which we are placed in this country, and that renders your advice doubly valuable."

Vergennes smiled. "I believe," he rejoined, "that it will not be displeasing to you if our meeting should result in something more concrete than mere advice. When our discussion has ended, perhaps you would care to have a word with Monsieur de Gérard."

As they took their leave Vergennes impressed upon Doctor Franklin that he would look forward with the very greatest pleasure to the prospect of frequent conversations with him. He would suggest, however, that such meetings should take place not in the official atmosphere of Versailles, but privately in Paris. If the Government, in spite of Lord Stormont's protests, had raised no objection to Monsieur Franklin's presence in the capital, it was because Monsieur Franklin, as had been reported to the Foreign Office, was staying there as a member of the Academy who was anxious to exchange ideas with his colleagues, and wished moreover to enable his grandsons to enjoy the fruits of French education.

Arthur Lee's glowering eyes never left Franklin's face. Would the old man calmly accept this insult, too? Would he carry his base opportunism to that extreme? He stared tensely at Franklin's massive countenance, which revealed no trace of indignation. On the contrary, the Doctor seemed to be slightly amused. "I quite understand, Count Vergennes," he replied. "In any case, one can talk more comfortably at the fireside in a pleasant environment than in a ministerial council-chamber."

At this, Lee could no longer contain himself. "I find it regrettable," he said in his shrill, wavering voice, "that the representatives of the thirteen United States of America should have access to the Foreign Minister of the King of France only by the backstairs."

"But, Monsieur—Monsieur," protested Count Vergennes, trying to remember the name of this excitable young man, which he had apparently forgotten.

Franklin intervened at once apologetically: "Monsieur Lee, my esteemed young colleague, has evidently not quite understood your French, Count Vergennes. He knows as well as I do that in a serious conversation the content is more important than the chairs on which one is sitting."

When the door had closed behind them the three Americans repaired to the office of Monsieur de Gérard, where they discussed figures and details. It appeared that de Gérard had received instructions to offer the envoys an immediate loan of two million livres, for an unlimited period and bearing no interest.

"Splendid!" said Silas Deane.

"A paltry tip!" said Arthur Lee.

Benjamin Franklin said nothing.

☆   ☆   ☆

Ever since his early childhood Franklin had had borne in upon him by both good and ill fortune that the actions of individuals and of society in general are determined to a great extent by economic factors. "A man without money," he used to say, "finds it difficult to remain honest. An empty sack won't stand up straight." The ultimate causes of the American Revolution were of an economic nature, as he was perfectly well aware. Now that he had himself reached a position of tolerable prosperity, he employed economic factors merely as a means, never as an end in themselves. By increasing the mobility of capital the middle classes were enabled to make swifter profits, and acquired an effective weapon in wresting from the feudal aristocracy privileges which had hitherto constituted a bar to progress. The economic factor therefore interested Franklin solely as a weapon. Otherwise he relegated it to the periphery of his thought and policy.

Unfortunately the greater part of his time during these days in Paris was taken up with matters in which the economic aspect predominated. The three emissaries knew that they could not rely upon

the receipt of funds from the Congress. They had to maintain a headquarters worthy of the country they were representing, they had been
entrusted with the task of ensuring a flow of supplies across the
Atlantic, and the money required for their several purposes had to
be found in France. Either they had to keep on going cap in hand to
the French Government, or they could issue letters of marque to
shipowners who were prepared to undertake the risky business of
privateering under the American flag in return for a share in the
profits.

The ships and cargoes taken in prize were not easy to dispose of.
Captain Lambert Wickes, for instance, the boisterous skipper of the
Reprisal, had brought in two further prizes and wanted to sell them
by public auction, but the French authorities intervened. France was
bound by solemn agreements to bar any foreign ship sailing under the
flag of a country at war with England from access to her harbours, to
say nothing of allowing it to sell its booty on French soil. Captain
Wickes, whose pride was hurt, did not understand what it was all
about. Here he was performing deeds of heroism, and instead of
giving him an ovation these French quill-drivers were asking him to
keep quiet and get rid of his spoil under cover of secrecy as if he were
a thief. He swore mighty oaths, travelled to Paris, and his blunt
sailor's tongue caused the narrow walls of the Hôtel d'Hambourg to
reverberate with curses and complaints.

Franklin spoke soothingly to the indignant sea-dog, explaining that
France had treaty obligations towards England. But Wickes refused
to listen to such landlubbers' babble. This was all red tape, and he
demanded that Franklin should bring those gentlemen in Versailles
to their senses.

The Doctor called on the French authorities and expostulated
mildly. It seemed to him absurd in principle to irritate the officials of
the Foreign Office because of such a trifling matter, but his colleagues
disagreed. Even Franklin's friend and admirer, Doctor Dubourg,
was unable to share his point of view. On the contrary, he was tempted
himself to go in for the business of privateering. When Franklin
gently teased him for his romantic piratical leanings, Dubourg was
hurt. Why, he inquired, should one scorn such a magnificent method
of financing the cause of liberty?

The French officers recruited by Silas Deane for service in the
American Army were no less of a worry than the captured English
ships. The Versailles Government forbade them to leave the country,
since this too would have been a breach of neutrality, and Franklin,
who was apprehensive lest the flooding of the American Army with
high-ranking French officers should be distasteful to the troops,
would have liked to seize the opportunity of cancelling their contracts.
Silas Deane, however, was proud of his acquisitions, with their

resounding names and titles, and he kept dinning into Franklin's ears
the urgent necessity of doing his best to obtain an exit permit for
them.

It was matters of this kind which absorbed Franklin's time, yet he
was convinced that they were doing more harm than good. Vergennes
was undoubtedly well disposed, but he had his own ideas on the
subject of when the right moment would have arrived to persuade
his ministerial colleagues and the King that the United States ought
to be recognized and a treaty of alliance concluded. It was inadvisable
to keep nudging him. Franco-American friendship was a tender
growth that might wilt at a clumsy touch. It must not be grasped too
roughly.

Vergennes's prediction of the effect that would be evoked by Franklin's presence in the capital was borne out by subsequent evidence. The
Duc de Choiseul, who had been First Minister under Louis XV, but
had fallen into disfavour with the young King, took pains to gain the
friendship of the American envoy, requested permission to call upon
him, and invited him to his house. Even Louis Philippe, Duc de Char-
tres, a cousin of the King who was zealously engaged in fostering the
old family hostility to the court, endeavoured to draw Franklin into his
circle and that of his handsome and gifted literary friend, Madame de
Genlis. The Doctor was courteous, but reserved. He did not think it
wise to enter into relations with the opposition. Lee, on the other
hand, wanted to show the King and the Government that they were
dealing with men who held power in their hands. He thought it would
be a good thing to ally themselves with the opposition and display
their claws. It was only with the utmost difficulty, and the exercise of
all his tact and cunning, that Franklin succeeded in dissuading his
colleague from committing acts of impropriety.

Apart from the disagreeable nature of these activities in which he
was forced to engage, Franklin did not find the Hôtel d'Hambourg a
particularly happy environment for his official duties. The offices occupied by the American delegation were very confined, and young William was partly justified in attributing the confusion which always
reigned in his registry to the lack of space. Franklin had never liked
the place, and as the weeks went by he grew more and more convinced that he would be well advised to live not in Paris itself, but
somewhere on the outskirts. Though he would not be wholly free
from tiresome visitors even there, yet their numbers would be fewer.

It was Doctor Dubourg who provided the solution. He had a friend,
Ray de Chaumont, who ardently favoured the American cause and
possessed a country house at Passy near Paris. Monsieur de Chaumont, explained Dubourg, felt lost in his vast, rambling mansion,
one wing of which was surrounded by a magnificent garden and
practically detached from the main building. If Franklin were willing

to take up his residence at the Hôtel Valentinois, Monsieur de Chaumont would feel delighted and honoured.

Franklin journeyed out to Passy and found that the wing in question was solid and commodious, well-furnished, and so embedded in its spacious garden that the occupier would be as hedged in and secluded as he could possibly wish. He fell in love with the garden the moment he saw it. Well-trimmed and laid out in an ornamental design, it merged gradually into a park in the English style, and terraces led down to the river with views everywhere of the city of Paris stretching into the distance on the further bank. The entrance to the garden-house could be reached through avenues and a gradually ascending path, but Franklin at once decided that whenever he managed to overcome his rooted inclination to take things comfortably he would go by way of the terrace steps. The more he inspected the place the more deeply he felt attracted to it. This was what he had dreamed of. He would practically be living in Paris, for Passy lay directly on the outskirts, yet at the same time he would be in the country. There was plenty of room for his books and all the odds and ends he liked to carry around with him. He could set up a workshop where he would be able to devote himself to his hobbies, and when he wanted to he could cut himself off from Silas Deane, Arthur Lee, and all the other tiresome people.

A little hesitantly he asked Monsieur de Chaumont what would be the amount of the rent. That gentleman replied that the garden wing was of no use to him anyway, and he would be honoured to place it at the great man's disposal free of any charge whatsoever. Franklin considered the matter for a moment. Monsieur de Chaumont had a finger in the supply of equipment to America, and he would no doubt expect to be recompensed in other ways for his kindness. Then, as he sat in the little belvedere tower and gazed out across the peaceful landscape, he thought of the noise and bustle in the narrow rooms of the Hôtel d'Hambourg and accepted the offer without more ado. Arthur Lee could write to his friends in America and tell them whatever he liked.

☆   ☆   ☆

On the following morning Franklin awoke and remembered that it was his birthday. At home in Philadelphia his family had always made it the occasion for great celebrations, with a cake, presents, a big family reunion at the dinner table, and the reciting of verses by his grandchildren. The Doctor wondered whether William would remember what day this was.

He lay in the wide bed, shut off behind the curtains of the alcove. In spite of the chilly January weather he had left the lattice window slightly ajar, for he liked fresh air, and he stuck one leg out of bed to feel the invigorating effect of the cold.

Seventy-one years of age! It was time he began to look after himself a little. Only too frequently did he think of his comfort more than his health. He ought to walk more and not allow his glass to be refilled too often. Life in France was very seductive. The women were obviously attracted to him, in spite of his seventy-one years. Perhaps he would even marry again. The Franklins were a lusty lot.

He could stay in bed no longer. He heaved himself up with an effort, grunting slightly. It was his custom to rise much earlier than the others and to read or work for an hour before breakfast. Putting on his dressing-gown he walked across to the sitting-room, where he kept his books. The room was warm, but full of smoke. These people did not understand how to keep a stove working properly. After fiddling about with it for a moment or two he threw off his dressing-gown and sat with nothing on, as he liked to do in the morning.

His books were packed too closely together in this confined space, one row behind the other, and it was difficult to find what one wanted. Things would be different at Passy. It would be six or seven weeks yet before he could move, since it would take that long to put the house in order, so he still had a couple of trying winter months in Paris ahead of him.

He pushed his chair across to one of the bookcases, a roomy chair constructed especially for his comfort which he had brought with him from Philadelphia. The seat could be turned up so as to form a ladder. Fetching down a number of books, he piled them around him and began to read. He would allow himself plenty of time today. He and his colleagues might arrive a quarter of an hour too late for their interview with Monsieur de Gérard, but that was a luxury a man could permit himself on his seventy-first birthday.

Breakfast was served at eight o'clock as usual, and the Doctor was greeted by young William with boisterous cheerfulness, to the accompaniment of joking comments that this time it was not he, but his grandfather, who had arrived unpunctually. Franklin confessed to himself that he had perhaps intended his tardiness as a reminder to the boy that this was his birthday. It saddened him to think that William had nevertheless forgotten it.

As some consolation he ordered buckwheat pancakes for his breakfast, which he normally did only on Sundays. The flour had been brought from America. He ate slowly and with enjoyment, conjuring up in his mind a picture of Philadelphia, with Christ Church, the Academy, Market and City Hall, the German Church, Government House, Carpenters' Hall, the great dockyard, Sassafras Street, Chestnut Street, and Mulberry Street.

After breakfast he started work. Dictated. Dictating, he walked to and fro, intent upon doing his three miles a day even if it could not be in the open air, and this meant striding six hundred times up and down the length of the room.

His mail, which lay opened in front of him, was copious, varied, and on the whole not particularly agreeable. A certain Chevalier de Neuville begged the loan of a few louis to save him from starvation. Doctor Ingenhousz, personal physician to the Empress Maria Theresa, asked his friend Franklin for information concerning some scientific experiments which the latter had been conducting. A Madame Hérissant requested the Doctor to discover the whereabouts of her son, whom she had reasons for believing to be in America. Arthur Lee wrote in a fair round hand, and in formal phraseology, to say that since Franklin had not reacted to his verbal protests he wished herewith to put on record the fact that he was continually being ignored and insulted by the gentlemen at the French Foreign Office, and if Franklin still declined to intervene in the matter he, Arthur Lee, reserved the right to take the appropriate steps himself. Fourteen sailors on the *Reprisal* complained about the intolerable treatment to which they were being subjected by Captain Wickes. Captain Wickes himself cursed in lurid terms and eccentric spelling the insubordination of his fourteen sailors. Monsieur Philippe Gueffier announced that he had composed an epic, directed against the English, which had made a deep impression on his friends, and he would be glad of pecuniary assistance for the purpose of publication.

These were the letters that engaged the Doctor's attention on his seventy-first birthday, but when he had finished with them he received his surprise present after all. The mail arrived from England. Despite the English secret service, some of his friends on the island had found ways and means of enabling messages to reach him. The London agents reported that the English Government had been rendered very apprehensive by the news of Franklin's arrival in Paris. The King had issued strict orders that every step taken by "that insidious man from Philadelphia" in the French capital was to be closely watched. Lord Rockingham, however, who had disapproved of the Government's policy towards the colonies from the outset, was telling everybody how greatly the chances of the Americans had been improved by Franklin's activities since landing in France. One of the agents had heard with his own ears the following remarks made by Rockingham in the presence of a numerous company. The disgraceful proceedings at the Privy Council, Lord Rockingham said, had not deterred Franklin from crossing the Atlantic. He had incurred the danger of being captured and dragged for a second time before an implacable tribunal. When the gentlemen who had taken part in that abominable scene pictured to themselves the spectacle of Franklin moving about at Versailles, they must feel as Macbeth felt when he saw the ghost of Banquo. Two of the gentlemen in question had been present when Rockingham talked in this manner, but they had remained silent.

Franklin was still reading his letters when Silas Deane and Arthur Lee appeared. They had come to fetch him for the conference with Monsieur de Gérard. Lee warned him peevishly that they were likely to be late. "Forgive me," said the Doctor amiably. "I was busy." He rose from his chair. "But now we are ready, my horses and I." Lee stared at him in pained surprise. Franklin was wearing his brown coat and gave no sign that he intended to change his costume. "Do you think I ought to change?" he asked with a suspicion of a smile.

"Frankly, I do," replied Lee. "But," he added morosely, "I know you well enough to be sure that you won't do it."

"You are quite right," said Franklin, and they set off.

☆   ☆   ☆

That odious Monsieur de Beaumarchais had been inquiring every other day when he might have the opportunity of calling upon the esteemed Doctor Franklin for the purpose of discussing American affairs. Silas Deane had persisted in his assertions that they would not be able to dispense with the services of the Frenchman who had done more to help the Americans than anybody else, and he had expressed astonishment at his colleague's continual refusal to receive him. Franklin realized that Deane, unfortunately, was right and that he must conquer his distaste for the dandified Frenchman. He could no longer put off meeting him and sent a message to the effect that he would expect him on the following day at eleven-thirty.

Early next morning the Doctor was sitting in his study, naked as usual, reading and writing, but he was unable to take any pleasure in poring over his books and papers. His gout was more troublesome than ordinarily, and the eruption on his skin seemed to itch with greater intensity. He decided grimly not to increase his discomfort by dressing ceremoniously for the interview, but to receive Beaumarchais in his dressing-gown.

Pierre, for his part, spent the morning alternating between hope and anxiety. He knew that there was no one on that side of the ocean who had rendered such valuable service to the Americans, and he looked forward eagerly to the coming discussion. Three ships belonging to the firm of Hortalez were at sea, and perhaps their cargoes were already in American hands. Further enormous stocks were being piled up in the warehouses, new ships were being built, additional contracts were being signed, and the Hortalez fleet would within a short space of time be second only to those of the King's Navy and the India Company.

He was puzzled at the attitude of Doctor Franklin, who not only displayed no interest in what he was doing, but even seemed to want to avoid meeting him. That he himself might be the cause of his aversion, that the Doctor might have conceived a dislike for his person, his way of living, and his writings, never even occurred to him. Probably his activity had been represented to the American in a false light. He was convinced that once he was afforded the opportunity of meeting Franklin face to face he would at once be able to scatter any doubts the latter might entertain of his sincerity.

He drove up to the Hôtel d'Hambourg in great style, sitting in his state-coach and attired with the utmost elegance. His first shock came when he saw the simple, shabbily furnished rooms in which the American lived. They reminded him of the lodgings occupied by some of his literary friends. What astounded him most, however, was Franklin's dressing-gown. He did not know whether this informal costume was to be taken as a sign of disrespect or whether it was a token of friendly confidence.

As they sat facing one another, the massive old man with his deeply furrowed visage, powerful jaw, and cold, searching gaze looked an imposing figure, in spite of his negligent dress. Pierre, for all his well-thought-out elegance and easy yet stilted manners, sat there like a supplicant. Franklin, possibly with a view to diminishing the significance that might otherwise be attached to the interview, had instructed his grandson, young William, to be present, and the boy inspected with the greatest interest every detail of the visitor's dazzling attire. This respectful homage paid to his reputation as an exponent of the latest fashions recompensed Pierre a little for the old man's frostiness.

He began by praising in rapid, melodious French the Doctor's merits and achievements. Drawing upon history for parallels, he extolled the vigour and craft with which the great American had wrenched the props from the English tyrant's throne. Franklin listened impassively, and Pierre was assailed by doubt whether he had understood what had been said to him in such choice French. After a time, however, the old man replied slowly, seeking the appropriate words in the foreign tongue, "When one contemplates an event of such tremendous historical importance as the struggle of the United States of America for their independence, one should not overestimate the services of a single individual."

For a fraction of a second Pierre considered whether this sententious dictum might be intended as a reference to his own activities, whether the old man wanted to imply that he was not so important as he imagined. But he at once cast the thought from his mind, and replied politely that such a philosophical attitude was only what was to be expected from a profound scholar like Doctor Franklin.

They continued to converse in the French language, and Franklin's laborious, halting manner of speech contrasted oddly with the flowing eloquence of Pierre. Nevertheless, the few words he uttered were imbued with more significance than all the witty embellishments of the younger man.

In preparation for the interview Franklin had carefully thought out what he should say to his visitor. The latter would have to wait a long time for his money, even for the first instalment of what was due to him. Franklin knew his Arthur Lee, and he knew his Congress. He was therefore not unwilling to gratify Beaumarchais with a compliment or two. They cost nothing, and he could see how the Frenchman was thirsting for them. Yet the strange repulsion he had felt when first hearing mention of his name was enhanced at the sight of Pierre sitting in front of him in his dandified get-up, perfuming the air around him, and evidently swelled with a sense of his own importance. The Doctor was unable to overcome his antipathy, and instead of the compliments he had intended to voice he confined himself to the dry comment, "I am glad, Monsieur, to see that so many worthy men on this side of the ocean are pledged to support our cause. It is a pleasure to me to have been afforded the opportunity of meeting one of them."

Pierre was far from gratified at being thus lumped together with many others, and he retorted in a slightly acid tone, "My endeavours to procure for the American Army the equipment and arms without which, as you are aware, a war cannot be waged, appeared to me a particularly honourable undertaking. I may, perhaps, be permitted to say that in view of the greatness of the cause to which I had committed myself, all the thoughts of the danger to which I was exposed by my activities melted away like mists before the sun."

"Danger?" queried the Doctor. He was uncertain whether he had heard the word correctly. "You mean the risk?"

"You may call it risk if you like," conceded Pierre courteously, speaking now in English. "I cannot weigh the various shades of meaning precisely. But I think that most of your compatriots and mine would not hesitate to define the situation as dangerous when one is faced by an opponent who is notorious for his quarrelsome, vindictive, and ruthless character."

"Do you mean a duel, Monsieur de Beaumarchais?" asked young William excitedly. "Have you been fighting a duel on our behalf?"

"Several," rejoined Pierre. "The last one was with the Marquis de Saint-Brisson, an impertinent lout who treated me to an exhibition of insolence when I was drawing a comparison between American liberty and the numerous abuses which the presumption of our hereditary aristocracy has brought in its train."

The Doctor was annoyed to think that a bourgeois writer like Pierre Caron should ape so childishly the pernicious customs of the nobility. "And did you succeed in convincing him?" he asked affably. "Did you manage to persuade this Marquis de Saint-Brisson, with the aid of your rapier, of the rightness of our principles? Does he believe in our cause now?" As Pierre was rather taken aback and said nothing, Franklin continued, "When one has reached my age, Monsieur, one no longer has faith in the practical uses of duelling." Then he began to relate one of those anecdotes of which he was so fond. "A gentleman sitting in a coffee-house requested a gentleman at the next table to move a little further away. 'Why so, sir?' 'Because you stink, sir.' 'That is an insult, sir, and you will have to give me satisfaction with your sword.' 'If you insist, sir, I will give you satisfaction with my sword. But I do not see what either of us can gain by it. For if you kill me, sir, then I too shall stink, and if I kill you, then you will stink, if possible, even more than you do now.' "

Pierre thought it bad taste on the old man's part to try to rebuke him by means of such a dull and homely story. In France, he declared stiffly, the fight against privilege had no doubt to be conducted in other ways than those customary in Philadelphia. Then, abruptly changing the subject, he spoke of the extraordinary difficulties involved in the provision and transport of munitions, frankly explaining the tremendous financial risk he was shouldering, and complaining of the taciturnity of the Congress which either refused to answer letters at all or else fobbed him off with noncommittal replies. Franklin suggested that Monsieur de Beaumarchais was no doubt referring to contracts that had been signed before his own arrival in France, and he thought that Versailles would not welcome any considerable discussion or correspondence about them. It would perhaps be advisable if Monsieur de Beaumarchais were to continue to arrange these matters with Mr. Deane, as hitherto. Mr. Deane had an excellent head for business and was a seasoned patriot. With that, Franklin came to a full stop, closed his lips firmly, and looked Pierre full in the eyes with a courteous and noncommittal air.

Pierre thought he understood perfectly. Franklin obviously believed that the Foreign Minister's desire for the utmost prudence must be humoured, and that was why the old man had displayed such reserve, not because of any personal disapproval of Pierre himself. That was consoling, and dropping the subject of Hortalez and Company he began to develop his ideas on the more abstract problem of human freedom. Even though, he suggested, the forms assumed by the struggle in America and France respectively might vary, yet it was fundamentally the same struggle. "My activities," he said, "have extended into a variety of fields, but in each of them, Doctor, I believe it would be true to say that I have borne myself like a soldier on the battlefield of liberty. I hope that one day even apparently irrelevant achievements, such as, for example, my comedy *The Barber of Seville,* will be recognized as successful battles fought on the path to victory."

Franklin continued to gaze at his loquacious visitor with the same keen but courteous expression on his face. "I am afraid I am not acquainted with your play," he replied.

Pierre was startled. He had never before met anyone who confessed ignorance of what was perhaps the most celebrated comedy of the century. With a wry smile he rejoined that he would feel honoured if he might be permitted to send Doctor Franklin tickets for the next performance of his comedy at the *Théâtre français.* Otherwise it would be difficult to procure a seat, for people often waited all night until the doors opened. Franklin thanked him politely, but said that he feared his health would not allow him during the winter months to go out in the evening except on the most urgent business. Young William, however, eagerly declared that if Monsieur de Beaumarchais would be so good as to send him a ticket he would be extremely obliged.

After some further conversation on trifling matters the Doctor rose as a sign that the audience was at an end. He dismissed his visitor with the formal assurance that America deeply appreciated the services of the friends of liberty in France, but his words sounded chilly, and Beaumarchais, though he did not betray his feelings, had little cause for satisfaction at the results of the interview.

☆   ☆   ☆

During the remaining days of winter Franklin continued to be plagued with tiresome negotiations. Silas Deane sent on to him contractors and shipowners who were anxious to offer their services, and persistently urged him to maintain closer contact with Beaumarchais. Doctor Dubourg also sent him contractors and shipowners who were anxious to offer their services, and persistently urged him to break off contact with Beaumarchais. They both sent people who wanted letters of recommendation to influential persons in America. Arthur Lee had some fault or other to find with every word he said or wrote. Franklin listened to Doctor Dubourg, he listened to Silas Deane, and he listened to Arthur Lee. To each of them he replied in amiable, but noncommittal, terms, and let things take their course.

Count Vergennes had stressed the advisability of his presenting himself to the public eyes as a man of science, not as a politician, and this he willingly did. He visited the numerous libraries, including the Royal Library, the Sainte-Geneviève, and the Mazarin, and everywhere he was received with the deepest respect. Then he put in an appearance at the Academy of Sciences. He was a member of this exclusive association, a distinction sought after by scholars throughout the world. No more than seven of its members were foreigners, and Franklin was the only American.

He had attended a meeting of the Academy once before, on the occasion of an earlier sojourn in Paris, but now that he had put his philosophy into practice and transformed words into deeds, his visit caused even more stir than it did then. He was introduced by Doctors Le Roy and Le Veillard. Thirty-one out of the forty members were on hand; they all begged to be presented to him in order that they might express the deep emotion and veneration with which they were filled. At the end of the session the Vice-President, Monsieur Turgot, moved a resolution that Franklin's presence on that occasion should be recorded in the minutes, and this was unanimously approved.

All these activities, whether enjoyable or, as was more frequently the case, depressing, took place during the cold, damp Parisian winter, and the cramped inconvenience of his quarters at the Hôtel d'Hambourg did nothing to alleviate his uneasiness either of body or of mind. He felt exhausted, and longed for the moment when he could move out to Passy, which he had already begun to call "his" Passy.

The news from overseas, at least, was cheering. General Washington had gone over to the offensive, crossed the Delaware, and gained a surprise victory at Trenton over strong enemy forces. A few days later he had defeated the English General Mawhood at Princetown and forced him to retreat on New York. Franklin was a skilful propagandist and knew how to turn this auspicious intelligence to the best advantage. Every journal in Paris, under his inspiration, published articles in celebration of the victory and drew the happiest auguries for the future.

Everywhere enthusiasm was unbounded, and the Doctor soon began to reap the fruits. Arthur Lee, who felt himself eclipsed in Paris by Franklin's mighty shadow, decided that the time was ripe for a journey to Spain, where he could work independently of his colleagues. Franklin hastened to provide him with passports and letters of recommendation, and when all was ready he shook Lee warmly by the hand, wished him a pleasant journey and a long, successful stay in Madrid, and breathed a sigh of relief as the carriage rolled away into the distance.

The news of the American victory did not fail of its effect on Franklin's relations with Count de Maurepas, the First Minister, at Versailles. Madame de Maurepas had not forgotten that Franklin, on his earlier visit to Paris ten years before, had made a special point of calling upon them. At that time Maurepas had not yet become the omnipotent statesman that he now was, but was living on his estates at Pontchartrain, whither he had been banished by the old King, Louis XV, as a mild punishment for having composed a malicious epigram on Madame de Pompadour. It was here that Franklin, who regarded him with sympathy on account of his liberal ideas, had made the gesture of paying him a special visit.

Maurepas made no attempt to conceal the friendly admiration he felt for Franklin, but the policy he pursued in the American question remained undefined, and for this there was good reason. Louis XVI was pious, and believed in the indissoluble union of the monarchy with God and the Church. Old Maurepas, however, was in his heart of hearts a free-thinker. He was tolerant in religious matters and accessible to liberal ideas.

On the other hand, he was now seventy-six years of age and with the passing of time he had grown more and more cynical. He had only one ambition left, and that was to die in office. He therefore prudently humoured the susceptibilities of the young monarch while taking care to maintain his own reputation as a man of progressive mind and, whenever possible, having regard for the opinions of the more advanced of the Paris salons. So far as the American question was concerned it was very difficult for him to look both ways, since the views of the King and those of his subjects in the capital were diametrically opposed. His own opinion vacillated. If he had been a private person he would probably have espoused the cause of the insurgents with a slightly ironic smile of benevolence. The attempt to build up a community on the principles of reason and natural religion was an interesting experiment, particularly when it was being carried out on the other side of the Atlantic Ocean. As a statesman, however, his attitude was by no means so clear-cut. It was, of course, desirable to support any action calculated to weaken England, but a victory won by rebels, whoever they were, could not be welcome to an absolute monarchy like that of France. Versailles was still in process of reorganizing its armed forces, and its aim must therefore be to fan the conflict between England and America until the French were strong enough to resume the struggle with their ancient enemy across the Channel. Versailles was consequently against England in her war with the colonies, but not for the rebels. Maurepas had therefore maintained a studied neutrality towards the rebels. One morning, however, a little unexpectedly, the Countess proposed that they should give a reception for Franklin. Maurepas pondered for a few moments. It was a bold suggestion that the First Minister of France should receive in his own house the American emissary whom Versailles could not recognize officially. On the other hand, Doctor Franklin was living in Paris as a private individual, he was a scientist of world renown, and he was moreover an old friend to whom they owed hospitality. So all in all Madame de Maurepas's idea was really very opportune, and the Minister was prepared to consider it.

They were both sitting at breakfast in the Palace of Versailles, in one of the small, but exceedingly comfortable, rooms which the young

King had assigned to his chief adviser in the proximity of his own apartments. The Minister was normally prim and formal, but on this occasion he had requested permission from the Countess to appear in his dressing-gown. It was a cold, wintry morning and he had taken the precaution to wrap his dried-up old body in a multiplicity of shawls, from which his bright, bird-like eyes darted quick glances at his wife. She was a good twenty-five years younger than he, and as she sat, her cat Gris-Gris in her lap, she was still very attractive, with her fine figure, and her black, restless eyes in her oval face.

"A reception for our Franquelin," he murmured thoughtfully, chipping away at his egg. "A charming idea. It raises one or two delicate problems, but a charming idea. And how were you thinking of arranging it?"

"It would perhaps be better," replied Madame de Maurepas, "if the invitations were issued in my name only, and not in yours. Doctor Franquelin is an old friend of mine, and the least I can do for him is to invite a few people to meet him. Of course I will ask my guests to come to the rue de Grenelle." It was in the rue de Grenelle that the town-house of the Maurepas was situated, a large, old-fashioned mansion called the Hôtel Phélypeau which was very little used.

"A charming idea," repeated the old Minister. "It is true that the Hôtel Phélypeau is a hideous setting for a party, and it is so difficult to heat, but after all Franquelin is the representative of a primitive nation and he is not likely to catch rheumatism. Perhaps," he sighed, "others may avoid catching it too."

"If I understand you aright, Jean-Frédéric, you will yourself put in an appearance at my reception?" she asked.

Maurepas carefully put his egg-spoon down in the saucer and kissed her hand with a show of animation. "It will give me much pleasure, Madame," he replied, "to greet our friend Franquelin."

So it was agreed that there should be a reception for Franklin. Madame de Maurepas expended considerable forethought on the drawing up of her list of guests, who were to include all the members of the higher aristocracy reputed to be favourable to liberal ideas. The fastidious salons of Versailles and Paris thought it frightfully intriguing of the Countess to present the brown-coated advocate of republican liberty to the proud aristocracy of France.

The Doctor realized at once why this fête was being arranged. He was going to be put on show as if he were a dancing bear. But he was also aware that it was not being done with any unfriendly intention. The whole of Paris was still excited about the victories of Trenton and Princetown, and it was advisable to strike the iron while it was hot. He would have liked to appear in fashionable dress like all the other guests, but it would have been discourteous to disappoint them of their expectation of seeing him in his Quaker coat.

The company assembled by Madame de Maurepas to greet the guest of honour was exceedingly select. Never during the months he had spent in France had Franklin seen so many bearers of ancient names. But the refined ladies of this aristocratic gathering formed a no less inquisitive circle round the celebrated foreigner than had the provincial and bourgeois ladies of Nantes; they plied him with questions that made an equal demand upon his patient indulgence, and they were equally thrilled by his grave, old-fashioned charm of manner. "Isn't he fascinating," they babbled, "our philosopher from the wild West? One has only to look at him and one senses the tremendous loneliness of those vast forests of theirs."

Maurepas himself arrived with deliberate unpunctuality. He wanted to demonstrate that he did not take the reception too seriously. The spindly little Minister and the massive American embraced and clapped one another on the shoulder, and then Maurepas proceeded to explain to everyone how agreeable it was not to have to fulfil the duties of a host, since he too was a guest that evening, the party being given by his wife. After listening to the praises sung in honour of Franklin, he said to the gentlemen, "Yes, he is a Seneca and a Brutus rolled into one, but let us hope that he will be luckier than those two politicians were." To the ladies he said, "I have a great affection for our Franquelin, too, but really, Madame la Marquise, if you continue to betray such enthusiasm you will make me jealous."

Shortly afterwards he declared that he would like to have his friend Franklin to himself for a while and, accompanied by Sallé, his secretary, he escorted the Doctor to his private apartments. Since he regarded the quarters assigned to him in the Palace of Versailles as his actual home, he devoted little attention to his rambling old town-house in Paris, which had fallen into neglect during his long banishment from the capital, and the only rooms he had fitted up comfortably were those reserved for his own use.

"I must show you the room," he said, "which I like best of all in this house," and he led the way to an elegantly furnished chamber of moderate size, the walls of which were covered with heavy silk curtains. "Please make yourself at home," he requested, and with a smile drew back the curtains, revealing finely executed paintings of nude, or mostly nude, women by contemporary masters. There was a Venus, just emerged from the waves, with her arms raised and the lower part of her silvery pink torso thrust slightly forward. Everyone in Paris knew who this Venus was. One of the old King's mistresses, Miss O'Murphy, appeared twice, lying naked on a couch with her delicate posterior curves turned towards the spectator. "When we, the young King and I," explained Maurepas, "inspected for the first time the private apartments of His late Majesty, to which we had not hitherto had access, we came upon these pictures. The young King is not exactly a passionate lover of art. The kind of pictures he likes best are maps, and he was afraid that these paintings might disturb him when he is working, so he asked me to have them removed. That is why they are now temporarily accommodated here. I have them on loan and only show them to such of my friends as are connoisseurs." The old art-lover allowed his eyes to rove appreciatively over the precious canvases.

Franklin was a scientist and had little understanding of art. He was more interested in the theory of sound than in the controversy whether Gluck or Piccinni was the better composer, and Newton's theory of colours appeared to him more important than the laws of painting as observable in Titian or Rembrandt. He liked to look at a pretty woman, and doubtless to kiss one too, particularly if she was of buxom figure, but he had no taste for the over-refined sensuality and seductive decadence of the pictures which Maurepas was gazing at with such fond pride. He did not wish, however, to hurt the latter's feelings and commented politely, "Remarkable! What light and shade! What amazing flesh-tones! I am honoured that you should permit me to see these treasures." The Minister realized with regret how little appreciation for real art the man from Philadelphia possessed, though he tried to conceal his disappointment.

With an air of joviality he changed the subject and broached the topic which he had brought Franklin there to discuss. "I do not like," he said, "being formal, especially here, where I can cast off my official cares. In these rooms I am no longer a Minister." Then he continued in a confidential tone, "May I ask you as a private individual, my dear Doctor, how you get on with my friend and colleague, Vergennes?"

"Excellently," replied Franklin without hesitation. "I find Count Vergennes perfectly sincere, and that is a quality I know how to esteem."

"I am very glad," said Maurepas, "to know that you take such an understanding view of our situation. Vergennes and I are in complete accord on the guiding principles of our American policy."

Franklin gazed abstractedly at the obscene pictures on the wall, the thighs of Venus and the shapely hips of Miss O'Murphy. Maurepas had obviously introduced him to his private picture gallery with the intention of drawing him into a confidential political discussion, and Franklin realized that this was not an occasion for confining himself to mere empty courtesies. He must take the offensive. "Frankly," he said, "I do not find it easy to bear patiently this period of inactive waiting to which Versailles has condemned me. To stand by passively is hard for the representative of a nation which has been tried beyond endurance and is now waging a struggle for its very existence. I have to take into account the fact that my attitude of caution may be misinterpreted at home, quite apart from the circumstance that my colleagues do not see eye to eye with me in regard to the necessity for such a policy."

Maurepas smiled. "Yes, yes," he commented, "we elder statesmen sometimes have our difficulties with the younger generation. It takes years and years before they learn that politics is a game that has to be played with the head, not with the heart," and with a sigh he drew the silken curtains over the old King's paintings.

Franklin was glad to have the portraits concealed from view. They were a disturbing element in the room, and in any case they seemed to him to be anatomically inexact. He remained silent, waiting to hear what else Maurepas had to say. After a while the Minister asked bluntly, "Do I understand that the two millions you have received from us are regarded as inadequate compensation for the caution which you are being compelled to observe?"

That was how Franklin did regard the two millions, and he rejoined, "It is as I have said. The Government's delaying policy is making our position here a little ridiculous."

"A Doctor Franklin can never appear ridiculous," replied Maurepas tactfully. "No foreign scholar has ever been paid such homage by the people of Paris as they have paid to you."

"We are grateful," said Franklin, "for the devotion and enthusiasm with which our cause has been greeted in your capital, but it had been our hope that the evident community of our interests would induce Versailles, too, to enter into closer relations with the representatives of the thirteen States."

Maurepas twisted his dry lips into a thin smile. This man from the West had earned a reputation for simplicity, but it was clear that he could be far from simple when he wanted to, and it was really not very seemly to introduce such banalities into a discussion with the First Minister of France. He sat and blinked at the American. What a massive fellow this Franklin was, full of peasant cunning, with his pretence of being a frank and honest bourgeois! The cause he represented might, perhaps, be useful to the world at large, but it certainly had its dangers for the French monarchy. This allegedly simpleminded American citizen must be made to realize that the French Government was not deluded either by him or his policy. "I am growing old," he said, "and I think it is time to record my experiences for the benefit of posterity. I have therefore begun to write my memoirs. That is to say," he corrected himself, "my trustworthy Sallé, who is the repository of my secrets, is writing my memoirs. Sallé's aim is to put on record my honest opinions. I have, however, no secrets that I would wish to conceal from my old friend, Doctor Franklin. Tell us, my dear Sallé, what we are writing in our memoirs concerning the relations between Versailles and the revolting colonies."

Franklin had already heard about these memoirs. The aged Maurepas had let everyone know of his intention to tell the unvarnished truth and to leave instructions that it was to be published immediately after his death. Whenever he wanted to intimidate either an enemy or a friend, he would threaten roguishly, "Have a care, my dear fellow, you might cut a sorry figure in my memoirs," and he would contemplate with glee the rather wry smile on the face of the person he was addressing.

Franklin had asked himself at the start why Maurepas had brought his secretary, and he now peered through his spectacles at the colourless individual who had hitherto been sitting there silently as if he were nonexistent. Both the Minister, who had reduced this man to a disembodied shadow, and the secretary himself, who had allowed himself thus to be deprived of his personality, exemplified the pernicious effect a despotic regime could have on human beings.

Monsieur Sallé's lips parted, and the voice that emerged sounded hollow and lifeless, as Franklin had anticipated. "We have grown old," the voice recited, like a clerk reading out a document, "and we have seen many things. We have seen men turn and twist with such shameless haste that we would not have believed such unprincipled chopping and changing possible if we had not ourselves experienced it and, to be quite candid, ourselves indulged in it. Only recently, for instance, the English colonists in America were carrying on a bloody war against us. They barbarously invaded territories in which we had settled and which we had civilized. And even more recently, when England found herself forced to allow a part of Canada to continue in its French way of living, these Anglo-American colonists overwhelmed the French regime, French manners, and the Catholic Church with savage imprecations. Now these same Anglo-American colonists are making overtures to us, smiling innocently and asking. 'Are we not friends? Have we not interests in common?' "

Franklin's wide mouth curved in a smile as he repeated, "Are we not friends? Have we not interests in common?" He stressed very slightly the words "are" and "have."

Sallé's faded voice went on, "The Kingdom of France and the English colonies of America have two mutual interests—the weakening of England and reciprocal trade between themselves. Apart from this, we see nothing but opposing aims. The absolute monarchy of France can have no interest in presenting its subjects with the spectacle of a successful revolution."

Franklin now knew why the old statesman had wanted to speak to him in private. He desired in this rather tortuous way to make it quite clear that he and Vergennes were giving their support out of pure good will, and that the American envoys were asking for a great deal without having anything to offer in return. Things, however, were not so simple as all that. If France were to stand idly by while England forced the Americans into submission, it could only be a question of time before both the English and the Americans together fell upon the French possessions in the West Indies, the rich sugar islands. This was not an argument of which Franklin could make strong use, but, if properly presented, it was bound to make some impression on Maurepas. The latter, however, seemed to think he had said enough to convince the other that he was not to be made a fool of. Before Franklin had a chance to reply he proposed that they should rejoin the rest of the company: "I have kept you too long from the Countess's guests."

During the absence young William had succeeded in focusing attention on himself, for it had not taken him long to discover that when the old man was about the best thing he could do was to play the affectionate grandson and remain in the shadow of his venerable progenitor. When the old man was out of the way, however, William emerged into the limelight. He was dressed in the latest fashion, he had learned how to pay compliments to the ladies, and he had been taught by experience that these compliments only gained in piquancy by his faulty French. So young William was now in his element.

And in the meantime another guest had arrived to stimulate the interest of Madame de Maurepas's aristocratic friends—Monsieur de Beaumarchais. It was most unusual to find a man whose title had been purchased and whose reputation was so dubious in such a select gathering, but the Countess had taken into consideration the fact that her "Toutou" was very closely concerned with American affairs, and she had not wanted to mortify him by omitting to send him an invitation. Yet though he had been pleased and proud to receive the invitation, he had hesitated before making up his mind to come. Franklin had studiously, if politely, ignored him, and he did not want to give the impression of running after the old man. In the end, however, he had decided to accept. The very difficulty with which he was faced in overcoming Franklin's resistance acted as a spur. He was a past master in the art of drawing reluctant collaborators into his net, and it would have been absurd to abandon his fish so soon.

Once at the reception he felt very self-confident; he was in good form, and found a ready audience for what he had to say about the victories at Trenton and Princetown. He spoke with warmth and appeared to have expert knowledge of the military situation.

Among those who listened to him was Lenormant. Their secret rivalry to see which of them would turn out to be right in his estimate of the Americans' chances had taken on a sharper edge and coloured both their personal and their business relations. Pierre's prospects had grown brighter with the American successes, and the fact that Charlot was among his audience stimulated him still further to display his wit. Lenormant listened quietly for a time with his customary air of friendliness, but he did not fail to notice the covert challenge implied in Pierre's comments. "I am delighted to see you so confident, my dear Pierrot," he said at last, "but I have just had an opportunity of exchanging a word or two with Doctor Franklin and he is not quite so optimistic as you are." There was an irritating smile on the corner of his lips, and Pierre felt a slight chill, but it quickly passed and he continued his exposition in a tone of even greater conviction which impressed his hearers.

Franklin and Maurepas had by now returned. The Doctor had not expected to see Beaumarchais at the reception. Even his friend Doctor Dubourg would hardly have had access to such an exclusive circle. But he controlled his feelings and greeted Pierre with a marked show of cordiality, to the latter's mingled pleasure and astonishment. Concluding that the old man had changed his mind and now regretted his former aloofness, Pierre proceeded to congratulate him on the recent victories as heartily as if Franklin himself had been personally responsible for them, and the two men were soon the centre of a crowd of interested listeners. Pierre was flattered at sharing an audience with Franklin, and in order to exploit his triumph over Lenormant he once more launched into a disquisition on the military prospects of the American troops, a subject he had carefully studied and on which he had sent detailed reports in his dispatches from London to the King and his Ministers. The Americans, he explained, could not be conquered, because their territory was so vast. The trained English regulars would be able to capture towns, of course, but they could not prevent Washington from withdrawing more and more deeply into the hinterland, the boundless, inaccessible forests where there were no roads and from which he could make constant sallies. The English generals would be faced with a war of attrition.

Franklin listened attentively. He had decided to be forbearing with Beaumarchais, whose rhetorical skill and agile wit he fully appreciated, and it had to be admitted that there was some truth in the views he was putting forward, though they were naturally coloured by the romanticism with which the French invested American affairs. There was no denying the possibility that they might really in the end be forced to organize a general withdrawal into the trackless hinterland. Yet though the Doctor envisaged such an outcome, he found it distasteful to listen to this dandified, perfumed Frenchman discoursing in such eloquent fashion about things that caused the heart to constrict. Despite his determination not to let impatience get the better of him, he could not suppress his old sense of irritation. "It would be a bitter experience, Monsieur," he said, "if we were compelled to wage war in the manner you have indicated. The cost would be heavy. A large proportion of our population lives in cities, such as Boston, Baltimore, New York, and Philadelphia. Philadelphia is the largest English-speaking city in the world after London. Just imagine what your own situation would be if you had to exchange your residence in Paris for a sojourn amid primeval forests."

Pierre was disappointed and angry. He had spoken from the deepest conviction, and what he had said could be justified in the light of reason. Yet Franklin had made him look foolish. He did not dare to catch Lenormant's eye, and it was only with difficulty that he managed to conceal his resentment. Then, however, Franklin looked him full in the face and his broad countenance expanded in an affable smile as he continued, "For the rest, Monsieur, you are right. England has three times as many inhabitants as we have, trained armies, a mighty fleet, and numerous hired mercenaries, but neither in the political nor in the military field has she any hope of victory. She will have to recognize our independence, and when the conflict is over she will be forced to admit that we are stronger than when it began." And he proceeded to relate one of his anecdotes. "An eagle, having spied a rabbit, swooped down and carried it up into the air. But it was a cat, not a rabbit, and it dug its claws into him and held on. The eagle loosened its talons and wanted to let the cat go, but the latter thought the drop too dangerous, clung on more tightly than ever, and said, 'If you want to get rid of me, eagle, you must be good enough to set me down at the place where you picked me up.' "

This was a homely parable for the Countess de Maurepas's guests, who had been brought up on the fables and frivolous *contes* of La Fontaine, but they saw the point and thoughtfully smiled their approval. They realized that the simple, patriarchal story embodied a deep conviction, and that if he had wished, the old man could have clothed his opinion in wittier words such as they were accustomed to hearing. Pierre could have contented himself with the reflection that Franklin had, after all, admitted his view to be justified, and he did indeed go so far as to clap his hands in applause, but as he chatted with his neighbour he was suddenly assailed by a feeling of helplessness, a sense of being no match for this American who put him so completely in the shade. For a moment he seemed to be falling into an abyss, on the verge of an unprecedented inner collapse. All his life he had been persuaded that what a man appeared to be was more important than what he was. *Pas être, paraître.* This was the principle on which he had based his whole existence, both his outward career and his secret thoughts. It was not what one admitted to oneself that mattered, but what one expressed in public; not the money one actually possessed, but the money one spent when others were there to see one spend it. The ideals a man carried in his heart were of no account compared with those he acknowledged to the world. That had been Pierre's credo. And now this American had come into his life, a man who made no effort to appear witty and spoke but little, even that little being the veriest homespun, and expressed moreover in halting French. Yet his mere simple, venerable personality made a deeper impression than he himself had been able to achieve with all his intellectual pyrotechnics. Pierre wondered why he had been so anxious all his life to play the strenuous role of a man who even in the most adverse situations smiled carelessly and, when danger threatened, passed it off with a witty *mot*.

This sudden onset of despair, however, passed in a flash, hardly taking the form of concrete thought, and while the consciousness of his inward emptiness began to gnaw at his mind his expression did not change. He continued to listen with an air of polite attention, and though he may not have heard everything that his companion, the Chevalier de Buysson, was saying, he had gathered enough to be aware that the young officer was one of the group who wished to go overseas to take an active part in the American war of independence. Shaking off the last vestige of the haunting fear with which Franklin had inspired him, he pretended to have been absorbed in what the Chevalier had been telling him, offered his hearty congratulations, and regained something of his normal verve as he assured the eager soldier that he would be only too happy to assist him in his preparations for embarkation.

Franklin sat tranquilly in his arm-chair, against which young William was leaning in a graceful attitude, and a number of the guests, including Pierre and de Buysson, had formed a circle round him. He could not help overhearing the Chevalier's remarks, which in any case had probably been intended more for him than for Pierre, and he interjected, "I too find your project very laudable, Chevalier. Nonetheless I would beg you, before coming to a final decision, to take into consideration the views of an old man who is familiar with conditions on the other side of the Atlantic. Monsieur de Beaumarchais was quite right when he pointed out a few moments ago that this war is being conducted in a very different way from European wars. I have been told that during the last French campaign the commander of your Army, before the opening of a battle, invited the English commander to fire first. In the war which we are now waging there can be no question of such an exchange of courtesies. Our war is not a sequence of brilliant, colourful, heroic battles, but rather an endless sequence of exceedingly unspectacular skirmishes, of physical hardships and dispiriting experiences. That is what it is like now, and that is what it will no doubt continue to be like in the future. Think of what I am telling you, Chevalier, before you cross the ocean."

There was a deep silence. Franklin had spoken without emphasis, as was his habit, but his words had been so impressive that the brilliant room and the gaily dressed throng seemed to melt away into a desolate vista in which there was nothing but squalor and devastation, hunger and sickness, and men dying miserably. The old man realized that he had stretched the bow a little far. He squared his shoulders, shook his massive head so that his sparse locks fell lower over his collar, raised his voice slightly, and declared, "But it will be all right. *Ça ira*. It will be all right."

Chapter Three

Louis and Toinette

❋ ★ ❋

With bright and colourful pomp the procession wended its
way through the Hall of Mirrors. Preceded by officers of the
Guards, and followed by the ladies and gentlemen of their
suite, Louis and Toinette walked between the ranks of deeply bowing
courtiers on either side, the mirrors reflecting the brilliant scene a
hundredfold. It was not easy to keep one's footing as one moved
along, for the parquet flooring was slippery; one had to take cautious,
gliding steps, one dared not lift one's feet from the ground; moreover,
the gentlemen were hampered by their swords, the ladies by their
voluminous skirts. Yet those taking part in the procession seemed to
have no difficulty, for they had had long practice, and there was a
light, festive air about this royal train, apart from the King himself,
who pushed his stout body along with an awkward, waddling motion.
Louis XVI had walked in this way through the Hall of Mirrors
innumerable times, on the way to mass and on the way back from
mass, but it was obvious that he still found it an ordeal. With an embarrassed smile on his flabby, boyish face he set one heavy foot before
the other with a maladroit movement that filled the courtiers lining
the route with apprehension lest he should topple over and bring
everyone in his immediate vicinity crashing to the floor.

The Queen, Toinette, who walked at his side, appeared all the more
airily graceful by contrast. Many of the spectators had more than once
indulged their spiteful wit at the expense of this haughty Austrian
princess from far-away Vienna, whose profligate ways and love of
gambling were no desirable asset to *la belle France,* but she looked so
young and charming as she glided along, tall, slim and radiant, every
inch the great lady, that malice was silenced and they were content to
watch. Her throat and shoulders, arms and bosom, were dazzlingly
white against the lace of her dress, her deep blue eyes, set in a long,
oval face, flashed beneath arching brows, her magnificent fair hair
was piled up high and gleamed above a lofty forehead. The slightly
aquiline nose and full, somewhat protruding under lip preserved the
face from what would otherwise have been a rather monotonous, if

harmonious, regularity. Her tall, elegant figure appeared to hover rather than to walk, and with her mingled air of youthful friendliness and royal pride she fitted perfectly into the role she had to play of daughter to Maria Theresa, sister to the Emperor Joseph, and wife to the King of France.

The thoughts agitating the brain behind that serene forehead were, however, far from agreeable. Toinette had enjoyed little sleep the night before. At a party given by the Princess Rohan she had played for hours and lost heavily. No doubt Count Mercy and the Abbé Vermond, the worthy counsellors whom her mother had inflicted upon her, were already aware of her indiscretion and she would have to submit to their reproaches. They would probably even report it to her mother in Vienna. In any case, she was now going to be short of funds and would again have to apply to Louis for money.

There had been many guests at the Princess Rohan's, too many, and some of them should never have been there. That Marquis de Dreneux and the Marquis de la Vaupalière, who had taken turns in holding the bank, probably had no right to the titles by which they had been introduced, and that Mr. Smith from Manchester was an Indian nabob, a very dubious character.

She ought to have stopped playing at midnight. She had indeed intended to do so and had already risen from the table, but she had allowed herself to be persuaded by Prince Charles, her brother-in-law, to sit down again and try to recoup herself for her losses. It was only after midnight that her losses had become really serious. But it was exciting. If she were to be quite honest with herself she had to admit that if the most exciting thing in the world was to win heavily at cards, the second most exciting was to lose heavily.

It was time to stop, however. She was now twenty-one and it would be foolish to keep on gambling in that reckless way. She had already firmly made up her mind that she was not going to play again tonight. She would join her circle of friends, since they would joke about her if she did not put in an appearance, but however much her brother-in-law Charles might chaff her, she would stick to her guns and no power in the world would induce her to play again.

They had reached the Queen's apartments and the cortège began to disperse. Toinette allowed her attendants to disrobe her and then, when she was alone, she breathed a deep sigh of relief, stretched her young limbs, and yawned loudly.

There were three hours in front of her before it was necessary to dress for supper, and her appointments included a conference with Mique, the architect. She had intended to have a thorough discussion with him about the replanning of her gardens at the Trianon. The Abbé Vermond had also asked for an audience, no doubt in order to read her a lecture on her mother's behalf. If he took his time about it she would have no more than an hour in which to rest. No, she would receive neither the Abbé nor the architect. She would sleep, sleep for three whole hours, so that she could be fresh in the evening and in a fit condition to resist the temptations of the card-table.

She was sitting in her spacious formal bedchamber, with its massive bed behind heavy embroidered curtains, and in her negligee she looked a healthy, lighthearted young woman, frivolous and pleasure-loving, very pretty, but at the moment very tired. She gazed with repugnance at the vast state bed, thinking of the ceremonies that took place around it every morning and evening, when she awoke and when she retired, of the ladies-in-waiting who handed her her chemise and her stockings and her washbasin, each presenting a different article in accordance with the strictest rules of etiquette, and for each of which attendants she had to have a friendly smile and a friendly word, since a hundred eyes followed her every movement.

With a roguish smile, and still wearing her slippers, Toinette tiptoed out of her formal bedchamber, ran along one of the dark passages that twisted and twined behind it, and along a second passage in the vast labyrinth with which she had become familiar, until she came to a small room which was never used except in the eventuality of the Queen's becoming pregnant. Then it was occupied by a lady-in-waiting, who spent the night there. Very few knew of its existence, and no one would expect to find Toinette there. After closing and bolting the door, she threw off her dressing-gown and lay down, completely naked, on the narrow, unpretentious bed. She stretched herself, gave a tremendous yawn, turned over on the other side, and drew up her knees. Then she fell into a deep, dreamless sleep, while the architect and the Abbé waited in the antechamber two corridors away for their audience with the Queen.

☆   ☆   ☆

When Toinette appeared in the apartments of the Princess Rohan, she was greeted as usual by the yapping of the Princess's little dogs and the screeching of her parrot. The Princess never allowed herself to be separated from her dogs, Chérie, Aimée, and Joujou, and she was never disturbed by the screeches of her parrot, Monsieur. The only thing he could say was, *"Les amants arrivent."* That was all he had ever learnt. He was a very ancient bird, having been alive, so it was said, during the Regency, when he grew up in a celebrated private hotel much frequented by the high nobility. Hence his peculiar form of greeting.

It was late and all the guests were assembled, a game having already started at the faro table, but no one interrupted what he was doing since Toinette had insisted that there was to be no ceremony when she was with her circle of intimate friends, who called themselves the Lilac Coterie. Princess Rohan and Gabrielle Polignac, Toinette's closest friend, came towards her. Gabrielle, in her soft, lazy voice, said, "Here you are, Toinette," but the Princess was loquaciously reproachful that she had come so late.

The Princess Rohan was a pretty woman, though her face, with its large, restless eyes, was a little too thin and harassed. Her speech and gestures seemed to be marked by some consuming obsession. Her husband, with whom she was passionately in love, neglected her atrociously, and she took refuge in communion with the spirits of the dead. She was rich, gave large parties at which her dogs and cats were always allowed to roam freely, could say startlingly clever things, never stinted either time or money for her friends, and her idiosyncrasies were accepted with good-natured irony by the cynical fashionables of Paris and Versailles. In spite of their free-thinking, most of them were actually tickled by her visions, and when they discussed among themselves the alleged utterances of the materialized spirits it was evident that for all their mockery they were not entirely sceptical.

Prince Charles greeted Toinette. "I am glad to see, sister-in-law," he said, "that you have taken my advice. Come along, let us have our revenge." Charles, the youngest brother of King Louis, was barely twenty, and whereas Louis and Prince Xavier, his other brother, were both very stout, he was slim and good-looking. He was a regular rascal, up to any kind of trick, of cheerful disposition and a welcome companion in Toinette's pleasures, of which indeed he was at times the moving spirit.

She cast a hankering glance at the gaming-table, where there could be heard the quiet chink of coins and the faint impact of cards being turned up, but she kept control of herself. "No," she said, "I am not playing tonight. I only came to see you all. It has been a strenuous day, with attendance at mass and the reception for the ambassadors, but here I am," and she looked around with a radiant light in her eyes. The sight of the card-table was, however, too alluring, and after a while she put her arm round Gabrielle's shoulder and went with her into a small adjoining room leading off from the salon.

The Marquis de Vaudreuil, the handsomest of the male members of the Lilac Coterie, was sitting on a sofa a little apart from the others with Diane Polignac, the sister of Count Jules and Gabrielle's sister-in-law. For a moment he thought of calling out some jesting remark to the two ladies as they slowly walked across the large room with their arms gracefully entwined round one another, but he decided that it would be in bad taste and refrained, resting content to follow them with his eyes, that were lit by a desire not belied by his slightly mocking smile. As he continued to chat with Diane Polignac his mind was busy comparing the contrasting charms of Toinette and Gabrielle, an occupation in which he often indulged. Toinette was young, vivacious, and gay, and every impulsive emotion, which she made no more attempt to conceal than a child, was reflected in her face. Vaudreuil was fascinated, yet almost angry, as he once more observed the strikingly haughty effect of the Habsburg features in an otherwise childlike face, the slightly hanging under lip and the bold, aquiline nose. Gabrielle, who was twenty-eight, had the same lofty forehead as Toinette, but her slightly slumberous eyes were set widely apart and were of a much deeper blue beneath their dark brows, her nose had a charming tilt, and her face gleamed palely under her jet-black hair. The innumerable admirers of Gabrielle praised the "divine purity" of her countenance, and Vaudreuil smiled to himself as he thought of what went on behind that angelic mask.

The two women sat down in the small cabinet. The curtains which closed it off from the salon were drawn back so that they were visible to the others in the larger room, and Toinette kept control of her features. From her smiling lips, however, there poured a stream of bitter complaint. She had sense enough, she said, to stay away from the cardtable, since that was what was demanded of her, but was it not an intolerable humiliation that she, the Queen, had no freedom whatsoever? Every step she took was hampered by this stupid etiquette, and even in her few leisure hours she was not allowed to do the things which gave her pleasure. Yet for all her restraint and self-sacrifice she earned nothing but reproaches. Really, any fishwife of the *halles* was better off than the Queen of France.

Gabrielle Polignac affectionately stroked her friend's lovely arm and her long, delicately plump hand. "Would you like to change places with a fishwife?" she asked in her lazy, mellow voice. Toinette laughed. "What quaint ideas you have, Gabrielle," she said.

Through the open doorway they could see Vaudreuil, who was still chatting with Diane Polignac. Gabrielle's sister-in-law was dark and thin, with a sharp nose, but plain though she was she had by far the most intelligent mind of all the Polignacs, and was in fact the cleverest member of the Lilac Coterie. "Why does he give so much of his time to her?" asked Toinette. Gabrielle did not reply, but her large eyes glided slowly over the pair. Toinette knew, as did everybody else, that Vaudreuil was Gabrielle's lover, though the two women hardly ever spoke about it. Abruptly she asked, "Are you never jealous, Gabrielle?"

Gabrielle, her eyes still on Vaudreuil and Diane, continued slowly, but with rather more pressure, to caress Toinette's arm. "I am not interested in anyone but you, Toinette," she said.

"But what is the real reason why he talks only to Diane?" Toinette persisted.

Gabrielle was silent for a moment before she answered, "I think he is worried. He does not let us see it, because he is too proud, but he can talk about it to Diane because she is not beautiful."

Toinette knew what the worries were to which Gabrielle referred. François Vaudreuil was rich, but money ran through his fingers like water. Diane Polignac had suggested to Toinette that she should revive a former court appointment, the post of "Superintendent of the Queen's Private Theatricals and Amusements." Toinette had need of such an officer in her household and the Marquis de Vaudreuil was the very man for the post, to which a considerable salary was attached.

She grew thoughtful. The appointment would involve her in a further expenditure of sixty thousand livres a year. Louis and his Finance Minister, Necker, would pull wry faces, and it would give Count Mercy and the Abbé Vermond the opportunity to indulge in more remonstrances about her expensive friendship with Gabrielle. Yet Gabrielle never demanded anything for herself. She had few wants. When Toinette had first discovered her, being attracted by her beauty and gentle charm, Gabrielle had been poor, so poor that she was compelled to spend the greater part of the year on her dreary, impoverished estate in a remote province, and could spend only two or three weeks at Versailles in order to show herself at court. She had, however, been unconcerned about her poverty, and it was only with the greatest effort and the employment of all her cunning that Toinette had managed to persuade her to accept the money which would enable her and her relatives to take up their residence at Versailles. The Polignacs were, to be sure, a numerous clan and as poor as church mice, and little as Gabrielle needed for herself she could not bring herself to refuse when her husband, Count Jules, and his sister Diane kept urging her to inform her friend of their financial distress. So at last she went to Toinette, blushing slightly with embarrassment, her slumberous eyes looking larger and more girlish than ever, and hinted that her family were once more in difficulties. Toinette could not bear the thought that anyone connected with her dear Gabrielle should suffer from lack of money, and she found a titillating pleasure in consoling her friend and helping her relations. According to a recent calculation by Count Mercy, as he had not failed to remind her, she had showered more than half a million livres a year on the Polignacs. It certainly sounded extravagant, but could she be expected to allow stupid figures to interfere with the only happiness she found in life, her friendship with Gabrielle?

"You are right," she said. "We must do something for our friend François. But he won't accept if I ask him to be the superintendent of my private theatricals and amusements. He has such a strangely exalted sense of pride."

"If anyone else were to make the suggestion he would reject it with scorn," replied Gabrielle. "You are the only one who can talk to him about it, Toinette."

Vaudreuil had meanwhile left Diane and was coming straight across the room towards where they were sitting. No other man would have dared to break in upon the privacy of the Queen and her companion, but he joined them with calm self-assurance and sat down, complimenting Toinette on the firm determination with which she kept away from the card-table.

It was in reality François Vaudreuil who dominated the Lilac Coterie, though in the salons of Paris and Versailles Prince Charles was generally thought to be the leading figure of that select circle. It was he who provided the Prince with his inspiration, but he did it so cleverly that no one, not even the Prince himself, realized it. Vaudreuil preferred to remain in the background, though he could not help attracting attention whether he wanted to or not. He was thirty years of age, of virile appearance, full-faced, with strong features, a bold, sensuous mouth, brown, rather gloomy eyes, thick, black brows and a high, arched forehead. He took an interest in intellectual matters, was acquainted with nearly all the French writers of repute, and was the most gifted and popular of all those who acted in the amateur theatricals of the aristocracy. There were countless rumours in circulation about him, and far beyond the confines of Paris it was said that the three Frenchmen who possessed the most fascination for women were the actor Lekain, the writer Beaumarchais, and the Marquis de Vaudreuil.

"You are right, François," said Toinette. "It is surprising that I am able to refrain from playing. There is nothing left to one but cards, for our other entertainments are so boring. The parties and fêtes I give seem to me to be amateurish. Gabrielle and I have just been talking about it, and I think I should like to re-establish the post of Superintendent of the Queen's Amusements."

The shadow of a frown darkened Vaudreuil's brow. He glanced from one of the ladies to the other, and it was astonishing to see the look of suppressed anger that had suddenly come into his eyes, a smouldering gloom that threatened to burst into one of those storms of uncontrollable fury that made people afraid of him.

Gabrielle rose hurriedly. "I think I ought to join the others," she said, and disappeared into the salon.

"Seriously, François," said Toinette when they were alone, "I need someone to superintend my entertainments, *that* you must admit, and there is nobody but you."

Anyone watching from the salon could see a smiling Vaudreuil sitting in a courteous attitude and apparently conducting a respectfully gallant conversation with the Queen. But Toinette realized that the smile was only on his face and that he could not banish the passion from his eyes. She knew her François. Their relations were of a complicated nature and caused agitation to them both. Louis XVI was her husband only in name. A physical defect prevented him from consummating their marriage, and though this could have been remedied by a simple operation, a form of circumcision, the sluggish young monarch had some kind of inhibition about it and refused to put himself in the surgeon's hands. They had been married six years. The Empress Maria Theresa and the old King Louis had escorted the Dauphin to the bridal chamber amid solemn ceremonies and laid him in the bed of the young Princess while all Europe looked on with interest, but there the matter had ended. Nothing more had happened during those six years. The French nation, filled with reverence for its anointed King, put the blame on Toinette, who had failed in her duty of providing an heir to the throne. The ladies of the *halles,* the fishwives of Paris, sang coarse songs about her, and the elegant writers of the day circulated obscene epigrams. At court, however, the circumstances were no secret. The gentlemen became more importunate and suggestive in their gallantries, while the pampered Vaudreuil made it his ambitious aim to sleep with the Queen of France, the daughter of the Caesars. Toinette, not as yet responsive to such desires, delighted in the homage paid her by the courtiers, flirted assiduously, and the bold flatteries of Vaudreuil, who was expert in such matters, excited her curiosity about a man who appeared to her in such a favourable light when compared with her husband. She submitted to the touch of his hands, to his practised caresses, and granted him a great deal, but she stopped short at the last favour of all. To his alternately persuasive pleas and violent demands she always returned the same answer, that she was firmly resolved not to foist an illegitimate Dauphin on the King of France. She was not prepared to run the risk of conceiving a child by another man.

Not a single one of Vaudreuil's friends would have rejected the offer of an appointment as Superintendent of the Queen's Amusements, but to Vaudreuil the proposal came as a blow. His gloomy eyes wandered up and down Toinette's face and figure, inspecting her from head to toe. She could see how difficult it was for him to maintain his conventional smile, and she could not help recalling how once, when he was in an angry mood, he had kissed her hand in the presence of many others and in doing so had gripped her wrist so fiercely that a bluish-red bruise had remained visible for days.

"You want to fob me off with a paid appointment," he muttered, making an effort to control his deep, mellow voice. "You are offering me charity. That is your confounded Habsburg arrogance. But you are not going to escape me so easily. I don't want your appointment, Toinette, I want something very different." There was bitterness in his voice, mockery, and a menacing, exciting note.

"Do be sensible, François," she begged. "What is there to be gained if one day your stupid creditors drive you into bankruptcy? All that will happen is that you will no longer be received at court and I shall not be able to see you any more."

"Then you will come and visit me at Gennevilliers," he retorted. "I suppose they will leave me one or other of my impoverished estates."

"But this is all very silly," she insisted. "I tell you that I have definitely made up my mind to restore the post I have mentioned. If you will not accept it, then I shall offer it to somebody else, dabblers though they all are."

"Listen, Toinette," he said. "I will willingly produce a play for you now and then, or arrange one of your fêtes, but please do not ask me to accept an official position in your household."

"You are amazingly conceited, François," replied Toinette. "The Marquis de Vaudreuil declines to accept anything from the Queen of France, yet he expects the Queen of France to accept favours from him. I beg of you," she urged, and regardless of the others in the next room she moved closer to his side, "do not refuse this appointment. Do not leave me in the lurch."

Vaudreuil was magnificently unconcerned about his financial difficulties. Money always turned up from some source or another. A François Vaudreuil without money was something beyond his powers of conception. He really did not want the lucrative office that Toinette was trying to induce him to accept, but she looked very charming as she exerted all her arts of persuasion and his desire for her was strong. "All right, Toinette," he declared. "I will think it over. Perhaps I shall decide to become the Superintendent of your Private Theatricals and Amusements. But let me tell you this straightway. If I accept, then I must be allowed to carry out my duties as I think best. If I should call upon the services of one of my knights of the pen, such as Chamfort or Marmontel or Beaumarchais, you must not say, 'Oh, I can't expect Louis to agree to that!'"

He escorted her back to the salon. *"Les amants arrivent,"* screeched the parrot, but nobody took any notice, since they were all used to his peculiar form of greeting. Prince Charles called from the card-table, "You have given us proof enough of your fortitude, sister-in-law. Don't be so dreadfully virtuous!" When she hesitated, he grew more insistent. "I have to pay Louis the Austere a call in any case to wheedle some money out of him. If you have bad luck I will see what I can get for you too."

From the card-table came the low, seductive chink of coins and the subdued cries of the gamblers. Toinette slowly drew nearer. Immediately Prince Charles and Jules Polignac jumped up to make room for her. She was still unable to overcome her reluctance and her face showed the struggle that was going on in her mind.

"Take my seat, Madame," invited Count Jules. "It has brought me luck."

"I will bet for you," cried the Prince. "Twenty louis to start with."

"Do stop jesting, Charles," she said, but she moved closer to the table and watched eagerly.

The Prince won, and the twenty louis had become a hundred. "Your money, sister-in-law," he cried gaily.

"No, no," she protested. Then she added hesitantly, "But you can lend me fifty louis. I did not bring any money with me so as not to succumb to temptation." She sat down and began to play.

They had been playing for some time when the Princess suddenly called out, "The dogs! Look at the dogs! Look at Joujou!" There was nothing remarkable about the dogs, except that they were yapping a little, but that was not unusual. The Princess was staring fixedly into space with a distraught expression in her eyes, her face was convulsed, and she asked in an anguished voice that seemed to be stifled before it reached her lips, "Can't you see her?"

"Ten of spades," said Toinette.

But Diane cried, "Please stop playing!" and Gabrielle inquired gently, "Who is it now?"

"Can't you see her?" the Princess repeated in an urgent whisper. "Don't you see that it is Adrienne?"

Adrienne had been a great actress, the greatest of a generation that had not long passed away. Though she was a calm and gentle creature, there had been some turbulent moments in her life, and she was supposed eventually to have been poisoned by a lady in aristocratic circles who had conceived a spite against her. When she died the Archbishop of Paris had refused to afford her honourable burial. Her fate had been the subject of countless pamphlets, one of the most famous of which, from the pen of Voltaire, had created a tremendous stir throughout France and Europe. This evidently was the Adrienne of whom the Princess Rohan was speaking, and though most of those present were inclined to scoff and were sceptical about the existence of God, they could not help feeling that perhaps the spirit of the dead actress really was in the room. They stood around with a chill shudder running down their spines. The Duc de Fronsac asked in a whisper, "What does she say?" And one of the ladies inquired a little fearfully, "Is she very angry with us?"

"She is not angry," replied the Princess. "She has no desire for revenge, but is only sad."

"But what does she say?" insisted Gabrielle.

"She is sad on our account," said the Princess. "She says that there was a bad beginning and there will be a bad end."

A brief silence ensued. Then Prince Charles said, "I think, ladies and gentlemen, that we can now return to our game."

"Ten of spades," called Toinette, and they went on playing.

☆   ☆   ☆

After her *lever* on the following morning Toinette dismissed her ladies-in-waiting more promptly than was her wont. They withdrew with respectful curtsies, but there was a peevish expression on their faces and they whispered indignantly among themselves. There had been forty-two ladies to assist Toinette in rising from her bed, while another hundred and eleven were in attendance upon her. To all these, the cream of the aristocracy, she had devoted exactly nineteen minutes. Yet for her dressmaker—and none of them doubted that she was now about to confer with her dressmaker—she would again be able to find two or three hours. And moreover Rose Bertin had not even access to the royal apartments. They had to turn and twist the rules of etiquette in order that she might be admitted to one of the "side-rooms," and the thought of these "side-rooms" made the ladies more indignant still. Who knew how many of them Toinette had opened up in the vast, almost endless labyrinth of the Palace of Versailles, and who knew what went on behind their closed doors?

Toinette actually did go straight from her *lever* to one of the side-rooms. Here she sat, closeted with Gabrielle and Rose Bertin, her dressmaker. She was in a radiant mood. She had won at cards on the previous evening. When she lost it was because fate had been unkind. When she won it was due to her own skill.

The dressmaker spread her treasures before the two ladies. A deluge of laces, ribbons, feathers, hats, gloves, fans, precious stuffs, finery of all kinds, overflowed the little chamber and was reflected tenfold in the numerous mirrors. Toinette and Gabrielle rummaged with pleasurable excitement among the expensive fripperies, while fat little Rose Bertin, her alert, pug-nosed, peasant features in odd contrast to her exquisitely fashionable taste, stood by to offer expert advice. It was a very agreeable way of spending a morning.

Meanwhile the Abbé Vermond and Monsieur Mique, the architect, were waiting in the antechamber to the Queen's apartments. She ought really to have received the Abbé first, but she was most anxious to go through his plans with the architect and did not want to spoil a morning that had begun so delightfully by what would no doubt be an unenjoyable interview with her mother's emissary.

Monsieur Mique was shown in, and they at once became absorbed in designs and models.

Toinette had thrown herself heart and soul into the project for reconstructing the Petit-Trianon and replanning its gardens. From the moment when she first saw the austerely elegant little château she had made up her mind that she wanted to own it. She was only fifteen at the time. Her life was bound up with the strict etiquette of the court, and wherever she might be she had to submit to its rules, but here she would be able to make her own rules. In the Trianon she would be not the Queen of France, but Toinette, a young woman who wanted to live in accordance with her heart's desire. As soon as Louis became King she persuaded him to make her a gift of the château and began to rebuild and refurnish it in her own way. She was whole-heartedly in sympathy with the new mode, which rejected the pompous designs of the previous generation and preferred simple lines copied from the models of classical antiquity. It was an elegant simplicity, suited to a refined taste, and it cost money to erect buildings that combined apparent fragility with extreme solidity, but she had set her heart on reconstructing her Trianon in this style, and the architects, decorators, and garden designers whom she employed soon realized that they were dealing with a woman who knew exactly what she wanted. She had ideas of her own, she would allow nothing to be done before she had inspected the plans, she tolerated no deviation from the ideal in her mind, she argued with the experts, and most of the suggestions she put forward met with their approval.

The house itself was finished, and it was now a matter of laying out the gardens. She loathed the stiff splendour of the ornamental parks surrounding the Palace of Versailles and wanted a natural garden in the English style. It was to occupy a comparatively small space and contain everything that appertained to "Nature"—a river with islands and bridges, trees and flowers, hills and dales, and of course a little village with real peasants and real cattle, a windmill, cowsheds, and a village green for rural festivities.

Toinette bent over the plans that the architect had spread before her and became immersed in the study of its details. "What a pity," she said suddenly, "that the model you promised me is not ready yet." Monsieur Mique explained apologetically that it was not his fault, since the money to pay for the making of the model had not yet been sanctioned.

Toinette was furious and sent at once for Monsieur d'Angivillers, the Superintendent of the Royal Residences. While they were waiting for him she continued to discuss the designs in an amiable, eager tone, but as soon as the official appeared she became the wrathful Queen. She would be infinitely obliged, she said with mordant politeness, if Monsieur d'Angivillers would be so good as to inform her why he had failed to carry out her instructions.

D'Angivillers paled at the quiet note of menace in her voice. "I have on several occasions," he replied, "ventured in all submissiveness to draw Madame's attention to the fact that my budget is exhausted. I have received the strictest orders not to issue any further sums without having previously obtained the express sanction of the Minister of Finance. Monsieur Necker has hitherto withheld his approval."

"Is Monsieur Necker the sole authority in this matter?" inquired Toinette. "Or has perhaps the King, too, something to say?" Then softly, but in an imperious tone that brooked no contradiction, she commanded, "See that the requisite funds are made available!" The Superintendent of the Royal Residences bowed and took his leave. "You observe, Monsieur," she said, turning to the architect with a merry laugh, "that it is very simple. One has only to speak in plain French."

It was not possible to postpone any further the disagreeable interview with the Abbé Vermond. Regretfully dismissing the architect, she ordered the Abbé to be shown in.

Vermond was deeply resentful at not having been received by Toinette at all on the previous day and at having been kept waiting so long on the present occasion, and his effort to conceal his annoyance was not wholly successful. Of humble origin, it had been an unexpected stroke of fortune when his superiors recommended him to the Empress Maria Theresa as a tutor for her daughter. In Vienna he had not only won the favour of the old Empress, but also the somewhat reluctant confidence of his young pupil, and when Toinette went to Versailles he remained her adviser. Her mother was insistent that she should consult the Abbé in everything she did.

His task was no light one. His cautious exhortations were usually received with some chaffing remark, such as, "Oh, the time will come, Monsieur l'Abbé, when I shall grow sensible, but until then I beg of you to let me amuse myself in my own way." Yet there were compensating advantages for the Abbé. Skilfully, though discreetly, he managed to spread the rumour that the real ruler of France was Toinette, and that the ruler of Toinette was the Abbé Vermond. He collected a little court around him, and it gave him great satisfaction to think that he, the son of a merchant in Sens, could hold a *lever* at which a queue of dignitaries waited to lay petitions of various kinds at his feet.

His position, however, was not invulnerable. The normally affable young King could not stand him. As the Abbé had been recommended to the Austrian court by the Duc de Choiseul when he was First Minister to Louis XV, he belonged to the latter's political party, and the young King, though he never spoke about it, was unable to rid himself of the suspicion that his father, the Dauphin, who had died under mysterious circumstances, had been poisoned by Choiseul's supporters, and that Vermond had been concerned in the alleged plot. In any case, as soon as Louis came to the throne he dismissed Choiseul without more ado and replaced him by Maurepas, while he neglected no opportunity to demonstrate his antipathy to the Abbé. He never addressed a word to him, and if Vermond had not possessed a strong prop in Maria Theresa he would long since have been sent away.

The ugly cleric, whose enormous mouth was full of irregular, yellow teeth, had brought his portfolio with him, and Toinette cast an uneasy glance at this repository for disagreeable documents. She knew from experience that the papers he drew from it were not calculated to cause her any pleasure. For the time being, however, he refrained from opening his portfolio, but contented himself with making polite conversation. He bent over the designs for the Trianon gardens which were still lying on the table, displayed deep interest in them, and praised Toinette's ingenuity and taste.

Yet she was aware of his resentful disposition, which did not allow him to forget an affront, and that he had certainly not forgiven her for having kept him waiting. In fact, after a while he inquired unctuously whether all these changes were not a little expensive, and when she answered merely with a careless shrug of the shoulders he spoke of the malicious gossip that was current in Paris about her extravagance. To which she rejoined innocently, "My dear Abbé, is there anybody about whom people do *not* gossip?" And she looked him straight in the eye as she smiled, thinking perhaps of the talk about the poisoning of her late exalted father-in-law, the Dauphin.

Vermond, however, was enjoying a bout of self-confidence that day, for in his portfolio was a document calculated to lend emphasis to his warning, and he ventured a step further. If she were only the Queen of France, he suggested, then she would certainly be justified in despising idle chatter. But God had imposed upon her the heavy, though blessed, duty of constituting a link between the two great Catholic reigning families of Europe, between the House of Habsburg and the House of Bourbon. Therefore even in her most harmless actions she must always bear in mind the possible consequences they might have for the policy of Her Sacred Majesty in Vienna. Paris was growing more and more hostile in its references to "the foreigner"; there was an increasing flood of pamphlets lampooning *L'Autrichienne*, "the Austrian woman." Toinette, with a charming pretence at being dumbfounded by what the Abbé was telling her, said it had really never occurred to her that Paris could get so agitated, or that the policy of the House of Habsburg might be seriously affected, by the transplanting of a few trees in the Trianon. She understood nothing about politics. Would the Abbé advise her to give up her plans for the Petit-Trianon altogether?

Vermond would have liked to be stern with her, but he did not dare. On two similar occasions he had threatened to resign his post, and on the second he had come within an ace of being taken at his

word. It was only by dint of the most tortuous writhing and twisting
that he had been able to set things to rights again. He was burdened
with a heavy responsibility, and God was putting him through a hard
trial. This confounded young King, who did not know how to appreciate the services he was rendering, was only seeking for a pretext to
get rid of him. The Queen, charming young creature as she was,
and despite all his efforts to lead her along the right path, was afflicted,
alas, with a frivolous mind and had been corrupted by the company of
scoffers. In matters appertaining to her pleasures she could be
extremely stubborn, and since she was now in a mood of that kind
there was nothing for him to do but beat a graceful retreat. So the
cavernous mouth with its irregular teeth began to pour forth soothing
words. He had only been endeavouring, he said, to tender her advice
of a general nature on the lines indicated by her royal mother, and it
was his cordial hope that her little château would turn out to be as
pretty as the dream on which her heart was set.

Then, and not without a certain malicious glee, he drew from his
redoubtable portfolio the document which he had come to present.
"I have the honour," he declared in formal phraseology, "to hand
to you a letter from Her Imperial Majesty, your mother," and he gave
her the sealed missive.

A letter from her mother always filled Toinette with apprehension.
She was aware that her mother had encircled her with a network of
spies and that every step she took was reported to the Empress with
all possible speed. In Vienna they knew all about her various
escapades, her style of dressing, her coiffures, her flirtations, her
gambling losses and her amusements, and a constant rain of well-
meant advice or stern rebuke showered down upon her.

Her attitude towards her mother was one of profound respect.
Maria Theresa was not only the first of all living mortals in point of
rank, but she was also the most outstanding. Her letters to her
daughter were steeped in wise counsel that came straight from her
heart, and Toinette regarded her with mingled fear, esteem, and
affection. She frequently felt very lonely at Versailles, abandoned
among strangers and hemmed in by a rigid etiquette. The only person
in whom she could confide without reserve was her mother. It was
therefore with mixed and contradictory feelings that she took the
letter handed to her by Vermond. She broke the seal, and before she
read it, she looked at the closely written page as a whole. The first
part was in the writing of a secretary; the second, however, was in
her mother's hand. Then it must be something of great importance
that her mother had to say.

She read. Slowly at first. Then unable to control herself longer,
she hurried to the end of the letter. Surprised, she read the whole

again, thoroughly. Then she let the page sink, and gazed into space, her face confused and deeply thoughtful.

What was in the letter filled her with terror and joy. Her brother Joseph, the Holy Roman Emperor, was coming to Versailles. Joseph, her handsome, brilliant brother of whom she had spoken so enthusiastically to her friends. Joseph, the eternal schoolmaster, who had so often scolded and jeered at her for her stupidity when she was still in the nursery and who, now that she was Queen of France, sent her reproachful, sarcastic letters every two or three months. Joseph, her dear brother Seppl, to whom she looked up with respect and affection, but also with a sense of guilt and a feeling of irritation. Whatever happened, his visit would contribute to strengthening her position at Versailles. After they had seen this dazzling brother of hers, the people of Paris would think of the Habsburgs in terms of the intellectual, tolerant, frugal Joseph instead of venting their spite on the pleasure-loving and extravagant Toinette. On the other hand, there would be a painful quarter-hour or two while he gave her a piece of his mind. In his letters he always treated her as if she were a schoolgirl who had not learned her homework, though it had to be admitted that he was often in the right. He was so uncomfortably clever, and after all he had her best interests at heart. He was a wonderful, insupportable person to have for a brother, and she knew that his biting, mocking manner would provoke her to fury.

She looked across at the Abbé, who was watching her with an amiable grin on his face. "You know what is in this letter, Monsieur l'Abbé?" she asked.

"Yes, Madame, I do," he replied.

"Is the King aware of its contents?" she asked further.

"Not yet, I think," was his answer. "He will probably not be informed until later. Your illustrious brother, Madame, is travelling incognito, and I am under the impression that he is not coming on an official mission." The Abbé's grin grew even more amiable.

A hot wave suddenly rushed through Toinette's body. If Joseph was not coming on an official mission, there could only be one reason, and that was a matter in which she was vitally concerned. Yes, that was what it was. Joseph was going to try to persuade Louis to undergo that little operation which would enable him to fulfil his marital duties in the interests of both the Habsburgs and the Bourbons. It was certainly not an official mission, but a private one, the most important, the most sacred mission in the world.

Joseph usually succeeded in what he set out to do. He had even wrested concessions from their mother, who was the most powerful person alive. There was no doubt that he would be able to induce the vacillating, irresolute Louis to permit the little operation and so remove the obstacle by which the consummation of their marriage had hitherto been prevented. And then? Then she would provide the people of France with the heir they demanded. Then she would have done everything that the House of Habsburg, the House of Bourbon, and God could justifiably require of her. Then she would in truth be Queen. Then she would be free, free to live in accordance with her own desires.

Her mind was filled with a maze of confused ideas. Pulling herself together, she said in her most stately manner, "I thank you, Monsieur l'Abbé. You will, I am sure, understand that after receiving this news I should like to be alone."

The Abbé withdrew very respectfully, but the grin had not entirely disappeared from his face.

☆   ☆   ☆

Louis sat at the little table in the bay window of his library. It was his favourite corner in the whole vast Palace, where he could sit and blink down with his short-sighted eyes into the courtyards and entrance drives—for the view from the window was extensive—and try to identify all the various people who came and went.

Today, however, his mind was occupied by no such conjectures. His flabby chin rested in his cupped hands, with elbows propped on the table, and he was deeply immersed in thought. He was dressed in green, for he had intended to go hunting, which together with riding was one of the few occupations that gave him any pleasure. His physicians had recommended him to go out on horseback as often as he could, since without this exercise his tendency to corpulence would be harmful to his health, and he felt particularly in need of exercise at the moment because he had been overeating, as he frequently did when he was absorbed in meditation and did not realize how much he was stuffing into his mouth.

He had cancelled the hunt when Monsieur Sallé, the Count de Maurepas's secretary, arrived on the Minister's behalf with a request for an immediate audience. If his mentor desired to speak with him in spite of the heavy cold from which the old man was suffering, it must be a matter of the most urgent importance and the King's private pleasure had to wait.

Whatever it was that Maurepas wanted of him, it was bound to be something disagreeable. Whenever anybody wanted something from him it was invariably disagreeable. The decisions he was asked to make were nearly always such as his instincts rebelled against. Yet it was so tiresome always having to resist, to keep on saying no. The others were never at a loss for arguments with which to assail him. They were false arguments, but it cost him an effort to controvert them. In the end he preferred to admit defeat and sign.

The stout young man heaved his unwieldy figure out of his chair and strode to and fro. His library was extensive, for he was fond of reading, particularly works of a geographical, historical, or political nature, and he had had the room reconstructed so that he might cram it full with the things he liked. There were globes, maps, clocks, and works of art of various kinds, especially porcelain. In his porcelain factory at Sèvres he had had statuettes made of the great writers of the past, such as La Fontaine, Boileau, Racine, and La Bruyère, and in addition to these he had adorned his library with bronzes and articles in wrought iron. These latter were something of which he possessed expert knowledge, for he himself worked in metal and he had a room at the top of the building, under the roof, which had been fitted up for him as a workshop.

As he stopped in front of the fireplace and stroked the finely wrought trellis-work, it was remarkable how delicately he touched the iron with his fat, clumsy hands. There was a far-away look in his eyes as they roamed over the fireplace. How much rather would he have devoted himself to his books than to the matters which his Minister was coming to discuss. What a laborious, uneasy, never-ending task it was to govern. Why had he not been born a simple country gentleman? How nice it would be if he could go hunting whenever he wanted to, or spend his time writing, reading, translating a little from the English, studying history and geography, and perusing the newspapers, especially the English journals which were banned in France. Instead of that he had to govern and make decisions, to ward off the greedy and ambitious, to act continually in accordance with expediency and not as wise reason dictated, against his own better knowledge and instincts.

His meditations were interrupted by the arrival of Prince Charles. Louis's relations with his brother were of a dual nature. After his grandfather's death and his succession to the throne, the good-natured King took his responsibility as head of the family seriously and felt that he was under an obligation to help and advise his brothers, but they both made things difficult for him. From childhood they had been accustomed to jeering at his awkwardness, and while Prince Xavier did it furtively, the less respectful Charles made no attempt to conceal his contempt even when others were present.

"I am expecting Maurepas," said Louis, when his brother entered the room, "and I have not much time. So please be brief. What do you want?"

"Money," replied Charles.

During the three short years of the King's reign Prince Charles had extorted from him not only an appanage befitting his rank and a château with a large, lucrative estate, but also on several occasions the payment of considerable debts. The last occasion of this kind had been no more than four months previously, when there had been a stormy altercation and Charles had recommended Louis to style himself not *Roi de France et de Navarre,* but *Roi de France et l'Avare.* Louis had finally paid the sum demanded, but Charles had been forced to promise solemnly that in future he would be more economical in his way of living.

Louis gazed gloomily at his brother. "You promised me," he began, but he did not finish the sentence. His voice was filled with a weary, despairing resentment.

"Then I must have lied," replied Prince Charles bluntly. "That is a matter which you can leave me to settle with my Maker. But you had better let me have the money, since you haven't any other alternative. There is no point in holding out, and I don't advise you to play at being Louis the Austere, for it doesn't suit you." When he was thirteen years old Louis had once asserted that it would be his ambition to go down in history as Louis the Austere, and it tickled Charles's sense of humour to remind him of it.

Louis pulled himself together. "I shall not give you any more money," he declared in a shrill voice. "I shall appoint a court of trustees, consisting of my Ministers, to look after your affairs."

"An excellent idea," jeered Charles. "The whole of Paris will want to know when you intend to set up a court of trustees to keep an eye on Toinette."

"I forbid you," he cried in a rage, "to refer to the Queen as Toinette."

"All right," said Charles calmly, with an insolent smile, "on *L'Autrichienne.*"

Louis wearied of the wrangle, which was leading nowhere. "How much is it this time?" he asked.

"Five hundred and eighty-seven thousand and a few odd hundreds," replied Charles. "But I shall be satisfied with a round five hundred thousand."

Louis sat limp and morose in his chair. "I will send de Laborde to you," he said, "so that he can come to an arrangement with your creditors." De Laborde was the controller of his privy purse.

"This petty mistrust is no more than I expected of you," rejoined Charles.

They both knew quite well that Louis would sanction the payment.

When the King was again alone he sighed, breathed heavily through his nose, and felt oppressed. Unbuttoning his coat, and loosening the waistband of his breeches a little, he felt slightly easier. He was always untidily dressed, frequently dirty, and both his valet and his hairdresser had a difficult time with him.

His whole day had been spoilt, and there was still the audience with Maurepas. The Minister probably wanted to talk about America again.

They never left him any peace with this confounded America of theirs. Doctor Franklin ought never to have been permitted to settle in Paris. There were free-thinkers and atheists enough in the city without fetching new ones from across the ocean. And they even wanted him to provide these rebels with money. It was not right. It certainly was not right. Yet when he said that to his Ministers they simply overwhelmed him with arguments, arguments, nothing but arguments.

He drew in a deep breath through his thick nostrils and exhaled it again noisily. They all came to him for money—Charles, Toinette, and the Americans. He sat humped together at his massive writing-table, a fat young man with a puffy face, waiting uneasily.

Maurepas arrived at last. Louis went to meet him with an assiduous display of courtesy, and he could move remarkably quickly despite his waddling gait. Though he had a heavy cold the old Minister had dressed carefully for the occasion. The Countess had urged him to have regard for his health and either to request the King to visit him in his apartments or at least to traverse the short distance in his dressing-gown, but he refused to deviate from the strict rules of etiquette. When it was a matter of discussing affairs of State he insisted on appearing before the monarch in ceremonial garb and in the latter's own apartments as was customary at court.

They seated themselves at the large table, where the porcelain statuettes of France's great writers were interspersed among writing-materials and piled-up papers, the untidily attired young King in an awkward, lolling attitude and, in consequence of his corpulence, looking much older than his twenty-two years, the Minister, thin and neat, looking far too youthful for a man of seventy-six and endeavouring to hold himself upright. His portfolio lay in front of him, and the short-sighted Louis squinted at it with his widely set brown eyes.

Maurepas began by stating that he had received a communication from his Austrian colleague, von Kaunitz, who submitted a detailed and very lucid exposition of the standpoint taken up by the House of Habsburg with regard to all questions still pending. If that had been all, however, then he, Maurepas, would not have ventured to trouble the King. Straightening himself up and smiling at Louis as if he were about to announce a joyful surprise, he said, "I will tell you my news at once, Sire. Your illustrious brother-in-law, the Holy Roman Emperor, is on his way to Versailles."

Louis's wandering eyes suddenly grew fixed, his mouth hung a little open, and he seemed dazed with astonishment. Behind his sloping forehead his thoughts slowly began to collect themselves, and his mind worked with a certain logic as he drew his deductions. He had known that Maurepas had disagreeable news to bring him. When Joseph arrived there would be a number of unpleasant things to discuss, and in particular that detestable problem of the Bavarian succession. It was true that Maria Theresa had denied any intention of putting forward a claim, but Joseph had been by no means equally reticent and things looked threatening from that quarter. Louis's Ministers had been pressing him for months to make it unmistakably clear to his brother-in-law that Austria could count upon no support whatsoever from France, and when Joseph arrived he would be forced to tell him so bluntly. Slow of speech as he was, he would have to face his brother-in-law, who was not only much his senior in years, but celebrated for his quick-witted eloquence and biting sarcasm, and attempt to take a strong line. Louis's heavy, rounded shoulders slumped still lower.

Maurepas continued to gaze at him with amiable expectancy as if he had been the bearer of wonderful tidings. The King's flabby cheeks twitched, his fingers plucked nervously at his sleeves, he fiddled with his coat buttons, but he remained silent. There was no sound in the room but the ticking of the clocks. Maurepas, guessing what was going on in the King's mind, cleared his throat noisily, drew out his handkerchief, and blew his nose. Alas, what a nuisance that cold of his was! "I believe, Sire," he said at last, "that this visit will be a very happy one, and will not be clouded by political argument. The Emperor is travelling incognito as Count Falkenstein and has requested that all ceremony should be avoided. He must therefore be coming purely for family reasons, and I assume that His Roman Majesty has not omitted on this occasion to obtain the sanction and the blessing of his illustrious mother. One brother-in-law is paying a visit to another; Joseph is coming to see Louis and to say 'How do you do?' to his sister Toinette."

Louis turned his gaze away from Maurepas and his fingers mechanically stroked the porcelain figures on the table. Then, with his chin resting on his hands, he once more became immersed in thought. His mind, working laboriously but logically, divined the reason why Joseph was journeying incognito, but he was unwilling to admit it to himself. Finally he overcame his reluctance and asked the old Minister, "Why is Joseph coming? What does he want?" When Maurepas said nothing, but only sat there with a slight smirk on his face, Louis cried suddenly in an unexpectedly shrill voice, "What does he want?"

Maurepas was not taken aback by the sudden outburst. He knew Louis and had a pretty good idea what he was thinking. The shy, inhibited young monarch had spoken to nobody but Maurepas and his personal physician about the difficulty which hindered the consummation of his marriage. It was not lack of courage which caused him to shrink from an operation, but a combination of pious or, as the free-thinker Maurepas secretly considered it, superstitious, belief and childish shame. And now he was going to have to discuss these things with the aggressive, rationalist-minded Joseph. The old cynic almost felt sorry for his pupil. With gentle courtesy he explained to Louis that Joseph was most probably journeying to Versailles in order to persuade his brother-in-law to undergo the very minor operation which had been mentioned by Doctor Lassone. Maria Theresa was no doubt hoping that such an operation would be conducive to blessings both for France and for Austria.

"Do they all know, then——?" asked Louis in dismay. He was a melancholy figure as he sat humped in his chair. All the various thoughts and emotions by which he had been agitated for so long on account of his physical defect surged through him in vague confusion. His marriage had been arranged for him when he was fifteen years old by his grandfather, the aged Louis XV, in order to create an alliance between France and Austria. It had been a "family compact," entered into on the advice of Ministers who were enemies of his father, the Dauphin. He had loved and respected his father, and the fact that his marriage had been brought about by men who hated the Dauphin, and had probably been the instigators of his early death, had inspired him from the outset with morose distrust of everything connected with the marriage. He was deeply religious, believed firmly in Divine Providence, and was haunted by the fear that a marriage which owed its origin to his father's enemies could not be pleasing in the sight of Heaven. Perhaps that was why God had created him with a physical defect of that kind, and if there was any truth in his assumption had he the right to intervene in the Lord's decree?

On the other hand, his marriage was an established fact and he was not the only one concerned. If he refused to submit to the surgeon's knife, was he not being unjust to Toinette? The thought of his wife filled him with deep embarrassment. She had been torn from her home and brought to a distant country in order to be mated with him, in order to bear an heir to the throne with the mingled blood of the Habsburgs and the Bourbons in his veins, yet he could not give her that to which she was entitled. If Joseph now appeared at Versailles and wrathfully insisted on his sister's claim to her rights, if he accused the House of Bourbon of having betrayed the House of Habsburg, that was only just and reasonable, and there was nothing that he, Louis, could say in answer to the charge.

Yet there must be some reason why God, through Whose grace he had been anointed and crowned, had made him physically what he was. He was entangled in a conflict of duties, and since he always found it difficult to come to a decision, he allowed things to drift. It was better to await the outcome than to sanction any irrevocable change. It was better to do nothing than to take action.

A prey to such thoughts and emotions, he sat limply at the massive table, tugged mechanically at his sleeves, and said nothing. Finally Maurepas inquired whether he might respectfully venture to offer a suggestion. Louis, anxious to hear what his Minister had to say, replied, "Yes, please speak, my mentor."

Maurepas then pointed out that there might perhaps be a way of exploiting Joseph's journey to their own advantage, and when Louis looked up in keen interest he suggested with a sly smile that the King should arrange matters with Doctor Lassone and undergo the little operation before the arrival of Count Falkenstein. His Roman Majesty would then have nothing further to do but tender his felicitations and return to Vienna, where he would report to his illustrious mother that they might really have spared themselves the trouble.

Louis admitted that this was excellent advice, but, he added with reddening cheeks, a king could not always allow himself to follow the dictates of reason. He must give heed to certain deeper stirrings of instinct. Maurepas knew that this was not mere idle talk on Louis's part, but sprang from profound conviction. Louis believed in the divine right of kings and regarded his instincts and impulses as guidance from Heaven which he must not resist. He would listen to sensible advice when it suited him, but when he appealed to his divine right as an anointed monarch it was best not to press him further. Only a short time before Maurepas had given the young King grounds for the melancholy reflection that his First Minister was lax in his religious views, and he thought it wiser on the present occasion to hold his tongue.

In any case he was feeling exhausted, and remembered the advice given him by the Countess not to overexert himself. He would have liked to withdraw, but unfortunately this was impossible since there still remained another topic to discuss. On receiving the news of Joseph's intended journey he had pondered on the possible results that might ensue as far as he himself was concerned. Toinette disliked him, Mercy and Vermond lost no opportunity to point out that he did not favour too close a connection with Austria, and the Lilac Coterie was conspiring to bring about his fall. If Joseph were to achieve his aim, if the operation were to take place and Louis entered into more intimate relations with Toinette, and particularly if she were to give birth to a son, then the chances of Mercy and Vermond would be enhanced and he himself would be directly menaced. It was true that Louis tried to keep politics out of the beautiful white hands of his Queen, but he was weak-minded and Maurepas, determined to die in office, was not anxious to take any risks. He had decided to combine his announcement of Joseph's visit with an attack on Toinette's defences.

So he fought down the weakness that was stealing over him, dabbed his face with his expensive handkerchief, coughed, and cleared his throat. Straightening his thin, elegant shoulders, he fixed his eye on the boorish figure that sat humped in the opposite chair.

Since he had been granted the honour of an audience with His Majesty, he began, he would like to permit himself the liberty of touching upon another question that was still pending. Monsieur d'Angivillers had transmitted to the Minister of Finance a further request for funds in connection with the reconstruction of the Trianon. In accordance with an arrangement entered into with the Queen, His Majesty had issued instructions to the competent officers of the royal household that the budgets already fixed were on no account to be exceeded. Monsieur Necker was therefore unwilling to authorize the required expenditure without an express order from the King.

Louis snorted uneasily. He himself was of an economical turn of mind, and he knew that Toinette's extravagance had created ill feeling in Paris. Hardly a week went by without his having to instruct the industrious but disapproving Necker, whom he could not endure anyway, to allocate supplementary funds to the Queen's household, thus running counter to the arrangements that had already been agreed. On the other hand, he fully realized that there was some excuse for Toinette's light-hearted way of spending money. He made no attempt to conceal from himself the fact that her wild plunging into a whirl of amusements was nothing but a substitute for the conjugal rights and pleasures with which he had failed to provide her. Conscious of his own responsibility, he treated her with the greatest indulgence, and while saving every franc he could on his personal expenditure he was almost glad to be able to recompense Toinette for that which he was compelled to deny her.

"How much is it this time?" he asked.

"300,000 livres," replied Maurepas.

"300,000 livres," Louis repeated to himself. He took up his quill, and on one of the sheets of paper lying about on the table he neatly put down: "300,000." Then he began to play with the figures and wrote: "60,000 x 5, 50,000 x 6, 25,000 x 12." He thought of the insolent references to Toinette made by his brother Charles a little while ago and wondered whether Charles had already been aware of this new demand of hers. He must have been aware of it, and Louis felt annoyed at this further evidence of his brother's intimacy with Toinette. "300,000 livres," he muttered again. Another 300,000 livres for the Trianon. It was a scandal, and there would be much talk about it.

Maurepas, rejoicing at the effect of his communication, drove the wedge in a little further. If he might venture to offer advice, he said, still very gently and very respectfully, he would suggest that His Majesty should authorize the expenditure on this occasion, but that at the same time he should request the Queen to exercise a little more economy.

"300,000 livres," muttered Louis. "25,000 x 12."

"317,634 livres, Sire," said Maurepas, "if you wish to know the exact figure. The sum itself is not excessive. But the standard of living, particularly in the rural areas, is tending to sink, and it is quite understandable if people are comparing the amounts spent by the Queen's circle with those to which they are compelled to restrict themselves. There are impudent scribblers who refer to everything which the Queen may do, including her most private affairs, as 'Austrian politics.' We are even at the present moment engaged in trying to suppress a lampoon in which it is declared that the Queen's extravagance prevents the Government from providing the necessary aid to America. It remains an indisputable fact that despite Necker's skill the financial situation is precarious, and my colleague, Count Vergennes, is dubious about asking your sanction, Sire, for the issue of the two further millions which the Americans have requested."

Louis brightened up now that Maurepas had brought the discussion round to a subject on which he could vent his spleen. "These Americans of yours!" he cried wrathfully, his voice rising to a high pitch while his incipient double chin trembled. "It's always these Americans! You are always talking about these rebels! And who is to pay for their rebellion? I am!"

Maurepas had gone into the American question with Louis on a number of previous occasions, and as he felt that his strength was giving out he was reluctant to enter upon a superfluous discussion during the present audience. He therefore limited himself to a résumé of the guiding principles which Louis had already been induced to accept. "I hope, Sire," he concluded in a rather sharper tone than he was wont to employ, "that I have correctly understood your views on the American problem. You have agreed with your advisers that it is in our interests to maintain the conflict between England and her American colonies for as long as possible, in order that England in particular, but the rebels too, may be weakened. You have instructed your Ministers to pursue a policy on these lines. You have issued orders to the effect that the rebels are to be kept going by a moderate degree of support until such time as we ourselves are ready to take up again our ancient struggle with England."

Louis was forced to concede that this was a correct appreciation of the situation. Maurepas and Vergennes had assailed him with their arguments, "logical arguments" that he was unable to refute, until in the end he had had to agree, but instinct told him that it was all sophistry, that he was right in his royal antipathy to the rebels, and that no good could come of this help afforded to the Americans. Yet what could he do? He sat morosely with eyes half closed so that they almost disappeared in the fleshy mass of his face. "How much do you want this time for your Americans?" he asked peevishly.

"Vergennes suggests two millions," repeated Maurepas patiently. "He would like to allocate them from his secret funds."

"*One* million," declared Louis angrily. "One million, not two. I will not give the Americans more than one million. My conscience would not allow it."

"Good. One million then," agreed Maurepas in a conciliatory tone.

"And he is to offer it in three instalments," ordered Louis cantankerously. "This Doctor Franklin of yours is so importunate, he is never satisfied, he keeps coming back."

"As you command, Sire," replied Maurepas, gathering his papers together. "May I now request permission to withdraw?" Then, to make sure that he had achieved his purpose, he said, "And will you be so gracious, Sire, as to speak with the Queen concerning the limitation of her personal expenditure?"

"Yes!" the King rapped out. He could see that it cost Maurepas an effort to stand up straight, and he added remorsefully, "I ought to thank you, my mentor, but you do not make things easy for me."

"I know, I know," said the old Minister consolingly. "But now you have got this tiresome audience over, Sire, and I wish you a happy day in the hunting field." He ceremoniously took his leave of the King and withdrew from the room with a strained effort to hold himself erect.

In the antechamber he nearly collapsed. His secretary and valet were waiting for him to come out and they almost carried him to his own apartments. Madame de Maurepas anxiously hastened to his side, and as he coughed and groaned she gently reproached him for disregarding her advice. He was put to bed, packed round with hot-water bottles, and given steaming broth.

Louis, too, was feeling rather low after the depressing interview with his Minister. The pleasure with which he had looked forward to the hunt was gone. He seated himself once more in the bay window and looked out across the avenues that led to the Palace entrance, but he saw nothing of the people who came and went. "300,000 for *L'Autrichienne,* the Austrian woman," he pondered, "1,000,000 for the rebel, 500,000 for the young scamp," and he continued to brood over the wearisome burden that had fallen to his lot.

☆   ☆   ☆

Louis awoke on the following morning with the dim consciousness that he had on that particular day to face some more than ordinarily difficult and uncomfortable ordeal. He slowly revolved the matter in his mind until realization came to him that he had promised Maurepas to see Toinette and remonstrate with her regarding her extravagance.

He lay drowsily for a while, breathing heavily through his nose. Then he tugged at a cord, the other end of which was attached to the arm of a lackey, whom he could thus summon at any moment. The lackey came hurrying in answer to the signal, and Louis laboriously heaved himself out of the bed in which he had slept and into the bed of state where he awoke ceremoniously for the *lever*. Louis had himself dressed in the presence of a hundred members of the high nobility, with whom he mechanically exchanged the customary meaningless phrases. Then he absent-mindedly devoured a large breakfast, his thoughts running on the coming interview.

His appointments that morning included an audience at which he was to receive Saint-Germain, the Minister for War. Louis liked Saint-Germain, and was convinced that his projected reforms were on the right lines, but he had recently been pressed from all sides to get rid of the old Minister. He still felt pricks of conscience when he recalled how he had yielded to the insistent demands of Toinette and her circle that Turgot, his excellent Minister of Finance, should be dismissed in disgrace, and he was determined not to let Saint-Germain go. Inwardly, however, he was not quite sure that he would be able to keep to his resolve. In any case, his talk with Saint-Germain was not likely to be very agreeable. The old man would overwhelm him with complaints and grievances, he would look at him with those devoted eyes of his like a dog waiting for a bone, and wait expectantly to be assured of help against his enemies. No, thought Louis, he needed all his energies for the forthcoming talk with Toinette. He would not receive Saint-Germain today. But he would recompense him by agreeing at last to inspect the Hôtel des Invalides, and moreover he would ask Toinette to accompany him. This had been a long-cherished desire of the Minister's, for he was proud of the way he had rebuilt it and restored it to order.

Pleased with this happy solution, Louis decided to spend the time so saved in his library. He loved to cram his excellent memory with facts and details, and the hours spent among his books were hours of rest that did him good.

He was greeted by the two librarians, Monsieur de Campan and Monsieur de Sept-Chênes. They were both quiet, unobtrusive men, always at hand when wanted and knowing when to keep out of the way if they felt that their presence would be disturbing.

Louis asked first of all for the latest journals. "Have any English papers arrived?" he inquired. It was his custom always to peruse the English journals, though they were officially banned in France. Sept-Chênes brought them at once. "I suppose you have been taking a peep at them too, Sept-Chênes?" Louis asked roguishly, wagging a threatening forefinger at the librarian, and he burst into a loud laugh. He

had a boisterous guffaw, "like a carter," as they said in the Lilac
Coterie. Monsieur de Sept-Chênes amiably entered into the humour
of the royal joke, to which he was accustomed.

Louis became absorbed in the English journals. They were full of
reports about the conflict with the colonies and they had a lot to say
about Doctor Franklin. It was, they suggested, remarkable that the
rebel leader should have been able to find asylum in Paris. Louis gave
a deep sigh. They were right. He read with pleasure the malicious
designations by which some of the English journalists referred to the
old rebel. They called him a "septuagenarian chameleon," a "profiteering Utopian," and a "charlatan." Louis slapped his thighs, summoned
the two librarians, pointed out the relevant passages, and read them
aloud in English. His pronunciation of the word "chameleon" was
not quite correct and Monsieur de Sept-Chênes ventured respectfully
to set him right. Anxious as he was to learn, Louis repeated the correct
pronunciation several times.

He liked to browse in a number of books at the same time, and he
had a whole pile brought to him, English historical works such as
Horace Walpole's *Historic Doubts on the Life and Reign of King
Richard III,* James Anderson's account of the trial of Mary, Queen of
Scots, and the stout volumes of Hume's *History of England.*

The two librarians had been struck by the fact that though he
always sent for the whole six volumes of Hume's work he never
looked at more than one of them, and it was always the same one.
He apparently did not want them to know that he was particularly
interested in this volume, which dealt with the life and reign of King
Charles I.

It was about a year ago that Louis had begun to take an interest in
David Hume's *History of England.* To be exact, it was in May of the
previous year. At that time he had dismissed Turgot in disgrace, and
Louis's interest in Hume's work was related to a letter that Turgot
had addressed to him immediately before his dismissal. In this letter,
Turgot had had the audacity to warn him that he was surrounded by
deceitful counsellors, that at the age of twenty-two he could possess
little experience or knowledge of men, and that he was standing on
the edge of an abyss. "Do not forget, Sire," the letter had said, "that
it was weakness which brought the head of Charles the First to the
block. People think you are weak, Sire." Louis had not shown this
letter to anyone, but had sealed it again and locked it away in the chest
where he kept his most secret documents. That very day he had sent
for Hume's great historical work for the first time and ever since he
had read over and over again, with unabating anger and astonishment,
the account of how the English criminals had revolted against their
King and cut off his head.

No, no. Whatever the logical arguments that might be adduced by

Vergennes and Maurepas, it was not right that the King of France should afford assistance to the septuagenarian chameleon and his fellow rebels; it could not turn out well in the end.

Louis closed his books, stretched his arms and legs, and undid a button or two. He was again feeling so congested. It was a thousand pities that he had been prevented from going out hunting for the second day in succession. He *must* get some exercise. There was still a quarter of an hour before he had to go across to see Toinette. Heaving himself onto his feet, he went up to his workshop in the room underneath the roof.

He was glad to find not only the sturdy, thick-set François Gamain, but also Monsieur Laudry, who was in charge of the difficult precision work carried out by the King's mechanics. Louis was not satisfied with the fastening of the chest in which he kept his private papers, and together with Gamain he had been working on a secret lock, but the craftsman did not possess sufficient inventive resource and the lock had not turned out quite as Louis had hoped. The excellent Monsieur Laudry discovered at once what was lacking, and Louis listened enthusiastically to his explanation of where they had gone wrong. The three of them set to work and in a short time the lock was ready.

It had taken, however, far more than the quarter of an hour that Louis had allotted, and he was going to be very late for his appointment with Toinette. Hastily stowing away the capacious piece of mechanism in the tail-pocket of his coat, he hurriedly washed the grease from his hands and made his way towards Toinette's apartments.

With his slow, waddling gait he ploughed through salons and corridors, the heavy lock in his tail-pocket banging continually against his behind. The corridors were alive with lackeys, guards, and gentlemen of the court in brilliant uniforms, who all sprang to attention and bowed deeply as he passed. Some of them could not help showing in their faces the contempt they felt in their hearts for the unroyal figure he cut, and Louis was well aware that the prescribed obeisance they made before the empty throne when they went through the throne-room was more sincere than the reverence they were now displaying in his actual presence. He again wondered gloomily why Divine Providence had not endowed him with an outward semblance more fitted to his sacred office.

He waddled across the room with the round window, the *œil-de-bœuf,* and reached the wing which contained the Queen's apartments. Suddenly a little boy about eight years of age came dashing out of a side-passage near the large painting of Jupiter, Peace, and Justice. He was neatly dressed, and his rapid movements, like those of a mischievous street-urchin, were in striking contrast to his rich attire. Louis knew that the lad was Pierre, the son of an assistant gardener named Machard, whom Toinette, following one of her whims, had adopted a year ago. When he saw the King he stopped his wild rush, stood against the wall to allow the King to pass, and bowed low as he had been taught to do. Louis went by with an affable smile, the lock still swinging against his thighs and buttocks.

All at once he heard behind his back an outburst of shrill laughter. Little Pierre had evidently been unable to restrain his mirth.

Louis was as good-natured as any man, but he was the King of France and Navarre, and he remembered the royal manner in which his late illustrious grandfather, Louis XV, used to stride along so that any whispering scandal about the dissolute life he led died away on men's lips as soon as he appeared. And he thought how in spite of her penchant for gambling, her masked balls, her frivolous amusements, Toinette radiated an air of royalty that silenced the scoffing even of the boldest. He was suddenly seized by a fit of raging fury. Turning swiftly around, he gripped Pierre in his great fists, shook the lad, who had gone pale with fright, as if he were a rat, and called for the guard in a voice which rose to a shriek. Lackeys came hurrying up, and while Jupiter, Peace, and Justice looked down upon the scene Louis handed Pierre over to the Swiss Guards and ordered that he should be kept in custody until further instructions were issued.

Then, with his emotions once more under control, he proceeded on his way.

☆   ☆   ☆

When he left Toinette's apartments two hours later, he looked like a man who had been relieved of a heavy burden. Beaming with content he returned to his own quarters.

His first action was to set about affixing the new lock to the chest. It was a tedious job extracting the old lock and replacing it with the new, but at last it was completed. Louis tried out his handiwork, opened the chest, closed it again, wiped the sweat from his brow, and rejoiced in a task well done.

Unlocking the chest once more he raised the lid and gazed tenderly at its contents. These were mostly of a very private nature, such as diaries, letters, and souvenirs of various kinds. They were now all safe from prying eyes. Delving into the mass of papers with the pleasure of a collector enjoying the touch of his treasures, and with a rather foolish smile on his face, his fingers came in contact with the letter that had been sent to him by Turgot and which he had resealed. Involuntarily he pushed it farther in among other documents, deeper and deeper, until it lay right at the bottom.

Then he began to delve again and fished out a letter from his mother-in-law, Maria Theresa. She had written it seven years ago when she sent Toinette to Versailles. Slowly his short-sighted eyes perused the missive: "Your bride, my dear Dauphin, has just taken leave of me. She was my chief joy in life, and I hope that she will bring you happiness. It is with this end in view that I have brought her up, for I have long been aware that she was destined to share your lot. I have trained her in those duties which she will owe to you, a tender affection and the capacity both to understand and to employ the means by which she will be able to find favour in your eyes. My daughter will love you, of that I am assured, for I know her well. Farewell, my dear Dauphin, may you be happy and may you make her happy. I am drowned in tears. Your devoted mother, Maria Theresa."

Louis continued to hold the letter in his hand. It was a good letter. He had not known at the time how he should answer it, since that was not a simple matter for a boy of fifteen. Finally, with the help of his tutor, he had composed a conventional reply in German with a few deliberate grammatical mistakes to make it seem like his own unaided work. The Austrian Empress's French had not been any better. In her short letter Louis had counted four mistakes in grammar and nine in spelling. "May you be happy and may you make her happy." It was easy for his illustrious mother-in-law in Vienna to talk. Now she was sending Joseph to have a word with him. "May you make her happy!"

It was a well-written letter. The Empress was not only a woman of superior intelligence, but she also possessed feeling. "My daughter will love you, of that I am assured, for I know her well."

Toinette had been very amiable just now when they had their talk together, and though neither of them had touched upon the possible reasons that might be bringing Joseph to Versailles they had conversed as if they had something in common. Louis had never experienced this before in a conversation with Toinette. The plans she had had prepared for the Trianon were truly splendid. She had ideas, and she had taste. She was beautiful, too. The fact that she seemed beautiful to him did not mean much, since he did not understand anything about women's looks, but Walpole, the author of that excellent book on Richard the Third, who was a good writer and therefore bound to know something about these things, had called her the most beautiful woman in Europe. If only she were not so quick-witted and so ready to burst out laughing. Her laugh always intimidated him.

It could not be said that the 300,000 livres for the Trianon was money thrown into the gutter. 317,634 livres—that was the exact figure, so far as he remembered, and he could trust his memory. He had made it into a round sum and promised her 400,000, though with a heavy heart. Yet it was only logical that the work already begun should be completed. It would be a waste to leave the place half finished. Moreover, she had promised that next year she would not go beyond the budget as far as the Trianon was concerned. So he would at least have one argument to fall back on when he told Necker to pay over the money.

In the matter of Saint-Germain he had been less successful. Toinette had refused point-blank to attend the inspection of the Hôtel des Invalides. And not only that. She had again urged him to dismiss the old man, whom she said she simply could not stand.

For the rest, she had been really sensible and easy to get on with, though there was one point, to be sure, on which she would brook no argument. She wanted to have a superintendent for her private theatricals and entertainments. Well, since he had agreed that the Trianon was her affair entirely, it was not altogether illogical that she should have her own superintendent.

"I have trained her in those duties which she will owe to you. Farewell, my dear Dauphin, may you be happy and may you make her happy." He stroked the letter with a tender touch that was remarkable in so heavy a hand, folded it, and put it away again neatly in the chest.

Then he drew out his diary, sat down in front of it, and thought over the events of the day to decide which of them were worth recording. He began to write: "Audience with Minister for War cancelled on account of difficult personal conference. Conversation with Toinette went off smoothly. Made a secret lock. Very effective. Did not go hunting." He put the diary back in the chest, closed the lock with a snap, and stood gazing at it with a satisfied smile.

Suddenly the smile died away. Something had occurred to him. Tugging violently at the bell-rope, he sent for the officer of the guard. "There is a boy being kept in custody," he said, "a certain Pierre Machard, a protégé of the Queen. He is to be released at once. And give him two francs' worth of sweets. No!" he corrected himself. "Make it five francs' worth!"

Chapter Four

JOSEPH

⚜   ★   ⚜

A FEW weeks later the Emperor Joseph was on his way to Paris. Joseph, the second of his name, was ruler of the Holy Roman Empire of the German Nation by courtesy only. His mother had elevated him to the rank of co-regent with herself, but in reality the old Empress retained complete power in her own hands. She was still very much alive and very decided in her views. These views, in the opinion of her son and co-regent, were in many cases merely prejudices. Maria Theresa was a deeply pious woman and felt at ease only in the bosom of the Church. Joseph was sympathetic to contemporary currents of thought, filled with distrust of the Church, which fostered superstition and protected bigotry, and ardently interested in the revaluation of ideas which had been undertaken by the century of enlightenment.

The young Emperor, who was no longer so very young, being thirty-six years of age, had no easy task. He burned to translate his conceptions into deeds, and thereby reform the world. When he announced his project to the world, the world listened, especially the younger generation. He was the joy and hope of youth everywhere in the Holy Roman Empire of the German Nation, but his power existed only in name. Action was the prerogative of his mother, who governed alone. So as the years rolled on he grew more and more embittered.

Since he was not allowed for the time being to reform the world, he decided to employ his involuntary leisure in getting to know it thoroughly. He therefore travelled. He travelled more than any other prince of his time, and he liked to remain incognito, convinced as he was that this offered the best chance of acquiring an unbiased picture of countries and peoples. Yet he had no desire to hide his light under a bushel, but was anxious that people should know about his efforts to study world affairs in this practical manner. When those whom he met on his journeys as Count Falkenstein showed that they knew him to be the Emperor, he would smile benevolently, and when the newspapers printed accounts of his travels he was not displeased.

Minute precautions had been taken to preserve the Emperor's incognito during his journey to Paris and also during his sojourn there. He entered Paris in a hackney-coach, alighted at the unpretentious Hôtel de Treville, and had the camp-bed that he had used on his campaigns, and which accompanied him everywhere, set up.

On the following day he went to Versailles. Toinette, as was only befitting, awaited him in her apartments surrounded by the ladies and gentlemen of her household, but she was unable to restrain her impatience and kept running to the window. When he came up the steps she hastened to meet him, and in front of the guards who were presenting arms threw her arms around him and covered him with kisses.

There was a strong resemblance between brother and sister. Like Toinette, Joseph had an open, expressive countenance, a lofty brow, lively blue eyes, a small mouth with rather protruding under lip, and a slightly aquiline nose. He was tall and slim, his movements were graceful and controlled. Nevertheless Toinette was disappointed when she looked at him more closely. In her memory was a picture of Joseph as she had seen him seven years before at Schoenbrunn, when he was the big brother whose gravity and schoolmasterly manner had intimidated her, though she could not help being filled with admiration for his knowledge and brilliance. She had spoken of him so enthusiastically on a hundred occasions to her friends at Versailles, and had told them that everybody was fascinated at the mere sight of him. And now there appeared a by no means distinguished-looking gentleman, plainly dressed, even a little shabby on the whole, and with hair beginning to get thin on top.

Yet it was pleasant meeting again after so long. Joseph had made up his mind for the time being to suppress the admonitory remarks that he would have liked to address to his sister. Instead he complimented her on looking so pretty and talked about the family in Vienna, especially about their mother. They spoke in French, but kept dropping into German, and Joseph had to help her every now and then to find the right German word, which induced him to comment amiably that she could speak neither correct German nor correct French. He was proud of his own fluent knowledge not only of German and French, but also of Italian, and of being able to converse in their native tongues with members of most of the peoples over which he ruled.

Holding Toinette's hand, he said, "Well, Toni, isn't it nice being together again after all this time?" She felt a surge of affection at the sound of his voice and the sympathetic look in his eyes.

With his brother-in-law too he controlled his urge to lecture, and as Louis made an effort to master his timidity everything went off better than either of them had expected. Louis showed Joseph his books and some of the articles he had made himself out of wrought iron, tried to talk a little German, laughed good-naturedly at his own awkwardness, and several times corrected his guest's French. This latter was not at all to Joseph's liking, and he insisted that there was nothing wrong with his pronunciation. The meticulous Louis, however, stuck to his guns, appealed to the authority of his librarian, Monsieur de Sept-Chênes, and even offered to submit the dispute to the Academy. Joseph could not but admire his brother-in-law's philological keenness and his clear, objective reasoning. The Austrian Ambassador, Count Mercy, had more than once respectfully, yet unmistakably, indicated that His Most Christian Majesty was a little simple-minded.

The following week the Imperial tourist devoted to an exploration of Paris and Versailles. At bottom he detested French ways and the French spirit, but he was conscientious and did not want to condemn the nation without having studied it thoroughly. So he poked his Habsburg nose into every nook and cranny of Paris, displaying a deep interest in small things as well as big. He visited every corner of the capital, the hospitals, tasted the soup that was distributed to the paupers, attended sessions of the courts of justice, inspected factories of all kinds, entered into conversation with numerous pedlars, noted down curious specimens of fishwives' slang, and sought out craftsmen in their workshops to listen to explanations of what they were doing. Everywhere he preserved his incognito, and everywhere he was recognized. The journals printed enthusiastic accounts of the inconspicuous way in which Count Falkenstein was pursuing his studies, his democratic bearing was the sensation of the city, he became the rage, and in many houses the portrait of the affable Emperor Joseph was hung beside that of the bourgeois sage, Doctor Franklin.

Above all he made a point of coming into contact with the great minds of France. He met scholars, writers, and philosophers as an intellectual himself, as a colleague, and expressed to them his regret that his occupation as a ruler left him so little time for scientific pursuits. With particular eagerness he visited the salons of the bluestocking ladies and even appeared in the salon of Madame Necker, whose husband was a heretic, a bourgeois, and a Swiss. The members of the Lilac Coterie received the news of the Emperor's visits to the "Swiss Cottage" with a mocking curl of the lip.

Joseph's exploration of Versailles, both of the vast Palace and of the customs of the court, was most detailed. He rummaged about in every corridor and corner of the great labyrinth and nothing escaped him, neither the little "side-rooms" of Toinette nor the workshop in which Louis exercised his hobby. He also attended the King's *lever* and *coucher,* hidden among the crowd of courtiers without Louis's knowing he was there. Shaking his head, he watched while Louis shamelessly had his shirt and breeches put on or taken off in the presence of a multitude of his subjects, his fat countenance displaying obvious boredom with the whole of the ceremonious proceedings. The

King's right side and his left side were attended to by different groups of nobles.

On one occasion Joseph observed that Louis, during the ceremony of being put to bed, strolled up and down the circle of courtiers with his breeches hanging down, stopped in front of the young Count Gramont, one of his chamberlains, stepped close up to him so that Gramont had to back up against the wall, and kept stepping closer until his fat belly was touching the young man's slim body, whereupon Louis burst into a boisterous guffaw and moved away from his apprehensive victim.

For at least twenty minutes every evening Louis had to undress before the public gaze. When he felt that it had gone on long enough he would signal to the pages, who then pulled off his boots and dropped them with a loud thud on the floor. This loud thud was part of the ritual, a sign to the aristocratic throng that they could now withdraw. Then, and only then, Louis was able to get into bed. Joseph thought with a feeling of pride how much more advanced his own simple court was, compared with this childish demonstration of Byzantine ceremony.

For the rest, he endeavoured to be fair and to regard with an unjaundiced eye all that was good in Paris and at Versailles. He was able to appreciate the magnificence of the Palace and gardens of Versailles, the imposing buildings of Paris, the beauty of the bridges and squares. But his eye was struck even more by the cobwebs that hung from the ceilings of the ornate rooms of the Palace, the broken frames of some of the paintings, the furniture that was in need of repair. He looked at the hawkers who raucously offered their wares at the noble approaches to the Palace and on the outside staircases. He did not fail to note the dirt, noise, and confusion that prevailed in the city of Paris, and the slovenliness evident in both the capital and the Palace made a stronger impression on him than the brilliance and splendour to which it was in such vivid contrast. It was with a certain satisfaction that he found so much of which to disapprove.

When people asked him what he thought of Paris and Versailles, he tried to be diplomatic and politely expressed his admiration of what he had seen, though his tendency to sarcasm occasionally got the upper hand and he would then indulge in pungent comments that made no attempt to conceal the superiority he felt. Neither the antiquated organization of the army, the chaotic condition of the street traffic in Paris, nor the general rottenness of what he regarded as a whited sepulchre escaped his criticism, and these occasional utterances of his were zealously put into circulation by those who heard them.

Every step he took was dogged not only by the agents of the Paris police, but also by spies in the pay of Count Mercy and the Abbé

Vermond. Both Maria Theresa at Schoenbrunn and Louis at Versailles received a continuous stream of detailed reports on the indefatigable efforts of Count Falkenstein to improve and disseminate his knowledge of the world.

Joseph possessed literary inclinations and he liked to formulate his impressions in well-chosen phrases. In a lengthy letter to his brother Leopold, the Grand Duke of Tuscany, whom he knew to be in agreement with his ideas, he wrote, "Everything in this city of Paris is based on show. The public buildings are magnificent and very imposing, but one must not inspect them too closely. They are fine outside, but disgusting inside. There is only a pretence of greatness. In this Babylon they are familiar neither with the laws of nature nor with those of a rational social order. Instead they cover everything with a veneer of politeness and ceremony."

He handed the letter to the Austrian Ambassador for dispatch by special courier to Ferrara, his brother's capital, but it fell into the hands of the French secret service, was copied by Monsieur Lenoir, the Chief of Police in Paris, before being forwarded to its destination, and the contents were communicated to the King.

Louis sat brooding for a long time over the biting criticism of his brother-in-law, which appeared to him unjustly exaggerated. All this was the result of Joseph's mixing so much with rebellious, godless philosophers. He had even had a long talk with Turgot, whose brazen audacity verged on treason. If Joseph looked down with pitying contempt on the nauseating servility which characterized the court of his adipose brother-in-law, the latter in his turn sincerely pitied the Holy Roman Emperor who had joined the ranks of the scoffers and was hazarding the salvation of his soul.

☆   ☆   ☆

Joseph was a passionate reformer. He believed that he had been born to set all things right that were out of joint, not only the world in general, but even such matters of detail as his sister's behaviour and his brother-in-law's procreative capacity. Years ago, when Count Mercy first began to send to Vienna his reports on Toinette's frivolous activities, Joseph had declared, "I must go along to Versailles and see what can be done about it." When the conscientious Ambassador, with respectful solicitude, informed the Empress of the young King's physical disability, he said at once, "I will go along and put things right. You can rely on me, Mamma."

Nothing must be left to chance. The first essential preliminary to his all-important interview with Louis about the little operation was to find out exactly what kind of a man Louis was. He had not yet been able to make up his mind about him. Sometimes Louis would make an observation that seemed to reveal remarkable acumen, at others he would betray a bluntness of intelligence that verged on cretinism. So in order to test his mental powers of resistance Joseph enticed him into a detailed political discussion.

At first everything went off harmoniously. Joseph explained his views on the Anglo-American conflict, asserting in a determined tone that he considered it wrong to show the Americans the slightest sympathy. He demonstrated with a great display of eloquence that true liberty was possible only under an enlightened monarchy, and in polished phrases that sprang from firm conviction he poured scorn on the dilettantes of freedom in Philadelphia whose activities were leading to nothing else but anarchy. Louis listened contentedly, nodded his heavy head now and then, uttered vague sounds of approval, and made a mental note of a number of Joseph's well-turned arguments in order to use them against Maurepas and Vergennes.

Then Joseph began to speak of the Bavarian succession. Warming to his subject, he elaborated on the possibilities that were opened up to the House of Habsburg by the prospect of the early decease of the Bavarian Elector. Was it not the House of Habsburg's sacred duty to seize the opportunity of protecting itself against the increasing threat from Prussia by taking over strategically important territory? This suggestion filled Louis with a dull sense of wrath. Did, then, the well-founded claims of Zweibrücken go for nothing in his brother-in-law's estimation? Was this enlightened and philosophical monarch, with his profoundly moral views, prepared to throw all morality on the dust-heap? Maurepas and Vergennes were right. The House of Habsburg was hatching megalomaniac plans for war, and France must not allow any family compact to drag her into the conflict. This brother-in-law of his, who was always talking about reason and morality, had abruptly revealed himself for what he was—a Romantic, an adventurer, an unscrupulous conqueror who wanted to gain world-domination for the House of Habsburg. In increasing bewilderment he sat and sweated as he listened to the presumptuous, godless words that flowed from Joseph's lips. Ought he not to reply? Yet how could he, who was so much younger and less experienced, preach on the subject of morality to the brilliant Emperor? The best thing was to stick to his original intention and evade the issue.

So he listened in silence, took a sheet of paper, scribbled, and when Joseph had come to the end of his discourse, he handed him the sheet and said, "Look here, Sire, there's the boundary line between you and Bavaria. Don't you think I drew it rather well offhand?"

Joseph debated within himself whether this young man who sat there with a smile of naïve pride on his flabby face was an idiot or whether he was indulging in some spiteful joke. He looked at the map, put it down on the table, and said calmly, "What is your opinion,

Sire? Do you adopt the same point of view as we do? May we rely upon your support in defence of our claims?"

"Let me see," replied Louis thoughtfully. "I think I can even repeat by heart the names of all the towns with more than two thousand inhabitants within the territories subject to the Elector of Bavaria." And he began to enumerate them.

Joseph gave up as hopeless the attempt to talk seriously with his brother-in-law, so he changed the topic to various matters of trifling importance and soon afterwards took his leave.

When, in his methodical way, he proceeded to draw his deductions from the interview, he decided that he had every cause for confidence. Louis was cunning enough to avoid giving a direct answer, but he had not the strength of mind to say "No" outright. Nonetheless it was going to be no easy task, and would demand great suppleness of argument before this tough, apathetic type of resistance could be overcome.

To Maria Theresa Joseph wrote: "Your son-in-law Louis, my dearest mother, has been badly brought up and he cuts an extremely sorry figure. But at heart he is decent. He also possesses an astonishing memory in which he has stored up a great deal of factual knowledge. For instance, he can repeat in alphabetical order the name of every town in Bavaria with more than two thousand inhabitants, though I do not see what use, either direct or indirect, such virtuosity can have for a monarch. For the rest, Louis suffers from a serious inability to make up his mind, and he has little defence against those who know how to intimidate him. I think, my dearest mother, that the purpose of my journey will be achieved."

This letter too fell into the hands of the Chief of Police, but Monsieur Lenoir preferred not to communicate its contents to the King himself. Instead he handed a copy to Maurepas. Maurepas read it and wagged his hoary head. Then he showed it to his secretary and asked, "What are your views on this, my dear Sallé?"

The secretary, in his ghostly voice, replied, "For a Holy Roman Emperor the Holy Roman Emperor is not a bad student of human nature."

Maurepas decided that for the time being it would be better to keep the letter carefully locked up and to make use of it only in case of special emergency.

☆   ☆   ☆

In his quiet house and garden at Passy, Doctor Franklin heard a great deal about the character and activities of the free-thinking Emperor. Those of his friends who had come into contact with Joseph—and there were not a few of them—praised his simplicity and found his manner sharp, alert, matter-of-fact, and at the same time amiable. The Doctor would have very much welcomed an opportunity to converse with Joseph. He hoped to convince him that the American question was at bottom a purely Anglo-Saxon affair and that nothing was further from the intention of the thirteen States than to instigate rebellion among the nations of Europe. He was confident of his ability to disperse the fears of Maria Theresa and her son that the American example would encourage European peoples to revolt.

He was therefore pleased when one of his friends, Condorcet of the Academy, informed him that his name had been mentioned during a discussion with Joseph and that the latter had intimated his willingness to make the Doctor's acquaintance.

The Abbé Niccoli, who represented the Grand Duchy of Tuscany of which Joseph's brother was the ruler, undertook to arrange a private meeting. He inquired of Count Falkenstein and of Doctor Franklin whether they would care one day to take a cup of chocolate with him, and he used the good offices of Condorcet to let each of them know that the other would be present.

When the Holy Roman Emperor received the invitation he felt for the fraction of a second that it would perhaps have been better if he had not expressed a wish to meet the American. Before leaving Vienna his mother had impressed upon him that if he must pay a visit to that corrupt city of Paris he should at least avoid coming into contact with certain "wild characters." He had forgotten the names of many of the "wild characters" she had enumerated. He was sure Voltaire and Rousseau were among them, but he had a vague remembrance of her having mentioned Franklin too. Be that as it may, however, the Holy Roman Emperor could not let his affectionate mamma lay down for him with whom he should speak and with whom he should not. Benjamin Franklin, rebel or no rebel, was one of the outstanding scientists of the age, a philosopher of the first order, and reputed to be a particularly stimulating conversationalist. Why shouldn't he seize the opportunity of entering into a discussion with such a man? Perhaps he could even convince the leader of the American insurgents, by courteous, objective argument that the masses were unable, by their very nature, to understand what was best for them and that an enlightened despotism was therefore the most rational form of government. Pleased with this bold and original intention, he told everyone about it.

The appointed day arrived and at nine in the morning, as arranged, Franklin called upon the Abbé Niccoli in the company of his grandson William. A few minutes later Condorcet appeared. They drank chocolate and conversed. Franklin took a second cup of chocolate and one or two of the excellent sweet brioches which the Abbé offered his guests. As they waited they continued to talk. The clock struck ten. It struck eleven. The Abbé served port, and Franklin accepted a glass of this excellent wine. They had no notion what could have prevented Joseph from turning up at the hour for which he had been invited. Franklin decided to give him another sixty minutes. The clock struck noon, and there was probably no point in waiting any longer. The party broke up and Franklin returned to Passy. He accepted the situation philosophically. No doubt it would have been quite helpful to the American cause if he had been able to have a talk with the Emperor. Well, he would have to wait for another opportunity.

What had happened to prevent Joseph from keeping his appointment was this. Count Mercy had received from Maria Theresa, who looked upon the old diplomat as one of her most reliable friends, a confidential letter in which she poured out her apprehensions concerning the visit that her difficult son Joseph was paying to the modern Babylon on the Seine. She had thoughtfully enclosed a list of the dangerous elements, the democrats, philosophers, loafers, and scoundrels, whom she desired the Holy Roman Emperor at all costs to keep at arm's length. The list was headed by the names of Voltaire and Franklin.

Count Mercy therefore received the fright of his life when he learned of Joseph's indiscreet intention, and he wrote straightway to Maria Theresa advising her to urge her son personally to refrain from carrying out his plan. A special courier was sent posting at break-neck speed to Vienna, another special courier came flying back, and in the early morning of the day when the meeting with Franklin was to take place a message was delivered into Joseph's hands. It was in German, written in his mother's own hand, and very touching. She sympathized with the curiosity which made him wish to see for himself what villains like the atheistic Voltaire and the insubordinate Franklin looked like, but she begged him at the same time to think of his responsibility before the tribunal of history. The letter was not very long and some of the words had been effaced by tears.

Joseph's eyes glided over the childish, laborious handwriting. His whole being revolted against the eternal tutelage to which Maria Theresa subjected him. Her fears were entirely without foundation. Did she think that he identified himself with the views of everybody he met? In any case, it had already been bruited abroad that he and Franklin were to have a talk together. It would be a most unroyal thing to do, and harmful to his prestige, if he were to call it off.

On the other hand, there had been a lot of questions still waiting to be settled when he left Vienna. There was that everlasting problem of the Bohemian Protestants, there was the reform of the schools, there was the matter of the Bavarian succession, there was the Russo-Turkish business. If he was to have any hope of persuading his mother to agree to concessions in a single one of these ticklish problems, he must be careful not to upset her. Which was more important, the reform of the Austrian schools or his meeting with the old Doctor? He heaved a sigh. Maria Theresa's letter had transformed a personal desire on the part of Count Falkenstein to see Franklin into an affair of state involving the destinies of the Habsburg monarchy.

Rather morosely he sought the advice of Count Mercy. To his great regret, he explained, it appeared that the Empress was anxious lest his conversation with Franklin should be open to misinterpretation. He had therefore decided, in principle, to sacrifice his personal thirst for knowledge to his mother's political scruples. He wished, however, to avoid any show of discourtesy towards Doctor Franklin. Had Count Mercy any suggestion? The Ambassador drew a breath of relief; he had a suggestion. Nobody could possibly take it amiss if, in consequence of an unexpected contingency—which there would be no difficulty in inventing—the Emperor were unable to keep his appointment to breakfast with the Abbé Niccoli at the exact hour arranged. It would therefore be advisable not to cancel the engagement, but to keep his host waiting a little, say for two or three hours, or perhaps even four. The Austrian Embassy had very efficient agents in its service who would inform Joseph of the earliest moment when it would be possible for him to pay his projected visit to the Abbé Niccoli without running the risk of upsetting the old Empress in Vienna.

That was why Joseph, when he called upon the Abbé Niccoli at twenty minutes past twelve, found to his profound regret that Doctor Franklin had just left.

☆   ☆   ☆

The Princess Rohan had issued invitations for one of those English tea-parties that were now the fashion. The leading members of the Lilac Coterie were going to be there, and the Emperor Joseph too had signified his intention of being present.

He had repeatedly told Toinette in plain words what he thought of her friends. He had even made stinging remarks to the ladies themselves.

In order to put a stop to such tactlessness, Toinette arrived very early at the Princess Rohan's apartments, but she found there only François Vaudreuil and Diane Polignac.

During the last few weeks there had been sharp arguments between François and Toinette. The nerves of François, usually so supercilious, had been set on edge by Joseph's presence in Paris. He regarded France not only as the most powerful, but also as the most civilized, country in Europe, and he was annoyed by the attitude of this Habsburg prince who, though he condescendingly admitted his appreciation of one thing or another, nevertheless made no concealment of his scorn for France, Paris, and the court in general. The qualities of the

royal brother and sister merged in Vaudreuil's mind. Joseph displayed
the same naïve arrogance that so frequently infuriated Vaudreuil in
Toinette. Though she had never discussed it with him, he knew why
she was so proud. She had been brought up to believe in the notion of
divine right, she held the view that a country was epitomized in its
King, and in her contemptuous sympathy for the loutish, impotent
Louis she identified him with his people. As a daughter of the Caesars,
of a long line of Holy Roman Emperors, she looked down with scorn
upon France, whose Queen she was. This innate and consuming pride
in both Toinette and Joseph wounded the pampered, haughty Vaudreuil to the quick, and it was with an even more intense mingling of
rage and pleasure that he meditated on ways and means of forcing
Toinette to become his mistress and thus bringing about her eventual
humiliation.

His chaotic emotions were confused still further by the purpose of
Joseph's visit. It angered him to think that the King of France needed
persuasion by his Habsburg brother-in-law before he could be brought
to deflower his consort. Whenever François was alone with Toinette
his violent nature spurred him on to mortify her as no one, not even
he himself, had ever dared to do before. Each tried to hurt the other
as much as possible.

While they were waiting for Joseph, he behaved towards her with
a ceremonious courtesy that irritated her more than open mockery
would have done. "What is the matter, Vaudreuil?" she inquired.
"Why are you acting like an ambassador at his first audience?"

"I have taken Count Falkenstein's criticism to heart," he replied.
"His Imperial Majesty has commented that our politeness is a veneer,
which serves merely to conceal our brutish and slovenly nature. I am
endeavouring to apply an extra coat of varnish." Meanwhile most of
the guests had arrived. "I hope," remarked Vaudreuil, "that Count
Falkenstein will not keep us waiting as long as he kept the Abbé
Niccoli."

"Why should Count Falkenstein keep *us* waiting?" rejoined Diane
Polignac.

Toinette pricked up her ears. When she had learned that her
brother's intended meeting with Franklin had not taken place after
all, she had not attributed any particular significance to the incident.
Her friends' smiles told her now that they regarded his unpunctuality
as deliberate and his failure to keep the appointment as cowardice.
With some bewilderment she noticed also that Gabrielle and Diane
were wearing little statuettes of Franklin in their towering coiffures.
Hitherto, in view of the fact that Louis and Toinette had held aloof
from the American envoy, court society had disdained to follow the
prevailing fashion and had likewise treated him with reserve. The two

Polignac ladies, however, had always claimed the privilege of freely
proclaiming their political opinions, and Gabrielle in particular always
stressed her independence, though in an indolent, matter-of-fact way.
So normally it would have attracted little attention if the two ladies
decided to demonstrate their sympathy with Franklin's mission. It was
customary for women to wear in their hair all sorts of emblems that
bore allusion to topical events. What rendered Toinette uneasy was
the circumstance that they should have chosen that particular day to
wear the statuettes and that François, moreover, should have made
the remark he did. It would have caused her no surprise if her intimate friends had sought an opportunity to avenge themselves for
Joseph's Teutonic bluntness, but she feared that by the incident of
the broken appointment he had revealed a chink in his armour. Her
curiosity was stirred and she wondered what her friends had in mind.

Count Jules, who was rather maladroit, had evidently not been initiated into the conspiracy, for he observed to Toinette a little clumsily,
"Don't you think, Madame, that my ladies are being somewhat more
liberal than is necessary?" Pointing to their Franklin emblems, he said
to them, "The outcome of your enthusiasm will be that this Franklin
of yours will set fire to Versailles and burn it down over our heads."
He was usually content to sit at the card-table with an empty expression on his handsome, though brutal, features, and his political opinions were not taken seriously. All Diane said was, "Our good Jules!"
and she smiled compassionately.

Gabrielle, however, with lazy self-assurance, replied, "I know very
little about America, but I find the Doctor delightful. On the two
occasions that I have met him, once at Madame Maurepas's and the
second time at the house of Madame de Genlis, he was simply charming. When he pays you a compliment it makes you feel important.
The Americans cannot be such iniquitous creatures as some people
think."

Toinette grew more and more bewildered. She had never been able
to find time to ponder much on the American conflict. Mercy and Vermond had impressed upon her that she must avoid saying anything
that might betray sympathy for the Americans, and she had not found
it difficult to follow their advice. Ought she perhaps to have given the
matter more of her attention? Was Franklin really so much the rage?
With amazement, and slightly worried, she noticed how warmly her
friends were entering the lists on his behalf.

Her thoughts were interrupted by the screeching of the parrot, *"Les
amants arrivent,"* and the announcement from a servant at the door,
"Count Falkenstein!" Joseph entered the room.

Tea was served in thin porcelain cups, and the company discussed
this new-fashioned drink for which the English cherished such an odd

preference. They talked of customs duties and monopolies, and expressed their surprise that such a weak, harmless brew should have been the cause of a revolt by the American colonies.

Prince Charles, pretending to be uninformed, asked Joseph what impression he had carried away from his meeting with the celebrated fur-capped and bespectacled apostle of freedom. Joseph, affecting a humorous tone, replied that when he arrived the impatient old man had gone. This astonished his hearers, since the Doctor was renowned for his mild and tranquil temperament.

"Will you not make a second attempt, Sire, to enter into contact with him?" asked Gabrielle innocently.

"In the first place, Madame," replied Joseph, "I would beg you not to address me as 'Sire,' and secondly, I have no intention of doing so." With a sarcastic smile he added, "Doctor Franklin can hardly expect me to run after him." That seemed to close the subject.

Gabrielle, with gentle insistence, refused to let the matter drop. "It seems, Count Falkenstein," she said, "that you do not share our esteem for the wise old gentleman."

"What else could you have imagined, Madame?" he returned dryly. "After all, I am a royalist by profession."

"Do you really think, Count Falkenstein," intervened Vaudreuil very politely, "that it was a sign of impatience on Doctor Franklin's part to have left before you arrived? He is a stickler for dignity. He represents a country that scorns our conventional and ceremonious ways, yet knows how to preserve its dignity."

Joseph raised his eyebrows and gazed at Vaudreuil. Was this man trying to read him a lesson? Vaudreuil returned his gaze with a well-simulated air of innocence. "It has not escaped my notice," said Joseph sharply, in a tone that brooked no contradiction, "that Doctor Franklin is being thoroughly spoiled by the people of Paris. Whether he possesses a sense of personal dignity or not, the ideas which he advocates are crazy and far from dignified. That is why I regret," and here he fixed his blue eyes sternly on the coiffures of the Polignac ladies, "to observe that an undiscriminating enthusiasm for this man appears to be infecting the Queen's circle. Liberal-minded as I am, I would not sanction the presence of Doctor Benjamin Franklin in my capital, and I would certainly refuse to tolerate an uncritical singing of his praises by those who attend my court."

This was not the first time that Joseph had brusquely rebuked the ladies and gentlemen of the Lilac Coterie, but never before had he been so blunt. There was an uncomfortable silence. Which was abruptly broken by the hostess, who said, "When this Franklin first appeared in Paris I tried to get into touch with Oliver Cromwell, but he did not materialize."

Nobody took any notice of the Princess Rohan. Toinette, painfully

surprised at Joseph's vehemence, had flushed slighty, Gabrielle smiled
a mocking, lazy smile as if she were only vaguely interested, Diane
stroked one of the Princess's dogs. They were all waiting expectantly
to see whether Vaudreuil would swallow the Emperor's retort or
whether he would have the audacity to accept the challenge.

He had. It suited his book quite well that this Habsburg should have
spoken to him so haughtily. He had set out to irritate Joseph, and his
bold, masculine features radiated an air of self-confidence as he prepared to pay the presumptuous Austrian back in his own coin. "You
must realize, Count Falkenstein," he said, "that in Vienna you are
accustomed to leading a simple life. Your conflicts are clear-cut and
easy to analyse. Here in Versailles, on the other hand, in the course of
our long history, with its increasing refinements of civilization, we
have become so over-cultivated, so artificial in our way of living, that
we long for anything that breathes of nature. In this venerable old
man, Benjamin Franklin, we see the epitome of those natural principles that are engaging the minds of our philosophers. You too have
heard, no doubt, of Jean-Jacques Rousseau. We are moved by the fact
that this simple old American combines within himself all the forces
of nature, we are touched by it, and we do not deny him our applause."

He paused for a moment as if waiting for a reply, but Joseph held
his tongue. Toinette felt uneasy and tried to turn the conversation by
a pretence of cheerfulness. "Nature!" she chattered. "When the Trianon is ready I will show you so much nature that you will lose all
interest in this Franklin of yours." She burst into a laugh, but nobody
joined in her laughter. They all still had their eyes fixed intently on
Joseph and Vaudreuil.

Since Joseph continued to remain silent, Vaudreuil resumed his
argument. "You may be right, Count Falkenstein. Perhaps it does
offend against our obvious interests, against those of the King and our
own, if we display such boundless sympathy for Franklin and do our
best to help him and his rebels. Nonetheless, there is perhaps a deeper
wisdom in our attitude than if we were to cover him with abuse and
to proceed to attack him from all sides. Since we cannot hold up the
progressive spirit of the times, we are assisting it in its advance. We
are sawing at the branch on which we are sitting because we know that
it is destined to fall." In contrast to Joseph's didactic tone, Vaudreuil
spoke in an easy conversational manner, stating his point politely yet
boldly, and his friends who were listening rejoiced at his success in
putting so aptly something of which they were all vaguely conscious.
Yet his audacity made them hold their breath and they wondered what
Joseph would say in reply, what he *could* say in reply.

Joseph was raging inwardly with impotent fury. In noble self-
restraint he had proclaimed and put into practice his ideas of tolerance,
and there were many who praised his attitude as the most courageous

in human memory. Now there came this wretched courtier, one of his frivolous sister's pitiful creatures, this pleasure-loving Frenchman, and tried to rap him over the knuckles by explaining proudly what it meant to stand up for Franklin and the brave cause of truth. The others listened with open mouths, defiantly displaying their sympathy for the Americans, while he, the Holy Roman Emperor, His Apostolic Majesty, stood before them as a cowardly fellow who did not dare to look the rebel leader in the eye. Yet was it any more than he deserved? He ought to have kept his appointment to breakfast with the Abbé Niccoli. It would have gone down in history as an event of historical importance if he, the enlightened monarch, had engaged in a discussion with the anarchist from the wild West and proved to him where true virtue and duty lay.

It was impossible, however, to keep silent any longer, and fighting down his anger he said coldly, "That is an outlook, Monsieur le Marquis, that I would not tolerate at my own court."

"I have never doubted that, Sire," replied Vaudreuil with a winning smile that drove Joseph to abandon all attempt of maintaining his self-control.

"If you mean by that, Monsieur," he rapped out sharply, "that there can be any comparison between your 'true' liberalism and my 'false' conception of the same ideal, it would appear that you have failed to understand me. Liberalism is not the equivalent of softness, it does not imply that one should allow oneself to drift, to be blown hither and thither by fate. Liberalism implies activity, the effective direction of one's energies. The goals that beckon to the man with a free mind are not revolt and anarchy, but order and authority based on reason."

"To be precise," said Diane sweetly, "enlightened despotism."

"Yes, Madame," answered Joseph tartly, "enlightened despotism."

"You may not be aware of it, Sire," commented Vaudreuil with his usual winning smile, "but you with your enlightened despotism are doing no less to saw away the aforementioned branch than we are. You too are abandoning privileges, making concessions to the spirit of the age. The only difference is that whereas you are doing so in grim earnest, we are making a virtue of necessity and getting a little fun out of it."

"That is pure cynicism. You can take nothing seriously—none of you," burst out Joseph irately. "You possess neither a sense of dignity nor a realization of your duty." Joseph's voice, raised in anger, disquieted the dogs who began to yap, while the parrot added its screeching to the hubbub. But Joseph, pointing his finger at Vaudreuil, outshouted the noise: "You are a more dangerous rebel, Monsieur, than Franklin."

Toinette firmly believed that royalty was a divine institution, and that this was a blessing for mankind. She entirely agreed with Joseph, and she considered Vaudreuil's last remarks criminal nonsense. It was more likely that the world would fly apart than that the institution of monarchy could disappear. Nevertheless, it was with a deep feeling of satisfaction that she listened to her overpowering and omniscient brother being contradicted on his own ground, and it filled her with an almost physical pleasure to watch him, though he was undoubtedly in the right, trying in vain to hold his own against the elegant, audacious François, her François. Joseph, the eternal schoolmaster, was at last himself being given a dressing down.

The matter had gone far enough, however, and she was asking herself whether it was not time to intervene with some soothing comment. Before she had time to speak, the Princess Rohan poured oil on the troubled waters by declaring firmly, "Now that will do, gentlemen. We are not in Madame Necker's debating club. We are here to drink tea and to talk about sensible matters." Amid general laughter the argument was closed.

☆   ☆   ☆

Toinette had invited Joseph to an intimate family dinner-party, at which only Louis and his two brothers with their wives were to be present. It was a very youthful gathering. Louis was twenty-three, his brother Xavier, Count of Provence, was twenty-two, and Prince Charles, Count of Artois, only twenty. Toinette at twenty-one was the oldest of the ladies. Joseph, who was thirty-six, felt an ancient in such company.

The conscientious Louis made a special point of preserving the common bond among the members of his family. His brothers had been assigned the most handsome apartments at Versailles and the three of them were often together. Yet it was a far from harmonious ensemble, for Louis was on no less dubious terms with Xavier than with Charles. Not that Xavier was as extravagant as his brother, or that he gave equal cause for public offence, but from early boyhood he had been unable to reconcile himself to the idea that the stupid Louis was destined to the throne rather than he himself, who learned easily and knew how to bear himself with royal dignity. It was with a sense of grim satisfaction that he learned of his brother's incapacity to provide himself with an heir. When Louis ascended the throne Xavier had become heir presumptive, receiving the title of "Monsieur" and being accorded the honours due to a Dauphin, but he had a long wait in front of him, a great many years perhaps, and to help kill time he amused himself by composing spiteful epigrams at the King's expense. Louis was aware of all this, yet it did not diminish his affectionate attitude towards his brother. He even used his full authority to defend Xavier against attacks from outside the family circle. This did not prevent the two brothers from saying things to one another privately that sounded as if they were meant in jest, but concealed a venomous barb. When Xavier was once playing the part of Tartuffe at an amateur performance, Louis commented with marked emphasis, "Excellent, Xavier. The role fits you like a glove."

Prince Charles was less furtive and mocked Louis to his face. Himself already the father of two children, he treated his impotent eldest brother with open contempt. Though his relations with Toinette were no more than those of a natural friendship between two young people, he deliberately tried, in order to mortify Louis, to foster the belief that he deputized for his boorish brother in his sister-in-law's bed.

With Joseph's arrival at Versailles the situation among the brothers took a sharper turn. Charles contented himself with cynical witticisms. Xavier, who saw all his hopes about to founder, was furious, dipped his pen in gall, and composed even more poisonous verses.

Such were the relations among the three young men who sat with Joseph at the family dinner-table. They discussed his wanderings through the city of Paris.

"Do you know, Louis," Joseph asked, "that you possess the finest building in Europe?"

"And which is that?" inquired Louis.

"The Hôtel des Invalides," was Joseph's reply.

"Yes," Louis agreed politely, "everybody tells me that it is a handsome structure."

"Do you mean to say," cried Joseph in horrified amazement, "that you have never seen it?"

"Did I not propose to you a week or two ago, Toinette," said Louis good-humouredly, "that we should do Saint-Germain a kindness and inspect his Hôtel des Invalides? He is so proud of it."

Toinette was annoyed. She was again being blamed because something had been neglected. It was always this Saint-Germain. Her friends had been urging her for ever so long to get the old fool dismissed. No, she was not going to submit any longer to being reproached on his account. While she chatted and chewed her mutton she made up her mind firmly and angrily that Saint-Germain must go.

Joseph talked of his tours of exploration, during which he had scrutinized the Palace from cellars to attics. "It seems to me, brother-in-law," he said, "that you have some magnificent things here that ought to be better looked after. I found some wonderful paintings hidden away in storerooms. They were leaning against the wall and were covered with dust. You really ought to have them sorted out and attended to."

"Yes," rejoined Louis, with obvious lack of interest, "there has been a great deal piling up since the days of Louis the Great. Plenty of immoral pictures too, by the way. I gave Maurepas instruction some time ago to have part of the stuff removed."

In his usual insolent way Charles commented, "Our Louis has never had much use for pictures." Then, turning to both his brothers, he said in a more animated tone, "Do you remember how we had to describe the painting with the pond and the swans when we were children? Louis gave an excellent description of it, only unfortunately he had not noticed that it was the same pond we used to pass every other day in our walks."

Louis laughed good-naturedly. "It was not exactly like that," he said, and continued eating. He ate very much, he enjoyed it, and again filled his plate. The others had finished and the servants were waiting to change dishes. Everybody looked as Louis ate all by himself, quite at his ease, deeply absorbed, and slovenly.

At last Toinette murmured reprovingly, "Louis!"

"Yes, my love, what is it?" he inquired. Then he looked round, allowed his plate to be taken away, and wiped his hands. Leaning back in his chair, he asked in a curiously mingled tone of anger and amusement, "Do you remember how once during a geography lesson that we were being given by the Duc de Vauguyon he slipped and fell on his nose? He had just been taking us through the rivers of the Iberian Peninsula, and I was the only one who knew them. You two had not bothered to do your homework. We were all punished because he had been tripped up." He paused for a moment. "You had stuck out a leg, Charles."

"No, I did not," retorted Charles with a mischievous smile. "The old idiot slipped."

"You stuck out a leg," repeated Louis, "but we did not give you away."

A hundred memories of childhood surged through his mind. He had been even more awkward then than he was now. Though he had frequently known quite well what to do or to say, he had been too shy to behave like a normal boy. His brothers knew less, but they were alert and full of spirit, so they had been regarded as the gifted ones while he was looked upon as the fool of the family and everybody, with Xavier and Charles in the forefront, used him as a butt. On one occasion, when he still bore the title of "Duc de Berry," they were all invited to spend the afternoon with their Aunt Adelaide. The other two romped about while he stood helplessly looking on.

"Don't stand there staring," his aunt had called to him peremptorily. "Show us that you can run, Berry. Say something, Berry. Make a noise, Berry." There was such a contemptuous and pitying note in her voice that he had never forgotten it.

When his father died so suddenly, and so mysteriously, things had taken a different turn. When he walked through the corridors the guards presented arms and cried, *"Vive le Dauphin!"* The first time this happened he had looked round stupidly as if the salute had been intended for someone else, though he was well aware that it was for him. The bitter-sweet feeling that his father, whom he had feared and loved, was dead and that he was now heir to the throne almost caused his heart to stop beating. Since he had assumed the crown his two brothers, the fat one and the slim one, hated him still more. Xavier, at least, confined himself to writing furtive epigrams. But that insolent, lascivious spendthrift Charles, who came to him every fortnight to extort money from him, went about telling everybody that he was making a cuckold of the King.

"I tell you, Charles," Louis insisted wrathfully, almost menacingly, "you stuck out a leg and tripped Vauguyon."

"There's no need to keep on repeating it," intervened Xavier, while Charles snapped out, "Oh, don't be so silly!"

"I am only saying what is true," muttered Louis stubbornly. Then he suddenly cried, "Do you want to deny it?" jumped up from his chair, and seized Charles by both wrists.

Charles laughed, though he was seething with anger, and tried to pull himself away, but Louis had strength in those coarse hands of his and Charles was unable to free himself.

"Please leave him alone!" demanded Xavier. Louis only held on more tightly.

"Messieurs! Messieurs!" exhorted Joseph, while the two Princesses uttered stifled shrieks.

At last Louis let go. "I am strong," he said, more to himself than to the others, with a foolish, embarrassed smile. Then he sat down again and went on with his dinner.

☆   ☆   ☆

In order to prove to himself and to the Parisians that his failure to keep the appointment with Franklin had not been due to prejudice, Joseph made a point of visiting a variety of personalities who were out of favour at court. He spent many hours with Baron Turgot and appeared more frequently than before in the salon of Madame Necker.

One evening he paid a visit to Madame de Genlis, the author of advanced books for the young, who also was very unpopular at Versailles. Her salon was conducted on rather informal lines. On three evenings a week her friends assembled, and Joseph went without announcing that he intended to be present. Among those he found there was Pierre Caron de Beaumarchais.

Pierre had frequently made fun of Joseph. The Holy Roman

Emperor, he used to say, had an easy task. He was only the mouthpiece of the monarchy, power being retained in the hands of the old Empress. She exercised a despotic regime, while her son played a liberal accompaniment.

It was hardly to be expected that Pierre should be entirely unbiased so far as the Habsburgs were concerned. Years before, when Toinette was still the Dauphine, he had hastened to Vienna in order to display to Maria Theresa a lampoon directed against her daughter. He had eloquently recounted at the Austrian court how he had succeeded, at the cost of great effort and after exposing himself to a number of hazardous adventures, in wresting the lampoon from its author. He had brought it with him, he read it to the Empress, and he offered to reduce the calumniator to silence. Of course, the fellow would have to be quieted with money. Here, however, the churlish Viennese police had a word to say. They alleged that the aforementioned adventures were fictitious, that the wounds received by Monsieur Caron in his struggle for the manuscript had been inflicted by himself with a razor, and that the histrionic skill with which he had read the lampoon was not to be marvelled at since he had written it himself. The Empress ordered his arrest, then changed her mind, decided to be generous, gave him a large sum of money, and sent him a valuable ring. This ring he still wore, and would occasionally refer to it casually as, "Oh, just a souvenir from the Empress Maria Theresa."

Joseph had a dim remembrance of Monsieur de Beaumarchais's exploit in Vienna and he hesitated before venturing on a conversation with a gentleman of such doubtful repute, but he was acquainted with his writings, he had recently seen a performance of *The Barber of Seville* and he could not withhold his grudging admiration for the Frenchman's wit. Moreover, he did not want to expose himself for a second time to the suspicion that he lacked the courage to talk with those people who were advocating French support for the American insurgents.

He therefore began with a laudatory word or two about *The Barber*, which made the self-satisfied Pierre even more self-satisfied. The fact that he was talking to a crowned head stirred all his bourgeois pride, and he addressed the Emperor as an equal, as one intellectual, whose achievements had already received recognition, speaking to another who still had to prove his worth. With beguiling impertinence, he even mentioned the assistance which a kindly destiny had enabled him to afford the old Empress, went into details about the lampoon in question, and quoted a few passages from memory, remarking at the same time that the author certainly possessed a sense of poetic form. In elegant phraseology he practically told Joseph to his face that he had made a fool of Maria Theresa.

Joseph did not answer. Since the fiasco of his projected meeting with Franklin and his argument with Vaudreuil he had learned caution. He even admitted to himself that there was a grain of truth in the lampoon which Monsieur de Beaumarchais was quoting.

Pierre, encouraged by Joseph's silence and enjoying the situation, went still further. He explained that it was a weakness of his beloved Parisians to say the most slanderous things about anyone merely for the sake of their wit and without caring whether there was adequate proof. He had himself had sad personal experiences in that respect, and a lady upon whom the eyes of the world were focused, like the Queen, must inevitably become the target for spiteful jests. Some of these were stupid and ribald, others achieved a more mischievous effect by their very delicacy. The most innocent whims could provide material for venomous attacks. For instance, there were the towering coiffures which the Queen, who was famous as a creator of fashion, had introduced and which were copied all over Europe. Pierre himself was flattered that they should be called *"Quès-a co,"* after a term he had used in one of his brochures, but there were calumniators who maintained that though this style of dressing the hair was admirably suited to the lofty brow and long profile of the Queen, it had a distorting effect on the round, more classical features of the Parisian ladies. It was said that the Austrian princess had introduced this type of coiffure out of jealousy, because she disliked all things French and wanted to make the ladies of Paris look plain. Pierre told Joseph how deeply he deplored the malicious gossip in which the world took so much delight.

Joseph was annoyed at this display of impertinence and felt that he ought to have avoided the possibility of being placed in such an awkward position. He had been making a lot of mistakes lately. First there was the contretemps with Franklin, and now there was this Beaumarchais. He had a clumsy touch in dealing with the American situation. A feeling of helplessness came over him, as if he were being thrust with bandaged eyes by some invisible hand onto a path that led to danger. In spite of his sincere intention to do what was right and useful, and though he felt that he had a great mission to fulfil, he seemed incapable of mastering the most simple problem.

Abruptly and simply he spoke out what was in his mind. "It is easy to possess a conscience, Monsieur, when one only needs to talk or write about it. But the man who has to act is constantly faced with the necessity, if he wishes to deal justly with one person, of being unjust to somebody else."

Pierre felt that the words had come from the very depths of Joseph's being, and he did not know what to say in reply.

☆   ☆   ☆

A week later Joseph decided that he was now ready for the decisive interview at which his brother-in-law was to be induced to consent to the operation.

They sat in Louis's library, surrounded by the books, the globes, and the porcelain poets. Joseph, plainly but neatly dressed, held himself very erect. Louis sat with rounded shoulders, rather dirty and untidy. While he had been working with Gamain in his locksmith shop, Joseph had surprised him and manœuvred him into this conversation.

When Joseph wanted to he could be very sympathetic, and he felt that this was the time for a display of sympathy. He spoke to Louis like an elder brother. Having briefed himself carefully by discussions with Doctor Ingenhousz, the Viennese specialist, and Doctor Lassone, Toinette's personal physician, he was able to explain to Louis with scientific exactness that there was no risk at all in the operation and that it was certain of success.

Louis liked to listen to men who had expert knowledge of the subject they were talking about, and Joseph's learned, objective way of speaking impressed him. From the moment he had heard of Joseph's impending visit to Versailles he had realized that evasion was no longer possible and that he would have to yield to his brother-in-law's persuasion. On the other hand, his every thought and emotion revolted against the surgeon's intervention. He wanted to leave things as they were. *Quieta non movere.* His innermost convictions urged him not to disturb that which was best left alone. He sat in heavy apathy, filled with a deep disquiet, his thoughts locked up in his mind. He kept his gaze averted from the man sitting opposite him, twisted helplessly, and tugged at his sleeves.

When Joseph had finished what he had to say, Louis remained silent for a long while. Joseph let him take his time. At last Louis pulled himself together and began to reiterate the old arguments that he had already employed in his talk with Maurepas. Much as he trusted the Minister, he had felt shy and inhibited when speaking to him of such intimate and delicate matters. Joseph, however, was a monarch by the grace of God like himself, and he would understand these deep and sacred stirrings of the soul. Louis could speak freely in front of him. Slowly he unburdened himself of his thoughts, and the arguments which had begun as a mere pretext developed into a revelation of his most secret feelings.

The body of a King was sanctified. If God had created him in the way He had done, with the physical disability which prevented him from fulfilling certain functions, then there must have been some reason for it. If therefore an attempt was made to intervene with the surgeon's knife, would this not be sinning against the will of God?

Perhaps God had destined him for a life of continence, just as He insisted on celibacy in His priests.

Joseph was fully aware of the sincerity with which the other spoke. It was difficult to refute arguments that sprang from the depths of a man's heart. But he had prepared his brief well. The crafty Count Mercy had been pumping Maurepas, and by this means Joseph had learned of Louis's scruples. He was equipped for his task of dispersing religious doubts.

The sober-minded Joseph disliked theological hair-splitting such as Louis employed to buttress his arguments. He hated everything that smacked of the priesthood, and if anyone else had displayed the superstitious hesitations that he observed in his brother-in-law he would have branded them with scorn and contempt, but he had made up his mind to be diplomatic. Having sought theological counsel from the Abbé Vermond, he was prepared to assail his brother-in-law's childishly Jesuitical scruples with equally childish Jesuitical counter-arguments. If he had astonished Louis with his medical knowledge, he was to astound him even more as a student of divinity.

Circumcision, as he explained to Louis, could not in any case, according to the theologians, be interpreted as an act committed against the will of God. Not only had God ordained it for His chosen people, but God's only begotten Son had Himself been circumcised, as could be read in the Gospel of St. Luke, Chapter II, Verse 21, and the foreskin was still preserved in a certain monastery in Italy. No doubt this relic was to be regarded as false, added Joseph wrathfully, as a swindle on the part of the priests, and the time would come when he would forbid it to be exhibited. Then in a gentler tone he urged, "Let the operation be performed, Louis. That is the only way in which you can be enabled to fulfil the biblical commandment, 'Be fruitful and multiply.' Now if," he added slyly, "you were to undergo the operation with a lustful purpose in view, if for instance you took after your late grandfather, then perhaps your scruples would be justified. But since your temperament is what it is, calm and controlled, by no means that of a young stallion, you can surely count on being able, even after the operation, to resist effectively any voluptuous temptations by which you may be assailed."

Joseph smiled, but Louis did not share his smile. He was picturing to himself the situation with which he would be faced when he met Toinette after the operation had been successfully performed. How should he let her know? How should he behave? The mere idea paralysed him. Breathing heavily through his nose, he sat humped gloomily in his chair and said nothing.

Joseph stood up, and Louis too had perforce to rise from his seat. Having overcome his brother-in-law's theological scruples, Joseph prepared to bring forward his main argument. Putting his arm round the younger man's shoulders, he walked with him up and down the room and spoke of the political consequences that must ensue if Louis should die childless. The crown would then go to Prince Xavier. He was convinced, continued Joseph, that on the family compact, on the political and marriage ties which had been established between the rulers of France, Austria, and Spain, there depended not only the whole future of those countries, but also the well-being of the entire world. If Prince Xavier were to become King of France the family compact would collapse, the alliance among the three great Catholic Powers would be jeopardized, and the consequences would be unpredictable. Louis must not permit this to happen. For the sake of world security he must put himself in the hands of Doctor Lassone and submit to the trifling incision. "Overcome your hesitations, Louis," urged Joseph warmly, and he held out his hand. "Let me inform my mother, our mother, that Toinette has at last found the happiness that we were entitled to expect."

Louis, reminded in this way of his duty and seeing the Emperor's hand stretched out towards him, could evade the issue no longer. "All right," he said apathetically, and feebly placed his coarse, rather dingy paw in the strong, slender hand of his brother-in-law.

"So I now have your firm and definite promise," said Joseph, summing up the outcome of their discussion, "that you will undergo the operation within the next fortnight." He continued to hold Louis's hand in his.

"Yes," replied Louis faintly. He drew back his hand. "But," he added quickly, "do not let us be precipitate. I will do it within, let us say, six weeks."

☆　　☆　　☆

Joseph was a well-intentioned man, who tried sincerely to help his family and friends and to be a model ruler over his people, but he had been forced to recognize that most of those whom he was anxious to benefit were obtuse and hostile, sick people who knocked the medicine out of the physician's hand. It was no wonder that he grew cantankerous, and things had gone so far that he felt happiest when he had an opportunity to be brusque and dogmatic.

It had tired him to play the role of the sympathetic elder brother to Louis for so long and he decided to take it out on Toinette. He would give her a piece of his mind and let her see how undeserving she was of the enormous trouble he had taken on her behalf.

Before informing her of the gratifying result of his interview with Louis, he proceeded to tell her bitingly what he disliked about her conduct, and that was not a little. There was her shameless habit of going masked to public balls and permitting herself to indulge in unbefitting and frequently frivolous conversation with complete strangers. The way she dressed was the talk of Europe. Her extravagance was driving the Government to despair. Her wild gambling had stirred the whole of France to anger. "I do not look forward," he concluded, "to the moment when I shall have to present my report to Mother."

Toinette was familiar with Joseph's brusque ways, but she had not expected him to let fly at her like this and she was indignant. "So now you have told me what's in your mind," she said, with an even haughtier and angrier expression than his own. "You are the great and famous Emperor who has come to scold his little sister because her frivolous conduct is putting him to shame. But perhaps you yourself are by no means so irreproachable as you imagine. I have heard quite a number of things about you. You like to make fun of our ways and customs. You crack jokes about our Army and our Navy. Do you really think that is likely to enhance the popularity of the Habsburgs in France? Do you think Mother will be pleased when she learns of the abusive language in which you allow yourself to indulge because you cannot control that censorious disposition of yours? You tell me that I give cause for mockery and criticism, but what about yourself? Who presented such a sorry example recently of vacillation and indecision, you or I?" Joseph stood staring at her completely nonplussed, and she concluded triumphantly, "Who was it that boasted to everybody of a talk he was going to have with the American, and then lost his nerve and stayed at home like a good boy?"

Even Joseph did not know whether he was more astonished than furious or more furious than astonished. He had come all the way to Versailles to extort from Louis, who liked nothing better than to sit on his backside, a promise that he would sleep with his wife and provide at long last the Dauphin whom she and Austria so urgently needed, yet all the thanks he got from her was open revolt. This was rank mutiny. Was he not her elder brother, and the Holy Roman Emperor to boot? Such behaviour was unheard of. And who was responsible for it? The circle she mixed with, those friends of hers, especially that insolent pimp Vaudreuil.

"You are a goose," he said bluntly. "You talk about things of which you haven't the faintest conception. You simply repeat what those fine friends of yours tell you. Those friends in whom you trust so implicitly. Haven't you any eyes? Can't you see what an irresponsible, cynical crew they are? Don't you realize that all they want to do is to exploit you? That you are a luscious bone for these hungry dogs? A juicy bone with plenty of meat and fat on it," he added scornfully. With malicious and meticulous accuracy he began to enumerate in detail the various lucrative sinecures she had procured not only for the Polignacs, but also for their friends and relations. Count

Jules had acquired the appointment of First Court Chamberlain, the Ministry of Posts, the customs administration, the estate of Fénestranges with a yearly revenue of 60,000 livres, and to crown it all a present of 400,000 livres for the payment of his most urgent debts. His father had been appointed Ambassador to Switzerland. His cousin, the Duc de Guiche, had been put in charge of the royal bodyguard. Another cousin had been made Court Chamberlain to Prince Charles. A third cousin was Chief Almoner in her own household. The list was endless. The Polignacs were drawing more than half a million a year from the royal treasury, without having anything to do in return except to keep Toinette company. Nor was this all. Toinette had succeeded in squeezing out of poor Louis a further 60,000 livres for her Vaudreuil, the elegant dandy who had filled her ears with that silly gossip about Doctor Franklin.

When he mentioned the name of Vaudreuil, Toinette nearly leapt from her chair. "Now you have come out with it," she cried. "Now I know why you have been abusing me in this vulgar way. You cannot forget that he made you cut a sorry figure. If you had only been able to summon up enough courage you would have gone to meet this American, and then you wouldn't have needed to come here and utter coarse slanders against men who have more sense of decency than all the fawning lickspittles with whom you like to surround yourself. François Vaudreuil has the cleverest and wittiest brain in Paris, and all the authors and philosophers you have been so anxious to meet are scrambling to enjoy his company. I am proud to have such a man as a friend. By the way, he has only made me a half promise. He is not interested in the money that Louis has offered him. You never leave off nagging me to cultivate literature and the fine arts, yet when I do so you come here and distort everything and overwhelm me with your mean accusations. Shame upon you. You are very different from the picture I had of you in my memory."

Joseph was completely taken aback by this outburst. The worst of it was that she probably believed what she was saying. "I do not deny," he conceded, "that this gentleman possesses a keen wit, but his wit only serves to mask an empty, unscrupulous nature. He is a libertine. You like to gamble, Toinette. Shall we have a bet on it that he will condescend in the long run to pocket the 60,000 livres? But you are blind. It is impossible to help you. Talking to you is like beating the air. It is not Vaudreuil alone that I am concerned about, but the whole rabble you have chosen for your friends. The salon of the Princess Rohan is nothing but a gambling den, or a brothel. Mamma and I have never considered you particularly clever, but surely you must realize at least that an Archduchess of Austria, the Queen of France, cannot behave like a Viennese washerwoman who has won the big prize in a lottery."

"The big prize," said Toinette mockingly. "The big prize," she repeated bitterly. Suddenly her pride evaporated, and her eyes filled with the tears she had been holding back so long. "Why did you send me to this country?" she asked in weeping accusation. "What am I here? What am I doing here? They all hate me. Everything I do is wrong. Why did you marry me to this man? This man of wood," she added in anger and contempt. "I so looked forward to seeing you. At last, I thought, there will be someone to whom I can speak freely. I believed you would want to help me, but now you are here and you too are trampling on me."

Joseph loved his sister in his own way. He understood what she was doing and why she behaved as she did. She had been only fifteen when she first came to Paris, where she had found both flatterers and enemies, where she was both spoilt and spied upon, and where she was tied to a husband who was her husband in nothing more than name. It was easy to realize that she was seeking an outlet for her emotions and a surrogate for that which was denied her. If she flung herself heedlessly into a whirl of silly amusements the reason was obvious.

"Toni," he said with a warmer sympathy than he was accustomed to display, and taking her hand, "I did not come here to scold you, but to help, and I think that I have been able to help you."

She looked up, and a slight flush crept into her cheeks. "You have been speaking to Louis?" she asked.

"Yes," he replied. "Everything is going to be all right. You can rely upon that. Within six weeks at the most," he added with a smile.

The flush on her beautiful face deepened, her eyes took on a darker hue, and she seemed to breathe more rapidly as she sat there with parted lips, a prey to conflicting emotions that surged up and merged within her. Louis would be coming to share her bed. He would lie beside her, skin to skin. She recalled how once, during her *lever,* she had sat half naked waiting for her chemise to be handed to her. It had so happened that every few seconds another lady of higher rank than the previous one had entered her bedchamber, and each time the chemise had to be handed ceremoniously to the newcomer by her predecessor of lower degree, while the Queen waited shivering and with a feeling of shame until at last she received her chemise. She experienced a similar premonitory feeling of shame as she pictured Louis coming to her bed, yet it was mingled with a sense of pride. One had to submit to that sort of thing when one had been singled out by destiny to be Queen of France. And her sense of shame and pride fused with a titillation of curiosity, with an impelling desire to laugh out loud like a little girl. Almost simultaneously the picture of Louis yielded in her imagination to visions of many other men, both members of the Lilac Coterie and strangers who had spoken to her at

masked balls, seized her by the arm, and put their faces very close
to hers. She thought of these men, then of Gabrielle, and again of
Louis entering her bed, and they all merged into a confused picture
which resolved itself into the pleasurable anticipation of the tremendous change that would ensue when she had duly given birth to a
Dauphin. The gossips would be silenced, scandal would no longer be
able to touch her, the fishwives would hold their insolent tongues, the
writers of lampoons would leave her in peace, in fact she would really
at last be the Queen of France. She would be the Queen, to do or
to leave undone as she pleased. She would be able to amuse herself as
she wished. Life, real life, had at last come within arm's reach. Everything that this world had to give would be hers. She would be young,
beautiful, a Queen, and a woman who was loved by many and could
herself choose whom she desired to love.

Slowly, and with a serious expression on her face that showed how
deeply his words had affected her, she walked up to Joseph, laid her
hand on his shoulder, and asked, "Why did you not tell me at once?
Why was it necessary for us to quarrel?" Throwing her arms round
his neck, she kissed him. "Sepp," she said, using the name by which
she had called him as a child, "Sepp, whenever I am at my wits' end
I can always rely on your being there to help me."

Joseph patted her neck and replied half jokingly, half in earnest,
"Well, Toni, the rest is up to you."

"You can scold me a little more if you like," she said happily, "I
shan't mind."

He almost regretted having to damp her joy by continuing to discuss affairs of State, but he had to take advantage of her softer mood
to impress upon her that she had a mission to fulfil. He had not had
the time to exact certain political concessions from Louis which were
essential for the welfare of the House of Habsburg, and this he must
leave to Toinette. She would in future be entrusted with a whole series
of similar duties, which would in fact occupy a considerable part of
her time throughout her life. After all, that was why she had been sent
to Versailles in the first place.

Holding himself as stiff as a poker, in accordance with his usual
habit when he was getting ready to deliver a lengthy lecture, he said,
reverting once more to French, "Listen, Toinette. I have something of
grave importance to discuss with you. Now that you are to become in
actual fact the Queen of France, there will be laid upon your shoulders
an even greater, an incomparable responsibility. You are the pledge
and link that bind together the Houses of Habsburg and Bourbon,
and the fate of Europe depends upon the way in which the alliance
between our two countries functions. The King is surrounded by counsellors who do not wish Austria well. It is your task, Madame, to
neutralize these noxious influences."

There was almost a note of injured pride in Toinette's voice as she replied, "There is hardly any need for you to elaborate on that. Have I not always acted in the way you indicate?"

"I admit," rejoined Joseph in a didactic, though kindly tone, "that you have followed to the best of your ability the advice transmitted to you on our behalf by Mercy and Vermond. But that is not enough. You must use your own initiative in attempting to find out what is afoot. You must make an effort to understand the projects that are being contemplated. You must read and converse with serious-minded men, even though they may not have the same elegant appearance as your friends. You must endeavour to comprehend the advice we shall offer you through the medium of Count Mercy and the Abbé. It may be that the King and his Ministers will now and then protest to you that the demands they receive from Vienna seem designed to further the interests of Austria, but not those of France. In certain cases they will be right in their assumption, but you must on no account ever agree that they are right, and you must have arguments ready to hand with which to refute the opinions of Louis and his Ministers. You must always be conscious, Toinette, of the fact that the welfare of Europe depends in the first place on the House of Habsburg, and only to a comparatively minor degree on the House of Bourbon."

"Of course," replied Toinette, assuming the expression of a well-behaved, attentive schoolgirl, but she was only half listening to what Joseph was saying, for she was still overwhelmed by the strange, half repellent, half fascinating thoughts and emotions that had taken possession of her a little while before.

"I should like to prevail upon you, Toinette," Joseph went on, "to do what you are told not in a merely mechanical way, but passionately and with inner conviction."

"But that is just what I do," declared Toinette eagerly. "I am more of a Habsburg than you are. Just look at my under lip and my nose."

"Please let us have no more of these childish remarks," snapped Joseph impatiently, and he continued with the lecture for which he had set the stage. He tried to explain to her the difficulties of the Russo-Turkish problem and the opportunities that were opened up for Austria by the impending decease of the Bavarian Elector. Toinette listened obediently, but it was clear to Joseph that her mind was far away and he attempted to strike a more appealing note. Was not playing at politics more absorbing, he asked, more exciting than sitting down to a game of faro at the Princess Rohan's? Did she not want to seize the opportunity of joining in?

"Oh, yes, of course," she agreed enthusiastically. "I always see to it that all important appointments are given to my friends."

Joseph stared at her, saw that she was being serious, and gave it up as a bad job.

Toinette, however, refused to let him go. He had spent so much time talking of his own affairs, about Bavaria and Russia and so on, and now he could stay and listen to something in which she was interested, namely, her plans for the Trianon. There was no one else to whom she could speak so freely about things that were close to her heart. She took him over to see the model, which was now completed and looked very attractive. Eagerly she explained exactly what she intended to do. Not a bush was allowed to be planted, not a nail driven in, without her previous sanction. Joseph saw that she knew precisely what she wanted, that it was all uniformly designed, that everything fitted in perfectly with her own personality, and that the whole scheme was in perfect taste. It was not without an inward sigh that he realized with what a degree of talent and enthusiasm she was able to devote herself to a matter in which she was really interested. It was a great pity that it was not Austria or France she was interested in, but only her Trianon.

Meanwhile she told him rapturously how it was here, in the Trianon, that she would be truly Queen of a realm in which she would rule without forced convention or ceremony. In the Trianon it was she alone who would set the tone. The servants would wear her livery, not the King's, with a colour scheme of red and silver. Invitations would be issued in the name of the Queen, and when she gave performances in her private theatre nobody would be allowed to attend except the people she liked.

She was very attractive as she babbled so light-heartedly about her plans. She seemed half woman and half child, and Joseph liked her when she talked in that way. He also liked the Trianon, but he could not help thinking of the new difficulties in which she was going to be involved. Those whom she excluded would try to make things unpleasant for her. She would create new enemies. And poor Louis, to say nothing of Monsieur Necker, would have to rack his brains to find the money for Toinette's expensive simplicity.

That evening Joseph wrote to his brother Leopold in Ferrara. "Our sister Toni," he reported, "is uncommonly pretty and charming, but she thinks of nothing except how to amuse herself. She has allowed herself to be infected by the extravagant tastes of this corrupt court. She does not possess an iota of affection for poor Louis, and has not the faintest idea of the duties befitting either a wife or a Queen. Her friends are a crew of hollow, greedy fellows whose minds are set on money and titles, and elegant harlots who think of little but dress. They only fortify her in her furious search for pleasure. I have done my best to implant more worthy ideas in her pretty, empty head, but I fear without success. If she should continue on this path I foresee for our sister a cruel awakening."

☆   ☆   ☆

Two days later, to Louis's great satisfaction and Toinette's mingled sorrow and relief, Joseph took his departure. His last evening was spent with them at Versailles.

They sat at dinner, Louis feeling very embarrassed, eating more than was good for him, trying to add to the cheerfulness of the atmosphere—"Say something, Berry. Make a noise, Berry."—by talking German and guffawing at his mistakes. As soon as the meal was over he withdrew. Stammering and blushing, he thanked Joseph for his advice.

Joseph said lightly, "I hope everything goes off all right."

Joseph stayed a little while longer alone with Toinette. Though they did not usually find any difficulty in knowing what to say they were both rather silent, and in this last hour together they spoke only German. Toinette's room, expensively but simply furnished, looked cosy and pleasant in the dim light of the candles, yet they were both in low spirits. Stroking her hand with unwonted gentleness he said, in contrast to the vehement optimism that he generally displayed, "Things are not easy for us, Toni. Not for you, either. But we shall manage." He put his arms round her, pressed her to him firmly and affectionately, and kissed her first on the forehead, then on the cheeks. She began to weep. With forced joviality he cried, *"Servus,* Toni!" and tore himself away. Toinette was violently unhappy at the thought that now she was once again alone.

In the hour of his departure Joseph had refrained from propounding any of his maxims, cracking any of his pungent jokes, or yielding in any other way to his didactic inclinations. On the following morning, however, Count Mercy had the honour to hand Toinette, on behalf of the Holy Roman Emperor, a booklet on the cover of which were written the words, *"Vade-mecum* for my sister, Princess of Lorraine, Archduchess of Austria, and Queen of France." It contained a number of rules and instructions, beginning with the exhortation to consult the booklet as frequently as possible.

Toinette was touched that Joseph should have gone to so much trouble on her account. She thought of the previous evening, when they had been in such close sympathy with one another, and started at once to read what Joseph had written. But it was a stout booklet. She read the first page or two, scanned the last couple of pages, went back to the beginning again and tried to study it carefully, yet she could not keep other thoughts from interposing themselves, thoughts of certain new shawls and hats about which Rose Bertin had been speaking to her. She thought of the solemn Mass that was to be celebrated on the following day and in which she would have to take part. It also occurred to her that once Louis had submitted to the operation, she would be able to assume a very different air when she met the amiable and impudent Vaudreuil.

Her eyes were still gliding over the carefully written lines of the *Vade-mecum,* but she had ceased to take in their meaning. She turned the remaining pages to see how much she still had to read. There were another thirty-two pages. Long pages at that. She yawned slightly and read one more page. Then she closed the book and locked it away in a drawer.

★ ❖ ☆ ❖ ★ ❖ ★ ❖ ★

PART TWO

THE ALLIANCE

★ ❖ ★ ❖ ★ ❖ ★ ❖ ★

We wish to preserve the fire of the past, not the ashes.

—JAURÈS

We must build up the present on the foundations of the past.

—LENIN

Fate? Fate is politics.

—NAPOLEON

Fate? The idea is mysticism, nonsense.

—STALIN

Chapter One

THE LONG WAITING

✤ ★ ✤

FRANKLIN sat idly under the great beech tree in the garden of his house at Passy. It was still early in spring and the young foliage allowed the light to percolate through. Franklin enjoyed the sunshine, which speckled the backs of his old hands and the top of his sparsely covered head.

The house and grounds merged pleasantly into the landscape. The spacious, comfortable old Hôtel Valentinois, particularly the wing in which he lived, was embedded in a green park, and the people called Franklin simply "the old man who lives in the garden," *le vieux dans le jardin.*

He sat bent forward, having taken off his steel-rimmed spectacles, and was scratching his bald scalp. His skin affection was getting better and his health generally had improved since he had allowed himself to relax in the country after the strenuous days in Paris. Perhaps he had even been overdoing the relaxation. Monsieur Jacques Finck, his newly engaged butler, had been called into conference on the question of what foods were to be served at each meal, and the menus that had resulted were undoubtedly too ample and toothsome for a man who had to look after his health, to say nothing of the pennies. So far as the latter problem was concerned, however, the eleven thousand odd francs he had received from the Congress were totally inadequate anyway.

There was a peaceful expression on his broad face as he gazed out across the lovely park, which dropped down towards the Seine in a series of terraces. As he contemplated the river and the silvery grey vista of the city on the far side, he thought of his resolution to climb up and down the steps of the terraces at least twice every day. Yesterday and the day before he had dispensed with this exercise, and he felt that he really ought not to be so lazy.

Monsieur de Chaumont passed by, bowed politely, and slowed his pace in the expectation that Franklin would speak to him. He lost no opportunity of displaying his joy at having been able to provide the Doctor with a congenial retreat, but though the latter was beholden to him for many kindnesses he did not wish to have his agreeable solitude disturbed at the moment and he returned Monsieur de Chaumont's greeting without addressing him.

It was delightfully restful at Passy. There were very few who ventured to invade his privacy, and the most obnoxious intruder of them all, Arthur Lee, was still in Spain.

Unfortunately, however, his other colleague, Silas Deane, too, refused to comprehend that the projected alliance with France could be achieved only by devious paths. The French Government could not be taken by storm, and overeagerness was more harmful than otherwise. Franklin had reconciled himself to a lengthy spell of waiting, and in a shed in the garden he had installed a printing press, primitive but efficient, where he amused himself by setting up brochures and other minor printed matter with his own hands. William was a great help to him in this hobby of his, for all the Franklins, even little Benjamin Bache, possessed an aptitude for the art of printing.

Life was good here in Passy. Even his neighbours were all agreeable people and very good company. With Doctor Le Roy, the Academician, and Doctor Cabanis he had a number of interests in common, the Abbés Morellet and de la Roche were men of education and wit, and when he took a little stroll with Monsieur Dussaul, the *maire* of Passy, there were a great many things to be learned.

He really ought to take some exercise and stick to his resolution to climb up and down the terraces. But it was so warm and pleasant under the beech tree and one could not tell whether the sun would shine so delightfully on the morrow. In order to make up for his omission he firmly resolved that on the first day when the water was not too chilly he would swim in the Seine. He was an excellent swimmer, and he smiled in pleased anticipation at the thought of how he would mention casually to Mesdames Helvétius and Brillon that he had just swum across the river and back again.

He had been a little hypocritical a moment ago when reviewing in his mind the charming neighbours in whose society he took such pleasure, for while he had included the Abbés and Doctor Cabanis he had omitted Madame Helvétius, in whose house these gentlemen lodged. Yet he would probably have felt far less at home in his garden if Madame Helvétius and Madame Brillon had not been living in close proximity. He had always been attracted to women, but it was only now, when he was entering upon his eighth decade, that he really had learned to savour them. It had taken him a long time to acquire wisdom, but now he was wise, and he knew that there could be no greatness in a man unmixed with eroticism.

No, he was not yet old. His senses were not yet blunted and he could still find pleasure in the motley variety of life, in science, women, success, nature, swimming, liberty, virtuous qualities, the differences between man and man, human strength and human weaknesses, the delights of solitude and the delights of sociability.

Young William came in sight, walking towards him along the foot-path. Franklin had given orders that he was to be fetched at this hour so that they might get down to work together. A handsome lad he looked, so slim and alert, as he came along between the trees. They went back to the house and began to go through the day's mail which, as usual, contained much of a tiresome nature.

The most important item was a communication from Count Vergennes. It was, of course, about that business of Captain Conyngham. Conyngham was of the same breed of old sea-dog as Lambert Wickes, only of even more formidable calibre. His latest venture had been no less than the capture of the Harwich mail-boat with the whole of its valuable cargo. This reckless or, as the English called it, insolent *coup* had infuriated the Government in London and King George himself had taken the matter up. Vergennes had been forced to promise that the English would be compensated and the guilty party punished. Conyngham had been arrested, but he was released soon afterwards on the protestations of Franklin and was now in command of a new ship armed with fourteen six-pounders and twenty-two smaller pieces of ordnance. The French authorities, however, refused to let him sail, though he had assured them on his solemn oath that he was merely setting out on a trading cruise, and Franklin had made a renewed protest to Versailles.

Vergennes's letter contained his reply to the American commissioners. It was couched in an exasperated tone and filled with grave reproach.

Franklin heaved a deep sigh. If he had been in Vergennes's place he would probably have written no differently. In well-turned phrases he replied that he profoundly deplored the improprieties to which the Minister had referred and offered his formal assurance that he would instruct Captain Conyngham to comply with the wishes of the French Government.

He went on with his mail. As usual there were many requests for letters of recommendation to Philadelphia. Enthusiasm in the cause of freedom may have been one of the motives which impelled these people to want to go to America, but many of them were undoubtedly adventurers and ne'er-do-wells. A large number of them gave as references men of whom he had never heard. After replying personally to two or three of these petitioners, he grew weary of the whole business and said to William, "I am going to dictate to you a model letter that we can use in future in all these cases."

He dictated as follows:

"The bearer of this, who is going to America, presses me to give him a letter of recommendation, though I know nothing of him, not even his name. Therefore I must refer you to himself for his character and merits, with which he is certainly better acquainted than I can possibly be. I recommend him, however, to those civilities which every stranger of whom one knows no harm has a right to; and I request you will do him all the good offices, and show him all the favour, that on further acquaintance you shall find him to deserve."

After composing this document Franklin decided that he had got through enough wearisome business for the day, and in any case he was expecting a visit from Silas Deane. So he sent William away and prepared to occupy himself with more agreeable matters, namely, the sifting of certain papers that he had brought with him from America. These consisted of manuscripts, drafts, notes of various kinds, letters from politicians, scientists, and friends, which he had been unable to sort out or reply to before his hurried departure from Philadelphia.

Among the letters in the varied accumulation was one in his own hand which he had refrained from sending to its addressee. He had a clear recollection of the circumstances in which he had written it, after hearing of the Battle of Bunker Hill, when he had felt that he must pour out his heart to his old friend and publisher William Strahan. The Doctor's large eyes scanned the hastily penned, yet legible, writing:

"Mr. Strahan:

"You are a member of Parliament, and one of that majority which has doomed my country to destruction. You have begun to burn our towns and murder our people. Look upon your hands! They are stained with the blood of your relations! You and I were long friends. You are now my enemy, and I am

> yours,
>> B FRANKLIN"

In the old man's eyes as he read there gleamed a reflection of the wrath that had filled him when he wrote the letter. It was an excellent letter. It expressed exactly the cold anger and contempt he felt for the man who had been unable to foresee the consequences of his actions.

He himself, however, *was* able to foresee the consequences of his actions, and he was glad that he had decided at the time not to dispatch the letter. William Strahan had been a good friend, and even now they remained in communication, in spite of the war. It was useful to have friends in London. It was a good thing that he had not allowed himself to be carried away by his wrath, and by his satisfaction at having composed a well-phrased letter. He had done well to leave the letter among the papers he had brought with him to Passy, instead of forwarding it to William Strahan.

While he was still engaged with his letters Silas Deane arrived.

The stout, cheerful gentleman had grown a little less cheerful during the last few weeks. He was worried by the strange attitude of the Congress, which continued to ignore both his own requests and those of Beaumarchais for funds, and his fleshy countenance had become somewhat lined, while his flowered satin waistcoat no longer fitted quite so tightly over his paunch; but he was as full of enterprise as ever and launched at once into a joyous account of the sensation created in Paris by the heroic deeds of Captain Conyngham. The attack on the English mail-boat, he declared, had furthered the American cause to a quite remarkable degree.

Franklin's only answer was to hand him the letter he had received that morning from Vergennes. Silas Deane, who still had difficulty with the French language, read it slowly. When he had digested its contents he refused to take the letter seriously. Warnings of that kind, he said, were mere diplomatic formalities. Vergennes was undoubtedly no less pleased at the capture of the English ship than he was himself. Insurance rates on the London market were rising from day to day and English merchants hardly dared any longer to entrust their cargoes to English bottoms. Franklin tried patiently to explain to Silas Deane that petty profits were no adequate compensation for the great political harm that was caused by the refusal to put a check on unrestrained privateering. It was not merely a question of capturing booty to the value of twenty or thirty thousand livres, but the commercial treaty and the alliance with France were at stake. Deane was almost affronted at this suggestion, and retorted that twenty or thirty thousand livres, when they accrued every week or fortnight, were not to be sneezed at, considering the precarious financial position of the Congress. "My dear Doctor," he begged, with the eloquent persuasion of a business man pointing out the urgent necessity for further capitalization, "please do bear in mind how great our needs are. You will not have forgotten the list sent to us by the Congress three weeks ago."

Franklin did not welcome this reminder. It had been a lengthy, an almost unending list. A country with an almost entirely rural population required an enormous inflow of industrial goods, and the imports which the Congress wished to draw from France consisted not only of guns, muskets and uniforms, but sheep-shears, padlocks, shoemaker's awls, sewing needles, medical supplies of every kind, opium, aloes and syringes, currycombs and groundsheets, band music and kettledrums. All these things were wanted in vast quantities, and it was the very scale of the demands which confirmed Franklin in his conviction that nothing could be done by petty means. In their desperate need they had to maintain a sense of perspective, to keep the ultimate goal in mind, that is to say, recognition by the French Government, the commercial treaty, and the eventual alliance.

This was what he endeavoured, by dint of logical argument, to make clear to his colleague, but Deane replied with sly affability, "Allow me, my dear Doctor, to confound Franklin by quoting Franklin. Did you not, in *Poor Richard,* assert that 'an egg today is better than a hen tomorrow'?"

Franklin changed the subject and spoke of other unnecessary burdens that Deane was placing on his shoulders. There were the applicants for appointments and jobs in Philadelphia who gave Silas Deane as a reference. If these people were sent to America, he suggested, they would only cause embarrassment to the Congress and bring disappointment upon themselves. Deane thoughtfully contemplated his elegant waistcoat. He did not share the view of his celebrated friend and colleague. It seemed to him that it would be a mistake, he declared modestly, but firmly, to rebuff French officers who were ready to sacrifice their position at home and in the Army because of their ardent love of liberty. Their active participation was kindling enthusiasm for America throughout Europe. "Or would you suggest," he concluded, "that Lafayette's departure for our shores has not carried us a tremendous step forward?"

This affair had created a considerable stir. The young Marquis Josèphe-Paul-Gilbert de Lafayette, after having received a commission in the American Army from Silas Deane, had told everybody of his intention to join the forces of General Washington. From the very beginning of the conflict the English had insisted on the principle that any assistance afforded to the rebels by French officers would represent a breach of neutrality on the part of the Versailles Government. They had therefore drawn the attention of Count Vergennes to the intentions of Monsieur de Lafayette and requested him to take the necessary steps. Even the Duc d'Ayen, Lafayette's influential father-in-law, despite his sympathy for the Americans, had expressed his strong disapproval of the action of the young Marquis, and in conjunction with Vergennes he had managed to obtain the issue of an order by the Cabinet forbidding his departure. These difficulties had only served to kindle Lafayette's eagerness to go, and he stubbornly announced his determination to defy the veto. For Franklin and his fellow commissioners the recruitment of Lafayette as an officer in Washington's Army thus became a matter of prestige, and the salons of Paris and Versailles were humming with excitement. Everybody was agog to see whether Lafayette would succeed in carrying out his intention. He did so succeed. With the help of Beaumarchais he fitted out a ship at his own expense and set sail secretly from a Spanish port.

The Parisians had greeted his departure for America with glee, and Silas Deane was right when he affirmed that the affair had been useful propaganda. Nor had Franklin himself been displeased. Unfortunately, however, his pleasure was not unmixed. Not only had he been constrained to appease the angry Duc d'Ayen, who suspected that the American envoys had assisted his rash son-in-law to circumvent the Government's edict, but it leaked out that Lafayette had taken with him a large number of other French officers who had likewise been issued commissions by Silas Deane. Franklin was worried at the thought of the wry faces of the American soldiers when it was proposed to place them under the command of these foreigners, many of whom were very young and arrogant. However, he did not waste his time trying to convince Deane that the Lafayette affair had its shady side, but contented himself with requesting his colleague not to issue any more commissions to Frenchmen, and Silas Deane, still a little surprised and hurt, gave his promise.

In return he had a favour to ask of Franklin. Whenever there was anything to be organized, he said, whether the procurement of supplies or the smuggling of Lafayette out of France, however great or small the occasion, they were always dependent on the good offices of the resourceful Monsieur de Beaumarchais. He had up to now been the only agent who had managed to transport an appreciable quantity of arms across the Atlantic, and without his aid Lafayette would never have got any further. Yet it appeared, suggested Silas Deane, or at least that was the impression he had received, that Franklin did not treat this useful gentleman with quite the consideration that his merits deserved. Monsieur de Beaumarchais held Franklin in high esteem and he was grieved to be afforded so little opportunity to lay before him an account of his activities.

Franklin could not help admitting inwardly that Silas Deane was right. Little as he liked the man, he would have to accommodate himself to the necessity of seeing him more frequently. "So long as I have not yet finished installing myself here," he said to Deane, "I receive only my intimate friends, that is to say, yourself and very few others. Later on, however, I shall be happy to seek another opportunity for a conversation with your resourceful Monsieur de Beaumarchais. He has ideas, of that there can be no question, and he is a man of business. He is what they call in this country a *débrouillard,* a fellow who can find his way out of any difficulty, and I by no means underestimate his services. Please tell him so as cordially as your command of the French language will permit."

He pondered for a moment. "At the beginning of July it will be a year since the Congress decided upon the Declaration of Independence, will it not?" he asked. "I think I shall invite our friends to a little celebration, and then of course we must not omit to include your ingenious juggler." It seemed to Silas Deane that July was rather a long way off, but he was glad of any crumb of comfort, thanked the Doctor most warmly, and took his leave.

☆   ☆   ☆

Later in the day, to his great delight, Franklin received a visit from Doctor Dubourg. During the past months he had grown more and more fond of this worthy, cultivated old gentleman, with his pompous and garrulous yet amiable ways. He sought his help in the polishing of the letters and minor things he wrote in French, listened to his comprehensive store of gossip, which was at times exceedingly interesting, and utilized his services in a number of ways. Nor did he forget that it was due to Doctor Dubourg that he had discovered his garden-house at Passy, and his balanced mind found a constant source of amusement in the Gallic vivacity with which his friend so rapidly worked himself up into a heated argument.

Dubourg announced with pride that Rouault, the publisher, was arranging to bring out a fourth edition of the translation of *Poor Richard* in a fortnight's time. He had recently, he said, been engaged in a long discussion with Baron Grimm of the *Encyclopédie* about his, Dubourg's, translation, a discussion he must confess which at times grew very animated. The newly created Baron had ventured to criticize the frequent repetition of the phrase "says Poor Richard," though it occurred only eighty-four times in seventeen pages. He had given the impertinent critic clearly to understand that it was not the translator's task to meddle with an author's work. Anything that emanated from the pen of so important a writer as Franklin must be approached by his translator with humility, reverence, and good faith, but these were presumably qualities which were foreign to the mind of Baron Grimm.

After a thoughtful pause Franklin said that on mature consideration he must admit that Baron Grimm's comment was not without justification. It was probable that in the more impetuous and witty medium of the French language such reiteration had a more wearisome effect than in English.

Dubourg stared at his friend in bewilderment. "You are surely not going to leave me in the lurch?" he asked indignantly. "You are not really going to admit that this upstart Baron is right, are you?"

"Perhaps," mused Franklin, "we ought to try to eliminate the phrase here and there."

A wily, beaming smile spread over the Frenchman's face. "Then I may take it that I have your consent," he said cheerfully. "You see, my dear friend, I did not want to give Baron Grimm a pretext to display his conceit in print, so I have already struck out the phrase twenty-six times in the new edition, and it now occurs only fifty-eight times. I am not one of those men of cork who always insist on floating on their own preconceived opinions. I have, in fact, subjected the new edition of my translation to a thorough revision, and I believe that it has been considerably improved in the process." Drawing the manuscript from his pocket he read out to Franklin the various emendations he had introduced. The latter could not see that there was any difference at all, but Dubourg, helping himself to pinches of snuff, worked hard to prove to him how much the translation had gained, until at last Franklin decided to humour his friend and agreed that there really was a great improvement.

Franklin then began to dilate upon the difficulties and dangers to which impassioned translators were at times exposed. He spoke of the blood and sweat that it had cost to produce the magnificent English translation of the Bible, instancing the case of William Tyndale who had composed beautiful versions in the language of the people of many parts of the Scriptures, such as the Twenty-third Psalm, but who had eventually been burned at the stake because he wanted to set up the logic of common sense in place of the not always logical views of authority. "Yes," he murmured thoughtfully, "the translator's path is often hazardous."

Dubourg looked at him uncertainly and changed the subject. In his naïvely conspiratorial way he told of the cunning manœuvres to which the privateers resorted in their efforts to capture valuable prizes under the very eyes of the English fleet and to dispose of them under the noses of the French authorities. Of course one could always rely on the latter to shut their eyes, however strictly the Versailles government might pretend to observe the obligations of a neutral.

There was, by the way, went on Dubourg, a favour that he would like to ask of his friend, Doctor Franklin. A certain Captain James Little had had the misfortune to cast anchor in a Spanish harbour which he had mistakenly assumed to be French, and the Spanish authorities had interned him. Being personally interested in the case, since he had invested a small amount of capital in Captain Little's enterprise, he wondered whether it would be possible for Doctor Franklin to intervene in Madrid.

Franklin looked at Dubourg, who was slightly embarrassed and played with his stick. At Madrid, he replied reflectively, the Americans were represented by his colleague, Arthur Lee, and it would be difficult to intervene without becoming involved in awkward complications. He believed, however, that there was in Paris a man who possessed many ties with the Spanish capital, namely, that celebrated *débrouillard*, Monsieur de Beaumarchais. Dubourg snorted uneasily.

Soon recovering his verve, however, he said that it had come to his ears yesterday at the Admiralty that a warship called *L'Orfraye* was being scrapped, a fine, big vessel fifty metres long and armed with fifty-two cannon. He proposed to organize a consortium for the purpose of acquiring this ship, having it overhauled, and putting it in service as a privateer. The undertaking would involve a considerable initial outlay, and perhaps Franklin would be willing to interest Monsieur de Chaumont, the owner of the Hôtel Valentinois, in the matter. He could, of course, have a word with de Chaumont himself, but if the suggestion came in the first place from Franklin, if, so to speak, the genius of liberty were personally to lend wings to the enterprise, the wind would be blowing from a favourable quarter. "O Ship, my Ship, now will a fresh tide bear thee out to sea," he concluded, quoting Horace.

Franklin heaved a sigh at his friend's reckless spirit of adventure. It would hardly be a fitting way to show his gratitude for Monsieur de Chaumont's kindness, he expostulated, if, in addition to despoiling him of his beautiful house, he were to try to hang a dismantled warship round his neck.

Dubourg felt slightly injured; nevertheless, he did not need much pressing when Franklin invited him to stay to supper. The butler, Monsieur Finck, had provided as usual an ample, appetizing meal and Franklin did full justice to it, but he observed with regret that his guest was not so good a trencherman as he had proved himself to be on former occasions. It struck him once more how his friend had aged, and not without a shock he came to the conclusion that his dear friend Doctor Dubourg had a Hippocratic face, that he was marked with the symptoms of early dissolution. The poor man had not long to live.

Franklin himself intended to live for a long time yet, but he was aware that the end might come unexpectedly and his mind was often occupied with the thought of death. He was not given to weak sentiment, he had seen many people die, both friends and enemies, and since the habit of authorship was in his very marrow he had felt impelled to express in words in his opinion both of those he liked and those he disliked. He had written numerous epitaphs, and he had gradually acquired the custom of composing these on friends and foes alike, on the dead and the living, and even on himself. So as he ate he searched his mind for apt words in which to clothe an epitaph praising the qualities of his friend Dubourg.

The latter broke in upon his thoughts by commenting with fussy solicitude, "It is good to see you looking so robust, my dear Doctor, but I note with some apprehension how heartily you eat. Should not men of our years be more prudent? The Pommard which your butler has set before us is excellent; none the less, and even though it is an atrocious thing to do, I would recommend you to put water into your wine."

"Odd," thought Franklin, "that this physician has no realization of his own *facies Hippocratica*." Aloud he said, as Dubourg reached out for the water-jug, placing his hand over his glass, "I am afraid, my

old friend, that you do not quote the Bible as accurately as you do
the classics. The Apostle Paul did not advise us to put water into
our wine, but wine into our water."

☆   ☆   ☆

On the following day, which was a Tuesday, Franklin drove over
to Auteuil with young William, in order to spend the evening, as he
did every Tuesday, with Madame Helvétius.

The house, as usual, was full of noise. There were cats, dogs, and
canaries, while Madame Helvétius' vivacious daughters and the two
Abbés, who like the physician Doctor Cabanis lived in the house,
contributed their share to the cheerful atmosphere. As at every meal
in the house of Madame Helvétius, there were also a few guests, for
the hostess possessed innumerable friends among statesmen, writers,
and artists.

Madame Helvétius gave the Doctor a resounding welcome, just
as she had done when he entered her house for the first time. He had
wanted to bring this influential lady, with her progressive ideas, into
closer association with his country's cause, and had gladly accepted
an offer by Baron Turgot to take him to see her. She had beamed
with pleasure when he came in, stretched out her attractively plump
arm in warm greeting, and cried, "Kiss my hand, and take your time
about it!" Very soon an intimate friendship had sprung up between
them.

She made him sit down as close to her as her capacious skirts would
allow and demanded with amiable severity whether he had not again
broken his promise and come in the carriage instead of on foot. Confessing that he had once more indulged his propensity to take things
easily, he gazed at her with a look in his eye that told how pleased
he was to be beside her.

To be sure, as he saw her filling her chair to overflowing, her rather
faded hair carelessly dyed, and her face negligently made up, he
recalled vaguely that some ladies likened her to the ruins of Palmyra,
but he himself tended to see her in the aura of her former brilliance.
Her impulsive good nature and sound common sense attracted him
deeply, as they did many other men, and he saw nothing out of the
way in her behaving, on the verge of sixty, like a spoilt beauty with
every man's heart at her feet.

While they chatted cheerfully about trifles there looked down upon
them the portrait of Claude-Adrien Helvétius, who had died six
years before. Franklin had made his acquaintance on his previous
visit to Paris and had esteemed him highly. Very rich, and a renowned
philosopher as well as a farmer-general of the taxes, he had married
the radiantly beautiful Marie-Félicité and they had lived in happy

union for more than thirty years. Portraits of him now hung in every room in the house and a reproduction of his tombstone, representing a woman weeping beside an urn, stood on the mantelpiece in the salon. Her beloved Claude-Adrien had urged Madame Helvétius on his death-bed to continue enjoying life to the utmost of her physical and spiritual powers, and in accordance with this desire his portraits and the reproduction of his tombstone formed a setting for the noisy cheerfulness which characterized the parties given by his widow and her pretty daughters.

After supper, while Doctor Cabanis and the Abbé Morellet, in company with the Abbé de la Roche, played a game of chess and William flirted with the young ladies, Franklin sat tête-à-tête with his hostess. "Have you been seeing Madame Brillon lately?" she asked him without beating about the bush. Madame Brillon, who lived near by, was young and beautiful, with an elderly husband in the Ministry of Finance.

"Of course," he replied without hesitation, and in his halting French he explained, "I have begged Madame Brillon to be with me as often as possible. She is helping me to improve my French."

"Your French is perfectly adequate, mon ami," retorted Madame Helvétius firmly, "and I am not at all pleased with the methods of instruction employed by your new French tutor. I have been informed that she sat on your knee in the presence of a number of people."

"Is there anything wrong with that?" he asked innocently. "Have your informants not told you that Madame Brillon, who was very attached to her late father, has adopted me as a parent in his place?"

"You old rascal," she said simply, and with conviction. "I admit," she went on, "that Madame Brillon is handsome, but don't you find her a little too thin?"

"Our Maker," replied Franklin, "has created beauty in various forms. I should think myself ungrateful if I were to attempt to specialize too narrowly."

"I don't like women," declared Madame Helvétius conclusively. "They are such vulgar gossips. Some of them tell everybody that I have a loose tongue and the manners of a washerwoman."

"If the washerwomen of Paris have the same manners as yourself, Madame," he said ceremoniously, in his halting French, "then they have the manners of a Queen."

This was the kind of conversation in which they always indulged. She was noisily energetic, throwing her arms round his neck and kissing him, while he would sit quietly, with an economy of gesture, but gravely attentive and courteous. There was a touch of ironic exaggeration in the compliments they bestowed upon one another, she in her flamboyant way, he with a more gentle discretion, but they were both aware of the genuine affection that lay behind their words.

Franklin was attracted by her assured worldly wisdom, her inexhaustible interest in men and things, her youthful appetite for life, her
unclouded naturalness, even her royal disdain for the accepted rules
of grammar and orthography. She for her part, who could not conceive of an existence without men and the homage they paid her,
found comfort in the evident admiration she inspired in a great man
whose qualities had been acknowledged even by her late husband and
by her friend Baron Turgot. It pleased her to think that he at least
placed her on a par with that skinny young Madame Brillon, and
when a fortnight ago he had cast formality to the winds and, instead
of calling her "Madame," addressed her in his melodious, caressing
voice as "Marie-Félicité," it stirred her blood.

Meanwhile Dubourg and Turgot had arrived.

Jacques-Robert Turgot, Baron de l'Aulne, a tall man in his late
fifties, looked older than his years. His handsome face, with its
shapely lips and straight nose, had deep furrows running down to
the corners of the mouth. He and Madame Helvétius had been friends
since youth. When she was still Mademoiselle de Ligniville he had
proposed to her, but since they were both penniless she had obeyed
the dictates of reason and refused him. When she later married the
wealthy and gifted Helvétius, Turgot stormily expressed his disapproval; nevertheless he remained on friendly terms with her and
saw her almost daily for thirty years. When her husband died they
were both of them rich and free to marry, but though he renewed his
offer she again turned him down. This second rebuff did not, however, deter him from seeing her frequently.

With his fundamental honesty of character, and passionately
devoted as he was to the cause of reason, Turgot enjoyed widespread
affection and respect. Even Doctor Dubourg entertained a sincere
liking for him and held him in high esteem, but he could never refrain
from reproaching him, in his ponderous, good-humouredly blustering
way, for the things he had either done or neglected to do while in
office. On the present occasion too he gave vent to his everlasting
grievance that Turgot had missed his opportunity to furnish the
American insurgents with a subvention of four or five million livres.
Turgot calmly explained for the tenth or eleventh time that he would
have jeopardized his plans for reform and offered his enemies an
opening for justified attacks if he had ventured to expend even a
single sou for any other purpose than his essential reforms. Dubourg
refused to be pacified and continued his taunts until Turgot was
driven to exasperation and gave him tit for tat. He had a loud voice,
Dubourg did not speak quietly either, the dogs joined in with their
barking, and the room was filled with hubbub.

Finally Turgot appealed to Franklin to bear witness that he understood the reasons for his policy and approved of them.

"To ask me to approve of them is rather too much," replied Franklin, "but I must admit that I find your attitude comprehensible."

He went on to say—and this was an opportunity he had been waiting for—that he had long desired to draw the attention of his two esteemed but disputatious friends to a story in the Bible which was not as well known as it ought to be. "My dear Abbé," he said, turning to de la Roche, "will you be so good as to relate to these gentlemen the story in Genesis which teaches the lesson of tolerance?" The Abbé pondered for a moment and then replied that he did not know which story Franklin had in mind. Nor did the Abbé Morellet have any recollection of the passage to which he had alluded. Franklin shook his head and remarked that it was odd how few people seemed to be familiar with the story, though it was one of the wisest of all those to be found embedded in the numerous barbaric and peculiar incidents recorded in the Scriptures. As he was aware of the intolerant disposition of his two dear friends, and had anticipated the renewal of their old argument, he had taken the precaution of bringing his Bible with him and begged the company's permission to read them the chapter in question.

Drawing a little Bible from his pocket he said, "It is the thirty-first chapter of Genesis," and he began to read how an old man, bowed with age and leaning on his staff, came to Abraham out of the wilderness: "Abraham sat in the door of his tent about the going down of the sun, and he arose and went towards the stranger, and said unto him: 'Turn in, I pray thee, and wash thy feet and tarry all night, and thou shalt arise early in the morning and go on thy way.' But the old man said: 'Nay, for I will abide under this tree.' And Abraham pressed him gently; so he turned, and they went into the tent, and Abraham baked unleavened bread, and they did eat. And when Abraham saw that the man blessed not God, he said unto him: 'Wherefore dost thou not worship the most high God, Creator of Heaven and Earth?' And the man answered and said: 'I do not worship the God thou speakest of, neither do I call upon His name; for I have made to myself a god, which abideth always in my house, and provideth me with all things.' And Abraham's zeal was kindled against the man, and he arose and fell upon him, and drove him forth with blows into the wilderness. And at midnight God called unto Abraham, saying: 'Abraham, where is the stranger?' And Abraham answered and said: 'Lord, he would not worship Thee, neither would he call upon Thy name; therefore have I driven him out from before my face into the wilderness.' And God said: 'Have I borne with him these ninety and eight years, and nourished him, and clothed him, notwithstanding his rebellion against Me; and couldst not thou, that art thyself a sinner, bear with him one night?'" Franklin closed the book with a snap.

"Not a bad story," commented Doctor Cabanis.

"It is strange," mused the Abbé Morellet, "but I really cannot recall the chapter." Nor could the Abbé de la Roche. Franklin handed the two clerics his Bible and they both bent over it. There stood the words *Genesis* and *Chap. 31* in ancient Gothic lettering.

"Tell me honestly," said Madame Helvétius, when she and Franklin were again alone. "Who wrote that chapter, God or you?"

"Both of us," he replied.

Franklin was glad to see that Turgot, too, enjoyed his hoax. He liked Turgot very much. Of course it would have been most useful if Turgot in his time had seen his way to allocate funds to the Americans, but Franklin respected him all the more for his refusal to compromise with his principles. It was certainly not the way to conduct practical politics, but it established clear, fixed ideals for the future and would read well in the schoolbooks.

With his instinct for authorship Franklin pondered how he could compress his opinion of Turgot in a single sentence, and while he carried on his animated flirtation with Madame Helvétius he hit upon the formula he was searching for. Jacques-Robert Turgot was not a statesman for the eighteenth-century, but the first of the nineteenth.

☆ ☆ ☆

Pierre was unusually deep in thought as he sat at his gorgeous writing-table. He could not conceal from himself the fact that there were grave difficulties ahead during the coming days. When he had asked his secretary, Maigron, that very morning for a paltry eight thousand livres from the firm's ready cash, the latter had only just managed to scrape the sum together, and when he finally brought him the money it had seemed to Pierre that his grey face was even greyer. If things were like that, how were they to carry on during the next weeks? The bill from Testard and Gaschet fell due in three days, the first quarter of a million had to be paid back to Lenormant on the seventeenth, and if he was to complete the contract for the purchase of the warship, the *Orfraye,* he would have to provide 100,000 livres in liquid funds at once.

The *Orfraye* was to be had for a song, and was he to give up all hope of acquiring her merely because he hadn't got the song at the moment? After all, he wasn't a fool. As soon as he had heard that the *Orfraye* was going to be laid up he had made up his mind to buy the vessel. He had fallen in love with the wonderful ship. A three-decker, fifty metres in length, and carrying fifty-two guns. She had such a splendid figure-head too. It warmed his heart to think of the great bird with its hooked beak flying ahead of his transports as they sailed across the ocean.

Yet he must have the money without delay. If he could not find at least 100,000 livres during the next twenty-four hours the ship would sail beyond his reach. His competitors were hot on the scent, as he knew from the information supplied by the reliable agent he had planted at the Admiralty. That fellow Dubourg was behind it all, but there was a disappointment in store for the scholarly, pompous old ass, who had nothing in his favour beyond the fact that he was a friend of Franklin's. Pierre knew exactly what he had to do if he was to capture the "sea-eagle." He knew where the palms were that were waiting to be greased.

It was ludicrous that he, the head of the firm of Hortalez, should have to rack his brains for the wherewithal to raise a petty hundred thousand livres or so. Yet who could possibly have foreseen that the American defenders of liberty would turn out to be such reluctant payers? Only that eternal pessimist Charlot had gone on with his croaking, and it really was absurd and disgraceful that for the time being his prophecies should have been proved to be right.

When the first three transports arrived at New Hampshire the Americans, beside themselves with delight, had received them with all honours, but they had brought back neither hard cash nor bills of exchange, only a few bales of tobacco covering less than eight per cent of the firm's invoice. Silas Deane, who had done his best, twisted and turned and suggested in his embarrassment that the tardiness in payment was due solely to the spiteful, slanderous reports sent to the Congress by Arthur Lee, who maintained that the consignments were to be regarded as a camouflaged gift from the French Government. "These Americans," muttered Pierre to himself as he scratched the head of his bitch Caprice. "Oh, these Americans."

He had only one American in mind as he uttered this lament, and that was not Arthur Lee. Lee's calumnies would have remained without effect if only a certain other American had taken the trouble to open his mouth. But Franklin did not take the trouble. He persisted in his incomprehensible, humiliating attitude of aloofness. He asserted that as the contracts had been concluded prior to his arrival in France, it was Silas Deane who was responsible and who must put the matter right. Yet Deane, for all his good intentions, was powerless without Franklin's support.

Pierre was accustomed to discussing his affairs frankly with his confidential assistants, but he never mentioned to anyone, not even to Paul, his unsatisfactory relations with Franklin. Now that he was anxious to acquire the *Orfraye,* however, he would probably have to talk over the whole situation with Paul and it would not be possible to avoid referring to this stupid Franklin business.

When Pierre told him of his intention to purchase the *Orfraye,* Paul's comment was, "You are playing for high stakes."

"Shall I leave the ship to the others?" demanded Pierre. "To Chaumont, Dubourg, and the rest of them?" Paul understood what he meant without his having to elaborate. There was more than a ship at stake. For the time being the firm of Hortalez was indispensable, and Pierre the only man who possessed enough supplies and transports to save the Americans from capitulation, but once his competitors, who were always hanging round Franklin, had enough arms and vessels to supply the insurgents, he would be squeezed against the wall and the firm of Hortalez would be reduced to a mere signboard.

"Maigron is astonishing," said Paul. "Nobody else could have managed matters in such a way that so far every bill has been met. But I am wondering how he is going to redeem the bills of Testard and Gaschet, and how he proposes to pay Lenormant's quarter of a million."

"We can rely on Silas Deane," replied Pierre.

"Yes," repeated Paul, "we can rely on Silas Deane." That was all, but it was enough to make Pierre realize that Paul was in the picture.

After taking leave of Franklin at Nantes, Paul had seen the American only twice, each time at a large party with many other people present. He was not normally of a shy disposition, but he had not ventured to approach him, since he was grieved and disconcerted at the Doctor's strange, almost insulting attitude towards his friend and employer. The fact that Pierre, who was generally so frank, kept his bitter feelings locked up in his breast showed how deeply Franklin's coldness had hurt him, and even in the present discussion he would not come straight to the point and admit that it was Franklin's attitude which was at the bottom of all the trouble. Paul resolved to see Franklin, without saying much about it to Pierre, and to ask the Doctor point-blank why he declined to collaborate with his friend.

Pierre was waiting for Paul to refer to Franklin's obduracy, and he was annoyed at his failure to do so. At last he said impatiently, almost angrily, "The Americans are bound to pay some day."

"Yes, but hardly before the last instalment on the *Orfraye* falls due," replied Paul.

"You seem very inclined to look on the dark side of things today," commented Pierre.

"If I were in your place," insisted Paul, "I would not count on any money coming in from America as far as payment for the *Orfraye* is concerned."

"I cannot imagine," said Pierre gloomily, "that the next five transports will return empty-handed."

"Hope is a poor counsellor," Paul replied, and he concluded bluntly,

"We can acquire the *Orfraye* only if Monsieur Lenormant either grants you a new credit or at least prolongs the old."

Pierre had realized from the start that his only chance of purchasing the warship lay in an approach to Lenormant with a request for postponement, but he had refused to admit to himself that there was no other way out. Now that Paul had put the disagreeable fact into words without any evasion, he remembered Désirée's warning.

Paul could see that the thought of asking a favour of Lenormant was a bitter pill for his friend to swallow, and he asked, "Shall I go see Lenormant?"

Pierre was tempted to accept the offer, but he said, "No, no, I will have a word with Charlot myself."

When Pierre informed Lenormant that he would like to call upon him, he was invited to dinner on the following day. Lenormant was giving a party to a small, select company, and appeared to be in a pleasant mood. When they rose from table Pierre buttonholed him. "Just a moment, my old friend," he said casually, still holding his glass of armagnac in his hand. "I believe that one of our bills is about to fall due shortly. May I assume that you will have no objection to renewing it for a month or two?"

Lenormant's veiled eyes gazed amiably at Pierre. He had long been expecting this request, and he had in fact probably granted the loan in the first place only because of his pleasurable anticipation of such a contingency. So his prediction had been fulfilled. The American enterprise had turned out to be an undertaking that a man could risk only if he was able to wait a long time for his money. He was a very gifted fellow, this Pierrot, a fellow of great charm, but he was not made for suffering, he was not made for experiences that went deep into a man's soul. Things had always gone easily for him, everything had come his way, and he took it as a matter of course that people should rival one another in showing him favours. There was Désirée, for instance. He, Charlot, had done everything he could to please her, he had suffered on her account, yet all he had reaped for his efforts was that she occasionally agreed to sleep with him. She belonged to someone else, to his friend Pierrot, whom she loved without his even taking the trouble to realize it. Now he had come to beg for postponement, postponement probably to the Greek Calends.

Lenormant had never quite made up his mind whether or not he would accede to Pierre's request when the time came. He did not even know what his reply would be when Pierre buttonholed him, but during the three seconds that elapsed while he gazed at the youthful, complacent countenance in front of him his decision became clear. His lips curved in that almost imperceptible smile which Pierre found so irritating, and in a calm, even voice he replied, "You have cracked some

excellent jokes this evening, Pierrot, but this is the funniest." With
a slight inclination of the head he went to join his other guests.

Pierre stood alone in the ornate, tastefully furnished dining-room,
where the smell of the guttering candles mingled with the fragrance
of the wine left in the glasses and the lackeys were beginning to clear
away the remains of the meal. Mechanically he took a sweetmeat from
a bowl and abstractedly nibbled at it. There had been little doubt in
his mind that Lenormant would agree to the renewal, and he had not
yet grasped the full significance of his refusal. Why had Lenormant
refused? Malicious pleasure in other people's misfortunes was completely alien to Pierre's nature.

The lackeys who were clearing away looked at him in surprise as
he stood there in deep thought, nibbling at a sweetmeat, but they did
not laugh. He was popular with the common people, who did not think
the worse of him for the luxury in which he lived, but were grateful
to him for taking their part against the privileged classes, and the
lackeys, waiters, and barbers in particular saw in the creator of
Figaro their poet and patron saint.

He pulled himself together and drove home. Sitting upright in his
carriage he presented an elegant figure as he returned the greetings
of passers-by, but his thoughts were elsewhere. Charlot wanted to
keep a stranglehold on him, to demonstrate to Désirée and to the world
that Pierre Beaumarchais was a braggart and a failure. Well, he
would show him that he was mistaken. He was more determined than
ever both to buy the *Orfraye* and to fling Charlot's paltry quarter of
a million at his feet.

He would show them all, damned aristocrats that they were, with
their supercilious stares. Vergennes too, for he was no different from
the rest of his class. Since Franklin had turned up in Paris the Minister treated him like dirt. The Count was apparently under the impression that he could cast him off like a worn-out glove, but he was
not worn out yet by any means. Did these gentlemen really believe
that a numbskull like Chaumont or an old donkey like Dubourg could
look after their interests? Monsieur de Vergennes imagined he could
trample on him because he was not an aristocrat and did not enjoy the
friendship of the great Franklin. Monsieur de Vergennes would find
that he had made a miscalculation.

With grim resolve Pierre drove to the Foreign Office. Not to the
building on the Quai des Théatins in Paris, but to Vergennes's quarters at Versailles, in great pomp, with his liveried footmen and his
Moorish page. He asked to see the Minister, but was received only by
Monsieur de Gérard, who informed him with the utmost courtesy that
the Minister was extremely busy and inquired whether he himself
could perhaps deal with the matter that had brought Pierre to Versailles. Pierre declared emphatically that he could not. It was a matter

not only of life and death as far as his own affairs were concerned, but involving also the most grave repercussions for the Crown. After some further demur he was admitted into the presence of the Minister.

If Pierre had believed that Vergennes was troubled with a bad conscience on his account, he was grievously mistaken. The Minister was an amiable sceptic. He was prepared to concede that Monsieur Caron was organizing the shipment of supplies to the rebels partly because of his ardent interest in the good cause, but he was pretty certain that his chief concern was the lining of his own pockets. The Government welcomed Monsieur Caron's activity and had provided him with considerable funds, but it was implicit in the original arrangement that he should himself assume a certain risk. That was only fair since he enjoyed the prospect of enormous profits. If the Americans were in arrears with their payments, it was up to Monsieur Caron to extract himself from his dilemma as best he could. Vergennes liked Pierre personally for his wit and brilliance, but was not unconscious of his less agreeable qualities. His conceit and inability to keep a guard on his tongue had embarrassed the Government sufficiently, and it was a stroke of good fortune that Doctor Franklin had arrived to take charge of American interests. So when Pierre entered, Vergennes gazed at him shrewdly and politely waited for him to broach the reason for his visit.

Pierre detected in the Minister's attitude the slight feeling of unease that he himself always felt when he was putting off a tiresome petitioner, and he grew even more grimly determined to pull Vergennes down from his heights of Olympian calm, and, by hook or by crook, to get his money out of him.

He began to talk of the financial difficulties in which he had become involved owing to the incomprehensible tardiness of the Congress in answering his letters and settling his accounts. He drew a dramatic picture of the way in which, at the cost of immense personal efforts and risks, of which the Minister was doubtless not unaware, he had succeeded in shipping vast quantities of war equipment across the ocean and delivering it into the hands of the insurgents. Apart from a bald confirmation that the goods had been received, not a single word had come from the Congress. In the deliveries which he had undertaken at the request of the French Government he had invested his all—fortune, honour, and talents. Now he was faced with the prospect of losing the fruits of his almost superhuman exertions. He was at the end of his resources.

Vergennes played with his quill and gazed at Pierre with an air of languid regret. "Why do you not apply directly to the Americans?" he asked at last. "They now have their representatives in Paris."

This too was a method of fobbing off a supplicant that Pierre himself had occasionally employed, but he had never done so when he was under such a deep obligation to a man as Vergennes was to him. Was not advice of that kind tantamount to sheer mockery? Franklin had referred him to Silas Deane. Deane had said, "Go and see Franklin." And now Vergennes had recommended him to apply to the Americans.

The Minister was still playing with his quill, and this harmless fiddling angered Pierre even more than his words. All the time he had been hesitating whether or not he should bring his most powerful weapon to bear. It was not a pleasant weapon to use, but these aristocrats were leaving him no alternative. Well, even if it was not pleasant, what did it matter? After all, *he* was no aristocrat.

It was not only his own money, he explained, that he had invested in the firm of Hortalez and Company in order to further the interests of France; in order to acquire vast supplies he had been compelled to undertake vast obligations, and some of these had now fallen due. He had come to his wits' end, he was faced with ruin, he did not know how to ward off impending bankruptcy and scandal, and he would find it difficult to justify his actions without being driven to indiscreet revelations that must inevitably create a sensation.

Vergennes looked up with a start, and for a moment his round eyes flickered with an angry light, but they at once resumed their former calm expression and as he continued to play with his quill he said, "We shall see to it that you are not driven to extremes, Monsieur." There was a note in his voice, however, that Pierre had never heard before. Without deviating one iota from his normal courtesy Vergennes had yet infused into his tone a disdain that verged on disgust, a sublimated haughtiness that drew a sharply defined line between the speaker and the man he was addressing, a repugnance that seemed to say *noli me tangere*. "We shall see to it that you are not driven to extremes, Monsieur," he repeated. "How much do you want?"

Pierre felt as if Vergennes had struck him in the face with his carefully manicured hand. He swallowed hard. It had been his intention to demand 350,000 livres, 250,000 for Lenormant and the remainder for the *Orfraye,* and he had been prepared for an attempt by the Minister to reduce this figure. "Five hundred thousand livres," he said, in the certainty that Vergennes would haggle.

Nothing of the sort happened. Vergennes merely replied in the same aloof tone, "Very well." He did not even say, "Very well, Monsieur." He simply said with polite disdain, "Very well." And after a short pause he inquired, "Is there anything further?"

No, there was nothing further. "I thank you, Count Vergennes," said Pierre. He tried to make his voice sound calm and matter-of-fact, but in spite of himself it expressed humility and relief. The immediate reaction in his mind was to think of an exceedingly opprobrious term that he would have liked to apply to Vergennes. How he hated and envied the man for that note of aloof contempt.

He took his leave and drove back to Paris with his liveried footman, his Moorish page, the promise of half a million livres, and a heart filled to bursting with a raging fury.

☆   ☆   ☆

The French word *bagatelle* had, and still has, a variety of meanings. It signifies a trifle, a bauble, something of minor importance, and the buffoonery which conjurers employ as an introduction and framework to their performances is known as *les bagatelles de la porte. Ce sont les bagatelles de la porte* signifies "Oh, but that's nothing. There is something far better in store." A further meaning of *bagatelle* is "hobby," and in particular it denotes a flirtation. *Ne songer qu'à la bagatelle* signifies "to think of nothing but making love."

There were two French terms that Doctor Franklin was very fond of using. One was *Ça ira,* the other was *Vive la bagatelle!*

During the early summer of 1777, when he had nothing to do but sit at Passy and wait, he passed his time with *bagatelles.* They were by no means useless, for while some of them concerned his relations with his friends, others were helpful in promoting the great cause. Since the victories of Trenton and Princetown little news had been received of the military situation, and he had good grounds for assuming that things were not going well. The English had dispatched considerable fresh reinforcements to America, shiploads of German troops, the so-called "Hessians" who had been sold by their princes as mercenaries, and this circumstance inspired Franklin to compose one of his bagatelles.

Early one morning he sat naked at his writing-table surrounded by books and writing a letter, a letter in French from an imaginary German princeling to an imaginary addressee. Lifting his pen for a moment, he read what he had written so far: *From Count de Schaumbergh to the Baron Hohendorf, commanding the Hessians in America. Rome, the 18th of February, 1777.* Yes, that was not bad. Count Schaumbergh was a good name for one of those German princelings. The date and place, too, were plausible. The news of the English defeat at Trenton could hardly have reached the Count before mid-February; and a prince who sold his subjects as if they were cattle was more likely to expend the proceeds in the agreeable environment of the Italian capital than under the wintry skies of his native Germany.

Franklin went on reading: "My dear Baron: On my return here from Naples I found awaiting me your letter of the 27th of December last. It was with great satisfaction that I learned of the bravery displayed by our troops at Trenton and you cannot conceive of the joy I felt on hearing moreover that of the 1950 Hessians who took part in the battle only 345 escaped with their lives. The number of killed therefore amounted to exactly 1605, and I cannot sufficiently urge upon you the importance of forwarding to my envoy in London a complete list of casualties. This precaution is all the more necessary in view of the fact that the official report to the English War Office gives the number of killed as only 1455. This would make 483,450 guilders instead of 643,500, which is the amount of my claim in accordance with our agreement. You will understand, my dear Baron, the extent to which such an error would reduce my revenues, and I do not doubt that you will make every effort to convince the English Prime Minister that his list is wrong and that mine is correct."

A deep smile of mingled satisfaction and anger extended the corners of Franklin's wide mouth. Then he continued to write: "The Government in London protests that about a hundred men were merely wounded and therefore can neither be included in the list nor taken into account when payment is made. I am relying, however, upon your having followed the instructions which I communicated to you before your departure from Kassel, and upon your not having allowed yourself to be misled by false and sentimental notions of humanity into preserving the lives of those unhappy creatures whose days could be lengthened only at the cost of an amputated leg or arm. Such a course would condemn them to an existence of idle vegetation, and I am sure that these people would rather die than continue to live in a condition that renders them unfit to do me further service. This does not mean, my dear Baron, that you are to make away with them. We must be humane. But you can indicate to the surgeons, with due emphasis, that a crippled soldier is a disgrace to the whole profession, and that when a warrior is no longer capable of bearing arms the best course is to let him die.

"I am sending you fresh recruits. Do not be too economical in your treatment of them. Remember that in this world glory is the supreme thing. Glory is the only true riches, and nothing degrades the soldier so much as avarice. The warrior must think of nothing but honour and glory, and glory can only be achieved in the midst of dangers. A battle won without great expenditure of blood is a battle won without glory, while even the defeated cover themselves with glory if they perish with their weapons in their hands. Remember the three hundred Spartans who defended the pass at Thermopylae. Not one of them came back alive. I should be proud if I could say the same of my brave Hessians."

Franklin went on composing his fictitious letter in this tone. He wrote rapidly in French, one barbed sentence following another in logical sequence, and when he could not think of the right French word he put it down in English. He approved of what he had written and smiled with malicious pleasure. Conscientious as he was, he made a fresh draft in more careful French, then, putting his manuscript away, he went off to his bath. He lay in the tub for a long time, rang twice for more hot water, scratched himself, and was happy.

During the afternoon the Abbé Morellet came over to see him. Exacting a vow of secrecy, Franklin showed him his letter about the Hessians and asked him to be so good as to help with the polishing of the French style. They sat down to work and it was delightful to see with what zest the Abbé entered into the hoax. Franklin was well content with the final version, and without calling upon young William for assistance he set it up in type with his own hand and printed off a few copies on the little press he had installed in a shed in the garden.

On reading it again in print it seemed to him that perhaps the squib was a little too virulent after all. It had been his intention to write it in such a way that the ordinary reader would not be certain whether it was genuine or not, and he feared that it was too pointed to achieve that aim.

When Doctor Dubourg called in the evening he decided to discuss it with him. Handing him one of the printed copies and taking another himself, he sniffed with pleasure the odour of the paper and the fresh printer's ink, and as he scanned once more his little opus he observed the expression on his visitor's face.

Dubourg read slowly and carefully, puffing out his lips as he silently formed the words, and it was clear that he was making a great effort to understand what it was all about. "Well," asked Franklin, when Dubourg had finished, "what is your opinion?"

The old Frenchman ponderously shook his large head. "I was aware," he said, "as was everybody, that these German princes are scoundrels, but I never thought that they could be quite so villainous as this."

Franklin rejoiced to hear this evidence of his literary skill, but he was sorry for his friend Dubourg. In his younger days he would not have been taken in so easily by a hoax. He was growing old, poor Dubourg, very old.

Dubourg, for his part, had also brought a present for his friend, a small, handsomely printed edition of La Fontaine's fables that had just been published. He had often heard Franklin praise the writings of La Fontaine, and the American was genuinely delighted with the gift, expressing admiration for the fine type and the author's charming worldly wisdom. Dubourg thought that Franklin, who had much in common with La Fontaine, would unfortunately not be able to appreciate all the finer points, since some of the more delicate shades of meaning must necessarily escape a foreigner even when he possessed the highly developed linguistic faculty of Franklin. "What suppleness," he enthused. "What elegance." And he began to read the verses aloud.

Having read one fable, with evident enjoyment of its easy grace and wit, he proceeded to read another, and eventually came to that which related the story of the coach and the horse-fly. Breathing heavily through his nose and accompanying the rhythm of the lines with an enthusiastic flourish of his fleshy hand, the corpulent Dubourg puffed out his lips as he recited the descriptive rococo verses.

The fable tells how six heavy horses are trying to draw a travelling-coach up a steep hill on a hot day. The occupants have alighted and everyone who can is helping to push. A fly hums and buzzes round the horses' heads, stinging first one and then another, and settles on one of the shafts or on the coachman's nose. Complaining that nobody else is doing anything to help the horses, but leaves it all the work to do, it whirrs hither and thither, assumes an air of importance, is in half a dozen places at the same time, and when the coach eventually reaches the top of the slope cries out triumphantly, "Now we can rest, my dear horses. I have managed to get you out of your difficulty."

A broadening smile had gradually been spreading over Franklin's expansive countenance. Letting the hand in which he held the book sink to his side, Dubourg declaimed the moral from memory.

> *Ainsi certaines gens, faisant les empressés,*
> *S'introduisent dans les affaires.*
> *Ils font partout les nécessaires,*
> *Et, partout importuns, devroient être chassés.*

Unobservant though he was, and absorbed in his reading, Dubourg could not help noticing that the far-away look in Franklin's eyes was not wholly due to the effect of the fable and his own impassioned recital, but that there was something else which must be occupying his friend's mind and providing him with amusement. Slowly a light broke in on him and he cried, "Why didn't I think of it before! La Fontaine's horse-fly is a portrait of our conceited Monsieur Caron!" And the two old gentlemen held their sides with laughter.

☆   ☆   ☆

On the following day an unexpected visitor arrived in the person of Paul Theveneau. Franklin did not normally receive callers without a previous appointment, but he directed that Paul be shown in at once. He liked the young man, who had seemed so anxious to be helpful at Nantes, and welcomed the opportunity to offset his neglect of Pierre by friendliness towards an employee of the firm of Hortalez. Paul, he thought, looked even thinner than when he had last seen him. His clothes hung more loosely on his frame and his shining eyes appeared larger than ever in his flushed face.

The Doctor was once more pleasantly surprised at Paul's sound judgment. This Monsieur Theveneau saw more clearly than had Arthur Lee and Silas Deane that final victory was possible only with the full support of the Versailles Government and the French Army. Though his main occupation was with the organization of supplies he realized that the co-operation of individual firms was not enough. The great political goal could be reached only by an alliance with France. The Doctor was deeply touched at this meeting with the courageous youth who had even less prospect than he himself, an old man of seventy, of living to see the fulfilment of their inmost aspirations.

For all his candour, Franklin kept his secret thoughts and feelings locked up in his heart. Though he did not doubt the end of the struggle, he feared that it would take many years at a sore cost in human life before victory was achieved. To the outer world he presented a bold front. Other men saw only the self-reliant old sage whose confidence in his cause was unshaken. They had no knowledge of the bitter anxieties behind his mask of calm serenity. But to this young fighter in the war of freedom, whose days were numbered, he opened his heart and spoke like an elder brother of the things which gave them mutual concern. He spoke of the military superiority of the English troops, of the political discord in the United States, of the numerous Americans who, whether from avarice or from stupidity, had thrown in their lot with the enemy, and of the precarious state of the Congress finances. He spoke of the long and arduous road that had to be traversed; spoke with loathing of war, and with quiet eloquence of his efforts to avoid it, spoke bitterly of the blind obduracy with which the men in London permitted this barbaric bloodshed to continue.

Paul greedily drank in Franklin's words. Profoundly moved as he was by the great man's complete sacrifice of reserve, he asked himself how it was possible after such a revelation to broach the subject of the Hortalez firm and its pecuniary difficulties. Were not these but the merest trifles compared with the load of responsibility that rested upon the shoulders of this venerable philosopher? Would it not be an intolerable impertinence to burden him in addition with his own personal worries? Yet, loyal friend as he was, he would not abandon his intention of pressing Pierre's claims. He tried to speak of the grievances that were the cause of his present visit, but his lips refused to utter the words. Torn this way and that by the thoughts that seethed within his mind, he listened with only half an ear as Franklin went on talking. At last he pulled himself together, banished all consideration of his personal troubles, and gave his undivided attention to Franklin. "How different things look," he heard the latter say, "from this side of the ocean."

These words thrust deeply into Paul's consciousness, and suddenly an idea seized hold of his mind and took complete possession of him. He would go to America.

That was the thing to do. The difficulties in which the firm of Hortalez had become involved could be solved in no other way. Franklin had given him the guidance he wanted. He must go to America, where he would be able to refute on the spot, in Philadelphia, the ridiculous charges brought by this Mr. Arthur Lee. The Americans on the other side of the ocean could not be expected to see the problem from the same angle as their supporters in Europe. Somebody who was thoroughly familiar with the course of events and devoted to Pierre must undertake the voyage to Philadelphia and put the insurgent leaders in the picture. That would be his self-imposed task, and how better could he spend the short time left to him? With quick resolve he told Franklin that he himself was going to America, on behalf of the firm of Hortalez. He intended, so he declared, to travel by the next boat dispatched by his firm.

Franklin gazed thoughtfully at the frail figure of the young man. Would he be equal to the hardships of the voyage? Would he be able to carry out the task he had set himself in a country which, as Franklin well knew, was at bottom hostile to the French? Cautiously he tried to dissuade him.

Paul realized that the old man was moved by apprehension lest his health should not be able to withstand the rigours to which it would be exposed, but he was now obsessed by this idea. He did not wish to die before having seen that for which his whole life long he had yearned so desperately. With modest determination he replied that his mind was made up and he intended to go. Franklin changed the subject. A sudden notion occurred to him. Handing a copy of the *Letter from Count Schaumbergh* to Paul, he said, "Please read this, Monsieur." Paul began to read, while Franklin watched his expression as, on the day before, he had watched that of Doctor Dubourg.

Paul had hardly read more than two or three sentences before a smile of mingled wrath and malicious triumph began to play about his lips. "That is the way I must have looked while I was writing it," thought Franklin.

"But it is magnificent!" cried Paul when he had come to the end. "You have hit off these people most uncommonly well, Doctor."

"What makes you think that I wrote it?" chuckled Franklin.

"There is no one else who can write like this," declared Paul warmly. "This was written by a man who loves his country as you love it and who hates and despises these people as you hate and despise them."

"I am glad you like my bagatelle," said Franklin. "I got a great deal of fun out of it."

"Bagatelle!" exclaimed Paul indignantly. "Fun! This letter will put as many Hessians out of action as did the battle of Trenton. It will prevent further reinforcements of Hessians being sent to America."

"I am afraid," commented Franklin, "that you overestimate the influence of literature."

☆ ☆ ☆

The money promised by that haughty dog of a Vergennes was paid over with insulting promptitude to the house of Hortalez. Pierre, though not in the seventh heaven as when he received his first subsidy from the French Government, nevertheless experienced a feeling of satisfaction that he, the *débrouillard,* had again succeeded in achieving what he had set out to do.

Though there were still two days to go before his debt to Lenormant fell due, he sent him his paltry quarter of a million.

Then he called upon certain officials in influential quarters, greased a number of itching palms, and acquired the certitude that the proud figure-head of the sea-eagle would lead his transports across the ocean and not those of a Chaumont or a Dubourg. Now in these years of his middle age Pierre was more imbued than ever with the zest of life, prepared to take what came his way and to revel in his strength and good luck. The varied and contrary emotions he stirred in people, whether admiration and affection or envy and hatred, the tumultuous excitement of his business affairs, the momentous nature of the cause for which he was working, the vast profits that beckoned despite his present embarrassments, all this turmoil kept him in a constant state of slight intoxication.

At the age of forty-five he was no longer the Figaro of his comedy. Though he still loved intrigue and gain for their own sake, he had acquired a more firmly based assurance of his own worth. He was no longer the mere buffoon. When he was kicked and made to dance, he could still laugh at himself and at fate; but now he laughed more bitterly and lustily at the stupid and criminal arrogance of those who kicked him.

Lenormant and Vergennes, believing that he had been cheated in the American business, had not only refused to help him, but had even laughed at him. Very well, gentlemen, he thought grimly. Perhaps I shall be the shorn lamb—the sucker in the American business; but if my attitude is ridiculous, then yours is ten times more so.

He had long carried in his mind the idea of writing a sequel to *The Barber of Seville,* and it now began to take shape. Striding up and down his spacious study, followed by the moist eyes of his bitch Caprice, he declaimed the lines as they formed in his mind, whistled, hummed, stood before the blank space of the wall where the portrait should have hung. He saw Figaro. Figaro had grown older, he had matured by experience, his spirit plunged into the depths, his wit was spiced with a more bitter savour. This new Figaro must be fixed in firm outline before the inspiration had time to disperse. Pierre sat down and wrote.

He wrote the speech in which Figaro addresses the great gentlemen for whom he has acted as pander and go-between in a hundred dubious affairs, and to whom he feels infinitely superior. It was his own story which he recounted, with its giddy ups and downs, its artfulness and glitter, its unbounded happiness and its unbounded distress, its wild whirl, its tragi-comic conflicts with the censorship and the courts of justice, and it flowed from his pen in elegant, barbed phrases that seemed to flash and dance in light-hearted mood.

"I am told," he wrote, "that there is now freedom of the press in Madrid, that I can say whatever I wish provided that it is submitted to two or three different censors and has no reference to the Government, religion, politics, morality, high officials or great lords," he wrote. "Friends procured me a Government appointment, for a man with ideas was wanted. I had ideas, alas! After a week I was replaced by a ballet-master," he wrote. "Because you are a great lord, Count, you imagine that you are also a genius. Nobility, titles, wealth, and appointments—these things make you proud. Tell me, Count, what have you done in return for the favours that have been showered upon you? You took the trouble to be born. I, however, sprung from the nameless crowd, have had to employ more knowledge and cunning merely in order to live than have been needed these hundred years to govern Spain and all her colonies."

He dashed off the whole lengthy speech without lifting his pen from the paper, and as he wrote there looked down upon him the busts of Aristophanes, Molière and Voltaire, the bust of himself, and his own portrait in Spanish costume. Before him was the empty space destined for the painting of Monsieur Duverny. His bitch Caprice gazed at him with devoted eyes, and the mirror reflected the man writing, thinking, laughing, working.

He read over what he had written. Yes, there was a bite to it. Abstractedly he stroked Caprice's head. Smiled happily to the man in the mirror, and the man in the mirror smiled happily back. He had hit the mark. He felt that he must show someone what he had accomplished.

He hastened to his father's room. The old man lay in bed, startlingly emaciated, but with eyes bright beneath his peaked night-cap, and as he greeted Pierre his teeth showed white and strong.

"I have written something, Father," said Pierre, "that will amuse you. I am composing a sequel to *The Barber,* and it is going to be even better. Just listen, and you will admit: it's great."

He began to read, while the old man listened eagerly. The mocking impertinence of the speech, with its fund of essential truth, stirred him more and more deeply as Pierre went on. He thought of his own past life, of the time when he was proud to be a bourgeois and a Huguenot; he sat upright in his bed and involuntarily pushed back his night-cap with his thin hand in order to hear the better. "I, however, sprung from the nameless crowd, have had to employ more knowledge and cunning merely in order to live than have been needed these hundred years to govern Spain and all her colonies." The old man drank in the words, savoured them; he listened raptly as he heard his own emotions vocal in his son's ringing and witty phrases. A raging, angry, uncouth hilarity seized him. A wild, uncontrollable fit of scornful mirth rose from his bowels to his heart, distended his aged, emaciated frame, forced its way through his throat and issued from his mouth in a hollow laugh, a rattling sound that shook him from head to foot and seemed as if it would never stop. Pierre gazed radiantly at the old man and joined in his laughter. The whole room rang with the noise of their merriment; it would not end.

Abruptly, however, it did come to an end. First, the old man's laughter became half a gurgle and half a groan. Then it ceased altogether and he lay back on the pillow without moving.

The sheets of paper from which he had been reading Figaro's speech dropped from Pierre's hand and he stared at his father. One of his thin, hairy legs stuck out stiffly from beneath the counterpane, his night-cap had slipped further back and revealed his bald skull.

Pierre stood and stared. Then, hesitantly, he stepped closer and bent down. The old man had ceased to move or breathe.

A dazed expression came over Pierre's face. He did not want to believe it, but he had to. His father had died from laughing Figaro's laughter.

☆   ☆   ☆

That same week Thérèse gave birth to Pierre's child. It was not Alexandre, but Eugénie.

Thérèse came through her ordeal well, and on the second day Pierre urged that the time had come for them to marry and live together.

She studied him with her clear grey eyes as he ardently tried to persuade her. During the past months he had looked after her with a tenderness that one would not have expected from a man with so tempestuous a nature, and now he was gazing with pride and tenderness at the tiny creature she had brought into the world. She knew that Pierre loved her, that he clung to her, that he was in deep earnest when he vowed that he wanted to live with her and the infant Eugénie. Yet she recalled how he had put off their marriage, and though she had not felt hurt, or rather had only felt a little hurt, she did not want to give him the opportunity of possibly reproaching himself later on for having acted too hastily. She preferred to wait until his rehabilitation, she told him, as he had himself once suggested. In any case she would feel even happier and less lonely out here in Meudon now that she had the company of her little Eugénie. He was somewhat disconcerted at her reply and continued his efforts at persuasion for a while, but desisted when it became quite clear to him that she had made up her mind.

Pierre was anything but superstitious, yet the strange way in which his father had died, so near the time when his child had been born, had bewildered him. He had shrunk from giving any indication to his friends of the peculiar circumstances of the old man's death, nor had he shown anyone the speech of Figaro which he would normally have displayed so proudly. The loss of his father had filled him with genuine grief, the birth of his child had brought him genuine happiness. He was almost glad that his preoccupation with the funeral and with looking after Thérèse gave him no time for mystical brooding.

The affairs of the firm were allowed to drift. He was not in the mood, he told Paul, to bend his mind to petty details and he would discuss only the most general matters.

This suited Paul very well. He had concealed from Pierre both his visit to Franklin and his intention of going to America, for he had not yet fully digested what had happened at Passy. It was strange that a man of Franklin's far-seeing wisdom and experience could not bring himself to forgive Pierre's weaknesses, but he had to accept the fact that the American by his very nature could not help feeling an antipathy to his friend. He had to reconcile himself to the situation.

Meanwhile a further convoy was being fitted out, and awaited only the latest news from Philadelphia before sailing. If Paul intended to travel with it, as he had announced so proudly to the Doctor, it was high time that he made his preparations. It was essential, above all, that he should have a word with Pierre.

He first paid a visit to Doctor Lafargue, his physician, who, on his return from the northern ports, had reproved him for his imprudence. Now the doctor wanted to send him to one of the high valleys in the Alps for the whole summer. When Paul informed him that urgent business demanded his presence overseas, Lafargue refused to hear of it. Although he tried tactfully to spare Paul's feelings, he made it quite clear that if he went to America, he would never return.

Paul sauntered through the bustling streets of Paris. He looked hungrily with his overbright eyes at the gay summer dresses of the women, heard the raucous cries of the hucksters, the curses of the draymen, saw the overflowing markets with their colourful piles of foods—he saw and heard and felt the light and sound and fullness of

the brightest and greatest city in the world, his father-city, Paris.
There were moments when he was at a loss to understand how he
could ever have said that he was going to America, that he should leave
this, his Paris, he who was so young, who had had so little from life
when he had wanted so much, he whose mind and whose every sense
could enjoy it as few were able to do—how could it ever have entered
his thoughts?

He went to see Thérèse, admired the baby. They spoke of Pierre.
His eyes had been sharpened in recent weeks and he recognized that
she, too, was less uncritical of Pierre than she had been, though her
realization of his faults did not detract in the slightest degree from
her devotion to him. It grieved Paul to think that though she understood Pierre so well, she had no inkling whatsoever of his own feelings, of what he wanted to do for Pierre, or rather what he had to
do for him.

In the meantime an astounding communication had arrived from
Philadelphia via Holland. A terse letter from the banking-house of
Grand in Amsterdam announced that they had received instructions
from the Congress to pay to the firm of Hortalez 4,036 livres and 7
sous for handkerchiefs, buttons, and thread which the said firm had
supplied to the Congress. This was sheer mockery. The firm had supplied guns, mortars, and munitions, tents and uniforms, for which its
claims were over 2,000,000 livres, and now a draft had been received
for 4,000.

The outrageous communication led to an immediate conference between Pierre and Paul. Pierre refrained from his usual eloquent complaints and execrations, and posed at once the blunt question, "What
are we going to do?"

The letter from Holland and Pierre's query constituted for Paul
the final spur. If he did not seize the present opportunity to broach
the topic of his projected visit to America for the purpose of adjust-
ing their difficulties, he never would do so. In that case he would never
undertake the voyage and Franklin would regard him as a braggart.

"There is only one way to get your money out of the Americans,"
he began. "Someone must go to Philadelphia to have a heart-to-heart
talk with these gentlemen and refute the lies that have been told them
by Arthur Lee. There will have to be someone who can receive our
cargoes in person and keep them under lock and key until the Congress has allocated either cash or goods in payment."

"And who should this someone be?" inquired Pierre.

"Myself," replied Paul.

Pierre had realized from Paul's opening words what he was driving
at. He had himself been playing with the idea of crossing the Atlantic,
for the thought of pleading his case before the Congress attracted him,
but, ardently as he sympathized with the aspirations of these men of

the Western World and shared their views, his experience with Franklin had been uncomfortable enough to make him feel that there was something disconcerting about the men themselves. He was afraid that if he were to go to America he might do his case more harm than good.

The next best thing would obviously be to send a capable representative instead. Paul, however, was the only possibility, and the thought of letting his sick friend cross the seas to his certain death was one that he had rejected as soon as it had occurred to him. Now Paul had come of his own accord with the same proposal, and Pierre was moved at his readiness to make such a sacrifice, but he unhesitatingly declined to discuss it. But Paul stuck to his guns, declared that he had already informed others of his intention, and announced that he was going on the *Amétie,* one of the ships in the next convoy.

"You have already informed others of your intention?" exclaimed Pierre in amazement.

"Yes," responded Paul. "I wanted to commit myself; I wanted to commit both of us."

"With whom have you been speaking?" demanded Pierre, thinking that it must have been with Maigron or Gudin.

"With Doctor Franklin," was the reply.

Pierre could hardly believe his ears. The American envoy had received this young fellow and even encouraged him to discuss his intimate affairs.

"You must understand, Pierre," said Paul, breaking in on his thoughts, "that there is no other course left to me. I must go to America. Otherwise I should look ridiculous in the eyes of Franklin."

This simple explanation only served to increase Pierre's feeling of bitterness. He himself evidently appeared ridiculous in Franklin's eyes for some reason that he could not discover, yet Paul was prepared to go to his certain death rather than incur the same misfortune. "I shall never permit you to leave," he cried vehemently. "Never!"

"I am leaving nevertheless," declared Paul with equal vehemence. "How are you going to pay for the *Orfraye?* How will you keep the firm on its feet unless someone makes the crossing and collects your money?"

"You can let me worry about that," snapped Pierre brusquely. Even if the house of Hortalez were to come crashing in ruins about his head he would never permit Paul to go to his death.

When the convoy sailed, and with it the *Amétie,* Paul was not on board.

☆　　☆　　☆

From Aix-en-Provence news reached Pierre that a date had been fixed for the hearing of the appeal for which he had been fighting with such grim tenacity throughout the long years. Vergennes had kept his word and Pierre was beside himself with delight.

His presence would be necessary in Aix for the duration of the trial. On the other hand, the complicated affairs of the Hortalez firm required day-to-day decisions in Paris, while the refitting of the newly purchased *Orfraye* demanded frequent visits to Bordeaux. Testard and Gaschet, in charge of the overhauling, were insisting on large payments on account, and if the proud vessel was to be placed in service without undue delay it was essential that a reliable and active agent of Hortalez should remain in continuous contact with the dockyards. It was arranged that during Pierre's absence the Paris office should be under the management of Maigron, while Paul went to Bordeaux.

Pierre then set off for Aix, taking with him the perfect travelling companion, Philippe Gudin.

Upon his arrival at Aix he paid the customary visits to the President and the other members of the Court of Appeal, and it became evident that this time his aristocratic friends had not left him in the lurch. The judges had obviously received a hint from Versailles, and they had made up their minds to help him to victory.

Assured, then, of a favourable verdict, he proceeded to invite those for whom he cared most in the world—Thérèse, Julie, and Paul— to Aix in order that they might witness his triumph.

But only Julie arrived. Thérèse wrote that she was unable to come as she did not want to leave the child behind yet could not expose her to the heat and fatigues of the long journey. As to Paul, he sent word that he must remain in Bordeaux. He deeply regretted his inability to leave, but he was experiencing new difficulties with the bureaucratic legal representatives of Testard and Gaschet. Now they even contested his authority to act on behalf of Hortalez and Company. He therefore had to beg Pierre to sign a general power of attorney which he duly enclosed.

Paul had been formally registered as the chief agent of the firm with full power to act, and this was perfectly well known to Testard and Gaschet. Pierre shook his head at this further attempt on the part of Testard and Gaschet to make things difficult for Hortalez and Company, but he told himself that Paul must know best what to do, signed the power of attorney and sent it off.

He soon forgot the matter, for the hearing at Aix was reaching its conclusion.

From every part of France lawyers had streamed in to watch the trial, and the newspapers were full of it. Innumerable people had come to hear the verdict promulgated, the tumble-down old monastery in which the tribunal held its sittings was packed with curious sightseers, the whole town was tense with excitement.

Pierre modestly passed the evening with Gudin and Julie at the lodging of his advocate in a secluded side-street. The night was far advanced before the verdict was at length made public. All the way from the hall where the court had been sitting, through the congeries of crooked streets that constituted the town of Aix, there rang out the cry, "Beaumarchais has won!" The narrow side-street where Pierre lived was bright with the flames of a torchlight procession, and the torch-bearers exulted, "Beaumarchais has won!"

Pierre had carried off many a victory in his lifetime, but never one that brought him so much happiness as this did. In the concentration of a single moment he realized more keenly than ever the weight of injustice that had been inflicted upon him. Innocent though he had been in all men's eyes, his highly born friends, who might have helped him, had been content to praise the brilliance of his pamphlets, to pat him on the back with a smile of amusement, and to let the very real disgrace stick to him. What did it matter? He had been born a bourgeois, so he had fought for justice not only for himself, but for all who had been born without privilege. It had been a good fight. A better victory could have been won by no man.

These were the thoughts that passed through his mind as the cry, "Beaumarchais has won!" rang in his ears. Throughout those six years he had never doubted that in the long run his fight would be crowned with success. Yet now that success was a reality it was more than he could bear. Excess of happiness swelled his heart to bursting and he fell to the ground in a swoon.

They rubbed his forehead with essences and brought him back to consciousness. As he sipped a glass of wine the sound of flutes, fiddles, and tambourines could be heard before the house. Another torchlight procession was coming along the street. A deputation of artisans offered their congratulations in improvised verses in Provençal. Gudin sat humped blissfully in his chair and gazed in admiring wonder at his friend. The most affected of them all was Julie.

When the travelling-coach drew up in front of his house in the rue de Condé, Pierre said simply, "It was a pleasant journey."

There was further glory to come when, as a sequel to the hearing at Aix, the Supreme Court in Paris sat to decide whether Pierre's civil rights should be restored. The proceedings were short. In three sentences the Advocate-General proposed that the judgment pronounced some years before should be declared null and void. After five minutes' consideration the bench of judges announced its decision. Pierre Caron de Beaumarchais would leave the court without a stain on his character and was to be invested with the offices and titles of which he had been deprived. Deafening applause broke out as Pierre bowed to the bench. Enthusiastic supporters bore him on their shoulders to his carriage. "Beaumarchais the Martyr" was accorded an ovation such as had not fallen to his lot even in the theatre.

A week later he received an official copy of the judgment promulgated by the court at Aix. The details were even more favourable than he had dared to hope. He was awarded all the sums of money to which he had laid claim together with a high rate of interest, as well as 30,000 livres compensation for the wrong that had been inflicted upon him.

Then they brought him the painting which the court had also declared to be rightfully his, the portrait of Duverny by the masterhand of Duplessis. Hooks were affixed to the wall and the space that had so long been empty was filled. There the picture hung, a token of what his tenacious and energetic optimism could do, and Pierre sat before it with a look of dazed happiness on his face.

☆   ☆   ☆

In the midst of all the turmoil and intoxication of the past weeks Pierre had been dimly conscious that no news had been received from Paul for a long time. Moreover, the last reports from Bordeaux had been signed not by Paul, but by Peyroux, the firm's resident agent. Now there arrived an urgent query from Peyroux that could have been answered by Paul on the spot. Profoundly disturbed, Pierre replied demanding to know with all possible speed what had happened to Paul, and by return of post Peyroux informed him in some surprise that Monsieur Theveneau had of course sailed for America with the last convoy.

Stunned by the news, Pierre sat in deep dejection, by turns accusing and attempting to exonerate himself. There was surely no blame attaching to him, in view of the sly means Paul had used to achieve his end. Had he not done everything possible to restrain his friend? Had he not forbidden him emphatically to leave his post in France? Had not Paul accepted his prohibition? He raged against himself, against Paul, and above all against the bad faith of the Americans.

Immediately after his triumph at the Supreme Court he had gone to see Thérèse and told her that now he had been rehabilitated there was no longer any obstacle to their marriage. He carefully formulated his words to make it appear as if it had been she who had insisted on the delay. They had agreed to wait until Paul's return from Bordeaux, since they were both anxious that he should be a witness to their wedding. Now, in uneasy agitation, yet not without a feeling of pride, he had to inform her of their friend's noble though incomprehensible action.

She grew pale, then flushed, her grey eyes darkened and her curved brows seemed to arch even higher. "You should never have permitted it, Pierre," she said. After a moment's pause she added, "It was a mean thing to do." She spoke more calmly than he had expected, but with a sharper note in her voice and as if there was nothing more to say.

Pierre was used to blame. Whether just or unjust, he had shrugged it off, and time after time he had got the better of his accusers, but the charge now flung in his face by the woman he loved best on earth was, to put it mildly, exaggerated. Overwhelmed as he had been by his legal affairs at Aix, he had perhaps failed to devote the attention he ought to have devoted to a rather odd letter from Paul. That was all. And now Thérèse was behaving as if he had been responsible for sending the lad to his death. A vehement retort was on the tip of his tongue, but he saw the expression of angry contempt on her face and the words were stifled before they passed his lips. Without allowing him time to collect his thoughts she rose and left the room.

Sitting at the table on which were still the remains of their meal, Pierre was oppressed by a sudden feeling of profound loneliness. The rebuff outweighed his victories at Aix and in Paris. It had been so unexpected, and particularly from Thérèse. He sat there with his thoughts still in confusion, gulping down a glass of wine. Then he got up and went to find her.

She was in her bedroom. He sat down beside her, but said no further word about the unhappy matter that had brought him out to Meudon. Instead he cautiously spoke of the various practical details to be attended to in connexion with their impending marriage. She merely shook her head, and when he gently took her hand she sharply withdrew it.

He was silent for a time. Then, knowing full well that it was the wrong thing to do, he began to speak of Paul and of the insistence with which he had ordered him to stay. Thérèse turned away and in a low voice, which yet brooked no demur, said, "Please go!"

With a deeper sense of defeat than he had ever known he stood up and left the house.

☆   ☆   ☆

When Arthur Lee returned from Madrid without having achieved his purpose, he could find no words too bitter or ironic with which to stigmatize the lazy, idle life that the Doctor *honoris causa* was leading at Passy.

Franklin was, indeed, paying but little attention to business during the whole of that spring and early summer, for he was convinced that any attempt to accelerate the negotiations with Versailles could only result in harm. There was nothing to do but wait.

There was little news from Philadelphia. Apparently more ships

were falling into the hands of the English than were arriving safe
and sound in European ports. Things were not going too well; so
much was certain. It had even become necessary to evacuate Philadelphia for a time, and the Congress had been meeting in Baltimore,
though since it had now returned to Philadelphia the enemy advance
must have been held up. Nevertheless the situation remained menacing. Arthur Lee considered this a reason for redoubling pressure
on the French Government, but that was nonsense. On the contrary,
until the military situation improved, the emissaries had to bide
their time.

Franklin was inspired by the deep repugnance of every man of
reason and humane feeling to such an unnecessary, stupid, atavistic
phenomenon as war. Throughout the whole lengthy conflict with the
Government in London he had taken infinite pains to avoid an outbreak of hostilities, and if he had been unsuccessful the fault was
certainly not his. Of all the foolish enterprises to which men had
recourse, the enterprise of war seemed to him the most foolish, and
it was shameful mockery on the part of fate that he should now be
forced by circumstances to long for a second Trenton or Princetown
with all the bloodshed and misery that it would bring in its train.

The Congress leaders evidently did not realize that an immediate
alliance with France was quite unobtainable. In their letters they
simply reiterated the words of Arthur Lee, and invariably ended by
impressing upon the commissioners in the most urgent terms the
necessity at all costs of accelerating the negotiations for a commercial
treaty and an alliance, for which the country was waiting as for rain
after drought.

Maurepas had spoken truly when he gibed in his cynical way at
the breakneck speed with which the men in Philadelphia managed
to forget the recent past. Some of the most vehement advocates in the
Congress of a French treaty had only a very short time before been
uttering thunderous denunciations of their hereditary enemies the
French, whom they branded as heretics, worshippers of idols, and
the slaves of tryants. All this had been forgotten in Philadelphia,
but not in France.

Nor had Franklin himself by any means cast from his memory
the struggle which the Americans called the French and Indian War
and the Europeans the Seven Years' War. He could understand the
view held in Philadelphia that the victory in that conflict was to be
attributed mainly to Anglo-American arms, but he could also sympathize with the belief cherished by the French that they had been
deprived of a sweeping triumph only by a singularly unfortunate
mischance. If, so they said in Paris, the Russian Empress had not
happened to die just when Frederick of Prussia was reduced to his
last extremity, with the result that her romantic idiot of a son suc-

ceeded to the throne, Prussia would have been defeated, France would have been able to dictate peace on the Continent, and the two Roman Catholic powers would never have been compelled to surrender their possessions in America.

Franklin had often pondered on how the English victory in 1763 had eventually turned out to the disadvantage of England herself. If the outcome had been different, the Roman Catholic colonies of France and Spain would still constitute a constricting girdle round the English possessions in the western world, and in order to maintain themselves against those two great powers the English colonies would still have to rely upon the military protection of their motherland. There could have been no thought then of independence.

Amused, yet saddened, the Doctor gazed in front of him. When one reviewed the course of events from a distance, as he was able to do in the fullness of his years, it became clear that mankind was after all making progress. Men were growing wiser, or at any rate less obtuse. History moved by very remarkable and devious paths. One could not always see what direction it was taking, but there did seem to be a goal and, so far as it was possible to draw deductions, a rational goal. But it was necessary to possess one's soul in patience.

While these thoughts were passing through his mind Franklin was sitting at his writing-table, and his wise resignation to the tardiness of historical progress did not diminish his uneasiness at the tiresome accumulation of correspondence which his laziness had once more permitted to pile up. He surveyed the mass of papers with a worried sigh. Then he resolutely pushed them aside. Though he would be laying himself open to another rebuke from Arthur Lee, he again put off the burdensome task of answering these letters. It would be more entertaining to write a note to Madame Brillon.

Madame Brillon was journeying in the south. The thought of her frequently occupied the Doctor's mind, and as he prepared to write his letter he had a clear picture of her sitting on his lap and nestling against him with her pretty face close to his. She had a pale olive complexion and dark hair, and her large, tender black eyes contrasted strangely with the almost imperceptible down on her short upper lip that afforded him such a pleasant tickling sensation. He could not have said whom he preferred, Madame Helvétius or Madame Brillon. They both at times called him affectionately their "old rascal," he shared his time equally between them, addressed them both with the same portentous, playful gallantry, and would not willingly have dispensed with either.

"I often pass before your house, my very dear Madame Brillon," he wrote. "It appears desolate to me. Formerly I broke the Commandment by coveting it along with my neighbour's wife. Now I do not covet it any more, so I am less a sinner. But as to his wife I always find these Commandments inconvenient and I am sorry that they were ever made. If in your travels you happen to see the Holy Father, ask him to repeal them, as things given only to the Jews and too uncomfortable for good Christians." He continued writing in this style, it amused him.

But when he had finished he could no longer find a satisfactory excuse for neglecting his official correspondence. Suddenly his leg began to hurt, and removing his shoe and stocking he massaged the gouty spots, groaning.

It was a pity, he thought, that he had not someone like Monsieur Theveneau to help him. Monsieur Theveneau was prepared to sacrifice himself for his frivolous-minded employer, on whose behalf he was going to America, while the representative of the Congress in France had not a single assistant on whom he could rely.

On the other hand, his assistants were not so unreliable as Arthur Lee maintained. Since his return from Spain his colleague had a new idiosyncrasy. He smelt spies everywhere. Everyone who came out to Passy was regarded with suspicion, such as Bancroft, whom Franklin sometimes employed for confidential secretarial duties, or the young clergyman John Vardill. Silas Deane, too, complained that Lee was accusing his two secretaries, Joseph Hynson and Jacobus van Zandt, of espionage. At the same time Deane himself thought that Arthur Lee's own trusted secretary, a certain Mr. Thornton, was by no means above suspicion. Deane and Lee had eventually had a violent quarrel on the subject, and Franklin thought with amusement of how he had had to intervene and make peace between his two fellow commissioners.

He was unaware of the fact that they were both right. The agents and secretaries in question were all of them, without exception, in the pay of either the English or the French secret service.

Reminded by the thought of his two colleagues and their mutual suspicions, he delved into the mass of papers on his table and picked out a letter that had been furtively delivered on the previous day. A mysterious Baron Weissenstein made tempting promises to the American leaders in return for their support in bringing about a compromise peace with England. Large sums of money, offices, and titles were offered in particular to Franklin and to General Washington.

Franklin considered it expedient to reply; he would deliver his message by a young man whom he suspected of being in the pay of the Paris police. It would do no harm for Monsieur de Maurepas to receive the impression that the American commissioners were not in principle averse from entertaining dealings with clandestine agents of the English Government. It might even help to persuade

the gentlemen at Versailles of the desirability of speeding up matters
a little.

☆   ☆   ☆

Franklin's popularity with the Parisians did not diminish. The old
sage and statesman who was so philosophically awaiting the course
of events in his rural garden remained for them a great symbol. The
unfavourable military situation, however, led him to fear that their
enthusiasm might not last much longer. It seemed to him that the
portraits which were still being sold in the streets showed him to
less advantage than formerly. Some of them gave him the face of
a wily, hard-bitten, calculating peasant lacking any trace of greatness or kindness.

In these circumstances he welcomed a suggestion made by Monsieur de Chaumont, who said that he would like to commission
Duplessis to paint Franklin's portrait. Duplessis, the most renowned
and highly paid portrait painter in France, knew how to invest his
subjects with an impressive dignity.

An awkward-looking man of fifty-five, with a Provençal accent
that Franklin had difficulty in understanding, he explained timidly
that he was a slow worker and would need a large number of sittings.
The Doctor did not find this an agreeable prospect, for he could
not bear to sit still for any length of time, but a portrait by Duplessis
would be worth the effort and he resigned himself to the inevitable
discomfort.

When the first sitting was over he was curious to see how the
work was progressing, but Duplessis did not like to have his pictures
inspected before they were finished. He was obviously a little over-
awed by the American, and at first he remained even more silent than
was his wont, but under the influence of Franklin's genial manner
he loosened up a little and spoke of his experiments in trying to
improve certain pigments, particularly madder and ultramarine.
Since the Doctor was evidently interested in these experiments and
asked intelligent questions about them, the painter was encouraged
to speak of other matters that occupied his mind.

There had been a tremendous to-do when he painted the Queen.
She was still the Dauphine, and the portrait was intended for her
mother, the Austrian Empress. Eventually she had condescended to
give him two and a half sittings, and though the connoisseurs thought
he had managed very well the Empress was dissatisfied. She declared
that it was not a good enough likeness, that the composition did
not set her daughter off to sufficient advantage, and that Toinette
was, in fact, more beautiful than the picture showed her to be.
Duplessis sighed and smiled. Then in mingled wrath and amusement

he told of his experiences with the King. It was almost impossible to persuade His Majesty to sit. Once he had been commissioned to paint a portrait of Louis that, so his instructions ran, must look particularly "magnificent," since it was intended as a gift from the *Compagnie des Indes* to the Rajah of the Carnatic. The King was to be represented with all the insignia of power, and the picture had to be done very quickly, as the ship was about to sail for India. The officials responsible for keeping the insignia safely under lock and key were reluctant to let them out of their charge and made difficulties about letting him use them as models, until finally Monsieur d'Angivillers ordered him to impose the head of Louis XVI on the body of His late Majesty Louis XV, utilizing for the latter purpose a painting by van Loo. The Rajah would presumably not notice the difference.

Franklin repaid the painter's stories with a few of his own homely anecdotes, but there were a great many sittings and their conversation gradually languished. The Doctor then invited one or two of his friends to come and talk or read to him, and Duplessis welcomed anything that would prevent the American from getting restless.

One day Maurepas dropped in unexpectedly. He had heard, he said, that Franklin was having his portrait painted and he had considered it his duty to come and keep his old friend company during that tedious operation.

Franklin sat on the dais in a comfortable, but dignified attitude, his waistcoat lumpy and wrinkled, his hair falling over the fur collar of his coat. The elegant Maurepas took a seat opposite him, and the two old gentlemen formed a strange contrast, the one with his air of simple dignity, the other dressed in the height of fashion and reeking of scent.

"Lately," the Doctor said good-humouredly, "I have often heard it said that I am shrewd and cunning. But I hope that it is not immodest for me to say that I have other qualities too, and perhaps some of them, such as patience, will show in the painting on which our esteemed Monsieur Duplessis is engaged."

Maurepas smiled politely. "Shrewd and cunning? You, my dear Doctor?" he exclaimed, speaking in English so that Duplessis would not understand. "No, with all due respect to your wisdom, I certainly would not call you artful. That manœuvre of yours, for instance, in the affair of Baron Weissenstein. You did not really expect us to be taken in by that, did you?"

Franklin chuckled inwardly. So that was why Maurepas had come. He had been wondering what they would be thinking at Versailles about his correspondence with the dubious Baron.

"However anxious you may be to make us think so," continued Maurepas, "we simply refuse to believe that you are the sly fox you pretend to be. I hesitated even to read your letter to this fellow Weissenstein." Franklin rejoiced to hear the Minister speak in this way, which was just what he had hoped and expected. "Please continue to negotiate with the English," went on Maurepas.

"Will it disturb you if I smile, Monsieur Duplessis?" asked Franklin.

"Not at all, my dear Doctor," replied the painter.

Franklin smiled broadly. "You must confess," he said to Maurepas, "that your policy is practically forcing us to negotiate with London. You keep us dangling for an unconscionably long time."

"A Franklin does not allow himself to be kept dangling," rejoined Maurepas amiably. "You do not find the waiting tedious, I believe. From what I hear, you have found agreeable ways of spending your time. And you will, I am sure, understand that your military situation does not render it any the easier for your friends at Versailles to speed up the conclusion of a treaty." Franklin was holding his head inclined a little to one side, as Duplessis had requested, but he could not prevent a rather grimmer expression stealing over his features than the painter wished. Before he could reply, however, Maurepas continued, "But I have not come to spoil your sitting. Let me assure you that your position here has not been fundamentally altered by the unfavourable news from America. We do not intend to sign a treaty with you before the time is ripe, but neither can we afford to leave you in the lurch. One thing is certain," he concluded courteously. "Unaffected by the fluctuating chances of war, America's strongest asset, my dear Doctor Franklin, remains your own popularity."

"It would be regrettable," replied Franklin, "if a great cause such as the establishment of the American republic were to depend upon the popularity of one man."

"We are both old enough, my friend," said Maurepas, "to know that the history of the world can be profoundly influenced by some such fortunate chance as that a nation happens to take a liking to a man's face. Or do you believe that the course of history is governed by laws, rather than by fortuity? I do not. The longer I live—please listen to what I am saying, Duplessis," he interrupted himself. He was now speaking in French. "You may profit by my experience—the longer I live, the more clearly do I realize that history has no meaning. The current surges and ripples first in one direction, then in another, while we merely splash about in it and are driven hither or thither." The atmosphere of the sunny room seemed to grow chill, and the matter-of-fact, conversational tone in which he spoke enhanced the gloomy effect of his words. Even Duplessis let his paint-brush sink and gazed uneasily at the sweetly smiling Maurepas.

Franklin, on his dais, did not stir. "I believe," he said quietly, "that

we are attempting to invest history with a meaning." There was no
hint of rebuke in his voice, but its note of confidence and conviction
dispelled at once the bleak breath of melancholy that had descended
when the other spoke.

"*You* are attempting to do so, Monsieur," replied Maurepas.

He stood up, stretched his arms and, with an agility that belied his
years, strode over to inspect the painting before Duplessis could
raise an objection. He stepped back a pace or two, moved closer,
stepped back again, and kept looking up to compare the features
of Franklin sitting on his dais with the painted features on the
canvas.

"Magnificent, my dear Duplessis!" he exclaimed at last. "Magnificent! It is even better than your portrait of Gluck." Then turning
to Franklin, he said, "Now one can see for the first time what sort
of a man you are. Or at least, I am seeing it for the first time. That
broad powerful brow!" he went on rapturously, as if the subject of
the picture were not with them. "One can almost see the thoughts
working behind it. And these furrows, so deeply etched, yet with
no indication of toil or effort. And what equanimity in the eyes. You
are going to give us a great deal of trouble yet, my dear Doctor,
a great deal of trouble—how much, I realize only now."

He again became absorbed in the portrait. "What a pity," he murmured to himself, "that I did not bring Sallé with me. Now my first
impressions will be lost to posterity." But at least he could hold
forth to the painter. "To the man whose semblance you have limned
upon this canvas difficulties are unknown. In his declining years he
finds the setting up of a republic not work, but play. All is play to
him, whether it be business affairs, the sciences, or mankind itself.
Par mon âme, s'il en fût en moi," he continued, quoting his favourite
line, *"Upon my soul, if I possess one,* you have no idea, my dear
Duplessis, what a masterpiece you have created here." And in a
renewed access of rapture he concluded, "Do you know what you
are, my most esteemed Doctor Franklin, do you know what you are,
both as you sit there on the dais and as you appear here in the picture?
You are a man! *Voilà un homme!*" Trying to translate the epithet
into English, he added, *"Behold a man!"* Finally he decided, "One
can say it only in Latin. *Ecce vir!*"

Franklin rose from his chair and stretched. "May I take a little
exercise?" he asked Duplessis, who stood blushing awkwardly at the
overwhelming praise lavished on his painting by Maurepas. Descending from the dais, Franklin walked up and down the room scratching
himself. "Count Maurepas is regarded as the first connoisseur in
the country," he said to Duplessis. "You really must have produced
a masterpiece. May I have a look at it?"

From the canvas there gazed at him a face that was familiar, and yet seemed strange. There were the pouches under the eyes, the double chin, and the furrows. The brow was powerful, the jaw strong and energetic, the eyes stern, searching, and just, the mouth wide and firmly shut. It was the mouth of a man given neither to complaint nor to despair. The face was old, yet not old; he knew it and he did not know it.

Duplessis looked at him a little apprehensively, for he had involuntarily assumed the stern, searching expression of the portrait. "You have done a good job there, Monsieur Duplessis," he said at last, and the artist was prouder of those few words than of the effusive praises showered upon him by the Minister.

"Will you paint a portrait of our Franklin for me?" asked Maurepas.

But Franklin protested, "I am not going to give any more sittings!"

"That is not necessary," explained Duplessis. "If I copy the picture with a few small changes the second or third version will be better than the original."

"That is agreed, then," declared Maurepas.

"But don't hang me among those nude ladies of yours," insisted the Doctor.

The Minister looked pensive. "Where to hang you," he said, "is something of a problem. I think it would be advisable for the time being to keep you from the eyes of His Most Christian Majesty. It would be better to hang you temporarily in Paris, at the Hôtel Phélypeau, not at Versailles. When the time is ripe I shall bring you to Versailles in the finest gold frame I can procure. My young monarch has little taste for feminine beauty, but he has a strong feeling for dignity and for a noble bearing. *Voilà un homme! Ecce vir!*" Maurepas savoured the significance of the epithet he had invented to describe Doctor Franklin's portrait.

☆   ☆   ☆

Pierre could not forget the angry contempt in Thérèse's voice when she said, "It was a mean thing to do."

He drove out to Meudon, but her maid curtsied and said, "Madame is not at home." He wrote to her, but received no answer.

He found her attitude inexplicable, though in his heart of hearts he knew what she was feeling and loved her all the more because she was what she was. Once more he assured himself that not a vestige of blame could attach to him.

He did not blame Paul either. The person on whose shoulders the responsibility must be laid was Franklin, whose hostile, senile whim had deprived him not only of the well-deserved reward of his labours, but also of his friend and the woman he loved.

It had long been his view that he had been the victim of calumny, that Franklin's peculiar attitude was due to some misunderstanding, but he had now cast aside any such illusion. He realized that Franklin simply did not like him. In contrast to Paul, he had found no favour in the old man's sight. That was something he found difficult to comprehend, for it was a new experience and he could not reconcile himself to it. Contrary to his normal loquacity, he kept his thoughts to himself, since he could not have borne the humiliation of mentioning them to others.

This was the situation in which he found himself when fresh news came from America to cause him further embitterment. For the third time one of his convoys had returned to France empty-handed, not only without money, but even without cargo. The Congress had found a new pretext for avoiding payment. Prompted by Arthur Lee, it refused to pay any sums on account of insurance on the grounds that Pierre had not arranged insurance with a third party but was carrying the risk himself. Until an understanding had been reached on this point, the Congress declared, all payments must be deferred.

Pierre was furious. It was customary in the French export trade for large firms to ensure their vessels themselves, and to make a considerable charge to cover the risk. On the other hand, they did not expect payment for cargoes that failed to reach port, and Pierre had not rendered an account to the Congress for supplies that had fallen into the hands of the English. Franklin was well aware of all this, and he ought to have refuted the base lies of Arthur Lee, instead of which his knavish silence had only confirmed the men in Philadelphia in their attitude toward the firm of Hortalez.

Pierre's whole fury was therefore directed against the old man in Passy, and he could no longer contain the resentment that filled his heart to bursting. Julie was the first to whom he unburdened himself. There was that fat, lazy spider, he raged, sitting in his garden and sucking everybody's blood, hoarding up all the glory that came his way. And who was his chief victim? Who was paying the piper? Who else but Pierre, the good-natured Pierre, the eternal idealist who was always being taken in? Julie joined him in his imprecations, told him how much she admired him, and expressed her firm conviction that he would overcome this misfortune as he had overcome others and show that malevolent old Doctor who was the better man.

In speaking to Gudin, Pierre was more cautious. He was aware that his loyal friend never forgot their conversations and probably kept a written record of them, for apart from his *History of France* he was also secretly engaged on a *History of Pierre Beaumarchais.* So in front of Gudin he repressed his wrath and assumed a mask of ironic resignation. He shrugged his shoulders as if he could well understand, bitter though the realization was, that these American soldiers of liberty were too preoccupied with their great task to remember to pay their debts, even though their remissness was ruining their chief supporter.

Gudin was deeply moved. He could see that though his friend pretended to be reconciled to the situation, he was consumed by a savage anger, a *saeva indignatio,* and he quoted the words that Euripides put into the mouth of Hercules in his frenzy, "I hate every man in whom gratitude has been extinguished," and other Greek and Latin authors. Gudin's erudition, however, brought Pierre no more consolation than had his sister's imprecations. Nothing could make up for his loss in not having Thérèse at his side. Nothing could make up for the absence of Paul.

A day or two later Maigron, with his grey face immobile as ever, reported to him at his *lever* that the total liquid capital at the disposal of the firm of Hortalez and Company amounted in all to 317 livres and 2 sous. For the fraction of a second a look of mingled rage and bewilderment appeared in Pierre's eyes. He seemed dazed by the news. But he had not lost his gift of passing an unwelcome experience off with a laugh after the first flash of anger. His life was a combination of the sublime and the ridiculous. His agencies and storehouses were to be found in every port of France and Spain, he was providing work for thousands of hands, he had procured and was shipping overseas ninety per cent of the requirements of the American Army, fourteen of his ships were at sea and nine others being made ready to sail, yet he could not pay his valet's wages.

He accepted the situation, however, and decided to ignore his worries and to cast business aside for some time. The most important part of the task he had undertaken in the interests of America and the fight for freedom was done. The Americans could now see how they managed without him for a few days. He ceased to put in an appearance at the Hôtel de Hollande and did not even ask for reports.

Instead he applied himself once more to the new comedy he was planning to write. Taking out of its drawer the monologue which in the first access of enthusiasm he had shown to his father, but to no one else since, he again felt the thrill of joy with which he had first sat down to it, and round this fragment he built up the play that was taking shape in his mind, the sequel to *The Barber,* the story of the great *débrouillard* who succeeds in extracting himself with a laugh from all sorts of unpleasant situations, who rebels against the stupidities and prejudices of the world and thereby overcomes them, the story of Figaro.

He unburdened his soul of its anger at a world that made life so easy for the blockheads who were born to privilege and so difficult for the geniuses who were not. With sure judgment he felt that rhetoric would be out of place. His deep anger was transmuted into couplets, into light but pungent songs. Never had his work been so effortless as now. The sentences seemed to write themselves, the dialogue streamed from his pen without his having to search for words. His light-hearted joy in a world that had so much to offer, his witty mockery of a world that refused so much, flowed easily onto the paper in words that sang and danced with graceful charm.

He read the play to Julie. Her admiration knew no bounds. Gudin listened with equal admiration, but more understanding. He savoured its wit and brilliance with the judgment of the practised critic, compared the author to Aristophanes and Menander, with Plautus and Terence, and expressed the opinion that Pierre had carried French comedy far beyond the point achieved by Molière.

Yet Pierre's pleasure in this sterling praise was marred by his longing for Thérèse. He yearned with all his heart and soul to watch the play of emotion reflected in her face as he read his play to her, but Thérèse had forsaken him. He sat about idly, sullenly.

In the midst of his brooding there arrived from the Hôtel Valentinois in Passy a neatly printed card inviting Monsieur de Beaumarchais to participate in a small celebration which Monsieur Benjamin Franklin was arranging for a select circle of friends on the fourth of July, on the occasion of the anniversary of the Declaration of Independence by the thirteen United States.

A wave of happiness flooded Pierre's whole body. Fortune was once more smiling on him. He had just dashed off his sparkling comedy, *The Marriage of Figaro,* and now the old man in Passy had at last realized that without the help of Beaumarchais the independence of the American colonies was inconceivable. Pierre read the card again and again, and his resentment at Franklin's former behaviour melted away.

Slowly, however, doubts began to enter his mind. Was this invitation more than a mere formality? Should he allow himself to be fobbed off by a politely worded card in lieu of the millions of livres that were due to him? He held the card in his hand and did not know what to think.

Now, if ever, he needed advice and there were only two people who could advise him. Paul was in America. He must see Thérèse. She could not refuse her help in a matter that meant so much to him.

In his dilemma he turned to Gudin. There had been, he said, a little misunderstanding between him and Thérèse, and he would be glad if Gudin would drive out to Meudon and let her know that he was anxious to ask her opinion on a point of importance. Gudin smiled with sly amusement. Pierre knew how to tackle women. "Perhaps you might tell her," continued Pierre, "that it concerns my relations with Franklin. Or say what you think best when you see her.

The old man has invited me, by the way, to visit him in his garden at Passy. They appear to have discovered that they can't get on without Pierre."

"And do you mean to say that you are going?" exclaimed Gudin indignantly. "With your absurd generosity you are always prepared to forgive and forget."

Pierre merely smiled. "Please drive out to Meudon, my dear fellow," he begged, "and don't come back until you have the answer I want. I am counting on your tact." Gudin was flattered and set out on his mission.

When Thérèse thought the matter over calmly, she admitted to herself that what she still regarded as Pierre's betrayal of his friend should have caused her no surprise. She knew his weaknesses as well as his good qualities, and though she did not regret either the brusqueness with which she had sent him away or her refusal to let him come and see her, she was aware of her inability to persist in this attitude in the long run. She could not do without him, for in his absence life had no meaning.

This was the mood in which Gudin found her. She and Gudin were good friends, she appreciated his honesty, his good nature, and his learning, and she knew how devoted he was to Pierre. He felt that he was being particularly tactful as he told her how he had gathered, from hints which Pierre had let fall, that there had been a slight misunderstanding between them, and he had considered it his duty, as a friend of them both, to see her at once without informing Pierre of his intention, for one should not allow a tiff to go on too long. At great length he explained that Pierre was in a difficult situation and urgently needed her advice. When she suspiciously inquired what he meant by "a difficult situation," he replied that it concerned Pierre's relations with Franklin. The two were not on the best of terms, and it was a pity that the chief representatives of progress now in Europe should be separated by mutual distrust.

Thérèse had already surmised that Pierre was taking Franklin's aloofness to heart, and when this was confirmed by Gudin the idea occurred to her that perhaps Franklin's coldness was a punishment for Pierre's shabby treatment of Paul. She told herself immediately, however, that this was nonsense. Paul had gone to America only because Franklin had left Pierre in the lurch, and it was hardly likely that God would punish a man for an action before he had committed it. Nevertheless, she could not rid herself of the notion that there was some causal connexion between Pierre's betrayal of Paul and Franklin's attitude toward him.

The fact that Pierre had sent Gudin to beg her advice seemed a good opportunity to make up their quarrel, and she declared her readiness to see him. When Gudin returned to Paris he reported with great satisfaction that his tactful efforts had been crowned with success.

When Pierre arrived at Meudon he made no reference to what had happened at their previous meeting, but confined himself to a plain, matter-of-fact account of his various attempts to bring about a fruitful collaboration between himself and Franklin, of the rebuffs he had experienced, and the old man's stubborn refusal to support his claims on the Congress. He then told her of Franklin's invitation and his doubts, whether it was an olive branch or simply a manœuvre to dissuade him from taking energetic action. Thérèse replied that it was probably nothing more than an act of courtesy. She did not think it likely that Franklin cherished hostile feelings towards Pierre. "In my opinion," she said, "he is far less interested in you than you are inclined to assume. It looks to me as if you have not made the same forcible impression on him that you make upon others, and that is all."

Pierre did not go further into this point, but asked whether or not he should accept the invitation. She replied that in his place she would have no hesitation in going. If he stayed away it would be an act of discourtesy and a childish way of declaring open war on Franklin, for whom he would be no match.

Pierre swallowed this pill too. He realized that he was being given sensible advice, and in any case he was tempted by the thought of being able to show off his brilliance at the American's party. So he answered shortly that she was quite right and he would do as she counselled.

After such a display of self-control, however, he was able to restrain himself no longer and launched into wild accusations against Franklin. His great enterprise, he declared, had been undertaken not from any thought of financial reward or gratitude, but on account of the cause it would help to further, and it was outrageous that the Doctor should be led by pure jealousy to treat him as he had done. Thérèse looked at him with her large eyes until he grew uncomfortable and broke off.

After a while he changed the topic and spoke of the play on which he had been engaged and which he thought was a good piece of work. He asked whether she would like him to read it to her while his mind was still full of it.

Thérèse had resolved that after this meeting she would not see him again for some time. She did not want to let him off too lightly. But it had been his writings that attracted her to him in the first place, and she was glad that he had now apparently returned to his right sphere. Whenever he had read to her from his works she had been carried away, raised to a higher plane, his petty weaknesses seemed to evaporate and she saw only the fiery spirit that animated him. He relived the process of creation as he read and she was able to share his creative experience. Consumed as she was with her eager desire to hear his new comedy, it cost her an effort to say calmly, "Very well, come back at the end of the week."

When he called again, armed with his manuscript, she was in a mood of happy expectation, though she did her best not to show it. She kept the baby in the room, but its crowing did not disturb him. He acted each part as he read the play, and he soon saw from her changing expression, in which each stirring of emotion was reflected, that he was achieving the desired effect. She laughed heartily, the child joined in with its crowing, and Pierre himself laughed at his own wit. He enjoyed no less than Thérèse the humour of his comedy, which sprang from no mere play of the intellect, which was no mere superficial coruscation, but had its roots in the sound common sense of the people, in the wit of the Parisians, and hit the mark with its pungent truths.

When he had come to the end she stretched out her hand towards him and said with simple sincerity, "That really is a good piece of work, Pierre." And he, boldly exploiting the moment, answered, "Now I will not listen to any more protests. We are going to get married."

Thérèse raised no objection, though she firmly declined to live under the same roof with Julie. Pierre, rejoicing that under the influence of his new play her resistance had at last broken dow , hit on a solution.

In the Faubourg Saint-Antoine, not far from his house, there was a piece of land, surrounded by a wall, which had frequently attracted his attention. It lay on the edge of the city where the rue Saint-Antoine broadened out into the Place de la Bastille and consisted of a large garden, which had been allowed to run wild, with an old house, half in ruins and standing alone, almost completely concealed from the street by the high wall and surrounding trees. On two occasions he had looked over the little estate, which was unlike any other residence in Paris. When one looked out from the upper story it was like being on an island in the centre of the teeming city. On the one side were quiet old houses, each surrounded by its private garden. On the other side lay the great square with the grim fortress of the Bastille.

The owner, well aware of its appealing charm, demanded an exorbitant sum. But Pierre, contemplating marriage, bought the place anyway. Other great gentlemen permitted themselves the extravagance of running two households, and he would do the same. So he commissioned the architect Le Moyne to relandscape the grounds, and to build on the old foundations a new house even more imposing than the one in the rue de Condé. He would keep on his present residence, which Julie would continue to manage, and in the second he would live with his wife and daughter.

Beaming with satisfaction he told Thérèse of his purchase. "Of course," he added, "we shall not wait until the house is ready. That might take years. If it suits you, we can get married next week."

And they were duly married.

★ ❖ ★ ❖ ★ ❖ ★ ❖ ★

Chapter Two

THE MEETING

❖ ★ ❖

THE company that assembled on the fourth of July at Franklin's house towards the cool of the evening was made up almost equally of Americans and Frenchmen. Silas Deane had asked permission to bring two of his sea-dogs with him, Captains Johnson and Smythe, who would be able to entertain the guests with stories of their privateering exploits. Arthur Lee was accompanied by a certain Mr. Reed, a gloomy gentleman from London who wished to demonstrate his respect for human rights and his contempt for the tyrants of the Court of St. James. Though the very emphasis with which he asserted his rebellious inclinations led Franklin to suspect him of being a spy, he raised no objections to his presence. The Franklin family was represented not only by the Doctor himself, but also by young William and little Benjamin Bache, who had come over from his boarding-school. The Doctor was afraid of spoiling his younger grandson and had made up his mind to send him to a school in Geneva that had a reputation for being particularly progressive, but meanwhile he wanted to see as much of him as possible, and the self-possessed little boy, now seven years of age, moved happily among the guests and chatted with everybody. Franklin noted with satisfaction that the child's French accent was already better than his own, and he looked on benevolently as Benjamin stuffed himself with the good things with which the tables were spread and even drank a little wine. The old man felt happy in the midst of his guests who had gathered in the garden-house—hot, noisy, and merry—talking both English and French, misunderstanding one another, and raising their voices in order to make themselves clearer.

It was a rather informal but very distinguished gathering. Apart from Monsieur de Chaumont and Doctor Dubourg, the publisher Rouault and Le Roy of the Academy, there were Baron Turgot, the young Duc de la Rochefoucauld, and the Marquis de Condorcet, whom Franklin held in high esteem as a philosopher, though he too was very young. And there was, of course, Monsieur de Beaumarchais.

Madame Helvétius had agreed to act as hostess, on condition that she should be the only lady present. Franklin suspected that her prohibition was directed against Madame Brillon, who, according to rumour, had dubbed her "the eternal thunderstorm." He thought it prudent to humour her, so there she was, looking pink and white, with her face carelessly made up, noisily happy and enthroned as the sole feminine element amid a multitude of males.

"Don't stand around looking so morose, Jacques-Robert!" she said to her old friend Turgot. "You surely don't have to wear that melancholy expression of yours on this of all days." Turgot, however, remained as taciturn as ever. Though he was convinced that mankind was moving towards the ultimate victory of the good and the useful, and therefore did not doubt the eventual outcome of the American struggle, he had learned from grievous personal experience that the paths taken by history were long and circuitous. The fight for progress brought bitterness and disappointment. Whether a statesman chose the right moment or not depended not only upon his judgment, but on the hazards of circumstance. If he found himself in a position either to delay or to accelerate the outbreak of an unavoidable armed conflict, he was no less subject to the whims of Fortuna than to the dictates of Minerva. Perhaps, brooded Turgot, it would have served the cause better if he had not tried to push through his reforms so rapidly. He envied Franklin his equable temperament, his ability to wait.

Captain Johnson, encouraged by Doctor Dubourg to refill his glass and tell his stories, recounted how he had captured a number of weavers' looms from an English merchant vessel and managed to tow the captured freighter into a French port. "I cannot remember its name," he said, "but it begins with Le H." He unloaded the looms and sold them under the noses of the French officials and the English spies. "It is an elevating thought," he concluded, "that in fighting for our freedom we Americans are able to provide the French population with cheap looms for the manufacture of articles of clothing at the expense of the English." His ruddy, tanned face expanded in a sly grin.

Captain Smythe, the other privateer, had captured two race-horses, which were not difficult to land, but prospective purchasers were dubious about acquiring them since the horses could be too easily identified. So they were dyed and renamed, one being called "Liberty," the other "Independence," and they had been entered for the next races arranged by Prince Charles. Silas Deane laughed at this story until his belly shook beneath its flowered waistcoat. Even Dubourg, who regarded everything to do with privateering as his own particular province, thought it amusing and found Silas Deane less revolting than usual.

Young William was listening meanwhile to Pierre's detailed account of the difficulties and dangers that he had taken upon himself. At least, he made an effort to listen, but he was more interested in the Frenchman's elegant gestures than in what he was saying. Others joined them, including Benjamin Bache, and the child stared in fascination at the splendour of Pierre's costume, the glittering gems he wore, and the lips which poured forth such a stream of eloquence. Pierre, who got on well with children, asked Benjamin what he was doing at school, and the oddly contrasted couple became engaged in an animated conversation that the others found vastly entertaining.

Fired by the attention he was attracting, Pierre turned to the onlookers. Having observed that most of the Americans understood French he kept lapsing into French himself, and was soon behaving as if he were in a French salon. Some of the others could not follow all the details of his pungent scandals or his witty epigrams on women and literature, and missed many of his allusions, but he continued to sparkle nevertheless.

He had started out in a rather uneasy frame of mind, for he did not know what effect he would be likely to produce among these Americans. When it became evident that they had taken to him, he cast off his sense of restraint and felt equal to the task he had set himself, namely, to show Doctor Franklin that he was being unfairly treated.

Franklin, for his part, had made up his mind to hide his dislike of Pierre, so he greeted him with an easy cordiality that was in marked contrast to the polite disdain which Pierre had found so aggravating. A weight fell from Pierre when he saw that the American was coming out of his shell, and, listening attentively to one of the old man's homely stories, he laughed appreciatively before proceeding to enter upon an analysis of the distinction between humour and wit, with discreet allusion to Franklin's special type of anecdote. Franklin smiled benignly.

Then, assuming a more serious expression, he inquired sympathetically after Pierre's young assistant, Monsieur Theveneau, who had sailed, so he understood, for America. Pierre replied that he was still without news of the ship on which Paul was travelling, and was not likely to have any for some time. They were both silent, engrossed in their thoughts.

De la Rochefoucauld had prepared a careful translation of the Declaration of Independence, which had been published by Rouault, together with a lengthy and well-written foreword, in time for the anniversary. Franklin was presented with a copy, and as he turned the pages of the handsomely produced little volume the young Duke's eyes were fixed eagerly on his face. He praised the translation, though his private opinion was that the noble phrases sounded some-

what flat in French, and then turned to Pierre and said he had heard
of the deep impression made by the latter's reading of the Declaration
in the park at Etioles. Pierre blushed, which was unusual for him,
and at that moment felt inclined to forgive Franklin for everything.
He regarded it as a happy dispensation of fate, he replied, and a
memory he would treasure till his dying day, that he had been the
first man in Europe to learn of the greatest event in the history of
the modern world and that he had been accorded the privilege of
imparting such a noble document to the most distinguished sons of
his own native land.

The thought of that day at Etioles put Dubourg in an ill humour.
It annoyed him intensely that Franklin should pay such a marked
compliment to an opportunist and profiteer like this man Caron, who
had snatched the *Orfraye* from under his very nose while he had
to carry on the fight for the good cause with inadequately equipped
privateers. Then he remembered how heartily Franklin had laughed
at the fable of the horse-fly and the coach, and he no longer took it
amiss that his wise friend should amuse himself by offering the
fly a little sugar.

The Marquis de Condorcet remarked, "By what feelings must you
not be stirred, sir, when you peruse this work of yours which has
changed the world."

To which Franklin replied tranquilly, "I regret the opinion, which
appears to be widespread in this country, that it was I who drafted
the Declaration. That is not so, as I have stated on a number of occasions. I would beg you, gentlemen, to accept my assurance and to believe me when I say that the resolution declaring the independence
of the United Colonies was moved in the Congress by Mr. Richard
Henry Lee, brother of Mr. Arthur Lee who is with us tonight, and
that the Declaration was drafted by a young colleague of mine, Mr.
Thomas Jefferson. All I did was to make certain trifling amendments
in the text."

Arthur Lee's lean visage clouded with annoyance at what he regarded as Franklin's overweening pretence at modesty, but Pierre
declared enthusiastically, "An amendment made by you, Doctor
Franklin, can never be considered trifling. In any case," he continued,
"whoever may have moved the resolution, the liberation of America
is your work. With all respect to Mr. Jeffersonne, you helped to draft
the Declaration and therefore it is your Declaration. The style of
Benjamin Franklin is unmistakable and can be recognized even in its
French translation."

Franklin gave up. He would never succeed in convincing these
Frenchmen that he was not the author of the Declaration of Independence, any more than he could manage to persuade them to say "*Jeff-*
erson" instead of "Jeffer*sonne*."

The Declaration, he pondered, would have run rather differently if he had been responsible for it. His own political views were also based on the ideas of John Locke, Montesquieu, and Vattel, and so far as the document's aims were concerned he was completely in agreement with Jefferson, who was a man of culture and an ardent advocate of progress; but he would have formulated both the general and the specific charges brought against the King in a calmer and more logical manner. On the other hand, a document destined for the eyes of the whole world ought not perhaps to be phrased too objectively. Ringing words, lofty rhetoric, were appropriate, and the Declaration was a capable piece of work. It was better adapted to the circumstances then prevailing than anything he could himself have put on paper, and it was fortunate that the right man happened to be available at the right moment when it came to the drafting.

He smiled inwardly as he thought of the debates that had been fought out in the Congress on the text of the Declaration. It had been a frightfully hot summer a year ago in Philadelphia, the afternoons were almost unbearably sultry in the State House, and the flies from the neighbouring stables kept on stinging and biting the legs. He still felt a slight amusement as he recalled how John Hancock and the tall, thin Samuel Adams, elegantly attired in thick garments and their hair dressed in the fashionable manner, had suffered particularly from the heat.

He himself had sat next to Jefferson who was a poor speaker as his voice did not carry very far. Jefferson had had to leave the defence of his text to the other Adams, little John Adams, an honest, hot-headed man who had done his job well. The fat little fellow had bobbed up every few minutes and fearlessly hurled his thundering insults to right and left. Many of the members present had felt the urge to add their own ingredients to the sauce, not always to its improvement, and if the weather had not been so hot the debate would probably have lasted another two or three days and very little would have remained of the original wording.

Young Jefferson had writhed as objection after objection was raised to this point or that, and Franklin retained a strong impression of the tortured look on the face of his lean, lanky, red-headed colleague as his text was so cruelly plucked to pieces. The poor author had repressed the rage with which he was inwardly seething, but he kept his fists clenched and was sweating.

Franklin tried to console him, as was his habit, with one of his stories. It was an instructive anecdote, and he could not restrain the impulse to repeat it to his guests at the anniversary party.

"During the discussions," he told them, "a large number of verbal changes were proposed by various members of the Congress and Mr. Jefferson was not overpleased with their suggestions. As I was sitting beside him, I thought I would try to keep him in a good humour and informed him that it was my own rule never to draft a document that had to be submitted to revision by a public body. This was a lesson I learned from a hatter of my acquaintance. He was about to open a shop and wanted a signboard with a suitable inscription. The inscription he thought of was: 'John Thompson, hatter, makes and sells hats for ready money,' with a hat painted below it. He showed his design to his friends. The first one thought the word 'hatter' superfluous, since his trade was obvious from the words 'makes hats.' So Thompson struck out the word. The second friend thought that the word 'makes' might also be omitted. The customers would not care who made the hats. If they were good hats, they would buy them. So this too was struck out. The third friend thought it unnecessary to put 'ready money,' because that was the local custom anyway. Thompson made the further erasure. The inscription now ran, 'John Thompson sells hats.' 'Sells?' commented a fourth friend. 'Nobody expects you to give them away.' So 'sells' was deleted, and as there was no point in retaining the word 'hats,' since there was one already shown on the signboard, all that was left was the name 'John Thompson' with a hat painted below it."

When they had finished laughing at this story, the Marquis de Condorcet said, "It would be a pity to strike a single word from the Declaration. As it stands it is an exalted manifesto, a simple and magnificent proclamation of those human rights which are so sacred, yet which mankind has forgotten."

"I consider it an honour," replied Franklin, "to be able to emphasize before this gathering how deeply we are indebted to the philosophers of your country for their share in the forming of our opinions. This Declaration could never have been composed if the works of Montesquieu, Rousseau, and Voltaire had not been published."

Arthur Lee could be heard gritting his teeth. So the shameless old man seized even this opportunity to flatter the French, who did nothing for the cause except make empty speeches.

Condorcet, however, went on, "It is true that the rights of man had already been proclaimed in the writings of philosophers and were probably also inscribed in the hearts of honest men. But what good did that do? Now they have been incorporated in this Declaration, in terms that can be understood even by the ignorant and the helpless, and they have brought forth deeds which mere philosophy could not inspire." His words were simple, but he spoke with ardour and gazed at Franklin. The eyes of all of them were fixed on Franklin, and Arthur Lee choked with anger at the audacity of this Doctor *honoris causa* who was reaping the glory not only for the books of Locke, Hobbes, and David Hume, but for the deeds of Richard Henry Lee and George Washington.

Franklin raised his hand and said, "I had not quite finished, Monsieur de Condorcet. There was another great son of your country whom I wished to mention and without whom our revolution would not have been conceivable, namely, Claude-Adrien Helvétius. His philosophy did not remain without effect. No, Monsieur le Marquis, that you cannot say. The echo of his book *De l'Esprit* can be heard in the Declaration drafted by my colleague, Thomas Jefferson. The ideas that we in America are transmuting into deeds are those of my dead friend Helvétius." The guests crowded round Madame Helvétius, and she, without being in the slightest degree embarrassed, asserted happily as she stretched out her hand for him to kiss, "That was well said, Doctor Franklin, and it is quite true."

Franklin went on, "If any man not only thought and wrote his philosophy, but lived it, that man was Helvétius. He revealed the secret of us all, namely, that we are every one of us striving for nothing but happiness, and he ordered his life in accordance with this principle. Of all the people I have ever known he was the happiest. He won the handsomest and cleverest of women for his wife, and he added to the store of reason and happiness of his fellow creatures."

"Yes," rejoined Madame Helvétius, "it's a pity he did not live to see this day. I should like to have you both beside me at this moment."

Turgot found all this a little exaggerated and in not particularly good taste. He had never entertained a high opinion of the writings of Helvétius, and had regretted that the insignificant thinker should have been elevated to martyrdom by the burning of his books. He shared Voltaire's view that these books were full of banalities and that whatever they contained in the way of original thought was either false or, at any rate, problematical. In a rather acid, didactic tone he expressed the hope that the American example would stimulate the rest of the civilized world to reflection and emulation.

"If it is not stirred by this example," cried Condorcet spiritedly, "then the rest of the world will not deserve to survive."

The butler announced that supper was served. Madame Helvétius had arranged a choice repast, which had cost a pretty penny, though she made Monsieur Finck account for the last sou. The butler had later complained to Franklin, protesting emphatically that he was an honest man. When Franklin repeated this to Madame Helvétius, he commented, "That is what Monsieur Finck always says, but I fear he is mistaken." At any rate, the menu had been tastefully prepared and the guests did full justice to it, talking animatedly as they ate and drank.

They spoke at length of the Marquis de Lafayette, for interest in his departure had not yet died down. No news of him had come from the other side and the hope was expressed that he was celebrating the day joyfully at Philadelphia. They drank to his health.

Later on toasts were drunk to America and liberty. Mr. Reed, Arthur Lee's English friend, his gloomy visage twitching with emotion, cried fanatically, "May the freedom and independence of America endure until the sun grows cold with age and the world sinks into chaos!" Franklin was taken aback at this excess of exuberance and cast a look at him that was filled with mistrust.

"The resolution proclaimed in Philadelphia twelve months ago," said Condorcet, "is a splendid illustration of the Greek poet's saying, 'There is nothing more awe-inspiring on earth than man.' Think of the courage it took to resolve that the colonies should be independent. We are told that many of these men are prosperous, that it would have been to their material advantage if they had continued at peace with their motherland. Yet they have hazarded their possessions, yes, even their lives, for the sake of the spirit, for the sake of freedom. And to think that the resolution was agreed to unanimously, that not a single one of them held himself apart."

Franklin sat quietly with a look of benevolent composure on his broad face. What the young Frenchman had said was true. The Declaration bore a heading that it had been unanimously resolved by the thirteen United States, and that was no lie. Yet what difficulties and stratagems had been involved before unanimity could be achieved. One of the delegates, Caesar Rodney, had had to be fetched in stormy weather from a distance of nearly a hundred miles in order to ensure the vote of Delaware. The delegates from New York had abstained from voting. His own conservative colleagues, Dickinson and Robert Morris, had cautiously stayed at home. During the three days they were occupied with the patching of Jefferson's draft not only greatness and sublimity of the human spirit had played their part, but also heat, flies, sweat, carping criticism, and petty conduct. Yet there was cause for rejoicing and confidence in the fact that so many men had been prepared to sign such a momentous and dangerous document. "When we appended our signatures," he told his guests, "I said to my colleagues, 'Now, gentlemen, the die is cast. We must all hang together, or we shall all hang separately.'"

Once more they drank to the future of America. Madame Helvétius threw her arms around Franklin, hugged and kissed him on both cheeks, and cried, "In you, my friend, I embrace all the fourteen States."

"Thirteen," he corrected her weakly. "Thirteen, my dear."

The party broke up before their exalted mood had dispersed, the Americans, however, remained as if by previous agreement.

When Condorcet had expressed the hope that Lafayette was celebrating that day in Philadelphia the city was in all their thoughts, but they did not know whether the Congress was still there. And even if Philadelphia had not been evacuated for a second time, and even if the anniversary was being celebrated there with ringing of church-bells and parades and fireworks, it must by now have become evident to the citizens that their freedom was by no means secure and that much blood and sweat would still be demanded of them.

It had been tacitly understood that the Americans should not mention their anxieties while the Frenchmen were present, but they had all felt a desire to remain together afterwards when they could be among themselves undisturbed by foreigners talking a strange tongue.

Now they sat around, a little weary and as if embarrassed by the emotion they were feeling. Even the two sea-captains had become silent, and perhaps they were thinking that their exploits were not so world-shaking after all. They were all conscious of the fact that their compatriots were going through a hard time and that there were harder times still to come. Each of them was glad not to be spending the evening alone. They smoked and drank and talked of unimportant matters. And even Arthur Lee felt no animosity towards the others.

It was a relief when Franklin at last made allusion to that which was occupying the thoughts of all of them. He did so in his usual roundabout way and only said two words. Moreover, they were in French: *"Ça ira."*

☆   ☆   ☆

Only those immediately concerned were supposed to be cognizant of Louis's decision to accept Joseph's advice and undergo the operation. Nonetheless, everybody was aware of what was impending, and in Vienna, Madrid, and London they were waiting anxiously for the day when the expected event would take place.

Prince Xavier tried to persuade himself that he was in no danger of losing the accession to the throne. Never, he declared, would Louis summon up the courage to submit to an operation. He worked himself into such a state of confidence that he offered to wager twenty thousand livres that in a year's time the expected event would still not have come to pass. His brother Charles accepted the wager. If Louis were to sleep with Toinette, he said, there would at least be some consolation in the twenty thousand livres.

Toinette passed the period of waiting in her accustomed way. She danced, gambled, gave parties, attended other parties, and pursued her various pleasures in Versailles and Paris. When Gabrielle or Vaudreuil ventured to make a veiled reference to Louis's intentions, she angrily bade them be silent.

Then, following upon a sultry day in August, there came a night destined to be writ large in the chronicles of Versailles. During that night, when the clock struck eleven, Louis of France left his bed-chamber and proceeded on his way towards the bedchamber of Maria Antonia of Austria.

Clad in his dressing-gown he waddled through the corridors of the vast palace which his great-grandfather had built, the largest edifice in the world. Beneath his dressing-gown he wore a costly nightshirt; his bulky feet were shod with comfortable slippers. He was preceded by an aged lackey in red, white, and blue livery, who walked with stiff solemnity as he had learnt to do during his forty years of service, and carried a six-branched candelabrum to light the King on his way. In this manner Louis traversed the corridors of Versailles, agitated, perspiring, trying to attract no attention, tremendously conspicuous. The corridors were alive with servants, Swiss Guards, and returning or departing dignitaries of the court. Embarrassed by their presence, Louis decided to construct a private passage leading directly from his own quarters to those of Toinette, and in order to divert his thoughts from what lay before him he pondered upon the technical details. The passage would have to be underground, and it would be best to take it beneath the room with the œil-de-bœuf. Working out in his mind the various points, with a far-away look in his eyes, past guards who presented arms and lackeys or courtiers who sprang to attention and bowed respectfully, he trailed his unwieldy body towards the apartments of Toinette.

When he appeared, the ladies in the antechamber sank to the floor in a deep curtsy. Louis, blushing with mingled pride and embarrass-ment, said, "Good evening, ladies!" Fingering the pockets of his dressing-gown he found a *louis d'or,* which he gave to his aged escort with a "Take this, my son." It would have been unbecoming to knock on the door of Toinette's bedchamber, so he scratched at it with a comb and disappeared within.

Five minutes later a whisper ran through the Palace: "The fat one is sleeping with her." The whispering grew, floated along the cor-ridors, from room to room, and out through the gates. Ten minutes later it reached the ears of Count Mercy, the Austrian Ambassador. In another quarter of an hour Señor Aranda, the Spanish envoy, learnt the news. After a further ten minutes Lord Stormont, the plenipotentiary of the King of England, was aware of what had happened. Secretaries were awakened in the middle of the night, all three ambassadors, Mercy, Aranda, and Stormont, dictated their dispatches, horses were saddled, the letters were hastily perused and sealed, and couriers galloped by the speediest routes to the east, the south, and the north, changing horses at every stage.

On the following day those who were most closely concerned wrote their several letters. Louis wrote to Joseph, and in his overflowing gratitude he poured out his heart in German. "To you, Sire," he said, "I am indebted for the happiness I now enjoy." Toinette wrote to the Empress, "This day, dearest Mamma, is the happiest of my life. My marriage has now been successfully consummated. Though I am not yet pregnant, I hope to be so at any moment." Here she made a blot.

Toinette did not normally like to be alone with her thoughts. This time she remained in solitude, even after she had finished her painstaking letter to her mother, and would see no one. She sat in an indolent attitude, suffused with vague thoughts and emotions, and meditated on what had happened. It had been very dark behind the heavy curtains of the great bed, through which only the faintest of rays from the night-light had been able to penetrate, and in any case she had kept her eyes tightly shut most of the time. Her thoughts had been washed away by an overwhelming sensation, but vaguely she wondered what it would be like if another man had been there instead of Louis. She had enjoyed many experiences, but never the ultimate one, and she found that this was really less than she had expected. She was disappointed, but not sorry. In fact she was highly content, for now she had fulfilled her destiny and become Queen of France in more than name. She was her own mistress and independent. The stupid jokes about the "virgin queen" would cease and the fishwives would no longer split their filthy mouths with laughter. But what would her friends say, Gabrielle, François? Though she was a little apprehensive, her curiosity was pleasantly titillated.

Everywhere in the palace at Versailles they were asking themselves maliciously whether, in the event of Toinette's becoming pregnant, it was Louis or one of her alleged numerous lovers who would be the father of her child. Particularly spiteful were the quips exchanged in the apartments of Prince Xavier, though the Prince himself entertained no doubt whatever that the event he so much dreaded had in fact duly taken place. He even conceded that Charles was the winner and paid over the twenty thousand livres he had wagered.

Louis went about in an aura of doltish happiness, letting everybody see how satisfied he was with himself and the world in general. He indulged more than ever in the coarse, good-humoured buffoonery that appealed to him, dug his gentlemen-in-waiting in the ribs, or thumped them vigorously on the shoulder. On one occasion, noticing that a lackey was stooping to pick something up from the floor, he gave him a resounding smack on the backside, laughing uproariously, and a *louis d'or* afterwards.

In his gratitude to Toinette he was almost obsequious. Without her knowledge he obtained a statement of her financial situation, and though it startled him he paid off all her outstanding debts without a word. Toinette graciously accepted these clumsy proofs of his love and admiration, and treated him affectionately as if he were a big, awkward dog, not letting him see how disturbing she found his weakness, his unroyal behaviour, and his lack of self-confidence.

Hitherto he had been indifferent to her friends, if not openly hostile, but now he put in an appearance at the apartments of the Princess Rohan, laughed at the parrot's screeching, fed it with birdseed, and allowed it to bite his finger. Then he inquired amiably after the Princess' dear departed spirits. He was a frightful nuisance, and they were all glad when he left.

Another time he benevolently teased Diane Polignac. Wagging a roguish finger, he boisterously declared that he had heard of her amorous dalliance with the old rebel of Passy. Her response was chilly, but he ordered from his porcelain manufactory at Sèvres an elegant *vase de nuit* with a portrait of Franklin and sent it to her as a birthday present.

Even the Marquis de Vaudreuil was not spared his importunate affability. Louis seized him by the lapel, brought his short-sighted eyes close to his face, and graciously expressed his views on Toinette's proposal that Vaudreuil should be appointed to superintend her entertainments. His household budget, he explained, was a little overdrawn at the moment, but since he had had cause during the past two or three weeks to look on the sunny side of things he had decided that the appointment should be sanctioned. Vaudreuil replied with icy politeness that he was delighted to hear that the King approved of Her Majesty's choice, but he was uncertain whether he was the right man for the honour and had therefore begged the Queen to allow him a short time to consider the matter. Louis gripped one of the buttons of his coat and said cheerfully, "Come, come, my dear Marquis. Do not stand on ceremony. Take the post. You will manage all right. All one needs is a little self-confidence."

The Lilac Coterie found these weeks rather too much for their nerves. The only one who remained unmoved was Count Jules Polignac, whose handsome, brutal features continued to display their wonted complacence. Despite their pretence at ironic calm, the rest of them were worried, for now that Toinette had shared her bed with Louis they were afraid the two might be drawn together in mutual sympathy. And what would happen then to their influence over the Queen?

The ladies and gentlemen of the Lilac Coterie assumed a more aloof attitude towards Toinette, allowing her to see that she had done something which had raised a barrier between herself and her friends. Vaudreuil felt greatly tempted to confront Toinette with an outburst of scornful indignation, but since he could not do this he vented his wrath on Gabrielle. She understood her François and realized the reason for his nervousness. He loved Toinette in his way and was mortified that her buffoon of a husband should be enjoying what he regarded as his own rightful due.

Toinette sensed the change in her friends and grew uneasy. She did not want to lose them. She tried to have a talk first with Gabrielle and then with Vaudreuil, but they both were evasive. Her longing for their former intimacy increased.

Gabrielle was less concerned than the others for the material fruits of their friendship, she was deeply attached to Toinette. So she finally surrendered and responded affectionately to the warmth with which Toinette embraced her. Vaudreuil, however, impatient as he was, continued to hold aloof, and when he at last condescended to a *tête-à-tête* with Toinette he made things as difficult as he could.

They met in one of the side-rooms, which had witnessed many a stormy scene of assent and refusal, as Toinette thought this the best setting for their heart-to-heart talk. He began by saying that her whole manner and attitude showed that she had achieved the goal for which she had so long been yearning. She looked as shamelessly happy as any woman of the *petite bourgeoisie*. Toinette did not take this amiss, for his anger only proved how much he loved her. "At last," she said, "the stupid obstacle has been got rid of that prevented me from being really Queen. I can understand why you are sad, François, but as my good friend you ought to be glad, as I am."

"You view the situation from a rather lofty eminence, Madame," he retorted sarcastically. "I would ask you to employ the same calm judgment in considering my position. You will then agree with me that there is no longer any place for me here. As you yourself have this moment said, you are now in very truth the Queen. You are therefore immeasurably far beyond the reach of the Marquis de Vaudreuil. He can only gaze up reverently to the cloud which floats high above his head—and take his leave. I have the honour, Madame, to ask your permission to withdraw. I intend to retire to my estates at Gennevilliers."

Toinette had expected an outburst of wild derision, even perhaps of violence. If he had seized her by the wrist as he had done once before, she would not have been surprised. At heart that was what she wanted him to do. His cold irony and gloomy air of resolve sent her into a panic. This was no mere empty talk. He was really going away. She thought of his stormy wooing in that very room and of the haughty self-assurance with which he had even made her brother Joseph cut a sorry figure. He must not go away. She loved him. She could not do without him.

"You are talking pure nonsense, François," she protested, her mind in confusion. "You don't yourself believe what you are saying. You cannot leave us like this. I shall not allow it. We belong together, don't we, you and I and the Lilac Coterie?"

"You are mistaken, Madame," responded Vaudreuil in the same chilly tone. "I am looking forward to a period of quiet contemplation, with no other company but my own. The experiences I have undergone here recently are not to my liking. Please do not permit yourself to succumb to illusions, Madame. My presence in this room is not intended as a clever move in a game of gallantry. I have come to bid you farewell. Have I Your Majesty's permission to kiss your hand?"

"Please stop this nauseous joking," she implored. She was now seriously upset. "This is the first time for I don't know how long that we have been able to have a talk together and you do nothing but torture me."

"You have tortured me, much more, Madame," he replied. "In any case, Gennevilliers is not so far from Versailles. I shall occupy myself with literature and with the theatre. Perhaps, when I produce a particularly virtuous play, I may have the honour of greeting you, Madame, and His Majesty as my guests?"

There were tears in Toinette's eyes. "Do be sensible, François," she begged again. "Do not let that wild and bitter mood of yours run away with you. What has happened is in your interest too. I have told you so often that the moment I become the mother of an heir to the throne I shall be free, and I intend to keep my word."

Vaudreuil looked her up and down. "Madame," he replied, "a man cannot pickle his feelings as if they were herrings. Love is impatient of stipulations." Low though his voice was, it seemed to fill the room with its deep resonance, and there was that savage look about him with which Toinette was familiar.

She started back in alarm, but it was a sweet alarm. This was how she wanted him to be, for she felt that she could handle him better when he behaved thus. She sat down and began to weep.

"Now she's blubbering into the bargain," he said disdainfully.

"I thought I was doing the best for both of us," she whimpered, sniffing back her tears. "I felt so free and happy, and now you've spoilt it all."

Without paying much attention he paced up and down the small room. Then keeping at a little distance, he stood still and looked at her. "Tell me," he said, "when it happened, did you think of me?"

She did not answer, but looked up at him shyly with a hardly perceptible smile.

"That too," he burst out indignantly. "I won't have it, do you hear? That is more than my duty as a subject demands. I refuse to act as your emotional stimulant when you want to have a Dauphin."

She had ceased to be afraid of him, however. When the wild look came into his eyes she was certain that he would not go away and leave her. "Don't always think merely of yourself," she begged. "Think of both of us. We have been waiting so long. Now the worst is over. Please have patience for just a little while longer." She stood up and pressed close to him. "François," she entreated, "stay here, François. I must see more of you than before, now more than ever. Accept the appointment that has been offered you. You must, François." She thought of the effort it had cost her to persuade Louis to sanction the sixty thousand livres, and now she had to beg François to take the post.

"You are asking a lot of me, Toinette," he said, and she breathed with relief at hearing him once more call her Toinette.

"Yes, I am," she gently agreed, "but you have told me that you love me. Please accept, François."

"I do not say no," was his reply, "but neither do I say yes." Seizing her in his arms he kissed her, still resentful, but prepared to forgive.

☆   ☆   ☆

Pierre sat at his writing-table facing the portrait of Duverny for which he had fought so tenaciously and a model of the *Orfraye's* figurehead. Since the party on the fourth of July he was confident that Franklin had been won over. After all, he mused, he ought not to have doubted that men like himself and the Doctor were bound in the end to come together. He scratched the head of his bitch Caprice and said, "Your master, Caprice, has been an ass. The cleverest of men acts like an ass sometimes."

As Emile helped him to undress he remarked, "Monsieur had not been looking very well this week or two."

"That may be," replied Pierre. "I was probably a little overworked. But, I am now looking my old self again, am I not?"

Emile cast a glance at his master's naked body, handed him his nightshirt, and said in a tone of satisfaction, "Yes, Monsieur is again looking no more than thirty."

His plans for the house in the rue Saint-Antoine grew more and more ambitious, and when the architect Le Moyne pointed out that his projects would be expensive to carry out his objections were swept away with a careless wave of the hand.

Yet the situation of the firm of Hortalez had by no means improved. There was still no news from Paul. Two ships had returned after a hazardous voyage with ridiculously small cargoes of American wares. Not that Pierre let this worry him. He was convinced that it would not now be very long before payment was received, and he refused to be perturbed by the fact that rumours were again in circulation about the precarious state of the firm's finances. Even when he was shown a particularly spiteful article by the journalist Métra, he merely shrugged his shoulders.

It occurred to him, however, that certain hints in the article could only be based on information from someone closely concerned with the firm's activities, and this made him thoughtful. When he pondered on the various possibilities his suspicions soon became centered on one man, and these suspicions hardened into certainty. Lenormant was angry at having had his paltry quarter of a million flung in his face before the loan fell due. He was angry because Pierre was now on excellent terms with Franklin. He was angry that Désirée—

Pierre smote his forehead. He had not seen Désirée for weeks. Amid all his preoccupations he had simply forgotten the existence of the best and cleverest of his women friends. It seemed incredible that he should not yet have shown her his new comedy. All thought of Lenormant vanished from his mind in a consuming desire to talk to her about his play. It would contain a part for her, the role of the lady's maid Suzanne. The part was merely sketched in, but he was sure that he could round the character out successfully.

He went to see Désirée. She greeted him as if they had parted only the day before. Her pretty tomboyish face, with its alert eyes and slightly tilted nose, lit up with pleasure at his visit.

He told her of the party at Passy and of his assurance that the Hortalez undertaking was now going to bring in profits, in addition to assuming an increasing political importance. She listened attentively with a puckering of the brow that produced a vertical crease above her nose, but she did not appear altogether convinced. When he spoke of his comedy, however, she believed without reserve. She knew more about the theatre than anybody else of his acquaintance, and he explained to her without undue exuberance how far he had gone with the basic plot, discussed the various roles, gave his views on technical details, analysed the pros and cons of particular aspects of the action, and emphasized a number of points in the characterization.

Then they read the play. Indications were sufficient for Désirée. She interrupted often, asked questions, pointed out now a contradiction, now a weak spot. Only now, looking at Désirée, talking with Désirée, he saw how the lady's maid Suzanne must be: shrewd, pert, witty, the very counterpart of Figaro. So they collaborated at length, grasping each other's half-words, perfecting the content, eying each other merrily, fascinated by each other's inventiveness.

When she at last said, "Well, that's enough," he wasted no time in thanks but simply seized her, and she flung herself into his arms. They laughed and were happy.

Only afterwards did it occur to him that in the character of Count Almaviva he had drawn a composite portrait not only of Vergennes and other people he knew well at Versailles, but also, and above all, of his dear friend Charles Lenormant d'Etioles.

Abruptly he said, "I paid Charlot his money before it was due."

Désirée was silent for a moment, then she replied, "That was not a very wise thing to do."

Her relations with Lenormant had become even more complicated. His friendship was important to her because it helped her in her career, but she was also attached to him in her own way. She suffered from his difficult temperament. If he had been stupid, or brutal, or vacuous as were so many of her aristocratic friends, she would simply have slept with him and not worried about him any further, but she was as much attracted as repelled by the knowledge of human nature combined with a profound misanthropy that characterized the melancholic epicure. He was undoubtedly in love with her, but instead of enjoying his love he referred to it with a touch of gloomy cynicism, and when he embraced her it was with a sigh of regret at once more succumbing to the temptations of the flesh. Sometimes she found it difficult to control her inclination to tell him straight to his face how deeply she despised the pampered, aristocratic complexity of his nature, but she knew that her power over him had its limits. The man who had refused to take back the penitent Pompadour would not forgive her if she trespassed beyond the bounds of what he considered permissible.

She was apprehensive of the consequences that might ensue from Pierre's thoughtless wounding of Lenormant's sensitive pride, but she could understand Pierre's action. Had she not herself played the role of Angélique?

They dropped the subject and returned to Figaro. When she complimented him on the skill with which he had contrived the plot, he thought of his father and remarked with a smile that one must have had experience as a watchmaker before one could make the cogs fit into one another so ingeniously.

With her practical sense of realities she began to consider whether it would be possible to present the piece in the theatre, and if so, where and how. It did not take her long to make up her mind. "I congratulate you, Pierre," she said. "You are the author of the finest and most audacious comedy that has ever been written. It is a pity that it will never be seen on the stage."

Pierre had already contemplated the prospect that there would be insuperable difficulties preventing the performance of his comedy, but when Désirée gave such blunt utterance to his own premonitions he declined to agree. "A thousand times they have cried against me, *'never!'*" he retorted. "But their cries have only shaken the air."

Désirée was perched on the table, with a teasing smile on her pretty face, and he knew what was passing through her mind. She thought him a presumptuous braggart to imagine that he could ever produce his play in defiance of the powers that be at Versailles.

At that very moment when he saw her looking at him so sceptically, he resolved: Nothing shall prevent Figaro from speaking his monologue on the stage. I shall fight for Figaro as I fought for my vindication, for America, for the *Orfraye* and for the friendship of the old man.

His resolve stood so firm that he did not even put it into words. "*Qui vivra, verra,*" was all he said.

He at once began to make plans to overcome the resistance of the aristocrats. There was only one way in which this could be done. They must be turned into ardent champions of his play. "You shall see," he declared triumphantly. "Our aristocratic friends will themselves help me to put Figaro on the stage. Are there not among them men so arrogant and so affected that they even find an aesthetic delight in being mocked? They feel themselves to be so high above the multitude that contemptuous laughter in the depths below spurts into foam at their feet."

"A pretty epigram," commented Désirée, "but is it a sufficiently solid assumption on which to base a plan of campaign?"

"Yes," asserted Pierre, "it is," and he sounded so confident that she almost believed him.

She pondered for a moment, and then asked, "Of whom are you thinking?" He racked his brains, but said nothing. "Of Vaudreuil?" she suggested abruptly. There was something in her tone that made him prick up his ears. Had she started a love affair with Vaudreuil? In any case, she was right. Vaudreuil was the very man. He was cynical and affected enough to take an interest in a play for the very reason that he was himself the butt of its attack, if only it had wit.

"Thank you, Désirée," he said, "for everything."

"I like you, Pierre," she replied. "Both you and your comedy are inspired by such agreeable and unambiguous ideals—money, humour, intrigue, and liberty."

"Don't forget love, Désirée," he retorted.

☆   ☆   ☆

For days, and even weeks, after his *tête-à-tête* with Toinette, the Marquis de Vaudreuil was possessed by a mood of grim satisfaction. He had achieved his purpose. His relations with Toinette had been placed on a more intimate footing, and the influence of the Lilac Coterie was more firmly founded than ever.

Considering it advisable to appear less frequently at Versailles, he spent most of his time in Paris consorting with writers and philosophers to whom he accorded his patronage. He had a taste for literature and did a little writing himself, though he usually destroyed straightway anything he had written. It was the process of writing that amused him. Any desire to achieve an effect by a finished work would have seemed to him vulgar. He did not wish others to share the fruits of his intellect.

Once it became known that he was living in Paris, people thronged to his *lever*. On one occasion Beaumarchais appeared.

Vaudreuil was in a mood that morning to show Pierre that his friendship for a clockmaker's son was to be regarded as a favour which could be withdrawn at any time. He merely acknowledged his presence with an indolent wave of the hand, and when Pierre tried to address him, ignored him.

Pierre swallowed the snub. He knew that Désirée was right and that of all the influential people at Versailles it was Vaudreuil who would be most in sympathy with the glittering brilliance of the sequel to *The Barber of Seville*. It was only by eating humble pie for the moment that he could succeed in his plan to enlist the aid of the leader of the Lilac Coterie. So he refrained from betraying any sign of mortification, and turned up again on the following morning.

During the night the Marquis had thought of a *bon mot* which struck him as particularly witty, and he had managed to restrain himself from communicating it to anybody, so he was in a very gracious and agreeable humour. When Pierre informed him that he had completed the greater part of a new play and would consider it a very great honour to be permitted to read it to Monsieur de Vaudreuil before showing it to any other living soul, in order that he might enjoy the benefit of Monsieur de Vaudreuil's advice, his request was granted without demur. Vaudreuil recalled the pleasure he had derived from former readings by his "court jester"; he had a taste for first-fruits, and now that he was about to assume charge of the Queen's entertainments he was doubly interested in being the first to make the acquaintance of a new play by the popular author. He therefore asked Pierre to send at once for his manuscript, invited him to stay for lunch, and then, when the meal was over, reclined lazily on a sofa in his dressing-gown and commanded, "Now, Monsieur, let us begin."

The exultation of being able to fling in the face of this conceited aristocrat the most insolent truths he was ever likely to hear spurred Pierre. His voice, capable of expressing every finest shade of meaning, was more supple than ever. While reading he felt as if he were creating each part anew. He did not merely read, he acted. The comedy took on colour and visual urgency such as it could hardly achieve on the stage.

Vaudreuil had more than once amused himself with raillery at the expense of his own class, but he questioned whether he ought to permit the same indulgence to this fellow in front of him, this clockmaker's son. He wondered whether he ought not perhaps to tear the manuscript from his hand and stuff it down his insolent throat. Before he could make up his mind, however, he found himself carried away by the dancing flood of words. It was a coruscation of wit such as he had never heard before, and he could only watch and listen in helpless fascination.

Pierre knew that this hour would decide the fate of his play. Everything depended on the reactions of the man lying on the sofa in his dressing-gown. If Vaudreuil decided in its favour, then Paris would see *Figaro* on the stage. If not, then the play might as well be locked away in a drawer to await the verdict of posterity.

He could see Vaudreuil's face, a little below the level of his own, a clever face, haughty and fastidious, with the haughtiness even more marked than the cleverness. Gradually the look of arrogance faded. Vaudreuil knew what was good theatre, and resolving to cast his doubts to the wind he gave himself up without reserve to the enjoyment of the comedy. He sat up, jumped from the sofa, paced up and down the room, and joined in the action. "Once more," he cried, "once more," and clapped his hands as if he were in an auditorium. His requests for the repetition of a passage grew more and more frequent, and asking Pierre to turn back a page or two he took up the cues himself. They could hardly speak their lines for laughing as they acted together in this astonishing charade, and neither could have said which was chaffing the other.

"It's a splendid piece of work, Pierrot," said Vaudreuil still breathless with laughter. "It simply knocks you over. It will knock Paris, it will knock the court, it's the finest piece written by a Frenchman since Molière."

"Do you believe there is any chance of its being done on the stage?" asked Pierre.

"Well," replied Vaudreuil thoughtfully, "the fat fellow can't stand me. The fat fellow doesn't understand anything about the theatre and he has no sense of humour. It is going to be a difficult job. But that is just why I am going to try it. Leave it to me, my Pierre, leave it to me."

☆   ☆   ☆

Philippe Gudin cherished a deep veneration for great men. He liked to read his Plutarch and it had pained him to see two men like Franklin and Beaumarchais, fighters in a common cause, unable to get on together. A weight dropped from his mind when Pierre told him of the party at Passy and the reconciliation that had taken place between Franklin and himself.

One day in the tavern known as The Fastidious Catherine, at a table frequented by writers and philosophers, he met Doctor Dubourg. Dubourg was one of the very few men whom the good-natured Gudin did not like. Not only had Dubourg stayed away when Gudin had read to a group of intellectuals some chapters from his *History of France,* but he claimed to have performed services on behalf of the American insurgents that rightfully stood to the credit of Pierre Beaumarchais, and Franklin's coolness towards Pierre was no doubt due in part to things that had been whispered in his ear by his French translator and friend.

Gudin was glad of the opportunity to impress upon Dubourg the fact that his spiteful gossip had in the long run failed to achieve its purpose. After an eloquent description of the enthusiastic manner in which Pierre had spoken of the party at Passy, he suggested that Dubourg must have been highly edified at being privileged to witness the friendly accord between the two great soldiers of freedom, Franklin and Beaumarchais.

Dubourg grumpily recalled that Franklin had indeed favoured Monsieur Caron with a display of unmerited cordiality. He had foreseen at the time that his American friend's geniality would be misinterpreted, and here was the proof. This horse-fly, this *mouche au coche,* was going to be more of a nuisance than ever now with his humming and buzzing.

It was in his mind to tell this scholarly simpleton of a Gudin a few home truths, and one or two vigorous aphorisms readily occurred to him, but he decided that it would be wiser not to allow himself to be provoked into saying something of which Franklin would probably not approve. So he merely answered dryly, "Yes, I remember having seen Monsieur de Beaumarchais at that little celebration. His presence, like that of so many of his fellow guests, helped to stress the greatness of Doctor Franklin and the cause he represents."

Gudin told himself that the sour comment of this pompous pedant only went to show how deeply he envied Pierre. He sat at his ease in the crowded noisy tavern, undid the top button of his breeches underneath his waistcoat, took a gulp of the excellent vin d'Anjou for which The Fastidious Catherine was celebrated, and remarked that it was instructive to see how the two men, with their contrasting qualities, complemented one another. The learned, sober-minded Franklin furthered the American cause with his philosophical observations, the ingenious and active Beaumarchais by bold action. Franklin was the Solon, or rather the Archimedes, of the century, whereas posterity would probably regard Beaumarchais as the Brutus of their age. Furthermore Beaumarchais was not only imbued with the democratic spirit of a Brutus, he had at his command the brilliant, deadly wit of an Aristophanes.

Doctor Dubourg, however, was sick of Gudin's sounding brass and tinkling cymbals. His eyes, already growing dulled with the physical decay evident in the pouched, sagging flesh of his face, lit up; he snorted, took a pinch of snuff, swallowed a mouthful of wine, and declared sententiously, "It sometimes happens that an historian who is able to interpret correctly the events of the past goes completely astray in his judgment of the present. That seems to be the situation in your case, Monsieur Gudin. I should be the last man to wish to minimize the merits of Monsieur de Beaumarchais. Yet it appears to me by no means fitting that in our appraisal of what is being done to further the American cause his name should be mentioned in the same breath as that of the statesman and philosopher, Doctor Franklin. When one listens to such exaggerated appreciation, it is comprehensible that certain people should be reminded of La Fontaine's fable of the horse-fly and the coach."

Gudin thought for a moment that in the babel of noise he had not heard correctly. But there was Dubourg gazing at him maliciously with his little eyes and puffing out his lips in obvious enjoyment of his triumph. Gudin felt the blood rushing to his head. Breathing heavily, he loosened his waistcoat and breeches a little more and asked, "Are there such people, Monsieur? Are there really people who dare to compare the author and statesman Pierre Beaumarchais with a horse-fly?"

"A plain question, Monsieur, deserves a plain answer," replied Dubourg. "Yes, there are."

The two corpulent gentlemen sat opposite one another, each of them snorting with indignation as he took up arms in defence of an admired friend. The other occupants of the table had begun to notice the argument, but there was so much noise going on that they could not distinguish what it was all about. "Are you perhaps suggesting, Doctor Dubourg," inquired Gudin in a low, but wrathful tone, "that when Beaumarchais's name is mentioned at Passy they are reminded there too of La Fontaine's fable?"

Dubourg hesitated for a moment, then he thought of the *Orfraye,* which had been snatched from under his nose, and of the letter in which he had been jeered at so unmercifully, and he answered, "Yes, Monsieur. Certainly, Monsieur."

Gudin's shoulders sank still lower. Reluctant as he was to believe what Dubourg was telling him, he could see from the latter's demeanour that it was true. He prided himself on his understanding of the human heart. In the writings of Seneca, of Cicero, and of Marcus Aurelius, in the characters of Theophrastus, he had read many a vigorous denunciation of envy, of jealousy, of want of thankfulness, of the depreciation of true merit. When Pierre first spoke to him about the peculiar way in which Franklin was behaving, he had himself deplored the prevalence of that most detestable of vices, ingratitude. Yet the look of triumphant animosity on Dubourg's face, the evidence he had just heard with his own ears of the outrageous injustice done to Pierre by Franklin, these shook him to his very depths. Doctor Franklin, esteemed on both sides of the ocean as an exemplar of honour and sincerity, the philosopher of virtue and reason, had flattered his rival before the public eye and then, behind his back, stooped to venomous calumny. Amid the cheerful hubbub of the tavern Gudin sat with bowed shoulders, his plump, good-humoured face clouded; he drank his wine but could no longer enjoy its piquant savour. "If it is true," he said, "that the philosopher in his garden at Passy, the Socrates of the Western Hemisphere, has permitted Beaumarchais, the author and pioneer of liberty, to be so grossly traduced in his presence, then— I must assert this with all due respect—then he has behaved in a most un-Socratic manner."

Dubourg had carried off the honours of the debate, but he could take no pleasure in his victory. He was haunted for days by the memory of Gudin sitting slumped in his chair with bowed head. As a man of science he strove to study problems objectively, and he could not deny that there was a grain of truth in what the rather obtuse though well-meaning historian had said about Franklin and Beaumarchais. His famous friend had laid the foundations of American independence, but since settling in Passy he had grown incomprehensibly sluggish and could not even summon up an interest in privateering. No wonder that such inactivity should be open to misinterpretation. Gudin was probably not the only one who was drawing unfavourable comparisons between the restless activity of Beaumarchais and the philosophic indolence of Franklin.

When Dubourg bent his mind to a problem, he always thought it out to its logical conclusion. Sitting alone over a bottle of Corton and a volume of Montaigne, he meditated on the argument that had taken place at The Fastidious Catherine. There was some advantage to be derived from the fact that Gudin with his *pinguis Minerva,* with the adipose tissue that constituted his brain, should have taken it upon himself to belittle Franklin, for a light was thereby thrown on a circumstance which he, Dubourg, in his capacity as a physician had indeed noticed, but which he had been reluctant to admit, namely, that Franklin's vigour was beginning to suffer diminution from age.

Something had to be done. Fortunately, mused Dubourg, though he was himself scarcely younger than Franklin, he was still in full possession of his energies. It was up to him to spur on his famous friend. That would be a mission that might influence the future history of the world. Franklin enjoyed tremendous renown and widespread popularity. Remaining modestly in the background, he, Dubourg, must induce his friend to exploit his popularity in some momentous undertaking.

He pondered on the various possibilities, searching his mind for an important project that he could submit to Franklin. A number of ideas occurred to him, but each was rejected in turn. He drank his wine and read a passage or two in his book, meditated on the problem once more, drank another glass, returned to his book. Then he went to bed, still without having discovered the solution.

On the following morning he awoke, and behold, the answer was there. While he slept, the Supreme Being had whispered the great scheme into his ear. What an astonishing stroke of fortune. Now it was within his power, before descending into the tomb, to do Franklin a service in the cause of freedom which posterity would not forget.

He ordered his carriage and set out on his way to Passy.

☆   ☆   ☆

At that hour Franklin was seated in his study writing to his friend Doctor Ingenhousz in Vienna a detailed report of a meeting he had with Lavoisier, the chemist. Lavoisier's treatise on oxidization opened up new prospects in chemical science, and the supplementary information he had received from the young Frenchman was deserving of the closest attention. Franklin was passionately interested in the lucid formulation of scientific problems. But today his trained mind could not concentrate. He let his pen sink and gave himself up to brooding on matters that had no connexion with experiments in the combination of certain atmospheric constituents with certain metallic substances.

He was feeling physically fit. The weather was marvellous and he had been swimming in the Seine, and keeping his resolution to climb up and down the terraces every day. His evenings with Madame Helvétius and Madame Brillon were exceedingly pleasant. Yet his mind was not at peace.

Mail had arrived from America, and he had at least been enabled to envisage the situation clearly. It was not an encouraging picture. If the official dispatches from the Congress contained a note of anxiety, the private letters from his friends were still more gloomy. Washington's army was short of men. The individual States were not providing the contributions to which they had bound themselves, either in men, material, or money. On the other hand, many thousands of citizens were engaged in privateering on their own account or were serving in ships that were so engaged. Administrative and economic difficulties were piling up. The money issued by the Congress was either only accepted at a high discount or not accepted in payment at all. There were incessant disputes between the States, confidence in final victory was melting away, and everything appeared to be disintegrating. If Franklin did not succeed in bringing about an alliance with France very soon, so his friends wrote to him, help would arrive too late.

One of the letters was from his daughter Sally. When the Congress had taken refuge at Baltimore, she and her husband, Richard Bache, had also fled and evacuated the Doctor's library. With the return of the Congress to Philadelphia they too had gone back to the house in Market Street with the books, pictures, and other chattels that her father treasured. Now, she wrote, it was rumoured that the city was again in danger. The Shippens, the Kearsleys, the Stansburys, and other Tories were once more raising their heads, while many of the Republicans were disposing of their properties far below value and were either preparing to fly or had already taken flight. This time, however, she was going to stay, and she proposed to keep her father's possessions in the house, for she was confident that everything would be all right.

Franklin thought of his daughter Sally, with her fair hair and robust, buxom figure, and the way she bustled about tackling her various tasks with her large, capable hands. She was a woman of sound common sense, and neither she nor her husband lacked courage. They had the bravery that goes with a want of imagination, but for that very reason their decision to stay was no proof that Philadelphia was free from danger.

His heart was saddened at the thought of the city he loved. It was the largest in America, yet comparatively small. Paris was more than twenty times the size. Philadelphia still bore a rural aspect, few of its streets were paved, and there were more gardens and green fields than built-up area, but it was a handsome, colourful city, sound and solid. Most of its inhabitants were comfortably off and one could see from their faces that they were contented with their lot. In Paris there were more people going about in silks and brocade, but it was best not to look too close, otherwise one saw that they were wearing the cast-off garments of the privileged classes that had been passed on to poorer compatriots. There was no such whitewashed poverty to be seen in Philadelphia. There were fewer carriages, it was true. Anyone who was too lazy to walk, as he was, used a sedan chair. On the other hand there was less dirt and privation, and a complete absence of the crooked alleys, stink, and swarming misery that he had observed in so many quarters of Paris. Even a poor man could live in the midst of gardens, as he did in Passy. It was hard for his friends to have to abandon their beautiful home town. It was hard for him, sitting so far away, to have to picture the possibility that English officers might be parading along Market Street or the redcoats and loutish Hessians swaggering in James's Coffee-House, at the City Tavern, or the bar of The Indian Queen. His old heart was filled with wrath at the prospect, and the sacks of buckwheat and maize flour that Sally had sent him so that he could enjoy his favourite dish did little to mitigate his chagrin.

Franklin had persuaded himself that he had grown wise with age and resigned to the gradualness of historical progress. Yet his patience did not penetrate deeply and the long ordeal of waiting was a long-drawn-out torment. The sands of his life were running out, but the cause to which he had dedicated the remainder of his days was not being advanced. He felt like Saint George in the picture, riding and riding yet never getting any further. It was true that he entertained no doubt of the final victory. America's independence was guaranteed by history and he had been permitted to make his own contribution to the eventual outcome. He had seen the promised land, but he feared that he would die without having entered into it.

It was a Franklin obsessed by unwelcome thoughts like these that Doctor Dubourg found when he came fussing in with an air of importance to submit the scheme that had occurred to him overnight.

They had, so he explained, been neglecting their chief asset. They had been allowing their capital to lie fallow.

"To what capital are you referring?" Franklin inquired.

"Your popularity," cried Dubourg triumphantly, and he pointed with his cane at Franklin. Ignoring the latter's sceptical smile, he proceeded to elaborate his views. If the alliance with the United States had not yet been concluded, the reason, as everybody knew, was to be found in the King's resistance to the pressure put upon him by his Ministers. Hitherto negotiations had been conducted only with the Ministers, but though these were favourably disposed they were unable to overcome the King's obduracy. There was only one person who could do that, namely, *l'Autrichienne,* Marie-Antoinette. Franklin must try to win her over to the American cause. The least he could do was to have a talk with her.

Franklin gazed searchingly at Dubourg. Then he replied amiably, "My dear old friend, you had better stick to your privateering."

Dubourg refused to be disconcerted, but went on to demonstrate the soundness of his plan. He had spent his whole life in Paris and understood the mentality of Versailles. If there was one thing that the court, and especially the Lilac Coterie, had set up as its idol, it was fashion. "You are now the fashion, Doctor Franklin," he declared with emphasis. "You must endeavour to arrange a meeting with the Queen. You will see that it will pay."

"There you go again, my romantic friend," replied Franklin good-humouredly. "You may perhaps recall that it was not possible even to arrange a meeting with the liberal Emperor Joseph."

"Toinette is a woman," insisted Dubourg. "She is not interested in politics. She is interested only in fashion."

"It is easy to talk of seeing the Queen," said Franklin, shaking his head. "The American commissioners may be popular in Paris, but at

court they hold their noses at thought of us. If I want to call upon
Monsieur de Vergennes, or even Monsieur de Gérard, I have to mount
the backstairs."

A sly smile appeared on Dubourg's sagging features. "How would
it be," he suggested, "if you were to meet the Queen by way of the
backstairs? According to my information, Louis has only recently
consummated his marriage. Marie-Antoinette has just entered upon
her womanhood. She is in a phase of life when women tend to be
emotional and easily tempted to indulge their idiosyncracies. At the
court of Versailles many things are possible. Listen just this once to
my advice, I conjure you, my very esteemed friend. Believe me, the
wisest course is to take the cow by the horns."

Petty intrigues such as Dubourg was trying to urge upon him were
foreign to Franklin's temperament. He believed in the immanent significance of history, and it seemed to him absurd to attempt to influence the course of events by childish manœuvres like the one
hatched out in the exuberant imagination of his old friend, who, alas,
appeared rapidly to be growing senile. Dubourg's scheme was probably no more than an idle notion that could not be put into practice,
and even if it could was hardly likely to achieve any effective purpose.
Franklin was accustomed, however, to examine an idea from all angles
before rejecting it. Could it do any harm if he tried to arrange a meeting with the Habsburg woman? There was, of course, no reasonable
possibility of his being able to "win her over to the American cause,"
as his naïve friend had put it, but there were very many influential
personalities who sympathized with America and were restrained
from manifesting their sympathy only because of the hostile attitude of
the royal couple, who insisted on the outward preservation of neutrality. If he were to meet the Queen and have a talk with her, the
mere fact might perhaps suffice to inspire the waverers to greater
boldness. Had not, as a matter of fact, old Maurepas himself indicated
that he was underestimating the practical use to which his popularity
could be applied? Why, indeed, should he not allow his capital to earn
interest? The military situation of the United States was unfortunately such that he could not afford to reject any project, however
adventurous it might seem, without having given it careful thought.
One had to grasp at any straw, even if it appeared in the shape of the
Devil's tail.

"Since you promise yourself such fruitful results from this idea of
yours," he said, "I will think it over. Whatever my decision may be, I
am grateful to you."

Dubourg had not yet left when Arthur Lee and Silas Deane appeared, and Franklin told them of the suggestion. Lee was emphatic
in his refusal to hear of it. The envoy of a free nation, he declared
severely, must not humiliate himself to the extent of flattering the

consort of a tyrant. Deane, on the contrary, was enthusiastic. It was incomprehensible, he said, that it should have taken them so long to hit upon such an excellent way of gaining influence at Versailles.

Lee flung in contemptuously that the unworthy project was doomed to futility from the very beginning. After their experience with the Viennese Pharaoh he could see no way in which a meeting with the consort of the Parisian despot could be brought about. Dubourg suggested that a Queen who was prepared to mix incognito with all kinds of rabble must surely be accessible to a Doctor Franklin. Whereupon Deane craftily reinforced Dubourg's argument with the opinion that, "If anyone can be relied upon to contrive such a meeting, it is the man who has so often got us out of a pickle, namely, our friend Beaumarchais."

Dubourg relieved his feelings in an angry snort. That was hardly what he had had in mind. Having indicated a way in which the coach could be dragged out of the mire, he found the horse-fly buzzing round his ears again. "You always bring up your Beaumarchais," he growled.

"There isn't anybody else," retorted Deane with a shrug.

"You see, gentlemen," commented Arthur Lee, "to what you are reduced when you even lend an ear to such undignified schemes. In order to flatter a female tyrant you have to enlist the services of an opportunist."

Franklin merely said soothingly, "If you want to turn a good bone button you must not mind if it smells a little."

Taking Silas Deane aside he asked him to have a word with Beaumarchais. "But please be careful not to let him know that the request comes from me," he added. "It would be unfortunate, after the fiasco with Joseph, if this plan too should come to nought, and discretion is not Monsieur de Beaumarchais's strong point. He must imagine it is a favour he is doing you personally. You can tell him it was just an idea that occurred to you."

"I don't like decking myself with Doctor Dubourg's feathers," objected Deane.

"Doctor Dubourg possesses the modesty that becomes a scholar," said Franklin consolingly. "I will take full responsibility."

"Very well," Deane agreed, but he could not refrain from adding, "I am glad to see that you too are beginning to realize the value of our *débrouillard*."

☆   ☆   ☆

When Silas Deane had his talk with Pierre on the following morning, the latter guessed at once who had sent him. "Tell me, my dear Mr. Deane," he asked him outright, though as if fully appreciating

that the matter was confidential, "do you come on behalf of our celebrated friend at Passy?"

Deane reddened, wiped the perspiration from his brow, and asserted emphatically, "Not at all. It was my idea entirely."

"A bold idea, certainly," acknowledged Pierre.

"Thank you," said Deane, feeling flattered.

Pierre was highly content, for this was glorious confirmation of
the impression he had taken away with him from the party on the
fourth of July. Franklin had realized that American independence
could not be attained without the assistance of Pierre Beaumarchais.

It was a tempting mission with which he had been entrusted. The
Queen was to be brought face to face with the rebel leader, however
much it might run counter to her instincts. That demanded the spin-
ning of an intrigue such as he had contrived in more than one of his
plays. He had already thought of a way in which it might be done,
and he rushed off with his half-conceived plan to consult Désirée, as
was his habit.

The two of them put their heads together, these wily, energetic
children of the Paris pavements, and considered how best to operate
their scheme against their haughty Versailles patrons.

It was clear that the first step was to approach Vaudreuil. He, as
the Queen's acknowledged favourite, could obtain her consent to
the meeting if he so desired. Furthermore, he was evidently prepared to accept the appointment the Queen had offered him and was
looking out for some form of entertainment that would create a
sensation.

Pierre went to the Marquis and told him that, since working on
his new comedy, he had once more fallen under the spell of the theatre
and had come to regard everything from the point of view of its suit-
ability as material for the stage. He had even been trying to build·
up a play round Doctor Franklin. The old man, with his brown coat,
fur cap, and steel-rimmed spectacles, was cut out for a comedy character. He would be a sympathetic figure, wise, patriarchal, and a little
ridiculous. Only it was confoundedly difficult, from the technical
aspect, to work out the plot. Though not usually lacking in invention,
said Pierre, he could think of no plausible way in which the protagonists could be brought together so that he might develop a dialogue
that should be at once witty and controversial. On the one hand
there was the old man from Philadelphia, on the other there was the
court of Versailles, and though the physical distance between them
was so small, they might for all practical purposes be oceans apart,
and he could see no possibility of bringing them together within the
framework of a play. It was a great pity that the unfeasibility of
providing a foil to Franklin should neutralize his potentialities as
a figure of comedy.

They were sitting at table. Vaudreuil appeared to have little appetite and to be listening with only half an ear, but Pierre as a student of human reactions realized that Vaudreuil's lack of interest was assumed. He was confident that he had him where he wanted him.

So confident was he in fact, that as he drove homewards he allowed his imagination free rein. In his mind's eye he saw Franklin calling at the house in the rue de Condé, sitting opposite him in the handsome study and tendering his thanks for the service that had been rendered. The old man would be ponderous, with a touch of mockery, as was his way, but when he got back to Passy he would dispatch a letter to the Congress in which he praised the efficiency of the firm of Hortalez and recommended that its justified claims, already overdue, should be settled with all possible speed. Then the firm's fleet of ships would come sailing back from America, each of them carrying remittances and loaded with an abundance of goods. He would at last receive the well-merited reward of his idealism and his dexterity.

Vaudreuil too was in a cheerful frame of mind. His court jester, the clockmaker's son, had provided him unwittingly with the idea for which he had so long been waiting. The impact of Franklin on the court. That would indeed be the sensation he wanted. A Monsieur Caron, of course, would find his path barred everywhere. Whichever way he looked he would find his path barred by insurmountable walls. But he, Vaudreuil, possessed the wings that would enable him to soar over any barrier. A meeting between the rebel leader and an influential personality of the court? Nothing easier. He, Vaudreuil, if only he wanted to, could arrange such an encounter, not with just *any*, but with *the* personality of the court.

He proceeded hilariously to build his bold and airy plan. It would be a joke worthy of Aristophanes, worthy of a Vaudreuil, a trick that would annoy the fat fellow and give the court something to talk about for weeks.

The setting must be a party at Gennevilliers, a masked fête so that Toinette could appear incognito. That much was clear. What he still had to think of was an adequate pretext for writing the old man. He must find a suitable play that had some connexion with the rebellion of these American Quakers. Rejecting one piece after another, he at last hit upon what he wanted.

There was an elderly dramatist of some repute named Antoine-Marin Lemierre who wrote plays in verse, elevated in style but somewhat tedious in content, that were remarkable for their defiant tirades against intolerant priests and despotic rulers. The scene was generally laid in ancient times and in some distant part of the world, such as Persia or India, and the censor, after some hesitation, had allowed them to pass. Then Lemierre produced *William Tell,* a play about the legendary hero of the Swiss rebellion. This was more than the censor could stomach. He declared that rebellious actions could be portrayed on the stage only after a chronological interval of at least a thousand years and if they had taken place at a geographical distance of at least two thousand leagues. The prohibition had created a considerable stir, the author had appealed to the King, and Louis had confirmed the decision of his censor. It struck Vaudreuil as a bold idea, not lacking in a certain piquant irony, to arrange a performance of this drama on his own private stage before a small and select audience. The parts would be taken not by professional actors, but by aristocratic amateurs, and he would have a good pretext for inviting both Toinette and the American.

He confided his design to his friends, Prince Charles, the Polignacs, and the Princess Rohan, explaining that it was planned not as a political demonstration, but as an aesthetic and social entertainment. There could be no question, of course, of taking seriously either the good Lemierre and his sturdy Swiss heroes or the homely patriarch from the land of the Quakers. They would merely be giving the rebels a friendly pat on the back and at the same time poking a little fun at them.

The others showed a lively interest in the scheme and were soon no less enthusiastic than Vaudreuil himself. The entertainment would be a masked fête, with the performance of *William Tell* merely one of many diversions, which were to include fireworks and a ballet. The preparations were to be kept secret so as to enhance the surprise effect. Prince Charles wanted at first to play both Tell who shoots, and the Habsburg Governor who is shot, but he contented himself eventually with the part of the Swiss patriot, the sinister Austrian being played by Count Jules, whose brutal cast of features was more fitted to the role. The only interesting part in the play, that of Tell's son who had the apple shot from his head, was given by Vaudreuil to a professional actress, Désirée Mesnard.

Diane Polignac undertook to arouse Toinette's curiosity, so as to make it all the more certain that she would accept an invitation when she told her in confidence of the plan and that Vaudreuil was wondering whether or not to ask her. Toinette understood at once that François wanted to demonstrate in this way the original manner in which he proposed to carry out his future duties at Versailles, and she was hurt that he should have doubted her courage. It would in fact amuse her to see the good-natured Louis thus harmlessly teased.

When she next saw Vaudreuil she said in a tone of bantering reproach, "What is this I hear, François? Are you not going to invite me to your masked fête?"

"Your presence, Madame," he replied, "would be an honour that I do not dare to entreat. I could not ask you to indulge in such an indiscreet act of courage."

"I do not remember," she retorted, "ever having given you cause to doubt my courage."

"I am going to produce a play," he said brusquely, "that annoyed the fat fellow intensely, Lemierre's *William Tell*. In view of your present relations with the King, I do not know whether it would be advisable for you to be present."

"I am obliged to you," replied Toinette, "for the solicitude you display in regard to my relations with the King. It is as tender as it is unexpected. I see no reason why I should not attend the performance of your *William Tell*. I am interested in Switzerland. In my little village at the Trianon I am installing a Swiss dairy, as you are well aware, and I find their national hero a sympathetic figure."

"The author of the play is going to be present," said Vaudreuil.

"What about it?" Toinette asked.

"There will also be a number of other interesting guests," he went on, "such as Doctor Franklin, for instance."

Toinette's arched brows arched still higher and a slight flush suffused her ivory cheeks. "What did I tell you?" said Vaudreuil with a smile. "It is easy to see that you are the sister of the Emperor Joseph."

Toinette was disconcerted. The adventure was not going to be quite so innocent as she had expected. Maria Antonia of Habsburg, Queen of France and Navarre, could not meet the old rebel printer from America. However boldly she might violate the normal ceremonial of the court, there were limits beyond which she could not go. It was not only that she would be embarrassing Louis, but she would be exposing herself to a sharp rebuke from Joseph, for though he had cut a sorry figure in his argument with François yet he was right in everything he said and thought about the rebel.

On the other hand, had not Joseph himself played with the idea of meeting Franklin? She was a woman, and had more right to do so than he had. In any case they were going to wear masks. If she conversed with the American at a masked entertainment, was that any worse than allowing herself to be addressed by total strangers at an opera ball, as she had so often done?

Vaudreuil was standing behind her chair, and leaning over the back he gazed down at her. The expression in his brown eyes beneath their thick black brows, the mocking smile on his virile features, told her more clearly than words what he was thinking, that she could talk boldly enough, but was not to be relied upon when it was a matter of incurring the displeasure of her husband or her brother.

No. She would not let him think she lacked courage. There suddenly returned all her angry resentment against Joseph, who had so often treated her to a dressing down, the eternal schoolmaster who wanted to regulate her life with that fat book of rules and precepts he had left behind for her.

Without altering his position, Vaudreuil said in a low voice, "Do you understand now, Toinette, that I wanted to spare you this test of courage? When people ask after you at my fête I can answer truthfully, 'Madame has not been invited.'"

This was too much for Toinette. "You are very impertinent, François," she rejoined. "I am hurt that you should have so little confidence in me."

It was the moment for which he had been waiting. "As you wish, Madame," he replied. Stepping forward, he bowed low and said, respectfully but with a mocking look in his eyes, "May I beg the honour of your company, Madame, at my little fête in Gennevilliers?"

Toinette bit her lip. Vaudreuil had moved back and was leaning against the mantelpiece, waiting for her answer. It was clear that she must refuse. She must not involve herself and Louis in difficulties, which might even bring harm upon France and the Habsburg dynasty, merely in order to prove François wrong and spoil his little triumph. It was easy for François, but she was Queen and had her responsibilities. She *must* say no. She *would* say no.

Vaudreuil still looked at her; his violent, fleshy face, filled with irony, seemed to say, *The sister of the Emperor Joseph!*

"I will come," she said.

☆   ☆   ☆

With a well-feigned air of unconcern, Vaudreuil explained his project to his friend and court jester, Pierre. "I would ask you, however," he commented, "to convey a cautious hint or two to your business friend at Passy that he must not overstep certain bounds. He will be expected not to reveal his recognition of the identity of the illustrious lady whom he will meet at the fête. I am anxious that our gentleman from the West should understand quite clearly that he is being invited to an agreeable social gathering, and not to a political meeting. You yourself, my dear fellow," he concluded graciously, "are, of course, also invited to witness the entertainment."

Pierre expressed his admiration and gratitude in suitable terms and offered his services in any capacity in which they might be useful. Inwardly he was filled with a grim delight. If the Marquis wanted to dance, he was sure that his business friend from the West would be willing to supply the tune, a discreet tune, but one that would be audible a long way off.

Though Pierre was well aware that he was not supposed to talk about the projected entertainment, he told Thérèse, Julie, and Gudin about it in the strictest confidence, not forgetting to emphasize the great service he was doing Franklin.

Gudin nearly exploded with rage. It was contemptible, he thought to himself, how these Americans were exploiting his noble, unsuspecting friend, only to jeer at him behind his back. Pierre was providing them with arms for the battle-field as well as diplomatic weapons, he was helping them to drag their coach out of the rut in which it had got stuck, and they called him a "horse-fly" for his pains. But Gudin felt that he could do no good by speaking, so he held his tongue.

Seated at his writing-table, however, he recorded in all the greater detail the events of which he was a living witness. Just as Procopius of Caesarea had worked in secret at his *Historia Arcana* with a view to exposing to the world the abominable truth about the character of the far-famed Justinian, so Philippe Gudin wrote down the true story of Doctor Benjamin Franklin and the thirteen United States. In vivid colours he painted a picture of his friend Pierre and the tremendous deeds he had performed. In ink of the deepest black he described the base ingratitude of the egotistic patriarch of Passy and his compatriots. From all the classic writers he gathered quotations to reinforce his indignation. He quoted Sophocles, "How swiftly doth the gratitude of man evaporate and turn to ingratitude." He drew upon Cicero and Seneca. And though Pierre was unaware of the malicious backbiting of which he was the victim, Gudin praised him for his noble bearing in that, as Plutarch had recorded of Alexander the Great, he "regarded with an indulgent eye the spiteful things said about him by those whom he had helped."

Such were the maxims and reflections of which the historian Philippe Gudin unburdened his soul as he set down in his chronicle the account of the deeds of Pierre Beaumarchais and the misdeeds of Benjamin Franklin.

☆　　　☆　　　☆

William entered the room while Franklin was sitting in his bath-tub, and from the look on his face he was obviously both pleased and impressed. "Look at this, Grandfather!" he cried. "It has just arrived." Seating himself on the wooden lid of the tub, he showed him an elegantly printed card. As Franklin carefully wiped his hands to avoid causing a smear, William went on, "It was brought by a lackey in olive-green livery. Do you think I might go too, Grandfather?"

The card was an invitation from the Marquis de Vaudreuil to a masked fête at his estate of Gennevilliers. There were to be fireworks, a ballet, and a dramatic performance. The motto of the entertainment was to be "An Evening in the Swiss Mountains."

Franklin was in no doubt that the invitation was connected with the adventurous project of the good Dubourg, and that same morning Silas Deane appeared with a wily smile on his broad countenance to talk about the illustrious personage whom his esteemed colleague would be meeting at the entertainment and whom he must be careful not to appear to recognize. He referred to the heroic revolt of those simple children of nature, the Swiss, under the leadership of their Washington, whose name was William Tell, and he did not omit to mention in glowing terms his friend Monsieur de Beaumarchais, who was so helpful whenever the Americans found themselves in difficulties. Franklin nodded his massive head, scratched himself thoughtfully, and commented, "Yes, the camel has once more passed through the eye of the needle."

He then paid a visit to Dubourg, who was now often compelled to keep to his room, and informed him of the invitation. Dubourg was happy and excited at having been privileged, before descending into the tomb, to perform such a great service on behalf of Franklin and America. He himself went into his cellar and brought up a dusty bottle of Corton 1761, of which noble vintage there were but two bottles left. In defiance of his physician's injunctions he helped Franklin to empty it, then went down and fetched up the other bottle.

Franklin smiled to himself, though not without being somewhat touched, at his friend's excitement. Nevertheless, he was looking forward to the meeting with a certain curiosity. He was not unused to intercourse with the great ones of the earth, and more than once had made fun of the ceremonial observed at royal courts. Yet now that he was to meet Marie-Antoinette he felt a little uneasy. There was only one way in which he was accustomed to converse with women, and he was not certain that his rather ponderous, slightly ironic gallantry would be quite in place with the Queen of France.

However, he had found himself in many strange situations in his time and had encountered all sorts and conditions of people. He had learnt to adapt himself and to make the best of men and events according to circumstances. He had mixed with candle-makers and diplomats, with printers, scholars, and slave-dealers, with writers, generals, farmers, and red Indians, and he had got on well with all of them. He was not the man to be put out of countenance by a person's outward garb, and he would no doubt strike the right note when he met Marie-Antoinette.

He had frequently amused himself by imagining how the happenings and personages of one age would appear if transplanted into the corresponding setting of another epoch.

Picking up his Bible he looked up the first chapter of the Book of Job and rewrote these verses.

6. Now there was a day, when the sons of God came to present themselves before the Lord, and Satan came also among them.

7. And the Lord said unto Satan, Whence comest thou? Then Satan answered the Lord, and said, From going to and fro in the earth, and from walking up and down in it.

8. And the Lord said unto Satan, Hast thou considered my servant Job, that there is none like him in the earth, a perfect and an upright man, one that feareth God, and escheweth evil?

9. Then Satan answered the Lord, and said, Doth Job fear God for nought?

10. Hast not thou made an hedge about him, and about his house, and about all that he hath on every side? thou has blest the work of his hands, and his substance is increased in the land.

11. But put forth thine hand now, and touch all that he hath, and he will curse thee to thy face.

6. And it being levee day in Heaven, all God's nobility came to court to present themselves before Him; and Satan also appeared in the circle, as one of the ministry.

7. And God said to Satan, you have been some time absent; where were you? And Satan answered, I have been at my country-seat and in different places visiting my friends.

8. And God said, Well, what think you of the Lord Job? You see he is My best friend, a perfectly honest man, full of respect for Me, and avoiding everything that might offend Me.

9. And Satan answered, Does Your Majesty imagine that his good conduct is the effect of mere personal attachment and affection?

10. Have You not protected him, and heaped Your benefits upon him, till he is grown enormously rich?

11. Try him; only withdraw Your favour, turn him out of his places, and withhold his pensions, and you will soon find him in the opposition.

He compared his version with the Authorized Version, and his mind was set at rest. He would be able to strike the right note when he met Marie-Antoinette.

☆ ☆ ☆

On the appointed day, which turned out warm without being oppressive, Franklin drove to Gennevilliers in the company of his grandson William. The boy, who was dressed in a shepherd's costume *à la mode,* looked well and was in a state of pleasurable expectation. Franklin wore his brown coat and looked the philosopher from the West, the Quaker, that the French liked to see in him.

His arrival created the usual sensation among the other guests, as he passed gravely through the throng of shepherds and shepherdesses, ladies and gentlemen in Swiss costume, gentlemen in dominoes, and ladies wearing masks.

Presently Vaudreuil's major-domo and other servants of his household came to invite the guests into the private theatre. The performance was about to begin.

Lemierre's drama seemed to Franklin a well-meaning piece of work, but rhetorical and divorced from reality. The Swiss peasants on the stage, portrayed by gentlemen in strikingly rich costumes, ranted of liberty in smouldering verses and thundered denunciation of the Austrian tyrants. Their charges appeared to him rather lacking in substance, and the general arguments they adduced would not in America have been sufficient to persuade a dog to come out from behind the stove, let alone to induce a farmer to leave his plough or an artisan his tools. While Lemierre's peasants continued to philosophize and bluster, Franklin made a mental note to look up the relevant authorities and find out what levies and taxes the Swiss had really been compelled to pay to the Emperor in the days of William Tell. That's the important point, my dear dramatist, he mused. The tempestuous flow of alexandrines, which was growing more than a little monotonous, was agreeably interrupted by the appearance of Mademoiselle Désirée Mesnard, in whose talent Franklin had already taken a benevolent delight at the *Théâtre français.* In her costume as Tell's son she was not only pleasant to look upon, but spoke her lines with a cheerful naïveté that did not prevent her from impressing upon the audience that the boy was really a young woman in disguise. She stood out from the other rather stilted figures of the play as a living character, full of vivacity, and when, towards the end of the piece, she gave utterance in resounding verse to the prophecy that the example of the Swiss Confederation would induce others to draw down the lightnings upon the tyrants, this obvious allusion to Franklin called forth thunderous applause. The Doctor stopped himself only just in time from joining in.

After the performance the actors, still wearing their stage costumes, mingled with the guests. A large group collected round Franklin and plied him with questions, some of them sensible, but most of them foolish. He was asked to autograph fans and dance programmes, and the general ardour for the American cause was only equalled by the general ignorance of what it was all about.

When Désirée joined the group, he paid her a compliment or two in his halting French. She replied that she was glad the Doctor had had an agreeable afternoon, adding with a roguish smile that she hoped he would find further cause for satisfaction in the course of the evening.

Pierre came up and praised the performance, though he concluded with the comment that in the reality of Doctor Franklin's presence even a good play like that of his colleague Lemierre paled. For how could the theatre compete with the tremendous spectacle that America was offering the world?

Franklin rejoined dryly, "Unfortunately the spectators do not pay for their tickets."

Pierre replied meaningly, "That is certainly true. Nobody likes to pay." Franklin saw his point and smiled understandingly.

Card-tables had been set up, and among the players Franklin noticed a lady dressed as a shepherdess in blue and wearing a mask of the same colour. He knew at once that it was the Queen. Though the upper half of her face was concealed by the mask, there was no mistaking the aquiline nose and short Habsburg under lip. The lady in the blue mask was not being treated with any special mark of respect, and it was clear to Franklin that a laborious attempt was being made to pretend that she was not recognized.

Rising from his seat, he strolled over to the card-table. He was politely offered a chair, but preferred to stand. The lady in the blue mask had glanced up quickly as he approached, but went on with her gambling and chattering without taking any further notice of him. He remarked with approval the delicate whiteness of her skin, the shapely contour of her arms, and her beautiful hands.

Someone explained to him the nature of the game that was being played. "Come on, sir," cried Prince Charles, in the tone of a gambling-booth proprietor at a village fair. He was still in the costume of William Tell and had set his crossbow on the ground beside him. "Try your luck. Place your stake, sir."

Franklin saw that the lady in the blue mask was looking across at him. Asking William to pass him some money, he put down a large silver coin, an *écu*.

"You must permit me, Doctor, to increase your stake," said Diane Polignac. "If you win, please accept this as a contribution to your great cause," and she laid down five golden louis beside his silver coin. The *écu* was lost, and with it the five louis.

Turning to William, Franklin said, "We will charge the *écu* up to the Congress."

He left the card-table and went back to his former seat, where the conversation turned upon the shooting of the apple from the boy's head and joking observations were made about the part that apples had played in history. There were, for instance, the apple in the Garden of Eden, the imperial orb of the Holy Roman Empire, which in German was called the imperial apple, the apple that dropped on Newton's head, and the poisoned apples used by the Borgias.

This reminded Franklin of one of his anecdotes, which he promptly proceeded to relate. A friend of his, a Swedish missionary, was once preaching to the Susquehanna Indians and told them a number of stories from the Bible, including Adam's eating of the apple and consequent expulsion from Paradise. When he had finished, an Indian orator stood up to thank him. "We are much obliged by your kindness," said he, "in coming so far, to tell us those things which you have heard from your mothers. What you have told us is all very good. It is indeed bad to eat apples. It is better to make them all into cider."

While he talked Franklin looked across at the lady in the blue mask. Vaudreuil was now standing opposite her, and at her side sat Gabrielle Polignac dressed as a Swiss peasant. The lady in blue was still gambling and chattering, but it seemed to Franklin that her thoughts were not on the game.

He was right. Toinette was ill at ease. She had proved to François that she did possess the courage he had so challengingly accused her of lacking. Having accepted his invitation, she had sat through the forbidden play and breathed the same air as the American rebel. Yet François stood there, paying little attention to the game and staring at her all the time in that impertinent way of his, obviously not yet prepared to admit defeat. Without his having to tell her in so many words, she knew that he expected more. What she had done was not enough. He was waiting for her to speak to the rebel. If she failed to do so, she would again have to face his cruel mockery next time they met, and her visit to Gennevilliers, which she had agreed to only after a hard struggle with herself, would have been in vain.

She touched Gabrielle lightly on the arm. "I don't want to play any more today," she said. "I am neither winning nor losing. Let us go across and join the group round your Doctor. I should like to have a closer look at him." She was quite pleased with herself at the casual way she had said this. Gabrielle smiled lazily and nodded assent. The two ladies got up slowly and made their way, again without any appearance of haste, towards where Franklin was sitting.

Chairs were brought for them by members of the group, which had now grown quite large. Pierre had again taken charge of the conversation, and the onlookers were all trying to act as if they were interested only in what Franklin and Beaumarchais were saying. Toinette, however, knew quite well that they were waiting to see whether she and Franklin would speak. Accustomed as she was to feel everybody's eyes upon her, she had learnt to maintain her self-possession, yet she was now more embarrassed than she had ever been in her life before. It was probably best to make some trifling remark to the rebel too, some quite conventional comment. Franklin was making it easy for her by refraining from turning his eyes in her direction. So she took advantage of a pause in the conversation to say lightly, "Were you sorry, Doctor Franklin, to lose the *écu* you staked at the card-table just now?"

They all laughed. Franklin turned his broad face towards her and regarded her benevolently. "An old man," he replied, "should rest content with his old vices and not try to learn new ones. But as I watched you playing, my beautiful lady, I allowed myself to share in your excitement. It was pretty to observe your emotions while you gambled."

Toinette's uneasiness evaporated. Under his searching, appreciative gaze, in which there seemed perhaps a touch of sensual enjoyment, she felt a pleasant titillation such as she had experienced at masked balls when strange partners pressed her body close to theirs. "Ah!" she thought to herself in amusement. "Our friend the rebel, who is looking at me in this way, is not so dangerous after all. I can twist him round my little finger."

"What emotions did you perceive?" she asked.

Franklin could feel a coquettish look fixed upon him through the slits in her mask. So he had hit upon the right tactics. This Queen was a woman such as he had met by the hundred in France. She was a little feather-headed and talked foolishly, but she did so with charm. In any case, he would treat this Queen in the way all the other women seemed to like, continuing to act the role of a half fatherly, half gallant old gentleman paying respectful, though slightly ironic, court to a pretty female.

"It is not a bad sign," he said sententiously, "when a woman occasionally indulges her inclinations and gambles a little. If one is tolerant towards oneself, one will also be tolerant to others."

"Do you think I am tolerant?" asked Toinette.

Franklin regarded her affably. "It is not any easier to see inside a human being than it is to see inside a melon," he replied, "especially when you can observe only half the face. Women are generally more tolerant than men, probably because they are closer to nature. It is a quality they have in common with the so-called savages. I must tell you," he went on, turning to the other listeners, "of a further experience of my friend, the Swedish missionary. He was once preaching to the Indians a solid, lengthy sermon, as is the way of missionaries, about the Christian truths and the parables to be found in the Bible. They listened to him attentively and when he had finished, like the well-bred people they are, they showed their gratitude by relating some of their own legends. Their stories were not so long as his had been, but they were by no means brief. Finally my friend lost patience and cried, 'Please stop! What I delivered to you were sacred truths; but what you tell me is mere fable, fiction, and falsehood!' The Indian, offended, replied, 'My brother, it seems your friends have not done you justice in your education; they have not well instructed you in the rules of common civility. You saw that we, who understand and practise those rules, believed all your stories; why do you refuse to believe ours?'"

"Excellent!" commented Prince Charles, and having hitherto tried in vain to find an opportunity of showing off his wit, he added, "And who possessed the better truths, your friend the missionary, or the Indians?"

"They both possessed their good half-truths," responded Franklin.

Toinette felt that his remark was meant for her. She was flattered at the attention he paid her, yet she was not altogether satisfied. He had let her see that he regarded her as a beautiful, desirable woman, but he was also making fun of her to some extent, and that she would not endure. She was not going to be treated like a schoolgirl. She would show the rebel that she was a match for him. "But you yourself, Doctor Franklin," she inquired craftily, "consider that you are in possession of the whole truth, do you not?"

He gave her a paternal look. Perhaps he could induce this woman, who seemed so anxious to demonstrate the intelligence she did not possess, to make some injudicious utterance that might assist the good cause, though she was so pretty that he almost felt sorry at the thought of getting her into hot water. "There have been times," he said peaceably, "when I have imagined my own opinion to be the only right one, but the older I grow the less do I indulge myself in that respect, and now I have travelled very far from the standpoint of the lady who once complained to me, 'I don't know how it is, but I have never met anybody who is always right except myself.'"

They were all listening tensely. Vaudreuil and Diane Polignac, Pierre and Désirée, each of them thought that he or she was the one who had started this interesting and exciting game. Vaudreuil followed with fastidious enjoyment every turn in the piquant passage at arms between the benevolent old rebel and the argumentative young Queen. Gabrielle had an uncomfortable feeling that Toinette was going to be worsted. "Wise as serpents and harmless as doves" was the thought that passed through her mind. Diane, on the other hand, watched with a certain malicious pleasure the beautiful and self-assured Toinette walk into traps of her own setting. Prince

Charles too found the situation amusing. He did not grudge Louis the harvest of trouble that Toinette was sowing for him.

Pierre observed with the appreciation of a connoisseur the skill with which Franklin led her on. He was playing with her as a great St. Bernard dog plays with a child, though the game was by no means harmless, while she innocently imagined that it was she who was playing with him. Pierre was happy, having brought all these people together and making them dance unwittingly to his tune.

In Désirée's amusement there was a grimmer tone. To her it was more than a game invented by Pierre and herself. Toinette stood in her eyes for the whole privileged caste of the aristocracy, and Franklin represented all the others, those who were born without privilege. In order to make life worth living she and Pierre had pushed their way into the circle of the ruling class, and were constantly forced to accept fresh trials and humiliations in order to maintain the place they had won. How she despised these great lords whose favour they courted. How stupid and blind they were, these great lords, in their arrogance. There they were, allured by Pierre and herself, smiling in their greed for ever new sensations, and vying to press into the hands of their enemies the weapons with which they would smash them. Young, daring, pretty, and lively, in her boy's costume, she sat at the edge of the large semicircle around Franklin, enjoyed the spicy and graceful sentences of the old doctor, and was glad to see what foolish part this proud pampered Queen was playing.

Toinette herself realized that the suavity with which Franklin was parrying her questions was putting her at a disadvantage, and she tried to think of something that would get below his guard. "Since you regard your own truths as only half-truths, Doctor Franklin," she said challengingly, "you probably also consider yourself only half a rebel?"

Franklin turned to face her directly, both surprised and amused. "A rebel?" he exclaimed good-humouredly. "I, a rebel? Do I look like one? Who told you so?" Then changing the subject abruptly, he went on, "How wonderfully that coiffure suits you. It brings out the lustrous purity of your brow. Will you not enlighten an ignorant foreigner as to what you call this style of hairdressing?"

Everyone breathed a sigh of relief at the tact with which he had trod out the fire before it had time to spread. Before Toinette could reply, Gabrielle said, "It is called the *coiffure Quès-a co,* Doctor Franklin."

And Désirée interjected, *"Quès-a co* means 'What is that? What does it signify?' It was a saying used by Monsieur de Beaumarchais in one of his brochures to make fun of the Provençal dialect of a clumsy adversary."

"Thank you, Mademoiselle," he responded, and with a slight bow to Pierre he added, "I see that you know how to appreciate literature in France."

"He is not going to escape as cheaply as all that," thought Toinette, and in a sweet voice she asked, "But you *have* rebelled just a little against your King, haven't you? Or have I been wrongly informed?"

"I think, Madame 'Quès-a co,'" he replied courteously, "that your information is not quite correct. There are many people who are under the impression that it is the King of England who has rebelled against us, not we against him."

The situation was threatening to get of hand, and Vaudreuil prepared to intervene, but Gabrielle anticipated him with the remark, "You have said such nice things about Madame 'Quès-a co's' coiffure, Doctor Franklin. Won't you tell the rest of us what you think of our costumes?"

Toinette, however, was not to be deterred. She had forgotten that she was the Queen and this old man the envoy of a rebellious people. She was merely a pretty woman who realized that a man admired her looks but did not sufficiently appreciate her intellect. "You are very learned, Doctor Franklin," she said, in the same low tone, "and I am sure that you can defend any thesis you wish to, whether it is true or false, far better than a mere ignorant woman. But do you not, in your heart of hearts, admit that the King of England after all has the divine right to issue orders to his colonies?" She spoke with a deep conviction.

Franklin had not wanted the argument to take this turn and once more sought refuge in evasion. "Madame," he asked, "do you really think that a man who looks like me can be a rebel?"

"Still waters run deep," she replied. "Why do you not answer my question?"

They were both talking in a quiet, conversational tone, but there was a tense hush, that was broken by a rather stupid laugh from Prince Charles who said, "Now this is really interesting," and leaned forward so that William Tell's crossbow fell to the ground with a clatter.

When the noise had died away, Franklin gave his reply. "Madame," he said, "on such a delightful evening and in the presence of such a beautiful woman I am reluctant to launch into a political lecture. Since, however, you insist on an answer, permit me to say that we Americans are not in principle opposed to the monarchical system of government. The idea of monarchy can, on the other hand, be carried too far, and that is where we disagree. A German professor once wrote to his sovereign, 'If God did not exist, it would be only right that His place should be taken by Your Serene Highness.' You see, Madame, on the other side of the ocean we think that is going too far. We believe that there is between a monarch and his people something like a contract. Your own philosophers, Madame, have taught us so. And we hold that the King of England has broken his contract. We can point to his having plundered our seas, ravaged our coasts, burnt our towns, and destroyed the lives of our people. That, we believe, is a breach of the contract that existed between us." As he spoke, a compelling power seemed to radiate from his patriarchal countenance and the words of the Declaration came easily and without bitterness from his lips, rendering them all the more impressive.

Count Jules, a domineering figure in his stage costume of the murdered Governor Gessler, broke the silence with his loud, blatant voice. "If that's what you call philosophy," he exclaimed contemptuously, "then philosophy is sheer mutiny."

"One could expect no other opinion," said Pierre quietly, "from the dead Gessler."

Toinette's eyes had been fixed on Franklin's face and she had been listening to the sound of his voice rather than to the meaning of what he said. She was sensitive to beauty and harmony, and the Doctor's rare combination of charm and power impressed her deeply. "It is not so simple as you think, my dear Jules," she said. "What Doctor Franklin has been telling us is not without its dangers, it is true, and we ought not perhaps to be listening to him. But when one looks at him and thinks how much music there is in his words, it is difficult to believe, in spite of everything, that such a man can be a rebel in his heart."

Prince Charles and Lenormant stared at her in astonishment. They had not thought it possible for the daughter of Maria Theresa to speak in such a manner.

Franklin, however, gazed at her benevolently and did not attempt to conceal his pleasure. Sitting there in a state of eager confusion as she tried to put her thoughts into words, and now again as she meditated on what she had said, she made a very attractive picture. "I am honoured, Madame," he replied, "that you should believe me incapable of harbouring evil designs and that you should have an ear for the music of our American sentences."

As he drove homewards through the night he thought over what had been achieved that day. The Queen had said that there was music in the words of the Declaration of Independence and had indicated her respect for the leaders of the American revolt. That was of the greatest importance. It would induce many waverers to acknowledge their sympathy with the cause for which the Americans were fighting. One thing was certain. Saint George had begun to ride out of his frame. Both horse and rider were in movement.

Young William sat beside him, sleepy-eyed, happy. The youngster too had enjoyed his evening. Smiling, he now said, "Grandfather, do you realize who the lady with the blue mask was?"

"Well, my boy," the Doctor answered pleasantly, "who was she?"

"The Queen," William retorted triumphantly.

"Was she really?" Franklin smiled.

Chapter Three

A BATTLE WON

IN Louis's library Monsieur Pourrat, the art director of the porcelain factory in Sèvres, showed the King the models which he had designed for the winter season.

There were hunting scenes, a shepherdess and a gamekeeper, and an author reading aloud to a companion. Louis contentedly inspected the attractive groups, and suggested further ideas of the same kind, such as a man immersed in a large book, or perhaps a smith forging a horseshoe, in short, *genre* scenes from everyday life.

His eager discussion was interrupted by the appearance of Monsieur de Campan. The librarian whispered that Count Maurepas was in the antechamber and begged an immediate audience. Louis's brow clouded. Whenever he was enjoying a quiet hour somebody was sure to break in and spoil it all. With a sigh he dismissed Monsieur Pourrat.

Maurepas entered in full rig, looking very grave. Early that morning news had reached him of Toinette's incredible indiscretion, and despite a feeling of fatigue and a particularly troublesome attack of gout, he had immediately requested an audience.

"Is the matter really so very important?" asked Louis ill-humouredly.

"Unfortunately, Sire, it is," replied Maurepas. He expressed his deep regret at having had to interrupt the scanty leisure enjoyed by the King who, as he well knew, was already over-burdened with cares of State. Then, however, with unusually bitter words, he spoke of the Queen's meeting with the rebel leader. He did not omit extenuating circumstances, but he mentioned them only in order, with all due respect, to throw into sharp relief the unprecedentedly indiscreet conduct of which Madame had been guilty. It was true that she had not conversed with Doctor Franklin as the Queen, but as a lady in a blue mask, but unfortunately she had attended beforehand the performance of a prohibited play and malicious people might claim that there was some definite intention behind the whole affair. Nor could it be denied that her utterances were in themselves perfectly harmless, yet they would without doubt be subject to political interpretation.

Louis made no attempt to conceal his agitation. As the Minister made his report he breathed heavily through his thick nostrils and exhaled again noisily, his flabby face twitched as if he were going to burst out crying, and when Maurepas had finished he sat for a time slumped silently in his chair. Then suddenly, in a high-pitched voice, he began to rage at the Minister. "I told you so from the start, you and Vergennes. You ought not to have let the old fox come here. Now you can see what you have brought upon yourselves. The most dangerous of our enemies is living here among us. I am being badly advised. Everybody is giving me bad advice. Why don't you say something?"

While he was being thus upbraided, Maurepas continued to maintain his dignified attitude. "The reasons, Sire," he replied in a tone of marked calm, "which argued in favour of our allowing Doctor Franklin to reside in Paris, and which Count Vergennes and I had the honour at the time of submitting for your consideration; these reasons are no less valid today than they were then. Our refusal to grant this permission to a great scholar, who is moreover a member of our Academy, would have been tantamount to taking sides in the conflict between England and America. It would have been regarded in Philadelphia as a hostile act and would have stirred up bad blood not only in France, but throughout Europe. Doctor Franklin is, in any case, behaving strictly in accordance with the injunction we impressed upon him. He is living quietly and in a patriarchal manner at Passy, carefully avoiding any action which might tend to cause us embarrassment. It is not he who is to blame for the disagreeable incident that took place yesterday evening."

Louis refused to be appeased. "He may be a scholar," he said, "he may be wise, whatever you like, but he remains a rebel and I have committed a sin in letting him come here." A vague, melancholy association of ideas was in his mind. This rebel had even started to lead his wife astray, she had sinned gravely by conversing with the reprobate, and now she would certainly not find favour in the sight of Heaven and would not become pregnant.

"He is a knave," said Maurepas, "for all his venerable manner, that I must admit." The phrase seemed to strike his fancy. "Yes," he repeated, "he is a venerable knave. But have confidence in me, Sire. I may not be so venerable as Doctor Franklin, but I shall have no difficulty in outwitting him."

Louis continued to look glum. He had been harder hit than Maurepas had expected, and the Minister thought it advisable to offer him some consolation. He began to explain the measures he proposed to take with a view to preventing political exploitation of the incident. Quoting Toinette's thoughtless remarks, which sounded strangely desiccated on the old statesman's lips, he proceeded to analyze them. Madame had indeed declared that Doctor Franklin was not a rebel. Luckily, however, she had had the wisdom to confine herself to the suggestion that he was not a rebel at heart. In other words, she had not expressed any judgment on Franklin's actions, but merely on his feelings, and this was necessarily and of deliberate intention nothing more than a statement of opinion, since nobody could look into a person's heart, neither a politician nor a journalist, but only God. Furthermore, Madame had said there was music in his sentences. That sounded serious, since he had been speaking of the American doctrine of rebellion, but if one studied the remark more closely it really turned out to be quite harmless. It obviously referred only to the form in which the American principles had been expressed, and it was therefore clear that Madame's pronouncement must be regarded as an aesthetic verdict, not a political one.

Louis listened abstractedly to his mentor's lucid analysis. Maurepas might twist and turn Toinette's words as much as he liked, but there was no doubt that they were ominous. He brooded over his unhappy lot. Was he the only person at Versailles with eyes to see? Were all the others blind and wicked? Did they not realize whither their thoughtless tongues and actions were leading them? Their very existence depended on the monarchy. The monarchy represented the ground on which they stood and the air they breathed. Yet they were doing all they could to destroy it.

Louis was shaken to his depths. His little double chin trembled and he suddenly cried in a shrill voice, "The waters of revolution are rising and will wash away the oil from the anointed head."

Maurepas was startled. "But, Sire," he remonstrated, "Sire, what possesses you? Nothing is going to be washed away. It is all very simple. You will pay Madame a visit. You will have the goodness to represent to her that it will in future be desirable if she inquires the names of the other guests before honouring any gathering with her presence. That is all." His tone was unwontedly concise and authoritative.

With weary irony Louis replied, "Yes, that is all. But it is not so simple as you appear to imagine." He realized that the interview with Toinette could not be avoided and had expected Maurepas to insist on it. From the moment when the Minister began to speak of the previous evening's incident the prospect of the interview had been haunting him.

Maurepas went on persuasively, "Your exhortations will not be the only ones, Sire. There can be no doubt that Madame will be warned most emphatically from Vienna that her behaviour is contrary to the interests of the family compact. Nor can we hesitate to believe that the communication Madame will receive from Vienna will be couched in a considerably sharper tone than anything that you may say to her. There will be a formidable wind blowing from that direction." The thought of Joseph and Maria Theresa raised his spirits, and as he was feeling tired and rather ill he so far forgot himself as to let slip the remark, "Upon my soul, if I possess one."

He nearly bit his tongue as soon as he had said it, but Louis seemed not to have heard. He had picked up Pourrat's drawings and was looking at them mechanically, with unseeing eyes, putting each one back again methodically, and he took no notice of his Minister's blasphemous utterance.

Satisfied that he had made the criminal thoughtlessness of *l'Autrichienne* sufficiently clear to the King, Maurepas requested permission to withdraw and departed to nurse his gout.

Louis, however, had not missed the remark and it annoyed him. He had long been aware that his chief adviser's attitude to religion left a great deal to be desired, and he felt that he ought to dismiss him, but he could not think of a suitable successor. He continued to stare glumly at the vacant chair.

A renewed surge of anger at Toinette welled up in him. He rose with a view to confronting her at once while his rage was still hot.

Yet before he reached the door his mind conjured up a vision of the scene that lay ahead. Toinette would stand there, her face twitching with fury, unable to grasp what the fuss was all about, and if one thing was certain it was that she would not yield. She was strong-willed, with that Habsburg stubbornness he detested, yet could not help admiring.

There was not much point in going to her now, without having prepared his brief. It would be wiser to put off the interview until the following day. He had better go out hunting this morning, as he had originally intended, and afterwards he would read a little and think the matter over.

☆   ☆   ☆

While Maurepas was demanding his audience of the King, Count Mercy and the Abbé Vermond were no less urgently demanding an immediate audience of the Queen. It rarely happened that the two emissaries of the House of Habsburg made a joint call upon Toinette. She knew why they had come, and was prepared for what they had to say.

The uneasiness she had felt during the first few moments after her meeting with Franklin had soon been dispelled by the praises of the Lilac Coterie, who had congratulated her on her courage. Now she was not only conscious that right was on her side, but convinced that she had performed a noteworthy deed.

The two gentlemen came in with gloomy faces. The Abbé, with his ugly mouth full of large yellow teeth, had no difficulty in looking severe, but Mercy, with his polished manners, had to make an effort and it amused Toinette to watch him.

The Ambassador began by referring to a more cheerful matter. She had told him of her desire to have in her bedroom at the Trianon some pictures she remembered at Schoenbrunn of scenes from her childhood. He had taken the hint and written to Vienna. Now he was able to hand her a letter from Maria Theresa and to inform her that certain paintings, two to be exact, would be arriving very shortly. Toinette was delighted and thanked him heartily.

Then he broached the subject of the fête at Gennevilliers, in the course of which, he said, an unwelcome incident had taken place that had given rise to numerous rumours, no doubt of an exaggerated nature. Toinette's expression changed to one of cold hauteur, but before she could reply the Abbé opened his great trap of a mouth and interjected, "We are really at a loss, Madame, as to how we are to explain this incredible episode to Their Majesties." Indignant at this blunt rebuke, Toinette raised her eyebrows, and Mercy hurriedly went on, "Would you be so gracious, Madame, as to give us your account of the affair?"

The little foot that peeped from beneath her voluminous skirts tapped impatiently. It was a habit into which she had fallen recently. "The affair?" she exclaimed. "What affair? You really oblige me, Messieurs, to ask myself to what you are referring." They both remained silent, though the Abbé's stern expression grew even more forbidding, so she continued with an air of sweet innocence, "Are you perhaps referring to the little conversation I had—incognito, Messieurs, for I was wearing a blue mask at the time—with Doctor Franklin? I hardly think he can be aware even now of my identity. I am sure he was not aware of it yesterday evening." As they continued to look at one another without speaking, she went on, "According to my information, Messieurs, my brother himself, the Holy Roman Emperor, entertained the idea of having a talk with the Doctor. And without a mask, Messieurs. He even arranged a meeting, though he failed to keep his appointment since he cannot always manage to be punctual. So surely there can be no objection to my conversing with such a nice old gentleman at a masked fête. In any case, it was the easiest thing in the world to handle him. If I had not known who he was I should never have suspected that he was a rebel, the way he told his homely stories."

Mercy was thinking that she looked particularly pretty and charming this morning, and that there was only one way to control a woman who was as foolish as she was attractive. She must be found a sensible lover who was himself amenable to control. The Abbé was thinking sadly and wrathfully that all his efforts and self-restraint for so many years had been in vain. But at least he now had a good excuse for giving her a piece of his mind. "You promised me, Madame," he reminded her sternly, "that you would behave discreetly if I refrained from interfering with your amusements. You will admit that though I regarded them with distaste, I did not reprove you on their account. And their name was legion. Yes," he ground out between his yellow teeth, "their name was legion."

The two gentlemen had arranged between them that if the Abbé should become too vehement Mercy should intervene, and he thought that he had better do so now. "It is not the Abbé's intention, Madame," he said soothingly, "to reproach you. He is only thinking, as indeed I am myself, of the anxiety that is bound to be felt at Schoenbrunn when they hear about this episode." As Toinette merely sat tapping her foot with an air of haughty unconcern, he went on to explain, "It is just because the Emperor avoided meeting the rebel that any friendly word on your part in favor of Franklin's principles will be construed as an indication that there has been a change in the joint Habsburg-Bourbon policy."

"A friendly word in favor of his principles?" she cried indignantly. "I? Who dares to suggest such a thing?"

"Everybody," snapped the Abbé brusquely.

"And you believe this?" she demanded angrily. "You really believe that I have betrayed the House of Habsburg to these revolutionaries?"

"May it please you, Madame, to keep to the point," he admonished her. "You have given utterance to certain expressions of opinion which it is open to the rebels to interpret to their own advantage. That is what causes such grave concern to Count Mercy and myself."

And Mercy added, "We are aware that the old Majesty, Madame your mamma, is oppressed by many worries. We are reluctant to afflict her still further, as we cannot help doing however we may qualify the report that it is our duty to send to Vienna."

Toinette's face had grown thoughtful, and for a moment it seemed as if she were on the verge of tears. "I know, Messieurs," she said, "that you are devoted to the House of Habsburg." But presently recovering her buoyancy, she continued, "I cannot possibly imagine how anything I may have said can lead to unfortunate consequences, and so long as you cannot prove to me that there *have* been unfortunate consequences you must permit me to be persuaded that I have not done anything wrong, nothing at all."

When Toinette was once more alone she gazed before her with an empty face. She thought of the lecture that was in store for her from Joseph and felt uneasy.

Then she picked up her mother's letter and broke the seal. "I have been informed by Count Mercy," wrote Maria Theresa, "of your wish to have some pictures of your childhood that you remember having seen at Schoenbrunn, and he has also given details of their size, where they are to be hung, and how they are to be lit. I am very glad indeed, my dear child, to be able to do you this favour, and I shall see to it that you do not have to wait seven years before receiving them, which is the time you have kept me waiting for your portrait that I am still eagerly expecting. I bear no resentment and shall at once forget my seven years of waiting when I see your dear features in the painting before me."

Toinette, vaguely distressed, thought of her ageing mother. Duplessis had been commissioned to paint her portrait for Maria Theresa, and everybody had said it was an excellent likeness, but the Empress had not been pleased with it. Toinette had not felt like sitting again, since she had so little time, and in spite of reminders from Mercy she had let things drift; but her Mamma seemed so bent on it that she would have to submit to the tiresome ordeal once more. It really was very nice of Mamma to send those pictures at once. As a child she had often looked at them. They were pictures of herself at the age of ten dancing and playing with her brothers and sisters, and as she grew older she had been fond of comparing herself with her earlier portraits. She was curious to see which of them Mamma had chosen, and she also wondered whether they would impress her as much as they had done when she was at Schoenbrunn. With her thoughts thus occupied she soon forgot the visit of her two guardians.

She thought that she would no doubt be receiving shortly a visit from Louis too, and she considered the clever replies she would give him. Nevertheless, she decided, it would probably be better to make one or two changes in the programme she was arranging for the twenty-third of August. This was Louis's birthday, and as part of the celebrations she had proposed to inaugurate the little theatre at the Trianon with a performance of *The Barber of Seville.* The fact that Louis did not like either the author or the play and would be a trifle annoyed about it would only have added a touch of piquancy to the festivities. After the to-do that had been caused by her meeting with Franklin, however, she felt hesitant.

When she saw her friends that evening, she asked, "Shall we keep to our original intention, and produce *The Barber* on the twenty-third?"

She had put the question lightly, and not as if there were a serious problem concerned, but Vaudreuil's face clouded. He had suggested the comedy for a very good reason. If the King attended a performance of *The Barber* on his birthday it would be much easier to persuade him later on to sanction the production of its sequel. So he replied sharply that the actors had already been told that they were to perform *The Barber,* and if owing to lack of courage the plans were now going to be changed both he and Toinette would be made to look ridiculous. Toinette hurriedly gave up the idea.

Vaudreuil, however, was not prepared to let her off so lightly. He went on to insist that now was the time to stick to her guns. She must not yield an inch. On the contrary, she must go over to the attack so that her meeting with Franklin would appear in its proper light as a deliberate first step in the assertion of an independent policy.

Toinette saw his point. She was developing a taste for politics. Joseph was right. The game of politics was more exciting than faro or lansquenet. She eagerly assured Vaudreuil that henceforth she would pursue a deliberate independent policy.

Suddenly Jules Polignac broke in. "An independent policy? Who? We?" he cried scornfully. "The others go in for politics—the foxes, our adversaries, Maurepas, Vergennes, and Necker. They are energetic fellows. They thwart us at every turn. And what do we do?" His friends exchanged amused glances at this unexpected outburst, but he went on, "Look how we stormed about that fellow Saint-Germain. We talked while he acted. Now the others—the rabble, the populace, the frogs—are being given the uniforms and the salaries. They are being made colonels and generals, while we sit here naked without a sou."

The members of the Lilac Coterie stared at him in astonishment. It was the first time anyone remembered having heard Jules Polignac talk for so long in coherent sentences.

"Those were good times," murmured Gabrielle dreamily, "when we chased Turgot out."

Toinette sat deeply thoughtful. Saint-Germain's name had been mentioned at a very opportune moment. She recalled all the harm he had done to her friends and the firm decision she had come to at the family dinner for Joseph to bring about the downfall of the stubborn, repulsive old man.

Her mouth, with its protruding under lip, curved prettily in a malicious, determined smile. She had found the right field for her activities. Now Louis could come and moan to her about the friendly word or two she had said to that nice Doctor Franklin. She would show him that this was merely the first step on a long road.

☆   ☆   ☆

On the following morning, in her smaller audience chamber, Toinette inspected the final model of the new Trianon. Gathered round her were the men responsible for the reconstruction of the château and the laying out of the gardens, including the architects. Mique and Antoine Richard, the horticulturists Bonnefoy du Plan and Morel, and, most important of all, the painter Hubert Robert, whose specialty was making buildings look old by adding touches of artificial damage.

The model she was now examining was the eighteenth, but it was to be the last and had been executed with infinite pains and ingenuity. The lake and the stream were represented by mirrors, the meadows and trees by stuffed and painted moss. The buildings were of wood and plaster. Every detail had been precisely reproduced, and with the aid of numerous plans, sketches, and coloured sheets Toinette was able to compare the three-dimensional model with the original designs.

Toinette had had a clear picture in her mind of what she wanted and now, finally, she was content. It was all as she had dreamed, extreme simplicity combined with supreme artistry. "You have done excellently, Messieurs," she congratulated them. "Our Trianon will be the pride of France. I thank you." She turned her eyes from one to the other with a radiant, childlike happiness in her face.

Then she added casually, "So I can rely upon everything being ready by the twenty-third."

They looked at one another, then at Toinette, and finally at Mique, who was in charge of the whole project. "On the twenty-third, Madame," said Mique, "the château will be ready for occupation and it will be possible to stroll about the park, but the Trianon will not by then be as we should like to present it to you and your guests."

Toinette raised her eyebrows. "But you promised me—" she said indignantly.

"Madame," replied the architect, "to us you are not only the Queen of France, but also our beloved and admired colleague. What was humanly possible has been done and will be done, but the date by which the Trianon is to be completed will depend not merely on our industry and our art. There remains, unfortunately, the question of money."

To which Morel added in further explanation, "We worked out our estimates very closely, Madame, and it was difficult even then to induce Monsieur d'Angivillers to supply the necessary funds. He will certainly not sanction further expenditure."

Though Louis had recently paid off her considerable debts once more, she thought it doubtful whether he would do it again after the Franklin episode, but she was proud of her Trianon and eagerly looking forward to showing her friends what she had achieved. There could be no more fitting opportunity than the twenty-third. "I have decided," she said haughtily, "to celebrate the King's birthday at the Trianon, and I have no intention of permitting the occasion to be spoilt in order that the Superintendent of the Royal Buildings may save a few livres. I will have a word with Monsieur d'Angivillers. But enough of these trifling details. Let us return to our work." The conference was resumed.

Suddenly the door was flung open and Louis came waddling in. Having succeeded in keeping his rage bottled up, he had waved away the lady-in-waiting who wished to announce his arrival, and now broke in upon Toinette's conference with a grim determination to take his guilty consort unawares.

He certainly did. His sudden appearance was the last thing she had expected, for her mind had been full of the Trianon and the coming birthday celebrations. After the first moment of astonishment, however, she decided that it was just as well, and the clumsy way he had interrupted her in the middle of a discussion of a party she was planning in his honour only helped to increase her self-confidence.

It was always a pleasure to see him, she said with a smile, though in a tone that left him in no doubt of her feeling that his behaviour was a little odd. But she was frightfully busy, and could he tell her whether his visit was connected with anything of a very urgent nature? The work on which she was engaged at the moment would, she hoped, provide him in the near future with a pleasant surprise.

The gentlemen had bowed low as the King entered and now stood at a respectful distance, smiling inwardly. Louis answered stiffly, "Certainly, Madame. What I have to say is of an urgent nature."

Toinette glanced at her group of experts, then at Louis, then at the model, and finally at Louis again. "Our occupation with the surprise that these gentlemen and I are preparing for you, Sire," she said, "demands our immediate and undivided attention. If, therefore, your communication is not *very* urgent . . ."

She stressed the word "very," without finishing the sentence, and gazed at him with an air of charming appeal, but with peevish obstinacy he insisted, "Certainly, Madame. It is *very* urgent."

She shrugged her shoulders and the gentlemen began to withdraw. "Please, Messieurs," she requested, raising her hand, "do not leave yet, but wait in the antechamber. I do not expect to keep you long." And they bowed themselves out.

Louis fixed his wide-set eyes on her, breathed heavily, and said, "Well, really, Madame—really—"

"What do you mean—really?"

"What have you been doing?" he burst out.

"What have I been doing?" she mocked. "I have been having a conversation with a great scholar. I exchanged a few words with him about trifling matters, as I have with other people on a thousand different occasions."

Louis, infuriated at such stubborn hypocrisy, began to boil. "Keep to the truth," he cried shrilly. "Do not imagine you can deceive me!

I know exactly what you did. You talked with him about politics. You told him you approved of his opinions."

"Please do not get excited," she returned haughtily. "Somebody has been stuffing you with nonsense. I talked with Doctor Franklin about music. I said there was music in his sentences. And there was."

Louis felt helpless when confronted with such a lack of logic. His anger began to evaporate and he lowered his bulk on to a fragile gilt chair. "Will you never realize, Madame," he asked sadly, "that you are no longer a child? You cannot allow yourself to indulge every whim. You are—"

"I know," she interrupted. "I am the Queen." She almost felt sorry for him as he sat there so gloomily, brooding on the wrong he imagined she had done him. She stepped towards him and touched him on the shoulder. "Do be sensible, Louis," she begged in a kindlier tone. "Come. I want to show you my Trianon." She led him over to the model.

Louis was really interested in craftsmanship and he could not help admiring the care and skill with which the elegant toy had been prepared.

"Is it not wonderful?" asked Toinette.

"Certainly, Madame," he agreed. "It is uncommonly pretty," and he fingered the various details with a delicate touch that was remarkable in such coarse hands.

Unwilling, however, to let himself be diverted from the purpose of his visit, he returned to the point. "Promise me at least," he begged, "that you will in future avoid such indiscretions." She again shrugged her shoulders, walked away from him, sat down on the sofa and tapped her foot sulkily. "Please do understand, Madame," he exhorted, "that these people are the arch-enemies of monarchy. You say he is 'a great scholar.' You talked with him about 'trifling matters.' You say there is 'music in his sentences.' That makes it all the worse." He began to rage again. "This man," he shrilled, "is a parasite in our country. He has burrowed his way in among us and is gnawing away our substance. He is our worst enemy, yours and mine. Not the King of England, but Franklin, that man Franklin. With our cousin at Saint James's we can find some common ground of understanding—with this rebel never."

Toinette looked him up and down as he squirmed in impotent fury. Her momentary feeling of compassion had vanished and left only contempt in its place. The letter in which she told her mother that she was going to bear an heir to the throne who would unite the Bourbons and the Habsburgs for ever, had been a premature boast. Louis had not yet fathered the Dauphin she needed to consolidate her position as Queen. It was truly time that she took a hand in politics.

"I find your attitude in the American question fundamentally false," she said didactically. Trying to remember as much as she could of the conversations of the Lilac Coterie, she went on, "Of course, we cannot publicly display our sympathy with the insurgents. Yet after all our essential interest lies in the weakening of England. It is a source of constant aggravation to me that the English are still at Dunkerque. Have you no blood in your veins, Sire? The very thought of it keeps me from sleeping at night. You really ought to pay more attention to my advice."

Louis was taken aback. It was difficult to reply to such an incoherent series of statements. "I wonder whether you have any idea where Dunkerque is," he said. Before she could reply he continued, "It has not hitherto been the custom for the Queen of France to intervene in State affairs." He was feeling affronted and defended himself with a deep sense of conviction. "Believe me," he assured her, "I know exactly what I am doing. I consider the matter from every angle, with my Ministers, with myself, and in my converse with God."

Toinette did not insist on the point, though she continued to speak as if she were laying down the law. "Though we have to remain officially neutral," she argued, "we should at least show the Americans, as I have tried to do, that we feel kindly towards them."

Louis made another patient attempt to explain his policy. Neither he nor King George wanted war. But the people of both nations were in a state of ferment, they were being stirred up by unscrupulous warmongers, there were questions of prestige involved, and if the governments did not proceed cautiously a conflict might spring up overnight from which there would be no way out. "England," he declared, "is anxious to avoid a war with us since she has her hands full already with the revolt in her American colonies. We are anxious to avoid a war with England because our finances do not permit it and we are militarily unprepared."

The final words of this logical exposition gave her the cue for which she was waiting. "If we are militarily unprepared," she retorted, "whose fault is that? Whose but that of your Minister for War? You have always talked to me so enthusiastically about the reforms of that obdurate old donkey. His reforms have caused my friends the greatest embarrassment and I have worried myself sick about them. Now you come to me and say, 'We are militarily unprepared.' So with all his reforms, which have demanded so many sacrifices from the country and from us, he has not even managed to reach the stage where we can look forward with tranquil minds to a war. Do you not think, Sire, that there is only one logical solution? The man ought to be dismissed at once."

Louis had jerked himself bolt upright on his little chair. His fleshy countenance was tense with wrath, and she realized that she had gone too far. "That is merely my opinion," she hastened to add, "but perhaps I have not studied the matter closely enough."

Louis, suppressing the anger that seethed within him, said as calmly as he could, "The equipping of the Army for a war with England is not child's play, Madame. It is not so easy as building a Château Bagatelle or even a Château Trianon." He noted with joy that his thrust had gone home. "The American Army," he continued, "is nothing to boast of. It is an undisciplined militia and very poorly equipped. If we become involved in a war with England we shall practically have to fight alone. Moreover, it will be a war that we shall have to wage only partly in Europe. It will be fought out mostly in distant territories. In America the English already possess armies and bases, and they have a fleet capable of transporting large contingents of troops overseas. So far as we are concerned—and I should like you to be quite clear about this, Madame!—it will be a matter of carrying everything, our soldiers and the whole of our supplies, across dangerous waters that are dominated by a powerful foe. Do you expect me to allow myself to be driven unthinkingly into such a war? I shall not do it, Madame. Never! And I shall permit nobody, not even you, to force me on to such a path."

Realizing that her plan to bring about Saint-Germain's fall must be put off to a more favourable opportunity, she decided to try another tack. "You treat me like a baby," she declared defiantly, "as if I believed every story people tell me, but I am better informed than you think. It is not true that the army of the Americans is not worth considering. The rebels are brave and have won a number of victories. I have forgotten the names of the battles, but I know that for certain."

"Well," conceded Louis, wanting to be fair, "to some extent you are right. They were successful. At Trenton and Princetown. But these were not battles. They were mere skirmishes, local engagements. In any case, these actions took place some time ago and we have since received reliable reports that things are not going well with General Washington's army. If we were not secretly assisting the Americans they would collapse at any moment."

Toinette felt that she now had Louis where she wanted him. If she could extract from him the promise she had in mind, she would be able to boast to her friends of a far greater victory than the dismissal of Saint-Germain would have been. Cautiously coming to the point, she asked, "So the main reason why you are unable for the time being to exploit the weakness of the English is that the military situation of the rebels is so precarious?"

"Yes," he agreed hesitantly, "that is one of the chief reasons."

Toinette prepared to launch her decisive stroke. "I tell you what,

"Louis," she offered. "I will promise in future to be as neutral as you and Joseph together if you in return will promise me one thing— that when the situation improves, that is to say, when the Americans have gained a great military success, you will conclude a treaty of alliance with them and open hostilities against England."

Louis perspired uncomfortably. "You are going too quickly," he said. "I must have time to think it over."

Toinette, however, was beginning to taste her triumph and was determined to press her advantage. "You told me," she urged, "that it is only the present military situation of the Americans that prevents you from helping them openly, and now you are trying to get out of it."

"Not at all," groaned the unhappy Louis. "You refuse to understand me, Toinette."

"I understand, at any rate," she retorted, "that you are not being consistent in your arguments."

"If the Americans," he said reluctantly, "were to achieve a military success, I mean a really important military success, it would certainly make a considerable difference."

"Would the difference be sufficient," she insisted, "to enable you to conclude a treaty of alliance?"

"Well, yes, I suppose so," he admitted unwillingly.

"Very well, Sire," she declared firmly. "That is agreed then. And now that we have made our political decision, let us return to our examination of the model of my Trianon."

☆ ☆ ☆

The twenty-third of August turned out very hot, and the select company of guests who had been invited to celebrate the King's birthday at the Trianon sighed a little apprehensively when Toinette proposed that they should join her on a tour of inspection through the park.

They soon forgot their fatigue, however, in their admiration of its beauty. There was none of the ornate and stilted style of the gardens at Versailles, which was ceasing more and more to appeal to contemporary taste. In its place they saw an artful representation of those natural surroundings which they had learned to appreciate from their reading of Rousseau, and they were duly ravished.

Dressed simply in a white linen frock Toinette led the way, gliding gracefully along the avenues, her lovely ash-blond hair welling from under her Florentine straw hat, her neck, shoulders, and arms dazzling white against the delicate lace embroidery. Accompanied by the host of architects and artists with whom she had collaborated in the planning of the Trianon, she enthusiastically pointed out its beauties, drawing the attention of her guests with naïve and undisguised pleasure to the various details or calling upon her experts to elaborate on the technical aspects for which they were severally responsible. The park contained eight hundred different species of trees and shrubs, which had been drawn from every part of the globe. There were red beeches from Germany, cypresses from Crete, cherry laurels from the Pyrenees and from China, locust trees from Virginia. Toinette stroked the cedars of Lebanon with her long, delicate fingers and proudly pointed out to Prince Charles how superior her tuberoses were to those in the garden of his own château of Bagatelle.

The aristocratic guests, who were normally so supercilious, found Toinette's ingenuous pleasure infectious. Prince Charles forgot to be insolent, Prince Xavier to be spiteful, and Vaudreuil to be arrogant. The most impressed of them all was Louis. What a miracle his radiant consort had worked. The Trianon was a tremendous success. He was happy to see that the others thought so too. And after all, wasn't some of the credit his, too? For who paid?

They came to the Chinese pagoda, where a merry-go-round actuated by invisible mechanism had been erected. The sculptor Bocciardi had designed the animals and birds, in the shape of dragons and peacocks, on which visitors were to ride. Toinette swung herself up onto one of the wooden dragons, looking very pert and attractive, and the others followed her example. To the accompaniment of silvery strains of music the merry-go-round began to revolve. Louis, perspiring cheerfully, took his seat on a peacock. It collapsed under his weight and he burst into a good-humoured guffaw.

Vaudreuil stood at considerable risk by the side of Toinette's dragon, clinging hazardously to the rope, and as he allowed himself to be carried around he murmured in a low tone so that she alone could hear, "This is our unique opportunity. Everything has gone off so well. You have never looked so lovely and alluring, Toinette. He is in a very favourable mood. You must get him to agree today."

"Agree to what?" asked Toinette, with a happy, vacuous smile.

"To the dismissal of old Saint-Germain," he whispered, and though he spoke softly there was an urgent note in his voice.

There was still a great deal to be seen, too much perhaps, for the guests were showing signs of fatigue. One thing, however, Toinette insisted on showing them before they returned to the house—her *Little Village,* her wonderfully realistic and charming little Swiss village. She had found her inspiration in the pastoral landscape to which the Queen of Golconda, the heroine of the Chevalier de Boufflers's *Aline,* flies for refuge. When the well-read Prince Xavier exclaimed, *"Mais mon Dieu,* this is the setting of *Aline!"* Toinette flushed with pleasure. Each of the eight little houses had its own little garden, partly kitchen garden and partly orchard. There were barns, wooden benches, threshing-floors, a poultry yard, a windmill, a cottage for the village policeman, sheepfolds, cowsheds, and a little market-place.

The cows were led forth, extraordinarily clean, well-tended cows. They lived in a shed that positively shone with scrubbing, the floor paved with white marble tiles, and the walls displaying cracks that had been specially designed by Hubert Robert. Toinette prepared to milk her favourite cow, which was called Brunette. The milk-pail was of the finest porcelain, manufactured at Sèvres in accordance with a pattern provided by Pourrat. They all looked on as Toinette's nimble fingers manipulated the cow's teats. "Neat," commented Prince Charles, "very neat," and the learned Prince Xavier quoted a line or two from Virgil's *Eclogues*.

Meanwhile d'Angivillers was telling those who were interested about the costs involved in the installing of the *Little Village*. It had been not so much the buildings as the occupants that made it so expensive. Madame's charitable intention was to populate it with needy peasants, but it had been difficult to discover suitable ones. Whenever they found one whose features met with the approval of Monsieur Robert, it appeared that the shape of his hands was not to the taste of Monsieur Mique, so he had to be adequately compensated for his trouble and sent back home again. One peasant after another was interviewed and found wanting, and when at last the artists were satisfied it was Madame who discovered blemishes.

Toinette produced her rustics for inspection. Her particular pride was the occupant of the third cottage, the village mayor, whose name was Valy, and did not Vercy, the village policeman really look like a genuine policeman? Toinette's little protégé Pierre Machard had been stripped of his decorative court costume and transferred to the village, where he was obviously finding it difficult to accustom himself to his long heavy coat and wooden clogs. She told her guests how she had impressed upon the schoolmaster that he was to pay particular attention to the dear little boy, who had now been dressed in the latest fashion in accordance with the principles of natural education laid down in Rousseau's *Emile*. Louis picked up the lad, one of whose clogs promptly fell off, and when he wept Louis gave him some sweets to console him.

"Where is our good Ulrich Schätzli?" inquired Toinette, and the guests pricked up their ears. The case of Ulrich Schätzli had stirred up considerable interest throughout the kingdom. He came from Uznach and had belonged to the Swiss Guard, where he proved himself a stout soldier and amenable to discipline. The Swiss, however, were passionately devoted to their native land—in the *Encyclopédie* patriotism was actually defined as a Swiss national malady—and one evening, after he had been sitting alone in a tavern endeavouring to drown his nostalgia in alcohol, Ulrich Schätzli went out into the Place

Louis le Grand and, to the great amusement of the passers-by, sang a number of the songs of his homeland, concluding with the melancholy strains of *Zu Strassburg auf der Schanz'*. His Most Christian Majesty's Swiss Guards were expressly forbidden to sing their native songs, and particularly this last one, which the French called *Ranz-des-vaches,* since it was feared that their homesickness might thereby be intensified, with the consequence that the temptation to desert from the King's service would become irresistible. There was even an ancient decree, which had never been rescinded, ordaining that any soldier found singing the *Ranz-des-vaches* was liable to the death penalty.

Louis, of course, had no intention of having Ulrich Schätzli executed, but he was at a loss to know what to do with him. He was therefore almost relieved when Toinette begged him to hand over the delinquent in order that he might be settled in her new village. Ulrich Schätzli was accordingly drummed out of the Swiss Guard with ignominy and honourably installed at the Trianon as one of the Swiss villagers.

He had been ashamed to show himself on the King's birthday, and no amount of persuasion on the part of the village mayor had availed to bring him out of hiding, but now he was ruthlessly summoned to appear before the Queen's guests. Deeply conscious of his guilt in having committed his dreadful act of insubordination, he arrived dressed in his Swiss peasant costume, a long coat of grey cloth and very short breeches, which had been designed by Hubert Robert from descriptions in the Alpine romances of the celebrated novelist Claris de Florian. Very tall, and in a stiff military attitude, he stood to attention for inspection by the ladies and gentlemen of the court. Louis blinked at him with his short-sighted eyes, and stared up into his wooden countenance. But Prince Charles walked right round him to examine him from every angle. When the company had moved on, Ulrich Schätzli continued to stand stiffly at attention.

The guests proceeded to inspect the house and its contents. The foremost painters and sculptors of France had collaborated in decorating the vestibule, the staircase, the antechamber, the dining-room, the large salon, the small salon, the tiny library and the spacious dressing-room, the boudoir and the bedroom. The bedroom especially attracted their interest. Not the elegantly designed furniture with its upholstering of blue silk, the mantelpiece with its magnificent clock, or the pictures by Pater and Watteau, but the three paintings that had been sent from Schoenbrunn. For not only had Maria Theresa kept her promise to forward the two she had chosen, but Joseph had added a third as a gift from himself.

The two pictures presented by Maria Theresa were even more charming than Toinette had remembered. They were by the painter

Wertmüller and showed her as a girl of ten. The little archdukes and archduchesses had performed an opera and a ballet on the occasion of the marriage of their brother Joseph. In one of the pictures Toinette, in a red bodice and frock of white flowered satin was dancing with her brothers Ferdinand and Maximilian. In the other she was dancing with one of her brothers and one of her sisters in a mythological ballet with a half-classical, half-English landscape as background. Her look of grave preoccupation was most attractive, and the picture delighted her guests as much as it delighted Toinette herself.

The most remarkable of the paintings, however, was the third. It depicted her Uncle Charles, her grand-uncle Maximilian, and the old Archduke Joseph Maria in monkish garb, digging their own graves. Toinette did not recall having seen it before, and her brother had probably sent it out of a sardonic sense of humour. Whereas the other two had been handed to her by Count Mercy, this one had been brought by the Abbé and she had been annoyed at what she regarded as a macabre joke, but then she had laughed and Vaudreuil too had thought it amusing. So she finally decided to hang it in her bedroom with the others, though her experts advised her not to do so since they did not think it of a sufficiently high artistic quality. Her guests found it interesting, but it made them feel a little uncomfortable.

Dinner was served early and the conversation was animated. At the end of each course the table sank into the floor and came up again loaded with fresh dishes, dumb-waiters did the rest, and they were able to dispense with lackeys. Louis displayed a voracious appetite and kept urging the others to do justice to the dishes. "Today, *Mesdames et Messieurs*," he said, "at the Trianon, we can forget our rank. We are just ordinary people, peasants in fact, so let us eat."

Vaudreuil had an idea. Taking advantage of Louis's good humour, he proposed that the musicians from the Opera, who were playing while the company sat at table, should be sent away and Ulrich Schätzli brought in to entertain them with his singing.

The Swiss was sent for. "You are no longer serving in the Swiss Guard, my good man," he was told by Vaudreuil, "and we should like to hear you sing your famous song."

Ulrich stood stiffly at attention, not comprehending what was wanted of him. "I beg your pardon, sir," he said. "What is it you wish, sir?"

"I wish," replied Vaudreuil, "to hear you sing the *Ranz-des-vaches*."

"It is forbidden to sing that song, sir," responded Ulrich.

"Nonsense, my dear fellow," said Vaudreuil. He took a coin from his pocket. "Look at this picture," he ordered, "and then look at this gentleman," pointing to Louis. "He is the one who commands whether anything shall or shall not be done. Ask him!"

Ulrich continued to stand as stiff as a poker, perspiring profusely. "Is it not forbidden, Your Royal Majesty, sir?" he asked Louis.

"It was forbidden, but it is now permitted," Louis replied. He was rather curious to hear the celebrated song, and also wanted to see how much he could understand of the German text. "So sing, my son," he commanded.

Ulrich, in his short breeches and long grey coat with its red piping, maintained strict military deportment, his legs straddled in the regulation manner, body erect, right arm stretched out rigidly with his hat clutched in his fingers. But obviously he was deeply moved, he breathed heavily, his rough-hewn face twitched, and suddenly he rapped out smartly and very loudly, "Yes, Your Royal Majesty, sir!"

He began to sing, in a deep, untrained voice and with a strong guttural accent:

> *Zu Strassburg auf der Schanz',*
> *da fing mein Trauren an* . . .

He sang the whole of the simple, melancholy song of the soldier who heard the Alpine horn across the river and, seized by homesickness, tried to swim across to his native land. He was captured before he could reach the other side, court-martialled, and sentenced to die. As he stood before the firing squad he made his last dying speech. The sound of the horn blown by the shepherd-boy was to blame for his attempt to desert. Bidding his comrades shoot straight, he commended his soul to God:

> *Oh Himmelskönig, Herr,* sang the Swiss,
> *nimm du meine arme Seele dahin,*
> *nimm sie zu dir in den Himmel ein,*
> *lass sie ewig bei dir sein,*
> *und vergiss nicht mein.*

Throughout the song Ulrich Schätzli kept his strict military bearing, but the tears ran down his cheeks. Louis was very touched. He had not understood the whole of it, but enough to grasp the general idea, and asking Ulrich to repeat a few lines he asked a number of questions about the meaning. Then he told the others what it was about.

"I have always maintained," commented Toinette with evident satisfaction, "that these republicans are not so bad. They are soft-hearted people and have a feeling for music." Turning to Ulrich she inquired, "Have you settled down comfortably now? Do you feel at home in my village? Is it not as good as being in Switzerland?"

Ulrich did not grasp what she meant and his eyes roved about in bewilderment. Then he answered hurriedly, "Yes, Madame!"

Louis held out a glass of wine. "Drink, my son," he said. "It will do you good. You did not sing at all badly." And he gave him a *louis d'or*.

☆   ☆   ☆

The actors from the *Théâtre français* who were to present *The Barber* were dining at the same time as the Queen's guests. The meal had been carefully prepared, the Queen herself having arranged the menu, as Monsieur d'Angivillers informed them at her request. There was a handsomely printed menu card, but as space in the château was limited and the actors could not with propriety be accommodated at the same tables as the royal company, they had perforce to eat with the servants.

There was no reason why they should consider this an affront. The guests were all pure-blooded aristocrats, each of whom could show a family tree dating back to the fourteenth century without a single bourgeois ancestor, and it was the custom to keep them apart from the common herd. Yet the ladies and gentlemen of the *Théâtre français* were piqued at being sent to dine with the lackeys, though they did not let their tongues reveal their feelings.

These lackeys were shrewd, sharp-witted fellows whom their masters found indispensable if ever they happened to be in a tight corner. They were their masters' confidants and acted as go-betweens in many a political, financial, or amorous transaction. It was their habit to call one another by the names of their employers, such as Vaudreuil, Provence, or Artois. It was wiser not to try to get the better of them, for they were very wide-awake, and it was certainly much more amusing to sit at table with them than to dine with Toinette's guests. Nonetheless, there was a slightly bitter taste to the choice dishes with which the actors and actresses were regaled.

At the table of the actors and the lackeys sat Beaumarchais, and grateful though he was to Vaudreuil for having arranged the performance of *The Barber,* since it was the first step towards the eventual production of *Figaro,* he too was suffering from a sense of humiliation and annoyance. The actors were fully able to appreciate what Toinette had achieved in building her Trianon, but this did not hinder them from cracking spiteful jokes and Pierre found a name for the Trianon that he knew would quickly go the rounds of Paris. He dubbed it *Little Schoenbrunn.*

They all had to admit, however, that they had never played in a prettier theatre. It was built in the form of a little temple with Ionic columns, decorated in white and gold, and upholstered in blue velvet. The balcony was supported on pillars with capitals in the shape of lions' heads, and the whole scheme had been carried out in the best of taste. The stage was provided with all the machinery and apparatus that the heart of an actor could desire.

While they were on the stage the actors missed the thunderous applause which always held up the play at intervals when they performed it at the *Théâtre français*. Louis's reverberating guffaw, it is true, almost compensated for the laughter of a packed house to which they were accustomed, but he was not very quick at seeing the point and sometimes he either did not respond at all or only after a time lag. Now that he had witnessed the piece on the stage, however, it seemed to him far more amusing than when he had read it and he told Pierre so. "Not at all bad, Monsieur," he commented graciously. "I found it very entertaining, and you no doubt heard me laugh. Continue to write like that, Monsieur."

"I shall, Sire," Pierre replied, and bowed deeply. Then he and the actors had to withdraw.

Toinette and her guests proceeded once more to the Swiss village, where they danced in the market-place. The peasants had been summoned to appear, and the King's musicians, who had had to give way to Ulrich Schätzli and his *Ranz-des-vaches* during dinner, were now afforded the opportunity of providing the music for rustic dances. Toinette led off with the village mayor, Gabrielle's partner was the policeman, and Louis chose the policeman's daughter, a buxom, embarrassed young woman who kept giggling.

Toinette had intended to spend her first night at the Trianon alone, while Louis and the others returned to Versailles, but he had been stimulated by Ulrich Schätzli's singing and his dance with the rustic girl and he remained behind. He stammered a little incoherently, but she understood what he was trying to say, and though she would have liked to have the place to herself that night she thought the opportunity of pressing home her demand for the dismissal of Saint-Germain was too good to be missed.

So she told him to wait and retired to the bedroom.

With his waddling gait, breathing heavily and perspiring, he wandered through the elegant apartments. When he thought that he had allowed her sufficient time, he scratched at the door of the bedroom. In a low voice she called, "Come in."

In the soft glow of the candles the blue room looked even prettier and more attractive than by day. On the wall little Toni danced with prim and dainty charm before a classical landscape. The most conspicuous article of furniture was the large, expensively simple bed. The late lamented Louis XV had slept in it, and occasionally Madame Dubarry. Toinette had retained it; for it was the most beautiful bed in the kingdom.

"Shall we put out the candles?" suggested Toinette.

"Shall we?" he hesitated. "Very well. If you wish." He began to blow out the candles and to snuff out the wicks with his fingers.

"That will be enough," she said, irritated at his slowness. He left two or three of the candles burning and their flickering light shone on the picture of the three exalted old gentlemen who were amusing themselves by digging their own graves. Methodically, one by one, he divested himself of his garments and then, without removing the last one, slid between the sheets. Toinette drew the curtains.

Later, lying behind the drawn curtains, Toinette told Louis that now she had not forgotten how often he had paid her debts without reproving her for her extravagance, and she deeply appreciated his kindness. From now on things were going to be different. With the completion of the Trianon her greatest desire had been fulfilled. She was going to stop playing faro and lansquenet, and in fact she intended to avoid all unnecessary expense. Resting her head on his breast she snuggled up to him. He growled contentedly and gazed at the faint, flickering shadows cast by the candles upon the bed-curtains.

She was silent for a while, then she began anew. "As I have made up my mind to meet your wishes in this respect, I assume that you will not be unwilling to do me a small favour." He snorted uneasily and muttered something unintelligible. "I want you," she said without more ado, "to get rid of that pernicious man, that old *crétin,* Saint-Germain. Who was it that was responsible for the last quarrel we had? Was it not he, and he alone? He is always the one who sows dissension between us."

Louis twisted uncomfortably. It happened every time. When they spent the night together, she invariably spoiled it afterwards. She always asked him to do something he did not want to do. The thought passed dimly through his mind that Dubarry had slept in this bed and that Toinette's behaviour now was lacking in royal dignity. He mumbled something and went on thinking of a variety of vaguely associated ideas, of the Army reforms, of military discipline, of his former Finance Minister, Turgot, and that in the morning he would look up Plutarch and read what he had to say about Antony and Cleopatra.

"Why don't you answer?" complained Toinette. "Are you annoyed at my asking a favour of you for once?"

He continued to brood without replying. Finding the darkness of the alcove oppressive, he pulled back the curtains. The room looked very peaceful and charming. "It was a very kindly thought of your mother's to send you these paintings," he said. "You make such a pretty picture dancing there. I am glad that we have them."

"You have yourself admitted," went on Toinette, "that Saint-Germain is not equal to his task. He has not been able to carry out the reforms for the sake of which he affronted me and the whole of the nobility."

"Don't you think," asked Louis, "that I ought to send your mother a personal letter of thanks?" Toinette sat half upright in the bed, blond, white, pretty, and forced him to bring back his wandering gaze.

"Please do not try to evade the issue," she demanded. "I want a straight answer. Are you going to dismiss Saint-Germain?"

"Well, well," said Louis, "we shall see."

"I want a plain yes," she insisted.

"Very well then," he growled. "Yes."

He got up and dressed himself again, but his mind was far away and he forgot two or three of his numerous articles of clothing.

It was very quiet in the park as he left the house. There was a faint light from the moon and a pleasant murmuring from the little stream and the fountains. He breathed in the fresh night air as he slowly walked back to Versailles and was happy to be alone. *"Zu Strassburg auf der Schanz', da fing mein Trauren an,"* he hummed to himself in the stillness of the night. Then he thought of Saint-Germain, who always held himself so erect. He saw the old man's grey, furrowed face, and as he hummed, *"Das Alphorn hat mir solches angetan,"* repeating the line several times, he reflected on the number of disagreeable people there were at his court and the fact that Saint-Germain was one of the few honourable characters among them.

When he reached Versailles he touched the heavy knocker. The Swiss Guard on duty peered through the grill, saw what he took to be an untidily dressed courtier, and cried brusquely, "You can't come in! Go away!"

Louis remembered that he himself had issued orders that nobody was to be admitted after midnight, and he burst into his loud guffaw. The sentry recognized him and gave a frightened start. "You are a good soldier, my son," said Louis approvingly.

Safely ensconced in his own bedroom, he was glad to see that there was still plenty of time before the official *lever*. There was no need yet to enter his state-bed, so he lay down on his comfortable, unpretentious cot, stretched contentedly, turned over on his left side, rolled onto his right, and fell asleep. He dreamt that he had a new pair of pliers in his workshop, a good, handy tool, but too heavy to use for long, so he picked up the old pair and could not manage with that either. The lock would not work, it was finished, he had tested it with Monsieur Laudry and with Gamain, but it still would not work, when he tried to insert the key he could not get it in. Nothing seemed to fit. The bill lay before him and it was much too high. The figures were confused. He was good at arithmetic, but he could not add up the bill, so he sent for d'Angivillers and de Laborde, each of whom made it come to a different result. He sweated profusely, was unable to make anything agree, and the lock would not work.

When his old valet came to wake him and warned him respectfully,

"Sire, it is time to enter the state-bed," he was glad to leave his comfortable cot and climb into the ceremonial bed that he loathed.

☆ ☆ ☆

After the *lever,* during which he was in a very cross temper, he went over to the apartments of Count Maurepas. Since he had committed himself to announcing the dismissal of Saint-Germain it was best to get it over with at once.

Maurepas guessed, as soon as his eyes lighted on his royal master, the errand on which he had come. Toinette had not invited him to the birthday party at the Trianon, and this had led him to suspect at once that she intended to utilize the opportunity to extract some promise or advantage from her consort. The Lilac Coterie had never made any secret of its determination to bring about Saint-Germain's downfall, and when Louis entered the room it was clear to Maurepas that Toinette had achieved her purpose.

He did not welcome the thought of his old friend's being ejected from office. If the whole of the court nobility had not conspired to throw difficulties in his way, the capable Minister for War would already have succeeded in providing the Army that was needed, and the Government's attitude towards England could have taken a different turn. But Maurepas had realized months ago that he would not be able to keep Saint-Germain. It was not only that the Austrian woman and her friends were against him, but Madame de Maurepas herself, his own wife, was anxious to see the War Minister's back. She had promised her dear friend and cousin, the Countess de Montbarrey, that the post should be given to her husband. Maurepas did not consider Montbarrey a suitable candidate, yet he in his turn had promised the Countess that when Saint-Germain went, Montbarrey should succeed him. Toinette hated the Count, and it tickled Maurepas's sense of humour to think of her face when she heard the name of the new Minister for War.

He was not feeling in very good shape that morning and was relieved that Louis had come over to see him, instead of his having to go over and see Louis. There was no need to change from the dressing-gown and slippers he was wearing into ceremonial garb.

Now that the crucial moment had come, Louis found it more difficult to say what he had to say than he had at first imagined. He was tormented by painful memories of what had happened when he dismissed Turgot. Turgot had been insolent, it was true, but he had also been thoroughly honest, courageous, and extremely efficient. Saint-Germain too was thoroughly honest and efficient, and he had a right to expect that the promises made to him when he was appointed should be kept.

Louis tried to put off the evil moment, inquired after his mentor's health, naïvely expressed his regret that Maurepas had not been present at the Trianon, and told him about the *Ranz-des-vaches* and how he had danced with the peasant girl. Then at last he came reluctantly to the point. He had been sleeping badly last night, he said, and to pass the time he had been reviewing in his mind the numerous complaints that had been coming in about Saint-Germain. He was aware, of course, that most of these charges were without any solid foundation, but it did seem to him that a man who was unfortunate enough to tread on everybody's toes was perhaps not the right man to occupy the position of Minister for War. He proceeded to enumerate the various objections that had been raised in different quarters to Saint-Germain's policies. There was the decree throwing open the senior ranks in the Army to officers of bourgeois birth. There were the old man's "Teutonic ordinances," which included, in particular, the introduction of flogging. There was that affair of the Invalides, and there was the trouble about the Jesuits. The list was endless.

The orders with which he was now reproaching his Minister for War had all been expressly approved by Louis himself, and he had promised Saint-Germain time and again that he could rely upon his support.

The cynical Maurepas, although secretly amused at the way Louis was trying to justify his action, listened with an air of grave interest. When Louis had finished, he began to defend his friend Saint-Germain. Since, however, it was clear that he was defending a lost cause, he took care that his arguments should be two-edged. The American conflict, he explained, had brought the Government face to face with the possibility that at any moment they might find themselves involved in a war with England. They should therefore think twice before deciding to dispense with the services of such a great soldier and efficient organizer as Saint-Germain. On the other hand, it could not be denied that his rigid, uncompromising nature had stirred up a host of enemies against him. The good fellow must have exercised an extraordinary degree of ingenuity to bring about such unanimity between normally antagonistic groups of people—the royal princes, the court, the *petite noblesse,* the common soldiers, the ladies of the salons, and the philosophers. Anyway he had certainly succeeded. They had risen against him as one man. And it must be admitted that the other Ministers found it difficult to work with their colleague. It was therefore comprehensible that Louis should in the long run have grown weary of continually having to protect a man to whom the Queen cherished such a rooted objection. Nonetheless, the very real danger of a war with England must be borne in mind and they must consider carefully before deciding to dismiss a Minister who had proved himself such a capable organizer.

Louis grunted, but said nothing. A line kept running through his brain, *"Das Alphorn hat mir solches angetan."* At last he muttered, "He is a loyal servant and has merited well of us."

"Undoubtedly," returned Maurepas. "On the other hand, Sire, there will be no need to search long for a successor. Montbarrey has been Secretary of State for some time and is well versed in the duties."

Louis looked up. He knew what lay behind Maurepas's suggestion, that Madame de Maurepas was pulling the strings, and he found some consolation in the thought that his supple chief adviser was likewise under the necessity of making concessions to his wife. There could be no question, continued Maurepas, of leaving such a responsible post unfilled even for a single day. The times were too dangerous for that. The duties must be taken over at once, and Montbarrey was the best man available. Though Louis could not stand Montbarrey, he thought it not a bad solution. By acting quickly he would prevent Toinette and the Lilac Coterie from presenting their own candidate. "H–m," he growled. "Well—maybe."

Maurepas thought it best to tie him down. "Then I understand, Sire," he said, "that you will inform Monsieur de Saint-Germain of his dismissal and appoint his successor immediately."

"Can't you tell him, old friend?" asked Louis.

"In my opinion," replied Maurepas, "it should be made clearly evident that the Crown itself is responsible for Saint-Germain's dismissal."

"You mean that I must personally—?" stammered Louis unhappily.

"If you command it, Sire," responded Maurepas helpfully, "I shall be present at the audience."

"Thank you, my mentor," said Louis gratefully.

"Then I will inform Saint-Germain that you wish to see him," suggested Maurepas. "Would three o'clock be convenient?"

"Let us say four o'clock," replied Louis.

"Your command shall be obeyed," said Maurepas. "Before Saint-Germain arrives I shall submit to you for signature Montbarrey's letters of appointment."

When Louis had returned to his own apartments, Maurepas settled down to the congenial task of sharpening the point of an epigram that had been running through his mind during the latter part of the interview. He was very fond of inventing epigrams and took great delight in polishing them. It had been on account of an epigram directed against Madame de Pompadour that Louis XV had banished him to his estates, but it had been a good epigram and well worth a quarter of a century's exile from Paris. He had, however, grown more cautious. Being firmly resolved to die in office, he was careful not to jeopardize his position a second time for the sake of an epigram, however exquisite.

The epigram on which he was now working pleased him mightily. It concerned that part of Louis's royal person which had failed to function before Joseph undertook his long journey from Vienna. Its pungent wit formed an excellent complement to his verses about the Pompadour, but it was too malicious to confide even to his secretary or his wife. He would not even dare to entrust it to his memoirs. A tremendous pity. But at least he derived an exquisite amusement from it himself. He wrote it out with trembling hand, held the paper as far as possible from his long-sighted eyes, read it through again, smiled, burst out laughing, crossed out and emended, cackled with mirth, and continued to file and polish. He was so deeply immersed that he almost forgot to give orders for the preparation of Montbarrey's letters of appointment.

☆   ☆   ☆

Towards four o'clock Louis was sitting in his library. He had remembered to ask for a copy of Plutarch and was reading the biography of Mark Antony, but his thoughts were elsewhere. His mind was haunted by a vision of Saint-Germain standing and looking at him questioningly with his faithful, dog-like eyes. The old man had not wanted to accept the post and had predicted that his reforms would meet with stubborn resistance, but Louis had been very much in favour of them and was resolved that they should be carried out. He had promised to protect his Minister against attack from any quarter whatsoever. "I shall stand by you," he had assured him. "Have no fear. I shall support you whatever happens."

Why, wondered Louis, did everybody always make it so difficult for him to do what he thought right? If he wanted to keep Toinette in a good humour, if he wanted to have an heir to the throne, he had to pay for it by constantly giving in to her against his will. Now he was being forced to dismiss this brave old soldier, Saint-Germain.

He tried to fix his attention on Plutarch's history of Antony and Cleopatra, but it was no good. Between his eyes and the printed page he kept seeing the letter that Turgot had sent to him after his dismissal. Though he had locked it away and not looked at it for a long time, he saw clearly every crossed *t* and dotted *i*, every twist and turn and every flourish. "People think you are weak, Sire." Nonsense. It was, of course, painful to have to break his promise and send Saint-Germain away, but did not the King stand above the laws that were valid for the common man? His conflicts were of a different order, and more difficult to resolve. After all, was it not more important that France should have a Dauphin than that Monsieur Saint-Germain should retain his post? Louis cherished the vague belief that if Toinette was angry with him she would not conceive his child.

Finally giving up his attempt to read, he left the book lying open on the table and rose from his chair. After pacing heavily up and down he seated himself in the bay window and blinked down into the court-yards and avenues to see whether he could glimpse Saint-Germain.

Maurepas, however, arrived first, elegant and erect as usual. Open-ing his portfolio, he withdrew the document which certified that Alex-andre-Marie-Léonor de Saint-Maurice, Count de Montbarrey, Prince of the Holy Roman Empire, Lieutenant-General, Commandant of the Swiss Guard of Monsieur, Secretary of State in the Ministry for War, was appointed to the office of War Minister and to be a member of His Most Christian Majesty's Privy Council. Louis peered at the edict with his short-sighted eyes, scanned it hurriedly, then pushed it aside muttering, "Yes, yes."

Maurepas exhorted him gently, "The Crown would find its task easier if it were to sign now." The Crown sighed and hesitated. Maurepas held out a pen, the Crown took it and continued to gaze at him, Maurepas nodded encouragingly, the Crown heaved another sigh, shook its head, and signed.

Saint-Germain arrived. He was feeling in better spirits than for some time and was in an expectant mood, hoping that Louis wanted to discuss two memoranda he had submitted the previous week.

Louis showed no anxiety to come to the point, so Saint-Germain began by referring to a matter of only incidental importance that had nothing to do with his two memoranda. He had the honour, he said modestly, to entreat His Majesty's advice in the affair of Colonel Esterhazy. The Colonel was quite an efficient soldier, but he was lack-ing in discipline. It had twice been necessary to call him to order, but each time the Queen had intervened and the punishment had had to be remitted. Now the Colonel had gone too far, and it was impossible to overlook his delinquency. He had stated in public that the Minister for War was intending to hand the Army over to the Jesuits. Discipline could not be maintained if the Minister's authority was undermined with impunity by his own officers. Saint-Germain therefore begged the King for his gracious assurance of support in case Her Majesty, as was to be feared, should again intervene on the Colonel's behalf.

Louis kept his eyes averted from the old Minister. They were in fact fixed on the Plutarch, which still lay open in front of him. "An-tony therefore returned to the City," he read, "shouting that he had been betrayed by Cleopatra to those against whom he had waged war for her sake." He read the words mechanically without grasping their meaning, for he was trying to think how he could work himself into a rage against the man who was standing before him.

"So this is the kind of business with which you trouble me, Count Saint-Germain?" he said slowly, his voice dragging strangely. "It is with such trifling matters that you waste my time?" His anger rose.

"What am I to do with a Minister for War who is incapable even of controlling his own staff officers? I expect England to attack us any day. How are you going to deal with the English army if you cannot even deal with this Colonel Esterhazy?" He had now worked himself up to the desired pitch. With his little double chin trembling, his voice shrill and harsh, he stared at the bewildered old man.

Saint-Germain's grey, furrowed face had lost its firm outline. His cheeks twitched as he protested, "I do not understand you, Sire. You have afforded me so many proofs of your confidence. You told me—" He did not repeat what Louis had told him. "If you are not satisfied with my services—" He did not finish this sentence either.

Louis gripped one of the little porcelain figures on his table so violently as if he wanted to squeeze it to fragments between his fingers, but suddenly he put it down again with unexpected gentleness. "Of course I am not satisfied," he said very quietly, once more averting his eyes. "I am receiving complaints from all sides. They may not be altogether justified, but I must insist on the gentlemen in my service settling their differences between themselves. You apparently find it difficult to get on with anybody, Monsieur, either with the nobility, with the troops, or with anyone else. The Queen is extremely displeased. What am I to do with a man who stirs up enemies everywhere?" He shrugged his shoulders and repeated, "Of course I am not satisfied."

Saint-Germain replied in an equally quiet tone, his voice hoarse with emotion, "Does that mean you want to get rid of me, Sire?" Louis studiously refrained from looking him in the eye and waited for him to go on, hoping he would say something that would provide a cue for further rebuke, but Saint-Germain remained silent. His silence forced Louis to meet his gaze, and he saw what he had dreaded to see, his old Minister's twitching face with its faithful, dog-like eyes, and he knew what was going on behind that lined forehead.

Saint-Germain was thinking how all his life he had dreamed of carrying out his decalogue of reforms. He had published his *Ten Commandments of Military Discipline,* and towards the end of his days Louis had summoned him to put his theories into practice. Delighted as he had been at this mark of confidence, he had been unwilling to undertake the task. He was a soldier, not a courtier, and feared that he would be no match for the intrigues at Versailles. But the young King had promised him every support. He had done his best to hold his own against the shameless, foolish demands of that cursed *Autrichienne.* Time and again Louis had renewed his promises. Now he sat there, Louis, young King of France, refusing to look him firmly in the eye and without even the courage to announce the decision to which he had evidently come, "Yes, Monsieur, you are dismissed."

Louis realized what was passing through the old man's mind and was seized by an almost unbearable pity for him, and an almost unbearable anger against himself. He could not bring himself to utter the word "Yes," but neither could he bring himself to utter the word "No," and he was furious with Maurepas for not coming to his rescue.

He was being unjust, however, to Maurepas. Maurepas was reliable, and he came to the rescue. Turning to his colleague he remarked in a light, affable tone, "I am afraid, my old friend, that you have interpreted His Majesty's intentions correctly. Is that not so, Sire?"

Louis growled, "Well, yes, I suppose so. If everybody wants it, what is one to do?"

Upon which Saint-Germain bowed low and said, "Then, Sire, may I crave permission to withdraw?" And he walked backwards towards the door in the prescribed manner. Louis kept his eyes averted. When he looked up again, Saint-Germain was no longer there.

"May I too be allowed to withdraw, Sire?" requested Maurepas, but Louis quickly answered, "No, do not leave me alone." Then he lapsed into a brooding silence. If they had not forced him to see Saint-Germain and tell him of his dismissal, the afternoon would have been spent hunting at Fontainebleau. There was nothing he liked better than hunting. The game was beaten towards him so that he could shoot it, and in the evening he recorded the bag in his diary, pretty high figures generally. In spite of all the animals he had killed he was always fascinated by the way they leapt up when they were hit and then sank in a heap. Yet he was sorry for the poor beasts. He felt singularly linked to them, he was himself both the hunter and the hunted.

When he at last jerked himself out of his absorption he saw Maurepas still standing in front of him, erect and respectful, a thin smile on his dry lips. "Are you still here?" he asked in surprise. But when Maurepas, obviously hurt, prepared to go, he held him back. "No, forgive me," he begged, and gripped him by the coat. Bringing his face close to that of Maurepas, he asked, "Was it not dreadful the way the old man looked when he went away? I believe there were tears in his eyes. He was such an excellent Minister and such a brave soldier. We have done him a grave injustice, my mentor. You ought not to have spoken to him so harshly."

For all his cynicism Maurepas was indignant at thus having the blame put on his own shoulders. But he showed no sign of it in his face. He was determined to die in office.

"We must make it up to him," Louis went on. "Of course he can keep on his residence at the Arsenal, and we shall grant him a pension equal to the full amount of his salary, as well as a lump sum in compensation."

"I admire your generosity, Sire," replied Maurepas. "I shall discuss the matter with Monsieur Necker."

Louis was already feeling consoled. "Please do, my dear friend," he said eagerly. "I should not like them to treat my Saint-Germain stingily. Tell Monsieur Necker that I said so. He is a miserly fellow, that Swiss. And I shall write personally to Saint-Germain," he decided, "to thank him for the great services he has rendered to me and to France."

☆   ☆   ☆

Franklin would have liked to deal with the greater part of his mail, which had arrived the previous day from America, before having to face the usual visit from Arthur Lee and Silas Deane, but the unreliable William had again stayed out beyond his allotted time. When he eventually turned up, however, he had an adequate excuse, for he brought from Paris news of an important event that he had thought it desirable to investigate. It appeared that Lieutenant Dubois and Major de Mauroy, two of the officers who, furnished with commissions by Silas Deane, had accompanied Lafayette to America, were back in Paris after having received an extremely cool welcome from the Congress. Even Lafayette himself had been greeted with a marked lack of cordiality. The two officers were now going about in Paris reviling the ingratitude of the Americans, their want of good manners, their niggardly attitude, and their arrogance. William had learned about the matter from de la Rochefoucauld, and afterwards from Condorcet. The whole city was talking about it.

Franklin listened impassively, but he was vexed and saddened. The Congress was not making his task any the easier. He had surmised from the start that the French officers would not be welcomed in Philadelphia, but he had not expected them to be treated with incivility. After all, they were in possession of credentials from one of the Congress's own representatives.

He had himself been making progress recently in his relations with the French. His meeting with Toinette seemed to be leading to fruitful results, and it was even rumoured that she had managed to extract definite promises from the King. Yet the people in Philadelphia had to choose this particular moment to let their ancient hostility to France get the better of them. Out of pure thoughtlessness and ill temper they had offered an outright affront to the court and the nation.

This was not the whole of William's tidings. He had heard that Maurepas and Vergennes proposed to be present at the opening of the Salon. The exhibition of Franklin's portrait by Duplessis was one of the topics of the day, and it was being said that merely on account of its subject it would put all the other exhibits in the shade.

Franklin looked forward with pleasure to the prospect of being able to view his portrait at the Salon, conscious as he was that the Parisians would be comparing it with the living model. It may have been vanity on his part, but was not vanity one of the most agreeable qualities with which the Supreme Being had endowed His creatures? In any case, the success of his portrait could only be helpful to the American cause.

He gazed benevolently at his grandson. The lad was a little frivolously inclined, no doubt, but he was shrewd and knew what was important. As he waited for his two colleagues to arrive, he decided to carry out an intention he had been cherishing for some time of appointing William to an official post. With a permanent appointment and a salary the lad would acquire a greater sense of responsibility. He would discuss the question that very day with his fellow commissioners. Lee would probably object and splutter something about nepotism, but Franklin thought that his services to his country warranted his claiming the right to look after his relatives. He had taken on the heavy burden in his declining years of representing the Congress in France, and it was probable that he would end his days in this foreign land. When the time came he wanted to have his eyes closed by one of his own kin, and he did not intend that the grandson on whom that pious duty would fall should idle his time away.

Silas Deane was the first to arrive. He had lost something of his former robust appearance. His cheeks were less puffy and his nose more pointed. The venomous Arthur Lee was probably giving him a bad time. Lee had been on a diplomatic mission to Berlin, but with no more success than he had been able to achieve in Madrid, and had grown even more embittered and morbidly self-assertive. Whatever his colleagues, and especially Silas Deane, did or omitted to do, he smelt some ulterior selfish motive.

As soon as Lee arrived, Deane began to talk about the reception accorded to the French officers in Philadelphia. Lieutenant Dubois and Major de Mauroy had called upon him with their complaints, and unfortunately their accounts were too clear and circumstantial to be doubted. Lafayette and his fifteen companions had reached Philadelphia after many hardships and reported themselves to Congress, expecting a warm welcome after all they had been through. They were received first of all by a Mr. Moose—presumably Robert Morris, suggested Silas Deane—who took their papers for examination and requested them to meet him on the following day at the entrance to the Congress building. They duly appeared at the appointed place and were handed over by Mr. Moose to another member of the Congress who spoke French and whose name began with an "L." This, thought Silas Deane, was probably James Lowell. He too said what he had to say in the open street. It was quite correct, he declared, that Mr. Deane had been authorized to send over French officers with a knowledge of military engineering, and some had already arrived who asserted that they were sappers, though they were not, as well as a number of artillery officers who had evidently never seen any service. It appeared, concluded the gentleman whose name began with an "L," that French officers were in the habit of coming to America without having been invited to do so. With that he left them standing in the open street before the red-brick Congress building and staring at one another in bewilderment. When Lafayette had first stepped upon American soil, he had bent down to kiss the ground and sworn that he would either march to victory with the American Army or die with his sword in his hand. Now all he could find to say as he stood in the street before the door of the Congress building was, *"Mille tonnerres!"*

This was the story that Deane told his fellow commissioners. He was deeply agitated, for since it was he who had recruited the French officers he regarded what had happened as a personal affront.

Franklin sat impassively and scratched. Lee smiled sardonically. As neither said a word Deane could not refrain from adding bitterly, "It cannot be said that the French asked us to come here, yet so far as I am aware nobody has told the Doctor that he ought to have waited for an invitation. Quite the contrary. Right now all Paris is talking of the honours it is proposed to pay him at the opening of the Salon."

"Yes," said Arthur Lee. "They give us fine words and a piece of canvas."

Franklin tried to find excuses for the behaviour of the Congress. Apparently, he suggested, the other Frenchmen had remained in Philadelphia. His letter recommending the young Marquis must have reached there by now, and no doubt General Washington would meanwhile have smoothed matters out.

"The Congress has disavowed all of us," stormed Deane. "It has refused to recognize the commissions that we made out in its name."

"That *you* made out," corrected Arthur Lee.

"I too," said Franklin, "was authorized to send over officers of the artillery."

Arthur Lee was standing by the fireplace, stiffly erect, with folded arms and chin pressed against his throat so that his forehead jutted forward. The lesson to be drawn from the affair, he declared with gloomy aggressiveness, was that nothing could be achieved by sending across a few muskets or a few French windbags with resounding names. They must go straight for the target, in other words, the alliance. They must be more active, the French Ministers must not be left in peace, they must have recourse to threats. The methods they had been employing hitherto would get them nowhere.

"If I remember rightly," retorted Silas Deane, "you employed your own methods in Madrid and in Berlin, but I have not yet seen any tremendous results. Here, on the other hand, something has been gained, and very recently too. Think of the Doctor's meeting with the Queen. Think of his portrait which is to be exhibited at the Salon."

"Please do not let us lose ourselves in generalities," exhorted Franklin. "Let us rather ask ourselves what we can do to avoid a repetition of such false moves in Philadelphia. My suggestion is that we address a joint letter to the Foreign Affairs Committee of the Congress, explaining that the French like a *No* to be served at least slightly sweetened."

"I am an American," said Arthur Lee, "and I intend to act like one."

Franklin sighed, dropped the subject, and asked what they thought ought to be done about the Prussian officer, Baron von Steuben.

Von Steuben had been on the Prussian general staff and aide-de-camp to Frederick the Great. After having fought with distinction in the Seven Years' War, he found the peace that had settled on Europe uncongenial and had offered his services to the Americans. His talent for organization was affirmed in reliable quarters, and he had made a favourable impression on Franklin. There was nothing boastful about him, he had demanded only a modest salary, and he was just the man General Washington needed to instil into his army the discipline that was lacking.

Franklin had been inclined to offer Baron von Steuben a commission, but the hostile reception accorded to the French officers now made him doubtful. Silas Deane had no such doubts. Lee, however, declared acidly that they ought to have learned their lesson by now and should refrain from wounding the feelings of experienced American officers by sending out foreign officers of high rank to be put over them.

"Formerly, Mr. Lee," protested Silas Deane in a tone of annoyance, "you only raised objections to the appointment of Frenchmen. Since your return from Berlin you are objecting also to the appointment of Germans. If you continue your travels much further you will try to prevent the appointment of everybody who did not enjoy the privilege of growing up in the family circle of the Lees."

"I must confess quite candidly, sir," replied Arthur Lee pugnaciously, "that I would rather see members of the Lee family here than certain other people."

"I should not like to read, sir," retorted Deane, "what you have been reporting about me to Philadelphia."

"I can well believe," said Lee, "that you would not find it palatable."

"Sir," intervened Franklin, "will you please be good enough to cease this recrimination. Your nerves are unstrung. You need a rest. If you will listen to an old man's advice, I would suggest that you put yourself in the hands of your physician."

"I do not see what my nerves have to do with the fact that I object in principle to the recruitment of foreign officers," grumbled Lee.

Franklin returned to the question of Steuben. "After what has happened," he said, "we cannot guarantee him a salary, however modest.

The most we can do is to assign him a piece of land, say two thousand acres, to be taken up after we have won the war."

"I am afraid," commented Deane, "that he is not likely to find the offer very enticing."

"If he is guided solely by the greed for gain," said Lee scornfully, "then I really think we can dispense with his services."

Deane pointed out that if they did not come to an arrangement with Steuben very soon, he would return to Germany. "I should be sorry to lose him," said Franklin. Deane suggested asking Monsieur de Beaumarchais for his advice. Franklin sighed inwardly. Unless they gave up hope of acquiring Steuben's services, this was probably their only course.

This problem settled for the time being, Franklin broached the subject of his plan to appoint William Temple as his secretary. The clerical burden was growing heavier and heavier, he said, pointing to the accumulation of papers on his desk. If a secretary was necessary, protested Lee, it would be better to appoint a trained and experienced man, not a boy of seventeen. Franklin had his answer ready. Whenever professional secretaries had been appointed for particular tasks, he pointed out, Mr. Lee himself had expressed doubts as to their political reliability. As far as William was concerned, presumably even Mr. Lee would hesitate to assert that he was a spy. Arthur Lee swallowed before declaring that the financial situation did not permit of new posts being added to the budget. "I had been thinking of a salary of 120 livres a month," explained Franklin. "80 livres would be placed to the account of the Congress, while the other 40 would come out of my own pocket."

"I consider the appointment of young Mr. Franklin an excellent idea," said Deane, "and of course there can be no question of the Doctor's being out of pocket in the matter."

"Then that is agreed," concluded Franklin.

"I wish it to be placed on record," said Lee, "that the appointment was made without my concurrence."

Franklin returned to the subject of the reception accorded to Lafayette and the other French officers in Philadelphia. "You are a man of judgment," he said persuasively to Lee, "and you certainly are aware that the behaviour of Messieurs Morris and Lowell is hurting our cause in France. Will you not add the weight of your approval and signature to the representations I am proposing to make in Philadelphia?"

"The way they have acted in Philadelphia is incredible," cried Deane indignantly. "And these officers have returned to Paris just at the very moment when preparations are being made to honour the Doctor at the Salon. Every Frenchman who looks at the picture of Franklin will see behind it Lafayette and the other officers standing in the street after the door of the Congress had been slammed in their faces."

Lee seethed inwardly. It was always "Franklin," never "America." The Doctor *honoris causa* was concerned solely for his own glorification. On the following day, or the day after, he would go to the Salon and stand in front of his idealized portrait, reaping the fruits of the renown whose seeds had been sown by Richard Henry Lee and George Washington and the thousands who had laid down their lives for liberty.

Franklin surmised what was passing through the mind of his embittered colleague and he turned to him with a kindly smile. "That is how he will smile," thought Lee, "when he looks at his portrait," but Franklin said, "After the humiliation suffered by our young French friends in Philadelphia, it will, I think, be best if we do not give the Parisians an opportunity to make the aggravating comparison. It will probably be wiser for me to stay away from the Salon."

Silas Deane's little eyes widened in bewilderment. "You are surely not going to reject the honour that is in store for you?" he asked.

"They recommended us at Versailles to be discreet," replied Franklin.

Lee took a deep breath. "If you are writing to the Congress," he said sullenly, "I am prepared to add my signature."

"I did not doubt," rejoined Franklin, "that an Arthur Lee would succeed in conquering his personal feelings where the cause is concerned," and Lee placed a limp hand in the hand the old man stretched out towards him.

☆   ☆   ☆

After the dismissal of Saint-Germain, Toinette received another joint visit from Count Mercy and the Abbé Vermond. Both gentlemen, of course, were perfectly well aware who had been responsible for the change at the Ministry for War, but they pretended ignorance and merely lamented that they had been no more able to prevent the removal of the gifted Saint-Germain, who was regarded with such high favour at Vienna, than they had been able to hinder the appointment of the incapable and notoriously self-seeking Montbarrey. Toinette merely shrugged her shoulders as if the matter did not interest her. Nevertheless, her joy had been short-lived. It was not an agreeable thought that in future, when she wanted commissions in the Army for her friends, she would have to enter into competition with Mademoiselle de Violaine of the Opera, who acted as Montbarrey's agent. She realized that she had won a very dubious victory during those few minutes in the alcove of her bedroom at the Trianon.

The two emissaries proceeded to a more personal and painful

topic. They informed her respectfully that they had unfortunately been right in their gloomy predictions. Certain friends of Madame may have assured her that her popularity would increase after the favour she had shown to the American rebel, but alas, this was far from evident. On the contrary. It was being asserted in the inns and coffee-houses that her extravagance had drained the national exchequer to an extent that made it impossible to assist the Americans in their war against the hereditary enemy of France. Her thriftless ways had forced the country to adopt a false policy dictated by weakness. When Toinette showed haughty incredulity, Mercy produced a pamphlet which was one of many that had appeared in recent weeks. Holding it in the tips of his fingers he read out to her a few passages. It mentioned fantastic sums that were alleged to have been expended on the Trianon, the *Little Schoenbrunn,* and it painted in dark colours the ominous influence of *l'Autrichienne* on the destinies of *la douce France.*

These warnings too were disdainfully rejected by Toinette, though she knew that they were not unjustified. The courage she had shown by her readiness to meet the rebel had either been forgotten or not sufficiently taken into account, and when she drove through the streets of Paris she could not help noticing that the crowds who had formerly cheered her now merely stared in hostile silence.

However, any uneasiness she might have felt was submerged in her occupation with a new project.

When *The Barber of Seville* was performed on the stage of her lovely theatre at the Trianon she had wished she were taking the part of Mademoiselle Mesnard or Mademoiselle Dumesnil, and she had felt that she could have spoken some of the lines with more point and charm than those celebrated professional actresses. Amateur playacting had become very much the fashion in society, and would it not be a shame if she too could not appear on her own stage in the most beautiful theatre in France?

Vaudreuil was very interested in her plan. Himself a gifted actor and passionately fond of producing plays, he found in amateur theatricals a matchless opportunity to impress others with his superiority. He told Toinette that as the superintendent of her entertainments he would permit her to appear on the stage only if she acted better than anyone else, especially since she really was gifted. Her French was still not wholly free from accent, and in particular her pronunciation of the letter "r" needed correction. She must study, and moreover she must take her studies seriously. Toinette eagerly agreed, and it was decided that she should take lessons in acting from Monsieur Michu and Monsieur Caillot of the *Théâtre français.*

For the rest, she adhered to her intention of presenting the nation with a Dauphin of whose legitimacy there should be no doubt, and Vaudreuil had perforce to wait. As his impatience grew, so did his will to domineer, and he continually renewed his attempts to involve her in a conflict with Louis.

One day he asked her accusingly why she had not yet visited the Salon. "I have promised Louis," she told him candidly, "to display the utmost reserve as far as the rebels are concerned."

"I know somebody," he replied, "who once complained bitterly that a Queen of France enjoyed less freedom than a fishwife of *Les Halles*. I can think of no reason why you should not go to the Salon."

"It will be looked upon as another act of defiance," she insisted.

Vaudreuil smiled, but said nothing.

A few days later the Salon was honoured by a visit from the Queen. Nearly all the artists who were exhibiting pictures turned up for the occasion, hoping for a word of recognition from her lips.

Toinette stood and gazed at the busts of Molière, Voltaire, and Rousseau by Houdon, though without much interest. She examined the pretty landscapes and ruins of Hubert Robert. Then she stood for some time in front of the vast picture executed by Robin for the city of Paris. It represented the young King Louis entering Paris for the ceremony of confirming the city's privileges. He was very much idealized and surrounded by figures representing Justice, Charity, Harmony, and Truth, and she would not have recognized him had she not been informed that it was the King.

Finally she came to the gallery containing the paintings of Duplessis, and Franklin's portrait was the first one to strike her eye, but she deliberately refrained from looking at it until she had been shown the others. Duplessis himself was present, looking rather odd and very shy in his ornate, ceremonial garb, which contrasted with his good-natured, peasant features. She graciously acknowledged his respectful bow.

The first portrait she inspected was that of Doctor Lassone, her own physician, who had also performed Louis's operation. Though Toinette and her friends liked to make fun of Lassone's conceit, his love affairs, and his greed for money, she cherished an almost superstitious awe of his cold, searching eyes and skilful hands. Duplessis had made no attempt to disguise the slightly flabby cheeks, but the mouth was hard, the eyes keen and dominating, and there was something menacing about the large, bony right hand that lay, with the little finger extended, on a pile of books. The portrait of the celebrated surgeon inspired her with an even deeper feeling of uneasiness than he did when he conducted the medical examinations which she looked forward to expectantly and yet dreaded.

Finally she reached the portrait of Franklin. The gallery was packed

and the crowd of inquisitive would-be onlookers stretched back as
far as the courtyard, but there was a deathly silence as she stood in
front of the painting.

The man gazing at her out of the frame was the same man that Toinette had seen at Gennevilliers, and yet he was very different. The
wide, commanding mouth was closed and did not by any means look
as if gallant phrases could emerge from it. The eyes beneath the
massive forehead were stern and just. Were they looking at her?
Were they looking beyond her? Were they looking right through
her? Toinette wondered at her courage in having entered into an argument with such a man. She was even a little afraid. Yet she was
once more attracted to him and proud that she had sought the meeting.

Duplessis was standing behind her and a little to one side, trying
to observe the impression his work was making on the Queen. He
seemed to see her face for the first time as it really was, pretty, not
clever though far from empty, vivacious, haughty, and with a royal
air. If he should ever have another opportunity to paint her, he would
make a good picture of it, but these mighty ones of the earth were
always so reluctant to give one the few sittings that were needed.
It was pleasant working with the American and his portrait had
turned out a success. The eyes had taken a lot of doing, but he was
satisfied with the result. This was the real Franklin, who looked at
you and at the same time looked beyond you.

Toinette stood before the picture in silence. The gallery was quiet,
oppressively quiet, and she knew that she was expected to say something, but she must be careful that what she said could not be misinterpreted even by the most malicious tongue. At last, turning with
a graceful movement to Duplessis, she commented, "Excellent. Really
an excellent portrait, worthy of our Duplessis." She was glad that she
had not said, "Worthy of our Franklin."

That evening she went to the Opera, where Gluck's *Iphigenia* was
being performed. She traversed the short distance on foot, and all the
way she was greeted with acclaim. On the last occasions when she
had appeared at the theatre the audience had risen on her entrance,
but they had remained silent. This time she received an ovation that
lasted for some minutes, and at the beginning of the aria in the
second act, "Sing praises to your Queen," Achilles stepped forward
to the footlights and faced Toinette's box as he sang. The audience
rose from their seats and twice demanded an encore.

Toinette had often in her young life had to acknowledge the homage
paid to her by a cheering crowd, but it had never inspired her with
such happiness as on this evening. Her oval face was slightly flushed
as she inclined her head with its magnificent high-piled coiffure first
to the left, then to the right, and again to the front in accordance
with the prescribed ceremonial. "Now let the Abbé come and tell

me again that I am unpopular in Paris," she thought to herself. The
simple but noble melody of the aria echoed in her heart, and she
regretted that she was not wearing Franklin's picture in her hair.

☆   ☆   ☆

When it came to Louis's ears that Toinette had been to inspect
Franklin's portrait, he was filled with a dull fury. Had she not
promised him to refrain from any manifestation of sympathy with
the Americans? If the people of Paris had afterwards accorded her
an ovation, that only confirmed the fact that her visit to the Salon
was regarded generally as a mark of favour shown to the rebels, in
other words as an encouragement to revolution. It was the spirit of
rebellion that had paid homage to Toinette at the Opera.

And he could do nothing about it but remain silent and sad. If he
were to reproach her with pampering the revolutionaries, she would
merely pretend not to know what he was talking about. He could
see her look of disdainful innocence. What had she done? She had
inspected the pictures of Duplessis, the court painter. Had that been
a wrong thing to do?

Prince Xavier came and spoke about the Salon. "There is a picture
of you there," he said, "that colossal daub of Robin's. They tell me
that he has very much idealized you, my dear Louis, and of course it
was necessary in order to make you look kingly. It would have been
a good joke if we could have gone there together to have a look at
Robin's masterpiece, but I suppose it wouldn't do since they've hung
the rebel's portrait there too. It appears, though, that some people
don't possess the same scruples. It is all a matter of taste."

Louis raged inwardly, but said nothing.

Two or three days later he received a print of the Franklin portrait,
and he sat studying with animosity the American's features. Duplessis
had of course suppressed all the baser qualities of the man. He was a
good artist, Duplessis; he had proved it in his picture of Louis himself, but it was a pity that art and virtue were so seldom found in
union.

He read the poetic caption beneath the engraved reproduction.
"Here are the glory and the power of the New World. The tides
of the ocean are hushed at his voice. He rules the thunder and bids it
cease at will. Does he who disarms the gods need to fear the kings?"
Louis read the verse a second time. So things had reached this pass!
People dared to publish such words in his capital city! This was more
than lèse-majesté. It was blasphemy. "He rules the thunder and
bids it cease at will." A coarse, angry sound issued from Louis's
throat. He rang the bell and ordered the Chief of Police to come and
see him at once.

When Monsieur Lenoir appeared, Louis thrust the print in front of his nose. "Have you seen this?" he demanded.

"It is the portrait of Franklin by Monsieur Duplessis," replied Lenoir. "It has been very favourably commented upon, very favourably indeed. The print is selling like hot cakes."

"Have you read the verse beneath?" demanded Louis again. "Read it!" he suddenly screamed.

"It is poor poetry," said Lenoir.

"And this is the kind of thing you allow to be sold in Paris!" Louis shouted. "This is the sort of thing that sells like hot cakes, at every street corner! Where are your eyes, Monsieur? Poor poetry, indeed! It is lèse-majesté, it is blasphemy. 'He bids the thunder cease.' Have you all gone crazy?"

Lenoir had turned pale, but he pulled himself together and said calmly, "The print is published by Monsieur Rouault, I see. I shall order Monsieur Rouault to remove the lines at once."

"This piece of blasphemy must be pulped," cried Louis, "and that fellow Rouault must be locked up."

"I would beg Your Majesty to consider—" the Chief of Police demurred.

"I *have* considered," interrupted Louis, "and you too should have considered before permitting this to be published. 'Bids the thunder cease.' Go!" he cried. "Carry out my instructions!"

Lenoir went, but he called first of all upon Maurepas and Vergennes. Then he arranged for Rouault to be informed that he had been ordered to arrest him, and it was only after the publisher had found safety in flight that agents were sent to carry out the King's instructions.

Meanwhile Maurepas was pointing out to Louis that at the present juncture, when Franklin's portrait was creating something of a sensation, the imprisonment of the publisher would not only be interpreted as a hostile act in America, but would be regarded as an affront to the people of Paris. After some hesitation, Louis ill-humouredly withdrew his order. "But those godless lines must be removed. They must disappear completely," he insisted with angry determination.

The print was sold henceforth without the offending caption, but there was plenty of empty space below the portrait and the people of Paris wrote in the lines themselves.

☆   ☆   ☆

Louis did not say a word to Toinette about her visit to the Salon or about the consequences of her visit, and she was glad that he said nothing.

There was, however, a feeling of disappointment, gnawing at her heart. She was restless and harassed by uncomfortable, humiliating thoughts. Week after week, month after month, had gone by and there was still no sign that a Dauphin was on the way. In all her mother's letters, in her reproaches at the meeting with Franklin and her extravagance in connexion with the Trianon she could sense the old woman's sorrow at the failure of her hopes.

In order to blunt the keenness of her disappointment she flung herself eagerly into her dramatic studies. She practised indefatigably the correct pronunciation of the letter "r" and even risked the danger of spoiling her celebrated "floating" gait by learning to walk like the ladies of the *Théâtre français*. Michu and Caillot were surprised to discover that she was prepared to work as if she wanted to become a professional actress.

All this, however, did not help her much. There were perpetual quarrels with Vaudreuil, who inquired scornfully how much longer she intended to wait for results from "the fat fellow." She ordered him angrily to leave her, and for two days she refused to see him.

In order, perhaps, to make her jealous, he attached himself more closely to Gabrielle. Toinette realized perfectly well what he was up to, but she grew more and more edgy, and since bitter retorts and reproaches had no effect on Vaudreuil she began to take her revenge on the gentle, easy-going Gabrielle.

It happened that Jules Polignac had promised an aunt of his who had lost her fortune, a certain Baroness d'Andlau, that he would help her. In his domineering way he demanded that Gabrielle should persuade Toinette to provide her with a pension. "A mere *pourboire*," he explained, "say, 6,000 livres a year." Gabrielle agreed without more ado, and when she next saw Toinette she casually passed on the request, not expecting that the latter would raise any objection.

Toinette had had a bad night. She remembered that in Paris they were associating her personal expenditures with the inability of the Government to provide immediate assistance to the Americans. She heard in her mind Joseph reciting with remarkable accuracy the long list of sinecures and annuities with which she had endowed the Polignacs. "How much would it involve?" she asked.

"500 livres a month," replied Gabrielle. It sounded an absurdly small amount the way she said it.

"I do not think I can make her this allowance," answered Toinette languidly.

"But it's a matter of 500 livres!" said Gabrielle in surprise, adding a little helplessly, "If I understood correctly, Jules has already promised her the money." When Toinette returned no answer, she concluded with a resigned shrug of the shoulders, "Well, in that case Aunt d'Andlau will just have to wait until Jules or I win at cards."

Toinette was annoyed that Gabrielle did not take her refusal more to heart. "By the way," she said, "I shall probably be announcing shortly that at my card evenings no higher stake will be permitted than 10 louis. I promised the King I would do so."

"Then you will have to come to me," replied Gabrielle with cheerful innocence, "when you feel like playing higher."

"I don't know," said Toinette slowly, maliciously. "Since moving into the Trianon I do not find any pleasure in meeting your Marquis de Dreneux or Mr. Smith from Manchester."

Gabrielle shook her head. "When I asked them to take the bank," she replied, still more surprised than hurt, "you were glad that they did so, weren't you? The rest of us were cleaned out."

In a sudden cold rage Toinette cried, "You are not venturing to tell the Queen, Madame, that it was she who induced you to invite this riffraff!"

"What on earth is the matter with you, Toinette?" asked Gabrielle in bewilderment. "Is anything wrong?"

"Everybody is trying to vex me," burst out Toinette. "They are all insulting me. Because I am kind to everyone, they think they can trample on me."

"Who is trampling on you, Toinette?" asked Gabrielle soothingly. But this query only served to incense Toinette still further.

"You are all trying to get what you can out of me," she cried. "Haven't you just demanded 6,000 livres for your aunt?"

Gabrielle realized that Toinette was taking revenge on her because her sarcasm and fits of fury had no effect on Vaudreuil. Goodnatured as she was, and sincerely fond of Toinette, she was prepared to put up with a great deal, but she herself was not particularly concerned about the material advantages her relatives derived from Toinette and she felt aggrieved at the latter's unfairness. "I can understand your being in a state of nerves," she retorted, "but I allow nobody, not even you, to dictate to me whom I shall receive in my house." Toinette did not reply, but maintained an air of icy hauteur, and the two parted without making any attempt at reconciliation.

For a couple of hours Toinette congratulated herself on having spoken her mind to Gabrielle. Then she began to feel remorseful. On the following morning Gabrielle was absent from the *lever,* and when she remained away for a second day, Toinette would have liked to go to her at once to beg her forgiveness. But her pride restrained her.

By careful questioning she discovered from Diane that Gabrielle was going to be present at a big card party in the Princess Rohan's apartments. After all she had said to Gabrielle, it would be humiliating to go to the Princess Rohan's that evening. Nevertheless she went.

The Princess's rooms were crowded, there was the usual thick atmosphere, the yapping of the dogs, the screeching of the parrot, the chink of money, and the subdued cries of the gamblers. Gabrielle was in the middle of a game, but when she saw Toinette she smiled with pleasure. Toinette sat down beside her, they chatted about clothes and other trifling matters, and it was as if they had never quarrelled.

Toinette began to play, though for not very high stakes. "If I win," she said casually, "I will grant your Aunt Andlau the allowance you asked for—though I shall do the same if I lose."

"Thank you, Toinette," murmured Gabrielle.

The game continued. Suddenly both wings of the double doors were flung open. "The King!" cried the lackey who was on duty outside. Louis entered, breathing heavily.

During the past week Louis had hardly seen Toinette except on official occasions. The Franklin print, the blasphemous verse, his order for the arrest of the publisher, and the subsequent happenings had made him more angry with her than ever, but he knew only too well that he could not do anything about it and he had held his tongue. Even when it came to his ears that she had broken her promise to cut down her expenditure and had resumed her frantic search for amusement, he said nothing. He took only one step to remedy matters. Subsequently to his night at the Trianon he had revived an old regulation, after consulting Toinette, to the effect that within the precincts of the Palace the highest stake permitted in games of chance was one *louis d'or*. When evidence reached him of Toinette's continued unreliability and disobedience he ordered the Chief of Police to inform him through his secret agents whenever a card game was in progress at which his decree was being flouted.

The news of the card party in the Princess Rohan's apartments, together with the information that the Queen was present, reached him as he sat poring over a volume of the Abbé Prévost's *General Account of Interesting Travels*. Monsieur de Laharpe of the Academy had been commissioned by him to bring out a new edition of this voluminous work, and he was taking a lively interest in the publication of the several volumes. It was in the eighteenth volume of these *Interesting Travels,* dealing with Kamschatka and Greenland, that he was so deeply absorbed when his studies were interrupted by the intelligence that his orders were being defied. Beside him stood a silver dish containing a piece of cold roast hare and a costly *saucière* of cranberry jelly. With his short-sighted eyes fixed on the printed page he dipped his piece of hare mechanically into the jelly, took a bite, tore a mouthful off with his teeth, swallowed it, and continued to read as he went on dipping and eating.

While the police agent, standing stiffly at attention, presented his verbal report, Louis stared at him and listened with his chunk of meat still poised in his hand. "Very good," he said. Then, before the police agent had time to reach the door, which he was approaching back-

wards, Louis hurled the piece of hare back onto the dish and shut
his book with a slam.

He was filled with a savage sense of satisfaction. Rising from his
chair, he proceeded, unescorted, towards the apartments of the Princess Rohan. Every now and then he wiped his hands on his coat tails,
and though the way was long his anger did not cool.

Even when he stood before the table where Toinette had been
playing, he was glad to note that his fury was unabated. The gentlemen had sprung up and bowed low, but he did not see them. He
had eyes only for what was on the table—cards, heaps of coins, and
a number of i.o.u.'s, glasses containing drinks, and small dishes of
sweetmeats.

"Good evening, Sire," said Toinette.

"Good evening, Madame," he replied in a high-pitched, agitated
voice. "I wanted to enjoy an hour of quiet conversation with you and
your ladies." He was breathing heavily and did not finish the sentence.

"That was a good idea, Sire," said the Princess Rohan, but Louis,
losing control of his voice, shrieked, "And this is what I see!"

"What is it that you see, Sire?" inquired Toinette. Beneath the
table her foot was beginning invisibly to tap.

Louis stepped close up to the table, gathered a small heap of coins
in his hand, and thrust them in front of the Princess Rohan's face.
"What are these, Madame?" he demanded. When she failed to answer
he shrieked again, "Are they livres? Are they sous or écus? No,
Madame! They are *louis d'or*. Not one *louis d'or,* but ten, eleven,
thirteen *louis d'or."* He flung the money back on the table. "On that
table," he shouted, "lies the budget of a whole province."

"You are exaggerating, Sire," said Diane Polignac with polite determination. "Even your poorest province could hardly manage on
such a small budget."

"Be silent, Madame!" he cried. "This is not a moment for
the display of wit. That which lies here on the table belongs to
the poor." Without addressing anybody in particular he issued his
orders. "I want a complete list of those who have been present here
tonight and a second list showing the amount of money on the tables.
I want the exact figures, tabulated according to the kinds of coin. The
list must be on my table by eight o'clock in the morning. Good evening, Madame. Good evening, ladies and gentlemen." He withdrew
with his heavy tread, snorting with satisfaction.

On the following morning Toinette sought him out in his library.
He thought she had come to apologize and was prepared to be magnanimous.

"It was kind of you, Sire," she said, "to take the trouble to visit me
in the circle of my friends. But the vehemence with which you reminded myself and my ladies of our charitable duties wounded me

deeply. It is not my impression that you have frequently found me wanting in this respect. I would recall to your mind the poor peasants whom I have provided with food and shelter in my village at the Trianon. Your coarse reproach—please permit me to speak bluntly—was indeed hardly necessary."

Louis stared at the book he had been reading. It was still the eighteenth volume of the *Interesting Travels*. He gazed at the words unseeingly, for he was completely disconcerted at such a display of naïveté on the part of Toinette, or was it, perhaps, impudence?

"I don't know," he stammered. "Really—"

"But you ought to have known, Sire," she said. "I had to spend the whole evening trying to comfort my ladies."

"You are not showing a good example to the court," he declared, pulling himself together, "when you gamble away in a single evening enough money to defray—"

"The budget of a whole province," she interjected mockingly. "I know. You said that yesterday. But do be fair, Louis. You must admit that I have been economizing recently. I am leading a simple rural existence at the Trianon and wear only linen dresses as they do in Alsace. I hear in fact that the silk manufacturers of Lyons are complaining because my example has reduced the demand for their materials. I have done my best to please you and even went to the Salon, though I am not particularly interested in paintings, because I did not want to hurt the feelings of the artists for your sake, Louis. I have had occasion, too, to realize that the people of Paris appreciate what I have been doing. Did you hear how tumultuously they greeted me at the Opera?"

Louis continued to stare silently at his *Interesting Travels*. He had given up trying to follow her chatter. "By the way," she went on, "talking of artists and pictures, it is time I saw to the decorating of the ceiling in my theatre. Lagrenée has already prepared some designs, Apollo and a few of the Graces, something very simple. But painters know how to charge these days and I have not yet authorized the work to be carried out. I know that I promised you I would economize. So, if you like, I will leave the theatre bare."

When she left, Louis had granted her another 100,000 livres for the Trianon.

☆   ☆   ☆

The two officers who had been returned from America, Major de Mauroy and Lieutenant Dubois, had gone straight to Pierre and told him about their unpleasant experiences in Philadelphia. He was very much upset, not only because he felt a certain responsibility for their departure from France in the first place, but because the chilly welcome they had experienced strengthened his premonition that the firm of Hortalez would still have numerous difficulties to overcome before its claims were settled.

Two hours later the American mail arrived with accurate and objective reports of the reception accorded to Lafayette and the other officers. The courier had at last brought the letter from Paul for which he had been waiting so long.

Locking the door of his study, and alone with his bitch Caprice, Pierre sat down to read through the extensive dispatch.

"Though I should have known better had I devoted more thought to the subject," wrote Paul, "I imagined when I was in Paris that the Congress of the United States would be something like the Roman Senate in its heyday, *an assembly of kings,* as the ancient authors called it. The reality in Philadelphia has turned out to be very different. To be quite candid, my dear friend, the Continental Congress of the United States can not even be compared, in point of either outward or inward dignity, with a provincial council in France. There is a constant pitiful squabbling over petty rights and duties, the thirteen States are always quarrelling among themselves, their representatives have only their particular interests at heart, and even the States themselves are split into Conservatives and Progressives. Profiteering and corruption flourish as they did in the days of despotism, only more blatantly. The adherents of the English King are more numerous and influential than is assumed in Paris, and deeply ingrained prejudices render even progressive Americans fanatical Gallophobes."

Paul went on to describe in detail the disgraceful way in which the French officers had been received. It appeared, however, that General Washington had meanwhile received the letter of introduction in which Franklin had recommended Lafayette, and he was doing his best to counteract the unhappy impression made by the Congress.

Paul then proceeded to analyse the prospects of the firm of Hortalez. Mr. Arthur Lee had several times declared in the most positive manner that the "loan" granted to Pierre by the French Government was an outright gift from the King not to Pierre, but to the Congress itself, and though Paul was exerting every effort to correct this distortion, the gentlemen of the Congress refused to listen. They deliberately insisted on misunderstanding the real situation. He was trying, however, at least to obtain payment of the claims that were not in dispute, though even in this case the gentlemen of the Congress were indulging in manœuvres which could only be described as subterfuges. Among the shabbiest of their excuses was the threadbare pretext that their sense of responsibility forbade them to pay anything at all until every item had been proved to be indubitably authentic. Such shifts were hardly worthy of a great freedom-loving nation, but the

mountainous financial difficulties of the Congress made them comprehensible.

Pierre read this passage twice, with a grim respect for his young
friend's objective attitude. "Comprehensible!" he mused bitterly. "The
subterfuges of the Americans are comprehensible! That is no doubt
correct. But I am the one who has to pay the piper."

To be quite fair, concluded Paul, in addition to many narrow-
minded shopkeepers the Congress contained also men of long vision
with a strong sense of honesty. A cargo of tobacco and indigo to the
value of 27,250 livres was on the way as a kind of token payment, and
he was confident that he would ultimately succeed in obtaining acknowledgment of the whole debt due to the firm. Nor had his belief
in the eventual success of the Americans been in the slightest degree
shaken by his experiences on that side of the ocean, much as they had
taxed his patience and his nerves.

Pierre propped his chin in both hands and for a fleeting moment
his courage melted away. "This is a pretty trap we've fallen into,"
he said to his bitch Caprice, "a pretty trap indeed." A surge of anger
welled up in him. So this was the sum total of Paul's efforts. For
the sake of a cargo of tobacco and indigo to the value of 27,250 livres
Paul had crossed the ocean and placed his life in jeopardy. Rogues,
shabby cheats who refused to keep their word, that was what they
were, these heroes who were allegedly fighting for freedom. It was
for such people that he was risking his money and ruining his nerves.
It was for such people that Lafayette had thrown his sword into the
scales. People who sought refuge in shifts and pretexts. If a single
item did not tally, then they rejected the whole account and declined
to pay. It would never be difficult to find such an item at which to
boggle. God damn them.

A look of repugnance came over his fresh-coloured, fleshy face.
He was ashamed not of his own credulity, but of the men on whose
behalf he had launched his enterprise. On the other hand, he would
not allow his interest in the great cause to be diminished in the slightest by the petty behaviour of individual Congress leaders.

He had an opportunity to prove this when soon afterwards Silas
Deane came and told him about the affair of Baron von Steuben. The
latter had returned to Germany, as he had said he would, and his
services as a seasoned soldier and organizer were irrevocably lost to
the insurgents.

Irrevocably? No! Was not Pierre de Beaumarchais still to be reckoned with? He sat down and conjured Steuben in a fiery letter to
return to Paris. All his resources, he said, would be placed at the
General's disposal and a ship was already lying at Marseilles ready
to transport him across the ocean. Was America, was the great cause
of liberty, to be denied the collaboration of such a distinguished

soldier merely because by some unlucky chance he had missed the opportunity during his sojourn in Paris of meeting him, Pierre de Beaumarchais? Such an unlucky chance must not be allowed to determine the course of history.

His letter was so persuasive that Steuben actually returned to Paris.

And within twenty-four hours Pierre had obtained his promise to join Washington's army even without the formality of a contract. Pierre saw to it that he was properly fitted out, sent him to Marseilles in his own comfortable travelling coach, provided him with a considerable sum of money, and handed him two letters for delivery on the other side, one addressed to Paul and the second to the Congress. He spared no effort to ensure that after Lafayette's unfortunate experience Baron von Steuben should be accorded an honourable welcome in Philadelphia. "Please do what you can," he wrote to Paul, "for this tried and trusty soldier whom I am proud to call my friend. If he should need money, furnish him with whatever he requires. It will be well invested. If it should be lost, it will be money well lost if only a man of his quality can be accorded the place he merits in America's fight for freedom. I can think of no better return on my capital than the deeds he will perform." To the Congress he lectured: "The art of waging war successfully demands a combination of courage, prudence, theoretical knowledge, and practical experience. All these are to be found in the great soldier whom I have the honour to send to you. He was a comrade-in-arms of Frederick of Prussia, at whose side he served for twenty-two years in a position of responsibility. Such a man will appear to you too, gentlemen, qualified to assist General Washington."

Furnished with these two letters of introduction, Baron von Steuben embarked for America. In order to ensure that the insurgents should not lose his services Pierre had spent 12,000 livres, almost half the amount that Paul had so far been able to extract from the Congress.

☆   ☆   ☆

The fact that Paul's letter had removed the last justified hope of receiving payment from Philadelphia within any foreseeable period did not deter Pierre from spending more and more money on the house he was building. It rejoiced his heart when the architect Le Moyne declared that it was many years since such a sumptuous edifice had been commissioned in Paris by any private person.

Thérèse, for whom the house was being built, showed little interest in it. She had only one desire, that the rooms in which she would live with her baby should be as simple as possible, like those at Meudon. Pierre was hurt, but eventually he agreed to her request.

Julie, on the other hand, eagerly assisted both in the reconstruction and the furnishing. Though she was highly affronted at Pierre's decision to spend part of his life in future with his wife instead of with her, this did not prevent her from having her say in everything the architect proposed to do or not to do, and when Pierre gently indicated that he wished to remove from the house in the rue de Condé a number of articles to which he was deeply attached, her indignation knew no bounds. He particularly wanted to transfer to his new house the massive writing-table in his study, the chest from the neighbouring little cabinet in which he kept his treasures, together with the broad divan that held so many pleasurable memories for him, and finally the portraits of Duverny and Désirée, as well as the copy of the figure-head of the *Orfraye*. Julie raised a fresh outcry at the mention of each item, even protesting against his proposal to take with him the portrait of Désirée, which had always been a source of irritation to her. He had no feeling for his family, she cried reproachfully, and if their father could see how he was leaving her in the lurch in her old age he would turn in his grave.

There was much gossip in Paris about the costly mansion being erected by Monsieur de Beaumarchais, whose financial position was known to be shaky. The firm of Hortalez, it was rumoured, was pitching and tossing like a ship at sea, and some people went so far as to declare that it was not a real house of brick and stone that was being put up behind the great wooden fence in the rue Saint-Antoine, but a mere façade for show. Pierre did not allow such gibes to disturb him. When the house was finished these gentlemen would be able to see for themselves.

The first to inspect it were the friends of Emile, Pierre's valet. The faithful servant had had to endure many taunts from his colleagues and he asked his master for permission to show two or three of them over the new residence. Pierre, knowing that the opinion of these lackeys had a great influence both at court and in the city generally, agreed.

So, accompanied by three of his friends, who were in the service respectively of the Duc de Richelieu, the Marquis de Vaudreuil, and the Count de Montbarrey, Emile drove in his master's carriage to the rue Saint-Antoine. They alighted and were guided by Emile through the domain. "These are our cascades," he explained proudly, though with an affectation of modesty, "and here is our Chinese bridge. Our original intention was to have a little Swiss bridge leading across the stream, like the one you have, Richelieu, but then we thought it not sufficiently modern. Our architect advised us that the Chinese style is now again all the rage, as it was fifteen years ago." All around was the white shimmer of statues and busts, partly of classical gods and goddesses, partly of Pierre's relatives and friends. The lackeys rowed on the tiny lake and seated themselves in the dainty arbours, that seemed made for lovers and were adorned with busts of Pierre's father and sisters.

The most striking embellishment to be seen in the park was a small temple that had been erected upon a mound. They ascended the steps leading up to it and Emile explained, "This is our Voltaire temple." Inside there was a marble bust of the philosopher, and on the dome gleamed a large golden terrestrial globe with a great golden quill pen stuck through one of the poles.

"Very neat, Beaumarchais," acknowledged the Vaudreuil lackey, "very apt. A really good idea of yours."

They read the motto: "From the eyes of the world he tore the bandage of error."

"Did your master write that?" asked the Vaudreuil lackey.

"No," Emile informed him, "it is by the other one."

From the temple, as from all the other points of vantage, they could see the sinister mass of the Bastille looming up on the other side of the square. "I don't like that so much," commented the Montbarrey lackey.

"You do not understand," explained Emile. "That is the most significant view of all, and it is the reason why we decided to settle here. We think the house and the view constitute a kind of allegory."

"Aha!" said the Vaudreuil lackey.

Emile took his friends round the house. Proceeding through the lofty entrance hall he led them up the elegantly curved staircase and through the fifteen rooms, of which the most imposing was the spacious circular salon with its great dome. It was decorated with pictures by Hubert Robert and Vernet, while the mantelpiece was supported by caryatids of Carrara marble. "This mantelpiece alone cost us 40,000 livres," said Emile.

The lackeys adhered to the same principle as their masters of not openly expressing their admiration of anything that impressed them, but in the case of Pierre's new house they could not help doing so and they spread its fame abroad.

When Pierre awoke after his first night in the rue Saint-Antoine, his *lever* was attended by all those whom he had hoped to see there— Baron de Trois-Tours, the Chevalier de Clonard, Monsieur Régnier of the Supreme Court, and the rest. Despite their malicious gibes at his extravagant love of ostentation, they envied a man who, though he had been bankrupt practically from the cradle, was able to indulge his taste for such luxury.

Maigron strolled through the magnificent rooms with impassive countenance, keeping his thoughts to himself. In his quiet, cautious way, more by his manner than by what he said, he had warned Pierre against assuming this new and heavy burden. Knowing as he did to the last sou what every single item had cost, he meditated

gloomily on the fact that, for instance, a statue of Ariadne had
involved an outlay that would have sufficed to meet Messrs. Roche's
bill for their consignments of sugar. Yet the more shaky the affairs
of the firm of Hortalez became, the more attached did the business-
like Maigron feel towards both the firm and its chief. It had been
hinted to him by certain people in the business world that a well-
known firm of sound repute would be glad to engage the services of
a man of his qualities, and he had reasons for believing that the offer
came from Lenormant. But so long as he remained the trusted assistant of Beaumarchais no offer had the power to tempt him away.

Lenormant himself was one of the first to call upon Pierre at his
new house. His small, deep-set eyes gazed with an air of melancholy
at the excessive pomp with which Pierre had adorned his home. Some
of the artistic treasures he had accumulated were undoubtedly worth
having, and Lenormant would have been glad to possess them. The
mantelpiece with the caryatids, for example, would look well in the
music-room of his Paris mansion, and the portrait of Désirée by
Quentin de Latour was just the thing for his dressing-room at Etioles.
In his low, oily voice he congratulated Pierre on the evident prosperity
of his American enterprise, which was clearly flourishing to a far
greater extent than he, Charlot, had ever thought possible. Only for
a fraction of a second, as he looked out upon the Bastille, did an
ominous vestige of a smile curve the corners of his mouth.

Julie's first reaction when he led her on a tour of inspection through
the completed dwelling was to indulge in spiteful witticisms, but then
she suddenly fell upon his neck in an outburst of mingled tears and
laughter and cried, "You really are the greatest and best of men,
Pierrot. Of course, you had to build this marvellous house. It is no
more than you deserve. And I do realize that Thérèse cuts a better
figure here than I could possibly do. If only Papa could have lived to
see this," she kept lamenting.

Pierre went about in a state of radiant happiness, anxious to share
his joy with everyone. He told his pretty sister Tonton to order herself a dress from Mademoiselle Bertin, and to his faithful Philippe
Gudin he presented not only a writing-table, made of precious wood
from the Islands and curved in the centre for the greater comfort
of his capacious paunch, but also a wonderful Chinese dressing-gown.
Furthermore he sent him a whole cartload of learned works. Touched
by such a display of friendship, Gudin sat down at his new writing-
table in his Chinese dressing-gown, with his stomach comfortably
fitting into the central curve, and worked with redoubled zeal at his
history of Pierre Beaumarchais. As the contents grew, so did the
title. It was now called, *A True Chronicle of the Life and Opinions
of the Writer and Statesman Pierre-Augustin Caron de Beaumarchais.*

Désirée was one of the last of Pierre's friends to visit his new acquisition. She wanted to wait until she could come with her fellow actors and actresses, for Pierre had dropped his original idea of giving a housewarming party to which the whole of Paris should be invited. At the suggestion of Gudin he had decided to celebrate the occasion in a more befitting manner by introducing his new comedy to the company of the *Théâtre français*.

So they assembled, proudest of the world's artists, to hear their favourite playwright read the sequel to *The Barber*. First they made a tour of the house, some of them being impressed, but the majority, who possessed more taste and judgment, not hesitating to express their criticisms freely.

The atmosphere threatened to grow frosty and Pierre was on the point of giving up the idea of reading his play. Then the very fact that the evening seemed to be turning into a fiasco made him decide that he would read it after all and show them what he could do.

At first it did not move smoothly, but then he got into his stride and the impressionable actors, who had been inclined to smile sarcastically, were soon carried away. They were unable to sit still, but kept jumping up to look over his shoulder at the script, or cried, "Again, Pierre, read that line again!" They grew more and more excited, and in the end the evening was a tremendous success.

They were all agreed, however, that there was no possibility whatsoever of *The Marriage of Figaro* being seen in the theatre.

"It will be produced," said Pierre with calm self-assurance.

"It will not be produced," said the actor Préville. "You are more likely to hear the Archbishop reading the memoirs of Casanova from the pulpit of Notre Dame."

"*The Marriage of Figaro* will be produced, Monsieur," replied Pierre, "and you will play the part of Figaro. That is as certain as that Versailles will recognize the independence of America. It is I, Pierre de Beaumarchais, who tell you so."

"Bravo!" cried the faithful Gudin with conviction.

"Shall we have a wager on it, Monsieur?" proposed Préville with the inimitable careless air for which he was celebrated.

"With pleasure," replied Pierre. "What stakes have you in mind?"

The actor meditated. "Shall we say—a bust by Houdon?" he suggested. It was well known that the sculptor Jean-Antoine Houdon never accepted a commission for less than 25,000 livres.

"The idea I should like to put forward is this," went on Préville. "If *Figaro* is produced I will order a bust of you from Houdon. If not, then you will order a bust of me."

"Agreed," said Pierre. "Ladies and gentlemen," he announced, "you have heard our Préville's promise to commission a bust of me. I hereby present it to the *Théâtre français* for the vestibule."

"Bravo!" cried Gudin enthusiastically.

They sat down to table. Pierre had spent the last fortnight arranging this repast. It was a long night, and between many wines they told one another many truths.

Towards morning, when the company was growing weary, Pierre drew back the curtains from the great window. Slowly the mass of the Bastille loomed up in the fading darkness. At first they were all surprised and attempted some lame witticisms. Then they fell silent; sitting or standing amid the stale fumes of the wine lees, in the flickering light of the guttering tapers, they stared at the grey, lowering structure whose sinister outlines became sharper in the rising morning.

"It helps me to write," said Pierre.

☆   ☆   ☆

Franklin drove from Passy to the Hôtel d'Hambourg to pick up his fellow commissioners for an appointment with Vergennes at the Foreign Office, which was situated in the Hôtel Lautrec on the Quai des Théatins. They had been instructed by the Congress to apply to the French Government for a further loan, and it had been impressed upon them that they should not set their demands too low. The moment seemed favourable, for the latest news from America was moderately satisfactory. General Washington had paraded his troops through the streets of Philadelphia, the population had greeted them with vociferous cheers, and a number of French officers, including Lafayette, had taken part in the procession. The trouble about the Frenchmen appeared therefore to have been settled and things looked more auspicious.

Unfortunately, however, during the two days that had elapsed since Vergennes had announced his readiness to receive them, the situation had changed for the worse, and as Franklin drove towards Paris in his comfortable carriage he pondered anxiously on the reports that had come in from Amsterdam and London. General Washington was said to have suffered a defeat near Philadelphia, and it was even rumoured that the city had already fallen. Moreover, the English General Burgoyne had penetrated deep into the territory of the United States from Canada and was threatening to cut off New England from the rest of the country.

When Franklin arrived at the Hôtel d'Hambourg he could see from the faces of his colleagues that the ominous rumours had received fresh nourishment. Monsieur de Gérard had just sent word to them that fresh dispatches had arrived from America and Count Vergennes wished to study them before receiving the commissioners. If the news they contained had been good, it was hardly likely that Vergennes would have postponed the meeting.

They sat in gloomy thought. In the circumstances it was doubtful whether there was any point in seeing Vergennes at all. Franklin suggested that it might be best to put off the interview indefinitely. Deane's view was that they should meet the Minister, but that instead of asking for the five million they had had in mind, they should ask for only three. Lee opposed this angrily. If they appeared too modest, he said, they would be giving the impression that they regarded the American cause as lost. On the contrary, they must put an even bolder face on the matter and demand not three or five millions, but the whole fourteen million that the Congress wished to obtain from France. Silas Deane retorted excitedly that if they were to approach a realist like Vergennes with such utopian ideas they would only make themselves appear ridiculous. To which Lee replied in equal excitement that if they applied to the gentlemen at Versailles for a petty amount like three million or five million, they would be looked upon as beggars and turned away contemptuously. After all, it was not Messrs. Franklin, Deane, and Lee who were treating with Count Vergennes, but one sovereign country dealing with another sovereign country.

"That is mere empty talk," pooh-poohed Silas Deane. "If we ask for three million we may get one million. If we ask for fourteen million we shall get nothing at all and only be laughed at for our pains."

"I ought to have realized from the outset," muttered Lee bitterly, "that I only have to make a proposal to be sure it will be rejected." He proceeded to work himself into a fury. "It drives me to despair the way I am treated here. You send reports to Philadelphia without showing them to me. I am expected to append my signature to accounts that I have been given no opportunity of checking. I am not supported when they rebuff me at Versailles. But this time I am not going to let you push me to one side. I insist that we ask the French Government for the whole fourteen million."

"I think it is quite hopeless to ask for such a sum," said Franklin very calmly, "but if you insist, I am prepared to go with you to Vergennes."

The interview with Vergennes accorded fully with Franklin's premonitions. The Minister, who normally exuded such amiability and charm, was neither amiable nor charming. He was, on the contrary, irritable and aggressive. "There is no need, gentlemen, for you to announce your request," he said. "I am already aware of its nature and am conversant with all the details. My informant was the English Ambassador." As they were too completely taken aback to utter a word, he continued in a sharper tone than they had ever known him to employ, "I must tell you candidly, gentlemen, that I am astonished at your lack of caution. We have warned you time and again not to let everybody obtain an insight into your affairs, but you are apparently still so heedless in all matters which, in your interests and ours, should be kept secret, that anyone who wishes can learn all there is to know. His Majesty is deeply annoyed. You are practically asking the English to share your secrets. I have even heard already of your plan concerning the *Robert Morris* which is now lying at Rotterdam, and in this case too my information was derived from English sources."

Franklin gazed in consternation from the Minister to his colleagues. "To what plan are you referring?" he asked.

"You see," replied Vergennes indignantly, and he turned towards the Doctor's two companions. "The English are aware of your intention even before Doctor Franklin knows about them. These gentlemen," he explained to Franklin in a tone of contempt that verged on pity, "wish to make a gift to the King of the American schooner *Robert Morris,* so that the vessel may be allowed to leave Rotterdam under another name without interference."

"Not a bad idea," commented Franklin.

"But there is no need to shriek it from the house-tops before you do it," said Vergennes.

"We admit that we have been lacking in caution, Count Vergennes," said Lee morosely. "We confess that we are to blame. On the other hand, I would ask you to bear one thing in mind. We are men of honour, unaccustomed to acting in a conspiratorial manner as if we were thieves, which is what appears to be expected from us here."

Franklin quickly intervened. "Permit me to assure you, Excellency, that we shall in future take care to be on our guard."

"We should indeed be grateful," replied Vergennes brusquely.

Franklin broached the topic that they had come to discuss. "Since you are already apprised of the reason for our visit," he said with a faint smile, "we shan't waste your time by elaborating our request."

Arthur Lee proceeded, despite the Doctor's observation: "The Congress is now in greater need of your country's help than ever. Not that we are unable to keep our heads above water without foreign aid, but in our war with England we have reached a point where assistance will be far more useful than it is likely to be later on. It will save thousands of lives, prevent our settlements from being burnt and destroyed, and reduce our eventual expenditure to the extent of millions of pounds."

Franklin, having promised his fellow commissioner that he would back him up, joined in with the tranquil comment, "Every gun you send us today will be worth five in twelve months' time."

The Minister played with his quill. "I should be happy, gentlemen," he said, "to help you, though our financial situation is not of the best. Unfortunately, however, the King is very upset at your want of care in maintaining the secrecy of your projects, and it is impossible for me at the moment to approach him with a request for funds. I would ask you, gentlemen, to help me in conciliating His Majesty. Please try to act with a little caution and reserve. Perhaps, when sufficient time has elapsed, we shall then be in a position to offer you not fourteen million, but at any rate one million livres. The essential condition is that you should preserve the utmost discretion."

On their way back to the Hôtel d'Hambourg, Arthur Lee broke into a fury of imprecations against the French. "This frog-eater said their financial situation is not of the best," he cried viciously. "And why isn't it of the best? That female despot, Doctor Franklin, your female despot from whom you expected so much, it is she who is spending our money on clothes and châteaux and voluptuous amusements. That's why there's nothing left for America and the cause of liberty."

"I warned you, Mr. Lee," said Silas Deane, "that in the circumstances it was crazy to ask for such a large sum."

"I could not foresee," snapped Lee venomously, "that your spies would be so quick in selling my plan to England."

"My spies!" cried Deane heatedly. "Who was it that discussed the individual items on which we were going to spend the fourteen millions with Monsieur Grand, the banker? Was it you or I? It was all your fault without a doubt. You have again done irreparable damage to our country by your eternal activities."

"Monsieur Grand is a man to be trusted," retorted Lee, "and I wish one could say the same about that boasting friend of yours, Monsieur Caron."

"I think that will be enough, gentlemen," begged Franklin. "In view of the bad news that has come from London we should have got no money out of Vergennes even if there had been no whisper abroad of our intentions. It was only a pretext." The rest of the short journey was carried out in tense silence.

On the following day Franklin received official dispatches from America. The Congress Army had been defeated on the Brandywine. Philadelphia had fallen. The Congress had fled to York. Prepared though he had been, it was a heavy blow to Franklin.

It was *his* Philadelphia, his handsome house in Market Street occupied by the English. It was a great pity that after having removed his books and pictures to a place of safety Sally should have carted them back to Philadelphia. Now some red-coated lout of an English officer might be lolling in the arm-chair in his library, and the various ingenious devices he had installed for the greater comfort of his house were at the disposal of these fellows who would not know how to use them properly. There was his portrait by Benjamin Wilson, not a great work of art, but he was fond of the picture and it was disagreeable to think of an English officer sitting in front of it with a grin on his face.

He felt tired and very lonely. If only Dubourg could come and keep him company. But Dubourg was on his last legs, poor faithful friend, and unable to leave his house. Franklin felt a strong desire to see him; he ordered his carriage and drove to Paris.

Dubourg was in bed, wearing his night-cap and propped up on numerous pillows. He was looking emaciated, but his eyes lit up as Franklin entered. "Next week," he said, "I shall be well enough to come out to Passy again." Franklin told him how much he had missed both his company and his advice.

"Well, well," he replied. "I have not been idle, even though I have had to allow myself a little rest in bed. I have taken to heart the exhortation of Poor Richard, 'Since thou art not sure of a minute, throw not away an hour.' What did you think of my idea of presenting the *Robert Morris* to the King?"

"So it was your idea?" exclaimed Franklin. "I might have known it."

"Yes," said Dubourg happily, "but I thought it better not to tell you about it beforehand. You are a great man, but you do not quite understand these little *finesses*. It was no simple matter to carry my scheme through and I had to proceed by devious paths, for I am not on the best of terms with Mr. Lee and Mr. Deane." Franklin now knew how the English had so quickly got wind of the plan.

He told Dubourg of his own worries, of the sore straits in which his countrymen found themselves, the loss of his house in Philadelphia, and the sadness with which he thought of his books and other personal belongings to which he was so attached. These were anxieties with which Dubourg could deeply sympathize, and he displayed such grief that Franklin at last had to comfort him. "Anyway," he suggested, "our military reverses cannot seriously jeopardize our position here at Versailles, for owing to your excellent idea we have at least secured the good favours of the Queen."

"Yes," replied Dubourg, "it is a great consolation to me on my bed of suffering that I thought of it so opportunely."

Franklin also spoke of the espionage to which he was being subjected. "Do you know who is to blame for that?" cried Dubourg, stretching out accusingly a large, pale, withering hand. "Always that horse-fly, always that *mouche au coche*."

"Maybe," said Franklin.

☆　　☆　　☆

While all those in Europe who had espoused the American cause were worrying about the fall of Philadelphia and the defeats at Germantown and Brandywine, the American troops had long since won a victory that wiped out these reverses and tipped the scales decisively in favour of the United States. This victory was due partly to General Gates and partly to General Benedict Arnold, but chiefly to the ineptitude of five Englishmen—King George; Lord Germain, the Secretary for War; and Generals Howe, Clinton, and Burgoyne.

On the thirteenth of December, 1776, at three minutes past five o'clock in the afternoon, according to his own account, King George gave birth to a plan for the ordering of the campaign in America during the coming year. General Burgoyne was to drive down from Canada towards the south, General Howe was to set out from New York and march to meet him, and when the two armies had joined forces they would have cut New England off from the other colonies. Lord Germain, the Secretary for War, had an appointment to go hunting, however, so he put aside the instructions that were to be sent to General Howe and forgot about them. Consequently General Howe did not march to meet General Burgoyne, and when the latter, after arduous experiences, had successfully fought his way through and reached a point far to the south, he found himself alone and facing an American force greatly exceeding his own in numbers.

John Burgoyne was a keen soldier, an able dramatist, and an ardent lover of fair ladies. He had distinguished himself in the campaigns in Portugal, made a runaway match with Lord Derby's daughter, written successful plays such as *The Heiress* and *The Maid of the Oaks,* won fortunes at the gaming tables and lost them again. Now he had marched from Canada with the flower of the British and German troops, an excellently trained army which was supported moreover by a large number of Canadian seamen, a strong contingent of pioneers, and a great many red Indian auxiliaries. Ticonderoga and Fort Edward had been captured, and he had pushed through extremely difficult territory deep into enemy country where he had expected to join the second English army.

Instead of which he encountered an overwhelming force of Americans. His communications with Canada were cut, Generals Howe and Clinton were unable to answer his calls for help, and his supplies would last for no more than fourteen days.

He attempted a break-through, but was flung back with heavy losses by General Arnold. He thereupon entrenched himself on the heights of Saratoga and held a council of war. In eloquent terms he explained to his officers the hopelessness of their position and inquired whether any of them was able to recall a case in the history of warfare in which an army in a similar situation to their own had refused to capitulate. At this point a cannon ball whistled over their heads and General Burgoyne divided his query into two subsidiary queries. In the first place, had they any other course but to capitulate? The officers answered that they had not. Secondly, would capitulation in the existing circumstances be in accord with the code of military honour? The officers answered that it would.

Thereupon Burgoyne wrote as follows to General Gates of the American Army: "After having fought you twice, Lieutenant-General Burgoyne has waited some days in his present position, determined to try a third conflict against any force you could bring to attack him. He is apprised of the superiority of your numbers, & the disposition of your troops to impede his supplies and render his retreat a scene of carnage on both sides. In this situation he is impelled by humanity, and thinks himself justifiable by established principles and precedents of state, and of war, to spare the lives of brave men upon honourable terms. Should Major-General Gates be inclined to treat upon that idea, General Burgoyne would propose a cessation of arms during the time necessary to communicate the preliminary terms."

The English officer who was sent forward to parley with the enemy, Major Kingston, met Captain Wilkinson of the American forces at the stipulated rendezvous, and they rode to the headquarters of General Gates. On the way they conversed about the landscape, which at that season of the year was spread before them in all its autumnal charm.

The capitulation agreement—which Burgoyne insisted on calling a "convention"—contained thirteen clauses, all of them very honourable, and it was duly signed. At ten o'clock on the morning of the seventeenth of October the English troops moved out of their entrenched positions, bearing their arms in accordance with the surrender terms, with drums beating and bugles blowing. Burgoyne, wearing full dress uniform and plumed hat, met Gates, wearing a simple blue tunic, at the entrance to the latter's encampment. They were introduced to one another by Captain Wilkinson, and Burgoyne raised his decorative headgear with the comment, "The fortune of war, General Gates, has made me your prisoner." To which Gates replied, "I shall always be ready to bear testimony that it has not been through any fault of Your Excellency."

That same day Gates wrote to his wife: "The Voice of fame, ere this reaches you, will tell you how greatly fortunate we have been. Major-General Phillips, who wrote me that saucy note last year, is now my prisoner, with Lord Petersham, Major Acland, and his lady, daughter of Lord Ilchester. If Old England is not by this lesson taught humility, then she is an obstinate old slut, bent upon her ruin." In a postscript he added that he hoped Mrs. Gates would by now have found some ruffles for her apron.

General Burgoyne was treated very considerately by his captor. Primitive though conditions were, the victorious general gave a banquet to the English general and his staff, at which they were regaled with ham, a goose, beef, and mutton, rum and cider being provided to wash the victuals down. There were, it is true, only two glasses available, one for the victorious and one for the defeated general, but Gates drank the health of His Britannic Majesty while the chivalrous Burgoyne drank the health of General Washington, after which, as was customary, an obscene toast was proposed amid acclamation.

In other ways, too, the captured English troops were well treated. When they laid down their arms no American soldier was allowed to be a witness to the scene.

Later on Burgoyne and his staff were quartered in General Schuyler's comfortable house in Albany. Mrs. Schuyler assigned them her best room and served up a first-class supper at which she herself played the charming hostess. Burgoyne had unfortunately been compelled some time previously to burn down General Schuyler's country seat, and his eyes filled with tears at such a display of kindness. With a deep sigh he protested, "Indeed, Madam, this is too much trouble to take for a man who has ravaged your country and burned your dwellings." On the following morning Mrs. Schuyler's seven-year-old son, excited at the strange guests, romped through the rooms, gazed in at the large chamber where General Burgoyne and his officers were sleeping, laughed joyfully, and cried with childish pride, "You are all my prisoners." This made General Burgoyne weep even more copiously than he had done on the evening before.

All those who favoured the English side were sad at the blow that had befallen them. The best of the English armies had ceased to exist and enormous booty had fallen into the hands of the Americans. Throughout the thirteen States the population was justifiably convinced that nothing could now prevent the ultimate victory of American arms.

Yet for a full seven weeks nothing of all this was known on the other side of the ocean. The last intelligence they had received was of Washington's serious defeats at Germantown and Brandywine and the fall of Philadelphia. The two chief cities, Philadelphia and New York, were occupied by the English and the country was facing a hopeless winter. The Americans in Paris and their friends were depressed and filled with a gnawing anxiety.

☆   ☆   ☆

Pierre too had received an accurate and detailed account of the Americans' misfortunes. Paul wrote that they were being attributed in great part to quarrels over precedence of rank between the American General Sullivan and the French General de Borre. At the moment when things were most critical each of them had claimed command of the right wing, and while they were still disputing they were surprised by the enemy. Though old de Borre had played a pitiful role, other

Frenchmen had distinguished themselves in the battle of Brandywine, Baron Saint-Ouary in particular and Captain Louis de Fleury, a kinsman of Pierre's. It was the Marquis de Lafayette, however, who had won special renown. Both he and Gimat, his aide, with complete disregard of their own peril, had done all they could to turn back General Sullivan's troops, who were fleeing in panic. Lafayette, though wounded, could not be persuaded to leave the forefront of the battle until General Washington gave him strict orders to make his way to the dressing-station. "Look after him as if he were my son," Washington said to the surgeons.

Everywhere, reported Paul, they were trying to make up for their former unfriendly treatment of the French officers, and there had even been prospects of considerable remittances being paid over to the firm of Hortalez, though unfortunately the recent defeats had given the Congress a further pretext for evasion.

Since, according to Paul's report, payment in hard cash was, for the time being, out of the question, Pierre wished to have at least some sort of spiritual recompense. He wanted both to show and to receive sympathy, and Paul's letter offered a good excuse to call upon Doctor Franklin for an exchange of views. He drove out to Passy.

The American reverses had cooled the enthusiasm of the Parisians, and particularly of Versailles. The heroes of liberty had become insurgents again overnight, and those who had the day before been loud in their avowal of support suddenly began to maintain an attitude of apprehensive reserve. The Doctor therefore welcomed Pierre's visit.

As though by tacit agreement the two men spoke only of the less unfavourable aspects of the situation, in so far as they were aware of them from their respective sources of intelligence. Pierre told Franklin of the exploits of the Frenchmen at Brandywine, and was informed in turn with ironical satisfaction that they had found time in Philadelphia to arrest a number of partisans of England and to take them away to Yorktown to be held as hostages who could be exchanged for such of their own supporters as had fallen into the hands of the English.

Since Pierre had expected to find a crestfallen Franklin, he was surprised and impressed by the Doctor's equanimity. He was stirred to meditation. "Generally," he said, "people face an historical event like children who are seeing a clock for the first time. They stare in fascination at the movement of the second hand, but do not notice that the minute hand and even the hour hand are moving too. We, Doctor Franklin, you and I, are of a different kind. The fact that an event touches us personally, we do not allow to make us regard it out of its context. We stand back, get the right perspective, and examine the picture as a whole. We know that a single reverse like the one along the Brandywine does not decide a war."

Franklin found the clock analogy not bad, and was amused at the
way in which Pierre pronounced the name of the river. He was glad,
he said, that Pierre shared his confidence. If France, which had already
contributed so much to the struggle not only in treasure, but also with
her mind and heart, should decide in future to contribute still more,
she would be displaying wisdom as well as generosity, since she would
thereby not merely be safeguarding her investments, but ensuring that
her capital would be repaid with interest.

Pierre interpreted this as meaning that Franklin intended to support him in pressing his claims on the Congress. Yes, he asserted
eagerly, France and America must advance together. If France represented the spirit of liberty, America was liberty's fist.

This metaphor was less to Franklin's liking, but he did not want to
hurt the feelings of a man upon whom one could rely even when
things looked bad, so when Pierre took his leave he invited him to
come to lunch on the following Sunday.

☆   ☆   ☆

On Sunday, the fourth of December, the weather was very cold and
foggy, but Franklin's house at Passy was well heated and cosy.

He had invited only a few guests, all sincere friends of America,
and Pierre was proud to be part of a company consisting of men like
Turgot, Leroy, de Chaumont, Condorcet, de la Rochefoucauld, and the
Abbé Morellet. Even the presence of Arthur Lee did little to dim his
pleasure.

Lee had come because he was consumed with anxiety, and with his
highly strung temperament he could not endure the thought of spending the day sitting in the Hôtel d'Hambourg surrounded by Frenchmen
who gloated at his country's reverses. At Passy he would find other
Frenchmen who for all their frivolous ways had taken the recent defeats to heart.

Franklin sensed that his guests were all hoping to hear words of
encouragement from his lips, and he told them: "I saw the beginning
of the revolution. Looking back now, I can not understand how it was
humanly possible for us to overcome our enormous difficulties. Everything had to be created out of nothing—laws, civil governments, an
army, a navy, arsenals—" and all this, he explained, had to be done in
the face of a strong English military force stationed in the country
and innumerable opponents, open or concealed, among their own
people. Many remained neutral out of timidity, while even some of
their friends were lukewarm. It had been a miracle that the revolution
had not sunk at once into chaos and anarchy. If, however, the improvised American Army had succeeded, circumstances being what they
were, in surviving its first hard winter and remaining in the field,

there could not be the slightest doubt that the United States, now strong and organized, would succeed in recovering from an isolated defeat without serious danger to their existence.

Franklin did not make a speech, but related his experiences as the only one present who had played a personal part in the opening stages of the revolution. He spoke simply and in a quiet tone, inspiring the others with his own conviction that what was still to be done weighed lightly in the balance compared with what had already been achieved. Even Arthur Lee was moved.

They spoke no further of America; they ate and drank and talked of eating and drinking, of French literature and the theatre. Pierre amused them with a variety of piquant stories and Franklin told some of his homely anecdotes. Yet they were unable to detach their thoughts from the anxieties by which they were haunted. They did not refer to them again, but every now and then there would be a pause in the conversation when it became evident that their minds were more occupied by that which was left unsaid than by that which was said. At last the atmosphere became so strained that their pleasure at being together changed to a feeling of uneasiness.

They were preparing to break up rather earlier than usual when a hackney-coach drove up. Monsieur Finck, the butler, seemed to be arguing. But the newcomer entered almost before the butler had time to announce: "Monsieur Austin." He was a stranger, a young man in travelling costume.

He looked round as if he were searching for somebody, then turning to Franklin he said, "My name is John Loring Austin and I come from Nantes, or rather from Boston. I crossed on the brigantine *Perch* and bring news from the Congress."

With a haste that was unusual in him Franklin demanded, "Has Philadelphia really fallen, sir?"

"Yes," replied Austin. "But my news is of greater moment," he added quickly. "General Burgoyne has surrendered." As the others stared at him incredulously, he went on incoherently, his words tumbling over one another, "Saratoga," he said, and he said, "General Gates and General Arnold." And he said, "The English General Fraser and the German Lieutenant-Colonel Breymann killed. And captured besides, General Burgoyne, Generals Hamilton and Phillips and the Brunswick General Riedesel. And captured Lord Petersham and the Earl of Balcarras and half a dozen members of Parliament. And 5,800 officers and soldiers and 2,400 Hessians. And taken 42 cannon, 5,000 muskets, and tremendous quantities of stores and ammunition."

The Americans who understood what he was saying, and the Frenchmen who did not, continued to stare at him. Arthur Lee went up to him, gripped him by the arm, and demanded hoarsely, "What is this you have told us? Who are you? 5,800 of the enemy taken prisoner, did you say? Did you say that General Burgoyne has been captured?"

But Franklin intervened. "Please be calm," he urged. "Repeat your story, Mr. Austin, and more slowly. Have you brought anything in writing?"

Austin, who all the time had been addressing Franklin, replied, "Here are my credentials, Doctor Franklin. And here is a letter from the Congress. It is very brief, because they did not want to delay the departure of the brigantine while the weather was favourable. I can tell you a great deal verbally, however, for I had a talk with Captain Wilkinson who brought General Gates' dispatch to the Congress."

Franklin perused the letter. Even the Frenchmen now grasped what it was all about, and Pierre exulted, "We have won a victory! Saratoga! What a beautiful name! My weapons, our weapons, have won a victory! What a stroke of good fortune that I did not permit myself to be deterred from sending ships and arms! Now they have won a victory, these weapons of mine, these weapons of ours, the weapons of liberty! Saratoga!" He rolled the resounding foreign word on his tongue, accenting it on the last syllable.

Silas Deane and young William, happy and excited, plied Austin with questions, and he elaborated his news with a number of details that increased their joy.

Franklin had not sat down again, but continued to stand there, a quiet, imposing figure. With one hand resting on the back of his chair and the other holding the letter, he read the brief dispatch and then let his hand slowly sink. For a moment he seemed to sway, yet still he did not sit down. His guests had swarmed round the messenger and they all began to ask him questions at once. Young William translated for the benefit of the Frenchmen and the room was filled with a cheerful hubbub, but Austin continued to address his replies to the Doctor.

Franklin listened with only half an ear. He was thinking that thousands of men, Americans, Englishmen, and Germans, had again died meaninglessly because of the obduracy of King George and some of his lords. Yet the picture of the wounded and dying was submerged in the overwhelming feeling of victory. He had spoken with great assurance a little while before when he was demonstrating that the Americans must inevitably win, but looming behind the logical conviction in his mind were the doubts and anxieties that troubled his spirit. Now all these doubts had ebbed away and the old man, who hated war and battles with all his soul, could think only of victory, of triumph, and he would have welcomed the killing of even more Englishmen and Germans. Then he recalled a gallant but artful conversation he had had with a lady in a blue mask, and the fact that this lady, as he had learned confidentially from Monsieur de Gérard, had afterwards extracted a promise from her consort. It had been a promise containing an important reservation, a contingent "if," and because of this reservation it had meant little. Now the contingency had suddenly been realized. The Battle of Saratoga implied far more than a success for American arms. It meant that the alliance was ensured. America and liberty were no longer merely ideals. They had become a reality. And over Franklin's broad, furrowed countenance there stole a look of radiant joy and pride that came from his very depths.

Lee stood a little apart from the others near the fireplace, stiffly erect, with folded arms and chin drawn in. He made no comment and asked no questions, but he had to hold himself so stiffly to prevent himself from leaping about like a young colt and flinging his arms around in a manner that would have detracted from his dignity. A load had dropped from his heart, and he felt a boyish happiness such as he had probably never known before in his life. He looked across at Franklin. Deep down within him there was a slight feeling of chagrin that the Doctor *honoris causa* should seem so completely oblivious of his presence, and he also took it amiss that Austin, whose message must have been intended for the three commissioners, had addressed himself to Franklin exclusively. These considerations, however, were soon effaced by an overwhelming exultation, and as he gazed at Franklin's radiant face there was in his heart neither jealousy nor rancour. "This Franklin," he thought, and, "Now he has done it, this Franklin, now he has done it for all of us."

Franklin seated himself in the comfortable capacious chair he had occupied when presiding at the meal. Coffee and dessert were still on the table. "This is a good day for us, my friends," he said in English, and then repeated his words in French. "This is a good day, for us, my friends, is it not?" They all shook hands and embraced, and there was a babble of cheerful, nonsensical talk. Jacques-Robert Turgot stepped up to Franklin and awkwardly put his arms round him, shyly and with tears in his eyes.

Franklin turned to the courier and said, "Well, Mr. Austin, perhaps you will sit down and drink something. You must be in need of a rest. It is a long journey from Boston to Passy, and in winter it could not have been very agreeable." He sent the butler down to the cellar to fetch up a few bottles of the best champagne, and Franklin clinked glasses with each of his guests.

One of them, however, had disappeared. Pierre had apparently rushed back post-haste to Paris. "Our *débrouillard* has already set to work," said Silas Deane, but Arthur Lee thought to himself, "He has gone to look after his speculations."

The Frenchmen told one another that the three commissioners would no doubt be wanting to attend to their affairs now that they had received such momentous news, and the gathering broke up, but Franklin asked the young Marquis de Condorcet, for whom he had a particular affection, to stay for a moment. "Please do not go just yet, my friend," he begged. "I should like to give you a message to take back to Paris." And before settling down to work with his colleagues he wrote a note to Dubourg telling him of the Battle of Saratoga and General Burgoyne's surrender. Sealing the letter, he asked Condorcet to deliver it as soon as he reached the capital.

Chapter Four

SIGNED AND SEALED

✤ ★ ✤

ON THE following morning, the fifth of December, Louis was sitting in his library in cheerful mood. He had risen early to go out hunting, and on his return had not bothered to change before resuming his translation of a chapter of Hume's *History of England*. Conscientiously he translated word by word and sentence by sentence, pausing every now and then to look up something in the dictionary, and as he pondered, polished, and perused what he had written he thoroughly enjoyed his work. He had eaten a hearty breakfast after the hunt, and there was a pleasant rumbling in his stomach as he bent over his books and papers.

It was a long time since he had felt such contentment of mind. The hunting that morning had been good sport, and translating Hume was amusing. It was only a pity that he would have to break off before long because he was expecting a visit from Vergennes.

When the Foreign Minister eventually arrived he was not alone. He was accompanied by Maurepas, and though they both looked as if they had brought news of happy import, Louis's peace of mind evaporated as soon as they entered. He knew that their appearance together boded no good.

"What is it you have to tell me, Messieurs?" he asked.

"Victory, Sire!" cried Maurepas, flinging out his right arm. "Victory!"

"Victory!" repeated Vergennes.

There was an exalted ring to the word as it emerged from the dry lips of the cynical Maurepas and the full lips of Vergennes, the man of the world. They told Louis of Saratoga and the thousands of prisoners that had been taken, including many important officers; in their eagerness they took the words out of each other's mouth. "It was French arms, Sire, that have achieved this success," they declared. "Arms supplied by Monsieur de Beaumarchais, whom you will recall our having recommended to you, so the money we invested in the fellow has paid us good interest. Here is a detailed dispatch from your Ambassador in London, the Marquis de Noailles. You will see, Sire, that the news came like a thunderclap to the English Government. The gentlemen in London cannot conceive how it was possible for their best army and their valiant General Burgoyne to capitulate so miserably. The Court of Saint James's is stunned."

Louis, too, was stunned for the moment. This sudden American victory was highly disconcerting, and his digestion, which had been behaving so admirably but a short time before, began to disturb him. The hereditary enemy had suffered a grievous defeat, and that was excellent, but his mind reverted to the tiresome consequences. Now it would be difficult to avoid the alliance to which he looked forward with such distaste. He at once decided craftily that he must find some way of frustrating it, or at least postponing the evil necessity as long as possible.

The report, he said, was probably exaggerated, as so often happened. The rebels were old hands at propaganda, and he could not bring himself to believe that a disorganized mob of mutineers had really defeated a trained English Army. "It is incredible, Messieurs," he declared. "It is quite inconceivable." He called for a number of geographical works and maps of the American colonies. He helped Campan and Sept-Chênes to carry the bulky tomes and charts, and while the Ministers continued to read out to him extracts from the reports he searched for the places mentioned—Saratoga, Bemis Heights, odd names, to be sure, and of course not marked on the maps. They had perhaps been insignificant encounters, mere skirmishes, which the rebels were trying to boost as happenings of historical importance so as to efface the effect of their reverses at Germantown and Philadelphia.

"These dispatches, Sire," replied Vergennes, "prove beyond all possibility of error that this is no rumour. The surrender of the English commander with the whole of his army is an indisputable fact." He went on to insist that it was essential for the treaty with the Americans to be concluded without delay. He enumerated once more the various considerations that rendered the alliance desirable, any one of which should have been adequate to prove his case. The time had come, he asserted, to realize the dream by which Louis had been inspired ever since he came to the throne, the conception of an epoch of justice, freedom, and human dignity under the dominion of France. This was the opportunity to re-establish French prestige, which had suffered so greatly through the peace of 1763.

Here Maurepas intervened. The alliance would help the country's finances, he said. It would lead to the conquering of new markets, and with a modicum of luck there was even some hope of regaining possession of Canada.

Vergennes took up the argument again with the suggestion that if they let this opportunity go by there was a danger that the colonies would grow tired of the struggle and make peace with their Mother-land. In that case France might even lose her West Indian possessions.

As the Ministers skilfully threw the ball to one another, Louis thought to himself that his worst anticipations had been fulfilled. They were again assailing him with the old arguments, good arguments, it was true, and not to be controverted, but his intuition, his inner voice, the voice of God spoke within him. "Do not listen to them, Louis," it exhorted. "Remember that you are the King of France."

He sat morosely humped in his chair. Then suddenly he burst out, "You have broken your word, Messieurs. You have left me in the lurch. You promised that you would support the Americans only suf-ficiently to keep them from collapse, but not to an extent that would enable them to gain victories. And now you see the result. The rebels have captured an English general together with his whole army. What is all this going to lead to? What are my people to think of the situation?"

"Your people, Sire," replied Vergennes with unexpected boldness, "rejoice at the tremendous blow that has been inflicted on the Eng-lish." Maurepas wagged his head in approval, and Vergennes con-tinued, "Your people, Sire, would fail to understand if we delayed any longer in signing a treaty."

Louis could not help admitting to himself that this was true. They all held the same views as his Ministers. The same views as Toinette.

Toinette. There was no doubt that she, too, would soon be coming to see him, probably that very morning, to remind him of his promise. If the rebels achieve "a military success," he had stipulated. *A mili-tary success*—that was a vague notion. This Saratoga was no military success. He did not want it to be. And in any case, one had to wait for more exact news.

He bent over the maps once more. "They are all rejoicing," he thought, "even my mentor. They are fools, blind fools, and do not understand what is at stake." He satisfied himself with grim determi-nation that Saratoga was not to be found on the map. "This misfor-tune is all your fault, Messieurs," he complained. "Revolution is an infectious moral disease, and we ought never to have allowed this leprous fellow Franklin to come here. I had my doubts at the time and hesitated to give my consent, but you succeeded in persuading me. You ought to have been even more keenly aware of the danger than I was, Messieurs, for you are older than I am."

The Ministers did not permit themselves to be intimidated by the royal wrath. Louis had sanctioned their American policy and his agree-ment was on record.

"We must act, Sire," urged Vergennes.

"You are not going to convince me against my will, Messieurs," protested Louis. "You are behaving as if our country's situation and that of the world in general had changed overnight."

"It has, Sire," replied Maurepas.

"Are then the reasons no longer valid," demanded Louis angrily, "which have hitherto spoken against an alliance? Is my Army more effectively equipped than it was yesterday? Is my treasury less empty?"

"Your Army, Sire," rejoined Vergennes, "is no more effective today than yesterday, but England's Army is less effective and England's credit is less sound."

"I will not fling myself into any adventures," insisted Louis. "I have no intention in present circumstances of launching upon a war."

"No responsible statesman," said Maurepas soothingly, "would support measures which might bring about the immediate commencement of hostilities."

"What we suggest, Sire," added Vergennes, taking up his cue, "is this. Let us transmit to Franklin our congratulations on the victory and indicate that we should welcome a resumption of the negotiations for a pact of friendship which he initiated some time ago. A considerable interval must elapse before such a pact can be concluded and hostilities begun, and we shall have time to strengthen our armaments."

Louis seized upon a single word in Vergennes's proposal. " 'Indicate'?" he retorted angrily. "You want me to 'indicate' something to these rebels?" He stepped close up to Vergennes and blinked at him indignantly with his bulging eyes. "Are you seriously suggesting, Monsieur," he cried in a high-pitched voice, "that your King should run after this Doctor Franklin? Nothing is further from my thoughts." Vergennes flushed and remained silent. Maurepas too said nothing. Louis was at once assailed by remorse at thus having mortified his faithful counsellors. "Congratulations, if you like," he said in a mollified tone, "but no more. Any further step would infringe our dignity."

The two Ministers exchanged glances and agreed tacitly that it would be advisable to rest content with what they had achieved. Doctor Franklin could be given to understand unofficially that the moment had arrived to renew his proposals for a treaty. The Doctor was a man to whom one could talk rationally. They bowed and withdrew.

Louis had not yet recovered from this upsetting audience when Toinette arrived.

She was radiant with happiness. The victory of the Americans was a confirmation from Heaven of her cleverness in winning over the leader of the rebels. It was now evident that the old man would be an important ally for France, with whose help a numbing blow could be inflicted on the hereditary foe. Her intuition, the inner voice that spoke to the Habsburgs, had counselled her well.

"My felicitations, Sire," she cried. "Is this not the greatest and most fortunate occurrence since we ascended the throne?"

"It is, of course, welcome," replied Louis without enthusiasm, "that the English should have suffered a humiliation. Yet we must not forget that a victory of this kind will encourage the rebellious spirits in my own kingdom. Everywhere in Europe discontented subjects will be raising their heads. That is to say," he added argumentatively, "if it really has been a victory. For that has by no means been corroborated, Madame."

Toinette had no difficulty in realizing what lay behind his words. Louis did not want to admit that the contingency on which his promise depended had become a reality. "In any case," she replied, "it seems to me that the time has come to remind you of a certain promise."

"Nothing is further from my mind," he rejoined, "than to avoid keeping my word. But it is my duty to discover whether the conditions have been fulfilled." His tone was more resolute than she had anticipated, and she had to be satisfied for the time being.

Hardly was he alone again, however, when he sank into his chair in a mood of deep depression. He knew that he could only delay the ultimate decision, but that there was no longer a way out. *Principiis obsta.* He ought to have resisted firmly at the start, instead of allowing himself to be drawn along a path that he was convinced could only lead to ruin. He had been pushed a step at a time until now he was overwhelmed with guilt and the divine grace had been taken from him. When he had been anointed at Rheims he had laid his hands upon three hundred sick people, and more than half of them had been healed. Heaven would certainly no longer accord him that blessed power. The shadow of Franklin had fallen upon the land and upon himself, and the world had become darkened.

There was no one to whom he could open his heart and unburden it of all the anxieties by which he was obsessed, except his mentor. Maurepas was shrewd and meant well, but alas, he had no soul. "Upon my soul, if I possess one!" Louis shuddered at the recollection. And Toinette did not know any better. She was blind. They were all blind, but they were all tugging at him, the only one who had eyes to see, and there were so many of them, all stronger than he was, conspiring to drag him down into the abyss.

It had long been his intention to collect the sayings of great writers in praise of order and authority, and he took up his notes. He had prefaced them with the ringing line from Homer, "It is not good that there should be many rulers. Only one shall be Master, only one shall be King." He had copied out many maxims from Plato, such as the comment made by Socrates to Glaucus concerning the inevitable decay of all democracies. He had even noted a passage from the dangerous *Esprit des Lois* of Montesquieu, "The populace is always either too quick or too slow. Sometimes it will throw everything overboard with a hundred thousand arms, and sometimes it will creep along on a hundred thousand legs like a caterpillar." As he perused his little volume of quotations his wrath and ill humour grew. It was with such people that he was expected to ally himself, with a "republic," a "democracy," a form of state that was doomed by its very nature to destruction.

He had no need to consult the wisdom of past ages in order to realize how unnatural was the alliance into which he was being drawn. For the Americans themselves had openly announced their principles with all the force and shamelessness of Evil. In their Declaration of Independence they had brought their charges against only one king, against his cousin of England, but they had ulterior motives, they wanted to sweep all divine authority from the face of the earth. And one of them had even said it straight out; they had greeted his words with acclamation, studying his poisonous book more devoutly than they studied the Word of God. Louis rang for Monsieur de Sept-Chênes and ordered him to bring the book by Thomas Paine entitled *Common Sense*. It was kept locked away in the cupboard reserved for dangerous works.

With darkened brow and fingers that turned the pages reluctantly, he scanned the textbook in which were laid down the principles of the nation with which he was expected to ally himself. "Monarchy," he read, "was the most prosperous invention the Devil ever set on foot for the promotion of idolatry. To the evil of monarchy we have added that of hereditary succession; and as the first is a degradation and lessening of ourselves, so the second, claimed as a matter of right, is an insult and imposition on posterity. One of the strongest natural proofs of the folly of hereditary right in kings is that nature disapproves it, otherwise she would not so frequently turn it into ridicule by giving mankind an ass for a lion. A king hath little more to do than to make war and give away places. A pretty business indeed for a man to be allowed eight hundred thousand pounds sterling a year for, and worshipped into the bargain! Of more worth is one honest man to society than all the crowned ruffians that ever lived."

No. It was too much to demand of His Most Christian Majesty that he should enter into a pact of life and death with a people who held such tenets. He underlined the passage and rang for Monsieur de Sept-Chênes. "Put this book back," he ordered grimly, "and see that you lock the cupboard carefully. This work contains the essence of all evil." He tested the lock himself to make certain that it held.

It held all right, for he had manufactured it with his own hands, but he continued to stand before the cupboard in anxious thought. He could lock Thomas Paine away so that nobody could read him, but when his troops returned from America there was no guarantee that they would not bring the vile volume with them and help to disseminate its poisonous doctrines.

An idea occurred to him, an idea that had been inspired by Paine's insidious, diabolical book. He would ally himself not with the rebels, but with his cousin in England. They would fight the rebels together, and as a reward the English would give Canada back to France. He would establish a holy alliance between himself and the two other rulers who were not yet sicklied o'er with modern ideas, George and Maria Theresa, and against such a union no revolution would be able to make headway. England's American colonies would be forced back onto the right path. There would be no difficulty in that, once the three European monarchs agreed to stand together, and it would serve as a wholesome warning to other prospective mutineers.

He drew himself up and stood erect. In his mind's eye he saw himself as Duplessis had painted him. It was a great scheme, worthy of the King of France, worthy of his ancestors.

Then he began to wonder whether he really was the man to carry it out. He feared that he had been idealized by the painter. He feared that in his soul he was quite different. Perhaps even his ancestors had been other than they appeared in their portraits. Perhaps they too had been idealized by the painters.

Nonsense. Louis the Great had dared to be what his portraits showed, had not shrunk from revoking the Edict of Nantes and expelling the heretics. He, on the other hand, Louis XVI, had been weak from the outset. He lacked the energy and vigour to set up a triple alliance against the rebels. In imagination he could see Maurepas's face when he told him of his great project. The old man would smirk and reply in that affable, soothing voice of his, "These are noble dreams, Sire, dreams of an Alexander."

☆   ☆   ☆

On the same day the American commissioners met again to discuss how they could exploit to the best advantage the victory that had been gained at Saratoga.

Arthur Lee proposed they should make it clear to Vergennes that they were now in a position to extract any terms they wanted from the English Government, and if Versailles did not conclude the alliance at once the French would have only themselves to blame for the consequences. Franklin tried to dissuade him from this idea. Such threats, he suggested, should be employed only as a last resort. It would be wiser, he thought, to allow the French Ministers to approach them of their own accord, rather than to exert pressure. The less eager they appeared, the better the terms that they would eventually be offered.

Lee declined to agree. They had already spoilt their chances by too great a show of phlegm, and they must not allow this further opportunity to go by default. Franklin remained silent, but gazed inquiringly at Silas Deane, who had hitherto said nothing.

Deane was looking sadly worn and grey. The ship that had brought Austin and his glad tidings had also brought orders for Deane's recall to America. In view of the machinations of Arthur Lee the blow was not unexpected, yet he was profoundly upset. He had been the first American to represent his country's interests in Europe, and he had represented them well, having brought about the happy association with Beaumarchais and thus ensured a steady flow of arms and war material across the ocean. Now, instead of thanks, all he got was a letter recalling him, and the Congress had hardly taken the trouble to conceal its mistrust and dissatisfaction.

At Franklin's silent inquiry he joined in the discussion. He generally displayed the greatest respect for Franklin's opinions and hardly ever opposed him, but today he supported Lee. He too thought that they ought to put pressure on the French Government by intimating that the Congress was likely to consider seriously the very favourable peace terms England would now be willing to concede. Silas Deane had need of haste. He did not want to return home before the treaty was signed and sealed.

Franklin knew that Deane was being recalled. He was sorry for his colleague and could understand his desire for some concrete achievement before he left, but he was convinced that covert menaces were inopportune. The commissioners had of course communicated the news of the victory officially to the two Ministers concerned, and he now urged his colleagues to wait patiently at least until a reply was received. Though they were still unpersuaded, they yielded to his wish.

When Lee and Deane had gone Franklin sat in his comfortable arm-chair with half-closed eyes, contented and relaxed, though somewhat tired, his mind agreeably empty, prepared to wait for weeks, even months. He was enjoying his indolence. Delving into the accumulation of papers on his table, he pushed aside all those that had to do with official business and picked out a report or two that he found entertaining. *Vive la bagatelle,* he mused.

He had been sent copies of the numerous manifestos issued by General Burgoyne in the course of the campaign that had ended in his capture, and he read with amusement a long document addressed to the American people. The General offered everybody who was prepared to resume his adherence to the King the assurance of his full support and clemency, while those who persisted in their insane and hopeless resistance were threatened with destruction. He would let loose his Indians upon them, thousands of whom were serving as auxiliaries in his army, and he would feel justified in the eyes of God and man in bringing down the whole vengeance of the state upon the stubborn miscreants who had placed themselves beyond the pale of humanity. There was also a manifesto addressed to the Indians in which Burgoyne declared that in accordance with their traditional customs, which invested such trophies of victory with honourable attributes, they would be permitted to scalp their fallen foes. To this the Indian chiefs had replied, "We love our father beyond the great water, and our affection and loyalty have sharpened our tomahawks."

In the peaceful retreat of his garden at Passy, Franklin studied the literary ebullitions of General Burgoyne and his red Indians. Then he sat down at his table and, with a grim smile of satisfaction, composed an article such as might have appeared in a newspaper.

A certain Captain Gerrish of the New England Militia, so his alleged report ran, had attacked an English detachment and captured considerable booty, including eight large packages containing American scalps. These scalps had been on their way to the Governor of Canada, who intended to forward them to London. The letter of the English officer accompanying the convoy was reproduced verbatim by the Doctor in the following terms: *At the request of the Senneka chiefs, I send herewith to your Excellency eight packs of scalps, cured, dried, hooped, and painted with all the Indian triumphal marks, of which the following is invoice and explanation. No. 1. Containing 43 scalps of Congress soldiers, killed in different skirmishes; these are stretched on black hoops, the inside of the skin painted red, with a small black spot to note their being killed with bullets. Also 62 of farmers killed in their houses; the hoops red; the skin painted brown, and marked with a hoe; a black circle all round to denote their being surprised in the night. . . . No. 4. Containing 102 of farmers; 18 marked with a little yellow flame to denote their being of prisoners burnt alive, after being scalped. Most of the farmers appear by the hair to have been young or middle-aged men, there being but 67 very grey heads among them all, which makes the service more essential. No. 5. Containing 88 scalps of women; hair long, hoops blue; skin yellow ground; a black scalping-knife or hatchet to mark their being killed with those instruments. . . . No. 7. 211 girls' scalps; small yellow hoops; white ground; hatchet, club, scalping-knife, etc. . . . With these packs the chiefs send to your Excellency the following speech taken down by me in writing: "Father, We send you herewith many scalps, that you may see we are not idle friends. We wish to send these scalps over the water to the great King, that he may regard them and be refreshed, and that he may be convinced that his presents have not been made to ungrateful people."*

Franklin read over what he had written, found it satisfactory, and printed it with his own hand in the form of an article out of the Boston *Independent Chronicle*. Then he dispatched copies to the *Affaires*

de l'Angleterre et de l'Amérique, the *Courrier de l'Europe,* the *Gazette
de Leyde,* the *Gazette Française d'Amsterdam,* and the *Courrier du
Bas-Rhin.*

As it turned out, his prediction that the French Government would
approach him before long was correct. Only two days after the receipt
of the news of Saratoga, Monsieur de Gérard appeared at Passy, solemnly presenting the congratulations of Count Maurepas and the
Foreign Minister. This having been done, he said, his official mission
was concluded, but he would like to add his own personal suggestion
that it might not be a bad idea if the American commissioners were
to renew their proposals for a treaty. There could be little doubt that
such proposals would now be listened to with the greatest sympathy.

Franklin thanked Gérard for his kind advice and at once proceeded
to draft the request that had been asked for. He reminded the French
Government that the United States had once before offered to sign
a pact of friendship with the King of France, that the commissioners
were invested with full powers by the Congress, and that they would
welcome the opportunity to negotiate the terms of such a pact.

When his two colleagues arrived at Passy that afternoon, Franklin
informed them with a smile that Versailles had come to Passy instead
of Passy having to go to Versailles. Then he showed them the draft
of his letter. Lee criticized a number of points and declared that the
document was too obsequious. Franklin promised to redraft it in accordance with Lee's wishes, but the latter insisted that he must see the
final version and that it must not go off without his and Silas Deane's
signatures, which caused a delay of two days.

Then William Temple carried the letter to Versailles.

☆   ☆   ☆

As soon as Pierre had heard the tidings at Passy he rushed straight
off to Paris. Having been the first to announce the American Declaration of Independence to his countrymen, he wanted also to be the first
to spread the news of Saratoga, and he ordered his coachman to hurry.
Besides, he was aware that the event would have its repercussions on
the stock exchanges of Paris, London, and Amsterdam, and the more
speedily he could exploit his knowledge in the money market the richer
would be his profits.

Winter had come early that year. Evening had already fallen,
and the roads were icebound. The coachman protested that he
had to drive cautiously. "To the Devil with your caution!" cried
Pierre. "I am making history and have no time for caution." The
startled coachman gritted his teeth and let his horses have the whip,
with the result that very soon the carriage overturned and Pierre was
flung out. He fell heavily, was unable to move his arm, and blood

was streaming down his face. The next carriage that passed by picked him up and took him home.

He was put to bed and Thérèse sent for physicians, who informed him that his arm was broken in addition to his other slight, but painful, injuries. While his wounds were still being bandaged he impatiently demanded that Maigron and Gudin should be sent for, and despite his high temperature and the inconvenience of the bandages he issued his instructions and dictated letters. Occasionally he would screw up his face in a smile of happiness, only to start groaning again with the pain of his scratches and abrasions.

To Count Vergennes he wrote that he had the honour to inform him from his bed of suffering that the noble mission with which he had been entrusted by His Majesty's Government had been fulfilled and the Americans enabled to achieve a victory which would be recorded for all time among the great victories of history. "Our children and grandchildren," he concluded, "will imprint upon their memories the name of Saratoga."

Julie came rushing to his bedside from the rue de Condé, lamenting that he must not overexert himself.

"Be silent, my dear," he requested. "This is a day that will live in history, and I would rise from my grave to share in its renown." He went on dictating.

Thérèse looked after her patient in the quiet, efficient manner that was characteristic of her, glad that Pierre had been privileged to contribute to the success of the Americans, but Julie thought her nursing inadequate and moved into the house in order to watch over her brother day and night. Thérèse raised no objection.

Pierre was a difficult patient and quarrelled with the physicians because they would not permit him to go to his office. Nor would he heed their warnings against receiving visitors.

Among the first to call was Lenormant. Pierre was magnanimous and merely hinted at the fact that his friend's fear that the Americans would not be able to keep their heads above water had proved groundless. Only for a fraction of a second did Lenormant display his ominous smile as he suggested that it had not been unknown in the past for victors to be led by the very consciousness of their strength into becoming dilatory payers. Pierre laughed, but he was unable to suppress a certain anxiety that gnawed at the back of his mind. He had done his utmost to bring about an alliance, yet once it had been concluded Vergennes would no longer have need of a secret intermediary. The Royal Arsenals would be in a position to supply the Americans openly, and hundreds of eager applicants would besiege the Government for war contracts, thus entering into competition with the firm of Hortalez.

For the time being, however, he had happy days to look forward to. For everybody came to condole with him on his mishap and to offer their felicitations on the success which had crowned his efforts. It was as if he himself had personally brought about the capitulation of General Burgoyne. Madame de Maurepas thought it redounded very much to the credit of her Toutou that, though three thousand miles away, he was able to display wounds received in the battle. Even the Marquis de Vaudreuil condescended to pay a call upon the clock-maker's son. He clothed his condolences in elegant phrases and spoke of the American victory with a touch of irony that did not altogether conceal his sincere acknowledgment of Pierre's achievement.

Vaudreuil's visit was evidently more than a mere act of courtesy. He stayed for some time, discussed the political situation, and flattered Pierre by lending an attentive ear to his opinions. For the news of Saratoga had acted as a stimulus to Vaudreuil. Not only did he too regard it as to some extent a personal triumph—had he not stood up for Franklin in the early days and brought about the meeting with Toinette?—but there were other reasons why it was welcome to him. The game he was playing with Toinette had lasted too long and he was beginning to find it boring. The gilded monotony of Versailles was palling upon him more and more, and he yearned for new sensa-tions. He had been reminded that the Vaudreuils had always been a warrior race which had distinguished itself in the naval battles of France. His grandfather had gained renown as Governor of Canada and one of his uncles was celebrated in the annals of the French Army. The victory of Saratoga was a clarion call to François Vaudreuil to carry on the tradition of his family and take a decisive part in the forthcoming war against England.

The first thing to do was to bring pressure to bear on the fat fellow so as to ensure that war would be declared. Louis was apathetic and stubborn, with his mind firmly made up that he was going to remain passive, but Vaudreuil was even more firmly resolved that with the help of Toinette he should not be allowed to remain passive.

So he listened with pleasure to the arguments with which Pierre proved that an immediate alliance was an urgent political necessity. He made a mental note of them and passed them on to Toinette. During the ensuing days he hardly moved from her side and neglected no art of persuasion that might induce her to extort from Louis the fulfilment of his promise.

☆   ☆   ☆

Spurred on by Vaudreuil, Toinette grew more and more determined to have a finger in the American pie. She even entered into collusion with Maurepas and Vergennes, and when the Ministers, after receiving the letter in which the American commissioners renewed their proposals for a treaty, requested a further audience of the reluctant Louis, she insisted on being present.

The Ministers explained to the King that his unwillingness to take the initiative in approaching the Americans was no longer a valid reason for delay, since Franklin himself had now requested the opening of negotiations, and if they were kept waiting for an answer there was grave danger of their coming to an understanding with the English. There was evidence from a reliable source, declared Vergennes, indicating a pile of voluminous documents he had brought with him, that the English Government was bombarding Franklin with offers of peace. Louis cast an uneasy glance at the documents, but did not touch them. "Any further postponement, Sire," asserted Toinette energetically, "will mean driving the Americans into the arms of the English."

Louis, however, had thought of a fresh pretext. "You forget, Madame," he rejoined with dignity, "as you also appear to do, gentlemen, that our hands are tied. Before entering into any undertaking that might evoke the danger of war, we must obtain the sanction of our allies. Am I to break my treaty with Spain?" he demanded angrily. "I refuse to launch upon any ill-considered adventures. I shall not conclude any pact with the rebels until I have received the unambiguous consent in black and white of my cousin in Madrid. I shall not break my word. You'll never get me to do that, Messieurs, nor you either, Madame."

Toinette tapped her foot, opened her lips as if she were about to reply, then changed her mind. Maurepas assured Louis that nobody had ever thought of signing such a momentous treaty without having secured beforehand the approval of Spain, and he begged permission to dispatch a courier to Madrid at once. "Very well," growled Louis.

Toinette, however, insisted that Doctor Franklin could not possibly be kept waiting until an answer had arrived from Madrid.

"I am under an obligation to Spain," declared Louis morosely, "and your Doctor Franklin will have to exercise the virtue of patience."

"May I make a suggestion, Sire?" interjected the supple Vergennes. "Can we not speak frankly to the Americans? Can we not tell them the truth, which is in effect that the Government has decided to conclude a treaty of alliance provided that no objection is raised by Spain?"

When Louis refrained from replying, but only sat peevishly humped in his chair, Toinette cried in a forceful tone, "Yes, that is undoubtedly the proper course to take."

Louis continued to brood in silence. "I thank you, Messieurs," he said suddenly. "I am now informed of your views." There seemed nothing left for the two Ministers to do but to withdraw without having achieved their purpose. They glanced at Toinette, as if seeking her help, and she came to their rescue by urging him in a persuasive tone, "Do not let us break up without having come to some decision, Sire. Instruct these gentlemen to give the Americans the answer that they have a right to expect from us. Please make your position clear, Sire."

"Very well, then!" said Louis. "Very well!"

Hardly had he allowed this concession to be wrung from him, however, than he added with angry haste, "But take care to impress upon these rebels of yours that our intention must be prevented at all costs from reaching the ears of the English Government. If, due to their carelessness, the slightest hint should leak out, I will break off the negotiations and inform them in London that the whole thing is a sheer fabrication. Mark my words, gentlemen, and see to it that the rebels mark them too. I shall break off the negotiations. I shall no longer consider myself bound by any promise that I may have made." By this time he had worked himself up into a fury. "That is all I have to say," he shrieked, "and from now on I do not wish to hear another word on the matter until an answer has arrived from Spain. I forbid anyone henceforth even to mention the Americans in my presence." He kept his eyes averted from Toinette as he issued this injunction. "I am determined to be left in peace."

The Ministers were satisfied and they hurriedly took their leave, but Toinette remained behind. "I am sorry, Louis," she commented ironically, "that you should have found it necessary to raise your voice in that manner."

"You do not realize what you are doing," he said wearily. "These gentlemen do not realize it, and you yourself have not the faintest inkling of what is at stake." She merely shrugged her shoulders scornfully, and he continued, "Have you ever tried to think, Madame, of the consequences for both of us if this treaty should be concluded?" She had no idea what he meant. "The first consequence," he explained vindictively, "will be that we, that is to say, you and I, will have to economize. This treaty means war. War means higher taxes. And if we demand higher taxes from the people, we must ourselves provide a royal example. I shall therefore, to my extreme regret, be compelled to ask you to reduce your expenses."

Toinette was taken aback. But she realized that it would be scarcely opportune to argue at the present moment, and she therefore replied with a display of charming determination that of course she would accept any sacrifice gladly if only it would serve the interests of France and help to weaken the hereditary enemy.

To this Louis rejoined that after all nothing had yet been decided and it would be weeks before an answer was received from Spain. When he gave her that promise, he said, he had not realized that he was

involving himself in such a dilemma, for he was under the obligation
of keeping his word not only to her, but also to the King of Spain.
He had reviewed the problem from every angle with his father con-
fessor. A promise made to a whole kingdom was weightier than a
promise made to a single person. If Spain did not reply unambiguously and unconditionally that she approved of the projected alliance,
he would be faced with a grave conflict of duties and would have to
settle with himself and with God upon the course he was to take.

Toinette now realized more clearly than ever that high politics was
indeed an exciting game. When anyone said "Yes," it did not by
any means signify "Yes." Her resolve to force this sluggish, ill-
humoured man to recognize the independence of the United States
and to declare war on England was strengthened.

☆   ☆   ☆

Before the day was out Vergennes had invited Franklin to a conference, but since he did not want to afford the reluctant Louis the
slightest pretext for withdrawing his sanction the meeting was veiled
in the utmost secrecy.

The Minister began by emphasizing a number of individual points.
France, he said, was not thinking of a war of conquest. It was not
the King's desire that the Americans should take possession of Canada
either for themselves or for the purpose of handing it back to the
French. Nor did he wish to acquire further colonies in the West Indies.
If he should decide to recognize the United States and to enter the war
on their side, he would do so purely from idealistic motives.

Franklin racked his brains for an answer to Vergennes's sententious
phrases. If the Congress had not been convinced, he replied, of the
King's humanitarian principles, it would not have sent the commissioners to Paris.

Vergennes bowed in acknowledgment of this courteous rejoinder.
Then he proceeded solemnly to inform the commissioners that the
Privy Council had decided to recognize the United States of America
and to enter into negotiations with them. In view, however, of his
previous agreements with Spain, the King was obliged to postpone
signing the treaty until word had been received from Madrid that the
Spaniards did not wish to raise any objection.

There was a momentary silence. Then Franklin said tranquilly,
"We thank you, Count Vergennes, for this very welcome communication." They all bowed.

"I must, however, stress the point once more," continued the
Minister, "that until France has reached an understanding with Spain
she will not be in a position to take any decisive steps. I would therefore beg you urgently to regard the negotiations as still of passing

through their initial stages and to maintain the strictest secrecy in
the matter."

"You have our promise," Franklin assured him.

When they were alone, Arthur Lee grumbled at the undignified
way in which the French had linked their agreement in principle
with the stipulation that it must be kept secret. "They are still treating
us as if we were thieves and conspirators," he rasped; but his two
colleagues refused to allow his soured comments to disturb their delight.

The day on which Count Vergennes announced the French Government's decision to the American commissioners was Saturday, the
seventeenth of December, that is to say, less than a fortnight after
the receipt of the news of the victory at Saratoga.

☆   ☆   ☆

Franklin was anxious to nail the French down to their promise, in
so far as this was possible, and he therefore wrote to Maurepas that
he had heard with pleasure of His Majesty's resolve to recognize
the independence of the United States and to conclude a treaty of
alliance in war and peace. He begged the Minister to transmit to
the King the thanks of the commissioners for his sympathetic
attitude.

When Maurepas had read Franklin's letter he shook his head.
Politically the letter fulfilled its purpose. It put on record that the
King and Government were bound by a solemn obligation. But what
a cold, dry, sober way to write. These people in the West had little
idea of manners. They did not know the meaning of elegance and
grace.

He mused on the way he himself would have composed such an
historical epistle if he had been in the American's place, and sitting
down at his table he began to draft the letter that Franklin ought to
have written: *The exceptional wisdom with which Your Majesty has
succeeded in wedding the interests of your country to the highest
dictates of humanity ensures the portrait of Your Majesty a place not
only above the hearth of every American, but also in the hearts of
those who dwell in the Western Hemisphere. Apart from the great
material benefits which Providence will certainly not deny to those
who are participating in this alliance between the two most progressive nations in the world, it may safely be asserted that the un-
dying affection of all friends of liberty will in itself constitute a
reward as noble as any monarch could desire. Though many thousand miles of land and ocean may lie between Your Illustrious Majesty
and the inhabitants of our continent, nobody is nearer to those inhabitants than yourself. Solomon was mistaken. All is not vanity. The*

love and gratitude which America cherishes towards Your Majesty are not vain.

That was the way the old man in Passy ought to have written. Yet how had he, in fact, expressed his sentiments? *I beg you, Monsieur le Ministre, to transmit to the King the thanks of the commissioners for his sympathetic attitude.*

Intrigued by Franklin's uncouthness, as well as by his shrewdness, Maurepas sought a meeting with the great barbarian.

When they met, Maurepas had Sallé, his secretary, with him. He first of all congratulated Franklin on his success, for if the alliance should materialize, he said, the credit would be due to Franklin alone. "It was your popularity," he declared, "which made it possible for us to convince the King of the necessity for an alliance. Without your masterpiece of strategy, when you stole your way into the heart of our charming Queen, we should never have been able to bring about a treaty."

"Thank you," replied Franklin.

"What I admire most in you," continued the indefatigable student of character, "is the way in which you have sublimated your ambition. What have we said on this subject in our memoirs, my dear Sallé?"

"Doctor Franklin," the latter recited in his hollow voice, "is not vain in the commonly accepted sense of the term. We, for instance, could never have denied ourselves the pleasure of inspecting our much-admired portrait at the Salon. Franklin's vanity is of a higher order. He possesses the, let us call it sporting, ambition to carry out difficult experiments, the most difficult of which is his last one of attempting in our century to establish a republic that will endure."

Franklin replied patiently, "You call it a sporting ambition. Others perhaps regard it as a convinced belief."

"Call it what you will," rejoined Maurepas in a conciliatory tone, "it still remains a highly individual and exceedingly whimsical display of *bravura* to turn a whole continent into a republic," and he went through the motions of languidly clapping his hands.

"Of course, your republic will be short-lived," he went on, casually but with an air of authority. "A state without a king is like a pair of breeches without a belt. It can't be kept up. Neither of us will be here to see it, but I am certain that before very long your American compatriots will yearn once more for the fleshpots of Egypt and plead either with their own Pharaoh or with ours to take them under his dynastic wing."

"It would be better not to say too much about that for the moment, Count Maurepas," responded Franklin, entering into the other's jousting mood. "Our Pharaoh would like nothing better right now than to make his peace with us."

"I know," replied Maurepas with a smile. "He is ready to compromise. Perhaps you would do better to conclude a pact with him rather than with us. Perhaps we too would be well advised to come to an understanding with King George. He is on the losing side and it would be easy to persuade him to make concessions. It is not unlikely," he added dreamily, "that he would even give us back our colony of Canada."

"If your heart clings so affectionately to Canada," suggested Franklin amiably, "why did you not conclude an alliance with us last year, when your help was so much more necessary to us than it is now? Then we, too, might have been willing to discuss the question of Canada."

"To discuss the question, no doubt," smirked Maurepas, "but would you ever have given it to us? You would never have accepted us on your frontiers. What was it that a certain Doctor Franklin once said in public about us Frenchmen?" he asked, turning to Sallé, and his secretary recited, "'I fancy that intriguing nation would like very well to meddle on occasion and blow up the coals between Britain and her colonies.'"

"Really," murmured Franklin thoughtfully. "Did I say that? How long ago was it?"

"Not very long," replied Maurepas, and his secretary added, "Doctor Franklin made the statement referred to on the 14th of August, 1767, that is to say, ten years and three months ago."

"Since then," said Franklin very calmly, "I have got to know my France better. In any case, I do not lay great store on always being consistent in my utterances. As a young man I traded in slaves, but later on I was the first man in the New Continent to publish books against slavery."

"If one does not die at a very early age," conceded Maurepas courteously, "one no doubt has to contradict oneself occasionally."

"You mentioned Canada," said Franklin. "I have been assured by Count Vergennes that His Majesty has no thought of possible conquests."

"The King is of very virtuous mind," agreed Maurepas, "but if by good fortune Canada were again to fall into our lap, I think Vergennes and I would be able to persuade him to accept it."

Franklin smiled imperceptibly and inquired with interest, "Tell me, Your Excellency. Are you still hoping to recover Canada?"

"My dear Doctor Franklin," replied Maurepas, "while there is breath there is hope, and perhaps hope remains even when the breath is gone. You are a free-thinker, and so am I. Nevertheless, neither of us would object to a cross being erected over his grave, the symbol of hope and of resurrection in the flesh. Why, therefore, should I not entertain the hope of recovering Canada?"

Franklin could enjoy a cynical comment as much as any man, but he believed in Providence. He was convinced that man's path through life had a meaning and a purpose, and this French Minister, who was so old, so empty, and so lacking in faith, a mere whited sepulchre, repelled him. He answered, "I am certain, Count Maurepas, that an alliance with us will be in the interests of France even apart from the question of Canada. In the long run America will prove to be a sounder and safer partner than England. Her people are more industrious, more simple, more skilful, more thrifty, and more capable." Though his voice was low and gentle, it was the Franklin of the portrait who spoke, the man with the stern, searching eyes, the broad, resolute mouth, and the massive chin, a man in every sense of the word.

When Franklin was alone, however, his face became gloomy. He hated the stupidity of war with all his heart, and was irritated and tormented by the thought that he and the other old man, both waiting for death, had sat together a long time and discussed ways and means of spreading this evil war farther and farther.

He sat down and wrote a story. It was a fable about a young angel who had been sent to earth, which he had not visited before, with an experienced old courier-spirit as his guide. When they came to the battlefield of Quebec and found themselves in the midst of the bloody fighting with all its misery and the groans of the wounded, the angel turned angrily to his guide and said: "You blundering blockhead, you are ignorant of your business; you undertook to conduct me to the earth, and you have brought me into hell." "No, sir," answered the guide. "I have made no mistake; this is really the earth, and these are men. Devils never treat one another in this cruel manner."

☆　　☆　　☆

It was a very hard winter that year. The roads were icebound and transport was hampered. Meat, bread, and milk came to be scarce and expensive in Paris, as well as wood for fuel. The poorer people were cold and hungry. The King and many of the great landowners gave permission for brushwood to be gathered in their forests, and it was taken even when permission had not been granted, so that the slippery streets were filled with people pushing handcarts and wheelbarrows or carrying packs laden with firewood.

The court and society took advantage of the weather to skate on the lakes and ponds, and go out on merry sleighing parties.

Toinette, restless as she was, thoroughly enjoyed these sleighing excursions. It was bracing to dash silently along through the chill air, accompanied by the whole of the Lilac Coterie, each vying with the others in the handsomeness of his or her equipage and the decoration of their horses. She kept thinking of new ways to adorn her sleigh, which glittered with gilt and was beautified inside with paintings by Boucher. The seat was upholstered in heavy red leather, the horses' trappings were of costly embroidery, and ostrich feathers nodded on their heads as they raced along.

The people of Paris, starved and shivering as they gathered their fuel under the watching eyes of the rangers, gazed timidly, but with anger in their hearts, at the glittering cavalcade. That was how *l'Autrichienne* was squandering the wealth of France. The popularity she had gained by her demonstrations of support for Franklin had disappeared, and hostile brochures were again being published. These sleigh rides, they said, represented one of the vices of decadent Habsburg society, and for the sake of the Trianon, her *Little Schoenbrunn*, *l'Autrichienne* was allowing America to go down in ruin.

As the misery of that winter increased, so did the embitterment, justified or unjustified, of the people, who collected in mobs to demand bread and looted the bakers' shops. Police and soldiers were called upon to drive the demonstrators from the streets.

One day as Toinette rode through the streets of Paris her coach was held up and the fishwives made use of their ancient prerogative of telling the Queen of France what they thought. In coarse terms they exhorted her to remember her duty and "drop a foal," as was only right and proper for any decent female, and especially for a Queen.

Toinette put as good a face on the matter as she could and replied with a forced jest, but she was filled with cold anger. She could understand how her failure to provide France with a Dauphin made them disapprove of her, but what glared at her from the angry eyes of the crowds was much more than disapproval—it was naked hatred, and this she could not comprehend. What did these people really want of her? Had she not spoken to the American for their sakes? Was it not on their account that she had paid a visit to the Salon? Had she not bought up all the dolls in Paris and presented them to the poor children of the city?

She had no ties of sympathy with the people of France. Though she did not admit it to herself, she despised the five and twenty million souls over whom her consort reigned. Yet she needed their homage and their affection. At her first solemn entry into Paris as the bride of the Dauphin, when she was still no more than a child, amid the thundering salutes of cannon and through avenues of flowers, banners, and triumphant arches, the streets had been lined with hundreds of thousands of sightseers who had cheered her to the echo. She would never forget how she had stood on the balcony of the Tuileries, deeply stirred by the enthusiasm of the populace. "How lucky are we who are of royal profession," she had written to her mother, "in being able so easily to win friendship and love. These things are so precious, as I have felt, understood, and will ever remember."

Now it appeared that she had once more thrown away the love of her subjects, and she was consumed with longing to experience again that wonderful sense of exaltation by which she had been uplifted as she stood in front of Franklin's portrait and listened to the ovation from the audience at the Opera. They were foolish, these fishwives, all the Parisians were foolish, but one had a feeling of chill when they did not greet one with cheers. She would force Louis to keep his promise. She would see to it that the alliance was concluded and war declared, then these stupid people of Paris would once more change their minds and greet her with enthusiasm.

She was always having to wait for what she wanted. The fishwives were quite right. It was absurd. Her fat husband was making her look ridiculous, even in the eyes of Vaudreuil. She had so long kept François on the tenterhooks of hope, putting him off so frequently with promises for the future, and she understood his occasional anger quite well. She decided to set herself a date. If she were not pregnant within two months, then she would not keep François waiting any longer.

Louis, on the other hand, had given orders that he was to be furnished with daily reports on the food and fuel shortage in Paris. The reign of Louis XVI, he brooded, would not be recorded as an age of well-being in the annals of France. The Plutarchs of the coming century would brand him as an unsuccessful ruler who had been deprived of heavenly grace. One great misfortune followed close upon the heels of another. It had all begun with his marriage festivities when there had been a panic in the Place Louis Quinze and numerous sightseers had been trampled to death. There had been bread riots when he ascended the throne, and now there was another famine in the fertile land of France.

He did his best to help the poor and needy. He sent them money and he gave them wood. When he heard of the difficulty they were having with their inadequate baskets and packs, as they tried to drag them along the slippery roads, he put his sleighs at their disposal, and it was a strange sight to watch the beggars and other tatterdemalions with their loads of wood being driven to their wretched hovels by liveried coachmen in the royal equipages. The Parisians made fun of him, but they did so good-humouredly, referring to him as *our good fat one*. The object of their detestation remained *l'Autrichienne*.

Louis read the lampoons directed against Toinette and was worried that she should be so hated. It was his fault, he brooded, for she was still waiting for a Dauphin to be born. Whatever he did, and with the

best will in the world, he was always at fault: he owed the nation an
heir to the throne, and he was linking the fate of the monarchy with
the cause of the rebels.

☆　　　☆　　　☆

Pierre had been right in his prognostication. The victory at Saratoga
had greatly enhanced his personal prestige. It had not, however, enhanced the prestige of the firm of Hortalez. Though his speculations
on the stock exchange had brought him in immediate profits that
helped him to tide over his most pressing difficulties, the business
world evidently shared his view that with the entry of France into
the war the most important function of the firm of Hortalez would
have come to a close. A secret intermediary would no longer be required for deliveries to America. The triumph that had fallen to the
arms supplied by Hortalez and Company led to the paradoxical result
that the firm's creditors insisted on their claims being settled at the
earliest possible moment. One day, when Pierre was still tied to his
room, Maigron appeared and once more announced in his dry way
that he was unable to meet the bills falling due in the coming week.

Pierre laughed, both amused and angry. To Désirée, the most
understanding of his women friends, he opened his heart on the
tragi-comedy of his situation. He had delivered to the Americans
the arms which had enabled them to gain the resounding victory at
Saratoga, and how had they rewarded him? On that day, the twentieth
of December, his claims amounted to more than six million livres,
yet over the whole period of eighteen months all he had received was
goods to the total value of barely 150,000 livres, and he was more
beset than ever by worries on account of his lack of liquid assets.

"It is the same old story," commented Désirée. She stroked his
hand sympathetically, but did not otherwise seem to be moved. But
she was moved, she was outraged, and her anger was directed in
particular against one man, Pierre's friend Charlot.

Lying on the sofa in her boudoir, her knees drawn up, rocking herself to and fro, a furrow between her brows, she squinted thoughtfully down her nose and there was an unwontedly grave look on her
roguish face.

Désirée had not become a celebrated actress of the *Théâtre français*
without having passed through sundry experiences that had rendered
her worldly wise. A realist, she was not surprised that Pierre's services to America had been rewarded with ingratitude. She would
indeed have been surprised had it been otherwise. She was, however, immeasurably indignant at the behaviour of her friend Charlot.

She drove out to Etioles, and during the journey her mind continued to work busily. For a man like Charlot, who was able to wait

for his money, there was no risk in granting Pierre the required credits even for years ahead. If he did not do so it was base conduct on his part, probably motivated by jealousy. She had endured as much as she could stomach of Charlot's crotchety, misanthropic whims. She would tell him plainly that she expected him to help Pierre, and if he continued to leave Pierre in the lurch she would break with him.

Casually she mentioned that Pierre was embarrassed and in need of a friend's help. "When hasn't he been?" said Lenormant. Désirée pictured in a few sentences how Pierre, a second Tantalus, was thirsting in the midst of plenty. "Thirsting?" asked Charlot. "Yes," Désirée answered, "and in the midst of plenty," and as a practised actress, she was able by a scarcely noticeable stress on these last words to indicate clearly to Lenormant that her hint was an ultimatum.

As a keen-sighted man of affairs, Lenormant had anticipated that the very success of the Americans would be an embarrassment to the firm of Hortalez, and he had contributed his share to intensifying Pierre's difficulties. If Pierre was refused credit wherever he applied for it, that was not altogether unconnected with the efforts of Monsieur Lenormant.

As Désirée explained to him that Pierre was again on the verge of bankruptcy, a scheme matured in his mind whereby he could meet her wishes and display his generosity while at the same time doing an excellent stroke of business and putting Pierre out of action for good.

He went to see Pierre and expounded his views on the situation in which the firm of Hortalez found itself. It had to meet considerable short-term obligations. The Americans' debts could not in any case be collected before the end of the war, if at all. Credits from normal sources were not available, since lucrative and immediate profits were now in prospect from other investments. A declaration of insolvency was therefore only a matter of time.

And what, inquired Pierre, would Charlot do in his place?

He had thought of a plan, replied Lenormant slowly, which would enable Pierre to reap adequate benefit while at the same time not involving himself, Lenormant, in too great a loss if he were lucky. The assets of the firm of Hortalez were of no value except to anyone who could afford to wait, who was possessed of influence, and who was ready to take a chance. There were probably no more than half a dozen men in the whole of France who came within that category, and in view of the tempting opportunities of profit opened up by the impending war it was hardly likely that any of them would choose the firm of Hortalez in which to invest his money. "But here I am," he went on, speaking still more softly, "filled with appreciation for the gifts and ideals of my friend Pierrot and feeling myself inspired by a moral obligation to help him. I should therefore like to make the following proposal. I will take over the firm of Hortalez lock, stock, and barrel, with its assets and its liabilities, and I will pay Monsieur Pierre Caron de Beaumarchais the sum of one million livres in cash."

Pierre did not speak. He was almost stunned at the offer.

After a momentary pause Lenormant continued, "There is no need for me to tell a man of your understanding that in view of the impending war a great deal can be done at the present juncture with a million livres. A million *livres Tournois* in this month of December 1777 will be worth three million in April 1778. But your friendship means more to me than a million livres, or three million livres, as the case may be. I should welcome it if you could see your way to letting me have two or three things from your private possessions as a makeweight, and also as a proof of your own friendship, such as, for instance, the mantelpiece here. If you were inclined to be particularly generous, you might throw in the portrait of our friend Désirée."

Pierre had turned pale at such a combination of insolence and magnanimity. Charlot had spoken the blunt truth about the financial standing of the firm. It was a tempting prospect to be rid of his debts and have a cool million in his pocket into the bargain, especially now that a million could be turned into three or even five overnight.

Lenormant had risen to his feet with an abrupt movement that made the bitch Caprice bristle up and growl menacingly, which she rarely did. *"Couche, Caprice!"* cried Pierre.

"Think over my proposal, Pierrot," said Lenormant calmly, gazing at him with veiled eyes. "No one else will offer you the same price, as you are well aware. But there is one thing I should like you to bear in mind. If you should turn down my offer, and then come to me in two or three weeks' time and beg me to take over the firm of Hortalez for a hundred thousand livres, or fifty thousand, or even for a fig, please do not take it amiss if I decline to give you the fig. One is not moved every day by a friendly impulse of such consequence."

In his mind's eye Pierre saw the fire-place in his room without its mantelpiece of Çarrara marble, bare of ornament, and a bare spot on the wall where now Désirée's portrait hung. A consuming fury surged up in his heart. He would have liked to throw Charlot out of the house with an obscene and brutal retort. Then he thought again: To be rid of all my debts, which total up to far more than a million, and to have a million in cash into the bargain. No! When there was so much at stake even a Beaumarchais could not afford the luxury of an outburst of rage and a sharp retort, however sparkling. With unruffled demeanour he replied in a somewhat casual tone, "Your proposal has taken me by surprise, Charlot, and you must permit me to follow an example I have learned from you. Let me sleep on it."

"Please do, my dear friend," said Lenormant, and he took his leave.

Alone again, Pierre sat in thought. "This is a problem," he told his bitch Caprice. "We are in a dilemma." If he accepted, it would be a triumph for Charlot. On the other hand he, Pierre, had achieved the ideal he had set before his eyes. The United States were about to be recognized and their independence assured. He had fulfilled his mission, he had secured his place in history, and he had the right to bring to a close his activities in the firm of Hortalez. He felt suddenly very tired. It would be a relief to be able to confine himself to his flourishing timber business, to politics, to literature, and to one or two unspeculative war contracts. He would be able to travel a little with his good friend Philippe. Yes, he had the right to leave the Americans to look after themselves and to devote himself to the refreshment of his own spirit.

Désirée, however, when he informed her of Lenormant's offer, saw in it nothing but spiteful misanthropy. This was not the way she had intended Charlot to help Pierre.

She drove out to Etioles in her sleigh. She was a great actress. She owed extravagance to her reputation; her sleigh could vie in brilliance with Toinette's. So, with golden bells tinkling, and filled with rage, she drove to Etioles.

They were all cynical, she, too—that was natural—but Lenormant's disdainful misanthropy was more than she had a mind to endure. The most despicable quality she found in him was the way in which he combined his vengeful jealousy with cold calculation of the profits he could extract from his acts of vindictiveness. No, it was better that Pierre should go down in a blaze of glory rather than that he should sell his achievement to Charlot in so humiliating a manner. Pierrot had done more than anyone else on the Continent to help the American cause, and now he was to be deprived not only the material rewards, but even of the credit for his courage and toil. If the firm of Hortalez fell into the hands of Charlot, the latter would soon see to it that he himself was accorded the honours due to the man who had delivered the arms for America.

The sleigh glided on its way, the bells tinkled, the horses' plumes nodded, and Désirée sat wrapped in furs, a small, dainty figure, resolute and angry. She had slept with Charlot and put up with his odd moods. He was a man of great capacities, dangerous and interesting. There had been moments when she felt very much drawn to him. It would be foolish to break with him. Yet she was determined to do so. That he wanted to rob and ruin Pierre out of pure hatred and caprice, because he was jealous, was something she could not be expected to tolerate.

She drove through the gateway with its inscription, *Vanitas, vanitatum vanitas,* and stood before Lenormant. He helped her out of her furs.

"Monsieur," she said, "you have behaved like a scoundrel to your friend Pierre."

Lenormant turned pale, but the smile did not leave his face. "I do not know what you mean, *mon amie*," he replied. "I offered our Pierre salvation from bankruptcy and a present of a million livres."

"You know exactly what I mean," retorted Désirée.

His round, deep-set eyes became even more veiled than was their wont. "I know that I am being misunderstood," he said, and added very softly, "I have often been misunderstood in crucial situations."

She was touched by his words, but his very sincerity and her realization that he was still tortured by the memory of Jeanne, which was responsible for the discordance in his nature, made her say, "If I mean anything to you—and I do believe that you are fond of me—you have indeed good reason for comparing the present situation with a certain other one. For this is the last time that you will see me here."

He did not doubt that she was in earnest. There she stood, insolent, young, and defiant, had him in the hollow of her hand, and knew it. Anger and resentment surged up in him and he longed to crush this pretty, shameless little reptile beneath his heel. But at the same time the old pain was eating away at his heart, the memory of that bitter, shattering moment when he learnt that Jeanne had left him and had gone to be the mistress of the King at Versailles. Désirée had not yet left him, but she had threatened to do so, and she would keep her threat. Jeanne had at least gone to Versailles, to the King, to a scoundrel of a King, it was true, but a man of magnificent appearance and one who was prepared to give her everything on which her heart was set—power, splendour, and wealth. Désirée was going to Pierrot, to the vain, ridiculous Pierrot, who was presumptuous enough to launch into enterprises that far outstripped his strength, poor swaggering starveling that he was. He had choked down his feelings and shared her with the wretched braggart; now she would not even let him share, now she was going to the starveling altogether and forever. But he would not let her go. When Jeanne had wanted to come back to him he had rejected her for the sake of his dignity, but he would not repeat the irrevocable mistake of sacrificing that which was part of his very soul merely because of his outraged dignity. Désirée was no Jeanne, but she was so radiant. Latin verses ran through his mind: *Ver vide./Ut tota floret, ut olet, ut nitida nitet. (Lo the Spring! How prodigally she blooms, how fragrant her breath, how radiantly she shines.)*

"Do not leave me, Désirée," he begged hoarsely, but she replied in a matter-of-fact tone, "Are you going to help him?"

"No!" he cried. The word shot from his lips, and after a second's pause he added, "But I want to marry you."

Rather she would have expected him to rush upon her and strike her with the first object that came to hand. "I want to marry you." It could not have been put into less words. What a triumph it would be to move into the Château d'Etioles as Madame Lenormant d'Etioles, to hold court there, to have her colleagues act on her stage for her entertainment and that of her guests. And Charlot was no longer young, she would not have to live with him for very long. Once they were married he would burn himself up with lust, rage, and grief.

"I will think it over," she wanted to say. Then she saw herself, hardly three hours ago, taking it as a matter of course that her friend Pierre should renounce riches and ease because he was unwilling to pay for them in humiliation. For Etioles she would have to pay in a little treachery to Pierre.

But Etioles was splendour—and what was a little treachery? "I will think it over," she started to say. Then she saw the fresh, shrewd, naïve, intelligent face of her friend Pierre, and, "No, Charlot," she said, "no, thank you, Charlot," she said, and left.

☆　　☆　　☆

When Pierre complained to Silas Deane of his disappointment and the injury that was being inflicted on him by the hostile indifference of the Congress, Deane for the first time candidly confessed that he was unable to help him. In view of Lee's intrigues, he said sorrowfully, he was powerless to do anything. He too had experienced the ingratitude of the leaders in Philadelphia. Pouring out his heart to Pierre, he declared that his most ardent wish was to append his signature to the treaty which he had worked so hard and endured so much distress to bring about, yet he was haunted day and night by apprehension lest a new commissioner should arrive to replace him before he had reaped the reward that was his due.

He lamented so bitterly that at last Pierre tried to console him. They had both reached the nadir of their fortunes, he said, but he was certain that this was rock bottom. The great day was about to dawn when the treaty would be concluded, and there could be no doubt that the historic document would bear the signature of Silas Deane. It was only to be regretted that Arthur Lee would presumably be a cosignatory to the treaty and thus deface a truly noble document.

Pierre interrupted himself in the midst of his eloquent condolences as a bright idea occurred to him. Since he was unable to get his money out of the Congress, he suggested, he at least had a claim to be present at the solemn act of signature. "Citizen Beaumarchais wishes to be a witness," he declared in ringing tones, "to the signing of the treaty between France and America by Citizen Franklin."

Silas Deane, considerably cheered by Pierre's words, promised to bring the matter to Franklin's attention as soon as an opportune moment should occur.

Pierre's fortunes did, indeed, seem to have taken a turn for the better. On the day after his talk with Deane he received unexpectedly favourable intelligence from America. The firm's prospects of payment, so Paul wrote, seemed to have improved, and he would be in a position to transmit goods to the value of between 180,000 and 200,000 livres by the next ship due to sail. The important thing was that he had succeeded in persuading the Congress to admit without reserve the outstanding nature of Monsieur de Beaumarchais's services, and this presumably meant that it also acknowledged his claims in principle. Pierre would receive confirmation of this in an official letter that was no doubt being carried by the same boat.

On the following day the official communication arrived, and it was signed by John Jay, the President of the Congress. In it the Congress of the United States of America acknowledged the extraordinary services performed on its behalf by Monsieur de Beaumarchais and assured him of its highest esteem. The Congress regretted the disappointments which he had suffered as a consequence of his support of the United States, but it had hitherto been prevented by unfortunate circumstances from fulfilling its obligations. It proposed, however, to take the promptest measures to acquit itself of the debt that had been incurred, and further assured him that the generous sentiments and the breadth of view which alone could have dictated conduct such as that of Monsieur de Beaumarchais reflected upon him the highest credit. His rare talents had gained for him the esteem of the young Republic and merited the applause of the New World.

Pierre's heart beat high. He had refused to let Charlot get the better of him; he radiated triumph.

What though he had not a sou in his pocket? He would use the flattering words of President John Jay to restore his fortunes.

Armed with the letter he went to Vergennes to ask for just one more little million.

Vergennes received him most amiably. In his audiences with Louis he had brought forward in favour of the alliance arguments drawn from Pierre's earlier memoranda, and he was duly grateful, so when Pierre asked for a further loan he replied that of course an old friend could not be left in the lurch. Pierre handed him the letter as proof that he would very soon no longer find it necessary to apply for money to the royal treasury, and as Vergennes perused it he fixed his eyes intently, and with visible pride, on the Minister's face.

To his shocked surprise, however, he saw that Vergennes's expression was changing as he read. The friendly, slightly ironic smile had vanished, to be replaced by an air of icy reserve.

Pierre realized in a bewildered flash that he had committed an unforgivable blunder. Vergennes had, of course, expected that a letter like that of the Congress President would be addressed to him, the responsible Minister, and not to his agent, whom he regarded as a mere tool.

Vergennes handed him back the letter. "Well, Monsieur," he said. "I congratulate you. It is clear that we have no need to exert ourselves in order to come to your aid." Both his words and the manner in which he uttered them revealed the haughty arrogance that Pierre so profoundly detested and admired in the born aristocrats. There was nothing for Pierre to do but take his leave.

When he had already risen from his chair, however, he referred once more to the reason for his visit. If he had understood Count Vergennes correctly, he said, he assumed that during the transition period, while waiting for the payments promised by the Congress, he could rely upon the continued support of His Majesty's Government.

"What kind of sum were you thinking of?" inquired Vergennes coldly.

Pierre had intended to ask for at least a million. "Four hundred thousand livres," he said.

"You are jesting, Monsieur," replied Vergennes. "I shall give instructions for you to be paid a hundred thousand livres. It must be strictly understood, however, that you will in future cease to make any claim upon His Majesty's secret funds."

John Jay's flattering letter in his pocket and red-hot anger in his heart, he set off homewards.

But when he was half-way there he ordered his coachman to turn the horses' heads and proceed to Passy.

Franklin read the letter and nodded his massive head appreciatively. "Very fine. You must have found this most gratifying," he said. But secretly he thought, probably the Congress regards their flattering words as a kind of payment on account, and Monsieur Caron's prospects of receiving ready cash during the next few months seem very dim.

Pierre broached the topic of his present anxieties. He had practically ruined himself, he said, in the process of providing arms for the Battle of Saratoga, and he needed credit until the payments indicated in the Congress letter materialized. Could Franklin perhaps let him have an instalment of the promised goods and drafts? He spoke of his difficulties in a half-humorous tone, which he thought was best calculated to produce the desired effect on the old raconteur, who, as he knew, liked his joke. *"Date obolum Belisario,"* he concluded in a well-simulated beggar's whine.

Franklin told himself that Monsieur Caron was not altogether unjustified in quoting the cry "Give alms to Belisarius!" since, like that great Roman general, he too had been to some extent beggared by his services to the State. But he found the undignified theatricality of this elegantly clad, almost dandified Frenchman repellent. He would have been prepared to accept the responsibility of paying a not too high advance on behalf of the Congress, but they were in difficulties themselves, and in any case it was no part of his functions to assist the man in obtaining his due.

"I sympathize thoroughly with your situation, my dear friend," he said, "but, you see, we commissioners of the United States are not bankers. We should be infringing our instructions if we were to assume such duties. The gratifying letter you have received from Philadelphia is sufficient guarantee that you may hope in the near future to be repaid for all your exertions." His tone was courteous and sympathetic, but his words left no more to be said and Pierre took his leave.

As he sat in the sumptuously furnished study of his great house with John Jay's flattering letter on the table before him, he murmured, "Empty words, Caprice, empty words!" and he locked it away in his chest together with the manuscript, the receipts, the treasured documents, and the love letters.

☆   ☆   ☆

The reply from Madrid arrived more speedily, and was couched in more definite terms, than was to Louis's liking. Though Spain did not intend for the time being to enter into an alliance with the English colonies, declared Charles, she would regard a pact between France and the Americans not only as not unwelcome, but even as desirable.

This disposed of the most cogent objection which Louis had put forward, and he was immediately faced with Toinette's insistent demand that he fulfil his promise. A further conference had to be called, at which he could not prevent her from being present.

There was great danger, Maurepas asserted, that continued delay would force the Americans to accept the English proposals.

"We should ask Doctor Franklin for a binding statement," suggested Vergennes, "that he will reject out of hand any offer from England which would involve reunion of the colonies with their motherland."

"Why should Monsieur Franquelin give us such a statement?" asked Toinette with a shrug.

"We think there might be a way," ventured Maurepas. To which Vergennes added, "If we were authorized to inform the Americans the King will enter into a solemn obligation to conclude the alliance, there can be no doubt that Doctor Franklin would be prepared, for his part, to enter into a reciprocal obligation."

They all now looked at Louis, waiting for him to speak. "Can one trust the word of a rebel?" he asked at last uneasily.

"It will not be the same as a royal word," replied Maurepas, "but Doctor Franklin possesses a world-wide reputation as a man on whom one can rely."

"In any case," said Vergennes, "there's no other way."

"You hear, Sire," said Toinette, and "Please let us have your views," she urged.

Louis fidgeted in his chair and breathed heavily. "Very well, then. Very well," he mumbled. The others sighed with relief.

Whereupon Louis added hastily, "But I will not agree to any definite date, Messieurs. It must be understood that there is no time limit and that my sanction is only of a general nature. So I must request you to be cautious in your negotiations with the rebel. There must be no precipitate action. Bear that in mind, Messieurs! Every single clause must be given mature consideration."

"You may have implicit confidence in us," replied Maurepas soothingly. "Your Ministers are not the kind of men to act rashly."

The very same day, however, Maurepas and Vergennes set to work.

Once more Monsieur de Gérard made a clandestine appointment with the three commissioners. Solemnly he announced that he had three questions to put to them. First, what assurances did the commissioners require from the French Government of its sincere devotion to the American cause in order that they might be dissuaded from listening to proposals from England? Secondly, what did they wish the French Government to do in order to convince the Congress and people of the United States of its devotion and to dissuade them from accepting proposals from England? Thirdly, what practical steps did the United States expect the French Government to take?

Franklin smiled benevolently and was about to reply when Arthur Lee bluntly interjected that such momentous questions could not be answered without due reflection. Monsieur de Gérard suggested that they had, after all, already had a whole year in which to consider these matters.

"That may be so," declared Lee implacably, "but we shall need one more hour to think them over," to which Gérard rejoined that with their permission he would withdraw and return in an hour for his answer.

Franklin sat down and began to draft a reply to the three questions, while Lee and Deane engaged in a violent argument. "A little more quietly, gentlemen, please," begged Franklin, and he went on writing.

When Gérard returned, Franklin read out to him the answer of the three commissioners. First, some considerable time had elapsed since the commissioners made their original proposal for a treaty of friendship and mutual trade. The speedy conclusion of such a treaty would remove their uncertainty, inspire them with adequate confidence in

France's good intentions, and make it possible for them to reject any peace proposals emanating from England which did not include a guarantee of complete freedom and independence. Secondly, a loan of suitable amount would convince the Congress and people of the United States of the French Government's friendship. Thirdly, the immediate dispatch of eight men-o'-war would enable the United States to protect their coasts and commerce, and eliminate any inclination to accept proposals from England.

Lee wished to add something verbally, but Franklin turned his face towards him and made a deprecatory gesture with his hand which, courteous though it was, effectively silenced him.

Gérard expressed his satisfaction with the reply and went on immediately to say, "I have the honour, gentlemen, to inform you that my Government is prepared to conclude the desired treaties." He rose from his seat and added casually, as if he were speaking of the weather, "I am empowered, gentlemen, to offer you His Majesty's word that we shall sign these treaties, the treaty of friendship and commerce as well as the treaty of offence and defence which will guarantee your independence. The only stipulation is that you, for your part, shall bind yourselves not to enter into a separate peace with England or voluntarily to surrender your independence."

Franklin succeeded in controlling his excitement. The two others, however, leapt from their chairs and Lee was again about to intervene, but a look from Franklin once more reduced him to silence.

Then, unhurriedly, Franklin rose and said calmly to Gérard across the table, "We give you this assurance, Monsieur."

"Thank you, Doctor Franklin," replied Gérard. "All that remains is for me to congratulate you and your colleagues on the happy issue of our negotiations. I hope that the association between our countries will be a lasting one and will confer benefits on both parties." With a deep bow to Franklin, and a bow less deep to the two other commissioners, he took his departure.

Only when he had gone did Franklin permit himself to breathe a profound sigh of satisfaction. He pressed Silas Deane's hand with unwonted warmth, and then shook hands with Arthur Lee a little hesitantly. Lee wished to speak. But, "Be still," said Franklin paternally, as if to an unruly child.

This took place on the eighth of January, thirty-five days after receipt of the news of Saratoga.

☆　　☆　　☆

Now that matters had progressed so far, Silas Deane recalled the desire expressed by Beaumarchais to be present at the signing of the treaty. He had hitherto been reluctant to make such a suggestion to

Franklin, but the ceremony would no doubt be taking place in the near future and he could hardly defer mentioning it much longer.

Franklin's face clouded. An essential condition, he pointed out, was the maintenance of secrecy. If Monsieur Caron were to be invited to witness the ceremony, they might as well send out heralds to proclaim far and wide that the alliance had been concluded.

Pierre's impudent request, however, inspired a train of thought in Franklin's mind. If among his French friends there was anyone who had helped to bring about the alliance, it was Dubourg, who had first suggested the meeting with the Queen, and if any Frenchman was to be invited to attend the signing, none was so deserving as Dubourg.

Having obtained the grudging consent of Gérard, he drove to his friend's house. He had not seen him for a whole week and found him propped up on numerous pillows, looking very emaciated, breathing with difficulty and perspiring, his night-cap tipped over his skull, and attended by an old servant and a male nurse. It was obviously a comfort to him to see Franklin, and, with his withered hand, he impatiently waved his two attendants out of the room.

Franklin realized at once that he had not been deceived when he thought that he could trace the signs of impending dissolution in his friend's face. It must now be clear to everyone that Dubourg had but a short time to live.

"Things are going splendidly," he said. "That excellent idea of yours has borne fruitful results. My meeting with the Queen was not in vain. It is practically certain that the treaty will be signed." Dubourg was overjoyed, breathed even more heavily, then croaked a line from Horace, *"Hoc erat in votis; this is what I have wished."*

Franklin had thought of something that would afford Dubourg great pleasure. The authoritative text of the Franco-American agreement was to be the French text, as was customary in all treaties between states. The commissioners had carefully examined every word and studied every shade of meaning. Franklin himself had consulted Madame Brillon and the Abbé Morellet as to the exact significance of certain turns of phrase. He knew, however, how passionately interested Dubourg was in problems of translation, so drawing the draft of the treaty from his pocket he said that he had a favour to ask. Would his old friend be good enough to give him his expert advices on the phraseology of various clauses?

Dubourg's reaction was just what Franklin had hoped. He became more animated, and as the text was read out to him he made an unsuccessful effort to sit more upright in the bed, breathed a little more easily, and listened intently. At one point he made a vehement gesture with his hand to interrupt Franklin and wheezed, *"de quelque nature qu'ils puissent être, et quelque nom qu'ils puissent avoir."* Franklin carefully noted down this amplification, though he thought it superfluous. Again he was interrupted by Dubourg, who amended impatiently, *"Les Etats du Roi."* He was dissatisfied with the words *"les dits Etats,"* which he evidently thought not sufficiently clear. He continued to suggest textual changes, and Franklin made a note of them all, expressing at the same time his deep gratitude, though they all seemed to him unnecessary.

Then he broke into loud self-reproach at his lack of consideration in thus importuning his sick friend. He only hoped, he added, that the effort had not tired Dubourg too much. For he must hurry up and get on his feet again, since the day was drawing near when the treaty was to be signed and of course Dubourg, who was the originator of the project, must be present to witness the official ratification of the alliance.

On hearing this, Dubourg stopped wheezing, succeeded in sitting up, and adjusted his night-cap with a trembling hand. "Are you being serious?" he asked. "You are suggesting that an old botanist like me should be present when you and the King of France—?"

"I don't suppose he will come himself," said Franklin, "but in any case I should regard your presence as more important than his."

Dubourg groped for his friend's hand and pressed it with all his strength. Even so, the pressure could hardly be felt.

☆   ☆   ☆

When, a few days later, Franklin came down to breakfast he found that the table had been festively decorated. It was his seventy-second birthday. William was a good lad after all and very attentive to his grandfather.

As a matter of fact, William would have forgotten his grandfather's birthday for the second time if Silas Deane had not reminded him. Deane's veneration for the greatest of his compatriots had been enhanced, if possible, by the recent successful negotiations with the French Government, but apart from that he was anxious to win Franklin's support in his difficulties with the Congress. He had therefore welcomed this further opportunity of showing his devotion before he returned to America, and had exerted himself to let everybody know that the Doctor's birthday was approaching.

Soon after breakfast—at which there were the buckwheat pancakes of which Franklin was inordinately fond, and to which he did full justice—Deane called to offer his congratulations and said with a mingling of humour and dignity that in view of their colleague's outstanding diplomatic success the envoys had decided to present him with a memento on his birthday. Two large cases were dragged in by burly porters and when the lids were removed they were seen to be filled with handsome, massive volumes bound in dark brown leather. Five, ten, twenty, there seemed no end to them. It was the famous *Encyclopédie,* the *Dictionnaire raisonné des sciences, des arts et des métiers,* twenty-eight volumes in all, plus three supplementary volumes and three volumes of engravings.

Franklin's broad face beamed. "This really is a joyful surprise," he cried, and he shook Silas Deane by the hand. "I have long wanted to possess the *Encyclopédie,* but I never dared even in my wildest dreams to think of buying it." It was a very expensive work. Though the censor closed an eye it was officially banned, and to obtain it from clandestine sources cost anything from 1200 to 2000 livres.

When he was alone again he gazed at the stout, heavy volumes and stroked them pensively, almost tenderly, with his hand. Some of his friends possessed copies which he had been able to consult, and he was familiar with the great work, which numbered among its collaborators personal acquaintances like Helvétius, Turgot, Marmontel, Raynal, and Necker, as well as others whom he only knew by renown, such as Voltaire, Rousseau, Montesquieu, and Buffon. The spirit of France and of Europe, everything that had been thought out and discovered since there had been a history of the human mind, lay enclosed between those dark brown covers. The editors, d'Alembert and Diderot, had had to overcome almost insuperable difficulties. Everybody knew that the Advocate-General of the Paris Parliament, the Supreme Court of France, had denounced the contributors and publishers as atheists, rebels, and corrupters of youth, threatening them with the most dire punishment. D'Alembert had then prudently withdrawn, but Diderot had tenaciously continued with his labours until eventually the work was printed and circulated with the tacit toleration of the Government.

Franklin had met Diderot years ago and had had the opportunity to observe how fanatically this great writer was obsessed by his work. In fact, a more useful and stimulating occupation could hardly be imagined. Standing with one foot in the Bastille, his comfort, his liberty, his very life at stake during the whole time, Diderot had fought unceasingly for the survival of the *Encyclopédie* against the Church, the State authorities, the Sorbonne, and the combined attacks of all the obscurantists in France.

Now it was completed, a concrete, tangible achievement, the textbook of the age, its Bible, the sum total of its knowledge. It was a storehouse of all the militant, progressive ideas, a gigantic, inexhaustible arsenal from which Reason could continually draw fresh weapons in its war against superstition and prejudice. These volumes were intellectual cannon with which to bombard the mighty fortress of privileged stupidity, the obsolete conceptions and moribund insti-

tutions of the past. The Advocate-General had been right when he
branded the contributors as men who were conspiring to establish the
reign of materialism and destroy religion, to corrupt the prevailing
morals, to unchain the spirit of independence throughout the world
and fan the flames of revolt. The independence of America could
never have been achieved without the intellectual equipment they
had provided, the array of ideas that had been marshaled within the
covers of the *Encyclopédie*.

Franklin's eyes wandered mechanically over the handsomely printed
pages. He was not conscious of what he was reading, for his mind was
filled with the concept of the omnipotence of Reason. As an author
himself he was proud of this tangible witness to the power of authorship, of this tremendous achievement that had already influenced so
effectively the history of the world and was continuing to influence it
with every day that passed. Benjamin Franklin was a sober-minded
man, but his heart sang within him: *Reason! Reason! Reason!* These
volumes that lay before him were a monument to Reason, more durable than brass.

His eyes took in the French words, but his thoughts were in English. With some amusement he meditated on the fact that the fundamental principles of the *Encyclopédie* had originated in England. It
had been one of his own race who first pronounced the dictum that
knowledge was power, the Englishman Francis Bacon. It was in the
atmosphere of England that the conception of the usefulness of
knowledge had germinated and flourished.

Yet it was remarkable what the French had succeeded in making of
the English ideas. Their keen, consistent logic, their emancipation
from the authority of the past, the dialectical brilliance of their intellectual attitude, these were peculiarly their own. "It will take us some
time to produce a Voltaire," he mused. "We must remain content
with a Franklin. None the less, we were the first not only to have
conceived these ideas, but also to have put them into practice. We know
how to wait for the opportune moment and to use it." *To every thing
there is a season, and a time to every purpose under the heaven. A
time to be born, and a time to die: a time to plant, and a time to pluck
up that which is planted. A time to kill, and a time to heal: a time to
break down, and a time to build up. A time to weep, and a time to
laugh: a time to mourn, and a time to dance. A time to love, and a time
to hate: a time of war, and a time of peace.* When as a boy he had first
read these profound and ambiguous words of the Bible, they had sunk
in deeply and become part of his very soul.

Whether those who had given utterance to the ideas of the *Encyclopédie* were English or French, theorists or men of action, he felt a
sense of kinship with them. They were all citizens of the world, tran-
scending the nations to which they belonged and constituting the Re-

public of Learning, a republic of which he himself, in pride and humility, was also a citizen.

Reason! Reason! Reason!

There was another link that bound him to these men: that was the blissful satisfaction with which he contemplated the quiet, wily way they had set to work. Diderot and his colleagues had needed all their patience and all their guile to lull the censors into closing an eye to the publication of the *Encyclopédie* despite the vicious attacks of the clergy and the veto of the Advocate-General. There had of course been concessions, which could not be avoided. Franklin turned over the pages of the articles in which the censors must have searched most meticulously for objectionable opinions, such as those on *Christianity, Soul, Freedom of the Will*. In none of these could the most orthodox theologian have found the slightest cause for offence. Elsewhere, however, under apparently innocent key-words, blunt truths were demonstrated with cogent arguments. Who would have expected to find under the title *Juno* scientific objections to the Immaculate Conception? Or under *Cowl* an attack on monks and monasteries? Or under *Eagle* the evidence against revealed religion?

Somewhere in the numerous volumes there must be guiding instructions as to how the reader could derive the greatest advantage from his study of the work. Franklin searched his memory. They were certainly not in Diderot's *Preface,* or in d'Alembert's *Introduction.* Ah! Now he remembered! They were to be found under the key-word *Encyclopédie.*

Franklin looked up the relevant passage. "In all the main articles," he read, "it is of course necessary to take into account both political and religious prejudices. To make up for this, however, it is possible to consult other articles, in less prominent positions, in which prejudice is countered by the pithy arguments of reason. In this way there is afforded an opportunity to knock down the whole obscene structure and scatter the worthless dust and rubbish. Such a method of enlightening mankind as to its errors offers no cause for annoyance, yet will not fail of its effect on those who are able to understand and will also influence imperceptibly and unawares those who are of a different frame of mind. If it is employed skilfully and according to plan, an Encyclopaedia can be invested with the power to change the whole way of thought of an epoch."

Franklin sympathized thoroughly with this form of strategy. The force of reason had to worm its way gradually into the minds of the more intelligent members of the community, whence it would slowly and quietly spread to the others. Any attempt to destroy the superstitious piety of the masses overnight was senseless. It would at most shake society to its foundations. He himself had employed similar arguments to those of Diderot in trying to dissuade an impetuous author who had written an aggressive book recommending that all church dogmas should be swept from the face of the earth. "Though your reasons are subtle," he said, "and may prevail with some readers, you will not succeed so as to change the general sentiments of mankind on that subject, and the consequence of printing this piece will be a great deal of odium drawn upon yourself, mischief to you, and no benefit to others. He that spits against the wind spits in his own face. Think how great a portion of mankind consists of weak and ignorant men and women, and of inexperienced, inconsiderate youth of both sexes, who have need of the motives of religion to restrain them from vice, to support their virtue. I would advise you, therefore, not to attempt unchaining the tiger, but to burn this piece before it is seen by any other person. If men are so wicked with religion, what would they be if without it?"

He smiled in amusement. These Frenchmen, like Voltaire and Diderot, were wily fellows, but old Benjamin was wilier. It had not been an easy task fixing up the alliance. That sluggish young monarch had realized from the outset that it would be a dangerous experiment for his dynasty to ally itself with the men who had established their state on the principles enunciated in the *Encyclopédie*. Diplomats like Maurepas and Vergennes saw only the advantages that might be derived in the immediate future, but for all their suppleness of mind they had no inkling of the hazards which lay in store for them. They had indeed unleashed the tiger. At the thought of the patience and guile with which he had induced the young King to sanction the alliance, the old Doctor was infused with a sense of deep satisfaction such as might have been felt by a horse-coper at the conclusion of a profitable deal. Now the ideas that lay within the covers of the volumes before him would take concrete shape in life, politics, history.

Reason! Reason! Reason!

He proceeded to put the volumes away among his other books, slowly and carefully choosing a position where they would be most handy, and in order to make room for them he rearranged his shelves, climbed up and down the ladder, dragged heavy tomes from one part of the library to another, stooped and stretched, and thus found in the *Encyclopédie* a useful opportunity to indulge in much-needed physical exercise.

Then he sat back in his comfortable chair, his eyes closed, somewhat fatigued. Now and then he blinked across at the new acquisitions. He was having a pleasant birthday. The alliance was ensured and would shortly be signed, the imposing volumes of the *Encyclopédie,* as handsome as they were useful, stood in orderly array on his shelves, and later on there was going to be a party in his honour at the house of his dear friend, Marie-Félicité Helvétius.

☆   ☆   ☆

Louis continued to hope in his heart, knowing full well the unreasonableness of his expectations, that something would happen at the eleventh hour to save him from signing the detested alliance. He therefore endeavoured to defer its formal conclusion as long as possible by carping at every trifling detail he could find to criticize. In every successive draft there was some word or turn of phrase to which he raised objections, and in the most harmless formulations he espied deceitful intentions on the part of the American signatories.

Though he was not aware of it, his delaying tactics were being reinforced by Arthur Lee. If Louis was suspicious and hard to please, Lee was even more pedantic and distrustful, and both wrangled at every word.

There was a series of stipulations in the treaty concerning the measure of assistance to be afforded by the French Government during the period when the Americans would still be fighting alone. Since it would undoubtedly come to open hostilities in the shortest possible time after England learnt of the ratification of the treaties, these clauses were really superfluous, but they provided both Louis and Arthur Lee with opportunities to display their acumen.

Every day Lee drove out to Passy. Every other day he showed his exasperation at not being received by Franklin at once. On one occasion he found a draft of the treaty lying about openly in a room where a French visitor was waiting for an interview, and he complained indignantly at the carelessness of Franklin's secretary, young William Temple. Franklin was disconcerted for a moment and sought to defend his grandson, but when he was alone with William he told him bluntly that he had been guilty of gross negligence, that he was a good-for-nothing, and that he deserved to be dismissed in disgrace from his post. William tried to get out of it with his usual display of charm, but Franklin ordered him to hold his tongue and glared at him so sternly that he turned pale and broke off in the middle of a sentence.

Lee's ceaseless grumbling drove Silas Deane to despair. He had set his heart on appending his signature to the treaty of alliance, yet more and more strongly he was assailed by the almost morbid fear that his successor would arrive before this could be done and that the new man's name would be attached to the document instead of his own.

Franklin too was anxious to see the treaty safely signed and sealed. The impression made by the victory at Saratoga was beginning to wane, and a speedy ratification had become a political necessity. Franklin therefore begged Lee not to exercise so much punctilio. He used the old-fashioned word "punctilio" because it seemed to him more mild and courteous, but it only served to enhance Lee's wrath. "Whom are you accusing of punctilio?" he demanded excitedly. "The treaty would have been ready long ago if you had not both of you made it a principle to reject every suggestion I ventured to offer."

At one point even Franklin's patience gave way under the strain. He had secured agreement to a clause in which France renounced all claim to territory on the American continent as well as to the whole of the islands within the American sphere that might be conquered by the allies. The islands mentioned were Newfoundland, Cape Breton, Saint John, Anticosti, and the Bermudas; the islands in the West Indies were omitted. On the following day Lee declared that the text was not sufficiently clear and insisted on the preparation of a precise list with the names of all the islands in question. Monsieur de Gérard raised no objection, but asked with a shade of annoyance in his voice whether Article IX could now be considered in order. Franklin hastily replied that it could, yet at their next meeting twenty-four hours later Lee again asserted that the text of Article IX was still unsatisfactory. He objected to the word *conquered* as incompatible with the sense of honour and virtuous principles of the United States. It was not a matter of conquests, since the islands to be occupied must be regarded as belonging naturally to the United States. He therefore put forward a new version, and a very complicated one, of the proposed Article IX.

Silas Deane was infuriated. "This is too much!" he burst out. And this time Franklin came to his help. Rising from his seat, he loomed massively over the slender figure of his fellow commissioner and thundered, "What is it you really have in mind, young man? Two days ago Monsieur de Gérard agreed to an important concession, which his Government was by no means obliged to do. Yesterday we requested an extension of this concession and it was granted, whereupon we made it quite clear that we were satisfied. Today you come here with a further display of punctilio. Do you want to make us look ridiculous in the eyes of our French friends?"

"I anticipated that you would support each other in your opposition to me," retorted Lee. "Punctilio, indeed! Suppose we should lose our islands on account of your lack of concern?" His colleagues maintained a frowning silence. "Very well then," he said at last. "I give in. But the responsibility rests solely on your shoulders."

"It does," agreed Franklin.

Meanwhile Vergennes had been giving reluctant consideration to the various objections raised by Louis, and after submitting to him no less than seven drafts, each time with numerous emendations, he hoped that the last petty criticism had been met. Louis, however, when the seventh draft was handed to him, announced affably, "Good! Now I am going to sit down for three days and study it all quietly." When, after three days, the Minister anxiously returned, there were twenty-three fresh points neatly noted in the margins which Louis wished to have revised.

Toinette, goaded by Maurepas and Vergennes, assailed by Vaudreuil, cornered him with a trenchant demand that there should be an end to further delays. The time had come to fulfil his promise. Louis fixed his eyes on her with a look in which craftiness was mingled with wrath and sorrow. "It is a pact with the Devil, Madame," he said, "into which I am about to enter. I have given you my word and I intend to keep it, but this alliance is no trifling matter. Every *t* must be crossed and every *i* dotted only after due reflection from the political, the juridical, and the moral angles."

"You have been reflecting for weeks and weeks, Sire," she replied heatedly. "These are mere pretexts. You are inventing something to carp at in every bagatelle. You persist in finding new *futilités, vétilles, babioles.*" She hurled at his head all the French words she could think of.

Louis was hurt. "This is something that you do not understand, Madame," he said, trying to look as royal and dignified as he did in Duplessis's painting. "This Doctor Franklin is a hard-bitten lawyer and schemer. He is seeking to lay a trap for me by every means he can devise. Had it been only a matter of myself, I should have yielded long ago, for I am worn out with his everlasting quibbles. But the fate of my people is at stake. The Americans have forgotten to mention one of my West Indian islands, though it is to be found on every map, yet among those that they want to wrest from the King of England they mention one that I cannot find on any map. Is it such tergiversations that you refer to as *futilités?* Do you expect me to put my name to such clauses? Furthermore, there are two separate occasions on which the 'whole course of the Mississippi' is specified. This river is to constitute the frontier between the rebels and the territory belonging to Spain. Yet the source of the Mississippi has not even been discovered. If I were to allow such things to pass, I should perhaps be depriving my cousin in Madrid by a thoughtless stroke of the pen of territories as large as Austria. *Futilités! Babioles!* You do not realize what you are saying, Madame. No, I will not put my name to such dubious stipulations. I cannot accept responsibility for them before God and my conscience." His little double chin was trembling.

☆　　☆　　☆

Suddenly there came news which put an entirely different complexion on the political situation. The Electoral Prince of Bavaria had died. The problem of his successors was agitating the chancelleries of Europe.

Count Mercy, the Austrian Ambassador, called upon Vergennes. The Emperor Joseph had certain claims to the major portion of Bavaria. These claims, however, had been acquired in an equivocal manner. They stood on paper, but it was common knowledge that Frederick of Prussia would never tolerate the cession of Bavaria to the House of Habsburg. Hitherto, while emphasizing in his conversations with Vergennes that his monarch was counting upon the assistance of France in obtaining recognition of his claims, Count Mercy had contented himself with drawing attention to the family ties that linked Schoenbrunn with Versailles and their existing treaty of alliance. Now that the question had reached its crucial stage, Joseph approached the matter more realistically and authorized Mercy to offer Louis a very tangible *quid pro quo,* namely, the Austrian Netherlands.

It had long been a dream of the Kings of France to incorporate in their realm the Flemish provinces that had been fertilized with generations of French blood, and Vergennes could not but admit to himself that the Habsburg Emperor's offer was both generous and shrewd. Yet what Joseph demanded in return involved the assumption of an enormous risk, the risk of a highly unpopular war with Prussia. Vergennes was therefore determined from the outset that the offer must be rejected. France could not afford a war on two fronts, and if she were to comply with Joseph's request she would be forced to renounce her ambition to weaken England by her support of the American insurgents. So Vergennes was not tempted by the Austrian offer.

What about Louis, however? Would he be able to resist the Austrian blandishments, reinforced as they would be by all the arts of persuasion that Toinette would bring to bear upon him day and night, and especially at night?

Maurepas shared the doubts of the Foreign Minister, and their chief apprehension was lest Louis should use the Bavarian question as a new pretext for postponing the signing of the American treaty.

When the Ministers approached Louis, he at once began to speak of the obligations imposed upon him by his treaty with the House of Habsburg, and it was evident that he was anxious not to rebuff, with an immediate blunt and unfraternal *no,* his brother-in-law, who had obviously set his heart on acquiring Bavaria. On the whole, however, Louis was inclined to agree with his Ministers, and nothing was further from his mind than to allow himself to be dragged into a conflict with Prussia. It would, therefore, be best, he said, to meet Count Mercy's demands by indicating that they had not yet resolved certain doubts, and to keep on inventing fresh grounds for hesitation as long as it was possible to postpone the eventual decision.

The two Ministers thought that this was inadvisable. Unless they refused firmly, and from the very outset, to help Joseph in any way, that energetic prince would occupy Bavaria without more ado and hostilities would have begun. He would then be able to assert, and

not without justification, that he would never have marched into
Bavaria if he had not been encouraged by the half promises of assistance that he had received from France. "Inform him without equivocation, Sire, that his proposal is unacceptable," urged Vergennes.
"Permit us to reject Mercy's offer courteously, but unambiguously."

Louis snorted uneasily and continued to wriggle. Blinking at his
colleague, Maurepas decided to have recourse to pressure.

The delaying tactics which Louis wished to employ were, so he
explained, exactly what his illustrious brother-in-law was counting
upon. If Louis did not say a firm *no,* then the Emperor was persuaded
he could intimidate him and win him over. There were reasons for
believing, went on Maurepas, that Joseph's whole policy was based
on the conviction that Louis was a tool in his hands.

Louis looked up in astonishment and with a wrinkling of the
brows as Maurepas delved into his portfolio and withdrew a document which, with a smile partly of triumph, partly of deprecation at
the wickedness of the world, he proceeded to hand over.

It was a copy of the letter in which Joseph had outlined for his
mother's benefit his impressions of Louis's character, and which had
been intercepted by the Paris police. It had been a good idea, thought
Maurepas to himself, not to make use of it at the time, but to await
a fitting opportunity. The right moment had arrived for Louis to
learn what his brother-in-law thought about him. "Your son-in-law
Louis," he read, "has been badly brought up and he cuts an extremely
sorry figure. He has stored up a great deal of factual knowledge. I
do not see what use such virtuosity can have for a monarch. For the
rest, Louis suffers from a serious inability to make up his mind, and
he has little defence against those who know how to intimidate him."

Louis read the letter through two or three times. It was clear that
it had wounded him deeply, but though he smiled bitterly he did his
best to preserve an air of detachment. "My brother-in-law Joseph
may be right," he said. "Perhaps I am not very bright. This much,
however, I do know. I must not allow myself to be drawn into his
war of conquest. I may suffer from an inability to make up my mind,
but this time he is going to learn that neither he nor anyone else is
able to intimidate me. You may rely upon that, gentlemen."

Vergennes quickly asked whether he was empowered to reject
Mercy's proposals. Louis hesitated for a second, breathed heavily,
and replied, "Very well. Very well."

Meanwhile the Austrians had not remained idle. Count Mercy and
the Abbé Vermond had called upon Toinette. Not for decades, perhaps not even for centuries, they declared, would there again be such
a favourable opportunity to strengthen the power of the Catholic
monarchies. The long-awaited hour had arrived when Toinette must
fulfil her destiny, to the greater glory of God, of Habsburg, and of

Bourbon. They told her of Joseph's magnanimous offer to hand over the Flemish provinces to Louis.

As she listened, Toinette recalled the last bitter-sweet conversation with her brother when he spoke of the duties imposed upon her by her birth. Now she would show him what she was made of. She had forced Louis to give in in the American affair; now she would get Joseph his Bavaria.

She set about her task in a transport of enthusiasm. If France did not intervene, she explained to Louis, Frederick of Prussia would forbid Austria to exercise her chartered rights to round off her possessions. Frederick would pose as the dictator of the whole of Germany. For seventeen years his despotic, violent nature had made him the scourge of Europe, and it was no less Louis's duty than that of Joseph to keep him within bounds.

Louis had been irritated from the moment when Toinette began to speak. She had managed to take him unawares in the American affair, but this time he was well prepared and did not intend to let her have her way.

In a dry tone he replied that Frederick would probably only be strengthened in his resistance to Joseph's claims if they were supported by France.

"On the contrary, Sire," rejoined Toinette eagerly. "If you declare yourself for my brother at once, that is the only way in which to frighten Frederick and prevent a war. If you sit with your hands in your lap, it will be tantamount to stabbing us in the back."

"*Us,*" said Louis bitterly. "*Us!* You speak of Frederick's despotism, of his violent character. What about you Austrians? After having fallen upon Poland, your family now wants to ravish Bavaria. You speak of *us*. I have always been aware, Madame, and I say it straight to your face, that your brother Joseph has the lusts of a tyrant and conqueror. Yet I would never have believed that his brutal schemes of aggression would find an advocate in the Queen of France." His fury rose. "Hold your tongue, Madame!" he cried suddenly. "Do not venture to contradict me! This time you will not find me weak." His voice grew shrill. "Not this time!" he shrieked in angry desperation. "Not this time! Not this time!"

Toinette saw that there was nothing she could do, and she retired to her own apartments.

☆   ☆   ☆

At their first audience Maurepas and Vergennes had prudently refrained from mentioning the American alliance, but now that Louis had rejected Joseph's offer they decided to use this very circumstance to obtain the King's signature to the American treaty.

They again requested a joint audience. Vergennes explained that further delay must inevitably lead Franklin to suspect that Louis was seriously considering intervention on behalf of the Habsburgs, which would prevent him from entering into an armed conflict with England. Such an assumption must force Franklin to make peace while there was still a prospect of being offered favourable terms.

Louis did not look at his Ministers, and remained silent. He abstractedly stroked the porcelain figures of the poets which stood on the desk between him and his ministers.

Maurepas then spoke. The refusal of the Habsburg proposals, he said, and his old voice had greater urgency than usual, was now determined. Louis, therefore, should cease his dangerous procrastinations and sign the American pact at once.

The arguments brought forward by his two advisers represented nothing new. Louis had long been turning them over in his mind. But now that he was finally to say *yes* to the pact with the rebels, his heart and his tongue failed him.

He rose from his chair, and the Ministers at once stood up respectfully. "Please remain seated, gentlemen," he begged. Pacing up and down the room, he finally came to a halt in front of the fire-place and passed his thick, clumsy hands tenderly over the graceful iron-work of the mantelpiece. "Did you have anything else to say, gentlemen?" he asked without turning.

For the hundredth time they enumerated the reasons which made it essential to sign the treaty as speedily as possible. He let them talk while he listened with his thoughts elsewhere. Then he returned to the table, sat down again, and cleared his throat. He had made up his mind to tell them frankly of his secret doubts and apprehensions. If the American adventure should turn out badly—and he was convinced that in the end it would turn out badly—he wanted at least to be able to assert before God and his conscience that he had raised a warning voice while there was still time.

Hesitantly at first, then gradually growing more eloquent, he spoke. Concerned as he was for the finances of his realm, he referred to the enormous expenditure that a war with England would bring in its train. He had instructed Monsieur Necker to estimate the probable cost, and it amounted to almost a thousand million livres. "A thousand million," he repeated, his tongue heavy. He rose from his chair once more, and with an almost violent gesture again motioned them to remain seated. Walking up to the globe, and with the words rolling slowly from his thick lips, he continued, "Can you conceive it, gentlemen? A thousand million! An unending stream of gold! I have attempted to calculate how far the line of sous contained in a thousand million livres would stretch if placed end to end. It would go twelve and a half times round the equator. Just think of it, gentlemen! All this money will have to be squeezed from my people, to support the rebels. Think of the hunger and deprivation it will involve for my subjects, for my sons. And if they should complain, if they should curse me, what am I to reply? A thousand million livres for Doctor Franklin."

The Ministers tried to disperse these gloomly predictions. Monsieur Necker, they suggested soothingly, tended to be over-cautious, and that was part of his business. He had probably exaggerated the sum involved and overestimated the duration of the war. In any case, England would have to pay for it all. Not only would France emerge from the conflict with her economy unweakened, but she would even be enriched by the new markets that would be opened up as a result.

Louis preferred not to argue this point. Returning to the table, he dropped heavily into his chair and painfully began to speak of his inner doubts. With flushed face and keeping his eyes averted, he confessed his constant secret apprehension lest the alliance with the rebels should stir up revolt in France. The officers and soldiers who had been fighting in the cause of this so-called liberty might come back with their minds and hearts poisoned to spread the plague in France, too. It was hard for Louis to put such despondent thoughts into words. He felt as if he were stripping himself naked before these gentlemen in the glaring light of day.

These gentlemen, after he had finished, sat in embarrassed silence. Finally Vergennes spoke up and proceeded to prove by detailed legal arguments that the recognition of the United States did not by any means imply acceptance of the principles enunciated in the Declaration of Independence. Maurepas went so far as to assert glibly a war with England would not only not stir up a rebellious spirit in France, but, on the contrary, such a popular war would be the best means to wean the populace from unruly thought.

Louis sat slumped gloomily in his chair. He had heard all the arguments in favour of the alliance, they had been repeated and threshed out time and again, and he admitted that there was considerable force in them. Yet he knew that they were false, he was convinced that the alliance would be a curse, and now he had even brought himself to tell these gentlemen of his innermost convictions. They refused to listen, these advisers of his, they were tugging and dragging him, and he had to yield. Yet he knew that he ought not to yield. He should never have let this Franklin enter the country. God was sending him signs and inflicting chastisements on him because he was so weak. It was because of his weakness, his sinful weakness, that Toinette had not become pregnant, and perhaps he was destined because of his sinfulness to be the last of the Bourbons. If he were now to make a show of strength and say *no,* there was the Habsburg Emperor standing at the other end of the rope ready to drag him into his

criminal war of conquest. Joseph wrote and Toinette talked and
between them they were drawing him into the vortex, and since there
was no way out, since he was condemned to lend a helping hand in
pulling the Bourbon dynasty down in ruins, since his Ministers were
waiting hungrily for him to say *yes,* he would yield without further
struggle and give them the answer they wanted even though he knew
better than they.

He still hesitated. He could not produce the *yes.*

"It is now almost a month, Sire," said Maurepas pleadingly, "since
you gave Doctor Franklin your word that you would sign the treaty."

"I believe," replied Louis, "that we are over-hasty. But since both
of you, and since the Queen, and since my city of Paris deem such
haste advisable, I renounce any further emendation of the fifteen
points that are still not in order."

"Then I may take it, Sire," said Vergennes, in order to clinch the
matter, "that we have your permission to inform the American commissioners of your willingness to sign the treaties in their present
form?"

"Yes," muttered Louis. "Yes. Very well."

He quickly added, however: "But I want to see the documents
before they are signed. And they are to be signed not by you, Count
Vergennes, but by Monsieur de Gérard. We do not need to lend an
air of too great importance to the ceremony. Moreover, do not forget
to impress on these American gentlemen that there must not be the
faintest whisper of the alliance before the treaties have been ratified
by their so-called Congress and the copies returned to us."

"Very well, Sire," said Vergennes.

☆　　☆　　☆

On the very same day Monsieur de Gérard informed the commissioners on the King's behalf that the treaties could be signed in
their present form. He had already handed the texts to Monsieur
Paillasson, the royal calligraphist, in order that two copies might be
prepared of each of the documents. Count Vergennes would then submit them to His Majesty for the last time and the act of signature
could take place presumably on the next day but one.

"Excellent," commented Franklin, and Silas Deane heaved an audible sigh of relief.

At once, however, Arthur Lee, interfered. "There must be some
misunderstanding," he declared with a frown. So far as his memory
served, the last draft had not yet been approved by the commissioners.
He, at any rate, had not given his sanction. Gérard replied in painful
surprise that if he had comprehended Doctor Franklin aright the
gentlemen *had* signified their agreement with the last version sub-

mitted to them. In that case, rejoined Lee, Doctor Franklin must have misunderstood him. Silas Deane snorted indignantly. It was very regrettable, suggested Gérard, making no attempt to hide his ill humour. It had not been an easy task to persuade His Majesty to accept the treaties in their present form. If they were now, at this late stage, to present the King with fresh amendments, it was to be feared that the whole alliance would be jeopardized. "That is not my fault," said Lee, breaking an uncomfortable silence.

"Will you be so good as to inform us of your further desires or objections, Sir?" Franklin dryly requested.

The others listened glumly as Lee proceeded to explain at length that if Articles XII and XIII of the treaty of commerce were studied closely it would be seen that they were not in accord with the principles of complete reciprocity upon which the treaties should have been based. These articles imposed upon the United States the obligation not to levy export duties on any products leaving their ports for the West Indies. France, on the other hand, bound herself merely to refrain from levying export duties on molasses. "Do you call that reciprocity?" he demanded.

"It was we ourselves who proposed the present text of the two articles," said Franklin. "I am not aware of any other important product that the West Indies could export to America."

"That may be the case today," responded Lee, "but no one can guarantee that it will always be so, and I was under the impression that the treaty is to remain in force for some considerable time."

The courteous Gérard lost something of his diplomatic calm. "I would point out once more, Monsieur," he said, "that the changes you wish to introduce at this late hour will place the treaty in jeopardy. It is by no means to be excluded that His Majesty may grow tired of the whole matter if he should be presented with new amendments on the subject of molasses, and I must tell you honestly that both Count Vergennes and Count Maurepas are also heartily sick of this continual haggling over petty details."

Lee stood with folded arms, his chin pressed in, his forehead thrust forward. "It is not a matter of molasses," he insisted, "but of the principle of reciprocity. The sovereignty of the United States is at stake."

"You will pardon me, Monsieur," replied Gérard, "but I believe that the King of France has offered sufficient proof of his good intentions in declaring his readiness to defend the sovereignty of the United States with his Army and his ships. I can assure you that it was not the King's purpose to use the clause concerning reciprocity in regard to the export of molasses as a means of disputing the sovereign independence of the United States."

Franklin, with a supreme effort at self-control, tried to pour oil on the troubled waters. "It is all my fault, Monsieur de Gérard," he said. "I ought to have afforded Mr. Lee an opportunity to discuss his objections beforehand with Mr. Deane and myself. They would then probably never have been raised."

"You are mistaken, Doctor Franklin," persisted Lee obstinately. "But in any case I shall not sign the treaty in its present form. The clause concerning the export of molasses—and I am speaking for the Congress of the United States—is unacceptable."

Gérard looked at Franklin with an air of respectful regret. It would be deplorable if the treaties, on which they had spent so many months of patient toil, should be wrecked through the unreasonable obduracy of this hysterical fellow with whom the Congress, in its lack of political wisdom, had seen fit to yoke the venerable Doctor Franklin. "I have an idea," he said. "You are afraid," he asked Lee, "that the Congress may take objection to the clause dealing with the export of molasses, are you not?"

"To be sure I am, Monsieur," declared Lee aggressively.

"Would you be content if, in a supplementary letter to be attached to the treaty, I were to assure you in the name of Count Vergennes that in the event of the molasses clause not being ratified by the Congress the remaining clauses shall nevertheless remain valid?"

"In that case," demanded Lee, "you would be prepared to conclude a separate agreement with regard to molasses?"

"We should," answered Gérard.

"You assume full responsibility for that?" insisted Lee.

"I do," answered Gérard.

"And you will state in this letter that the said letter is to constitute an integral part of the treaty?" asked Lee.

"I shall," said Gérard.

"Let me see if I understand you correctly," said Lee, summing up the results of this exchange of question and answer. "Even if the Congress, as I fear will undoubtedly be the case, should decline to surrender its rights to levy export duties on all our products in return for your abolition of the export duty on molasses, the remaining clauses of the treaty of commerce will not thereby be affected, to say nothing of the treaty of offensive and defensive alliance, which will then retain its validity in its present form despite the deletion of Articles XII and XIII, that is to say, the stipulations concerning molasses? That is your intention, Monsieur, is it not?"

"That is exactly my intention, Monsieur," replied Gérard. A trifle impatiently, he added, "Approved and agreed."

"Then I am satisfied," declared Lee, and he unfolded his arms.

"Well," said Franklin, "that is another matter of punctilio successfully settled."

Gérard promised to let them know when the documents were ready

for signature and suggested that they should be prepared for the ceremony to take place on the next day but one.

"You see, gentlemen," said Arthur Lee when they were again alone,
"even the greatest difficulties can be surmounted by the exercise of
a little patience and perseverance."

☆   ☆   ☆

Two days later, on the fifth of February, Franklin drew forth
his suit of heavy blue Manchester velvet. It was the same that he had
worn four years before at the Privy Council when Wedderburn, the
Attorney-General, had so shamefully abused him and none of the
thirty-five members had uttered a word in his defence.

Wearing this suit, and accompanied by young William, he drove
to Paris, where his first call was upon Dubourg. On the previous day
he had sent William to inquire whether his sick friend would be in
a fit condition to rise from his bed and drive to the Foreign Office.
The physician had pulled a doubtful face, but Dubourg insisted on
going, and now he sat waiting, with his physician, nurse, and servant
in anxious attendance, dressed in ceremonial garb and looking pitifully shaky.

The sight of the solemn, blue Franklin excited him. "One must
make an effort," explained the doctor, "to select the right clothes
for particular occasions and for the particular company in which one
will find oneself. I learned that from Charlemagne. When he went
to be crowned at Rome he changed his appearance from that of a
simple Frank to that of a Roman patrician." He told the story of
his blue coat and added, stroking the heavily quilted velvet affectionately, "You see, my friend, I owed this coat a little revenge." Dubourg
smiled, nodded his head vigorously, and fell into a fit of coughing.

Once more the physician warned him not to venture out on such a
wintry day, but Dubourg crossly waved him away and they prepared
to leave the house.

Suddenly, however, a messenger arrived from Monsieur de Gérard.
He was out of breath, having been first to Passy whence he had rushed
post-haste to catch up with Franklin. Gérard regretted that the act
of signature would have to be deferred until the following day for
reasons that Doctor Franklin would find in the letter the messenger
carried. The disappointed Dubourg was undressed again and put to
bed, Franklin promising to come and fetch him next day, though it
was evident that after his present exertion it would be impossible
for him to rise from his bed again and make the journey.

The reasons for the postponement were as follows. Monsieur
Paillasson had prepared two copies of each of the documents, using
the costly parchment that was always employed for state treaties and

writing out the text with the extreme care for which he was renowned. When Louis looked them through, however, he discovered that in the treaty of amity and commerce, on sheet 3, line 17, there was a full-stop that might be taken for a comma. He ordered the sheet to be recopied and submitted to him again. Thus he gained a day, in the course of which he hoped that something might happen to save him the necessity of signing.

Nothing happened. Monsieur Paillasson carefully copied out the sheet again so that even the most critical eye could not take the full-stop in line 17 for anything other than a full-stop, and Vergennes once more entered the King's presence to request his signature. Louis heaved a sigh, muttered, "Very well, then. Very well," and signed. Vergennes hurriedly handed the documents to Gérard together with the authorization to sign and seal in his name, and therewith in the name of the King, the state treaties numbered respectively 1778/32 and 1778/33.

On the sixth of February, punctually at five o'clock in the afternoon, the three commissioners, accompanied by William Temple, called upon Gérard at the Hôtel Lautrec. Franklin was again wearing his blue suit, but Dubourg had been unable to come.

The two treaties lay ready on the table, and beside them had been placed the King's seal. At another and smaller table Gérard's secretary stood waiting. "Well, Doctor Franklin," said Gérard, "the moment has come. If you are agreeable, we can proceed at once to the act of signature."

Arthur Lee raised his hand in a determined gesture. He looked at Franklin, and when the latter remained silent, he demanded, "Should we not first exchange our credentials?"

"Have we credentials?" asked Franklin in a low voice, and William began to grope in his portfolio.

Gérard, very coldly, said to his secretary, "Please show the gentleman my letter of authorization, Pêcheur."

Lee read the document through carefully, then handed over his own credentials.

"Thank you," said Gérard, without glancing at them.

Lee, however, continued rather stiffly, "I would beg to inform you, Monsieur de Gérard, that I am in possession of two letters of authorization. I am here both in my capacity as plenipotentiary of the Congress at the court of Versailles and in my capacity as plenipotentiary at the court of Madrid. Would you consider it correct, Monsieur, after having signed the treaties as a whole, for me to append my signature to the secret clause concerning the eventual entry of Spain into the alliance, or would you consider it sufficient if I sign the treaties and note after my signature on the treaty of alliance the fact that I am acting in a dual capacity?"

"Note the fact that you are acting in a dual capacity," Franklin suggested jovially.

"Yes," agreed Gérard, "that will be sufficient."

"Then that is settled," said Lee. "But now there is the question how I can best translate my title of 'Graduate Counsellor-at-Law' into French. I think it would come nearest to the English if I simply put 'Conseiller des Droits.' "

"Permit me to assure you, Monsieur," replied Gérard, "that His Most Christian Majesty will not dispute the treaty in whatever form you sign."

"Thank you," said Lee. "In that case there remains only one further preliminary to be settled. Will you be so good as to submit the document which, in accordance with our agreement, is a supplement to, and an integral part of, the treaty of commerce, that is to say, the letter concerning the eventual establishment of reciprocity in the matter of the export duties on molasses and so forth."

"Please submit the document, Pêcheur," said Gérard.

While Lee was studying the letter, Gerard addressed himself to the other two commissioners. "I am instructed by Count Vergennes," he said, "to impress upon you once more most urgently the importance of allowing no hint of our alliance to leak out before the treaties have been ratified by the Congress. We shall thereby be deferring the outbreak of war for the few weeks which are essential for the completion of our preparations. You will perhaps permit me to repeat that the assurance of your silence and discretion was and continues to be a prerequisite condition of the alliance. Count Vergennes does not ask for your promise in writing. Your word will suffice, Doctor Franklin." Franklin inclined his head slightly. Arthur Lee said nothing. He merely walked to the fire-place and folded his arms.

"If you are agreeable, gentlemen," said Gérard, "we shall now proceed to sign." The table on which the documents were lying was not very large. Gérard sat down in a small arm-chair at one of the narrow sides; Franklin stood opposite him with both hands resting on the table; Arthur Lee retained his pose near the chimney piece, with Silas Deane beside him; and William Temple took up a modest position near Pêcheur, who was heating the sealing-wax and allowing it to drip upon the parchment. Gérard impressed his seal and signed the first copy.

Franklin cast a glance at the clock which stood on a console-table by the wall. The hands pointed to twenty-two minutes past five.

With his large ruddy hands propped lightly upon the table, his sparse locks falling upon the collar of his blue velvet coat, he watched the movements of Gérard's white, well-tended hand as he made the four impressions of the seal and signed his name four times. His heart was filled with a great joy. This was the moment, the precise

moment, for which he had been waiting so long. February 6, 5:22.
Outside there was a drizzle of rain and snow. Within the room there
was a bright fire burning, the candles gleamed cheerfully, Pêcheur
was heating the wax, and Monsieur de Gérard was alternately impressing the seal and signing his name. It was for this moment that
he had undertaken the arduous voyage across the ocean, for this
moment that over a period of fourteen months he had played his role
of the rustic philosopher from the wild West in fur cap and brown
coat, patiently answered a thousand stupid questions, and entered
into a wily though foolish conversation at Gennevilliers with a pretty
though foolish woman in a blue mask. And now this man was signing,
and then he, Franklin, would sign, and then many French ships would
put to sea with many cannons and many men, and many Frenchmen
would die so that England might recognize America's independence.
The King on whose behalf this elegant French gentleman was
appending his signature to the treaties was not very bright, but he
had realized the danger of an alliance with the young republic that
was the enemy of all despotic authority. The obese young monarch
had resisted the advice of his Ministers with might and main. He had
not wanted to recognize the independence of the thirteen United
States, whose citizens he looked upon as rebels, and he had said *no*
over and over again. The King of France was an absolute monarch,
not responsible to any Parliament, subject only to his own will. Yet
it was clear that he was after all subject to something other than his
own will, that he had to do what he did not want to do. That which
was commonly called world history was stronger than the King of
France and compelled him to obey its dictates. There must therefore
be some meaning in history, some purpose which drove men in a
certain direction whether they wished it or not. And the old Doctor
watched how Monsieur Gérard's white hand wrote and sealed, and
wrote and sealed, and he was very happy.

Gérard had signed and sealed the last of the documents, and he
said politely, "If you please, Doctor Franklin." He motioned towards
the large arm-chair that had been placed at one of the longer sides
of the table, but Franklin seated himself in the smaller chair that
Gérard had just vacated. Pêcheur heated the wax and was about to
let it drip onto the parchment, but young William Temple eagerly
pushed his way forward to take his share in the ceremony. Franklin
impressed his seal and signed. He neatly inscribed the letter *B,* and
linked it artistically with the letter *F.* He wrote with many flourishes
and used his own signet-ring with its decorative design composed of
ears of corn, two lions, two birds, and a fabulous animal. Gérard
stood opposite to him and looked on in silence. Messrs. Deane and
Lee stood by the fire-place and also looked on in silence.

Then came the turn of Silas Deane. With hasty step he walked cheerfully to the table and seated himself in the arm-chair. Young William Temple assiduously lent his aid, heating the wax, and handing him the quill. Each time Deane returned a hearty "Thank you." As he sealed each document he wrote his name in thick, clear letters, then gazed blissfully at the treaty and his own signature. He had swallowed many a bitter pill during the past months, but he was richly recompensed by the sweet delight of that moment. That malicious man, his colleague, who was now staring so gloomily at his signing fingers, had harried him like ten devils and traduced him with a pen dipped in venom, yet he had not been able to prevent him from sitting here as the treaty partner of His Most Christian Majesty, and signing the most important treaty of his country and of his century. He impressed his seal and wrote his name, and there it stood for all to read—*Silas Deane*.

Then, with measured tread Arthur Lee strode towards the table. He sat stiffly erect with an expression of morose resolve. William Temple prepared to assist him, but he said sharply, "Thank you, Mr. Franklin, I can manage without your aid." It took him some considerable time to furnish the four documents with his seal, his signature, his title, and the statement of his dual capacity. He did it all most carefully, for these Frenchmen were slippery customers and he would not trust them an inch. Arthur Lee at any rate was going to do his best to ensure that they would not be able to find any loopholes. His fellow commissioners, instead of watching the act of signature as was their duty, were chatting with the Frenchman, and the only one who appeared to be taking any interest in the proceedings was that officious young lout of a grandson, William Temple. They were not only not watching, but they were even disturbing him in the solemn performance of his duty by their idle babble and whispering.

Against his will he had to listen. "You have had a long path to travel, Doctor Franklin," Monsieur de Gérard was remarking. "It has been an arduous journey for you and your compatriots and I am glad that you have at last attained your goal with the conclusion of our alliance."

Franklin replied, "It was not I who brought about the alliance. The credit for that is due to the victory at Saratoga." As he wrote the words, *"Conseiller des Droits,"* Arthur Lee bit his lip contemptuously at such a show of false modesty.

Gérard went on, "No, no, Doctor Franklin. Without your wise reserve and the extraordinary tactical skill with which you conducted your conversation with the Queen, we should never have succeeded in inducing the King to give his sanction." Arthur Lee jabbed his pen on the parchment as he crossed the *t*. These Frenchmen were always identifying Franklin with America. As if the old libertine were a fitting representative of the young and virtuous republic. If any single American was to be taken as a symbol of the whole country, who could be more suitable than Richard Henry, his brother Richard Henry Lee, who had introduced the resolution declaring that the united colonies were, and of right ought to be, free and independent States? Arthur Lee's pleasure in signing the treaties that meant so much for his country was spoiled by the presumption of the Doctor *honoris causa* and the lack of judgment displayed by these Frenchmen.

It was over. They all looked on silently as Pêcheur elaborately and conscientiously affixed the King's Great Seal to the four documents.

Gérard handed to Franklin the two copies intended for the Congress, and the Doctor passed them on without more ado to his grandson. Lee would have preferred to have them in his own safe-keeping, but he had to acquiesce in this entrusting of the precious parchments to a thoughtless youth. "The letter," he said in a hoarse voice. The others gazed at him inquiringly, and he explained, "The letter concerning Articles XII and XIII." But for him they really would have forgotten all about this momentous supplement to the molasses clause.

There were many people about in the corridors of the Hôtel Lautrec when the commissioners emerged from Gérard's room, but Silas Deane, ignoring the attention he was attracting, seized Franklin's hand and shook it warmly. "A great day," he cried. "An historic day. Thank you, Doctor Franklin. America is under an infinite obligation to you." There were tears in his eyes. Arthur Lee, disgusted at such a display of false sentimentality, could not bring himself to remain any longer in the company of his two colleagues. Declining Franklin's invitation to accept a lift in his carriage, he went off on foot.

After taking Silas Deane home, Franklin drove not to Passy, but to the house of Doctor Dubourg. Taking the treaties from William, he bade his grandson wait for him in the carriage.

Dubourg had taken an appallingly sad turn for the worse since his exertion and excitement of the previous day. He could hardly speak, and it cost him an effort to turn his head as his visitor entered.

Stepping softly up to the bed, Franklin held the documents out towards him and said, "We have done it, my old friend." Dubourg stretched out a hairy, waxen hand, but could not keep his grip on the parchments, which fell onto the coverlet. Franklin picked up the treaty of alliance and held it close in front of the sick man's eyes. Dubourg again stretched out his hand, and though he could probably not read the words his fingers felt for the great royal seal.

Franklin did practically all the talking. He praised his friend and gave him the chief credit for the happy conclusion of the alliance. In a low voice, with his lips close to Dubourg's ear, he spoke very distinctly in French so that the sick man should be able to understand with less effort, but Dubourg, enunciating the words with difficulty, whispered, "Please speak English."

Seeing that his visit was draining Dubourg's last reserves of strength, Franklin collected the treaties with a view to taking his departure and allowing his friend to doze off in peace. But Dubourg restrained him with an impatient gesture. Passing his fingers once more over the parchments he whispered with ghastly pathos, *"Quod felix faustumque sit*— May it bring happiness and blessing."

He still would not let Franklin go. There was apparently something further that he wanted to say. *"Eulogium Linnaei,"* he mumbled. Franklin understood. Dubourg, whose favourite preoccupation had always been with botany, had told him of an article he was writing on Linnaeus, the great botanist, who had recently died. "Shall I take the article? Do you want me to translate it?" he asked.

Dubourg's head moved slightly as if he were trying to nod.

"I shall be very happy to do so," said Franklin. His friend had translated many of his writings, and Franklin was glad to have the opportunity of repaying him for his devotion. "As soon as you are feeling better," he continued, "you can let me have the article and we will go through it together, word for word." He knew that this would never be possible, but he was resolved that whatever happened he would publish an English translation of the article.

Dubourg, however, knew that this was the last visit he would receive from Franklin and he wanted to make sure. Again motioning Franklin not to go, he indicated that he wanted the manuscript brought to him. Franklin and the two attendants had to search for it, and only when the *Eulogium* was safely in Franklin's hand did Dubourg rest content.

Franklin turned over the pages. "It is very clearly written," he assured the sick man. "I will print it myself both in English and in French." An inner radiance seemed to illumine the sallow, emaciated face that Franklin knew he was seeing for the last time.

With the two treaties and the eulogy on Linnaeus in the pocket of his blue velvet coat, Franklin drove back to Passy.

★ ❧ ★ ❧ ★ ❧ ★ ❧ ★

PART THREE

THE RECOMPENSE

★ ❧ ★ ❧ ★ ❧ ★ ❧ ★

The convulsions in France are attended with
some disagreeable circumstances; but if by the
struggle she obtains and secures for her nation
its future liberty and a good constitution, a few
years' enjoyment of those blessings will amply
repair all the damages their acquisition may have
occasioned.
—FRANKLIN *on the French Revolution*

Young man, first get your facts, then distort
them as you please.
—MARK TWAIN (*to Rudyard Kipling*)

Chapter One

VOLTAIRE

✢ ★ ✢

ON THE same day that the treaties were signed a very old man, small of stature and strikingly ugly, set out on a lengthy journey from the village of Ferney on the Swiss frontier. The whole of his domestic staff had gathered round the roomy, old-fashioned travelling-coach that stood before the spacious mansion, and the old man climbed painfully into the vehicle with the help of two lackeys who supported him on either side. The servants appeared to be deeply affected by his departure, and their master, leaning out of the window, exhorted them to dry their tears. They were behaving, he said, as if he were leaving them for ever, but he did not intend to be away for long, under no circumstances for more than six weeks. The driver pulled on the reins and the coach moved off.

Scarcely had it reached the village square, however, before it was held up. Practically the whole population had turned out to bid the traveller farewell. When the old man had first come to settle at Ferney and had built his château there it had been a squalid hamlet, but in response to the old man's invitation more and more people from the near-by city of Geneva had taken refuge there from the puritanical severity and persecution of the Calvinist clergy. He had provided them with work and shelter, built up an extensive industry for the production of clocks, lace, and textiles, and Ferney had developed into a large and flourishing place, one of the most prosperous for its size in France.

The old man—his name was François Arouet, but the world knew him as Voltaire—was journeying to Paris. The *Théâtre français* was about to present his latest play, the tragedy *Irène,* and he wanted to take charge of the rehearsals.

It had been many years, twenty-seven in all, since he had last seen his native city. Though he had not been expressly forbidden to enter Paris, the late King, Louis XV, had declared that his presence in the capital would be unwelcome. But now there was a new King on the throne, and the old man was regarded with admiration by Toinette and the Lilac Coterie.

Nevertheless, he had hesitated for a long time before making up his mind to set out. His faithful friend and secretary, Wagnière, who was accompanying him, had advised against it. Voltaire was eighty-three years of age, he was able to live and work in greatest comfort at Ferney, and it seemed ludicrous that he should undertake the arduous journey to Paris. The people he wanted to see were only too glad to look him up in his distant village. If there was anything in Paris that he desired to have it was brought to his door. Both verbally and by letter he was kept informed of everything that was happening in the capital, whether publicly or behind the scenes, and living in his Ferney he had a better conspectus of French and world affairs than the King's Ministers at Versailles. So what was the point of giving up the well-ordered life he was leading at his house in the country in order to plunge into the harassing whirl of Paris?

Voltaire admitted that his secretary was right. His physicians, too, had given utterance to their doubts. Madame Denis, his niece and confidante, represented to him, however, that since he was yearning for a sight of Paris and had long wanted to supervise the production of one of his plays on a great stage, he ought not to miss the wonderful opportunity. Another member of his household, in the person of the Marquis de Villette, the husband of his adopted daughter, plied him with similar arguments, and Voltaire willingly allowed himself to be persuaded. On the other hand, he did not ignore the equally cogent dissuasions of Wagnière. So he was pulled this way and that, and after having decided in the quietness of the night that it would be foolish to leave his beautiful Ferney, on the following morning he would say to himself that he must not leave the first performance of *Irène,* the tragedy of which he had such high hopes, to the inclination of actors who were interested only in their own personal glory.

He told Wagnière that his chief reason for going to Paris was to achieve a reconciliation with Versailles and thus remove hindrances to the circulation of his writings. He spoke also of his consuming desire to see Paris once more. Having spent over a quarter of a century in the solitude of exile, he wanted to experience again before he died the colourful hubbub of his native city.

Wagnière, however, who knew his employer's strength and weaknesses, was well aware that the ultimate reason for this nonsensical journey was not Voltaire's nostalgia, but Voltaire's vanity.

Vanity was a quality that the old man despised. He was sated with fame. Ferney had become the intellectual centre of the world. From his country estate Voltaire reigned over the republic of the mind more absolutely than any sovereign monarch reigned over his subjects. Whoever laid claim anywhere in Europe to intellectual distinction called upon him, entered into correspondence with him, or sought his advice, and among these were two great rulers, Frederick of Prussia and Catherine of Russia, who looked upon Voltaire as the wielder of power equal to their own. He mocked at his fame as if it were the mere tinkling of cymbals, for he knew—and the world never tired of confirming—that he had erected for himself a monument more durable than brass. His reputation had long since ceased to depend on the approval or disapproval of his contemporaries. It was subject only to the verdict of posterity. Yet in the evening of his years he was assailed by the urge to harvest the fruits of his present glory, to feel its physical presence, to absorb it within himself, to drink in the thunderous plaudits of the multitude. He thirsted for the eulogies of the city that had cast him out. He wanted to hear his achievement corroborated once more by the jubilation of the city in which he had been born.

Against the advice, therefore, of his most loyal friend, his physicians, and his own better judgment, he left the comfort and satisfying environment of his country home to travel along the wintry roads of France towards the noisy bustle and fatigue that awaited him in Paris.

He was the owner of many titles—Count de Tournay, Seigneur de Ferney, Chamberlain of the King and, last but not least, Voltaire. On this journey, however, he used none of them. En route and during his first few days in Paris he wished to remain incognito.

He had not reckoned with the fact that his features were as familiar as those of the King on the nation's coins. Wherever he appeared he was besieged by crowds anxious to do him honour. The postmasters at the halting stages, normally so insolent, hastened to provide him with good horses so that he might continue his journey without undue delay, and when he put up at an inn the news of his presence spread like wildfire and people collected to catch a glimpse of him.

At Moret, not far from Paris, he was met by the Marquis de Villette. This young gentleman, who had long enjoyed the reputation of being one of the most dissolute libertines in Paris, had paid a visit to Ferney originally to contribute his quota of homage to the greatest writer of the age in accordance with the prevailing fashion. Before that he had been in the habit of indicating to his friends that Voltaire and his mother had been close intimates, and if he felt so deeply attracted towards the old man there might perhaps be a very natural reason for this. Voltaire had given him a warm welcome and the young Marquis had remained at Ferney. He had had good grounds for absenting himself for a time from Paris, where he had been boxed on the ears in public by a dancer.

Among those living in the château of Ferney at that time was a young lady named Reine de Varicourt, a pretty girl of unusual good nature and simple ways. Voltaire, who had saved her from entering a convent and who treated her as if she were his daughter, believed that

he had succeeded in converting Villette to intellectual interests, and as
the young aristocrat had obviously found favour in the girl's eyes Voltaire indulged his fondness for match-making and sponsored their
marriage. Whether or not he was really Villette's father, he became
officially more or less his father-in-law.

The Marquis had done his share in persuading Voltaire to undertake the journey to Paris, for in the long run he had found Ferney
rather dull. Together with his wife and Madame Denis he had gone
on ahead to prepare his house for the old man's reception, and he had
now come to escort him on the final stage of his journey, anxious as
he was to demonstrate to his friends the close relations that existed
between himself and the most famous man of the epoch.

When they reached the outskirts of the capital, Voltaire was asked
whether he had brought any forbidden articles. He grinned and replied, "Only myself." The customs official stared at him and cried,
"Mon Dieu! But it is Monsieur Voltaire!" A crowd collected at once
and the Marquis de Villette rejoiced in his feeling of self-importance.

Villette's mansion was situated in one of the best quarters of the
city, at the corner of the Quai des Théatins and the rue de Beaune.
Voltaire was received with a gush of welcome by the obese Madame
Denis, and his adopted daughter escorted him to his suite of rooms,
which were dark and not so comfortable as those at Ferney. It was an
old-fashioned house. With the help of his valet he changed his clothes,
donned his accustomed dressing-gown and slippers, and covered his
skull with his beloved night-cap. He had promised the Marquis to take
a little rest, but his mind was busy working out new ideas for the
improvement of *Irène,* and he began to dictate to Wagnière.

His dictation was soon interrupted. Though it had been agreed that
Voltaire was to relax during his first two days in Paris, Villette had
informed a score or so of friends in the strictest confidence that he
was expecting a visit from his father-in-law on Friday, the tenth of
February, and an unending stream of visitors began immediately to
call to pay their respects. This was exactly what Voltaire had desired.
He wanted to see people, as many people as possible, and he received
them all in his dressing-gown, slippers, and night-cap. His memory
was excellent, he remembered old friends even when he had not seen
them for decades, and he had a warm and witty word of personal
greeting for each of them.

Among the callers was Monsieur de Beaumarchais. He regarded
the old man with veneration. Voltaire had lived for eighty-three years
as Pierre himself wished to live, his days filled with passion, great
literature and small intrigues, success and glory, finance and the theatre, victorious campaigns in the cause of liberty and reason. He was
now a lord of the manor, surrounded by faithful retainers, treated by

an Empress and a great King as their equal, with a name that re-verberated across continents and oceans. His victories in the fight against injustice and the stupidities of privilege had become merged into history, and the old man could say to himself that if the world, now he was about to leave it, had acquired a little more understanding and sense of justice than it had possessed when he first entered it, this was in no small measure due to his efforts.

It was with a feeling of exaltation that Pierre recalled how Voltaire for many years had placed him on a par with himself, writing him ex-tremely flattering letters about his *Mémoires*.

Now, too, the old man singled him out for special honour. Passing through the crowd of callers who respectfully made way for him, he embraced Pierre and greeted him as "My very dear friend and col-league." Pierre escorted him back to his sofa, paying him every at-tention.

He was deeply affected by the sight of Voltaire. There the incred-ibly meagre, dwarflike old man was sitting, enveloped in a dressing-gown that was far too capacious for his figure, his ugly visage grotesquely framed in a night-cap, but his eyes shone with shrewd good humour and an enormous vivacity, and this bundle of bones and parch-ment-like skin housed the keenest intellect then to be found on the whole planet.

A delegation from the Academy was followed by a group of players from the *Théâtre français,* and even the hard-boiled actors and ac-tresses were moved at seeing in their midst this, their foremost writer, who had become to them almost a legend. He had begun the play they were about to perform when he was eighty-two years of age, and, re-hearsing this play, they realized that Voltaire had lost nothing of his former skill and strength. *Irène* was filled with the same power-ful hatred of bigotry. The shrunken, toothless old man was still a 'bundle of energy, a great angry flame directed against the forces of evil.

In the course of an eager discussion he listened to their opinions, accepted some of their suggestions and rejected others, and it was finally agreed that rehearsals should be held in his room since it would be too much of an effort for him to attend the theatre as frequently as would be required. He proposed that he should read the play through to them on the following day, and before they left he recited a number of passages with an effect that was not diminished by his toothless delivery and his gown and night-cap.

As further visitors arrived they reported that the whole of the rue de Beaune and the Quai des Théatins were crammed with inquisitive sightseers, consisting not only of those who were interested in litera-ture or ardent theatre-goers, but for the most part of workmen and shop assistants, people who had come from the cafés and taverns to see not the author of the *Henriade,* or of *Candide,* or of *Mérope* and *Zaïre,* but the man who had fought on behalf of the innocent Calas family and the Sirvens and Madame de Bombelles, for poor Martin and his dependents, for the unjustly condemned Montbailli, his wife, and his unborn child, the man who had denounced the desecration of the corpse of the actress Adrienne Lecouvreur, who had abolished the hated taxes on his estates and in his village, who had seen to it that those who lived and worked at Ferney should be more enlightened, more prosperous, and more happy.

Pierre could not tear himself away from the spectacle of Voltaire holding court in Paris. With unwonted modesty he stood on the edge of the circle surrounding Voltaire, listening and watching in silence. The symbol of the little temple in his garden at home was an allegorical expression of an evident truth. It was by dint of his pen that Voltaire had achieved an abundance of fame and power such as few monarchs had enjoyed by possession of their crowns. Pierre was glad to feel that he was linked to this man by fate and by kinship of mind.

On the following day Voltaire received no less than three hundred callers. On the day after that the number was increased to four hundred. Among those who came to pay their respects were Madame Necker and Madame Dubarry, Condorcet and Turgot, and the famous musician Gluck, a very proud man who had yet deferred his departure for Vienna in order to have the honour and happiness of meeting Voltaire. Shortly afterwards there appeared Gluck's great opponent and rival Piccini, the Marquis de Vaudreuil, and the two Polignac ladies, Gabrielle and Diane. There was every writer in Paris, "the whole of Parnassus from miry base to summit," as one of them expressed it.

There was also Doctor Franklin.

Franklin had come partly from curiosity and partly out of admiration. He and Voltaire had been in friendly correspondence for many years, Voltaire had always been full of praise for him, and, above all, had done more than anyone else to disseminate the ideas upon which a free America had been constituted. In almost festive mood, and accompanied by young William, Franklin called to greet his great colleague.

There were about twenty people in the room, and Voltaire was lying on a couch with a slight temperature, his deep-set eyes over the large, pointed nose shining more brilliantly than ever in his emaciated face. He was about to rise as Franklin entered, but this the American would not permit. Walking straight up to the couch, he gently but firmly pressed the old man back upon his pillows.

Voltaire said that he was happy to have the opportunity of congratulating Franklin personally on the victories won by American arms. He spoke in English, and Franklin replied that every American interested in literature saw in Voltaire the father of the American republic.

"If I were as young as you, my dear sir," rejoined Voltaire, "I would cross the ocean in order that I might set eyes upon your fortunate country." Voltaire's niece, speaking for all the others present, protested against the conversation being conducted in English which none of them could understand. "Pray forgive me," begged Voltaire, "for having yielded to my vanity in wishing to speak Doctor Franklin's language."

Young William, who had modestly held back, was called forward by Franklin and introduced. He bowed deeply and Voltaire, after gazing at him searchingly for some time, said finally in French, "You may esteem yourself lucky, my dear lad. It will be your lot to live in a great country and in a happy age. Bend a little lower," he continued, and placing his hand upon the youth's head he said in English, "God and Liberty." He repeated the words in French, and everybody was deeply moved.

An hour later Voltaire received the English ambassador, Lord Stormont.

Still more visitors arrived and Voltaire chatted, directed rehearsals of his play, worked hard at its revision, read his letters, dictated detailed replies, and thought out further plans for the future.

Amid all this bustle and turmoil the faithful Wagnière grew more and more uneasy. He was not only worried by fears of his master's health, which was visibly deteriorating, but he was even more oppressed, if possible, by anxieties which sprang from another cause. Wagnière was an ardent and implacable believer in reason, but Voltaire had little sense of the dignity of martyrdom. It was one of his maxims that there was no point in making a martyr of oneself, since truth could be spread, if necessary, by equivocal means. He never hesitated to deny his authorship of certain works, and was even prepared to attack his own productions when there was danger that they might do him harm. Now that Voltaire was in Paris, Wagnière was afraid lest he might be induced to disown not merely isolated writings but the whole of his literary output and the fundamental truths it contained.

Carefree as he pretended to be, and void of bigotry as he undoubtedly was, Voltaire was yet haunted by the idea that his corpse might one day be flung on the public rubbish-heap as that of a heretic. This was what had happened to Adrienne Lecouvreur. At Ferney there would be ways and means of avoiding such a humiliation, but if he were to die in Paris without having recanted, the Church would refuse him honourable burial and Wagnière was certain that he would be ready for any sacrifice, even for the disavowal of all his principles, if only he could thereby preserve his body from desecration after death.

Wagnière's apprehensions were increased when an increasing horde of black-robed priests thronged round the great heretic, spurred on by the ambition to achieve his conversion. Monsieur de Tersac, Dean of Saint-Sulpice, a portly and dignified figure, was followed by the Abbé Mignot, Voltaire's nephew, who employed all his gentle but persevering arts of persuasion. With a certain Abbé Gaultier, who came armed with letters of recommendation, Voltaire talked for a long time and with evident pleasure. "A good man that," he commented to Wagnière when the Abbé had taken his departure. "He is amiable and simple-minded, and when the time comes he won't make confession and recantation too difficult. We must make a note of his name."

"*Ecrasez l'infâme*" had been Voltaire's motto for decades, and the vile thing that had to be crushed was the fanatic bigotry and intolerance of the Church. It was in his master's passionate, unyielding struggle against superstitious prejudice that Wagnière saw his supreme service to humanity, and he was wounded to the very soul by the tone of Voltaire's remarks. Jesting though they might sound, he feared that they were meant seriously and that the old apostle of reason would not be disinclined in his last hours to renounce the fundamental principles by which his life had been guided. He implored him to prepare a written declaration which, while satisfying the Church for the time being with the prudent and guarded terms in which it was couched, would yet not betray the fundamental truths of philosophic reasoning. Voltaire grinned. "You can have your declaration straightway, my dear fellow," he said, and sitting down he wrote in his clear hand, "I die venerating God, loving my friends, without hatred of my enemies, and detesting superstition." Wagnière joyfully took the document into safe keeping.

A few days later, a fortnight after his arrival in Paris, Voltaire was attacked by a violent fit of coughing during which he brought up blood. "The time has come to summon our good Abbé Gaultier," he panted, and managed to grin though the blood was pouring from his mouth and nose. When the Abbé arrived, Wagnière was told to show him the declaration and Voltaire asked whether it was sufficient to ensure him honourable burial. His eyes were fixed anxiously on the Abbé's face, but the Abbé answered, "Unfortunately, no. Our little transaction must be conducted on a firmer basis."

At Gaultier's request Voltaire confessed. Then, in the presence of his nephew, the Abbé Mignot, a second cleric, and Wagnière, he wrote out a document in which he stated that having made his confession to the Abbé Gaultier he died in the Roman Catholic faith in which he had been born.

Gaultier perused the document. "I think it will suffice, won't it?" suggested Voltaire with sly apprehension.

The Abbé, however, shook his head. "Unfortunately, no, my dear sir," he said.

"What else do you want me to write?" inquired Voltaire.

"Write as follows," ordered the Abbé gently, but firmly. "Write: 'And if I have ever caused offence to the Church I beg forgiveness from the Church and from God.' " Wagnière grated his teeth.

"Must I write that?" asked Voltaire.

"Have no fears, *cher maître,*" replied the priest persuasively. "A little document like this hurts nobody."

Voltaire wrote. Wagnière watched his thin hand as it passed over the paper. The words did not seem to come easily from his pen. "And now," said the Abbé, turning towards the witnesses, "will you please bear testimony by appending your signatures to the fact that Monsieur de Voltaire has written this declaration in his own hand, of his own free will, and in full possession of his faculties." The two priests signed their names, Wagnière sullenly refused.

When Voltaire was once more alone with his faithful secretary he made an effort to justify his action. "You see," he explained, "after all, this is a pretty good piece of business I have just done with the Church. I have written fifty thousand pages at least, and for each single one of them the clerics would like to fling me to the dogs, yet at the cost of three short lines I have forced them to afford me honourable burial." Since this simple calculation made no impression on Wagnière, Voltaire continued, "When you have reached my age, my dear fellow, you will appreciate the truth of Henry IV's dictum that Paris was well worth a Mass." Wagnière, however, remained sullen.

Meanwhile the Abbé Gaultier had hastened with his precious document to his superior, the Dean of Saint-Sulpice. The Dean, enraged because the conversion of the great heretic had been achieved by the insignificant Abbé and not by himself, asserted that the declaration was too lukewarm to be accepted as an adequate recantation of so much stark heresy and such great offence. The Abbé, annoyed but persevering, hurried back to the house of the sick penitent in order to extract a stronger declaration.

But Voltaire was feeling better and would not see him. When the persistent priest called again on the following day Voltaire was feeling better still, and again the Abbé had to go away. On the third day the sick man felt so much recovered that when the Abbé once more asked to be admitted, he was informed that Voltaire was going to be very busy during the next few months and would have no time to spare.

Voltaire recovered with such amazing rapidity that he was soon receiving throngs of visitors again, writing, dictating, rehearsing with the actors, in short, working as indefatigably as he had been doing before his attack. It was not long before he was out of bed and returning the visits of a number of those who had called to pay their respects.

Richly dressed in slightly outmoded fashion, his thin form wrapped in shawls and furs, he was carried in a sedan-chair through the streets of Paris. The day was bright, but very cold; nevertheless he ordered the curtains to be drawn back so that he might see the streets and the people, the whole bustle of his Paris. Everywhere they went he was at once recognized, men stopped, bared their heads, and cheered.

On his return journey both the Seine bridges, the Quai des Théatins, and the rue de Beaune were so densely packed with sightseers that it was impossible for Voltaire in his sedan-chair to reach his residence; the police, partly by persuasion and partly by less gentle methods, had to force a passage. Thus Voltaire was borne along between serried ranks of cheering people, his cheeks flushed by cold and pleasure.

☆   ☆   ☆

Since her meeting with Franklin Toinette had felt that it was her vocation to patronize the cause of progress, and she would very much have liked to arrange an equally sensational meeting with Voltaire. The whole of the Lilac Coterie shared the fashionable enthusiasm for the great writer, who had indeed been concerned for years to establish friendly relations with Toinette. He had composed a little gala play in her honour and made unmistakably flattering references to her in more than one of his works. She was by no means insensible to these attentions, but she realized clearly enough that if she were to receive Voltaire officially at Versailles it would be interpreted throughout Europe as a political demonstration.

It was the shrewd Diane Polignac who thought of a solution. Would it not be possible, she suggested, to place at Voltaire's disposal the box at the *Théâtre français* which was normally reserved for the gentlemen-in-waiting? Since this box was next to that of Toinette herself, it would not be difficult to arrange an informal interview.

Louis burst into a fury when Toinette broached this project. "I forbid it, Madame!" he cried. "Do you hear? I forbid you to pollute yourself by any contact whatsoever with this arch-heretic!"

"Monsieur de Voltaire," retorted Toinette, "is the greatest writer in your kingdom, Sire, and presumably in the world."

"And presumably," scoffed Louis, "there is music in his sentences. Nevertheless, Madame, I forbid you to listen to his music."

That same day Maurepas said to Louis, "Have you heard, Sire, that Monsieur de Voltaire is paying a visit to your capital?"

"I thought," responded Louis coldly, "that the gentleman had been banished from Paris."

"Not exactly banished," said Maurepas. "But be it as it may, Sire, you would not consider it appropriate that the old gentleman should be expressly ordered to withdraw his presence from his native city?"

"That, unfortunately, is hardly feasible," conceded Louis gloomily.

"I am even inclined to ask myself," continued Maurepas, "whether it would not be proper to offer Monsieur de Voltaire, who is after all the most esteemed writer in Europe and very advanced in years, some small token of honour in the land of his birth."

"No!" snapped Louis brusquely. "It is my duty to protect the faith and morals of my subjects. I really ought to have the old blasphemer driven from my capital with contumely, and it seems to me that if I am willing to ignore his presence that's honour enough for literature."

Louis was angrier than he allowed his words to reveal. When Maurepas had gone he morosely surveyed the books and pamphlets of Voltaire that were safely locked up in his poison cupboard. There were a great many of them. They had been printed in Amsterdam, in Leyden, in Hamburg, and in London, but they could not be kept out of France any more than one could keep out the wind. Frontiers were no protection against them. It was a warning from on high, a divine chastisement, that the author of these writings should have come to Paris so soon after the conclusion of the treaty with the rebels. Now he had both those wicked old men clinging round his neck. With shameless insolence they had settled down in his capital like Baal and Beelzebub, and both his wife and his Ministers burned incense at their feet.

☆   ☆   ☆

On the eleventh of March the English Government recalled its ambassador, and Versailles followed suit on the thirteenth.

On the same day Vergennes informed Doctor Franklin that henceforth the American commissioners would be recognized as the fully accredited representatives of the thirteen United States at the Court of Versailles, and he requested the honour of being permitted to present the three gentlemen in this capacity to His Most Christian Majesty.

The invitation was welcome, but a source of considerable embarrassment. The ceremonial costume to be worn at court was highly ornate and there was only a bare week in which to give orders to the tailor. Franklin decided to appear in the brown coat which he would no doubt be expected to wear even on such an occasion, but he agreed at least to don a wig. Every wig, however, that was tried on him turned out to be too small. At last the *perruquier* cried out in despair, "It is not the wig that is too small, Monsieur. It is your head that is too large." The whole of Paris laughed at the *mot* and repeated, "His head

is too large." Franklin ceased to bother any further about the instructions of the chamberlains and masters of ceremonies, but made up his
mind to garb himself with simple dignity and ignore their insistence
on court fripperies.

So on the twentieth of March, Benjamin Franklin, tallow-chandler,
printer, bookseller, swimming master, dealer in second-hand goods,
publisher, slave-trader, physicist, merchant, doctor *honoris causa,* inventor, bank-note engraver, author, philosopher, and commissioner of
the United States of America, went to see Louis de Bourbon, King
of France.

The approaches to the Palace of Versailles and the great courtyard
were crowded with sightseers, all anxious to know whether Franklin
would venture to appear in his normal costume. They would have been
disappointed if he had not done so, yet when he actually did arrive
with neither wig nor sword, wearing his brown coat and breeches, the
steel-rimmed spectacles on his nose, and the carefully combed white
hair falling on his shoulders, completely à la Quaker, they were spell-
bound at such a display of dignity and audacity. It was probably the
first time in history that any man had ever gone to court in the dress
of an ordinary citizen. But it was also, to be sure, the first time that
the representative of rebels had been received in audience by a Most
Christian King.

Vergennes took charge of the party and escorted the commissioners
up the great outside staircase. The drums rolled, the sentries presented
arms, the double doors leading to the royal apartments were flung
open, and the Colonel of the Swiss Guard announced, "The envoys of
the thirteen United States of America!" The inner antechamber was
thronged with courtiers, bishops, diplomats, and high legal dignitaries,
who all stood aside to make a path for Franklin and his companions
and bowed deeply as he passed. The ladies, too, rose and curtsied as
Franklin came by.

The envoys were led into the King's bedchamber. Louis, who detested having to receive them, was seated at his toilet-table wearing a
dressing-gown over an open-necked shirt, and his slovenly appearance
was obviously deliberate. His hairdresser was hovering busily around,
the six gentlemen-in-waiting were hovering around, one stiffly and
ceremoniously holding the royal breeches, the other the stockings.

Vergennes introduced the Americans. Louis glanced up with an eye
that looked past rather than at them. So this big, massive fellow was
the leader of the rebels, he thought. He did not show in his face the
diabolical thoughts that he carried in his heart, but what a rebellious
and insolent way to dress. And he stood there without humility, as if it
were his inalienable right to attend the toilet of His Most Christian
Majesty.

Louis snorted slightly, and said, without looking at the envoys, "Very well, then. Very well. So here we are. Please convey to the Congress, gentlemen, the assurance of my favour. I am not dissatisfied with the manner in which you have hitherto conducted yourselves in my country." He spoke indistinctly and did not raise his voice, but the Americans understood every word, for there was a complete hush in the room and no one stirred. One of the chamberlains continued stiffly to hold out the King's breeches and the other his stockings.

Franklin calmly contemplated the corpulent young man who was sitting so awkwardly at his toilet-table. With his bold nose he looked like all the other Bourbons whose images were stamped on the nation's coins, yet his face was undeveloped like that of an infant. There was something unnatural in his obesity, which was obviously due to a disturbance of the circulation or of some other internal function of the body. The sixteenth Louis seemed sluggish and clumsy, but he did not look unintelligent. He was nothing of an orator, that was certain, and what he did say did not sound very friendly, yet on the whole it was appropriate to the occasion and Franklin accepted the cue. Bowing deeply he replied, "I thank you, Sire, in the name of my country. Your Majesty may count upon the gratitude of the Congress and upon its readiness faithfully to fulfil its pledges."

"Very well, gentlemen," responded Louis, and the audience was over.

Vergennes gave the commissioners an official banquet which was attended by the whole of the nobility of France. Now that Franklin had been received by the King everybody was anxious to meet him. He took in to dinner the aged and highly respected Marquise de Créquy, who noted with astonishment the details of his dress, the whole effect of which was to make him a study in brown—his coat and waistcoat, his breeches, even his hands. His neckcloth was of linen. Most amazing of all, she thought, were his table manners. He ate asparagus with his fingers and melon with a knife. He broke eggs into a glass, added butter, salt, pepper, and mustard, and proceeded to eat the mixture with a spoon. Since she knew him to be a famous philosopher she asked him whether he believed in a personal God and in the immortality of the soul. Sipping his strange concoction he replied emphatically that he did. The Marquise told her friends later that the Quaker had the manners of a backwoodsman, but his opinions seemed respectable.

Louis spent the evening with Toinette at the Trianon. Having kept his promise to the last iota, and having even submitted to the humiliation of speaking to the rebel in the presence of his court, he wanted at least to reap the reward she owed him, an agreeable night.

"I regret to hear, Sire," said Toinette, "that you were so rude to Doctor Franklin."

"The old boor did not even wear a wig," grumbled Louis. "He had the insolence to stick out his bare skull at me. Did you expect me to smile in appreciation?"

"I shall be all the more amiable to him tomorrow," declared Toinette. "You may be sure of that."

"I cannot stop you," muttered Louis peevishly. "I find Versailles perfectly intolerable," he suddenly flared, "since this rebel has begun to come in and out as if he were at home here."

"Yes," replied Toinette sweetly, yet with an air of triumph, "I have managed to bring a little fresh air into the place."

Louis had no wish to start a quarrel. His visit to the Trianon was due to quite different motives, so he ate and drank with zest, enjoyed the company of his beautiful wife, and stayed the night as he had intended, taking his pleasure under the eyes of his Austrian kinsmen who were digging their graves in the garb of monks.

☆ ☆ ☆

For Silas Deane the reception at Versailles signified the end of his mission. John Adams, a well-known politician and an active member of the Congress, had been designated as his successor and was already on French soil. There was nothing left for Deane to do but to return to America, and he went with a heavy heart. Not only was he embittered at the ungrateful way in which he had been treated, for he was being recalled in disgrace, but he was leaving his best friends behind in France, men who were fully aware of the services he had rendered to his country, whereas at home he would find only people whose minds had been poisoned against him.

Franklin was sorry that he was going. Though he had had his difficulties with him, the man in the flowered satin waistcoat was well-meaning and an undoubted patriot, and he had always in the end yielded to reason. Franklin promised to do his utmost to help him in his relations with the Congress and declared that he would often think of him, particularly when his eye fell upon the precious volumes of the *Encyclopédie*. For all his sadness Silas Deane smiled, and when the moment came to say good-bye he could hardly tear himself away.

It had not been his intention to take leave of Arthur Lee, but to his surprise Lee came to call upon him. Lee was simmering with fury. The French Government had appointed Monsieur de Gérard as ambassador at Philadelphia and had consulted both Franklin and Deane but not him, Arthur Lee. He strongly suspected that this affront was due to some sinister manœuvre of his two colleagues.

He had no conclusive proof that his suspicion was justified, but he did possess solid reasons for complaint on other grounds. Among the files that had been handed over to him by Silas Deane there were important documents missing, and he demanded with gloomy accusation why they had been extracted. Deane replied that they were papers which he intended to submit to the Congress in defence of the charges that had been laid against him, for he had cause to believe that certain persons had been calumniating him in Philadelphia.

"Among the files that you are being kind enough to leave behind," continued Lee, "there appear to be a number of rather doubtful items. Under the heading of the commissioners' expenses, for example, there is included a sum of 1470 livres for the purchase of the *Encyclopédie des arts et des métiers,* delivered to Doctor Franklin. I should be glad if you would be good enough to explain."

"With pleasure," replied Silas Deane politely. "You and I presented this great work to Doctor Franklin on his birthday."

"You have had the audacity," rasped Lee, his voice quivering, "without consulting me you have had the audacity to make such an expensive gift in my name? At a time when the citizens of the United States are having to pay almost a Congress dollar for a copper penny, you present Doctor Franklin at the country's expense with books to the value of 1470 livres?"

"I did not ask your consent," said Deane with aggressive calm, "because I knew that you would refuse in any case. So far as the Congress is concerned I am covered, since the *Encyclopédie* was purchased on a majority resolution."

"How do you mean, a majority resolution?" inquired Lee, a little dazed.

"I did not, to be sure, request Doctor Franklin's approval beforehand," explained Deane, "but I am as certain that he would have said yes as I am that you would have said no."

"It is with French sophistries such as this," cried Lee angrily, "that you have damaged all along the good name of America."

"It is with French sophistries such as this that Doctor Franklin has succeeded in saving America from ruin," replied Deane.

Arthur Lee folded his arms and thrust his head forward. "When you return to Philadelphia, sir," he said menacingly, "they will show you there what America thinks of you."

When Silas Deane took leave of Beaumarchais, the latter tried to hearten him. "Tell the Congress frankly what is in your mind," he urged, "both on your own behalf and on mine. Tell these gentlemen to their faces how pettily and ungratefully they are behaving. Have no fear, my dear Mr. Deane. France leaves no man in the lurch to whom she has promised her support. Put your trust in the King and the firm of Hortalez and Company."

☆   ☆   ☆

Arthur Lee did not cease to press his grievances, and in his attitude he was reinforced by two other envoys from Philadelphia who had meanwhile arrived in Paris, his brother William Lee and Ralph Izard.

Ralph Izard was a wealthy man of thirty-five who had studied in England and enjoyed the friendship of leading English statesmen and writers. As a young gentleman of position from the colonies he would have been presented to the King, but in accordance with court ceremonial he would have had to bend the knee, and Ralph Izard's principles forbade him to bend the knee to any mortal. Therefore he declined to be introduced at court, and later on, when the conflict with the colonies developed into an open break, he returned to America and ardently espoused the insurgent cause. He had now been appointed envoy to the Court of Tuscany, but as that country had not yet recognized the United States he had been instructed to remain in Paris for the time being where he could be of assistance to Franklin and Lee.

The other envoy was a true scion of the thin-faced, gifted, suspicious, and argumentative family of the Lees. He had been appointed to represent the Congress in Berlin, but the United States were no more recognized in Prussia than they were in Tuscany, so he too was ordered to cool his heels in Paris and meanwhile to afford Franklin the benefit of his counsel.

The two new arrivals at once made common cause with Arthur Lee. They were all three young and impatient, and Franklin's mild way of going about things appeared to them merely the sluggish weakness of old age. Now that the treaty had been signed, they saw no reason why the French Government should not continually be pressed for more and more money, troops, and ships. Franklin's refusal to concur in this plan they regarded as criminal negligence.

Into the midst of their first disagreeable altercations with Franklin came the man who had been designated by the Congress as Silas Deane's successor, John Adams.

Franklin and John Adams had worked together for years, and had both been concerned in the preparation of the first draft of the Declaration of Independence. Each of them was fully aware of the other's good qualities, but there was no love lost between them. Adams was forty-five years of age, a lawyer by profession, and accustomed to express his opinion in resounding terms with many analogies drawn from Scripture and the classics. Having grown up during the war against the French and Indians, he was a passionate patriot, and he had once

asserted that if the Americans succeeded in driving those aggressive
Frenchmen from the Western Hemisphere they would, before another
century had passed, exceed all other nations of the earth in numbers
and put Europe completely in the shade. In the view of John Adams,
the old continent was decadent, and from early youth he had cherished
the dream of a mighty American Empire founded on virtue.

There were great political achievements standing to his credit. If
the Declaration of Independence had entered into force, this had been
in no small part due to his efforts. His untiring energy was held in
high esteem at Philadelphia, and when the anxiously awaited news of
the signing of the French treaty of alliance was delayed day after day
and week after week he was nominated to succeed Silas Deane in
Paris in order that he might at last bring the alliance into being.

When he arrived in Paris he found that the treaty had already been
signed, so there was really nothing for him to do in Europe. His restless urge to activity, however, would not allow him to remain idle and
he proceeded to study the files.

John Adams was a short man, corpulent and temperamental, with a
broad, bald head whose broadness was emphasized by copious tufts
of hair on either side. As he read through the files of the commissioners this pate of his was continually in movement, shaking with
surprise and disapproval. He set about bringing order into the chaos
which he had discovered, and when he saw Franklin smiling benevolently and not without a certain amusement at his efforts, he explained,
"You may call my methods bureaucratic, if you like. The Romans
called it discipline. Without such 'bureaucracy' nothing great can be
achieved; this much is certain. How do you think we are going to
build up a great country that will outstrip the continent of Europe if
we cannot keep order in our little house at Passy?"

Adams was living in the garden house at Passy, which was looked
upon as the headquarters of the American representatives, and he was
thus in a position to observe Franklin's way of life from a point of
vantage. Their relations were founded on mutual courtesy and respect,
but as the days passed Adams grew more and more disapproving. Despite his years and the gout which troubled him, Franklin ate and
drank as he wished. Though there was every reason to economize, he
kept a luxurious carriage, was surrounded with servants, and his house
was lavishly furnished. The fact that he had already passed the biblical
age did not prevent him dangling round women like any Frenchman.
All in all, thought John Adams deprecatingly, Franklin was an epicurean.

Adams had not been many days at Passy before Madame Helvétius
paid an unannounced call, sweeping into the house as if she were at
home there. Traces of her former beauty were still evident, but she

was carelessly dressed with her hair in disarray, a soiled kerchief had been tied round her little straw hat, and over her shoulders she wore a black shawl that kept slipping off. In the presence of John Adams she kissed Franklin heartily on both cheeks and on the brow, and sitting between the two gentlemen at dinner she frequently had an arm on the back of each of their chairs, while every now and then she leaned over to embrace the Doctor. The scene was described by Adams in a detailed letter which he wrote to his adored wife Abigail, to whom he was attached with a chaste and devoted affection.

Mr. Adams refrained from reproaching Franklin in rancorous terms, as his younger colleagues did, but used his influence to conciliate the parties. In their more serious disputes, however, he reinforced by his silence the opposition of the brothers Lee and Ralph Izard.

So, for instance, in the case of the conflict over William Temple:

During the process of putting the archives in order, it was discovered that the letter concerning the molasses clause drafted by de Gérard at Arthur Lee's request as a supplement to and integral part of the Treaty of Amity and Commerce had been either lost or mislaid. There was no doubt in any one's mind that the agreement would be ratified by the Congress, or might even already have been ratified, whether this appendage was attached thereto or not, and the lost document therefore was of merely academic or historical interest. Nevertheless—and this was emphatically insisted upon by Izard and the two Lees—a person who was capable of allowing such a document to go astray was not to be regarded as a suitable occupant of the post of secretary to the Congress representatives. A youth of seventeen could never, in any case, have been the appropriate choice for such an office. Had he not in other cases proved himself to be negligent and dilatory? Had he not, for instance, permitted the draft Treaty of Alliance to lie about under the eyes of indiscreet Frenchmen?

"Was it really necessary," asked Izard, summing up the reproaches levelled at Franklin by the other two, "was it really necessary to appoint Mr. William Temple Franklin as secretary to the embassy?" He stressed the young man's first Christian name, and they all realized to what he was referring. The English journals had recently been loud in their praises of young William's father, Governor William Franklin, who in defiance of persecution by the rebels had remained loyal to his King, and they poured out their scorn on the insurgent leader, Doctor Benjamin Franklin, who had been unable to convince even his own son of the righteousness of his cause.

Franklin had hitherto listened tranquilly to the recriminations of his colleagues. But hearing this last argument, he rose in anger. "Would you rather I had left the lad in his father's charge?" he demanded, and there was such grief and wrath in his voice that the others were silenced.

At last John Adams intervened. "You have allowed yourself to go too far, Mr. Izard," he commented rebukingly, and Izard at once apologized. "I am sorry," he said, "if I have hurt Doctor Franklin."

The incident was closed by Franklin's resolving to pay William Temple's salary out of his own pocket and to appoint a second secretary recommended by his colleagues. This latter was a young Frenchman, Monsieur de la Motte.

☆   ☆   ☆

Since the conclusion of the alliance, with everybody glorifying Franklin, the services of Pierre de Beaumarchais seemed to have been forgotten in Paris, and this gnawed at the heart of his faithful friend Philippe Gudin. Wrapping his bulky form in the dressing-gown which had been a gift from Pierre, he ensconced himself within the semicircle of his costly desk and took up his pen. He was composing an essay entitled *Provisional Sketch of the Life of a Great Contemporary*. Without mentioning names he described the services rendered to America and the cause of liberty by his friend's activities in the spheres of statesmanship, literature, and commerce, and there could be no doubt on the part of any initiated reader as to who was meant and what these activities were. Due appreciation was expressed of the contribution made by the "old man in the garden," but obscure allusions were made to certain dangerous qualities of this same old man. The respective achievements of the two protagonists were compared, to the advantage of the *great contemporary,* and the essay concluded with the prediction that the day would come when history would distribute light and shade more justly than was now being done.

Reading over what he had written, Gudin was satisfied. Though he had been compelled, like Heraclitus or Lucretius, to speak in veiled terms, without possessing the gloomy power of those philosophers, he felt that at any rate his little work would bear comparison with the histories of a Rollin.

It was not likely, he thought, that Pierre would approve of the publication of the *Provisional Sketch,* since his generous nature would wish to spare the old man such an exposure, so he had it printed at his own expense and on his own responsibility, without saying a word about it to Pierre, and sent copies to all those he thought would be interested, including the "old man in the garden" himself.

Then, proud and happy at what he had accomplished, he presented the little volume to his friend, in whose honour he had written it.

Pierre's heart warmed to Philippe as he turned the pages. At last there was somebody who had taken the pains to enumerate his services and to estimate them at their true worth. Pierre was touched, but he could not help realizing that even a veiled account of the activities of the firm of Hortalez might involve him in unpleasant consequences, and he suggested that the brochure should for the time being be kept to themselves.

"I have taken steps," said Gudin, "to ensure that your modesty shall not again play you a scurvy trick. Copies have already been sent to those concerned." His good-humoured countenance beamed with pride at the cunning and knowledge of human nature he had displayed. Pierre thumped him on the back, shrugged his shoulders, and said no more.

Shortly after this one of Pierre's ships, the *Gloire de France,* arrived at Lorient, bringing a cargo of rice and indigo from America. The accompanying bill of lading was addressed to Messrs. Franklin, Deane, and Lee, but the cargo was undoubtedly intended for the firm of Hortalez, being the consignment which had long since been announced by Paul. If it had been addressed to the American envoys, that was only in order that the firm of Hortalez should not again be compromised if the ship happened to be captured by the English. The *Gloire de France* had sailed before the signing of the Franco-American Alliance had become known on the other side of the Atlantic.

Arthur Lee, however, smelt a rat and demanded that until matters were cleared up the cargo should be placed at the disposal of the addressees, that is to say, the American envoys, and of no one else. But the captain of the ship refused to hand the cargo over to the Americans, who thereupon held a consultation at which Lee vehemently insisted that his colleagues must no longer allow the notorious Monsieur de Beaumarchais to lead them around by the nose. This was probably not the first cargo, he suggested, which had been consigned to them from Philadelphia in Beaumarchais ships and permitted by Silas Deane to fall secretly into the hands of the Hortalez firm. This time, fortunately, the bills of lading had reached the right persons, and he proposed that the master of the ship, who was obviously in league with Beaumarchais, should be forced by law to surrender the cargo.

Had the affair happened a week earlier Franklin would probably have opposed such a step. Two or three days previously, however, he had received a brochure entitled *Provisional Sketch of the Life of a Great Contemporary,* in which some learned donkey with a wealth of classical quotation made spiteful allusions to *the old man in the garden* and in ponderous phraseology ascribed the chief merit for the victory at Saratoga and the achievement of the alliance to Monsieur Caron. It was not normally Franklin's custom to take lampoons very seriously, but in this case the author was evidently familiar with numerous details that he could have learned only from Monsieur Caron himself or his intimates. The publication of the brochure was therefore to be regarded as an act of hostility on the part of Monsieur Caron, and in view of this Franklin did not feel called upon to defend him. Together with Lee he drafted a petition to the maritime court at Lorient requesting that the master of the *Gloire de France* should be ordered to deliver up his cargo to Messrs. Franklin and Lee, the rightful consignees.

Pierre turned pale with astonishment and rage. This was his reward for having effected the old man's recognition as ambassador of the United States. His first official act was to rob him of his property. Never before had he experienced such vile and barefaced treachery. Tartuffe was put in the shade by this *Bonhomme Richard*.

And why had the old man behaved in this way? To be sure, the Americans were short of money. Yet they were not so desperate that they had to rob a poor man of his one ewe-lamb. Franklin's motive must be personal.

It was the brochure that had stirred up Franklin, that unhappy, tedious production of Philippe's. They were all working together to bring about his ruin, his friends as well as his enemies. His pent-up fury and disappointment were discharged upon the head of Philippe Gudin.

They were sitting in Pierre's study, and Pierre was pacing stormily up and down the room as he hurled denunciations at his wretched friend. Philippe listened patiently for a while, then he too began to stride to and fro with heavy step as he panted for breath. "Do at least sit still when I am talking!" raged Pierre.

Gudin stood still. "I am prepared to hold my tongue," he said, "and to bare my breast to all the spears that are waiting to pierce it, like that Swiss martyr. But you are doing me an injustice. It did not need my little book to turn this Franquelin into your deadly enemy. He has always been that. In my *Provisional Sketch* I applied to him a line from *Antigone,* the line about 'the man with the insidious lips,' which was how Sophocles referred to the tyrant Creon. The old man in the garden is more spiteful than Creon, I tell you; he is a veritable Thersites. Of all calumniators and detractors he is the blackest. He has— but no, I will no longer fan your wrath. Continue to believe that it was my feeble words that kindled the vengeful lust of that rancorous old man. Continue to believe it."

"What do you know?" demanded Pierre imperiously. Gudin remained stubbornly silent. "What else has Franklin said or done to damage me?" cried Pierre in agitation.

"Pray calm yourself," begged Gudin. "Do not ask me to repeat those dreadful words."

"What did he—" Pierre's voice broke and he could not finish the sentence.

"He compared you," said Gudin reluctantly, almost in a whisper, "with the horse-fly in La Fontaine's fable, with that conceited and annoying little insect that kept buzzing about the horse's head."

"With the horse-fly?" asked Pierre in bewilderment. "The horse-fly and the coach?"

"Yes," said Gudin. "The horse-fly and the coach."

Pierre groped for a seat, he felt weak and dizzy. He had sacrificed years of his life and his fortune for America, he had sent the arms for Saratoga, he had obtained the meeting between the old man and the Queen, and through that, the treaty. And the old one had nothing for him but cheap and brattish laughter. The horse-fly and the coach. Slowly he shook his head, crushed.

Never had Gudin seen his friend like that; it tore his heart. Silently and pitifully he stood there and could do nothing but gaze at him. "I can't understand it," Pierre said after a while in a strangely low voice. "I just can't understand it. What have I done to him? Isn't it true? Did I not send ten million livres worth of arms to America? And did I get anything for it?" He kept on shaking his head.

☆   ☆   ☆

When he told Thérèse of what had happened, her face clouded. She possessed a keen sense of justice and was deeply mortified that Pierre's merits and achievements had been so badly rewarded.

Without saying a word to Pierre, she drove out to Passy.

After the greetings and small talk, Thérèse said that she had never before intervened in her husband's business affairs, but this was more than a mere matter of business. She regretted that the envoys of a country which had received such tangible proofs of her husband's friendship should have behaved towards him with such unconcealed hostility. There were many Frenchmen who would be surprised and saddened that no attempt had been made to come to an amicable understanding before having recourse to the courts.

Franklin could not help admitting to himself that she was right. Even before she had come, he had repented his step. He had often been irritated at the tactless and prejudiced way in which his compatriots dealt with foreigners, and yet, instead of following the dictates of reason, he had himself yielded to his impulses and acted like an Arthur Lee.

He replied that the unfortunate situation might have been avoided if Monsieur Deane, who had been in charge of the negotiations with Monsieur de Beaumarchais, had not been obliged to return to Amer-

ica. The matter was somewhat involved. Monsieur Deane's successor
had not yet had sufficient time to study all the relevant documents, and
it was the custom in America, when the facts of a case were not clear,
to have recourse to the courts. It was far from the intention of the
envoys, to say nothing of his own, that their action should be interpreted as hostility, or even unfriendliness, towards Monsieur de Beaumarchais. He certainly did not underestimate the services which her
husband had rendered to the United States, and so far as he was aware
these had already been acknowledged by the Congress in a letter
couched in the most flattering terms. But business was business. Figures and contracts had neither heart nor manners. In any case, it was
his opinion that Monsieur de Beaumarchais would find judgment delivered in his favour, and nobody would be happier about it than he
himself. While Franklin was speaking he kept his old, calm, large eyes
fixed on Thérèse, and took care to address her with the utmost respect, yet, in spite of his effort, he knew his argument sounded
chilly.

Thérèse returned home assured that Pierre's property would soon
be released, and probably even before the maritime court had delivered its judgment, but she was equally sure that Franklin's dislike of
Pierre was too strong to be overcome.

Franklin, for his part, sat for a time thinking. It was odd that the
vacuous-minded Monsieur Caron, who inspired him with such distaste, should be capable of attracting the affection of a woman such as
this wife of his, and of a young man such as that Monsieur Theveneau who had gone to America on his account.

He pressed and massaged his gouty foot. His talk with Thérèse had
spoilt the day for him. Despite the numerous friends with whom he
was able to enjoy both serious and amusing conversation, despite
Madame Helvétius and the other women who so tenderly sought his
society, despite the companionship of the handsome, light-hearted
grandson whom he loved, he sometimes felt very lonely and exiled in
a foreign land.

He missed his old friend Dubourg. He took up the *Eulogium Linnaei* with which the dying man had entrusted him. It was a good piece
of work; Dubourg had been a sound scholar who had sought knowledge for its own sake. Franklin had already translated it with loving
care; he walked across to his printing-press and proceeded to set up
the manuscript.

☆   ☆   ☆

After his triumphal procession through the streets of Paris,
Voltaire had suffered a relapse and was again unable to leave his bed,

though that did not prevent him from continuing to direct the
rehearsals of *Irène*. Raising himself up on his cushions, he repeated
the lines over and over again, the words issuing passionately from
his toothless mouth. But at last the rehearsals proved too much for
him in his enfeebled state, and there could be no question of his being
in a fit condition to attend the first performance.

Yet even without his presence the opening night was a great event.
With the exception of the King, the entire court attended. The whole
audience, including Toinette and the Lilac Coterie, was determined
to let itself be carried away. And again and again they interrupted
the performance with wild applause.

Toinette was genuinely moved by certain passages. When Zoë
lamented the hard lot of her Empress, were not the lines an evident
allusion to her own fate? "To slavery hast thou been born. Thy
radiance and thy splendour, what are these but tokens of eternal
suffering and restraint? Thou art our ruler, it is true, but in no more
than name, and the perilous burden of thy dignity holds thee in
wretched duress. Thy people's prejudices, their custom and tradition, chain thee more firmly than could any tyrant." As Toinette
listened to these lines she almost stopped breathing, burningly conscious of the presence of Vaudreuil standing behind her chair.
Voltaire was a great writer who knew how to give utterance from
the stage to her most secret feelings.

Sitting modestly in the body of the house was Pierre. This time
he had come to the theatre not to be seen, but to see. Sensitive as he
was to great spectacles, he was carried away no less by what was
happening in the auditorium than by the incidents on the stage.
The sight of Toinette and the court paying homage to the genius of
Voltaire was merged in the representation of Irène's tragic conflict, and he forgot any criticism that might have been levelled at
the play, the characters, or the acting. He was transported by the
ringing verses and the tumultuous applause. He was intoxicated by
the storm of prejudice that overwhelmed Irène, the struggle waged
by Alexis against tyranny and the domination of the priests, the
jubilant excitement of the spectators, the blissful feeling that literature was such a potent force in the world, the whole noisy splendour
of the occasion.

As he sat there a project began to ripen in his mind that had been
vaguely haunting him during the past few days. Monsieur Pancoucke, the most distinguished publisher in France, had for some
time been considering the idea of issuing the *Complete Works* of
Voltaire. It would be a costly undertaking, and a risky one, for it
had become evident particularly since Voltaire's sojourn in Paris

that in view of the King's stubborn hostility it would be practically impossible for years to come to achieve an adequate circulation. Monsieur Pancoucke had therefore finally abandoned the scheme, and now, under the intoxicating influence of the brilliant opening night of *Irène,* Pierre decided that it was he himself who was destined for the bold enterprise. In an endless series of magnificent volumes he would erect a national monument to the memory of Voltaire.

Voltaire meanwhile lay at home in bed, coughing and perspiring, pretending to be calm, but in reality as excited as any young author on the opening night of his first play. One messenger after another arrived hot-foot from the theatre to report on the audience's reception of each individual scene. His pretence at equanimity broke down, his curiosity was insatiable, and he eagerly put question after question about the way in which this passage or that had been received. When he was told that the line denouncing the obscurantism of the priesthood, "I will hurl your temple down," had had to be repeated three times, he giggled blissfully, "I was sure of it. I know my Parisians. *Ecrasez l'infâme!*"

When the performance was over his nearest friends, Pierre among them, hastened to the author's house to tell him of the events of the evening and to offer their congratulations. The servants could not hold them back and they thronged into his room.

Voltaire was obviously a very sick man, but he grinned under his night-cap as he drank in their enthusiastic praises. Calling Pierre to his bedside, he said, "You are the best connoisseur of the theatre in France, my friend. Tell me all about it," and he stroked Pierre's hand. Pierre allowed an occasional trifling criticism to slip into his narration to heighten the triumphal effect, and the old man beamed. "Since it is you who tell me this," he said, "it must all be true."

Pierre could control himself no longer. With an eagerness that he made no attempt to restrain he begged Voltaire to grant him permission to publish a complete edition of his writings. "You may rest assured," he declared, "that I shall spare no effort and no outlay. I shall seek the collaboration of the best minds in France to help me with the work of editing, and I shall have a type designed such as this country has never seen before."

Voltaire's darting eyes shone more brightly than ever. Clasping Pierre in his wasted arms he called him "My good friend!" and declared, "Now I can die in peace. My work has been left in strong and tender hands."

Pierre's heart beat to suffocation. The insults levelled at him by *the old man in the garden* faded into the distant recesses of his mind, together with the anxieties caused him by the ill-will of his defaulting debtors beyond the seas. The greatest genius of the century had acknowledged him as a brother and heir, and all Paris was witness.

☆   ☆   ☆

When Voltaire's condition continued to deteriorate, his physician, Doctor Tronchin, declared that he refused to tolerate any longer this long-drawn act of suicide.

Tronchin was an old man himself, and he and Voltaire were close friends. On the very day of Voltaire's arrival, Tronchin had told him bluntly what he thought of his incredible idiocy in exposing himself to the fatigues of a visit to Paris, and now he insisted that Voltaire must return without delay to Ferney. "You are eating up your capital," he declared grimly, "instead of living on your interest. You do not imagine, I suppose, that you have very much of your capital left? To stand the kind of life that you are leading here you would need a body made of steel. Return to Ferney," he urged, "while there is still time." He wrote himself to Ferney ordering Voltaire's travelling-coach and servants to be sent to Paris for the journey home.

Wagnière rejoiced at the prospect of having his master back home again where he could attend to his real work and follow a fairly sensible routine. The Marquis de Villette, however, did all he could to dissuade his famous guest from leaving Paris. He was revelling in the self-satisfaction of having his house looked upon as a centre of the Paris social world, and his pleasure in this fact was so undisguised that Maurepas felt moved to compose an epigram on the subject. "Little Villette," he wrote, "you have reached the height of fame—the fame of a dwarf exhibiting a giant at the fair."

The most effective resistance to the return to Ferney came from Madame Denis, the stout niece, who hated living in the country and far preferred the bustle and whirl of Paris. While admitting that her esteemed uncle was unable to enjoy the quiet and comfort he needed at the house of his son-in-law, she insisted that this could easily be remedied. It would not be difficult to find another domicile, and she negotiated for the purchase of a property in the rue Richelieu.

Voltaire himself was pulled both ways. He felt a nostalgic longing to be back at Ferney, and he knew that Tronchin was right. Paris was shortening the few days that were left to him. Yet there was work that could not be carried out elsewhere. The Academy had just elected him as its President, and this provided an excellent opportunity to realize a plan that he had long cherished, the revision of the *Dictionary of the French Language*. There were, moreover, innumerable details to discuss with this excellent new friend of his, Beau-

marchais, concerning the publication of his *Opera Omnia,* and among
the thousands of other people who were anxious to have a word
with him, he ought at least to see a couple of hundred or so with
whom there were important matters to talk about.

While he debated the matter, the travelling-coach arrived, together
with his devoted old servants and his bitch Idamée. There were tears
in the servants' eyes as they kissed his hand, and Idamée was unable
to contain herself for joy. "It seems that you are all yearning to have
me back at Ferney," said Voltaire. He decided to return.

Then came news of a fresh assault that had been launched against
him by the leader of the clericals, the Abbé Beauregard. After having
thundered his denunciations in the Cathedral of Notre Dame, the
great preacher had announced from the pulpit of the chapel at the
Palace of Versailles that the time had come to prepare a crusade.
"All the writings of these so-called philosophers," he had preached
before the King and his court, "have as their sole aim the destruction
of the Throne and the Church. Yet we are imprudently permitting
these works to be published, and homage is paid to authors who are
deserving of condign punishment. The owl of the heathen goddess
Minerva has settled upon our city of Paris, spreading its shameless
wings and receiving the unholy incense of its devotees. The idol of
the heretics is carried publicly in a litter through the streets of the
capital of our Most Christian King. From the public stage the
philosophers proclaim their intention of hurling down the temple of
the Lord. In their criminal hands they already wield the hammer and
the axe, and they are only waiting until the time is ripe for them to
destroy both Throne and Altar. Have those who are most nearly concerned forgotten that even indulgence must have its limits? Are
they not aware that tolerance is merely weakness if it fails to punish
blasphemy?"

When Voltaire heard of this sermon he at once cancelled his decision. So the priests wanted to drive him out of Paris? No, he was
not going to yield to their scorn. He was stirred by a great wrath.
Ecrasez l'infâme! Rejecting the urgent advice of Doctor Tronchin
and the entreaties of Wagnière, he signed the contract for the purchase of the house in the rue Richelieu. "The old fool has signed his
death-warrant," commented Doctor Tronchin.

Since in Ferney pressing matters had accumulated, Voltaire sent
his devoted secretary back. They parted with heavy hearts.

So nobody was left in Paris to keep the old man's energy within
bounds. He received callers, went out, attended ceremonies in his
honour.

Now, too, he complied with his friend Beaumarchais's request
that he visit him. Pierre was eager that the contract for the publica-

tion of Voltaire's collected works should be signed at his house in the rue Saint-Antoine.

He received his guest at the entrance to his estate, where a sedan-chair was held in readiness. When Voltaire had taken his seat, Pierre walked reverently beside him, showing him the garden and the court-yard. Voltaire was touched and smiled his acknowledgment of the apt allegory of the little temple that bore his name. A breeze was blowing and the globe rotated, as if moved by the quill-pen. Pierre was filled with pride and humility.

Thérèse was introduced. She remained almost silent, but her expression and attitude revealed the deep veneration she entertained for the man who throughout his long life had fought for justice with an ardour that excelled even that of her Pierre. The names of those whose freedom he had achieved or whose memory he had rescued from unwarranted infamy lined his life's path like tablets of honour. Thérèse inclined her head in homage.

Then Pierre requested his visitor to append his signature to the contract in which were enumerated the rights and obligations of the man who had undertaken to publish the authorized edition of his collected writings. It was a short document, but it laid a heavy burden on Pierre's shoulders. Voltaire raised his *lorgnon* and carefully pe-rused the various clauses. "An excellent contract," he commented, "and very clear."

For a brief moment Pierre thought of Maigron's calculation that the venture would require the investment of more than a million livres. But wasn't he Voltaire's heir and brother? And having made such sacrifices for an ungrateful America, should he shrink from the hazard of spending a paltry million on the greatest intellectual achieve-ment of the age? He seized the pen and signed. So did Voltaire. And one next to the other, there stood the two names: Beaumarchais — Voltaire.

Through the wide window they saw the great grey mass of the Bastille looming, which twice had confined Voltaire, and which threat-ened the printer of his works.

☆   ☆   ☆

At last Voltaire felt strong enough to attend a performance of *Irène*.

With his thin little figure decked out in old-fashioned stylishness and enveloped in the sables that had been a present from the Empress Catherine, he drove to the *Théâtre français* in his blue star-spangled carriage. Everywhere in the streets he was greeted and cheered; the vestibule and corridors of the theatre were packed to suffocation, and it was only with difficulty that a path could be cleared for him until he reached his box. The people kissed his hands and tore strands of hair from his furs to keep as souvenirs. When at last he appeared in his box the whole audience sprang to its feet, shouting and clapping and even stamping on the floor-boards until the auditorium was filled with a dense cloud of dust.

The curtain rose and the performance began. It was for this that he had made the journey to Paris, and it was a more significant occasion than he had originally expected. After the militant sermon of the Abbé Beauregard, the resounding verses in which he denounced Throne and Altar had assumed an even greater portent. They were the answer given by Reason to the charges and abuse levelled against it by superstition and the Church. That was fully realized by the audience too. The lines were greeted with tumultuous applause.

At the end of the play they all remained standing in the stuffy, dust-filled theatre; the curtain rose once more, revealing a pedestal on which had been set a bust of Voltaire. The actors, still in costume, were crowning it with a wreath. The tide of applause ebbed and flowed and seemed as if it would never end. This was what Voltaire had dreamed of. It was more than he had dreamed. He laughed and wept for joy, and was, at the same time, disillusioned. Was this all? Was this why he had come to Paris? Was it for this that he shortened his life? He wished that he could dictate to his Wagnière at this moment a line or two of proud, ironic verse.

A few days later, when he drove to the Louvre to assume the presidency of the Academy, his sense of triumph was dampened even more poignantly by consciousness of the vanity of success.

Again some thousands of people had assembled to catch a sight of him, and their cheers re-echoed far across the Seine. The members of the Academy came to meet him in solemn procession across the great courtyard, an honour that had never been accorded to any prince, and they escorted him into the hall.

Among those present was Doctor Franklin. He had brought John Adams, who sat in the audience. D'Alembert delivered the welcoming oration, to which Voltaire replied, bowing at the conclusion of his speech to Franklin, who joined in the applause of the others.

There was a demand that the two great men should appear together on the dais, and this they did. "You must embrace," shouted the whole audience, "you must embrace and kiss. That's our custom."

The two old men hesitated. They were both aware that theatricality, resounding phrases, and spectacular gestures were indispensable concomitants of fame, but Franklin was large and corpulent, Voltaire small and scraggly, and they both feared that they would look ridiculous. But both also felt that the request was justified; each had contributed his fair share to clearing the way for the American revolution. So they complied, and, clasping each other, each kissed the other's leathery cheek.

"What actors we are!" thought Voltaire to himself. "But it is an effective scene and there is much significance in the gesture." Franklin's thoughts were much the same. It was Voltaire who had torn down the prejudices that would have barred the way to the establishment of the United States. He had long ago given utterance to the principles from which the American revolution had sprung, and he had formulated them so effectively that they had seized upon all men's imagination. There passed through Franklin's mind the bold remark of Monsieur Caron that if France represented the spirit of liberty, America was liberty's fist. So they stood upon the dais, Voltaire and Franklin, and the onlookers cheered, and cried "Behold! Solon and Sophocles!"

John Adams, as he watched and listened, also had his own thoughts. "The popularity of this Doctor *honoris causa*," he mused, "is our strongest asset in Europe." And he thought, "The world wants to be deceived. Here am *I* sitting in this hall, yet these Frenchmen insist on regarding the old Epicurean as the epitome of Arcadian virtue."

"You must not, my dear Mr. Adams," explained Franklin as they drove home to Passy, "take this exaggerated and extravagant display of homage on the part of the Parisians amiss. They are a people who have been brought up under the influence of monarchist ideas, and they are accustomed to seeing greatness personified in one man. They believe that great deeds are the work of a single individual, and they are unable to comprehend the fact that it needed the combined efforts of many stout-hearted men to realize an achievement such as the United States of America."

For a brief moment John Adams was touched by such modesty and asked himself whether he would have said the same in Franklin's place.

That evening he sat down to write a long letter to his wife Abigail. "Franklin's reputation," he informed her, "is more universal than that of Leibniz or Newton, Frederick or Voltaire. There is scarcely a peasant or a citizen, a coachman or a footman, a lady's chambermaid or a scullion in a kitchen who is not familiar with his name. They consider him as the friend of all mankind and seem to think he is to restore the golden age. His face and name are as well known as the moon." He then described the scene which had taken place that afternoon at the Academy. "They really did embrace each other," he wrote.

"They hugged each other in their arms; they kissed each other—
two aged actors upon the stage of philosophy and cynicism."

☆ ☆ ☆

A carriage stopped in front of Pierre's old house in the rue de
Condé and a young man in travelling costume inquired of the servant
who opened the door, "Is Monsieur de Beaumarchais at home?" The
servant informed him with an arrogant air that Monsieur de Beaumarchais now lived in his new house in the rue Saint-Antoine.

"Of course," replied the stranger. "I ought to have thought of
that."

The inquisitive Julie, who came to the door at that moment, cried,
"Monsieur Paul! It is you!" A horrified look passed over her face for
a fleeting instant, but she immediately suppressed it. "You will stay
here, of course," she declared. "I will send for Pierre at once." Pressing him to come in, she showed him to his room and went off to see
to his luggage.

Paul's appearance was pitiful. His large brown eyes shone as brilliantly, as ever, but he was worn almost to a skeleton and seemed to
be living on his last reserves. Yet he was surprisingly animated and
talked incessantly.

When Pierre saw his friend he could hardly manage to conceal
his shock. Paul told him that with the conclusion of the alliance there
had been little left for him to do on the other side, so he had thought
he could be more useful to the firm if he came home. This was nonsense, and they both knew it. Paul had come back because he did
not want to die among strangers in the Western World, but in the
Paris that he loved.

Perhaps it was to divert his thoughts that he talked so copiously.
He spoke of the influence possessed by the Lees and their adherents
at Philadelphia and throughout the country. It was to be feared that
Silas Deane would not be able to hold his own in the face of their
intrigues. The firm of Hortalez was also likely to have many difficulties
to contend with though there were now many members of the Congress who had been made to see clearly the part played by Pierre.
The firm's claims would undoubtedly be met in the long run, but
it would take some time. Paul then entered into a detailed account
of the political and economic situation in the United States.

In the afternoon Paul paid a visit to his old physician. After examination, Doctor Lafargue said that his patient's condition had
deteriorated as he had predicted. But now, since he was in good
hands he would soon be in better shape. The physician spoke in a
tone of confidence and authority, and Paul did not believe a word.

He then went for a walk alone through the streets of Paris. It was for this that he had returned to Europe. Though he met many an old acquaintance on his way, he avoided speaking to them by disappearing into the crowd. It was hardly necessary for him to take this precaution, for few would have recognized him. He stood for a time on the Pont Neuf and the Place Louis Quinze, where the traffic was at its densest; he was jostled and cursed by the hurrying passers-by, and enjoyed it; he sat down in a smoky café, and later in the tavern of Père Ramponneau; the people drank and laughed and sang old melodies and new, sentimental songs and ditties that were cheerfully obscene, and he smiled with satisfaction at the discovery that the Parisians were still whistling and humming the opening air of *The Barber of Seville.* They smoked and bawled, some of the customers became troublesome and were thrown out, others linked arms and swayed to and fro as they chanted the old canon, *Frère Jacques, Frère Jacques, Ding, dang, dong, Ding, dang, dong.* Then he went out into the streets again and listened to the hawkers crying their wares. The vegetable women cried, "Fresh watercress, fresh watercress, there is nothing more healthy than fresh watercress! Buy my chicory, little wild chicory!" The cheese-sellers praised their "Good ripe stinking Livaro, Camembert all ripe and fruity!" The plaiters of cane-chairs called, "Chairs to mend, ladies! No need to sit on the ground!" The flower-girls chanted, "Sweet-smelling violets! Make yourself smell nice, pretty lady! Sweet-smelling violets!" He watched the men, who always seemed in a hurry, and the women, who always had time to return a glance. He was hearing, seeing, and feeling in every fibre the busy life and bustle of Paris, and a faint, foolish hope stirred in his breast that perhaps Doctor Lafargue had not been lying to him, since it was unimaginable that all this would continue to be, and he would cease to be.

He was suddenly overcome by an attack of dizziness, and beckoning to a hackney-coach he drove to Pierre's house.

Before they sat down to dinner, Pierre took him on a tour of the house, but Paul showed little interest. Even the project of publishing the complete works of Voltaire failed to stir his enthusiasm, and the only subject for which he displayed any real concern was Pierre's connection with the great historical events of the day. He was much agitated when Pierre told him of the incomprehensible hostility manifested by Franklin but when Pierre launched upon details of the involved state into which his business affairs had fallen he again lapsed into apathy. Pierre realized in a sudden flash that his young friend had settled his accounts with many living things, so that henceforth they were dead for him and he for them, and that among these things were, for instance, the affairs of the firm of Hortalez.

On the following day, without saying a word to the others, Paul drove to Passy.

Franklin received him in the open air, under the beech tree. "I am afraid that I am disturbing you," said Paul apologetically.

Franklin, however, invited him to sit down beside him, and his welcome was all the warmer because he was so touched by the imprint of doom on the sick man's face. "Let us have a bottle of madeira," he ordered the butler.

The old man and the young one sat together gazing out over the beautiful park which stretched down towards the Seine, with the silvery grey haze of Paris on the far bank. They were sprinkled with the mild sunshine that penetrated the early foliage of the great beech and Franklin, who had taken off his spectacles, was playing with his stick. Though they cast only an occasional glance at one another, each was vividly conscious of the other's presence beside him.

Franklin asked Paul about his impressions of America, and Paul spoke openly of his disillusionment. The American Tories were not only more numerous than the patriots, but there were also among them a much greater number of cultured and refined people, so that the Republicans had to fight both the English and a formidable front of educated and propertied compatriots. Paul was speaking in English, slowly but without hesitation, and he suddenly broke off to interject with a faint smile, *"Mais ça ira!* Anyone who has spent his life in Europe," he went on, "can hardly realize, unless he has been to see for himself, what it means to live in a continent that is not burdened with the traditions of centuries. It is not only that there are no ancient castles in America, but even before the revolution the people were far less hidebound by a system of caste and privilege. We were, of course, aware of that, but experiencing it in the way I did the impact of it struck me afresh every day. The relations between your citizens and the authorities, between your soldiers and their officers, all this was for me a marvel which I still find it difficult to grasp in its entirety. And there is one further point. It is only after one has crossed the ocean that one realizes the vast extent and emptiness of this America of yours with its three million souls. Europe is so crammed full with princes, peoples, and privileges. It is true that we of the old continent have both formulated and argued the case for the establishment of the State on the principles of Reason, but it was only in your country that such a State could really be constituted. I realized what Leibniz meant when he said, 'This land is a blank sheet of paper, on which anything can be written.' "

Franklin listened attentively, taking an occasional sip at his madeira or drawing figures in the sand with his stick. Stealing now and then a furtive glance at Paul, he noted how swiftly the symptoms of his malady had become aggravated, and he gazed down at his own brown weather-beaten hands and thought of the decay of his own body, and that life was from the very outset merely a long-drawn-out process of dying, and the phenomenon of old age was still a mystery despite all the efforts that had been made to explain its physical mechanism.

Paul had come to the end of his story. "You have been a keen observer," commented Franklin. "The Tories among us are numerous, and they are to be found mainly among men of education. Yet even more dangerous are those lukewarm citizens of ours who are neither friends nor foes. We Americans, who have not only to observe, but also to fight, have only one course available to us. We must not allow ourselves to be confused by the varying aspects that each problem assumes. Here in Paris you are enabled by the prevailing conditions to take into account the subtle ramifications of each particular question, but a nation that is engaged as we are in a struggle for survival must strive to think on more simple lines. I am not always"— and here a smile appeared at the corners of his broad mouth—"the rustic philosopher that your people like to see in me, but when I wish to obtain a clear picture of the situation in which my country finds itself I try to see things simply as they present themselves in their general outline." He had turned his massive head towards Paul, and in his wide eyes there was a look of almost stern tranquillity.

Paul was gratified at being addressed by Franklin with such friendly confidence, and thinking aloud he asked abruptly, "Why did you have Monsieur de Beaumarchais's cargo confiscated, Doctor Franklin?"

He was immediately horrified at his boldness, and Franklin felt a momentary surge of wrath at the audacity of the young man who had dared to beard him in this way. His anger ebbed, however, before it showed in his face. He had encouraged his visitor by his own display of candour, and there was no one more justified in asking such a question than this young man on the verge of the tomb who had shortened his already numbered days for the sake of America and Monsieur Caron. Paul was apparently unable to understand how a man reputedly wise could have acted with such lack of wisdom. Franklin was unable to understand it himself. "My action," he conceded, "was somewhat precipitate. I was carried away by impulse."

Paul's heart warmed to these words and the way they were said. The great man's admission that he had allowed himself to be swayed by an emotion of the moment, ignoring the dictates of reason, brought him down from his chilly height to the common human level. A statue at which one had stared in admiring wonder had turned to flesh and blood. Yet at the same time Paul recognized with painful clarity that there could be no bond linking Franklin and Pierre. The

American's distaste sprang from impulse and temperament; reason
had no say in the matter. Paul's feelings and thoughts were submerged in a profound sense of gratitude to the old man who had
permitted him to catch a glimpse of the dark stirrings within his
breast, and he felt close to him.

Franklin himself remained sitting beneath the beech tree with
mixed emotions. It was good to feel the mild rays of the sun as one
gazed across at the beautiful vista of Paris. When one considered
that before twelve months had passed this young Monsieur Theveneau
would no longer be here, while one's own gouty self would still be
sitting beneath the beech tree relaxing in the warm sun, one was
moved by emotions in which pain and pleasure were curiously
mingled.

☆   ☆   ☆

It was shortly after this that Thérèse begged Paul to tell her about
his experiences in America and what he sincerely thought of that
country.

Simply, but with conviction, concealing nothing of the disagreeable
experiences he had encountered, he spoke of the infinite difficulties
that had to be overcome by the young American nation. Their numerous setbacks had tried the temper even of the most equable and
made them far from easy to get on with. Most of them had in any
case not yet learned to mask a temporary surge of anger by a display
of good manners. Egotism took no pains to disguise itself, but was
manifested in all its naked ugliness.

Nevertheless, despite the many unhappy symptoms that were so
much in evidence, there was gradually being built up a noble and
fascinating entity. Though there might be something petty about most
of the Americans, they were being carried along, by their great
cause, by their striving for Reason, for a rational ordering of the State.
However regrettable might be the behaviour at times of individuals,
the nation as a whole, in defiance of the serious blows it had suffered,
was possessed by a stubborn self-reliance, a calm and most admirable
power of perseverance.

"When negotiating with some quarrelsome and suspicious member
of the Congress," he said, "or when talking to one of General Washington's rough-tongued soldiers, I could not understand how men of
such insignificance had been able to realize such a great ideal and to
set up their republic of Liberty and Reason. Then I would attend one
of their meetings and I did understand. In England or in France,
when you are in the midst of a crowd of people, you have perhaps
a feeling of warmth and comfort, but never more than that. In

America there is always a moment when it seems that some tremendous flame is being kindled. To expand with a crowd into something that is greater than oneself, to be carried off one's feet, to become merged in the mass without being ashamed of thus losing one's individual identity, this is something that can be experienced only in America. We Frenchmen," he concluded, "have our great men, we have our Montesquieu and Helvétius, our Turgot and Voltaire and Jean-Jacques, and I may even perhaps mention my friend Beaumarchais, yet for all her heroes, writers, and philosophers, France has been unable to wrench herself from the pitiable condition in which she exists today, whereas these simple citizens and farmers have succeeded in shaking off their English lords and exploiters."

☆   ☆   ☆

It was in the garden, not far from the Voltaire temple, that Paul had his last, fatal hemorrhage. Doctor Lafargue said that he would not outlive the day, and though Pierre and the others could not but have expected the end to come in this way they were stunned when it happened.

During his last hours Paul remained fully conscious. Pierre and Thérèse were at his bedside, and Pierre had to keep a tight hold on himself not to burst into a fit of weeping. "At least," said Paul, "there are now some people in America who know that the United States could not have been victorious without your aid." Later he said, "I am glad I crossed the ocean, so let nobody regret my going." Then he added something that caused Pierre to stare at him in stupefaction. "Doctor Franklin was sorry that he had your cargo confiscated."

"You went to see Franklin?" stammered Pierre. Paul nodded, and the shadow of a crafty smile flitted across his face.

Pierre wept without restraint as he stood before the dead body of his friend. He had never learned to curb his emotions. It was as if he had lost the better part of himself. He would never again find such a friend as Paul. There was no one who, while recognizing all his faults, had yet maintained such steady faith in his plans and ambitions. He gave loud and uncontrolled utterance to his grief, blaming himself bitterly for not having prevented Paul from going to America.

Then he abruptly turned on his heel and left the room.

He washed his face and then sat down at his writing-table, attentively observed by his bitch Caprice. It irked him that Paul's last act had been to visit Doctor Franklin. It had been done for his sake, he knew, yet he was hurt. The world seemed cold and bleak, and there was a feeling of emptiness in his heart such as he had never known before.

He wanted to arrange a pompous funeral for Paul, but Thérèse dissuaded him. Her tone was gentle, but there was a look in her eyes that made him give up his plan. Very few friends were informed when the funeral was to take place. But the news must have spread quickly. The coffin was escorted to the grave by a large number of carriages, among them that of Doctor Franklin.

☆   ☆   ☆

Vaudreuil was playing tennis with Prince Charles at Gennevilliers, where he had had the courts extended and modernized.

In recent weeks he had been going in a great deal for sport of all kinds. When he rode, hunted, or chased tennis balls it was easier to throw off the feeling of restlessness that consumed him. He regarded the coming war as his war. It was he who had brought it about and he was impatient for it to begin. He wanted to get away from Versailles, to play his part on the military stage, and yet Louis was still doing all he could to delay the outbreak of hostilities.

The continued waiting was fraying Vaudreuil's nerves. He was sick to death of Versailles and the court. The prospect of sharing Toinette's couch had lost its charm. The Trianon and the Lilac Coterie had become dull and insipid. He was sickened by the whole atmosphere of artificiality and affectation, and scarcely took pains to conceal his ill humour beneath his wonted air of condescending amiability.

Prince Charles, who copied Vaudreuil in everything, was infected by his passion for tennis and trained zealously. Vaudreuil, however, was by far his superior in strength and skill. So long as the Prince was useful to him he had allowed him to win occasionally, but now he had no scruples in showing him what a bungler he really was.

Désirée was watching from the gallery, and it was perhaps due to her presence that Vaudreuil was handling the Prince with particular ruthlessness.

During the past weeks he had become more and more deeply attracted by Désirée. He consorted with many women, women of the most varied types; this was the custom of the time, this was also in accordance with his inclinations, and at first he had merely regarded Désirée as one of his many. But the more he wearied of Versailles and of Toinette, the more strongly did he feel drawn towards Désirée. She never bored him. In everything she did and said there was a vigorous element of healthy vulgarity. Moreover, the rumour had got around that she had declined an offer of marriage from Lenormant, and Vaudreuil was not averse to being regarded as her official lover.

During dinner Prince Charles referred to the preparations for the amateur dramatic performances at the Trianon, for in the very next weeks Toinette would be ready to make her appearance on the stage of her private theatre, and they were rehearsing six short plays, with the intention of producing two each evening. While they discussed these rehearsals, Vaudreuil's ill humour vanished. The performances at the Trianon were the only events at Versailles in which he took any real interest. He had set his heart upon the achievement of a very high standard.

Toinette, as both gentlemen agreed, was attending rehearsals assiduously, but this, Prince Charles suggested, was not enough. She had not yet acquired the requisite technique, and the two old actors who tutored her were not adequate for the task. "You ought to give Madame, my sister-in-law, a little advice, Désirée," he said jokingly.

Désirée merely smiled, but she took the humorous remark more seriously than its author could have expected. Through Vaudreuil and her other friends of the Lilac Coterie she had heard a great deal about Toinette's passionate enthusiasm for her theatre at the Trianon, and it had already occurred to her that, as coach to Toinette, she would have entry into the royal circle. She realized, however, that such an ambition could be achieved only with the aid of complicated intrigue and that whatever happened the suggestion must not come from herself. Now that Prince Charles had given utterance to the same idea, she found the prospect more tempting than ever.

It had not been easy to work her way up to the position of a *Sociétaire du Théâtre français*. She was small of stature and her acting did not conform to the classical style of the ensemble. There were many who thought her too "modern," and in recent weeks the hostility towards her had become sharpened. The actor Lekain, who had always stood up for her, was dead now, and the Duc de Fronsac, who had governing control over the *Théâtre français* and on whose support she had hitherto been able to count, had suddenly turned against her. She had little doubt who was responsible for his change of attitude. Monsieur Lenormant was friendly with the Duc de Fronsac; it was he who was stirring the duke up.

If she could manage to gain the good will of the Queen, then she would be able to snap her fingers at her enemies. Neither Charlot nor the Duc de Fronsac could do anything against the wishes of Toinette. Prince Charles had been jesting, but there was a grain of seriousness in his jest, and Désirée made up her mind that she would give the Queen lessons in acting. She would set her plan in motion that very evening.

Désirée liked Vaudreuil, who was not so empty-minded as the other aristocrats she knew and less shallow both in loving and hating. His wild tempers had their fascination, and there was a naturalness of gesture in his extravagance. But he, too, like all his class, moved in a dense cloud of conceit and prejudice. He had not, for instance, any inkling of the trick that she and Pierre had played upon him when they arranged the meeting at his house between Franklin and Toinette. It simply never occurred to him that anyone could be making fun of the Marquis de Vaudreuil, Grand Falconer of the King and Superintendent of the Queen's Entertainments, and it was this quality in him that lured Désirée into trying out her inherent bourgeois superiority over his aristocratic arrogance. She enjoyed using him as an unconscious tool.

If she were to ask him to assist her in inveigling herself into the good graces of Toinette he would certainly refuse without more ado. She must contrive things so that it was he himself who invited her to coach the Queen, and it could be done only in a roundabout way.

Luckily, as soon as Charles had gone and they were alone together, he returned to the subject of the plays he was producing at the Trianon. It was expected that Louis would be present on the first evening, and Vaudreuil explained that he wanted to choose two pieces containing witty allusions to the King himself, allusions whose malicious intent should be clearly evident without its being possible to prove that they were deliberately aimed at him. For this purpose the programme would be made up of Sedaine's *The Unforeseen Wager* and *King and Peasant*. Désirée remarked casually that it was a pity the choice of plays for the Trianon was so restricted, which meant that his productions could not help being affected by the tedious atmosphere of the court. Vaudreuil was hit upon the raw and retorted that he thought it by no means tedious, but on the contrary very piquant, to taunt Louis in public with mocking references to his passion for the locksmith's trade or to assail his ears with the enlightened truths of the freemasons.

"Of course," answered Désirée, "political witticisms of that kind are quite charming. But they are a little thin, aren't they? Don't you think they are rather like lemonade compared with the champagne that is served elsewhere?"

"Where?" asked Vaudreuil.

"Well," replied Désirée, "my former friend Lenormant, for ex-ample, offers more heady liquor at his little theatre than you do at the Trianon."

At the mention of Lenormant's name Vaudreuil's thick black eye-

brows knitted more closely together. None of the great ladies with
whom he consorted would have been bold enough to compare a venture of his with that of a former lover. For a fleeting second he had
a mind to have Désirée shown the door by his valet Baptiste, but he
knew that if he did, she was not the woman ever to come through
that door again. She had just proved this in the case of Lenormant
himself.

Moreover, there was a grain of truth in what she said. The noble
actors and actresses at the Trianon had an ineradicable tendency
to lapse into conventional ways when they were on the stage, and
as producer he himself was not quite sure of his technique. In short,
he was afraid that in spite of the political allusions his amateur
theatricals at the Trianon would exhale a faint aroma of faded laven-
der. If there was any person qualified to disperse the insipid fragrance, that person was Désirée. With an effort at self-control he
shrugged his shoulders and begged in a subdued voice, "Don't let
us argue, Désirée!" Then he went on, "I thought of putting on the
two plays together because it seemed to me that it would be amusing
for me personally. I have a pretty wide range as an actor, and it will
be fun, in two different roles, to tell the fat fellow what I think of
him. In the first piece I take the part of a nobleman, in the second
that of a country bumpkin." Assuming the attitude of the peasant
Richard who does not recognize the King, he began to speak his
lines with a broad accent, "Do you know, Monsieur, since we have
been speaking about the King, that I have seen something a King
never sees?" "And what might that be?" he asked, changing his
voice to represent that of the King. Again assuming the tone of the
peasant, he replied slyly, "Human beings!"

"I don't think I did that too badly," he commented in his natural
voice. Désirée looked thoughtful for a moment before she replied,
"Not too badly for an amateur."

Vaudreuil swallowed. "What is there amateurish about the way I
spoke?" he demanded.

She tried to explain. "You put the lines across as our good old
Michu used to do, with a broad and obvious striving for effect as if
you had to bring the point home to every simpleton in the audience.
I would speak them without emphasis. There is no need to stress the
meaning." And she showed him how she would have done it.

Vaudreuil saw at once where he had gone wrong. "That was wonderful, Désirée," he admitted, and he meant it honestly. "You know,"
he went on, "that was not perhaps such a bad idea on the part of
our friend Charles. How would you like to coach Toinette for a bit?"

"He has taken the bait!" sang Désirée triumphantly to herself.
"*Ça y est.*" Aloud she murmured pensively, "It might be all right

working with you, François. You have a gift for acting, and if you
were not François Vaudreuil you would probably be a *Sociétaire du
Théâtre français*. But *l'Autrichienne* is a different pair of shoes."
She screwed up her face as she always did when she was thinking
hard. "Isn't she frightfully capricious? And one hears she is very
haughty. If she can't make a success of her part, isn't she likely
to put the blame on me?"

But Vaudreuil cried impatiently, "Come, come! Don't be so difficult!"

Désirée was rejoicing inwardly, but she continued to put forward
objections. "I suppose Madame is going to play the part of the Marquise? I find it uncongenial and I don't think I can help her there.
The role is far too tedious for even a professional actress to make anything of it, let alone an amateur. I prefer the soubrette, though it isn't
such a fat part. I never envied Molé being given the Marquise to play."

"Who told you that Toinette is going to play the Marquise?" demanded Vaudreuil heatedly. "I have been thinking for some time that
it would be better to give her the soubrette. It would be much more
piquant."

Désirée's success had been greater than she had dared to expect.
Monsieur le Marquis was making a laughing-stock of himself without
knowing it. He was letting her cast his play for him. She took care,
however, not to let him see that he had fallen into her trap.

He grew more importunate. "You must do it, Désirée!" he insisted.
"I want you to coach Toinette. Please do it for my sake! I will give
Toinette the part of the soubrette."

She squinted down her nose with a perfect pretence at giving way
only reluctantly. "But you must make it perfectly clear to your Toinette," she demanded at last, "that she has got to take the thing seriously. And you must let us have sufficient time. If you promise me
this I will do my best—for your sake."

☆   ☆   ☆

Toinette's relations with Vaudreuil had grown somewhat less acri-
monious. They still quarrelled violently, but they were both anxious
that the productions at the Trianon theatre should make their mark in
the history of the French stage.

She was not ungifted and really did take rehearsals seriously, discussing details with Vaudreuil and the members of the company,
working several hours a day with the two actors Michu and Caillot,
and slowly learning to control her refractory *r*. Nor did she have any
illusions that her talents were wholly on a par with those of the ladies
of the *Théâtre français* or the *Comédie des Italiens*.

When Vaudreuil suggested to her that she should take lessons from Désirée, a slight flush came into her cheeks. Her reaction was one of mingled embarrassment, eagerness, and proud disdain. She was aware, of course, that Désirée was one of Vaudreuil's mistresses, and his proposal stirred her at first to indignation. It was not easy for her to pretend ignorance of the fact that he and Gabrielle, her best friend, discussed her affairs together in bed, but it was sheer impertinence on his part to expect her to consort with the Mesnard woman. On the other hand she realized that the Lilac Coterie would laugh at such bourgeois scruples, and in any case there could be no doubt of Désirée's outstanding qualities as an actress. Her technique was much more attractive than the outmoded style of Messieurs Michu and Caillot, and the prospect of being coached by her was very tempting.

"Do you really think, François, that I can work with Mademoiselle Mesnard?" she asked. Involuntarily she slightly stressed the personal pronoun. Vaudreuil understood her meaning. What she intended to say was, "Do you really expect me, the daughter of Maria Theresa, to breathe the same air as this harlot of yours?" He knitted his brows.

"As the Superintendent of your Entertainments, Madame," he declared, "I have to inform you that the time has now come to decide who is to play the Marquise and who the soubrette. The soubrette is the more thankful role, but the more difficult one, and Madame de Polignac is less capable of undertaking it than you yourself would be. A Madame de Polignac who had been coached by Mademoiselle Mesnard would, however, be more fitted for the part than a Queen who had been coached by Monsieur Michu. The decision rests with you." Suddenly his self-control broke down and he burst out, "We have all worked hard on this production and I am not going to let it be ruined by your prudish scruples."

Toinette bowed her head, and on the following day the Superintendent of the Queen's Entertainments and Amusements wrote to Mademoiselle Mesnard informing her that she was invited to appear at the Orangery at Versailles on the ensuing Tuesday morning at ten-thirty o'clock.

The letter was couched in terms that verged on discourtesy; it was a command rather than a request. Vaudreuil apparently did not want to admit to himself how much he was depending on her co-operation, or to let her see what an effort it had been to persuade Toinette. But Désirée did not take it amiss. She was content to savour her triumph.

There was a long wait at the Orangery on the following Tuesday morning. When Toinette eventually arrived she apologized somewhat perfunctorily and was charmingly condescending.

Though Toinette had made a close study of Sedaine's comedy and had seen it performed both at the *Théâtre français* and the *Comédie des Italiens,* it was not long before she realized, under Désirée's tuition, how much had escaped her. She learned the importance of emphasis and the importance of emphasis omitted. She understood quickly and showed enthusiasm and naïve admiration for Désirée's accomplished technique. Désirée politely thanked her, but did not conceal the fact that she was accustomed to such homage.

During the ensuing days Désirée continued to coach her pupil assiduously while avoiding any personal relationship. Toinette frequently kept her waiting and just as frequently retained her long beyond her normal hour of departure. On one occasion Désirée pointed out that if she did not leave at once her part that evening would have to be played by Madame Molé.

"You will be recompensed, my dear," said Toinette.

"There can be no recompense, Madame," replied Désirée dryly.

Toinette continued to make no concealment of her naïve admiration for Désirée's art, but the actress allowed herself to be no more affected by a display of friendship than she was by a display of haughtiness. She would amuse herself now and then by showing the Queen what hard work really meant. After making her repeat a passage a number of times, she would discover that the text ran differently and Toinette would rack her memory in vain for the exact wording. Finally she asked, "Does it really make much difference if I say *'alors'* instead of *'ainsi'?"*

"Yes," replied Désirée determinedly, "it does. The author's text is sacred."

"How ever did you manage to sharpen your memory in that way?" Toinette asked.

"When I was a student," replied Désirée, "I had to learn fifty lines of Corneille, Racine, or Molière by heart every day."

"Your time was not so taken up with ceremonial, my dear," sighed Toinette.

"No, Madame," said Désirée. "I was an errand-girl at Madame Meunier's lace shop. Monsieur Robecque used to give me lessons without charge. We were both of us overworked and I was often tired, while he was generally in a bad temper. He could be very disagreeable when I failed to learn my fifty lines correctly."

"Did he punish you?" inquired Toinette.

"Instead of fifty lines," said Désirée, "I had to learn a hundred for the next day, and more than once he would give me a box on the ears." She did not tell Toinette that there were other unpleasant things she had had to put up with while training for the stage. That she was expected to sleep with her teacher she had regarded as a matter of course, but Madame Robecque had been jealous and her emotions had found vent in scratching the face and tearing the hair of her husband's pupil. She had been beaten too by her mother, whose moral sense was outraged at the liberties taken by Monsieur Robecque.

"Well, it seems to have been astonishingly effective in developing your memory," commented Toinette. "I shall learn twenty lines of Racine or Corneille every day and I hope it will do the same for me."

Désirée's common sense had always told her that a woman remained a woman even though she wore a crown. "There are certain parts of a queen's body which look the same as those of a serving wench," they used to say in the French taverns, and Désirée was well aware that Toinette, for all her natural charm, was rather a foolish woman and obsessed by an almost insane pride. None the less, Désirée had never been able wholly to rid herself of the feeling of awe and veneration which, as a consequence of the efforts of the Church, the schools, and the secular authorities, was associated with the conception of king, queen, court, Versailles. The close-up view, however, which she had recently been enjoying of the ways and doings of the Lilac Coterie, showed her that behaviour in court circles was even more primitively human than she had suspected.

If it amused Désirée to make the Queen of France play a lady's maid, it amused Toinette even more to be the maid. Small though the role was, it gave her the opportunity of putting in the shade her friend Gabrielle, who was to play the more important part of the Marquise. It was also entertaining to show that she was not only receiving the homage of her French subjects, but that she also understood their ways and was really one of them.

On the stage she had to serve dishes and press the breeches of the *valet de chambre* Lafleur, so she took lessons from her own maid in serving dishes and pressing breeches. The idea that she, descendant of Habsburg, she, Queen of France, pressed and served, pleased her enormously. She proudly demonstrated her skill to Désirée, who promptly dampened her enthusiasm by patiently pointing out that on the stage what mattered was not using a smoothing-iron correctly, but giving the impression that one was using it correctly. It was the appearance that was important. Toinette was dreadfully disappointed, but she understood.

Vaudreuil watched with eager interest while Désirée applied herself to her task. His ambition was spurred on not only to achieve striking stage effects, but also to achieve credibility. The two parts he was going to play, that of a nobleman in the first piece and a peasant in the second, must be equally authentic. Désirée praised his efforts in her shrewd and unexaggerated way. With each rehearsal her feeling of grim satisfaction increased. How they sweated, these aristocratic amateurs. Even François Vaudreuil forgot that he wanted to be the Queen's lover, forgot his dream of leading French armies to the shores of England, and was intent only on being an actor, though for all his painstaking efforts he could not in his best moments achieve the level of mediocrity reached by the least of the actors at the *Théâtre français* at their weakest. How blind they were, this royal lady and her noble friends.

☆   ☆   ☆

Count Mercy faithfully reported to Schoenbrunn that Toinette had taken up a new hobby, but the old Empress was not unduly perturbed. She replied that play-acting was a less expensive amusement than card-playing, and it was cheaper to give the Polignacs parts on the stage than sinecures in the Government.

Louis was himself interested in the theatre and raised no objections to Toinette's indulgence in her new pastime. He even attended some of the rehearsals. Before rehearsing certain scenes, however, Vaudreuil begged him to be so gracious as to retire, since they wanted to surprise him. Louis fully appreciated their desire to keep back a few plums for the opening night, and said good-humouredly as he went out, "Very good. I will return to my work. But I insist on one thing, my dear Marquis. If you are going to have songs, you must let me hear my favourite air." They all knew what his favourite air was. It was "The Song of the Goat."

The rehearsals went on without respite. Toinette struggled with her articulation of the letter *r*, Vaudreuil consulted Pierre on certain minor alterations in the text, the most celebrated composers in France orchestrated the music that was to accompany the songs, and in order that Louis should have no fault to find with a door-lock that played such an important role in *The Unforeseen Wager*, expert advice was sought from Gamain.

At last everything was ready and Toinette went through her part with Désirée for the final overhaul. "I have learned an enormous amount from you," she said happily, and in a sudden surge of sincere emotion she put her arm around Désirée's shoulders, a token of intimate affection that was normally reserved for Gabrielle.

When the evening of the performance finally arrived, there were only twenty-three guests assembled in Toinette's dainty little theatre. Count Mercy would very much have liked to be present, so that he might send an eye-witness account to Toinette's illustrious parent, but Toinette wanted only spectators of royal blood. None but members of the royal family were admitted, and no exception could be made for the Austrian Ambassador.

Decorated in white and gold, the ornate yet discreet elegance of the small auditorium shimmered in the glow of innumerable candles,

the boxes and *fauteuils* seemed to offer a dignified but cordial welcome to the guests to seat themselves in comfort, and the lions' heads
on the columns supporting the balcony indicated that one was in the
private apartments of the Queen.

The guests took their seats and waited excitedly, though not without
some scepticism, for the curtain of heavy blue velvet embroidered
in gold to rise upon the scene. The orchestra, recruited from the
King's best musicians was ready. There was a certain amount of coming and going between the boxes and a subdued hum of conversation.

Behind the curtain there were signs of stage fright. Prince Charles
was drinking rather heavily, and even the abstemious Toinette took a
glass of champagne. "Feel how cold my hand is," she whispered several times to Vaudreuil. Suddenly she declared that the emptiness of
the theatre made her feel nervous. Moreover, the acoustics were not
right unless the auditorium was full.

"You should have thought of that before, Madame," rejoined Vaudreuil, who was looking more handsome and virile than ever in his
blue and red colonel's uniform.

"I want more people in the theatre," insisted the lady's maid Nanine, now by no means maid-like. "Order Swiss Guards and servants
to occupy the empty seats."

"You expressed a wish, Madame," said Vaudreuil peevishly, "to
have none but members of the royal family in the audience."

"Swiss Guards and servants are not audience, but people," retorted
Toinette.

"Toinette is right," interjected the Marquise de Clainville, otherwise Gabrielle Polignac, gently, and Jules Polignac growled indignantly, "Audience forsooth, *ces espèces!*" Vaudreuil himself was a
little worried about the acoustics, so he submitted and issued the
necessary orders.

Presently the heavy tread of the Swiss Guards could be heard, and
there they marched in, under the command of an officer. At sight of
the King they stood stiffly at attention. "At ease," cried the officer.
"Take your seats! Quick march!" The soldiers, abashed and trying
to make as little sound as possible, squeezed their massive hind-
quarters into the elegant arm-chairs, clattering noisily. In among them
pushed a crowd of female servants.

Then there came the three thuds on the floor-boards, the curtain
parted, and there stood, in a dainty, expensively designed lady's-
maid's costume that revealed the legs half-way up the calf, with a pair
of breeches flung over her bare arm, Marie-Antoinette, Queen of
France, who said to her brother-in-law, Prince Charles, the *valet de
chambre* Lafleur, "You see, we servants are always complaining—"

Before she could tell, however, what they were complaining about, she was interrupted by the reverberating guffaw of Louis. "Splendid, Madame!" he cried, and clapped his hands. "You really look like a genuine lady's maid, and you speak like one, too. Splendid! Bravo!" Turning to his neighbours he asked, "Don't you agree with me, ladies and gentlemen? Splendid! Encore!"

The curtain descended with a rush and Vaudreuil came to the front of the stage. He was boiling with fury, but managed to keep his self-control. "Ladies and gentlemen!" he announced. "We are about to make a fresh start and I must beg you earnestly not to interrupt the actors."

"That's all right, Vaudreuil," said Louis good-humouredly. "No harm meant. I thought Madame so astonishingly good that I couldn't help applauding. I promise you I won't say another word."

The curtain parted once more and this time the performance was allowed to proceed without interruption. Everything went as smoothly as they could have hoped, and the princely observers soon became absorbed in the presentation of a little episode in the married life of the de Clainville couple. There was only one further slight disturbance when Louis, despite his firm resolve to restrain his exuberance, was overcome by the sight of Jules Polignac making an expert examination of the door-lock. "You must let me have a look at that later on, Jules," he cried.

The soldiers, lackeys, and maidservants in the audience had been so startled at the sudden invitation that for some time they were unable to take in what was happening on the stage. They were confused both at finding themselves in the auditorium and at seeing the Queen and the King's brother behaving in such a strange way. Why, they wondered, should she take such great pains to act a lady's maid? And it was very improper for them both to conduct themselves like clowns and comedians. Gradually, however, they overcame their embarrassment and enjoyed the whole thing. It was not easy for them to follow the elegant dialogue, but what they did understand was that the author sympathized with the people more than with the aristocracy and was making fun of the stupid dalliance with which the privileged classes sought to forget their ennui. They appreciated the insolence of Nanine and Lafleur, which was their own insolence, and the fact that it came from the lips of masquerading royalty spiced the joke, but they dared not yet show their amusement without restraint. Their laughter sounded uneasy and was stifled at birth. After all, their capricious masters might suddenly decide without rhyme or reason to take things amiss.

Then, however, Vaudreuil sprang his first surprise. He stepped up to the footlights and sang. In his deep melodious voice he sang the daring old sailors' chanty with which they were all familiar, and which, now that the war with England threatened, was invested with dangerous political implications. He sang of the English frigate which was sighted by a French ship while on its way to Breslau. The French Captain asked his second-in-command, "Lieutenant, do you think you can board that ship?" The proud and valiant Lieutenant replied, "Aye, aye, sir!" and heaving to, they made the Englishman see the light of reason with the aid of pikes, muskets, and grappling-hooks. "And now," sang the Marquis de Vaudreuil, Grand Falconer of the King and Superintendent of the Queen's Entertainments, "we'll drink a toast to the Captain and one to his gallant Lieutenant. We'll drink a toast to all sweet lovers and one to the King of France. And *merde* to the King of England, who made war on us."

The illustrious guests in the boxes were put out of countenance. France was not at war with England, and it was very odd that Monsieur de Vaudreuil should sing this old coarse ditty in the Queen's theatre. The soldiers and other common folk in the stalls, however, *ces espèces,* were unable to contain themselves any longer. They applauded vigorously and cried, "Bravo! Bravo! Encore!"

Vaudreuil glanced at the King's box. He had hesitated up to the last moment whether or not he should risk it, but he was glad now that he had done so. It had been an audacious trick to play on the eternally temporizing monarch, but it had come off and Vaudreuil was wonderfully well pleased with himself. It had also been a good idea to fetch in the common people, for now the story would soon be all over Paris and it was he, François Vaudreuil, who would be given the credit of having declared war on England.

Louis's good spirits were damped as soon as the insolent Vaudreuil struck into the chanty. It had been a stupid song even during the last war, to which it owed its origin, since in the first place the French had unfortunately captured very few English ships and there had been little cause for jubilation and the drinking of toasts. In the second place, it betrayed an astonishing ignorance of geography on the author's part when he let the English ship sail to Breslau. And in present circumstances the song was not only stupid, but also highly offensive. It was most unseemly of this fellow Vaudreuil to stand there and bawl such a ballad.

He sat slumped in his chair and fidgeted uneasily. When the people in the stalls began to applaud vociferously and to demand an encore he was filled with melancholy. Poor fools, he thought. They wanted war. He had a vision of these men, robust and chubby-cheeked as they sat squeezed into their *fauteuils,* being stowed into the holds of ships and later drowning like rats in a trap, or perishing miserably in the forests of a mutinous country in the proximity of villages that were not even marked on the map. Yet that impertinent fellow had the audacity to gaze up at him and look him straight in the eye with a mocking smile on his lips. For a fleeting moment Louis was impelled by the urge to cry, "Stop! Curtain! I don't permit this to go on!" But he told himself that if he did that he would be transforming a childish incident into a public scandal, and he decided, "No. It is best not. This is a private entertainment, it is a family affair, I will ignore the words and do not wish anyone to attach any particular significance to them. It is just a song. Since a ship can't sail to Breslau it can't be captured, and the whole thing is simply a piece of irresponsible nonsense." So he sat there with a silly smile while Vaudreuil bowed his acknowledgments and sang the song again.

The second play, however, the comedy *King and Peasant,* was very much to Louis's taste. He liked the hunting-costumes, the cheerful sound of the horns, the pert and charming appearance of his Toinette as a rustic maiden, and the acting of his brother Charles as a clownish ranger who arrested the whole company of huntsmen including the King and his suite. As a bumpkin, Vaudreuil was simply magnificent. When he spoke his celebrated lines, "I have seen something a King never sees—human beings," Louis simply refused to take umbrage, but interjected loudly, "Very good! Very good! Excellent!" and Vaudreuil was once more disappointed. The people in the stalls, of course, were very appreciative, but this time they did not dare to applaud. They only gazed up affectionately at their good King Louis.

Then came the high light of the evening for Louis, the interpolation of the song for which he had asked. Prince Charles, as the clownish ranger, presented "The Song of the Goat" with a boisterous effect that stirred his royal brother to enthusiasm. "We had a goat, an aged goat, a goat of fourteen years," he sang. "A clever goat she was, forsooth, and ate Jean Bertrand's cabbages. But Jean Bertrand, he caught her in the act and had her arrested by eighty gendarmes. A clever goat she was, forsooth, and when she appeared before the court she lifted her tail so daintily and sat down in the dock. She lifted her tail, sat down in the dock, and let off a petard in the nose of the magistrate. A clever goat she was, forsooth, and scattered a whole basketful of currants on the floor of the dock for the gentlemen of the jury. And then she rammed her horn up the backside of the worthy magistrate. A clever goat she was, forsooth, a clever goat she was."

This was the song the princely ranger sang, and while he sang, the soldiers, lackeys, and maidservants felt the same embarrassment stealing over them that had held them in restraint before. It was a good song, the song of the clever old goat, and it contained a number of home truths, but it was out of place in the Queen's theatre and hardly becoming on the lips of a prince of the blood. And that he should sing

it for them was really unimaginable. But there he stood and sang.
They sat and listened, yet they refused to believe it. Nor did it become
any more credible even when they saw and heard how evidently Louis
was revelling in it. He had begun by humming the refrain softly and
then joined loudly in the singing.

Vaudreuil was more than satisfied with the success of the evening.
He was walking on air. Yet he pretended that he felt cheated of his
reward by Louis's thick-skinned complacency. With a show of irritation he said to Toinette, "We ought not to have let him come. It was
scandalous the way he behaved. He interrupted the performance twice
and kept laughing in the wrong places. I am really ashamed to look my
valet de chambre in the face."

Toinette could not understand what he was so bothered about. In a
state of pleasurable excitement herself, she thought that everything
had gone off extraordinarily well. There had not been a single hitch of
any consequence, she was well satisfied with the effect of her own performance, her guests had entered wonderfully into the spirit of the
evening, Vaudreuil had surpassed himself, and he must surely have
noticed what a hit he had been. Her praise was so obviously heartfelt
that he threw off his pretence of ill humour.

Later that night, as Baptiste was helping him to undress, he observed from the man's face that he seemed anxious to say something.
"What is it, Baptiste?" he asked. "Is anything the matter?"

His valet handed him his warmed nightshirt and replied with respectful enthusiasm, "Begging Monsieur's pardon, but you really
were magnificent."

"Thank you," said Vaudreuil, with a depreciatory wave of the hand.
"Thank you, Baptiste." But when he was ensconced between the
sheets, behind the drawn curtains, a smile flitted over his features.

☆   ☆   ☆

Toinette lay upon her bed, being examined by Doctor Lassone. Despite his years the physician was reputed to be a lover of the ladies,
who certainly spoilt him, and Toinette was unable to rid herself of a
feeling of embarrassment though she tried to look upon him merely as
a medical practitioner carrying out his professional duties. His cold,
searching eyes and skilful hands inspired her with a sense of discomfort mingled with a titillated curiosity; she was vaguely conscious that
he was comparing her naked body with those of other women. At the
same time she waited with almost unbearable tension for his verdict.
For some days there had been a faint dawning of hope.

Gently Lassone drew her shirt down over her abdomen and then
stepped back. She kept her eyes averted from him and did not ask any

questions, but he bowed low and said, "My most humble congratulations, Madame."

Toinette raised her head with a jerk and stared at him. She could hardly find her voice. "Can there be no doubt, Doctor?" she asked.

"There can be no doubt, Madame," he assured her, and he repeated, "My most humble congratulations."

She still did not dare to believe him. "Then I can write to Vienna?" she asked again. "I can tell Louis?" It was the first time that she had referred to the King as "Louis" in the presence of Doctor Lassone.

"There can be no doubt, Madame," he said again, infusing a little more emphasis into his tone.

When he had gone she lay for a long time with eyes closed, in a happy daze. An enormous weight had fallen from her. All her petty worries seemed washed away and there was room in her heart only for a sense of blissful fulfilment. She was more than Toinette; she was Habsburg, she was France; in her rested the past and the future of these two countries.

She lay alone for a long time. Then she rang the bell and sent for Count Mercy.

While waiting for him, she wrote a letter to her mother in a mixture of German and French. "How grateful I am to you for having given me birth," she wrote. "I could never have thought it possible that there could be such happiness in this world. I wanted to write to you a few days ago, and am now sorry that I did not do so. But I was afraid that you would grieve too deeply if my hopes had turned out to be false."

Count Mercy arrived. He had been startled when Toinette's summons reached him, for he scarcely remembered ever having received such an urgent request from her before. She must have done something alarming. Then he saw her, her face transformed, soft, strangely relaxed; she seemed about to cry. As he bent to kiss her hand, she said, "You must be the first to hear. You are my closest friend. You are Vienna." She began to speak in German. "I am going to have a child, Mercy. I am pregnant." Then she changed over to French again. "I am going to give birth to a Dauphin." She embraced the old Ambassador, who, hardened man of the world though he was, could himself scarcely restrain his tears. He was already pondering the quickest means of dispatching the news to Schoenbrunn, while Toinette went on blissfully, "You must keep a closer eye on me now. The fate of France depends on my taking great care of myself. Do you think I had better give up riding?" He was thinking, however, that precautions of a very different nature would now be necessary, precautions against the treacherous Prince Xavier whose hopes would be dashed by the prospective birth of an heir to the throne.

While the courier was making ready to carry her letter and Mercy's dispatch to Schoenbrunn, she went across to Louis's apartments, but he had gone to his workshop under the roof leaving instructions that he was on no account to be disturbed.

Standing with legs wide apart, alone with Gamain, he was hard at work. He was in no pleasant frame of mind. The Bavarian complications, and the imminent threat of war with England, filled him with a depression that he could cast off only by strenuous physical activity. Standing there in his shirt-sleeves, with breeches belt loosened and sooted countenance, he vigorously swung the hammer and banged away at the iron. Oh, if this were only Franklin! If it were only Joseph! He swung his arm and struck the metal, with a look of gloomy joy on his puffy features.

Toinette could hear the vulgar clatter from a distance. Only once before had she paid a visit to the top floor, years ago when Louis proudly brought her to inspect his workshop. She had loathed the place and had never come again. In the Lilac Coterie they made jokes and composed epigrams about Vulcan and Venus, and she herself had occasionally indulged her wit in this connexion, but the thought was far from her mind at the present moment. She pushed open the low, heavy door. And there Louis stood, with his clothes soiled and rumpled, his face, hands, and shirt covered with soot, with knitted brows and sweating copiously, just a blacksmith, not much more than an animal.

He glanced up and saw Toinette standing in the dim chamber, illuminated by the flickering light from the forge. If she had come at any other time he would no doubt have been glad to see her, though her unexpected visits were nearly always concerned with some unwelcome request. Today, however, he was absorbed in his work, and as he slowly collected his thoughts there was no room in his mind for anything but irritation and annoyance at being disturbed when he had given orders that he was to be left in peace.

"Good afternoon, Louis," said Toinette.

"What can I do for you, Madame?" he asked. "You see that I am busy," he added involuntarily, in a surly tone.

"Send your man away," she begged.

"Can I not finish what I am doing?" he demanded. "It will take me another ten minutes."

"No, Sire," she declared firmly. "I will not give you a single minute." And Gamain had to withdraw.

"What is the matter, Madame?" inquired Louis peevishly.

She gazed at him radiantly. "I have not come alone, Louis," she said.

He stared at her suspiciously. "You have brought somebody with you?" he asked.

"There are two of us here in front of you," she burst out. As he continued to stare at her stupidly, she went on, "Haven't you guessed yet?"

He racked his brains and then muttered hesitantly, "You are pregnant, Madame?"

"Yes! Yes! Yes!" she cried exultantly.

"You are really pregnant?" he asked again, still unable to grasp the fact.

"Lassone says there can be no possible doubt," she assured him.

At last he believed what she was telling him. A light spread over his face, his wide-set brown eyes blinked, his fat cheeks quivered, his little double chin trembled, he flung his hammer into the corner with a loud clatter and slapped his thigh. "We are going to have a child!" he cried. His voice cracked, he slapped his thigh once more, and then gave Toinette a resounding smack on the back with his sweaty, sooted hand. "A child!" he shouted again. "You and I, a Dauphin!" He burst into his loud guffaw, stamped up and down, broke into a dance. Seizing her by the waist he kissed her and called her by her German name, "Toni! Toni!" Then circling round her, he gazed incredulously at her voluminous skirts, pointed his thick finger at her abdomen, and said with a broad smirk, "Louis the Seventeenth."

They sat happily together for a long time, and she did not care that now her skin and clothes were covered with soot too. "You will have to look after yourself now," he warned her with an air of importance. "A bath every day. But not too hot, mark you. And not too cold. You will have to go to bed early. No excitement. No talk of war or budget. You must think only of our child, of the Dauphin."

"Yes, of course," she agreed. "I shall not need much persuading."

She told him that she had been trying to work out when it was that she had conceived. It must have been that day when he treated Doctor Franklin so brusquely and then came remorsefully to see her at the Trianon. "Don't you think it is a good omen?" she asked. "It seems to confirm that my course of action was right and pleasing in the eyes of God. Otherwise He would not have granted me such an abundance of happiness." Louis said nothing, but continued to caress her bare shoulder and make it even sootier than it was already. "And to think," she went on, "that my old uncles were watching us that night from their picture. It is all very strange and wonderful, and there must be some significance in it." Louis did not pursue the subject, but said that he would write at once to her mother. "I will write to her with my own hand, and in German," he declared proudly. "And I shall donate ten thousand livres to the poor."

Toinette then proceeded to inform her most intimate friends. Gabrielle shared her friend's happiness, though she said little. She needed time to think out the implications, both favourable and unfavourable, of the sudden tidings.

Then Toinette talked to Vaudreuil. Radiant and unembarrassed she told him that she was about to bear the Dauphin for whom France and the world were waiting. So filled was she with the significance of her news that she entirely forgot the relations between them and the promise she had given him. She regarded it as a matter of course that everyone, that literally the whole of France, would share her joy.

Vaudreuil controlled himself sufficiently to reply calmly, "My most cordial congratulations, Madame." But he was permeated with cold anger, and at that moment the last vestige of his desire for her passed away. So the fat buffoon had managed it after all. And Toinette was rejoicing at the prospect of her swelling belly like any *petite bourgeoise* who had scraped together enough sous to provide a nurse for her baby. It really was time that he got the war started so that he could quit Versailles, and he must do so before Toinette's figure became too repellent and made him ashamed of them both.

He told Désirée of his intention. He was sick of Versailles, he said, and the fuss that was going to be made about Toinette's pregnancy would make life there more intolerable than ever.

Désirée screwed her face up thoughtfully. "I suppose that Madame will now give up her idea of memorizing twenty lines of Racine a day," she murmured with mocking regret.

The tone in which she said this reminded Vaudreuil forcibly of the six plays he had been preparing to produce at the Trianon. There were still four to come, and each of them contained a part which suited him down to the ground. "Well," he replied, "things won't go so quickly as all that. I think, Désirée, that you will still be able to coach Toinette for a while."

Maria Theresa's reaction to the joyful news became known at Versailles within a remarkably short time. The courier from Vienna brought three letters, one for Toinette, overflowing with touching sentiments of affection and happiness; one for Louis, couched in dignified terms and offering heartfelt congratulations; one for Count Mercy, filled with apprehension. "I must tell you frankly," she wrote to her old friend and confidant, "that I am deeply worried about both mother and child. In a country where freethinkers are allowed to flourish as they do in France, the people do not shrink from the blackest crimes. I fear the intrigues of Prince Xavier and that Italian wife of his. If I were not consoled, my dear Mercy, by the knowledge that you are at hand to help my daughter and look after her welfare, I should be even more beset by anxiety. I try to forget the numerous

horrifying misdeeds that have stained the annals of France and place
my trust in God's kindly providence."

Two days later the Empress wrote a further letter to Toinette containing advice on both prenatal and postnatal hygiene. "Do everything
the doctor tells you," she exhorted. "Infants must not be swaddled too
tightly or kept too warm. And above all, look round straightway for a
good, healthy wet-nurse. You will not find one in Paris, and it will be
difficult even in the country, owing to the corruptness of French
morals."

It was assumed generally at Versailles that Toinette's influence in
political matters would now increase, and consequently suppliants for
favour focused their attention more than ever on the two emissaries
of the House of Habsburg, Count Mercy and the Abbé Vermond. At
his *lever* the Abbé's dressing-room was more crowded with dignitaries
than before. When the Marquis d'Aubespine called to entreat his good
offices in connection with certain negotiations then pending with Tuscany, Vermond condescended to receive his visitor while sitting in his
bath and the Marquis did not even appear to be surprised at the unusual *venue*. The Abbé thought of his father, the little tradesman of
Sens, and was sorry that he had not lived to see this day.

☆   ☆   ☆

Voltaire, perhaps in order to numb his sense of remorse at not having returned to Ferney, worked with redoubled zeal. He sorely missed
his faithful secretary Wagnière, but, setting his lips firmly and drinking a greater quantity of coffee than usual, he wrote and dictated without intermission.

Not only was he engaged on a tragedy, *Agathocle,* for which the
Théâtre français was waiting and which still wanted a number of
scenes, but he was busy on a new plan of far more ambitious scope.

Voltaire and the French language were indissolubly linked. It was
the tool of his trade, the soil from which he drew his nourishment, the
only mistress of whom he had never wearied. He had proposed to the
Academy that the out-of-date *Dictionnaire* of the French language
should be completely revised, a suggestion that was received very luke-
warmly since it would be a thankless task demanding long and concentrated labour.

Realizing that his plan could never come to successful fruition if
these gentlemen set to work with such dubious enthusiasm, Voltaire
began to prepare a manifesto in which he sought to explain the important function that the modernized *Dictionnaire* he had in mind
would fulfil in the life of the nation. He also demonstrated the method
to be employed, and with a view to providing examples, he himself

started to work on the difficult and multifarious items included under the letter *A*. He wrote with passion, for it was his aim to inspire even the dull and the sluggish with enthusiasm for the vigour and elegance of the French language. He informed the Academy that he would read his manifesto on the revision of the *Dictionnaire* at the meeting to be held on May 11.

When the day came, however, he felt too weak to go out and had to retire to bed, so the reading was postponed for a week.

By the following morning, May 12, his condition had worsened. His servant Morand wanted to call in Doctor Tronchin, but the sick man refused to allow this. He did not want to face the old physician whose wise advice he had disregarded. Meanwhile his friend, the aged Duc de Richelieu, came to see him, and when he saw Voltaire writhing in pain he recommended a certain opiate that he had himself found helpful in similar circumstances. Voltaire took a large dose, but the only result was that his pains increased. He fell into a kind of delirium and called for Wagnière.

"Wagnière is not in Paris," Madame Denis informed him gently. "You sent him to Ferney."

But Voltaire continued to cry, "Wagnière! Wagnière! Why don't you come?"

They had at last to summon Tronchin, who gave him an antidote to the opiate he had taken. When Voltaire had regained consciousness, he murmured sadly, "You were right, my friend, I should have gone back to Ferney." As Tronchin was leaving he told Madame Denis and Villette that there was no hope. Voltaire had but two or three weeks more to live.

On May 17 the Academy inquired whether it could count upon Voltaire's being able to give his reading on the following day. "Ask them for another week," he said. "I shall be ready on the twenty-fifth."

On May 25 Tronchin announced that Voltaire could not live the week out.

☆　　☆　　☆

Voltaire's relatives made every effort to ensure that he should be accorded the solemn burial for the sake of which he had been prepared to accept such humiliation. In order to avoid the issuance of instructions by the Church authorities that he was not to be interred in holy ground they kept his condition secret.

Meanwhile Voltaire's nephew, the Abbé Mignot, who was titulary incumbent of the Abbey of Scellières, was negotiating confidentially with Monsieur de Tersac, the Dean of Saint-Sulpice, begging him to dispense the last consolations of religion to the dying man, who had after all made a Christian confession of faith. The Dean replied stiffly that he had already expressed his dissatisfaction with the so-called confession of faith submitted to him. It was therefore impossible for him either to grant the dying man the last consolations or to consent to Christian burial. The Abbé Mignot replied that this was a very austere and perhaps narrow-minded conception of their religion, and Monsieur de Tersac would be called upon to justify it before the Archbishop and the Supreme Tribunal. "I assure you," he said, "that I shall appeal to these authorities."

"As you wish, Monsieur l'Abbé," the Dean rejoined curtly.

Mignot then turned to the amiable and simple-minded though crafty Abbé Gaultier. Perhaps the latter could extract from the dying man a more comprehensive and precise declaration that would meet the demands of the Church. Gaultier promised to do his best.

As soon as Mignot had left him, however, the Dean of Saint-Sulpice recalled to mind the considerable and painful stir that had been excited when burial was refused to the actress Adrienne Lecouvreur. He feared that if an unfavourable wind should blow up from free-thinking quarters the Archbishop might leave him in the lurch, and he began to regret his firmness. He requested the Abbé Mignot to call upon him once more.

Mignot informed him that Gaultier was going to make another attempt to obtain a more detailed confession from Voltaire. The Dean was silent for a while, then he politely announced that though he was forced by clear and unambiguous precepts of the Church to refuse Monsieur de Voltaire Christian interment within the precincts of his own authority, he would refrain from exercising his right to retain the corpse.

"Does that imply that I may arrange for honourable burial elsewhere?" asked Mignot.

"That is a matter beyond my jurisdiction," replied the Dean.

"But you grant me permission to remove the corpse from Paris?" insisted Mignot.

"Yes, Monsieur l'Abbé," the Dean agreed.

"Would you be so kind," requested Mignot, "as to let me have your sanction in writing?"

"If you wish it," said the Dean a little touchily, and he wrote out the required licence.

Reflecting that the Abbé Gaultier had already had a modicum of success with Voltaire, and apprehensive lest the simple but crafty priest might after all succeed in extorting a sensational confession, since dying men were wont to talk and luck was sometimes with the stupid, the Dean decided himself to make a final attempt at converting the great arch-heretic. In very large letters he wrote the words, "I,

Voltaire, believe in the divinity of Christ." He proposed to hold this document before the eyes of the dying man and would be satisfied if it were signed only with the initial *V* in the presence of witnesses. Hastily summoning Mignot and Gaultier, he drove with them to the house where Voltaire was occupied in dying. "Merely the initial *V*," the Dean explained to his companions on the way. "One down stroke, and one up stroke. Let no one say the Church is not tolerant."

Voltaire himself had passed far beyond such worries. Pain clutched his entrails, burned him, twisted and stabbed him. Sometimes he plunged into merciful unconsciousness, but never for long. Doctor Tronchin wondered whether he should administer an opiate to ease his friend's death. On the other hand, he thought that a man who throughout his life had willingly accepted every experience, whether good or ill, would not wish to miss his last hours however grievous. Tronchin also hoped that the intolerable pain might at last induce the scoffing atheist to reveal remorse at the foolish way he had spent his life. Yet when the agony abated, there was no sign of tortured regret on the withered old visage. On the contrary, with disappointment and uneasy astonishment Tronchin gathered from the mumbled words issuing from Voltaire's lips that the latter, instead of recalling his sins, was conversing in a tone of cynical humour with dead friends, making mocking observations about dead enemies, or composing an article on the term *ad patres* for the *Dictionnaire*. This term was employed with reference to one who was being or had been gathered to his fathers, that is to say, who was dying or was dead.

When the Dean and the two Abbés entered the room, there were assembled at the bedside Doctor Tronchin and Morand, the Marquis and Marquise de Villette and Madame Denis.

Stepping up to the bed, the Dean said, "Monsieur de Voltaire, the time has come. Do you repent? Do you believe in the divinity of Jesus Christ?"

The dying man looked at him with unclouded eyes, but said nothing. The Dean bent lower and Voltaire raised an incredibly thin arm in an effort that seemed to take his last ounce of strength.

The Dean smiled, thinking the heretic raised his arm in greeting and repentance. Softly, but very clearly, he repeated, "Monsieur de Voltaire, do you believe in the divinity of Jesus Christ?"

This time, however, the arm moved in a gesture that could not be taken for anything but an attempt to ward off the questioner. Then Voltaire sank back with a harsh whisper, "Let me die in peace."

As he left the room the Dean muttered grimly to the Marquis, "Why did the Abbé Mignot interfere? Why did you invite the simple-minded Gaultier? If you only had left it to me I could have arranged it easily."

The members of the household stood at Voltaire's bedside for a further two hours. He continued to ask for Wagnière. At four minutes past eleven he whispered to his servant, "Adieu, my dear Morand, I am about to die." At thirteen minutes past eleven he drew his last breath.

With him there went uncounted unborn dramas, epics, and brilliant essays; there went an intelligence of flashing keenness, a boundless impulse to mockery and a mastery of the art, an unconquerable and naïve urge to self-assertion; there went a mind that in many small things was beyond measure egoistically deceitful and in all great things was beyond measure militantly sincere; there went a being compounded of paltry avarice and heedless extravagance, capable of shameless greed and sublime beneficence; there went a vast knowledge and an astounding capacity for building bridges from one intellectual sphere to another; there went a burning desire to disseminate enlightenment throughout the world, a flaming hatred of intolerance, superstition, ignorance, and injustice; there went a mind fashioned to radiate its influence into the farthest distance and to the most distant ages. At thirteen minutes past eleven on the thirtieth of May all this shrank into a gnome-like corpse.

While this shrunken gnome-like thing could still reason and write, it had written as follows: *I knew a man who was firmly convinced that when a bee is dead it ceases to hum. He compared a human being to a musical instrument that gives forth no further sound when once it is broken. He asserted that a human being, like all other animals and like plants, is manifestly created to be and then not to be. And when this man had grown as old as Democritus, he behaved like Democritus and laughed at everything.*

Now this man reasoned no longer, and laughed no longer, and he no longer cared what was happening to him.

There were, however, others who did care. The Dean of Saint-Sulpice had considered it his duty to report at once to the Archbishop. The Archbishop surmised that Voltaire's relatives would carry his body to Ferney, and the Bishop in whose diocese Ferney lay was instructed that even at Ferney Christian burial was to be prohibited.

The Abbé Mignot had foreseen this contingency, and had thought out a plan whereby his deceased uncle would be assured of the honourable interment for which he had wished and the Archbishop cheated of his revenge on the heretic. Voltaire's death was therefore kept secret. A trusted surgeon and two assistants embalmed the body, rouged the cheeks, and gave it the appearance of life. It was placed in a travelling-coach by night and seated in a comfortable position. Looking as though he were asleep, the great Voltaire was conveyed in stealthy silence through the streets of Paris and so out of the city that he had entered amid the plaudits of the multitude but a few months before. With him there went a servant, who saw to it that he remained in an upright position, and the Abbé Mignot. Speeding through the night in a southeasterly direction, they at last reached Romilly on the Seine, some hundred and ten miles away, where the Abbey of Scellières, of which Mignot was titular head, was situated.

At Scellières the Abbé explained to the Prior of the monastery that in accordance with his uncle's wishes he was conveying the latter's body to Ferney for interment, but it appeared that the corpse was not likely to withstand the long journey. He therefore requested permission to provide his uncle with a last resting-place in the church. The flattered Prior, after having glanced at the confession of faith that had been made in the presence of the Abbé Gaultier, gave his sanction without more ado and the necessary preparations were put in hand. During the afternoon the body lay in state in the choir of the church and masses for the dead were sung. During the night the body remained in the church, illumined by torches and guarded by reverent watchers. On the next morning, the second of June, the remains of Voltaire were laid in sacred earth in the presence of numerous ecclesiastical and secular dignitaries with all the pomp of religion, precisely as he had planned and arranged it in the childish and mischievous spirit of his last months.

Three hours after the ceremony the Prior of Scellières received a letter from his superior, the Bishop of Troyes, instructing him that in no circumstances was the body of Voltaire to be furnished with Christian burial.

☆   ☆   ☆

Louis firmly approved the Church's refusal to bury the heretic. The freethinkers, and especially Voltaire himself, had praised Tolerance with many high-sounding phrases, but Louis was not allured by the sweet babble, which only masked with fine words the crime of being lukewarm. He was determined to show an iron Intolerance. The throne must not lag behind the altar.

It was his wish, he sternly informed Lenoir, the Chief of Police, that no honour should be shown to the deceased heretic. The journals were forbidden to publish obituaries, or even to mention the fact of his death. The Academy was instructed that there must be no attempt to hold a meeting in his memory, the theatres that his plays must not be performed, and the schools that his works must not be read.

Yet these measures met with little success. The people of Paris refused to be deprived of their right to honour the memory of the greatest genius that France had produced during the century, and the attempts to outlaw the dead man enraged the citizens. Hundreds of pamphlets appeared in the streets scorning and reviling the authorities who tried to kill immortality. Never before had Voltaire's works been read with such burning interest, and for the very reason that they were proscribed thousands of youths learned by heart during these weeks the words of the prayer with which Voltaire concluded his *Treatise on Tolerance:*

To Thee, God of all creatures, of all worlds, and of all ages, I address my petition. Thou hast not given us hearts so that we may hate one another, and hands that we may slay one another. Grant that the trifling differences in the clothes with which we cover our frail bodies, in the inadequate tongues we speak, in our absurd customs, in our imperfect laws, in our meaningless convictions, grant that all these trifling distinctions which appear so vastly important to us and are so insignificant in Thy eyes, grant that they may not become tokens of hatred and persecution. Grant that men may learn to abominate and outlaw tyranny over souls as they abominate and outlaw robbery and violence. And if wars may not be avoided, grant at least that we may not hate and tear one another in the midst of peace, but that we may employ our existence, in a thousand tongues yet in one united feeling, from Siam to California, in praising Thy goodness which has given us the brief moment that we call life.

The priests, for their part, knew no bounds in their attacks on the dead man. "In his abominable frenzy," wrote one of them, "this shameless blasphemer dubbed himself the personal enemy of the Saviour. He plunged into the mire, wallowed in the mire, revelled in the mire. His imagination was kindled by the flames of Hell, and it was from Hell that he derived the strength to stride through the realms of evil unto their furthermost frontiers."

Though the people of Paris were forbidden to honour openly the memory of Voltaire, the rest of the world made up for the omission. In the United States of America, orators and newspapers celebrated the man whose ideas had contributed so much to the establishment of their Republic. In Petersburg the Empress Catherine mourned Voltaire's passing in terms that revealed her profound sorrow. "Now that he is dead," she lamented, "the world is void of intellect and of true wit. All the thoughts of which I am capable," she confessed, "I owe to him." King Frederick of Prussia, who was President of his own Academy, arranged a memorial meeting and himself delivered the oration. It breathed contempt for the narrow-minded, bigoted priests of France and the news of it spread throughout the length and breadth of Europe. Frederick also ordered that in all the Catholic churches of his kingdom masses should be said for the dead writer and philosopher.

Sooner than could have been expected, Versailles was forced to raise its ban. When the *Théâtre français* performed his posthumous tragedy *Agathocle,* the audience appeared dressed in mourning, refrained from applause, and dispersed in silence. It was the same when the Academy met to honour his memory. Thousands of people dressed in mourning assembled in the courtyard of the Louvre and thronged the surrounding streets, standing bare-headed and silent in the rain while d'Alembert pronounced the eulogy.

Chapter Two

THE VETO

✻ ★ ✻

AFTER Voltaire's death, Pierre set about the publication of the *Opera Omnia* with consuming energy. A *Société Littéraire, Typographique et Philosophique* was founded, which consisted solely of Pierre Beaumarchais. This *Société* purchased type from the famous printing house of John Baskerville in England, enlisted the services of particularly skilled type-founders whom he brought from Holland, and set up paper mills in the Rhineland. There could be no thought of printing the works of Voltaire on French soil, so the *Société Littéraire, Typographique et Philosophique* leased from the Margrave of Baden the deserted little township of Kehl on the French border and there it established its printing presses. It amused Pierre hugely to print the works of the arch-heretic under the walls of the French fortress of Strasbourg.

It was not long before attacks on the enterprise were launched from all sides. The Prince-Archbishop of Strasbourg, Cardinal Rohan, celebrated throughout France for his worldly way of life, conjured his "cousin," the Margrave, not to tolerate upon his territory the activities of so dubious a character as the notorious Beaumarchais. He feared that the souls of his pious flock in Strasbourg might be placed in mortal danger if the poisonous writings of the deceased heretic were permitted to be printed in such close proximity to their city. A judge of the Supreme Court in Paris issued a militant pamphlet entitled *Lament and Weep!* in which the dead Voltaire was denounced as Antichrist triumphant, for whom his chief apostle, Pierre Beaumarchais, was now engaged in setting up a throne.

The publication of the *Opera Omnia* was in itself an expensively risky and complicated venture, but Pierre's other business commitments were becoming no less involved and speculative. The forests and sawmills left to him by his first wife had been an inducement to establish ship-building yards, and in order to finance these ship-building yards he had founded a discount bank, which in turn had to be financed by a company floated for the purpose of manufacturing modern fire engines as well as other enterprises of a similar nature. On the conclusion of the Franco-American Alliance the shipping offices controlled by the firm of Hortalez had undertaken considerable deliveries and transports for the Government, particularly to the West Indies. Pierre's other businesses too, his sawmills, his ship-building yards, his discount bank, were expanding in all directions. The only man who could find his way about the entangled ramifications was Maigron, who informed his chief in a dry and gloomy tone of voice that during the past three years the turnover in all his businesses had amounted to the sum of 54,044,191 livres.

Pierre told himself that an entrepreneur through whose hands such vast sums were passing could not afford to be petty in his everyday dealings, and he did not stint himself in helping others either with money or with advice. He granted loans to impoverished aristocrats, provided inventors with the means to exploit their patents, assisted people whom he believed to be unjustly persecuted, procured permission for the Calvinist merchants of Bordeaux and La Rochelle to become members of the Chambers of Commerce, accorded his patronage to gifted actresses of the *Théâtre français* and the *Italiens,* and supported a petition of the Prince of Nassau to the ecclesiastical authorities for the legalization of his marriage with a Polish divorcée.

The greatest of all his enterprises, America, continued not only to bring him no profit, but to enhance his indebtedness, though acknowledgment of his efforts was not lacking. A Mr. William Carmichael, evidently a distinguished American statesman, inquired what had happened to Paul Theveneau. Mr. Theveneau, he wrote, had succeeded in convincing him that the claims of the firm of Hortalez were entirely justified, and he proposed to exert all his influence to see that they were met. A certain Mr. Thomas Jefferson—whose name seemed faintly familiar to Pierre in connexion with the Declaration of Independence—wrote to express his sincere regret that the firm of Hortalez should be suffering loss through the tardiness of the Congress and the devaluation of the American currency. Monsieur de Beaumarchais had deserved particularly well of America and had earned the deepest respect of its citizens by his efforts to further the rights of man, by his genius, and by his literary achievements.

Pierre read these letters with delight, and was profoundly touched that Paul's activities should still be bearing fruit even after his death.

Lenormant continued to maintain friendly relations with Pierre and was a frequent visitor to his house. As Désirée's successor he had chosen another actress of the *Théâtre français,* the youthful and pretty Sophie Olivier, with whom Pierre had for a short time been on ardent terms. Doctor Lassone, too, had been an admirer of hers, though an unsuccessful one, and the denial of her favours to the physician, as well as the fact that she had granted them to Pierre, increased Lenormant's pride in being her acknowledged lover. When Mademoiselle Olivier set her heart upon playing roles that were the prerogative of Désirée, he did what he could to assist her in attaining her ambition.

As far as business affairs were concerned, Pierre and Charlot remained on the same footing of bantering amiability with its slight undertone of menace. Now and then Lenormant would inquire in ironic sympathy when Pierre expected to receive any considerable payments from Philadelphia, and Pierre would reply with assurance, "In six months at the most."

"Your months have many days," Lenormant would comment, with a shadow of an ominous smile on his lips, whereupon Pierre would assert, "You have yourself admitted that nobody has predicted more clearly and accurately than I have myself the course of American events. Do you really think that a man with such keen judgment in political matters can be completely blind where his own business is at stake?"

"It has been known to occur," suggested Charlot with a pensive smile. Pierre's arguments only served to confirm his conviction that the firm of Hortalez would fall into his hands in due course.

When Pierre told Désirée of these conversations with Lenormant, she listened calmly. She understood the ways of the world and took it as a matter of course that Pierre should wish to retain Lenormant's friendship though she herself had broken with him. It was she herself who had been foolish in rejecting Lenormant's offer for Pierre's sake. There had been no doubt in her mind at the time that such an opportunity could never recur, and that she was turning an influential friend into an implacable enemy, yet she would do it again if necessary. She shook her head at her own odd behaviour. Wont as she was to draw a sharp line of distinction between life and the theatre, it seemed to her childish to experience in actuality the emotions that she expressed so convincingly on the stage. She had never been prepared to admit that her affection for Pierre was other than good companionship with an occasional titillation of the senses, but now she was being compelled, with a certain amused bewilderment, to recognize that there was more to it than that.

There was something ridiculous about her Pierrot, with his homely love for his wife Thérèse and his boundless conceit. He had done great historic deeds, he had written dramas that could vie with Voltaire's. But not content with allowing others to praise his achievements, he insisted on blowing his own trumpet to the full extent of his lungs. The world found it ridiculous, and the world was right. His extravagance, too, was absurd, his ostentation, centering around

worthy, bourgeois Thérèse. And most absurd of all was the fact that
his whole way of life was nothing more than an eternal, gilded bankruptcy.

For all Désirèe's keen-sightedness, however, she was helpless. She
never said "Au revoir" to Pierre without in the next moment longing
for him to be back again with all his weaknesses and strutting poses.

☆   ☆   ☆

Franklin watched as his new secretary, Monsieur de la Motte,
sorted the mail. Besides many letters in French, there was a fresh
post from America.

There were numerous communications of a trifling nature, some
melancholy, some comic, all of them wearisome. A variety of poets
extolled the cause of American freedom in verse, both rhymed and
unrhymed, and each of them expected a reward of anything from
two to ten livres in accordance with the amount of artistic effort
that had been expended. The Duke of Burgundy complained in
courteous though vigorous terms of the difficulty he was experiencing,
owing to the latent state of war, in obtaining certain English hounds
without which he could take no pleasure in his hunting. He hoped
that Doctor Franklin, who was no doubt still in touch with influential
personages in England, would be able to assist him in his predica-
ment. A physicist named Jean-Paul Marat enclosed a confused though
apparently not uninteresting essay on the nature of fire and electricity,
which he requested Franklin to read with a view to recommending
it to the notice of the proper quarters. A Dutch philosopher submitted a plan for the establishment of permanent peace. A Swiss
judge offered to draft a model constitution for the thirteen United
States on the lines of the Swiss Confederation with its thirteen can-
tons. Monsieur de la Guarde, a retirêd colonel, forwarded for consideration a project whereby a thousand hussars, disguised as tourists,
would be able to capture a hostile city. The French, unfortunately,
had scruples about employing such a bold scheme, but a young nation
such as the Americans would have no difficulty in putting it into
execution.

De la Motte then handed Franklin a booklet that had come from an
unknown gentleman in Philadelphia named Ritchie. It was a biography of the Reverend William Smith, written by the latter's son.
The Reverend William Smith had been a leader of the party of
landed proprietors who were hostile to Franklin, and he and Smith
had had frequent sharp differences in which the late clergyman had
not refrained from personal invective. He had, for example, asserted
without the slightest proof that Franklin had stolen his ideas on

electricity from Ebenezer Kinnersley. Franklin had controlled his
temper and conducted himself with philosophic calm, but on one
occasion, when the Reverend William Smith published a sanctimoni-
ous brochure on the blessings of charity and kindness, he had been
unable to restrain himself from applying to this publication some lines
of the poet Whitehead:

> *Full many a peevish, envious, slanderous elf*
> *Is in his works benevolence itself.*
> *For all mankind unknown his bosom heaves,*
> *He only injures those with whom he lives.*

Franklin turned the pages of the dutiful son's biography and saw
that Smith junior had not pulled his punches. *Doctor Benjamin
Franklin,* he read, *has told the world in poetry what, in his judgment,
my ancestor was. His venerable shade will excuse me if I tell in prose
what Doctor Smith was not. He was no almanack maker, nor quack,
nor chimney-doctor, nor soap boiler, nor printer's devil, neither was
he a deist; and all his children were born in wedlock. If his descend-
ants cannot point to his statue over a library, they have not the
mortification of hearing him daily accused of having been a fornicator,
a hypocrite, and an infidel.*

De la Motte read out the covering letter of the unknown Mr.
Ritchie, who was apparently also a clergyman. With malicious solicitude Mr. Ritchie drew Franklin's attention to the fact that the
asseverations of the younger Mr. Smith were unfortunately not
exaggerated. There were indeed disagreeable rumours to be met with
throughout America concerning the epicurean mode of living of the
envoy of the United States in Paris at a time when his compatriots
at Valley Forge went cold and hungry. It was being said that Doctor
Franklin dwelt in a magnificent palace where he revelled in the
delights of a groaning board, that his house swarmed with servants,
and that he drove abroad in a four-horse carriage. He was furthermore alleged to be surrounded night and day by ladies whose manners
and morals were not compatible with American views on virtue. Mr.
Ritchie himself, the letter continued, was fully persuaded that this
was all mere lying gossip, but in the interests of the United States,
of virtue, and of liberty, it was very much to be desired that Doctor
Franklin should offer tangible proof that there was no basis of truth
in the evil reports.

The hollow absurdity of this letter was enhanced by the flat tone,
with its slight French accent, in which de la Motte raced through it,
but Franklin was hardly listening. It was not the first communication
of the kind he had received, and even in the reports that reached him

from sincere friends about the atmosphere at home there was much talk of the increasing hostility and mistrust with which he was viewed. More and more of his fellow countrymen were unable to forgive him for being the father of the traitor William Franklin, for the respect in which he was held by foreigners, for adapting himself to the ways of the French, and for not keeping the Sabbath holy.

"What shall we reply to the Reverend Mr. Ritchie?" inquired de la Motte when he had reached the end of the letter. "I think, my friend," said Franklin, "that I can leave that to you. Let us thank him politely, but in noncommittal terms, for his amiable advice."

Young William entered. He had been in Paris interviewing the sculptor Houdon, who had asked Franklin to sit for a bust he wished to present to the Americans on the occasion of the second anniversary of the Declaration of Independence. Franklin did not know a great deal about art, but he realized that the great sculptor's offer could not be ignored. A bust by Houdon would make an impression even in America.

William reported that the sculptor had received him very warmly and that they had arranged times for the various sittings. Houdon did not think he would need very many. William had also brought back two or three volumes that had arrived for Franklin at the bookshop, as well as a print that had been on sale since the previous day. It was an engraving of Voltaire's tomb. On the one side Ignorance, represented by a vigorous, buxom female with bandaged eyes, was thrusting forward; gigantic bat's wings sprouted from her shoulders and in her right hand she brandished a flaming torch. On the other side of the tomb stood figures representing the enlightened intelligence of the four corners of the world, and that of America bore the features of Franklin. He was very sparsely clothed, but wore his fur cap and was rather furry generally, and in his hand he held something that might have been either a switch or a palm-branch which he was lifting threateningly against the buxom lady. With a humorous sigh Franklin gazed at the robust arms and thighs with which the artist had endowed him, and he rubbed his gouty foot.

"We must put it in the portfolio," said William to de la Motte.

"What portfolio?" asked Franklin. "What have you two been hatching out now?"

The secretary looked with an inquiring grin at William, who replied, "Well, I think the portfolio is full enough to be shown to Grandfather."

Contrary to Franklin's expectations, the two young men got on very well together, and he himself had acquired an affection for the French secretary, whom his colleagues had insisted on engaging for him. De la Motte was evidently well trained in the methods of work favoured by John Adams and Arthur Lee, and he had taken little pains to conceal his astonishment at what appeared to him to be slovenly indolence on Franklin's part. Gradually, however, he had come to realize the sagacity that lay behind Franklin's calm and apparently remiss way of setting about things, and to appreciate his quiet, humorous kindliness. Abandoning his air of passive opposition, he never missed an opportunity of letting the Doctor see in what profound respect he held him.

With portentous pride the two young men brought along a large portfolio and placed it on the table.

It contained numerous pictures of Franklin, some good, some bad, some complimentary, some otherwise. He appeared alternately as a complacent bourgeois, a mythological hero, a crafty man of affairs, an epicure, and a philosopher, but they all appeared to be designed to do him honour.

There were the portraits by Duplessis, by Madame Filleul, by Charles-Nicholas Cochin, by Greuze, by Jean-Martin Renaud, and by Carmontelle. There were the grave, aloof portrait by de l'Hospital and the brilliant, strangely attractive one with the twisted mouth and the inscription *The American Socrates* by Fragonard: Most of them were framed in verses or had verses printed below, usually of a very florid nature. There was also the engraving by Martinet, for which Dubourg had supplied the accompanying lines of poetry. Franklin shook his head again as he read the exuberant praise: *He wrested the lightning from the sky; in the country of the savages he caused the arts to flourish. In the forefront of her sages America has placed him. Had he been born in Hellas he would have been counted among the gods.* Well, well, mused Franklin, the late Dubourg was a little inclined to exaggeration.

William and de la Motte took one picture after another out of the portfolio to show him, and after the portraits came the symbolical and allegorical representations. One woodcut depicted the globe, with America clearly marked and above it a bust of Franklin being crowned with a wreath by Liberty. On another print was Diogenes holding his lantern in his left hand and pointing with his right to a handsomely framed portrait of the *man* whom he had been seeking all his life and had now at last discovered, and behold, the *man* was none other than Benjamin Franklin.

This touching if rather childish collection had evidently been made by the two young men to offset their indignation at the stupid ingratitude of his fellow countrymen, and if they had chosen this particular day to present it to the Doctor it was because the latest intelligence from America had demonstrated the foolish spite with which he was being rewarded for his reprehensible audacity in being a great man.

As the Doctor looked upon the pictures his heart warmed within him at the thought of the devotion with which he was regarded by the younger generation, the younger generation of America and of France.

His grandfather had now seen enough, suggested William. It was time for him to rest. The other envoys were expected during the afternoon in order to discuss the latest dispatches from home.

Franklin, however, did not feel tired, and instead of lying down he proceeded, as soon as he was alone again, to reread a letter that had arrived some time ago from his friend Ingenhousz in Vienna. Doctor Ingenhousz informed him of some new experiments in which he had been engaged, and in contrast to the scientific ingenuity of these experiments he spoke of the sluggish obtuseness of the masses. He also referred to the war with Prussia which, to his pain, he considered to be inevitable.

As he read this letter once more, Franklin thought again of the Reverend Mr. Ritchie and the deceased Doctor Smith, of Arthur Lee and his own son William, the traitor. Sitting down at his desk he replied to his friend Ingenhousz: *The rapid progress true science now makes occasions my regretting sometimes that I was born so soon. It is impossible to imagine the height to which may be carried the power of man over matter. We may perhaps learn to deprive large masses of their gravity, and give them absolute levity, for the sake of easy transport. Agriculture may diminish its labour and double its produce; all diseases may by sure means be prevented or cured, not excepting even that of old age, and our lives lengthened at pleasure. O that moral science were in as fair a way of improvement, that men would cease to be wolves to one another, and that human beings would at length learn what they now improperly call humanity.*

☆   ☆   ☆

The conference that afternoon with John Adams, the brothers Lee, and Ralph Izard took place in the "Brown Library," which was the room that Franklin found least to his taste. It was used for storing the files and such books as he had no particular use for, and for some weeks there had been hanging on its walls a picture which the painter Prunier had presented to the envoys. This work of art depicted General Washington standing on a battlefield that was strewn with corpses and cannon under a blood-red sun. The Doctor did not like it, but he had allowed it to be put up here since otherwise his colleagues would have written to Philadelphia complaining that owing to his jealousy of General Washington he was permitting gifts from French artists to gather the dust in a lumber-room, thereby not only affronting the patriotic feelings of his compatriots, but offering a gratuitous insult to the art of their Gallic allies.

The envoys appeared with worried faces. The winter had not started off so well as might have been expected after the great victories that had fallen to American arms. The official report from the Congress, couched though it was in dry and cautious terms, was grave in tone, and the confirmatory information contained in private communications revealed even more clearly the seriousness of the situation.

In many parts of the country people were refusing to accept the paper currency issued by the Congress and individual States. The producers who brought their goods to market, so Mrs. Abigail Adams had written to her husband, simply rejected the Congress money, and Ralph Izard had heard that his father had had to pay a silver shilling and three paper dollars for a pair of slippers.

Worst of all, the Army was deteriorating owing to the increased cost of living. Franklin had received a lurid account from an Army surgeon of his acquaintance, Doctor Waldo. Supplies were not reaching the troops and they were getting no pay. At their wretched winter quarters in Valley Forge the men were cold and hungry, and they were unable to sleep, since there were no beds and few blankets. They were without soap, but in any case there was nothing to wash, for they were going about in rags. Not many of them had boots even. They were being ravaged by epidemics, but there were no drugs. At Valley Forge there were only famine and frost, sickness and death, mutiny and desertion. And the Congress left them in the lurch. No help came from the Congress.

Arthur Lee defended the men in Philadelphia. "The fault lies here," he declared. "It lies in France. A few millions are all we need, but the French are as miserly as they are rich."

This brought them to the purpose of their meeting, for the burden of all the letters that had come from America was the need for money. Once they had good French gold in the treasury, say five and twenty million livres, there would be an end to all their difficulties. It was a considerable sum, to be sure, and it was left to the discretion of the envoys how much they should ask for and when they should ask for it, but money they must have. Unless a loan was forthcoming they were lost. The sober members of the Congress waxed poetical as they tried to put into words the urgent need for a loan. They thirsted for it "as a parched field thirsts for rain," they panted for it "as the hart panteth after the water brooks."

It was clear that the nature of the French alliance was not properly grasped in America, or at least that they were reluctant to understand its significance. When the news of the signing had arrived, everyone had breathed a sigh of relief and it had been celebrated with

pompous speeches and rejoicing, but—and this was all too evident
from the reports—there was a strong party in the Congress which
thought it humiliating that they should have been compelled to seek
the assistance of the French. These gentlemen both overestimated and
underestimated the importance of the pact. While pouring scorn on
their new allies, they expected from them the impossible.

In Franklin's opinion it would be unwise at the present juncture
to press for a loan. There had been a number of minor incidents
recently which had led to the perceptible cooling of French enthusiasm
for America. The Chevalier de Buysson, who had gone to enlist in
the United States Army, had returned in a mood of disillusionment
with many stories to tell of the ridiculous and vexatious behaviour of
the Congress, the soldiers, and the citizens generally. A number of
wealthy Frenchmen had offered funds for the creation of a Chair of
French at Yale College and the establishment of a French library, but
the President of the College, Doctor Stiles, had yielded to the persuasion of influential Puritan clergymen and had hesitated to accept
the papistical offer, to the deep annoyance of the would-be donors.
And above all, Franklin had been reliably informed that the King
was seriously disturbed at the unexpectedly high expenditure on armaments and hardly in a frame of mind to sanction any considerable
loan to the "rebels." Franklin realized, however, that his fellow envoys
would refuse to listen to arguments of this kind. Their nerves were
on edge, and he feared that their feelings would overcome their sense
of logic.

The Lees launched out into complaints about the conduct of the
French Ministers. These gentlemen, they asserted, had turned deaf
ears to discreet hints as to the enhanced value of a loan in the present
emergency. Such an attitude had been positively insulting. It was a
good thing they were now in a position to state that official instructions had come from Philadelphia to apply for a loan.

"We can now force these questionable allies of ours," declared
Izard triumphantly, "to say yes or no without equivocation."

Arthur Lee commented frowningly, "It is France's duty to grant
us this loan, but I shall not be surprised if the Government tries to
shirk its obligations. After all, the French have broken their treaties
with England by the very fact that they have recognized us and
signed the alliance. A nation like that will not boggle at betraying us
too if it suits their book."

Franklin found it difficult to control his temper at such a perverse
display of logic. In order to preserve his calm he fixed his eyes on
the painting that hung on the opposite wall and tried to concentrate
on an interpretation of its symbolism. What sort of a sun was that
above Washington's head? Was it rising or setting? The painter's

intention was by no means clear. He must remember to ask Monsieur Prunier about it.

Slowly he proceeded to invalidate the illogical arguments of his colleagues. "I would beg you to bear in mind, gentlemen," he urged, "that the alliance was concluded between unequal partners—on the one hand, a nation of twenty-five millions, with a powerful fleet, the best army in Europe, and a diplomacy celebrated for its flexibility and skill; on the other, a country of less than three millions, half its territory occupied by the enemy, possessing no commerce, no industry and only a weak Government. It can hardly be asserted that Vergennes was exploiting the unfavourable situation in which we found ourselves. You must concede, gentlemen, that we would have accepted less advantageous terms than he has given us. In my view, France has treated us well, even generously."

Arthur Lee protested vigorously; France, he insisted, had entered into the alliance from purely selfish motives, and soon the envoys were engaged in a general discussion of the French character and French politics. Izard and the two Lees were suspicious of everything that France did, seeing in her actions nothing but greed, empty promises, pretence, and fraud.

Franklin replied that he was firmly convinced of the genuineness of the French people's enthusiasm for the American cause. "It contributed not a little," he declared, "to the overcoming of the strong objections which existed in influential quarters to the conclusion of the alliance."

"If it had not been for our victory at Saratoga," retorted Arthur Lee, "we should never have had the treaty."

"Do not forget," rejoined Franklin, "that there would have been no victory at Saratoga if we had not received munitions from France."

John Adams had hitherto held his tongue, but it was clear from his expression that he was preparing a weighty speech, and this was the moment he chose to deliver it. There was no doubt, he said, that there were many fine words to be heard in Paris about America and the ideal of liberty, but French babble was of a very different order from the glowing ardour, the *saeva indignatio,* of the American nation. What one heard in Paris was at bottom no more than carping criticism and the pin-pricking gibes of a refractory population. Little else, indeed, was to be expected. The French nation was corrupt to its very roots.

"I have, for instance," he went on to explain, "been afforded the opportunity of examining the statistics concerning the increase in the French population. The figures are horrifying, gentlemen. During the past year, the year 1777, the number of children born in Paris amounted to 19,855. And do you know how many of these infants

were exposed? No less than 6918! More than a third of the total number. Just think of it, gentlemen! 6918 infants exposed, 6918 in a single
city! You will never be able to convince me, Doctor Franklin, that
a nation in whose capital so many infants are abandoned by their
parents can truly be said to have embraced the ideals of liberty and
virtue. Admittedly the French have prepared the soil on which we
were able to build, admittedly they have helped to shatter certain
prejudices that stood in our path. But at the same time they have
torn down many things that were good. Their sole achievement has
been destruction, nothing but destruction. This man who died recently,
your Monsieur Voltaire, Doctor Franklin, what else did he do
throughout his life but destroy one thing after another? It is we who
have done the building up. He was no more than the spirit of negation. Let us proudly give credit where credit is due, gentlemen!
There is only one great positive achievement in the world today, and
that is America."

His younger colleagues had listened breathlessly; now they were
silent, profoundly moved.

Franklin reflected that his own moral outlook and way of life must
inspire the strongest aversion in a man who held the views of John
Adams. As the well-formed phrases dropped from the well-formed
lips of his fellow envoy, he had kept his eyes fixed upon the broad
head with its luxuriant tufts of hair, wondering whether the time
would ever come when it would be possible to deduce from the shape
of a man's skull the nature of the contents that lay within.

When John Adams had finished speaking there was a slight pause
while Franklin gazed at the picture of General Washington, with
whom he knew himself to be of one mind, and then at the colleagues
who were with him in the flesh and with whom he found it so difficult
to come to an understanding. "Perhaps you will permit me," he said,
"to relate a little story. A man was sitting on the Pont-Neuf a short
time ago offering gold coins for sale, *louis d'or* both old and new,
for which he asked two livres apiece, in other words a tenth of their
value. Many of the passers-by stopped to listen, they examined the
coins, which had the authentic ring, yet the man did not succeed in
selling a solitary one of his *louis d'or*. Not a single purchaser could
be found who was willing to risk a couple of livres in order to acquire
a whole louis."

"Well," asked Ralph Izard in a depreciating tone, "what about it?"

"The *louis d'or* were genuine," replied Franklin. "It was all part
of a bet. The man won his wager, for he had asserted that people are
so suspicious by nature that they will not even accept real gold if it
is offered them cheaply."

"I still do not understand what you are driving at," insisted Izard, but Arthur Lee demanded, "Are you seriously suggesting, Doctor Franklin, that the French people's enthusiasm for liberty is to be taken at its face value?"

Franklin gazed at him calmly. "Yes, Mr. Lee," he rejoined. "I do."

"And do you also suggest," inquired William Lee challengingly, "that a nation with so many foundlings is sound and not decadent?"

"The French nation," replied Franklin, "is no less sound and no more decadent than any other." His colleagues stared at him in silent indignation, but he went on, "It is by no means excluded, in fact it is even probable, that during the next few years the number of foundling children will continue to rise. I am practically certain that a definite relationship exists between the level of taxation and the number of infants who are abandoned by their parents. Since you wish to argue on the basis of figures, I will reply with figures. I have been informed by Monsieur Necker that the war in which the French are about to engage—in our interest as much as in theirs, mark you—will cost the nation something like one thousand million livres unless it can be brought to a conclusion within two years. One thousand million. The foundling statistics will show a proportionate increase."

"It is easy enough in Paris," said Arthur Lee, carefully refraining from looking Franklin in the eye, "to indulge in economic and philosophical reflections, while at Valley Forge our troops are starving."

"You consider the French a nation of egoists, gentlemen," replied Franklin slowly, "and you take their idealism for mere bombast. Yet there are not a few Frenchmen who look upon us here in Paris as parasites who are sucking France dry. We demand money, arms, and ships, a great deal of money, and very many ships. What, I would ask, are we offering them in return?"

"We are offering them," answered John Adams, "the greatest moral spectacle the world has ever seen." Quietly, but with emphatic confidence, he added:

"The Eastern nations sink; their glory ends,
And Empire rises where the sun descends."

Franklin would have liked to reply that for the time being the Empire that was rising in the West needed a loan from the sinking East, but he suppressed the impulse. It was clear that there was no hope of obtaining any further deferment of the request for a loan. "Let us return to our agenda, gentlemen," he suggested.

"We have been instructed by the Congress," said Arthur Lee stiffly, "to apply for a loan of twenty-five million livres."

"Up to twenty-five million livres," corrected Franklin.

"Since the war is in any case going to cost the French a thousand million," commented William Lee, "Monsieur Necker is not likely to worry very much about another twenty-five million."

"If you will take my advice," said Franklin, "you will agree to postpone the application. I would beg you to remember the sharp rebuff that we encountered when we asked for the fourteen million. We shall have public opinion against us this time too. The expenditures of the French treasury for armaments are tremendous. New taxes were announced no more than three weeks ago. We shall again be unsuccessful, and all that will happen is that we shall put the Cabinet in an ill humour. Everybody in France is aware that the loan will be tantamount to a free gift."

"The French," replied Arthur Lee, "are holding back their men and their ships and leaving it to us to carry on the war. They can at least hand over a few sacks of gold, which God knows will weigh lightly in the balance compared with the streams of blood that we are being compelled to sacrifice. I think it should be possible to make this point clear to the French gentlemen. I move that we ask for a loan immediately."

"Agreed," said Ralph Izard.

"Agreed," said William Lee.

"And you, Mr. Adams?" inquired Franklin.

"If Doctor Franklin feels that we should not act too precipitately," replied Adams, "I have no objection to waiting another fortnight."

"Another fortnight will not help very much," said Franklin.

"It will perhaps be prudent to entrust Mr. Adams with the conduct of the negotiations for the loan," suggested Arthur Lee. His brother, Ralph Izard, and John Adams exchanged glances, but none of them spoke. Neither did Franklin, though he smiled slightly. "We are all agreed?" asked Arthur Lee. They were all agreed.

When the meeting was over Franklin's four colleagues went home and wrote long letters to their friends in America, in which they each expressed the opinion that there was little prospect of further fruitful collaboration with the Doctor *honoris causa*. It was not so much the debate on the loan as the discussion on the moral state of France which had convinced them of the futility of continuing to work with a man of so repellently different views. They therefore put forward the proposal, each in his own way, that instead of three commissioners there should be appointed one single plenipotentiary to represent the United States at the Court of Versailles. John Adams regarded it as a matter of course that the choice would fall upon himself. Arthur Lee had no doubt that the Congress realized by now that he, Arthur Lee, was the only possible candidate.

Franklin reflected that his potential successors were now going to scuffle among themselves like dogs round a bone, but he did not intervene. He waited calmly, ready to accept whatever might eventuate.

☆   ☆   ☆

That early summer was a good time for Louis. Toinette was too occupied with her preparations for motherhood to bother her head about politics, and he shared assiduously, in her solicitude for her own health and the well-being of the expected Dauphin. He anxiously took note of numerous symptoms that were not symptoms at all, and consulted Doctor Lassone as to their significance, while in correspondence with the old Empress in Vienna he discussed the precautions that were to be taken. Doctor Ingenhousz was frequently called upon by Maria Theresa to add his opinion to that of the Versailles physicians.

Louis was indeed happy. Casting all thought of politics to the winds, in so far as this was possible, he passed the time studying history and geography, translated a little, visited his porcelain factory, rode out hunting, and concerned himself with the health and comfort of his beloved wife.

Early that summer he had additional cause for rejoicing. Jean-Jacques Rousseau, the philosopher, the rebel, died. Louis was sitting before the table in his library, in front of him the great dead writers, La Fontaine, Boileau, Racine, and La Bruyère, whose statuettes he had had manufactured in Sèvres. These were writers after his own heart; their work had been created in the belief in God, and continued to further the belief in the divine order of things. What a pity that there existed no longer great authors of that kind. Yet there was one consolation. Of the three rebellious spirits who had been sent to plague him, Voltaire, Rousseau, and Beaumarchais, two at any rate were safely dead and buried.

Nevertheless his cup of joy was not unmixed. He had been seduced by his Ministers into playing with fire, and the war into which they were forcing him might break out at any moment. Though he realized well enough, and there was no lack of people to confirm him in the realization, that the breaking off of diplomatic relations was in itself equivalent to a declaration of war, he employed every art and stratagem he could think of to defer the evil day and possibly avoid altogether the almost inevitable hostile clash. Using Spain as his intermediary, he offered assurances in London that his recognition of the United States was not intended as a political measure, but solely as a commercial expedient, and though the Court of St. James's maintained a contemptuous silence he would not allow himself to be deterred from proposing, with a wealth of circumstantial detail, that the two countries should enter into a mutual pact of non-aggression.

He was glad now that he had appointed the Count de Montbarrey to be his War Minister, for the latter was proving of the greatest help in his tenacious passive resistance to the designs of his other advisers. Montbarrey could also be appealed to in his refusal to entrust the hot-head Vaudreuil with a military command. The times were too serious for important posts in the Army to be given to men other than those who were known for their caution and prudence.

Whatever he gave away with the right hand he took back with the left. At the urging of his Ministers he agreed to dispatch a strong fleet to American waters, and a considerable military force was mobilized on the French coasts. But at the same time he issued orders that no provocation was to be offered and that in no circumstances was any of the French ships to fire the first shot. Plans were worked out for the invasion of England. In Normandy and in Brittany his officers were dreaming of the capture of the Channel Islands, then it would be but a jump to the Isle of Wight, Portsmouth would fall, and in a day or two they would land at Harwich. Yet no word of command came from Versailles. The King's Regiment of Guards was expecting orders to be ready to march at short notice. The Marquis de Biron, their colonel, was asked whether his troops would be able to set off within two weeks. He drew his watch from his pocket. "It is now one o'clock," he said. "We shall be ready to march at four." But they did not march at four. And Louis took care that they did not march even when the two weeks were up.

Despite all his efforts, however, he could not prevent the inevitable. When the first vague reports reached him of a clash between English and French ships, he sat slumped in deep meditation. "War," he thought. "It has all been useless. We are at war. They have pushed me into war." Then there came more precise intelligence of what had happened and he brightened up. He was innocent, and his people were innocent. It had been the English who fired the first shot, falling wantonly upon his good ship, the *Belle Poule,* whose captain had behaved impeccably, manifesting peaceful intentions while at the same time preserving a bold demeanour. The *Belle Poule* had held her own against overwhelming hostile force and had reached the port of Brest with colours flying. In this preliminary skirmish God had favoured the French guns. The spirit of the Bourbons came over Louis. "I am at war with England," he mused, "and the first victory has fallen to my arms."

News during the ensuing weeks was equally good. The might of Louis's navy and of his armies was inspiring England with fear.

The population of Cornwall and Devon was fleeing into the interior. His cousin George was having to assume an even greater burden of debt than he himself, and England's national credit was sinking even more rapidly than that of France. God was on the side of His Most Christian Majesty, King Louis XVI. God, who could see into the hearts of men, knew that Louis was doing his best to stem the tide of rebellion and atheism.

Yet the world did not share this knowledge. Louis was filled with a dull rage at the realization that he was being celebrated as the patron of the rebels. On his table one morning he found a wood-cut entitled *The King of France recognizes the Independence of the United States.* The rude print depicted him as a youthful hero in armour trampling upon broken chains. A number of awkward figures in peasant costume were raising their hands to receive from him a roll of parchment on which could be discerned the word *Liberty.* A lady of majestic proportions, wearing a Phrygian cap, was approaching from behind to set a wreath upon his head, and the scene was completed by ships with pennants flying, a palm tree, and a few soldiers in full retreat, evidently Englishmen.

Louis wrinkled his receding brows, and his fat cheeks twitched. He had no desire to be crowned with laurel by the lady in the Phrygian cap. He did not wish to be regarded as the protector of the mutinous riffraff. He did not wish to be regarded as the originator of this stupid, suicidal war. He gave Vergennes instructions to vindicate him by letting it be known that from the very outset French policy with regard to America had been directed towards preserving the freedom of the seas.

Vergennes and his staff prepared a draft manifesto, but when it was laid before the King he made no attempt to conceal his disappointment. It all sounded wrong and lacked the force of conviction. Taking up his pen he strewed the broad margin of the lengthy document with detailed and peevish comments. *There is no point,* he wrote, *in declaring that France has no concern with the disorders in the English colonies. It would be better not to touch upon this ticklish question at all. We are indeed responsible for the fact that the United States have been able to assert their independence, for if we had not recognized them the national sovereignty of America would have been impossible of realization.* And further, *Monsieur de Vergennes is fond of words like "infamous," "perfidious," "hypocritical." The employment of such terms is not compatible with French courtesy.* Finally he wrote, *Reference to the assassination of Charles the First and Mary Stuart can at the most serve to incite our own malcontents, such as the Protestants or the Separatists in Brittany. And please delete the name of Cromwell. The English are perfectly justified in continuing to reproach us for having recognized the Government of this wicked man.*

Louis perused once more his marginal comments and saw that while he had removed objectionable phrases, he had not added anything. He pondered on the most effective way of putting England in the wrong in the eyes of the world, and then proceeded to write, "When I observe how my subjects in India, and even in Europe, are oppressed by the English, how they are physically ill-used and chastised, then I see that it is my duty to punish England for her conduct. These are the arguments you must employ, my dear Vergennes, for it is such arguments that make an impression. When the Spaniards once cut off the ears of an English fisherman, the whole of Europe was seized with anger."

Even toned down as it was by these emendations, the manifesto made a deep impression, though only on those who had already been convinced.

☆   ☆   ☆

Since Voltaire's death Pierre was more determined than ever that his *Figaro* should be produced on the stage.

At his request the *Théâtre français* submitted the manuscript to the Chief of Police, applying for a licence for performance. Within a week the *sociétaires* were informed that a licence could not be granted.

This was what Pierre had expected, and Désirée too. She was, in fact, almost glad. Now it was up to her to fight for the production by using her influence with Toinette.

With patient guile Désirée had succeeded in drawing more and more closely to the Queen. By her very aloofness she had gradually managed to make herself indispensable to Toinette, who sensed in the actress something different from herself, something ironic and menacing, which fascinated her. Désirée was a part of that *people,* whose ovations, ridiculous though they might seem to her, she could not do without.

Despite her pregnancy, and probably because she wanted to have Désirée with her as much as possible, Toinette went on with her studies, learning by heart her twenty lines of Corneille or Racine a day as Désirée herself had once done. Désirée suggested that as a change from these classic dramatists Toinette should memorize modern prose, which was more difficult, but would be more useful. Toinette agreed at once, and on the advice of Désirée she studied first of all the part of Rosine in *The Barber*. In this way there was

created an opportunity for Désirée to talk about *The Marriage of
Figaro,* in which, as she explained, there were three female roles,
each as splendid as the others. She herself had been offered the part
of the soubrette Suzanne by the author, but she was wondering
whether she would not prefer the page Chérubin.

Toinette was flattered by the actress's unwonted confidence and
showed an eager interest in the problem. "You must get me a copy
of the play to read, my dear," she begged, "and I should be glad if
you would let me advise you."

"There is nothing I should like more, Madame," replied Désirée,
"than to have the advice of a judge in these matters on whose good
will I can rely. Unfortunately, I shall have plenty of time to decide,
for there are certain difficulties to overcome."

"Difficulties?" queried Toinette.

"Yes," replied Désirée casually. "I hear that there are some scruples
in official quarters. Something to do with the censorship, I think,
though I am not quite certain."

Toinette raised her eyebrows. Then, smiling graciously, she said,
"You can play Suzanne or Chérubin, my dear, whichever you like
and whenever you like. I think the objections in official quarters will
disappear if I wish to see the play performed."

"If you help to have this comedy produced, Madame," declared
Désirée, "you will have done a lasting service to the French theatre."

"I rejoice, Désirée," rejoined Toinette, using her Christian name
for the first time, "at the opportunity to do you a service."

She informed Louis that Monsieur de Beaumarchais had written
a new piece. "It is said to be very good indeed," she suggested. "At
the *Théâtre français* they feel that it is the best comedy of the age."

Louis replied dryly, "Actors tend to exaggerate. My information
is that Monsieur de Beaumarchais's comedy is improper. Monsieur
Lenoir has banned it."

Toinette looked a little surprised and was silent for a while. "Perhaps we ought to have the play read to us," she said tentatively. "It
really is supposed to be a wonderful comedy, and Monsieur Lenoir is
sometimes inclined to be overscrupulous."

"I haven't much time, Toinette," replied Louis uneasily. "The
war—"

"I should like to have the play read to me, Louis," she insisted,
"and I do not want to hear it alone. Please do me this little favour.
You must remember my condition. I am sure Monsieur de Beaumarchais will be happy to read it to us himself."

"I won't have anything read to me by that man," declared Louis
crossly.

"If you think it would be doing him too much honour, Sire," she proposed, "it could be read to us by somebody else, by Vaudreuil, for example, and Mademoiselle Mesnard."

Louis twisted unhappily in his seat, but he was anxious not to excite unduly the mother of his child. "Very well, then," he muttered. "Very well."

☆   ☆   ☆

When Toinette triumphantly announced to Désirée that by the King's desire she and Vaudreuil were to read to him Monsieur de Beaumarchais's comedy, the actress was radiant. It was wonderful that her voice would be a weapon to overcome the aversion of the mightiest man in the kingdom against her friend and his best work.

Vaudreuil too felt that it would be a pleasant interruption of his enforced idleness to tell the fat fellow a few of the home truths contained in *Figaro*.

The two of them began to rehearse together. It was essential that the dangerous passages should be glossed over and emphasis laid on the cunning intricacy of the plot, but if they were to succeed they would have to make some revisions.

The Désirée who was now collaborating with Pierre was not the Désirée who had been unable to conceal her delight when she first encountered the comedy. The astounding discovery she had made that she possessed a heart had rendered her more exacting. She wanted the play to be the acme of perfection, a masterpiece not only of humour, reasoning, and audacity, but also of feeling, music, and poetry.

She had no difficulty in convincing Pierre, who realized that there was too much accusation and too little poetry in his comedy, and they sat down together to revise it.

Though the scene was set in Spain, the local colour had been painted on too thinly. He now recalled the Spanish period of his career. It had been an exciting and enjoyable interlude and he was able to draw upon his memory for colour, music, and radiance. The château, that might have been situated anywhere in Europe, was turned into the country seat of Aguas Frescas near Seville. Characters that might have been at home anywhere else in the world became authentic Spaniards. And the important monologue was changed from a mere insertion to be spoken by one of the actors in front of the footlights into an essential part of the action. Figaro was now a real Spaniard, hovering between fear and expectation as he strolled through a grove of magnificent chestnut trees, a grove that was well known to Pierre, for it really existed not far from Seville and he had himself spent a memorable hour there, a prey to hope and fear.

Vaudreuil, who collaborated in the work of Pierre and Désirée, was well content. He had been irritated at first when he was told that he should emphasize the part of the Count Almaviva and take away most of the verve and insolence of the part of the rebellious valet Figaro; for Vaudreuil had confidence in his histrionic ability to portray even a member of the mutinous mob. Now, however, he began to identify himself with the Count Almaviva.

Pierre had originally intended Almaviva to symbolize nothing more than the puffed-up arrogance of the aristocracy, and he had used him as a means of venting his spleen on Vergennes, Lenormant, and probably Vaudreuil himself. But with Vaudreuil so manifestly eager to help, Pierre turned Count Almaviva into a rounded figure with attractive human qualities, and supplemented the Count's haughtiness and sensuality with a goodly share of charm, elegance, dignity, and tact, even in the bitterness of defeat. Vaudreuil did not fail to notice how the character was being transformed into a portrait of himself. He found it astonishingly true, and felt flattered. He came more and more to regard *The Marriage of Figaro* as a comedy of his own making, to which he had magnanimously permitted his protégé Beaumarchais to append his own signature.

When Désirée had told Toinette that she was undecided whether to play the soubrette or the page, it was more than mere artful pretence. It was true that she had first seen herself only in the part of the sophisticated Suzanne, which she had herself helped to write, but she had gradually felt tempted to play the role of Chérubin. The character was still shapeless, but from the beginning she had sensed alluring possibilities in it. She visualized Chérubin as a youth just awakening to life, filled with the stirrings of adolescence that he did not yet comprehend, lured by every woman he met and naïvely flitting in an intoxication of the senses from one to another.

Pierre was taken aback when she suggested that she should play the page. He gazed at her slim petite figure with its roguish charm, and the pert, slightly tilted nose, and could not see her in any part but that of the soubrette. Then she acted for him the role she had in mind, and he realized that she was right. Man of the theatre as he was, he saw at a glance the possibilities of Chérubin. The part could be taken only by a girl, and Désirée was the only girl who could be entrusted with it. With keen insight he grasped the whole confused tangle of emotions that she wanted to instil into the character. But he still had no conception of what was passing through the mind and heart of the real Désirée. All he saw was the actress who was to play his page Chérubin.

"Oh, how stupid these clever people often are!" thought Désirée, in the words of Figaro.

With keen pleasure, not unmingled with a certain bitter irony, she

set about the task of helping Pierre to create the character of Chérubin, and the page took shape as she had seen him in her mind's eye;
naïve gaiety and the natural confusion of very young emotions were
in him, and about him there was an air of tender and sweet frivolity.
Then Pierre hit upon the little popular song for which he had long
been searching and which had sense only if it came from Chérubin's
lips. They were to be very simple verses, and he succeeded in making
them simple. The ballad was bound to appeal to everybody, it came
out of the people, as had Pierre himself, despite his air of being a man
of the world. Désirée picked up Pierre's guitar and strummed and
sang and everything fit.

> *Mon coursier hors d'haleine,*
> *Que mon cœur, mon cœur a de peine!*
> *J'errais de plaine en plaine,*
> *Au gré du destrier.*

Pierre then hit upon another verse; Désirée found the missing
word, and then a third verse came.

The ballad was to be sung to the tune of *"Malbrouck s'en va-t-en
guerre,"* and it was this rhythm that inspired Pierre's verses. The old
war song had recently come into vogue again through the war in
America, and Pierre smiled as he mused that the Americans had in
this way at least partly repaid the debt they owed him.

☆   ☆   ☆

The reading took place in Toinette's Yellow Salon.

Both Désirée and Vaudreuil were aware that they were taking a
great risk. The effect of their reading might be to confirm the suspicious Louis in his objections to the play, but they were none the less
confident of success. Louis would be in a minority of one against three
enthusiastic admirers of the piece, and moreover he had to bear in
mind Toinette's delicate condition.

Louis was in a cheerful mood and looking forward to a pleasant
evening. Having decided to please his dear wife, he intended to sanction the play unless it should turn out to be too shocking. If Toinette
were upset, it might harm the Dauphin. In order to help preserve his
good humour while he listened, he had dined well and copiously and
had furthermore ordered a piece of cold hare pasty and some sweetmeats to be set at his elbow.

It was a summer evening and still light, but the curtains had been
drawn and the tapers kindled. After assisting Toinette to assume a
comfortable position, Louis seated himself in a massive arm-chair
and announced, "You may now begin, *Monsieur et Madame.*"

Vaudreuil and Désirée began to read. In accordance with their pre-arranged plan they glossed over whatever might have given the King offence and the long first act passed off satisfactorily. When they came to Chérubin's ballad in the second act, Louis even showed a considerable degree of high spirits and hummed the tune to himself. When Désirée had finished singing and read the line spoken by the Countess, "It is so simple and full of feeling!" he interjected with unwonted vivacity, "Quite right! Very true! A most charming song! I like it." He repeated the refrain, *"Que mon cœur, mon cœur a de peine,"* and turning to Toinette declared emphatically, "This is a ballad that you ought to sing, Toinette."

Throughout the whole of the second act Vaudreuil kept himself in check, making the most of the Count and toning down the sauciness of Figaro. Désirée grew more confident than ever of success.

In the third act, however, it became obvious that Vaudreuil was finding it more difficult to observe her instructions. It seemed such a pity to drone out Figaro's witty speeches in such a pale and colourless way. After all, he was acting a part and had a right to achieve his effects. He thought of the enormous amusement he had felt when Pierre first read the play to him, and it was in bad taste to take all the spice out of the comedy. It would be a base action to deny his own child. Moreover, he enjoyed the piquancy of the situation. There was not likely to be a second opportunity to tell the phlegmatic fat fellow certain truths. The tone in which Pierre had read particular lines had made a deep impression on him, and he now proceeded more and more to copy that tone. Soon he was speaking the lines with all their original emphasis and point.

Louis shifted uneasily. Now and then he would take a morsel of his hare pasty and chew it vigorously to cover his annoyance. He had made up his mind not to take offence too easily, and there were certainly some rather fine passages in the play, but the character of the fellow Figaro turned out to be more and more indecent. It was certainly by no means agreeable to have another man wanting to take your place in bed beside your newly wed bride before you had slept with her yourself, but if the lascivious, hot-blooded Count was an unsympathetic fellow, the mutinous and crafty valet was simply repulsive. He was an impertinent creature whose speech and action both completely lacked the charm of comedy. Spurning all authority, as he did, he resembled his author; he was his author, that venomous fellow, Monsieur Caron.

By glance and gesture Désirée tried to warn Vaudreuil that he was going too far, but the Marquis had allowed himself to be carried away, and when he saw that Louis was growing agitated he completely forgot the purpose of the reading in his glee at the fat fellow's increasing fury.

Toinette was also becoming disquieted, though for the first time for many a day she had again fallen under Vaudreuil's spell. How menacingly the lightning flashed from his eyes as he knitted his thick brows, and how cleverly he spoke his clever lines. What an actor he was. What a man. Both the Count Almaviva and Figaro were incorporated in his person, and once she had safely given birth to the Dauphin she would not forget either François or the promise she had made to him.

Désirée was incensed at the haughty aristocrat's lack of self-control, which deprived the whole plan of its point. Yet as she listened to Vaudreuil she seemed to hear the voice of Pierre, and for all her irritation she could not help being amused that her Pierre should be telling the King through the mouth of one of his first noblemen what he and Paris thought of him.

Louis frowned more and more grimly. He picked up a sweetmeat to calm his feelings, but put it back on the plate untasted. Then he picked it up again and stuck it in his mouth. He rose from his chair. He strode to and fro chewing. He shook his head. He muttered, "Very bad. Very bad." And, "Poor taste. Poor taste. Nothing but a caricature." Désirée stopped reading. Louis sat down again, but this time on a little gilt chair, his behind overflowing the edges massively. "Do you feel all right, my love?" he asked Toinette, and when she nodded he said to Désirée in a courteous but decided tone, "Read on, Madame."

They continued with the play, and as he listened to the deep voice of Vaudreuil and the clear, high voice of Désirée, he thought with dull resentment of the self-assured Monsieur Caron. It would be crazy to let the Parisians see this comedy. It was quite enough, forsooth, that an unhappy concatenation of political circumstances should have forced him into waging war as an ally of the rebels of the Western World. He could not be expected into the bargain to permit seditious sentiments to be proclaimed from the stage in his own capital city. Monsieur Caron was evidently bent on becoming the Catilina and the Gracchus of Paris, in emulation of Doctor Franklin in Philadelphia. They were working hand in glove, those two, trying to overthrow not only England but France as well. He reflected wrathfully on all the injuries this fellow had already done him. He had published seditious memorials against the administration of justice. He had supplied the rebels with arms for their cursed victory at Saratoga. It was he, this Caron, this impudent, rebellious valet, this Figaro, who had harassed him and driven him, against his will, into the American adventure. And now, on top of all this, Monsieur Caron was daring to make fun of him to his face and in the presence of the Queen.

The fourth act was over. This time Louis managed to remain on his little chair, breathing heavily but controlling his temper. "I do not think we can allow this play to be performed," he said with dangerous calm. Nobody spoke. The only sound to be heard was that of Louis's snorts.

"Please wait until you have heard the rest," entreated Toinette after a while. Louis had quite forgotten her condition, and he pulled himself together. "As you wish, Madame," he replied.

Désirée began to read the fifth act. Vaudreuil took up his cue, and they came to the great monologue. They had thought it best to cut this monologue down to a few lines, but as he began to speak Vaudreuil thought to himself that since all was lost in any case he might at least get what amusement out of it that he could, and boldly laying aside the script he proceeded to deliver the monologue from memory just as Pierre had written it. He invested each point with its original emphasis, and the sharply filed phrases came tumbling from his lips: *My book was banned, and at the same time that they barred to me my publisher's door, they opened for me the doors of the Bastille. For six long months I was provided with free board and lodging, and this economy was the sole financial profit that I derived from my literary activities.* And: *It is only little minds that fear little books.* And: *Because you are a great lord, Count, you imagine that you are also a genius. Nobility, titles, wealth, appointments—these things make you proud. Tell me, Count, what have you done in return for the favours that have been showered upon you? You took the trouble to be born.*

Louis had risen again and shuffled heavily to and fro. His snorting was so loud that Vaudreuil had to raise his voice. Désirée realized that they had not only achieved nothing, but that everything was irreparably lost. Nevertheless she sat tranquilly in her chair, seeing her Pierre in the place of Vaudreuil and listening to Pierre's laughing voice, his glorious voice, telling the King impertinently to his face what he thought of him and his court.

I, however, went on Pierre-Vaudreuil, *sprung from the nameless crowd, have had to employ more knowledge and cunning merely in order to live than have been needed these hundred years to govern Spain—*

He did not finish the sentence. Louis knocked sharply with his ring on the edge of the mantelpiece. "Thank you," he said. "That will be enough. I am now in the picture."

Toinette had been reclining in a negligent attitude, but as Vaudreuil began to recite the monologue with such an intensity of passion she had moved into a more upright position.

"The play does not please you, Sire?" she asked sweetly.

"It is abominable," declared Louis. "It is improper from beginning

to end." He fixed his bulging eyes angrily on Vaudreuil, shifted them
to look at Toinette, and then stared back again at Vaudreuil.

"Yet it is very witty," Toinette suggested.

"Yes," retorted Louis venomously. "There is music in the words.
But I do not wish this music to become popular. I do not wish anyone
to be ensnared by it. I am one of those with little minds, and I do not
like little books. I tell you, Madame, that I will not permit this play
to be performed. I have had enough of making concessions," he
shrieked suddenly in a high-pitched voice, "and enough of compromises. The Bastille, forsooth! The fellow dares to scoff at my Bastille!
I would give orders to tear down the Bastille before I permitted this
play to be performed."

There was a deep silence. Then Vaudreuil, with what might have
been deliberate insolence, closed his manuscript with a snap. But in a
politely ironical tone that was different from his usual wont Louis
said, "I thank you, *Monsieur le Marquis*. You read your part very
effectively. And you, Madame Mesnard, are a great artist."

☆   ☆   ☆

Pierre was less disappointed than were the others. He had become
accustomed to everything being made difficult for him, and destiny
had apparently singled him out to be a fighter.

The first thing to do now was to make everybody curious about his
comedy. Beginning with the Lilac Coterie, people began to whisper in
surprise and indignation that the King himself had forbidden the performance of Monsieur de Beaumarchais's new piece, a charming little
thing, out of sheer peevish prudery.

At the parties given by Vaudreuil, the Polignacs, and other members or friends of the Lilac Coterie, Pierre was invited to discourse on
his celebrated play and to read extracts from it. It would be discovered
that he happened to have the script in his carriage and it was sent for.
Bound in blue leather with silk ribbons, it was a dainty volume to hold
in one's hand, and as Pierre prepared to read the passages he had
chosen he graciously begged the company not to allow themselves to
be disturbed in what they were doing, whether they were absorbed in
the card-tables or chatting in a corner. Amid the hum of a cheerful
social gathering, with coins softly chinking and people laughing or
gossiping in subdued tones, he would read a couple of scenes. He knew
how to sense the mood of his listeners, and to grip them by constantly
changing means. Soon the gamblers would leave their tables, flirta-
tious couples would break off their gallant conversation, and everybody
gathered round him. Then, when the atmosphere of happy excitement
was at its pitch, Pierre would murmur with a smile, "Well, that will

be enough," and closing the volume he would return it to his portfolio, nimbly tying the blue silk ribbons, and nothing could induce him to change his mind and go on reading. "A comedy needs a stage, ladies and gentlemen," he would say. "Or do you not think so? I wrote this play to be produced in the theatre, not to be read."

Thus Pierre read a few scenes of *Figaro* in the salons of Madame de Genlis, of the Princess de Lamballe, of the Princess Rohan, invariably breaking off when the interest of his audiences had been sufficiently aroused and they clamoured for more.

There was one scene, however, he always included, namely, the fourth of the second act, which he called *Conversation in Spanish* after the picture by Van Loo. It was the scene in which Chérubin sang his ballad; Pierre sang it, hummed it, acted it, and it never failed to sway the listeners.

From the salons of the great lords and ladies the song spread to the city. "Where does that come from?" people would ask, and the gentlemen's servants would answer, "From Monsieur de Beaumarchais's new piece *Figaro*." The pedlars who came to the door would say, "It is from *Figaro*, by Monsieur de Beaumarchais, which the King has forbidden to be performed." In the taverns and cafés they told one another, "It is from *Figaro*, which the King refuses to let us see." Everybody was humming, *"Que mon cœur, mon cœur a de peine,"* and talking about *Figaro* and Beaumarchais and saying, "They have banned him again."

At a reception given by the Duchesse de Richelieu—she was the third wife of the doddery old Duke, a young woman whom he had married chiefly to annoy his son—there were several high ecclesiastical dignitaries present when the hostess persuasively begged Pierre to read a scene or two from the comedy that everyone was talking about. "Let us have the *Conversation in Spanish* and the scene where the page conceals himself," she entreated. "The Duc de Guines told me that he still bursts out laughing every time he thinks of them." Pierre demurred, pointing out that the Archbishop and other prelates were among the guests and would probably take offence. But Monsignor de Virieu inquired with polite indignation whether Monsieur really thought that being an ecclesiastic meant being a hairy pillar-saint. Had not Cardinal Bibbiena asked Machiavelli to read to him his *Mandragola?* Had not Chigi, the Papal Legate, been present at the reading by Molière of *Tartuffe?* So Pierre complied with his hostess's request, and the prelates were no less amused than the rest of the company, joining in the applause and humming, *"Que mon cœur, mon cœur a de peine."* Monsignor de Virieu wagged his finger at Pierre and said, "You are a rascal, my dear sir!" and they were all astonished that Louis refused to permit such an agreeable comedy to be produced in the theatre. The young King's notions were too strict, commented Monsignor de Govone, and it was a pity that he did not have more sympathy for the weaknesses of the flesh.

It was at this time that the heir to the Russian throne, the Grand Duke Paul, was paying a visit to Paris. He was warmly welcomed at Versailles. Vaudreuil and his friends found little difficulty in stirring his curiosity about Beaumarchais, for they had witnessed a performance of *The Barber* at St. Petersburg and the Grand Duchess had read his pamphlets with considerable interest.

A meeting was arranged in the salon of Gabrielle Polignac, and the Russians were charmed with Pierre. The Grand Duchess and her first lady-in-waiting thought him perfectly delightful. Such writers as had previously come within their purview had been awkward fellows, unable to hide their embarrassment and lacking in conversational facility, but this man was amusing and of elegant appearance, more courtly than most courtiers, and with a gallant or witty reply to anything that was said to him. He was pressed to read a few scenes from his new comedy, and the enthusiasm of the ladies knew no bounds.

The Grand Duke Paul had an idea. How would it be if Pierre's comedy, which was apparently having difficulties to contend with in Paris, were to be produced at St. Petersburg? In any case he proposed to tell the intendant of the Imperial Theatre, Monsieur de Bibikoff, all about it and to instruct him to get into touch with Monsieur de Beaumarchais with a view to its eventual performance.

Pierre's heart swelled. It was a happy chance that the Grand Duke should have made this proposal in the presence of his fellow authors, Chamfort, Marmontel, and Sedaine. The worthy Gudin was right. He, Pierre, was spreading the fame of France throughout the globe, as far as the Arctic regions. He had in very truth entered into the heritage of Voltaire.

☆   ☆   ☆

News arrived of a naval battle that had taken place off the Breton coast near an island that the French called Ouessant, and the English knew as Ushant. It was at first announced as a great victory, then as having been broken off without decisive results, and finally it appeared that it had been a defeat rather than a victory.

There were two different theories current at Versailles as to how the war should be waged. One school of thought cherished the idea of an invasion of England, the other wanted to dispatch an expeditionary force to America. Louis frowned on both projects, though he found the suggestion of an expedition to distant shores beyond the seas less distasteful than the plan of an incursion upon the nearer shores of

Britain. The victory that his fleet had failed to gain at Ushant caused him to regard the experiment of an invasion of England with deeper repugnance than ever.

Vaudreuil had set his heart upon England's being invaded, and looked upon himself as the man destined to lead the expedition. The blunders committed by the admirals at Ushant only served to strengthen his indignation at being condemned to involuntary idleness at Versailles, and the chief object of his fury was the Minister of War, the Count de Montbarrey. The latter's incapacity for taking bold decisions had been the principal cause of the disaster. A man like Montbarrey would never entrust the command of an expeditionary force to an audacious soul like François Vaudreuil. Montbarrey must go.

There was only one way to compel him to go, and that was through the intervention of Toinette.

So long as Vaudreuil had been filled with desire for Toinette, he had not found it difficult to use her for his own advancement, but now that she left him cold it cost him a considerable effort to approach her with a request for favours. Nevertheless, the command of the expeditionary force that was to set sail for the English coast was well worth such an effort.

So he had a conversation with Toinette in one of the "side-rooms." He acted in his usual way, scoffing, flattering, enumerating innumerable arguments, stroking and embracing her, seizing her wrists in a brutal grip; and finally he demanded that she should have Montbarrey dismissed. Toinette, desiring and fearing his hands and eyes, promised to comply, and went to Louis.

But Louis, hesitating as ever, supported Montbarrey, whose delaying war tactics he liked.

Then, quite involuntarily, Emperor Joseph came to the help of his old enemy Vaudreuil. Since Joseph threatened to enforce his claims on Bavaria by military means, Frederick of Prussia invaded Bohemia, and Toinette, instructed by Vienna, pressed Louis to give Joseph armed aid in accordance with his pact with Habsburg.

Louis's only reply, however, to her protestations and demands was, "What am I to do? What *can* I do?" Toinette, without admitting it, understood very well that now, in the midst of waging war against England, he could under no circumstances expose himself to the dangers of a second front. But since Louis was unable to help the mother of his child in the all important Austrian cause, he would at least have to grant her other favours. And she decided to seize this opportunity, and to obtain by all means the fulfilment of François's patriotic wish. This time, she would procure the dismissal of that Montbarrey.

She pleaded and she threatened, she pouted and she flattered, she

spoke of her pregnancy and the danger to the Dauphin, till at last
Louis yielded, promising he would discuss the matter with Maurepas.

"Please do so at once," Toinette insisted.

"Send for Maurepas. We shall see what excuses he can find for his
protégé."

When Maurepas arrived she let fly at him before he could utter a
word. "I am given to understand that the King has resolved to relieve
Monsieur de Montbarrey of his duties, unless you can submit convincing reasons why he should be kept in office."

Maurepas could hardly conceal his bewilderment. He had already
foreseen that he would have to drop Montbarrey, but he was unprepared for this broadside from the pregnant *Autrichienne*. Madame de
Montbarrey was his wife's cousin and her closest friend. He had disagreeable visions of what he would have to suffer at meal-times if he
allowed Montbarrey to be dismissed.

"Is it really your intention to replace the Count, Sire?" he asked.

"You have heard what the Queen has said," returned Louis uncomfortably. "I leave the decision in your hands, Monsieur."

Seeing that Louis was still undecided, Maurepas determined to put
up a fight. "With your well-known love of peace, Sire," he said, "you
commanded your Minister of War to avoid the outbreak of hostilities
with England for as long as this might be possible. There is none of
your officers, so far as I am aware, Sire, who would have exhibited
such exemplary caution in holding aloof from conflict as the Count
de Montbarrey."

"Yes," cried Toinette heatedly. "The whole of Europe is laughing
at us because of the feeble manner in which your protégé is carrying
on the war. And I am blamed for it. It is perfectly outrageous!"

"Do not excite yourself, Toinette," urged Louis. "You are taking
the matter too seriously." A sudden fit of anger swept over him at the
endless difficulties that were put in his way. He was angry with
Joseph, angry with Franklin, angry with Monsieur Caron, angry with
Montbarrey, and angry above all with Maurepas, who was unable to
protect him from all these petty worries as it was his duty to do.

"What reply have you to make to the Queen, Monsieur?" he demanded sternly. His voice cracked and he concluded in a shriek, "It
was on your advice that I took Montbarrey! Or was it not?"

Maurepas paled beneath his paint. "I am seventy-seven," he thought
to himself, "and I haven't much longer to go. I must stick it out to the
end. When Louis flies into a rage he looks like a good-natured savage
who has donned a war-mask in order to frighten the enemy. But he
can't take me in." The simile pleased him, he decided to use it in his
memoirs, and became again mild, sceptical, and calm. Accepting the
fact, he made up his mind to drop Montbarrey as elegantly as possible.

"The Count de Montbarrey," he said, "is an ideal War Minister in time of peace. When I suggested his name to you, Sire, we *were* at peace. Now, unfortunately, we are at war." He shrugged his shoulders expressively.

Louis had at once regretted his outburst. Dragging his bulk up to Maurepas he whispered in his ear, "Do not desert me, my mentor."

Yet Toinette went on. "So you have no arguments in defence of Monsieur de Montbarrey, Your Excellency?" And since he was silent, she added, tapping her foot, but very polite and haughty, "Then be pleased to inform Monsieur de Montbarrey of the King's desire."

Maurepas gazed inquiringly at Louis.

"Very well, then," said Louis. "Very well." Maurepas bowed. "As you command, Madame," he murmured, and withdrew respectfully, uneasily and mortified, to dictate to Sallé, his secretary, a maliciously accurate record of the pitiful trio that had just been sung by the King of France, and *l'Autrichienne,* and himself.

☆   ☆   ☆

The Countess de Maurepas had a variety of ways to show her husband her discontent. When Montbarrey was dismissed, she became monosyllabic, and this was the worst thing she could do to punish the companionable Maurepas. He regarded the breakfast hour as the most agreeable period of the day, and he sorely missed her piquant conversation.

For three days she allowed him thus to feel the weight of her displeasure. On the fourth morning she opened her lips. As he was sadly dipping his crispy croissant into his chocolate, she said suddenly, "How would it be, Jean-Frédéric, if I invited our Toutou to read his *Figaro* at one of my receptions?"

Maurepas was so startled that he allowed the tip of his croissant to remain steeped in the chocolate longer than he had intended, so that when he took it out again it had become so softened that it splashed back into the cup. Carefully wiping the spurts of chocolate from his dressing-gown he spooned up the soggy fragments of croissant while he thought of an answer.

His dear Countess expected some recompense for the damage he had done to her feelings, and he was quite ready to make it up to her, but what she was asking now was a bit stiff. If the wife of the King's First Minister were to arrange a reading by the author himself of a play that the monarch had not only declared distasteful, but had even banned, it would be tantamount to open mockery of the King's judgment. To the well-meaning it might appear as a harmless little joke, but those who were maliciously inclined would see in it a challenge bordering on sedition.

He swallowed the remains of his croissant and coughed a little to clear his throat. "You wish to ask our Beaumarchais to read his charming little piece to us, my dear?" he murmured. "Would it not be going the slightest bit too far?"

"It is about time, my dear Jean-Frédéric," she replied, fixing her alert black eyes full on his face, "to invest our entertainments again with some spice. They have become very insipid of late."

Above her head, and facing Maurepas, hung Duplessis's portrait of Franklin, which the old Minister had brought to Versailles after the signing of the alliance. His dear Countess had displayed the right intuition with regard to the rebel from the backwoods, and she would probably also prove to be right in the matter of her Toutou. It was really very stuffy of Louis to have prohibited the play, and he would have to withdraw his veto in the end. In the enlightened eighteenth century one could not take too seriously a little comedy that made fun of an attempt that went amiss to exercise the *droit du seigneur*. Maurepas felt that he owed it to his posthumous fame to show that he did not see eye to eye in this respect with his royal pupil. Louis could hardly venture to think ill of him for it, for after the humiliation to which he had subjected him in the presence of *l'Autrichienne* he must be suffering from pricks of conscience.

Taking a fresh croissant, he offered a piece to Gris-gris, the kitten, who sniffed at it and turned away. "So you wish to invite your Toutou once more to the Hôtel Phélypeau?" he said aloud, but as if he were revolving the problem in his mind.

"No, no," she said decisively. "Not to the Hôtel Phélypeau. It is far too dusty and antiquated to provide the proper setting for a play with so much verve and *esprit*. I shall ask him here, of course. To this very room, and he will read, sitting where you are sitting now, my dear Jean-Frédéric."

"Upon my soul, if I possess one!" exclaimed Maurepas to himself, and he involuntarily jerked a little to one side. He knew his Countess, and had realized from the outset that she intended to have the reading at Versailles, in close proximity to the tedious young monarch.

"You always have such original ideas," he sighed.

"I knew it would please you," she responded. "I am sure you will have a delightful evening."

The old man was taken aback. "I beg your pardon, Madame!" he ejaculated. "Are you counting upon my presence? Would not His Most Christian Majesty be bound to interpret that as an act of overweening audacity on my part?"

"It is your bold spirit, Monsieur," she rejoined sweetly, "that causes you to be held in such high estimation by the world and by myself."

He raised her hand to his lips. "If my work permits, Madame," he said, "I shall look forward to the pleasure of appearing for a quarter of an hour."

Pierre's joy knew no bounds when he received the invitation to read his play at Versailles, within a stone's throw of the King's apartments, and in order that the occasion might have its chronicler he asked his hostess's permission to bring Philippe Gudin with him.

In fact, Pierre read as he had never read before, and made his comedy so vivid and clear that one could watch it as if on a stage. With voice and gesture he painted the situations and gave individual life to each of his characters. The guests were carried away, they applauded, they called out comments, and he had for each of them his own witty, hitting answer.

Gudin stood by in an intoxication of delight, evolving in his mind stately phrases for incorporation in his *Chronicle of the Writer and Statesman Beaumarchais*. What a poet! What a mind! What an actor! This was what it must have been like when Homer sang his rhapsodic cantos to the inhabitants of a Greek island, or when Horace recited his immortal odes to his friends.

Maurepas did not put in an appearance until the reading was far advanced. He had made an elaborate toilet, but wore a dressing-gown and affected surprise at seeing such a large company. "I merely wanted to say good night to you, my dear," he explained. "I had no idea that you were giving a party!" Allowing himself to be persuaded to stay, he sat down and listened. "Charming! Perfectly charming, my dear Pierre!" As a passionate theatre-goer he could appreciate the polished perfection of Pierre's play, its blending of intellect, frivolity, and wit. And while Pierre went on reading, the old Minister found the attitude adopted by his royal pupil more and more reprehensible. Generally Louis was docile and good-natured, but he could be unexpectedly stubborn and difficult to handle. This time he had worked himself up into a state of moral resentment against this pretty comedy and was making his old mentor look ridiculous in the eyes of posterity, instead of thanking his gods for having endowed his reign with such a brilliant literary production. No, the veto must be withdrawn. It might have to remain in force for a little while longer, since Louis had set his obtuse mind upon depriving the stage of a masterpiece, but not for very long. For he, Maurepas, determined that he would yet attend the performance of this very sweet comedy at the *Théâtre français*.

The Countess had watched his evident interest with pleasure. Accompanied by Pierre, she approached him and inquired, "Do you not think, Jean-Frédéric, that this excellent comedy deserves its place on the stage?"

Maurepas felt the same youthful vigour and audacity with which he had been imbued when, having barely reached the age of seventy, he had accepted the chief office under the Crown. A man who had dared to break a lance with the Pompadour could surely not be worsted in a skirmish with Louis the Sixteenth. "Madame," he declared gallantly, "I am entirely of your opinion." Meditating for a moment, he turned to Pierre and suggested in the wily phraseology of the skilled diplomat, "Now if, for instance, two or three of your illustrious friends were to arrange for your charming piece to be performed before a select audience, it seems to me that our gracious Sovereign would shut his eyes to an accomplished fact, just as he was pleased to ignore the presence of the heretic Voltaire within the precincts of his capital."

"You advise me, then—?" queried Pierre anxiously.

"I advise nothing whatsoever, Monsieur," interjected Maurepas. "I was merely giving utterance to the passing thoughts of a private person who knows how to appreciate the graceful play of an impudent wit. Today, alas, it is only we old men who possess such appreciation. You may recall, my friend, that I once accepted banishment for a quarter of a century because of an epigram I had composed. That was a wonderful epoch. We believed that a certain boldness of spirit was an essential ingredient in all literary achievement. Your *Figaro* recalled those times to me for a brief moment, my dear colleague."

☆   ☆   ☆

Vaudreuil willingly agreed to help Pierre. He was in the best of spirits, for the new Minister of War, Count Ségur, had promised him the command of the forces in Brittany in the very near future and he welcomed the opportunity of staging what would undoubtedly be the sensation of the season before he left Paris.

The whole Lilac Coterie set to work eagerly. The performance of *Figaro* was to take the form of a private celebration of the birthday of Prince Charles. Gabrielle succeeded in inducing the director of the Opera to place at their disposal the Hôtel de Menus Plaisirs, which contained one of the finest halls in the realm. The fact that the little palace belonged to the King only added zest to the joke.

Pierre made it his concern not only to direct the rehearsals, but also to attend to the business details. He even took a hand in preparing the invitation cards, arranging for them to be printed on costly handmade paper specially manufactured at his own paper-mills. On the front was a drawing of Figaro in a rather dandified and amusing costume, bowing with an elegant air and holding a guitar in one hand, his hair gathered up in a net and a red silk fichu wound negligently round his neck. A caption from *The Barber* announced with cheerful mockery, *"Eh, parbleu, j'y suis. — Well, here I am."*

The invitations were handed to the chosen guests with significant smiles and the actors, as well as the guests, were exhorted to preserve the secret, with the inevitable result that all the bustling about and confidential whispering soon made the whole town privy to what was afoot. And that was exactly what they were intended to do.

The Chief of Police was faced with a problem. The forthcoming production was not, to say the least of it, in accordance with the King's wishes, nor had the required permission been applied for. On the other hand the Superintendent of the Queen's Entertainments had engaged the actors of the *Théâtre français* and the rehearsals were taking place with the full knowledge, and probably at the express desire, of the Queen. Anyone who was bold enough to intervene in the pleasures of the Lilac Coterie was likely to burn his fingers. So Monsieur Lenoir had cause to be worried. Whether he permitted the performance or prohibited it, the probability was that a royal quarrel would be made up in the end by his own dismissal.

Meanwhile rehearsals were going ahead at the Menus Plaisirs, and at many of them a number of ladies and gentlemen of the court who were on terms of close friendship with the members of the Lilac Coterie were allowed to be present. Seated quietly in an inconspicuous part of the auditorium was Lenormant. He felt in his very bones the fascination of the play and its performance; he felt it to be thoroughly indecent, sinful, wickedly stirring the senses and the reason. Lenormant watched with keen appreciation a performance which both stirred his senses and appealed to his intelligence. He gazed at Désirée in her white page's costume embroidered with silver, her pert, boyish features beneath the plumed hat, the flimsy blue cloak flung across her shoulder, he saw her transformed into a girl and listened as she sang the ballad in a voice that roused deep instincts in him. His liaison with Mademoiselle Olivier seemed ridiculous in comparison with his former friendship with Désirée. He was consumed with raging desire for her, and at the same time with a wild longing to spring on the stage and strike her down.

On the following day he called on Maurepas and broached the subject of the rehearsals for *Figaro*. "It is remarkable," he commented, "how effective the comedy is on the stage. It excites emotions in the audience such as must have stirred those revolutionaries at Boston when they boarded the ships carrying their cargoes of tea and pushed us into the war with England."

Maurepas cackled. "I really cannot bring myself to believe, *mon cher,"* he replied, "that such a charming comedy is likely to incite the Lilac Coterie to go out and ransack tea-shops. Our Pierre employs a touch of political piquancy among his other artistic effects, and why should he not do so indeed? If our blasé lilac friends are amused by the agreeable thrill of horror that it gives them, they are welcome to it so far as I am concerned."

"If we were living in times of peace," protested Lenormant, "then I should be in complete agreement with you. Now that we are involved in a war on behalf of America, such scenes are a veritable incitement to revolution. I would beg Your Excellency to mark my words."

"I regret," smiled Maurepas, "that I am unable to share your opinion. Doctor Franklin and Figaro, the barber—the combination is really too bizarre."

"But they do belong together," insisted Lenormant. "History has harnessed them together. They belong together, like war and pestilence."

As Maurepas continued to grin with polite incredulity, Lenormant went on to elaborate his thesis. "The King," he explained, "is apprehensive lest the alliance should help to transplant seditious ideas from the West. You have yourself told me so, Your Excellency. If a play like *Figaro* should achieve widespread popularity, the King will see in this a proof that his fears are well grounded. I am sure that you would realize the force of my argument if you were to attend one of these rehearsals."

Maurepas gazed at him smilingly. "You will figure in my memoirs," he said, "as a man of really remarkable caution."

Yet the smile disappeared as soon as Lenormant had gone. Though he had not been willing to admit it, his visitor had made him feel uneasy, and he shivered a little despite the wraps and shawls in which he was enveloped. In the solitude of his country seat at Pontchartrain a display of boldness had not appeared incongruous, but here in Versailles a wise circumspection was more fitting. It had been from a proper sense of prudence that he had deserted his friend Turgot and his friend Saint-Germain. Compared with such sacrifices it did not seem that it would be of any great consequence if he postponed for a little while longer the pleasurable duty of persuading the King to permit the performance of *Figaro*.

On the other hand he was no reactionary and had no desire to be taken for one. Nor would it be seemly that he should stand in the way of a performance which he had himself been instrumental in bringing about. To say nothing of the vexation that he would thereby be causing the Countess!

The wily old diplomat sought for a way out of his dilemma, and he found it.

When he next reported to the King, there slipped from his portfolio the invitation card for the entertainment at the Menus Plaisirs. The short-sighted Louis absent-mindedly picked it up, played with it mechanically, cast a fleeting glance at the coloured picture, regarded it more attentively, and then read the caption. *"Eh, parbleu, j'y suis,"* announced Figaro.

Louis frowned. "What is this?" he inquired.

"So far as I can gather," replied the Minister innocently, "it is an invitation to a celebration in honour of the birthday of Prince Charles."

Louis was about to make an angry retort, but he swallowed the words before they reached his lips. He merely asked, "May I borrow this invitation for a while?"

"It is a very pretty card," said Maurepas. He was well content with the result of his strategy. He had fulfilled his obligation both towards the cause of progress and towards his loyalty to the young monarch.

When Louis was alone he examined the card closely. *The artists of the Théâtre français—the Countess Polignac—on the occasion of the birthday of His Royal Highness Prince Charles—at the Hôtel des Menus Plaisirs—* Eh, parbleu, j'y suis. He stared at the portrait of Figaro, his motley garb and guitar, his Spanish coiffure, the red silk fichu, the impudent expression on his features. At the Menus Plaisirs, he mused. In my own house. What a crew. What a rascal. In my own house.

He summoned the Chief of Police and thrust the invitation in front of his nose. *"Eh, parbleu, j'y suis,"* read Monsieur Lenoir.

The Chief of Police explained that he had not been unaware of the celebration that was being planned in honour of Prince Charles. His first impulse had been to forbid it. On the other hand, the entertainment in question was designed to take place within a select and illustrious circle, evidently with the approval of Her Majesty the Queen, and it was clearly his first duty to take into consideration Her Majesty's delicate state of health. He had therefore been faced with a problem which it was beyond his competence to solve. If the King had not summoned him to his presence, it had been his intention to request an audience with a view to submitting a humble appeal for His Majesty's advice.

Louis was silent. The reference to Toinette's pregnancy was displeasing to him.

"May I then forbid the performance, Sire?" inquired Lenoir after a while.

Louis hesitated for the space of three seconds. Then he snapped morosely. "What a silly question, Monsieur! I said *never,* and I meant *never.* My Chief of Police should be aware of that."

Lenoir bowed low preparatory to withdrawing.

"Wait a moment, Monsieur," commanded Louis. "Wait a moment."
In my own house, he mused. "Do not be over-hasty in issuing your
veto," he ordered vengefully. "Leave it until the last minute."

"With pleasure, Sire," replied Lenoir.

When Lenoir had withdrawn, Louis paced up and down the room
with a stern expression on his face. Gradually his face became slack
and sad. Seating himself at his writing-table, he stared abstractedly
at the porcelain statuettes of his poets, and told them: "And he will
get his way in spite of me, this Monsieur Caron."

☆   ☆   ☆

The sightseers who gathered in front of the Hôtel des Menus
Plaisirs on the evening of the performance had no reason to regret
the trouble they had taken. A double row of lackeys in the Polignac
livery stood before the Palace, the guests were received at the grilled
gate by Gabrielle's major-domo, the carriages were festively decorated, and the occupants who alighted bore the greatest and most
ancient names in France.

Through a chink in the curtain Désirée inspected the audience.
With the exception of the royal couple the whole brilliance of the
court was assembled, and she was seized with a wild delight at having
succeeded by devious methods and with a final stroke of luck in bringing the performance about. It was great and solemn fun to play this
comedy for those lords and ladies, against those lords and ladies.

She was proud, too, to be Chérubin and not the soubrette Suzanne.
She knew that today nobody in France but she was capable of por-
traying the nostalgic, confused, and burning amorousness of Chérubin; she knew how graceful and alluring she looked in the costume of
the page, she knew that she could add the grain of sauciness that
would save the figure from sentimentality.

In one of the boxes she spied Lenormant, who naïvely and in-
solently had brought Mademoiselle Olivier with him, pretty empty-
headed little goose that she was. He wanted to demonstrate that he
had got over his grieving for Désirée. Poor Charlot. Poor, embittered,
helpless Charlot. She was happy that she had committed the most
stupid blunder of her life in rejecting the offer to make her entrance
into the Château d'Etioles through the gateway with the sculptured
inscription *Vanitas, vanitatum vanitas*.

Ten minutes had passed since the hour announced for the rising of
the curtain, and the audience was beginning to grow impatient. The
actors were evidently still waiting for Prince Charles, in whose honour
the entertainment was being given. Here he came, youthful, insolent,
mischievous, and he was greeted with laughter and applause.

The show could now begin. Yet a further five minutes went by, and some of the spectators stamped their feet. "What's the matter, darlings?" cried the Prince, in his clear, insolent voice.

At last one of the actors appeared before the curtain. It was Préville, who was to take the part of Figaro, in the costume they had all seen depicted on the invitation cards. Was there to be a Prologue? There was a perfunctory clapping of hands and then silence.

There was no Prologue. In a voice that long practice enabled him to keep level, yet with little attempt to conceal his indignation, he made the following announcement: "We request your attention, Messieurs et Mesdames. There has just reached us a written communication from His Majesty the King. This communication forbids us, under pain of His Majesty's displeasure, to take part in any performance of the comedy entitled *The Crazy Day, or The Marriage of Figaro,* no matter by whom such a performance may have been arranged. Our entertainment cannot, therefore, be presented. We entreat your indulgence, Messieurs et Mesdames."

There was a deep hush. Suddenly a shrill whistle was heard, from the lips of Prince Charles—and a loud, brutal voice cried, "This is unheard of! It is veritable tyranny!" Jules Polignac was giving vent to his feelings.

Then the whole audience, all those festively clad lords and ladies, began to boo and whistle, and again and again they shouted, "Oppression! Tyranny!" But Pierre cried above the tumult, "Calm yourselves, ladies and gentlemen! The curtain has not yet fallen on this 'crazy day.'"

It had cost the Duc de Richelieu a great effort to come to the Menus Plaisirs, for he was very old, but the events of the evening had an invigorating effect on him. As he escorted his youthful wife to the exit, he remarked to his sixty-three-year-old son, the Duc de Fronsac, "You see, my lad! Under the fourteenth Louis we kept our mouths shut. Under the fifteenth we indulged in a little grumbling. Under the sixteenth we are kicking loudly against the pricks."

A large number of sightseers were still waiting in front of the theatre and they took up the cry that came from the disappointed guests within. The air reverberated with shouts of "Oppression! Tyranny!" and later that evening the taverns and cafés rang with angry protests: "They have banned our Beaumarchais! Despots! Oppressors! Tyrants!"

Chapter Three

FIGARO

D URING that early summer Doctor Franklin satisfied the desire
that he had felt at his first sight of the Hôtel Valentinois and
its garden. He moved into the main building.

In future the peace and comfort of his abode would no longer be
disturbed by the presence of strangers.

When he seated himself on his favourite bench beneath the great
beech-tree, gazing out contentedly at the river and the silvery grey
city of Paris, he would no longer have to anticipate with apprehension
the prospect of being involved in a lengthy and polite exchange of
meaningless conversation with his host. Moreover, he now had sufficient space in which to house himself, his books, and the numerous
articles that contributed to his comfort without being compelled to
consult somebody else's convenience. He no longer needed to enter
the Brown Library except for conferences with his colleagues, and he
was able to save himself the constant irritation of having to face the
wretched portrait of his esteemed friend General Washington standing on the bloody field of battle.

Even for the whole house Monsieur de Chaumont asked only a
paltry rent. There had been no difficulty in coming to terms with him,
though John Adams had thought it unseemly that the representatives
of the virtuous new republic should install themselves in such luxury.
Nevertheless, he had pocketed his objections, for he respected Franklin despite the difference of outlook between them.

So the old man was able to enjoy the amenities of his garden house
and the beautiful weather in peace. He sat beneath his beech-tree and
meditated. He read his books. He went strolling in his garden with
Madame Helvétius and Madame Brillon. He received long and interesting letters from Erasmus Darwin, from Doctor Ingenhousz, from
John Pringle, and from many other friends, which he did not fail to
answer at equal length. It seemed to him good to be on this earth,
despite his fellow envoys, despite the Congress at Philadelphia, de-

spite the ingratitude and lack of understanding on the part of his compatriots in particular and the fathomless stupidity of the inhabitants of this planet in general.

The pleasant quiet and spaciousness of the house awakened in him the longing to see his younger grandson, Benjamin Bache. He could continue his studies with advantage at Passy. The Doctor wrote to the headmaster in Geneva requesting him to send the lad back in charge of a reliable grown-up.

During that summer he looked after his health, climbing up and down the terraces and swimming in the Seine. Three times a week he soaked for two hours in a hot bath. Then either young William or Monsieur de la Motte would come, and the two youngsters would sit on the wooden lid of the bathtub, and quietly, and sometimes a little maliciously, all three of them would talk about the affairs of The Garden and of the world, and the old man would enjoy the warm water and the conversation.

One evening, while William was seated on the lid of the tub and chatting with his grandfather, it soon became obvious that he had something on his mind, and he needed little urging to confess that he was on terms of intimacy with a very attractive young French girl. Well, commented the Doctor, the fleshly appetites undoubtedly constituted the strongest of our instincts, and one ought to exercise a certain measure of self-restraint, nevertheless one could not be expected to restrain one's erotic impulses on every occasion. The young man looked attractively embarrassed and explained hesitatingly that unfortunately there was more to it than that. Blanchette was pregnant.

Franklin pondered. "Blanchette?" he inquired. "Who is Blanchette? Do I know her?"

"I believe you do," responded William. "It is Blanchette Caillot."

His grandfather received this information with mixed feelings. Monsieur Caillot, the father of Blanchette, was an employee of the tax farmer Fromentin, who was one of the contractors supplying equipment to the United States. The family was a respectable one, and the thing was going to be awkward. He had been in somewhat of a hurry, had young William. He himself had been twenty-three when he became the prospective father of his own son William, and the latter about twenty-eight when he sired the youth now sitting on the lid of the bathtub. Young William was not yet nineteen and had already proceeded to make him a great-grandfather. However, this was France.

Franklin would have been very unwilling to see his youthful grandson marrying a French girl of little means, but he decided that if young William insisted he would yield. "Let me ask you a blunt question," he said. "Is it absolutely necessary for you to make babies?"

William was silent for a moment before replying, "She is so pretty, Grandfather."

Franklin was worried. The lad would want to marry the girl. "What do you propose to do now?" he asked.

"Do you think I shall have to marry her?" William asked miserably. "I am not nineteen yet."

Franklin breathed a secret sigh of relief at his grandson's display of common sense. But it was going to cost a tidy sum if scandal were to be avoided, and his recent domestic expansion had already involved him in considerable outlay. "What then do you propose to do?" he repeated.

"It was our idea," said William, "that Blanchette should have a word with her mother. It won't be easy for Blanchette, but it seems the only recourse. Then we thought that Madame Caillot could come and see you so that you could both discuss what is to be done about it."

"Are you not making it a little too simple, my boy?" asked Franklin. "You and the young lady have all the fun and leave the rest to be settled by Madame Caillot and me."

William looked uncomfortable, but not really worried: "What can I do if you won't help me?" he demanded. "And what should Blanchette do? She's such a charming girl and has even learned a little English."

"Very well," sighed Franklin. "Send Madame Caillot to me. But be sure to impress upon her how very saddened and angry I am." He smiled as he uttered the words of warning.

When William had gone the old man pondered with a kind of grim complacency on the remarkable way in which history had repeated itself in the Franklin family. His son and grandson had followed his own example. Always the sons presented the fathers with illegitimate offspring, and always the sons brought heartbreaking sorrow upon the fathers.

For heartbreaking sorrow had been brought upon William, the traitor, too, by his son. Franklin thought with vengeful satisfaction of the way in which young William had repaid his father for the affliction which the latter had heaped upon his own parent. When young William was about to accompany his grandfather to France, he had not found it easy to take final leave of his father, and many tears had been shed at their parting in Perth Amboy. Later, however, just before they sailed, young William had of his own accord sent his father a clear and decisive letter of renunciation. He had rejected him with the same determination as that with which William the traitor had rejected him, old Franklin, the year before.

The Franklins were provided by their sons with male grandchildren, but they had no other luck with these illegitimate offspring of theirs, even though they afterwards adopted them legally. *The gods are just, and of our pleasant vices / Make instruments to plague us.* Franklin had not much use for Shakespeare, but these were good lines full of truth.

Two days later he received a visit, as arranged, from Madame Caillot and Mademoiselle Blanchette. Blanchette really was most attractive, and her mother too was not unappetizing, though rather plump.

Madame Caillot opened the proceedings by explaining that after a sleepless night she had at last managed to reconcile herself to the situation. In any case she had no alternative. Nevertheless, she had not yet dared to inform Monsieur Caillot of the dreadful disaster that had befallen his family. One of his cherished hopes would be nipped in the bud and he would be torn between rage and grief. Madame Caillot's cheeks twitched, her ample bosom heaved, and she wept copiously. Remembering, however, that Monsieur Caillot was employed in the offices of Fromentin, the tax farmer, who was engaged on the fulfilment of large contracts for the United States, she hastened to assure Franklin that of course her husband, in spite of what had happened, would continue to glow with ardour for the American cause.

With great eloquence she declared how deeply upset she was at owing the honour of an interview with the celebrated Doctor Franquelin to such a sad occurrence. Yet melancholy as the occasion was, it might be transformed into a cause for happiness. It seemed to her that a speedy marriage would be the most satisfactory solution. She would be overjoyed at the prospect of being able to welcome young Monsieur Franquelin, who was such a delightful and promising young gentleman, as her future son-in-law, and her resentment at his premature course of action would soon be forgotten.

Franklin replied amiably, though in a decisive tone, that the young man would in all probability soon be returning to America, and he himself could not under any circumstances consent to Mademoiselle Caillot's separation from her devoted parents for the rest of her life. Madame Caillot replied that her daughter might perhaps succeed eventually in mastering her grief at such a separation, but the Doctor insisted on his point and after some vain counter-argument she abandoned the project. It was Franklin's impression that Madame Caillot was a sensible woman and would allow her distress to be offset in some degree by the fact that it was Doctor Franklin's grandson who had been the author of the trouble.

Blanchette herself said little, but continued to gaze at her lover's famous grandfather with tender admiration. She obviously had no regrets. On the contrary, to judge from her somewhat roguish, self-satisfied smile, she apparently felt that she had put something over.

After considerable discussion it was agreed that Blanchette should in due course, that is to say in two or three months' time, retire to the country. A sister of Madame Caillot lived not far from Le Havre, and she would be able to look after the girl. The idea of confessing the situation to her sister induced a fresh flood of tears in Madame Caillot, but the silent Blanchette now found her tongue and sweetly begged Doctor Franklin to allow her William to visit her as often as possible in her rural retreat.

Madame Caillot then broached the subject of the material difficulties with which she would be faced. She spoke in rapid French of which Franklin could make little, but from various allusive references he gathered that it was a matter of money and he replied that he would of course meet all financial obligations. He estimated that the cost of board and lodging in the country, together with expenses incurred during the first three years after the child was born, would not amount to more than eight hundred livres in all, though he was prepared to go to a thousand if required. Madame Caillot lamented the painful necessity of such material considerations having to be discussed between herself and the liberator of America.

The interview had lasted well over an hour. Madame Caillot again wept abundantly on taking leave, while Mademoiselle Blanchette affectionately kissed the old man's hand, made a deep curtsy, and thanked him prettily in English.

☆   ☆   ☆

By the next mail Franklin received news that Eliza Franklin, née Downs, the wife of his son William, the governor, the traitor, had died. She had not seen her husband during the years of his imprisonment, and he must have been bitterly grieved that she should have passed away in forlorn solitude.

The Doctor was himself deeply affected. He had been fond of his daughter-in-law. Her marriage with William had not turned out well. She had come from the West Indies, where her family was well known and respected, and with her good looks, sensible ideas, excellent manners, and handsome dowry she had been a good match for his son. Yet when William's reckless conduct had forced the Congress to cast him into gaol he had left her badly provided for. The old man had sent her a little money, a mere matter of sixty dollars, and he remembered the sum exactly since if he had sent her more it would have given rise to malicious talk. He also remembered the letter he had received from her in acknowledgment, a modest, moving letter full of respect and gratitude in which she timidly interceded for her husband. Now she was dead and William, behind his prison bars, was alone in the world.

William could have avoided letting his wife die alone and forsaken. He had been treated leniently by the Congress for his father's sake, but he had practically forced the leaders in Philadelphia to adopt sterner measures by his arrogant defiance. Having been freed on parole he had got drunk with a number of friends who shared his political opinions, indulged in foolhardy abuse of the thirteen States, and when the watchmen courteously warned him to be quiet he had threatened them with the gallows. If he had not been included in an exchange of prisoners of war during the past two years, he had only his own stubborn recklessness to thank for it.

Litchfield gaol was not a very pleasant place, and William must have been filled with black, bitter thoughts when news reached him of his wife's death. If he set himself to draw up a balance-sheet of his life, he was bound to admit that he had wasted and played away his life. He had had the best prospects—far better than his father's; he had had high office and titles while still very young. If he now was so miserably in the mire, there was no one to blame but himself.

Benjamin Franklin was a just man who always tried to see the point of view of others even when their conduct was distasteful to him. But when it was the case of Americans adhering to the party of the stupid English King and his equally stupid Ministers, he could not remain impartial. And in the case of his son, his boy William, the traitor, he did not even want to be impartial. He was no longer a boy, his boy William. He was getting on for fifty, and should have known better. We were all only human and therefore liable to make mistakes. Men's opinions were mostly shaped by outward circumstance. He had himself, brooded Franklin, used his influence to secure his son's appointment as Governor by the King, and it was comprehensible that the boy should wish to remain loyal to the man whose bread he ate. But he could have adopted a neutral attitude and refrained from taking up arms against his father.

Conflict between parents and children were not unusual at that time. The daughter of his friend Otis had eloped with a Major in the English Army; that had been an unpleasant thing, too, for old Otis.

Franklin was sorry for his son William, but his grief and sympathy were swept away by his anger. He loved his son, and he hated him as he hated no other human being in the world. It was not his way to force his advice on anyone who had rejected it, yet he had tried to do so in the case of his son. He had argued with him till he was hoarse, but neither sage counsel, well-meant expostulations, nor angry warnings had been of the slightest avail. William had refused to listen. He was a thorough courtier, filled with a puffed-up conceit like any of the dandies at Versailles. A courtier, this William, his William, his and the serving-wench Barbara's William; it was to laugh and to cry. The foolish, swaggering cockerel. He deserved to be sitting in Litchfield gaol while his wife was dying at Perth Amboy.

In a sudden flash the old man recalled his friend Dubourg uttering a Latin quotation: *Acerrima proximorum odia*— Nothing more bitter than hatred between those closely akin.

Did his son hate him? He did. Otherwise he would not have made such a to-do when he went over to the enemy. He had wanted to demonstrate to the world that he was different from his father and wanted to have nothing to do with him.

Had he, Franklin, deserved such treatment? He had taken William into his house a small child, adopted him legally, and given him the best possible education in England, far better than would have been available in America. He had given him the opportunity of taking his degree at Oxford, he had procured titles and offices for him, he had from the very outset conversed with him not only as a father with a son, but as one friend with another.

Many people had told him how much the lad resembled him, and their intention had been flattering, for William was a fine-looking fellow. He possessed a natural elegance that was lacking in his father, though in other respects he had received at birth and had acquired through continual intercourse with his father many qualities that were characteristic of the latter. William was even in the habit of relating the same anecdotes, and in the same tone of voice. Obscene and rather daring as these sometimes were, their effect was enhanced on the lips of the elegant Governor. William had so much in common with him, in his gait and general bearing, in a variety of small gestures and the way he spoke, even in his attitude towards many matters of minor importance, yet when it came to the decisive problem he had behaved so abominably, a traitor, a coward, a blockhead, a wicked egotist. Both the resemblance and the dissimilarity to himself fed the Doctor's resentment against his son. He did not like rhetoric, but he thought: "He has trampled on my heart. It serves him right, if his own heart hurts. He has trampled on my heart."

That evening Franklin drank more than was his wont, more, in fact, than was good for him. He did so in order that he might sleep, but he passed a bad night, and in the morning his gout was troublesome. "This, too, is William's fault," he thought, but with a smile on his face.

☆   ☆   ☆

Young William came dashing in with an air of importance. "It has arrived," he announced with a cheerful air. "They are bringing it along." Franklin knew what he meant. It was his bust by Houdon.

The impressive piece of sculpture, together with its pedestal, was carried into the Green Library, which was the room in which he most loved to sit. The three of them, Franklin, young William, and Monsieur de la Motte, stood before it, but no one spoke. Words seemed unnecessary. Then, as though by prearrangement, the two young men withdrew and left Franklin alone.

Though not large, the bust dominated the room. It was a realistic piece of work with the massive cranium and the deeply furrowed brow, the strong jaw, the baggy double chin, the tufted eyebrows, and the creases beneath the eyes. The artist had not ennobled the features, but neither had he indulged in petty details. This was the Benjamin Franklin acclaimed by Paris. In every inch of the face there was a great and noble simplicity.

Franklin sat in his comfortable arm-chair, slack, feeling in every joint and muscle the aftermath of a sleepless night. The two heads faced each other, the one of white marble with eyes that for all their look of meditation seemed alert and watchful, the other with face of ruddy hue and eyes that were clouded. Which was the real Franklin? The marble one with its air of clear serenity, or the gouty old one, with the flabbiness and decay of his flesh, and the fatigue and confusion of his heart?

The marble did not tell the whole truth. The marble lied. Old Benjamin Franklin had by no means attained to a pure serenity of mind. His heart was not filled with a sovereign dignity. He was a prey to troubled longings and passions.

He had believed on the previous evening that he had cast off for ever all tormenting thoughts of his son William, but they had plagued him throughout the night and even now gave him no rest.

The years he had spent in gaol and the death of his wife must have taught William a lesson and made him a wiser man. He would behave less arrogantly for the time being, and when the next exchange of prisoners took place he would be set free and conveyed to a part of America held by English troops. Then he would once more vent his fury on the "rebels," of whom his father was one. The English journals would again be filled with praises of the vigour with which Governor Franklin was defending the King's cause, and they would say how tragically comic it was that the old rebel had not even been able to win his own son over to his side. And William would be filled with grim satisfaction.

Yet his satisfaction would be based on nothing, for Benjamin

Franklin would have erased his son's memory from his mind and from his heart.

He *had* already erased it. By strenuous effort of will he endeavoured to banish all thought of William. He sat more erect, his eyes grew keener, he pressed his lips together, and involuntarily he assumed the expression of the bust.

But he soon relaxed again. His foot hurt him, and, taking off his shoe and stocking, he massaged it, groaning a little.

It was absurd to try to put all the blame on William. With the sculptured eyes resting on him he realized that when he was wroth with his son he really was being wroth with himself. He had treated the boy very well, like a father, like a friend, and he had meant well when he concealed the identity of his mother from the boy. But it had been a mistake, a grievous mistake.

It was not pleasant to remember this mother, William's mother, Barbara, the serving-wench. Her wages had been ten pounds a year, and he had added another two pounds with the warning that she must never under any circumstances reveal to the child that she was his mother. When he recalled her clumsy, unattractive appearance and her stupidity, he could not imagine how it could ever have been possible that he had wanted to sleep with her. He had had affairs with quite a number of women of her type in his youth, when his erotic longings had made him indiscriminate, but they had been brief, secret intimacies, and none of these serving-wenches or harlots had ever made more than a fleeting appeal to him. On many a morning after a lustful night he had determined that he would in future restrain his desires, but when evening came he again had run after them. He had been ashamed of Barbara because he was ashamed of himself. Moreover, there had been a cogent reason of a different kind for his concealing his relations with her. According to the law of the time, he was liable to a sentence of twenty-one lashes at the pillory in Philadelphia. Even without this inducement, however, he would have done his best to keep Barbara in the background, for he had strutted around in pride and cockiness in those days.

It had been in March 1730 that he got her with child. He had slept with her four times that month, and he could still remember the anxiety and distress of those weeks just before and after her confinement in the following December. Barbara had humbly agreed to carry out his instructions. She could hardly have done anything else, since she was entirely dependent on him. Accepting the two pounds addition to her wages, she obeyed his orders and held her tongue. Nevertheless, some rumours had been spread abroad, and on several occasions unambiguous references had been made to his way of life, so that taking it all in all he felt a great relief when

Barbara died. He had been fond of composing epitaphs, but he never wrote one for Barbara, either in prose or in verse. He had set no stone upon her grave; she lay in a piece of earth, unmarked and forgotten.

He had not wished his son to know who his mother was, but he had been powerless to prevent his wife Deborah from coarsely abusing the boy when she was roused to anger. She had called him a bastard and screamed that little was to be expected from the son of such a baggage, such scum, such a whore. Things had smoothed over eventually, for in her heart of hearts Deborah had been a kindly woman, and when his son was no longer living in the house the two had got on well together. If William had been forced to suffer as a child and to hear himself scolded as a bastard, his father had more than made up to him later by the titles and honours he had procured him. Yet the bastard had not forgotten, and when asked to give up his offices and honours he had stubbornly clung to them.

The marble Franklin gazed at the living one with a wise and patriarchal tolerance. Man's senses had been given to him in order that he might take delight in them, if he could do so without inflicting harm on others. Without lust, without eroticism, there was no great man imaginable, no statesman, no scholar. Yet though he, Franklin, had mastered all his other instincts, and kept them within reasonable bounds, this one urge, this blessed and cursed one, remained beyond his powers of control. It had tormented him since his early youth, and at the age of seventy-two he had still not learned to bridle it. His massive head might sometimes resemble the marble one before him, but that which went on behind the living brow was not always fit to be revealed to the world.

When Eliza died, William must have been reminded of the death of his stepmother, Deborah, his, old Benjamin's, wife. She, too, had died alone, when he, Franklin, was on the other side of the ocean. In informing him of Deborah's death William had written, "I heartily wish you had happened to have come over in the fall, as I think her disappointment in that respect preyed a good deal on her spirits."

He had married Deborah for practical reasons, so that he should not continually be driven from one sordid adventure to another by the fleshly desires he was unable to conquer, and also because he needed someone to look after his household and his accounts. It had not been an unhappy marriage, for each had been indulgent towards the other's failings. She used to call him Pappy, a nickname which was eventually taken up by the whole of Philadelphia, but he never mentioned a word to her of the vexation this caused him. He put up with it as he put up with other faults of hers. On the other hand, he had done many things that must have caused her pain. She certainly did not like his staying away so long when he went on his frequent journeys. He had always offered to take her with him, however, and if she was so afraid of seasickness it could hardly be said that he was to blame. It was true that he inwardly rejoiced at her preferring to remain at home. His Deborah was not suited to society life and her presence with him in London and Paris would hardly have been advantageous to the business on which he was engaged. Yet he had never allowed her to glean the faintest hint of the thoughts that were at the back of his mind. He had, on the contrary, made every effort to show how much he was attached to her.

Suddenly there recurred to him the lines that he had once applied to his enemy Doctor Smith: *For all mankind unknown his bosom heaves, He only injures those with whom he lives.* But this was absurd. Never had he given his Debby grounds for doubting the sincerity of his feelings. It was quite impossible that she could ever have cherished the suspicion that he might be ashamed of her.

It was really remarkable how his own experiences had been repeated in the case of his son William. Now William's Eliza had died alone, just as Deborah had died. The old man uttered a faint, uneasy sound as if to ward off his painful thoughts.

The inscription on the bust consisted of the name *Benjamin Franklin.* That was all. Houdon had not considered it necessary to add any of the usual inflated epithets. *Benjamin* signified *the son of the right hand* according to the Bible. The world thought he had done honour to his name. He had indeed done most of the things in his life with his right hand, but inwardly he had only rarely been so blessed as the sculptured countenance seemed to indicate.

He was an old man, was Benjamin Franklin, plagued by his small frailties, though he was enjoying much success and was wiser than most men and probably also more virtuous, according to common standards. Yet he was more wicked, for when he disguised his vices before himself he was well aware that he was doing so.

Was the bust the true Franklin?

Socrates was certainly not always the Socrates presented to us by Plato and Xenophon. If Socrates corresponded *occasionally* to the portrait that has been drawn of him, that was in itself a great deal. And *if* he occasionally was like that, then the Socrates of Plato and Xenophon was the true Socrates and what he might have been at other times was of no importance.

Nothing of what Benjamin Franklin had once been had vanished. It continued to live in his crumbling body, his brittle bones, his leathery skin. The lecher who had secretly lain with Barbara, the serving-wench, tormented by pricks of conscience; the avaricious slave-trader who had dealt in the souls of his fellow men; the glutton who had devoured a second portion of whipped cream though he knew that it was harmful to him—all of these were still active in the man of the world, in the honoured philosopher, in the wily, affable old gentleman who had conversed gallantly with the lady in the blue mask, and in the dignified envoy of simple habits who had signed the great treaty of alliance between his country and France. Yet the shadows did not darken the light, while the light shone into the darkness. Franklin had no need to lower his eyes before the marble bust.

Seating himself at his writing-table in the presence of the bust, he composed his epitaph:

> The Body of
> B Franklin Printer,
> (Like the Cover of an old Book
> Its Contents torn out
> And stript of its Lettering & Gilding)
> Lies here, Food for Worms.
> But the Work shall not be lost:
> For it will, (as he believ'd) appear once more,
> In a new and more elegant Edition
> Revised and corrected,
> By the Author.

☆　☆　☆

The Franco-American Alliance was still in its early days, but it was being put to a hard test. The fleet which France had sent across the Atlantic had arrived too late to intercept Admiral Howe's squadron. The Americans were loud in their complaints at the French failure, there was constant friction, and Admiral d'Estaing reported angrily to his Government that collaboration with the Americans was impossible.

By an unhappy mischance John Adams chose this juncture to din into the ears of the French Ministers his demand for a loan. Franklin anxiously watched his fellow envoy's frowning mien and waited expectantly for the querulous report that he knew was bound to come.

It was not long before Adams came to see him. "I was quite right," he declared. "These Frenchmen are haggling shopkeepers. I told Vergennes so to his face."

Franklin was taken aback, but composed himself. "And did you then receive the loan?" he inquired blandly.

"Not at all," responded Adams angrily and with some embarrassment. "Things have reached the stage where I, an accredited Minister of the United States, am not allowed to show my face at the Quai des Théatins. Even my letters remain unanswered."

The conference was taking place in the gloomy Brown Library, and Franklin glanced up at his friend Washington, who had his own difficulties with members of the Congress and would no doubt sympathize.

"It's a burning shame," Adams continued with heat, "that the United States have been forced to enter into an alliance with such a nation and such a court."

Franklin thought it wiser to ignore this comment. "What do you think should be the next step?" he asked. "The simplest thing would be for *you* to take over the negotiations," replied Adams. "You know how to get on with this crew better than I do."

"I am afraid," rejoined Franklin, "that with things as they are, there does not seem much point in trying to negotiate a loan just now."

"But at least," insisted Adams vehemently, "these frog-eaters must be taught to preserve the elementary rules of courtesy in their dealings with us. I should be extremely obliged to you, Doctor Franklin, if you would draw their attention to this matter."

"I will do the best I can," Franklin answered.

Count Vergennes received him amicably. His Ambassador in Philadelphia, Monsieur de Gérard, had reported to him in detail concerning the reception he had been accorded by the Congress, and he told Franklin about it with a faint smile of amusement. The discussions with reference to the ceremonial to be employed had lasted almost a fortnight. The Congress members who came from the South had wanted an outward display of pomp in order to stress the fact that the greatest of republics was receiving the envoy of the mightiest of European monarchs. The members from the Northern States were afraid of being thought obsequious and recommended republican simplicity. There had been disputes with regard to the number of horses that should be assigned to Monsieur de Gérard's carriage, the number of steps leading up to his seat of honour, and the cut of the neckcloths which the members of the Congress were to wear at the reception.

Franklin returned the Minister's smile. "At all events, Count Vergennes," he commented, "it must be clear to you from the welcome offered to your Ambassador that the importance of the alliance is fully appreciated in Philadelphia."

Vergennes's eyes became veiled and he assumed his air of aloofness. "I fear," he replied, "that such an inference would hardly be correct. Unfortunately the reports I have received from Monsieur de Gérard are not wholly taken up with details of an entertaining nature. He informs me that Philadelphia is rent and torn on almost all questions of Franco-American policy. There are many of your countrymen who are not at all inclined to acknowledge the generosity of our sovereign. They are filled with suspicion and jealousy. Naturally, after the conclusion of the treaties, we had expected that their first request would be for us to dispatch an auxiliary corps overseas. But because of their cursed lack of confidence in us, Philadelphia sent no such request. All your countrymen really want from us," he concluded with bitter contempt, "is money."

"Monsieur de Gérard," replied Franklin cautiously, "cannot have failed to inform you that your reproach can apply to no more than a small fraction of the Congress leaders. I would beg you to bear in mind our pressing financial anxieties. Is it not, perhaps, comprehensible if these anxieties have disturbed the sense of judgment of some of my countrymen?"

"The King," said Vergennes ungraciously after a short pause, "feels that he has already done a great deal for your country. That you should use this particular juncture, when he has assumed vast new burdens on behalf of the United States, to approach us once more with demands for financial aid, appears to him, to put it mildly, lacking in modesty. Your Monsieur Adams has just requested a further loan of fantastic proportions and for an indeterminate period. And he minced no words in telling me into the bargain that the feelings entertained towards us by your countrymen are far removed from those sentiments of gratitude which we feel entitled to expect. Nor was that all. He saw fit to adopt what I can only describe as a menacing tone in lecturing me upon my duty to grant these millions to your country. I am prevented by the ordinary conventions of courtesy, as we understand it in France, from stigmatizing such behaviour in the terms that I should otherwise be tempted to employ. Let us say that it was malapropos."

Franklin was silent. Vergennes continued, but his tone became a little more conciliatory. "I am a sincere friend of your country, as you well know, Doctor Franklin, and for that reason I have given the King no more than a general indication of the tenor of my distasteful conversations with Monsieur Adams. It is not my wish, however, to expose myself to further experiences of the same kind. They are injurious to my health, and I have resolved in future that I shall not be at home to Monsieur Adams."

Franklin thanked the Minister for his candour and expressed his regret that his fellow envoy should have been so maladroit. The loan, however, was of the utmost importance for the United States, and he hoped that the last word had not yet been said on the subject.

Vergennes played thoughtfully with his quill. It was the King's opinion, he said slowly, weighing every word, it was the King's opinion that he had been more than generous already and that it was now time to call a halt. Only the most pressing and cogent reasons could induce His Majesty to reconsider his decision. He, the Minister, could do nothing in this direction without the powerful support of Count Maurepas. Maurepas, on the other hand, was disinclined to take the risk of drawing down upon himself the King's anger, and the indiscreet language which Monsieur Adams had seen fit to employ had been seized by him as a welcome excuse for refusing to take action. "As things are at present," Vergennes concluded, "I am the only member of the Cabinet who wishes to proceed with negotiations for a loan to the United States. Upon me, my dear Doctor Franklin, you may assuredly rely, though you are fouled with your Messieurs Adams and Lee.

A few days later Franklin met Count Maurepas informally in a tavern called The Redoute Chinoise.

The recently opened Redoute Chinoise was a new type of restaurant and place of entertainment. It stood on a narrow, elevated piece of ground in the Place Saint-Laurent. An artificial grotto had been built into the hill, galleries led up the slope, and it was remarkable how much of the Far East had been reconstructed in such small compass. There were a caravanserai, a bazaar, a café, clumps of exotic trees in an exotic landscape, even a merry-go-round and a tiny theatre. Chinese lanterns furnished a subdued light, while the porters, waiters, and other attendants were either real Chinese or dressed to look like Chinese, and they all wore pigtails.

In this strange setting the two old politicians met. Sitting in the caravanserai, tasting the Chinese dishes and sipping the rice wine and the China tea, they conversed agreeably. Franklin remarked *en passant* that he hoped Monsieur de Maurepas had not dealt too harshly with his colleagues, Mr. Adams and Mr. Lee, when inditing his memoirs. Maurepas, visibly delighted that Franklin should have made mention of his memoirs, leaned back comfortably and prepared to deliver one of the witty lectures in which he loved to indulge.

"You gentlemen of the West," he began, "apparently like to be noisy and to go about in crowds. We are a nation of twenty-five millions, but we sent you only one single envoy. You are a nation of three millions, yet you have tied no less than three plenipotentiaries round our necks, to say nothing of a couple of counsellors with high-sounding titles. Do you not think that is rather overdoing it?"

Franklin tried to manipulate a morsel of meat with his chop-sticks. "You see, we want more from you than you want from us," he replied with modest candour.

Maurepas went on lecturing him. "There is a variety of methods by which Versailles can be induced to grant its favours: cunning, deceit, gentle threats, blackmail, humble petitions oft-times repeated, sheer impudence that charms by its very boldness. But there is one method that will never succeed, and that is, virtuous bleating combined with menaces."

"My late friend Dubourg," commented Franklin in polite agreement, "used to quote Aristotle's maxim: Too much virtue is no less harmful to a Government than too much vice."

"Seriously speaking, Doctor Franklin," continued Maurepas, "your colleagues are becoming a real nuisance. They appear to feel that noisy manners are an essential attribute of freedom. We think it odd in France when gentlemen put their feet up on the table." Franklin gazed at him thoughtfully, and under the spell of his large, tranquil eyes Maurepas waxed confidential. "Yes, my dear Doctor Franklin," he said, "if only we had you alone to deal with, we should not take long in coming to an understanding about a number of matters that are still pending. I have good cause to realize that. Every morning, when I am breakfasting with my dear Countess, I see your portrait before my eyes and each time it is impressed upon me with renewed force, *Ecce vir*. And with a *man* we can come to an understanding. Count Vergennes is at one with me in this opinion, and if I am not mistaken he has thrown out a hint to Monsieur de Gérard in this connexion. I have no doubt that our Ambassador will do his best to inform the gentlemen in Philadelphia of our point of view."

The half-light of The Redoute Chinoise helped Franklin to conceal his emotion. Perhaps they would now realize in Philadelphia that certain envoys would be better employed elsewhere than in Paris. Monsieur Malaprop's efforts to negotiate a loan had had an unexpected, if welcome, result. "The sympathy," he replied, "with which you regard my country is most gratifying, Count Maurepas."

When Franklin left The Redoute Chinoise he felt in good trim. The more he thought of what Maurepas had told him about Gérard's intervention at Philadelphia, the more pleased he felt. Now he had it from the lips of Versailles's leading statesman that the mere presence of Messrs. Lee and Adams in Paris was jeopardizing the relations between the United States and the French Crown. He now had a duty to perform, a duty from which he had hitherto shrunk. The procrastinating Congress must be persuaded that the recall of his two fellow envoys was a matter of the utmost urgency. Otherwise, he must himself be recalled.

Next morning he wrote a letter to Mr. James Lovell, the Chairman of the Foreign Affairs Committee of the Congress.

After reporting on various transactions of the Commissioners, he went on: "Speaking of commissioners in the plural puts me in mind of inquiring if it can be the intention of Congress to keep three commissioners at this court. We have indeed five with the gentleman intended for Tuscany, who continues here and is very angry that he was not consulted in making the treaty, and the envoy to Vienna, not being received there. The necessary expense of maintaining us all is, I assure you, enormously great. I wish that the utility may equal it. All the advantages in negotiations that result from secrecy of sentiment and uniformity in expressing it, and in common business from dispatch, are lost. In a court, too, where every word is watched and weighed, if a number of commissioners do not every one hold the same language in giving their opinion on any public transaction, this lessens their weight. And where every one must be consulted on every particular and one of them is offended if the smallest thing is done without his consent, there is certain to be dissension and delay. The delay might be less if all the commissioners could live in one house. But it is almost impossible to find three people whose tempers are so good, and who like so well one another's company and manner of living and conversing, that they can manage to live in harmony. In consideration of the whole, I wish Congress would separate us."

Rereading what he had written, he found it dignified and lucid. There could be no doubt that the Congress would have to make up its mind to recall two of the envoys, and it was quite in the cards that either Adams or Lee would be left in Paris as sole plenipotentiary. Each of them had a strong party behind him, and all the people of self-righteous stupidity to be found in the United States. Behind him stood only his achievements and Reason, two forces whose supporters normally remained in the minority. At any rate, the arguments of the French Ambassador would give the opposition something to think about. He closed his letter and affixed the seal. Whatever the eventual decision might be in Philadelphia, he had done his part and was prepared patiently to await the outcome.

☆   ☆   ☆

It was therefore a calm and cheerful Franklin who greeted his guests on the fourth of July of that year, 1778, the second anniversary of the Declaration of Independence.

The situation of the United States was different from that of twelve months before, and Franklin's anxieties were correspondingly decreased. There was still a long way to go, but one thing was certain: the thirteen States had won their independence. An America dependent on England was no longer conceivable. His son William would never again be Governor of New Jersey. For the term of his life he would remain *the former Governor*.

The envoys had thought it proper, now that their country was recognized, to celebrate the national day on a fitting scale, and Franklin had invited a large number of guests. The whole house was festively decorated, the American flag and the Phrygian cap were everywhere in evidence, and attractive presents had been provided as a surprise for the guests. A colourful, talkative throng dispersed throughout the rooms and gardens, and there was an absence of stiff ceremonial, for on this occasion too the arrangements had been in the hands of Madame Helvétius, who possessed the gift of imparting her own air of sociability to any gathering. The whole house took on something of her own boisterous, untidy personality, and everywhere could be heard the loud, cheerful voices of herself, her daughters, her abbés, and her dogs.

This time she had to tolerate the presence of other ladies, and there were many handsome ones among them, including Madame Brillon, the young and beautiful Princesse d'Enville, and the Countess d'Houdetot.

Count Vergennes had not been able to bring himself to face a meeting with the unmannerly John Adams and Arthur Lee, but he had sent Monsieur de Rayneval, Gérard's successor at the Foreign Office, to represent him. This time Franklin had invited no aristocrats save those who had espoused the American cause from the outset, such as Turgot, Condorcet, de la Rochefoucauld, Noailles, and Madame de Mouchy; on the other hand, he had asked French bourgeois from all over the country to participate in celebrating the great anniversary of free America. There was one of the leading lights of the city of Nantes, and from Marseilles had come a Monsieur Marius Leroucas, a jovial gentleman who told how a club had been established that met once a month to glorify the victories and virtues of the Americans. Arthur Lee again appeared in the company of the gloomy Mr. Reed, so that even the freedom-loving section of the English people was represented. Most numerous were the philosophers, scholars, and artists, among them Houdon, Le Roy, Duplessis, and practically all the intellectual leaders of France. "We could hold a session of the Academy here tonight," commented Turgot jokingly.

There had been unfavourable rumours emanating from America recently, but none of the guests revealed any sign of shaken confidence. It might be some time before the alliance with France, the most powerful country in the world, would show results, but the mere fact of the alliance had rendered victory certain and Franklin's guests showed no less tranquillity of mind than he did. *Ça ira.*

Turgot missed his friend Dubourg and the quarrelsome discussions on the ethical motives that had caused him to refuse credits to the Americans while he was in office. For he liked to argue that the purity of the American cause should not be corrupted by the money of a decaying monarchy. Now, with Dubourg dead, and the alliance an accomplished fact, he expressed his dissatisfaction to a group of young

Frenchmen. He was glad the alliance had been concluded, he explained, but he also found reason for regret in that the moral prestige
of the United States would be diminished thereby. He was not a man
who liked compromises, and he would have preferred America to
liberate herself by her own strength. It was only to be hoped that the
United States would not suffer from the defiling contact. "Today,"
he declared warmly, "the American people are the hope of the human
race. They must become an example for all mankind. They must
prove to the world by deeds that men may be free without losing their
calm strength and self-control. The tyrants and charlatans of every
creed have declared that the welfare of mankind depends on ties, on
constraint, on subjection to kings and prelates. America must demonstrate that it is possible to be free of fetters and to flourish for that
very reason. America owes it to herself and to the world that she
should become the asylum of liberty in all its forms. She must grant
refuge to the oppressed of all nations and thus furnish comfort to the
earth. Then liberty will reign throughout the world. The fact that
their people have access to such a place of refuge where they can
escape the clutches of an evil Government will compel all Governments to comply with the demands of justice and enlightenment."

Franklin was displeased with Turgot's speech. Such utterances, he
felt, were hardly calculated to improve relations between Philadelphia
and Versailles. Even less did he like the talk that was being indulged
in by the vivacious Monsieur Leroucas of Marseilles, but luckily Monsieur de Rayneval was pretending not to hear what was going on.
Leroucas was just then reciting to a number of fanatical-looking
young gentlemen gathered round Mr. Reed his rhymed *Letter to the
Men of Boston,* which Franklin had already had to listen to once. "I
myself," declaimed the man from Marseilles, "observe with envy how,
despite the clamour of those whom you oppose, you are pillorying the
Caesarian despotism which in our country has set the clock back two
thousand years. Disloyal rebels that you are, without a pope, without
kings or queens, you dance while the rest of mankind is rattling its
chains. As you calmly destroy the traditions of others, you have the
audacity to laugh in the world's face and to be free."

Mr. Reed applauded with gloomy appreciation, an example which
the others copied. Pierre too joined in the clapping, though not without a touch of benevolent irony at the well-meant but somewhat
wooden verses of the Marseilles rhymester.

This year Pierre was accompanied by Thérèse, as the Doctor had
expressedly asked him to bring his charming wife. Pierre had forgotten any resentment he had ever felt towards Franklin. He had
always known that a man like Franklin could not continue to hate a
man like Beaumarchais.

In a cheerful mood he wandered about the great house, of which he had already heard so much and which David Hume, the philosopher and historian, had described as being one of the twelve most beautiful mansions in Paris. Eventually he came to the Green Library and saw Houdon's bust. Given as he was to quick impressions, he was lost in profound admiration of the marble head. He realized that he had only once in his life encountered a greater man. That greater man was now dead. Now Benjamin Franklin was the greatest living man. Whatever Franklin had done to him, it had been no wrong. This man could do no wrong.

He suddenly recalled his wager with Préville. Houdon would be ready for the sittings in a few days, but was it not presumption, mused Pierre to allow his likeness to be modelled by the genius who had created the bust of Franklin?

With a wave of his fleshy, well-manicured hand he cast away his scruples. There might be men who were greater than he, but the author of *Figaro* owed it to posterity that he should leave behind a representation of his features by the first artist of the day.

He returned to the drawing-room, where he was caught up in a circle that had gathered round Franklin. The Doctor was explaining the mechanism of a stove which he had had built for this room, and when the talk turned to other inventions Pierre told how in his earlier years he had worked out an improvement in the "resistance" of clockwork mechanisms, a technical refinement which had subsequently been adopted generally. As had always happened in his career, he had at once been involved in a dispute. A certain Monsieur Lepaute had tried to claim the invention as his own, with the result that there had been lawsuits, polemics in the newspapers, and reports by the Academy before Pierre's right to the invention was recognized.

In response to Franklin's request for further details, Pierre described how he had been invited to demonstrate his invention to the King and the court. That had been a quarter of a century ago, when he was twenty-one, spurred on by all the ambition of youth. He had endeavoured to make the best possible impression on the King at that time, but now that he had Franklin as an audience he was more determined than ever to show his mettle. As one master-craftsman to another, he explained with extreme preciseness of detail how the mechanism had been improved and what the invention had involved, using both Franklin's watch and his own for the purpose of practical demonstration. Franklin revealed his genuine interest by the questions he asked, and he felt an unwonted respect and sympathy for the watchmaker Caron who so well understood his craft. "You are very versatile, Monsieur," he commented flatteringly.

"No more than you are yourself, from all I hear," rejoined Pierre.

"That may well be," remarked the Doctor. "I have practised many trades in my time. I have been merchant and politician, author and printer."

"I have been all those too," said Pierre, "as well as a lawyer and shipbuilder, to say nothing of a watchmaker and musician."

"Have you ever been a soap-boiler?" queried Franklin. "Or a swimming-instructor? Have you ever been a designer of bank-notes? You see, I am more than a match for you. But there, you are still a young man."

Franklin moved towards another group where a disputatious Turgot was facing an argumentative John Adams. "No!" Turgot was saying. "I do *not* like the constitutions you have cobbled together for your various States. In Pennsylvania a man has to swear a religious oath before he can enter the House of Representatives. Is that what you call freedom of conscience, Monsieur? Elsewhere, I believe in the Jerseys, a candidate even has to testify to his belief in the divinity of Christ. No, Monsieur! That is not my idea of what is meant by freedom of thought. You simply lack the courage to place your trust in the sound common sense of the people. You simply have no faith in them. Otherwise you would not persist so thoughtlessly in copying English institutions. Why do you not entrust power entirely to a single popular Chamber? I will tell you why, sir! Because England has a King, and a House of Lords, and a House of Commons, that is why every one of your thirteen States must have its own Governor and its own Senate and its own House of Representatives. I call that a fine way to trust the people!" Adams opened his mouth to reply, but Turgot would not let him speak.

Here they were discussing Monsieur de Sartines, the recently deceased Naval Minister. Monsieur de Chaumont expressed the view that without the Minister's talent for organization France would not have created the fleet which was now proving its worth in war. Condorcet and de la Rochefoucauld, on the other hand, had only hard words for the late Monsieur de Sartines, whose unscrupulous activities, so they asserted, had been responsible for the present state of the national finances. On the pretext that ships must be built whatever the cost, he had helped profiteering business men to denude the royal treasury.

De Chaumont took up the cudgels on behalf of the departed Minister. "Surely the important thing," he declared, "is that we have the ships! And that was his work. The honest men were less successful."

"Whatever Monsieur de Sartines may have done," commented Monsieur de Rayneval with a smile, "he did it with grace and the most polished of manners. He was a nobleman even in his thefts and robberies."

"I am reminded of an epitaph," interjected Franklin, "which my friend Erasmus Darwin once showed me in England, when we were visiting the cemetery at Lichfield. There was a tombstone bearing the inscription: 'Here lies Roger Jackson, a politician, and a man of honour.' I asked Doctor Darwin whether there was so little room in the graveyard that they had to bury three men in one grave."

"You do not appear to hold the profession to which we both belong in very high esteem, Doctor Franklin," smiled de Rayneval.

"I may be a politician," protested Franklin, "but my methods are very unpolitical." With a chuckle he whispered confidentially, "Do not betray my secret, Monsieur de Rayneval. I always tell the truth, and then nobody believes me."

Feeling a little tired, Franklin stole away, and, noticing that the Brown Library was empty, he went in and sat in a chair. General Washington looked down at him from the bloody field of battle, and as Franklin stared back at the long nose and wooden face with which Monsieur Prunier had endowed the military hero he silently lamented the circumstances which compelled him to tolerate such a daub in the house where Houdon's bust had been installed. "I shall put it in the attic," he decided. "When the others have gone, that is the first thing I shall do." He closed his eyes. "I am really very tired," he thought. "I ought, I suppose, to be looking after my guests. But I'm not going to bother. I have a right to feel fatigued. It has been a busy year, and on this fourth of July there are no faint hearts to be comforted. Ça ira."

Steps approached the library. They were those of Ralph Izard and the brothers Lee. They were probably drawn by habit to the room where they had so often enjoyed long hours of argument.

Franklin thought it his duty as host to exchange a few words with them and asked whether they did not, like himself, rejoice at being able to greet such a numerous company on the occasion of their celebration of America's independence.

There seemed to be plenty of people present, replied Izard, but if one judged by the quality of the guests and not merely by their numbers it was regrettable to note how many gentlemen from the distinguished old families of France had preferred to remain at home. It only served to confirm his opinion of the hostile scepticism with which the French aristocracy continued to hold aloof from the American cause. "Your interpretation of these gentlemen's aloofness is not correct," remarked Franklin affably. "They are not here simply because I did not invite them. Now that the alliance has been signed, it seems to me more important that the world should be reminded continually of the adherence to our cause of men like Turgot, Condorcet, Morel-

let, Houdon, Duplessis, and," he concluded with a faint smile, "the
author of *Figaro*."

Arthur Lee folded his arms across his breast, thrust his head forward, and prepared to launch into one of his usual bitter speeches. But Franklin checked him. Pointing to Washington's picture, he inquired with a smile, and an air of preoccupation, "Tell me, Mr. Lee, what do you think? Is the sun rising behind General Washington, or would you say that it is setting?"

Lee could hardly conceal his disgust. "You will pardon me," he answered dryly, "but it seems to me that the representatives of the United States Congress have more important problems to solve."

☆   ☆   ☆

Maigron refused to be put off any longer with consolatory phrases. Though Pierre was closeted with Gudin, he insisted on being heard. Pierre complied with a sigh, but he ordered Philippe to remain. "It will keep Maigron from getting too prosy," he said.

The bitch Caprice, which could not stand Maigron, growled her disapproval. "Be quiet, Caprice," Pierre commanded. "What is it this time?" he demanded, turning to the secretary as he drummed on the table with his fingers.

Maigron explained without any embroidery that the firm of Hortalez was unable to meet bills amounting to 112,000 livres which were to fall due on the following Friday. The firm's revenues were already mortgaged for a long time ahead, and it was impossible to borrow money on the strength of its American credits.

"Is that all?" asked Pierre.

"Yes," replied Maigron, and despite his faded expression he seemed to stand there like a looming fate.

"What have you to suggest?" Pierre inquired again.

"I advise you to allow the firm to go bankrupt," said Maigron.

Pierre meditated for a brief moment. "The *Compagnie Industrielle de Chinon* will advance you the 112,000 livres you require," he decided with a grandiloquent air.

"That would be unwise," commented Maigron. "The *Compagnie Industrielle* represents the most solid of your assets; in fact it is the only one that is really solid, and it was always our policy to keep this company separate from the rest of your undertakings. It would be foolish to involve it now." His tone remained impassive and he did not raise his voice.

Gudin felt impelled to illumine the situation from the philosophical point of view. "When the philosopher Thales of Miletus was very poor," he said, "he bought up all the olive-presses in Miletus on the instalment plan, so we are told by Aristotle, and then charged monopoly prices for their use. Through this he grew rich. He did it, he said, only to show that philosophers could make money if they wanted to, and that if they remained poor, it was because they chose to occupy themselves with more important things than chasing after profit."

"Your philosopher, Monsieur Gudin," replied Maigron calmly, "was in a more favourable position than Monsieur de Beaumarchais. I'm afraid that Monsieur de Beaumarchais will be unable to find the money to buy olive-presses on the instalment plan."

Pierre sat down and wrote. "Here," he said, "are your 112,000 livres. This is a draft on the *Compagnie Industrielle*. Now leave me in peace."

"I have already told you," rejoined Maigron, "that such a solution would be unwise." Slowly and deliberately, without moving a muscle of his face, he tore the draft into little pieces. The bitch Caprice growled.

"Perhaps," said Pierre ironically to Maigron, "you would permit me to sell my old house in the rue de Condé in order to keep the firm's head above water?"

"I have never ventured," rejoined Maigron, "to intervene in your personal affairs, but I should like to point out that the sale of your house will involve you not only in a financial loss, but also in considerable domestic annoyance."

Pierre could already hear the wails of his sister Julie when she learnt that she would have to leave the old house and share her reign in the new one with Thérèse. But the firm of Hortalez was more important, and the house in the rue de Condé was duly disposed of.

As he had expected, Julie was loud in complaint. "I am glad that father did not live to see the day," she lamented, "when you would drive me away from our home where I cared for him until his dying day." He tried to pacify her with the assurance that she would be far more comfortable in the new home. How nice it would be for them all to be living harmoniously under one roof, and such a splendid, noble roof!

Julie thought it over and decided that she possessed sufficient force of character to be able to manage Thérèse. Pierre ought to be properly looked after, light-hearted as he was and in need of tender affection, and whatever Thérèse might have to say Pierre was going to be looked after. She pictured to herself how she would run the house in the rue Saint-Antoine. It was a lovely house, Pierre was right there, and it was very big. It should not be too difficult to persuade the easy-going Thérèse to keep to one part of it. Julie was inwardly reconciled to the change, but she continued to scold her brother. "The worst of it is," she cried indignantly, "that I shall again have the portrait of that creature staring me in the face all day long, that Mesnard woman who has never brought you anything but misfortune."

☆   ☆   ☆

When Toinette, despite her delicate condition, insisted on continuing with her theatrical studies, Louis had ordered Doctor Lassone to be present during her lessons and to see that she did not exert herself unduly. This enabled the physician to make the acquaintance of Désirée, and he very soon forgot Mademoiselle Olivier, who had left him for Lenormant. He attended rehearsals assiduously, lost no opportunity to sit beside Désirée, and never ceased to assure her in his pedantic and somewhat old-fashioned phraseology of the fascination she exercised for him.

At first Désirée was only amused by her new devotee, but gradually the aged physician came to interest her more than many of her younger and more dashing friends. There were numerous stories circulating in Paris about his conceit, his amorous affairs, and his avarice, but she possessed sufficient judgment to realize that these qualities, which he took little pains to conceal, were dominated by intelligence of a high order. It amused her to think that this convinced rationalist was unable to resist the magic spell she cast over him, and she was not repelled by his domineering old eyes, his tight cruel lips, and his big, bony, menacing hands.

With cool and shameless persistence she plied him with questions about his personal affairs until he was reluctantly forced to reveal to her everything that she wanted to know about his character and his outward circumstances. He had gained scientific successes which none but scholars were in a position to appreciate, he enjoyed titles and dignities which impressed the general public, and he was a man of wealth. He was a miser and loved pomp and extravagance.

It soon became clear to her that he was only waiting for a modicum of encouragement to make her an offer of marriage. The news she had recently received that Pierre was having to sell his old house made her thoughtful. If she were to become Madame Lassone, she would probably be able to purchase the property and let Pierre continue to enjoy possession of it. Furthermore, if she married Lassone it would be she who had condescended to take him for a spouse and she would therefore be less beholden to her husband than if she were to accept some young scion of the aristocracy. In any case, she would have no difficulty in managing a husband like Lassone. What's more, he was an old man.

☆   ☆   ☆

Meanwhile the French fleet, under Admiral d'Estaing, had gained a resounding victory in the Caribbean Sea, near Grenada, and without knowing it Pierre had made a vital contribution to this naval success.

Early in July a convoy of ships belonging to the firm of Hortalez, consisting of twelve heavily laden vessels under the escort of the man-o'-war *L'Orfraye,* had reached the Caribbean Sea, where Admiral d'Estaing, struck by the war-ship's stout appearance, immediately assigned her a place in his line of battle, leaving the unlucky merchantmen to their fate. The *Orfraye* put up a glorious fight in the ensuing encounter with the enemy, but she was pierced by no less than eighty cannon balls, her masts were shot to pieces, and her captain was killed. Admiral d'Estaing himself sent Pierre a personal report in a flattering letter, in which he congratulated him on having made such an outstanding contribution to the success of the King's arms and expressed his intention of seeing to it that Pierre's interests did not suffer.

Pierre exulted. He sat down and wrote a letter to the King in which he expressed his burning pride that one of his ships should have been permitted to co-operate in the chastisement of the arrogant English. Lovingly he gazed at the model of the *Orfraye's* figure-head. He had been right to sink his last resources in the vessel. In the end courage and brains force fortune to be their servant.

Maurepas offered his congratulations and asked what reward he would expect. Pierre replied that all he asked for was a memorial service in honour of his First Captain, who had fallen in the fight, the Cross of St. Louis for his Second Captain, and for those of his seamen who had particularly distinguished themselves, enrollment in the Royal Navy.

"Your demands are more moderate than I had anticipated," commented Maurepas.

"I shall, of course," went on Pierre, "expect Monsieur Necker to treat my claims to compensation with the same generosity that I am myself accustomed to show in similar circumstances."

The victory in the West Indies was celebrated by the Parisians with fireworks and other public entertainments, and since Admiral d'Estaing could not be present they chose Pierre Beaumarchais as the hero of the day. Once again and more frequently than ever, the people of Paris whistled and hummed and sang the tenderly martial ballad of Chérubin.

Pierre's lively rounded face, with its clear brow, shrewd, merry eyes over the straight, sharp nose, and full, arched lips, radiated animation. He felt it to be a most fortunate combination of circumstances that Houdon should at this moment be working on his bust.

He was floating on a fresh wave of optimism. The compensation he would receive for the damage to the *Orfraye* would keep the firm of Hortalez going, and Court and town were pampering Pierre as never before.

There was only one thing that clouded his joy. *Figaro* was still banned from the stage, and it irked him to think of it. The veto must be withdrawn. With the whole of Paris at his back he would demand that his comedy be allowed to be performed. Louis would have to abandon his stubborn attitude. He would wrest from the King of France the repeal of his veto as he had wrested from the King of England the tyrannous power he had wielded. The fame of the statesman and warrior Beaumarchais would be crowned by the glory of the greatest playwright of his age.

☆   ☆   ☆

Vandreuil had received the news of the victory at Grenada with mingled feelings. Though he was patriot enough to be glad, he had been waiting in a frenzy of impatience for the moment when he would be able to depart for Brittany as commander of the army that was assembled there for the invasion of England. The victory in the West Indies had now supplied a cogent argument to those naval and military leaders who supported the plan for dispatching an expeditionary corps to America. One thing was certain. He was doomed to continue hanging about at Versailles until he could induce Louis to set the seal of his approval on the contemplated invasion.

This was the mood in which Pierre and Désirée found him when they spoke to him about *Figaro*. When Désirée, half jokingly and half in earnest, mentioned her regret that the Marquis should be leaving Versailles without having carried out his design of producing *Figaro,* he welcomed the reminder. He was no *petit bourgeois* and consequently no stickler for keeping promises, but there had been many witnesses to his assertion that he intended to produce the comedy despite, and even because of, the royal prohibition, and it had become a matter of prestige. Furthermore, the production of *Figaro* would enable him to set off in a blaze of glory for the brilliant military career which was to start in Brittany. "Do not worry, Désirée," he said. "Nor you, either, Pierre. My plans for the attack on England have not driven *Figaro* from my mind."

He went to see Toinette. He felt repelled by the changes that her pregnancy had made in her appearance, the heavy gait, the sagging face, and he was glad that before very long he would be leaving Versailles. He wanted to have no more to do with this woman who was rejoicing in her prospective motherhood like any shopkeeper's wife.

He was at a loss to comprehend how he could ever have desired her.

He took care, however, to hide his revulsion. In restrained terms he said how sorry he was to be leaving her, and expressed his regret at not even having been able to carry out his task as her superintendent of entertainments. It had been his ambition to ensure that her name was handed down to posterity as a patroness of the French stage; he would have liked to see *Figaro* produced under her auspices, but he had been unlucky.

She replied hesitantly that he could not be unaware of the stupid stumbling-blocks that were in the way. Forcing himself to assume a softened look, he said that at any rate it would have been a touching memorial to their years of friendship if they had been able to work together on the project that had so obsessed his mind. He was not inclined to be sentimental, but there was after all no certainty that he would return. "Do not talk such nonsense, François," she cried, her lips twitching.

He laughed and replied light-heartedly, "Anyway I don't want to live or to die without *Figaro,* and it's worth while attempting a last throw. We could not wish for a better excuse than the victory of the *Orfraye.* Paris demands that this foolish veto should be withdrawn. Speak for the people of Paris. The fat fellow can hardly refuse."

Though she did not reply he was certain that his words had made an impression and he changed the topic, lapsing once more into a mood of tender melancholy.

That same day Toinette went to Louis's apartments.

Louis had received the news of the naval victory with the pride of a Bourbon. What cheered him particularly was the fact that it would weaken the arguments of those who were clamouring to have an army thrown against the English coasts. His Ministers and Generals would be wanting to accelerate the dispatch of an expeditionary corps to America, and since two such momentous enterprises could not possibly be undertaken simultaneously the invasion would have to be postponed indefinitely. The idea of his soldiers fighting in America might fill him with loathing, but the thought of an attempt at invasion was ten times more repugnant. Wars in the true sense of the term could be waged only in Europe, and as long as he was able to avoid any serious military encounter in Europe it was still not a real war. So he was proud and pleased at the news which reached him from the West Indies.

There was, to be sure, a touch of gall mingled with his satisfaction. He was annoyed that the ship which the notorious Monsieur Caron had cheated him out of should have played such an outstanding part in the battle. It irritated him to read in the secret police reports that the *Figaro* ballad had been adopted as a kind of national anthem. The troops were said to be singing it on the march, and there were rumours that the sailors of the *Orfraye* had died with it on their lips.

However, these were minor dissonances in his general mood of harmony, and Toinette found him in cheerful spirits. With a broad smile he inspected her figure and observed contentedly that it was already growing rounded. To his inquiries as he clumsily caressed her she answered that she could not have felt better, though she *was* a little sad at the thought that one of her dearest friends, the Marquis de Vaudreuil, would soon be leaving Versailles. Louis commented dryly that if his memory was not at fault it was she herself who had insisted on his being entrusted with command of the army in Brittany. She replied that of course she was prepared to sacrifice her friends when the interests of France were at stake. She had, by the way, granted Vaudreuil a final wish that he had very much at heart, and she hoped that Louis would not stand in the way of her fulfilling her promise. The Marquis was anxious to crown his period of service as her Superintendent of Entertainments with a production of *Figaro*.

Louis's face darkened. Here they are, he brooded, pulling and tugging at me again from all directions, just as it was before the alliance. They are all blind. They are digging their own graves and I can't stop them.

"Vaudreuil," went on Toinette, "is not alone in his desire. Monsieur de Beaumarchais's fleet has won such a glorious victory and now all Paris wants to see his play."

Louis snorted wrathfully. "That is the whole point," he snapped. "If it were only a matter of a performance at Versailles I should not care a fig. The ladies and gentlemen of my court have long been beyond spoiling. But I refuse to allow the good people of Paris to see such an indecent comedy. I knew exactly why I said *never*." He tried to infuse a note of authority into his voice.

Toinette sulked. "Maybe, Sire, you have heard somewhere or other that women in my condition are subject to whims, and that if they are not humoured it can be bad for their health. Doctor Lassone will tell you whether this is true or not. You really must think of the Dauphin, Louis. I have set my heart on affording Vaudreuil the last pleasure he is likely to enjoy at Versailles before he goes away."

After a while Louis said weakly and maliciously, "And where does he want to produce the play, Monsieur your Intendant? At the Menus Plaisirs again? Or perhaps at the Trianon?" He stared at her challengingly.

"Of course not," she answered quickly. "It is to be quite private and only for my most intimate friends. In his Gennevilliers, I think."

Louis sat with his brow knitted in deep thought. "Listen, Toinette," he urged. "It really would not do, it really would be highly improper, if the Queen of France were to attend a performance of this comedy after I have said *never*."

"I shall not be present if you do not wish it," she agreed. Then she put the question bluntly, "So Vaudreuil can put the play on?"

"Very well, then. Very well," said Louis.

At once, however, he made reservations: "On condition that all unseemly passages are deleted. On condition that there shall be no more than one single performance, that performance being given at Gennevilliers and only for the intimate friends of the Marquis de Vaudreuil. On condition that you, Madame, shall not be present. On condition that once the performance has taken place nobody ever mentions another word to me about this *Figaro*."

"Agreed," said Toinette.

Then she added sweetly and radiantly, "I knew that you would not refuse a favour to the mother of your son, my dear Louis."

☆   ☆   ☆

The day of the performance turned out very warm, and in the small theatre at Gennevilliers where Désirée had once played the son of William Tell it was almost intolerably stuffy, for even the corridors and passages were packed.

Hitherto Pierre had complacently accepted invitations from certain of his aristocratic acquaintances which did not include his wife, but this time he had insisted on bringing with him Thérèse, Julie, and his friend Philippe Gudin, and all four of them were occupying one of the small boxes in full view of the audience. Thérèse, in her simple blue frock waiting for the curtain to rise, was the focus of much interest. Nearly everyone in the audience knew everyone else, but few of them had ever seen Thérèse before. "That is Madame de Beaumarchais," it was whispered, and some of them remembered with surprise that Pierre was married.

Once more Désirée, wearing her page's costume, peeped through the chink in the curtain. At last she had brought it off, despite Charlot and despite the King, and she was not going to be cheated a second time of the reward for her wiliness and the humiliation to which she had been exposed.

She saw Thérèse sitting in the box with Pierre standing behind her chair and leaning over towards her. It was rather remarkable and even a little ridiculous that Pierrot, who for all his idealism was so cynical, should yet in his heart of hearts love only this Thérèse of his, to whom he showed the devotion of a large, faithful dog. It was she,

Désirée, who had released in him the genius that enabled him to give form and speech to the awakening emotions of the boy Chérubin, yet his own emotions were centred not on her but on the woman in the box.

The three thuds were heard on the floor-boards and the curtains parted. Préville was seen in the role of Figaro measuring the dimensions of the room. "Nineteen by twenty-six," he said.

Pierre sat and watched and listened, he was as in a dream and at the same time wide awake. *Figaro* was actually being performed. The curtain *had* risen on *Figaro*. Victory was his; Louis of Bourbon had raged in vain. They had gathered, all these Princes and Dukes and Counts and Marquises, and he was telling them to their faces what he thought of them. They had even demanded to hear what he had to say, for they knew that there was no other playwright in France who could speak from the stage with such wit and ease. There he sat in his box with his beautiful and beloved wife, on the stage his brilliant and much-admired friend Désirée talked and acted, and in the audience the great lords and ladies of France sat and listened intently.

The aristocratic audience may have come in the first place merely in a laughing spirit of rebellion against the King, but this was soon forgotten in their unreserved delight at the charm and overflowing richness of the comedy. They possessed wit and taste, as well as a sense of the theatre, they appreciated to the full the shrewd impertinence of Figaro, the haughty, slightly morbid elegance of Almaviva, and they were no less astonished than touched by the acting of Désirée Mesnard. They would never have thought that she could portray the enamoured youth with such moving sincerity.

In the *parterre,* where there was only standing room, old Doctor Lassone was wedged in among a suffocating throng of spectators, and young though he may have felt, it could not have been good for him to submit to such physical and mental strain. He knew that every man in the auditorium was gazing at Désirée with lustful eyes, and that probably most of the women had their senses stirred by the boy Chérubin. It is stupid of me, he thought, but I am going to marry her. She loves none but that empty-headed fellow Caron, and she even prefers that conceited cockerel Vaudreuil to me. She will deceive me to the top of her bent and humiliate me and cost me the whole of my fortune. But it will be the last of my stupidities and well worth the cost.

Vaudreuil too succumbed to Désirée's spell. She belonged to him. All this belonged to him. It was a good evening for Vaudreuil, it constituted the link between his brilliant past and his even more glorious future. Everything that had filled his life and furnished him with delight was concentrated in this one evening. Through his protégé

Pierre he had created the spectacle that they were all now enjoying, he had forced the fat fellow to withdraw his veto, he had given this comedy to the French nation as Louis the Fourteenth had given it the comedies of Molière. He was the master of the man who had thought out the dialogue and shaped the characters, of the woman on the stage who was weaving her magic spell, of the Queen who had wheedled a reluctant promise from her consort. And the piquant thing about it all was that he did not care a fig. He was abandoning this world where he ruled supreme and going off to the wars.

In one of the boxes sat Maurepas, priding himself on the liberal outlook which had inspired him to procure, or at any rate to permit, the performance of his court jester's play. He did, it is true, yield at one or two passages to the foreboding that all those who were now listening with such amusement were sawing another deep notch in the branch on which they were sitting, and for a fleeting moment he felt an uneasy sensation in the pit of his stomach. But he told himself that the branch would certainly last out his lifetime, and for the rest of his evening his pleasure in the charming comedy was unspoiled.

The others, this whole assembly of the noblest of the French nobles, were untouched by any premonition that had passed through the mind of Maurepas. They were delighted and laughed, seeing themselves so truly presented on the stage, their frivolous attitude toward life, their polished manners, the dreary waste of their brains and hearts. The strongest effect was produced by the unspoken lines for which Pierre had substituted gestures and lengthy, significant pauses, for many members of the audience knew these deleted lines by heart and recited them aloud. The applause waxed and grew to a deafening clamour as the great lords and ladies thanked Figaro for telling them to their faces what they were.

A few writers and philosophers had been selected for attending the performance, and during the interval they formulated the judgments which were to be repeated on the morrow by all Paris. A truly encyclopaedic comedy, pronounced Chamfort. Baron Grimm, the redoubtable critic who had reviewed Pierre's earlier plays with biting scorn, was the most laudatory of all. Observing the sincere enthusiasm of the influential audience, he decided that his previous verdicts were mistaken and confessed his error in orotund phrases. The piece, he declared, presented a bold and ingenious picture of the manners and opinions of the ruling class, painted by a man who knew how to mix his colours and to wield his brush. The play consisted of nothing but the intrigues centring around a night of love, yet it mirrored a whole epoch. It was therefore indubitably the creation of a genius.

Then came the last act with the great monologue. It was the longest monologue that had ever been delivered on the French stage, and it remained to be seen whether, after having listened to nearly three hours of witty dialogue and complicated plot, the public would accept such a protracted soliloquy.

Figaro paced to and fro beneath the Spanish chestnut trees and spoke and meditated and spoke. Yet the audience gave no sign of unrest. They did not even cough, but followed intently the meanderings and spasmodic transitions of the soliloquy.

Désirée was standing in the wings, wearing her officer's uniform. She forgot how provoking and alluring she looked; she was waiting for the wonderful lines in which Figaro-Pierre, concluding the monologue, would speak of his life and career in words more apt than either his admirers or those who envied him could have drawn upon. And now they came, these lines:

Forced to follow the path upon which I entered unknowingly, as I shall quit it unwillingly— Préville took the risk of speaking softly, yet he was listened to with bated breath— *I have strewn it with as many flowers as my good humour allowed. I say my good humour, yet I know not whether it is mine any more than the rest, or even what is this I, this shapeless assemblage of mysterious constituents, with which my thoughts are occupied. A pitiful fool, a sportive little animal, a young man chasing ardently after pleasure. Today the master, tomorrow the servant, as fortune decides. Ambitious from conceit, industrious from necessity, but indolent—by inclination. With a talent for eloquence when danger threatens, for poetry when I need diversion, for music when opportunity offers, for love when the crazy fit befalls me. There is nothing that I have not seen, nothing that I have not done, nothing of which I have not taken advantage for my own enjoyment.*

The play drew to its close. The verses of the *Vaudeville*, the music of the final ballet, were submerged in the waves of frantic applause. The actors came forward to make their bow and both they and the author in his box received an ovation. He too made his oft-repeated bows, but not, as other authors were in the habit of doing, with a feigned air of blasé disinterest. He made no attempt to disguise the genuine pleasure he felt.

Désirée was proud. By guile and sheer force of acting she had achieved a victory for her Pierre. Yet it was with a faintly ironical and bitter smile that she observed how Pierre, though he applauded her and the other actors, kept leaning towards Thérèse with a tender affection which he was at pains to emphasize.

Later on, in Désirée's dressing-room, Vaudreuil said to Pierre, "Well, we've done it, *mon cher*. And tomorrow I set out for Brittany to bring England to her knees."

☆   ☆   ☆

From the four hundred or so Americans who were held in captivity in England came loud complaints concerning their wretched condition, and the envoys resolved to send them money and such other assistance as might be feasible. The man entrusted with this mission, which would not be without its dangers, must be reliable and have his wits about him. The two candidates for the post put forward by Franklin were unknown to him personally, but they had been recommended by men in whose judgment he had confidence and they looked honest. Arthur Lee, on the other hand, urged the appointment of a business man from Maryland named Digges, whom he had known for some years, insisting with his wonted gloomy vehemence that he could guarantee both the man's upright character and his aptness for the task. "I'm prepared to vouch for the man," he repeated several times. Franklin was not very favourably impressed by Mr. Digges, whose oily eloquence and shifty eyes inspired him with distrust. Lee and Adams, however, overruled his objections, and Mr. Digges was duly dispatched on his mission to London.

Franklin had long realized the distaste with which John Adams regarded him, but he was also aware that his colleague was trying to be fair. He was therefore all the more painfully surprised when he learnt that the envenomed atmosphere of the long period of waiting had induced even a John Adams to demean himself by making some particularly unfriendly references to him in conversation with Monsieur Marbois, one of the French Foreign Minister's secretaries. Franklin was both angered and saddened that an envoy of the Congress, an honourable man, had blackened a colleague's reputation in the eyes of an important French official.

He longed to be rid of the others. He warned himself against entertaining false hope, but in his secret heart he was counting upon being appointed sole plenipotentiary.

Across his prospects was cast the shadow of his son.

William had been behaving with circumspection during the past few months, and in consequence he had been duly included in an exchange of prisoners and set free. Now he was in New York on English soil presiding over an *association of loyal Americans,* advising the English officers and officials, and announcing in grandiose speeches that the majority of the colonial population adhered steadfastly to His Britannic Majesty. The English journals seized upon these speeches and exploited William as a national hero whose inviolable loyalty stood in such striking contrast to the knavery of his rebellious father. There could be no doubt that these English articles were very welcome to Franklin's enemies in Philadelphia, who saw in him not the man who had helped to bring about the French alliance, but only the father of the traitor. His opponents had fresh weapons in their armoury and the Congress a further pretext for deferring its decision.

Young William and de la Motte did not mince their words at the delaying tactics, the reprehensible procrastination, of the people in Philadelphia. Franklin, however, kept both ill humour and impatience locked within his heart. One day when he was lying in his bathtub while the two young men, sitting on the lid, indulged in wrathful resentment against the Congress he told them the story of the rabbit and the tortoise.

The rabbit, he recounted, had broken a leg, and said to its friend the tortoise, "Please be so good as to run to the doctor and ask him to let you have a few medicinal herbs." The tortoise nodded and the rabbit lay in pain waiting for his friend's return. He waited a long time, for it was not until the evening of the following day that he saw the tortoise again. "Could you not get to the doctor's sooner?" moaned the rabbit. "If you talk to me like that," replied the tortoise, "I won't go at all."

The old man had one deep source of joy amid these vexations and delays. Little Benjamin Bache had returned to Passy. The boy had made astonishing progress, and Franklin listened with delight to his fluent French. With an alert interest in all he saw, and a mature judgment that belied his years, he became absorbed in his grandfather's printing press and very soon picked up as much of the art of printing as the old man had time to teach him. Madame Helvétius at once took the child to her heart and never tired of pointing out in her cheerful, boisterous way how closely he resembled his grandfather.

Little Benjamin reminded Franklin of his son Francis, his favourite son who had died at the age of four. And during these weeks he often thought of his dead wife Deborah, Franky's mother.

He could see her clearly in his mind. With a proud, embarrassed smile on her plump pink-and-white face, she stood and looked at him. She had called him to breakfast, and to his surprise he found his milk served in a porcelain bowl with a silver spoon. Hitherto he had used a tin spoon and a twopenny earthenware bowl. She had bought the expensive articles, without telling him about it beforehand, for twenty-three shillings, and when he grumbled a little at the cost she replied that she could see no reason why her husband should not have a porcelain bowl and a silver spoon like his neighbours. She was a buxom woman, more than a little rustic in appearance, it was true, but what a fine resolute female she was, and who knew better how to humour his many little whims and fancies than she did? How proud he had been at the time of the Stamp Act at being able to go about clad from head to foot in wool and linen that she had woven with her own hands. And when she bought rags for his paper mill, what a keen bargainer she had turned out to be. He had always preached economy, but it was not part of his nature to be economical, and if she had not kept an eye on his accounts the money would have flowed through his hands like water.

It would be good to have somebody like Deborah with him now. Life without women was a dreary business. He was as conscious of that at seventy-two as he had been at seventeen. So it was. The urge had been implanted in one by the Supreme Being, and if there were moments when one felt it to be humiliating, then the feeling was false. He mused with a smile on the blunt jests in which he had from time to time given vent to his lusty humour, such as the hearty letter in which he had impudently twisted the Latin of Thomas à Kempis. *"In angulo cum puella,* or as the case may be, *in angulo puellae."* His essay on the reasons for preferring an elderly mistress to a young one had not been without its merits either, to say nothing of its logic. He did not believe in romantic love, but he believed in platonic love still less.

A man alone was an incomplete being, like half of a pair of scissors. Franklin felt tired and lonely. And if he were to be recalled to America, to his homeland where he was regarded as a lecher, a hypocrite, and an atheist, would he not feel even more lonely?

Here in France he was loved and honoured. The lads had already started to fill a third stout portfolio with eulogies in both prose and verse, as well as flattering drawings. He did not want to leave France, and it might be as well to equip himself with new relevant arguments beforehand so as to be ready in case the Congress should deprive him of his present ones.

☆ ☆ ☆

He spent the evening at Auteuil with Madame Helvétius, at whose untidy but amply loaded table he felt more at home than he did in his own house. There they devoted themselves to looking after his needs, humouring his weaknesses, and anticipating his wishes. When the other guests were served with roast veal he was offered a tasty dish of minced chicken, which was more suited to his scanty and somewhat sensitive teeth. With the dessert and pastries he had whipped cream, just as he liked it, thick and sweet.

When the meal was over the Mesdemoiselles Helvétius sang his favourite Scottish ballads, the abbés joked in their affable way, he himself related a number of anecdotes, and everybody thoroughly enjoyed his own company and that of the others.

Later on in the evening he sat chatting with his hostess by the fireside, the two of them alone together as was their wont. She was in her late fifties, her figure more than amply filled her arm-chair, her fading blond hair was carelessly dyed, and her complexion of roses and lilies was equally carelessly made up, but in the Doctor's eyes she was still the brilliant beauty that she had been in her youth. As she babbled on in contented self-assurance, her cheerful voice and impulsive gestures, in fact the whole boisterous ensemble, stirred Franklin to a deep delight. She was a wonderful combination of the qualities he had so esteemed in his homely Deborah and those which attracted him in the smart Parisienne, Madame Brillon.

Disregarding his painful foot he stood up and went across to lean over the back of her chair. With a sense of amusement, not untinged with embarrassment, the thought flitted through his mind that as he stood leaning over Madame Helvétius, with her puppy on her lap, they formed together a little group such as was to be seen on one or two of the gallant engravings with which the walls of the room were adorned.

"How would it be, Marie-Félicité," he asked abruptly, "if we were to do a little marrying?"

She looked up in undisguised atonishment. "Are you being serious?" she inquired.

Searching laboriously for the French words, he replied, "If you mind, then I am not speaking seriously, but if you don't mind, then I am in earnest."

She was silent. There was a strange look of reverie on her painted countenance as she mechanically caressed the puppy that was lying in her lap. Gazing at her plump arm and small, childlike hand, Franklin explained to her, in a low, dispassionate tone, almost casually, his present situation. "If, as is not at all unlikely," he said, "I should be recalled from my post in the near future, I shall be faced with a grave problem. Am I to go back to Philadelphia? Am I to quit the shores of a country where I have met with so much sympathetic understanding, where I have found such great comfort, both material and spiritual, to warm my heart? The country in which you are living, Marie-Félicité? One small yes from your lips would solve my problem."

Slowly she swept the puppy from her lap and rose from her chair. With an embarrassed smile that made her appear much younger than she was, and evidently profoundly moved, she pointed to one of the numerous portraits of her late husband, Claude-Adrien Helvétius.

In a more animated tone than was usual with him, Franklin said, "Your husband, my friend Helvétius, was a great man. He, of all men, would understand why I long that you should share your life with me. He would approve of my desire and support it with the whole weight of his philosophy. Have you not yourself told me, Marie-

Félicité, that with his dying breath he begged you to enjoy your life?"

Still smiling, but with her eyes averted, she replied, "Do go on talking, beloved and esteemed great man. I like to listen to you."

Speaking in light, gallant, reasonable words, he pointed out that they appreciated the same things, the same people, and the same way of living. Then a little impatiently he broke off with the lament, "How I regret my poor French. I wish I could say all this to you in more adequate language, and less bluntly."

"Your French is not at all bad," she commented. "Madame Brillon has been a very efficient tutor," and hesitantly, with a deepening smile and as if she were savouring the syllables, she addressed him for the first time by his Christian name, "Benjamin." None of his French friends had ever used it and he did not at first recognize his own name in its French pronunciation, but her expression and attitude told him more than her words and he thought that she had already yielded to his wooing. With a devoted if rather portentous air he raised her hand to his lips.

Her heart was beating rapidly at the thought that this man, whom all her friends regarded as the greatest of living mortals, had succumbed so unreservedly to her fascination. "It all sounds very marvellous, *mon ami*," she said, "and it pleases me deeply, I must admit. But I know what a sly old gentleman you are, for you have often told me yourself that without actually lying you are able to put your words together in such a way that people readily accept them. So I must consider everything thoroughly, and you must allow me time."

She went to see her friend Turgot and told him of Franklin's proposal. "It is only one of his jokes," declared Turgot without hesitation and disapprovingly.

"Oh no, Jacques-Robert," she protested vigorously. "He meant it absolutely seriously."

Turgot thought of the two occasions when she had rejected his own offer of marriage, once when he was young and poor, and a second time when he was rich and famous. He still smarted at the memory.

"What did you say to him?" he demanded, his handsome, furrowed face darkening still more.

"I insisted that I must have time to think it over," she replied.

"What?" he burst out angrily. "You did not turn him down without more ado? Time to think it over? Have you gone crazy?"

"You are always so rough, Jacques-Robert," she protested plaintively. "Don't you think I should feel honoured and tempted by an offer of marriage from Doctor Franklin?"

"Honoured?" he snapped. "Tempted? I find it tasteless. It is perfectly absurd. It is utterly ludicrous. Supposing some other man of his years and appearance were to make you the same proposal, a

Mr. Brown or a Mr. Smith, you would laugh at the mere idea, wouldn't you?"

"But he isn't a Mr. Brown or a Mr. Smith," she replied. "He is Doctor Franklin."

Turgot strode wrathfully up and down the room. "When I hear you talking like that," he declared, "it seems incomprehensible to me that I should sometimes have tried to conduct a rational conversation with you. Can you not see for yourself how preposterous it is to waste a single word on the matter? But I see," he concluded bitterly, "that you are easily dazzled by fame. Having married the man whom you regarded as the most celebrated philosopher, you now want to marry the most celebrated statesman in the world."

She looked very meek and youthful as she sat in her capacious armchair. "But I should so like to live with him," she sighed. "Please explain to me, Jacques-Robert, why you think it so preposterous."

"If you marry him," he explained, "you will have to change your whole way of living. Has that ever occurred to you?"

"How do you mean?" she queried, somewhat taken aback. "He likes the same people as I do, and we share the same tastes."

"The American Ambassador," he commented, "even though he may disregard the conventions as Franklin does, must refrain from inviting to his house many people whom you would like to see there and he has to invite many whom you would not wish to meet. You will have to renounce many things and many friends, Marie-Félicité. At every step you will have to ask yourself, and to ask him, whether it is correct. A strong-minded woman like yourself will certainly resent her salon being turned into the European agency of the United States."

She looked thoughtful. "Perhaps the Doctor will be recalled," she suggested hopefully. "And if the office he holds should stand in the way of our inclinations, he can resign of his own accord."

"What is this foolish chatter?" he retorted rudely. "Do you seriously believe that a man like Franklin would hesitate for a single moment in making his choice between you and America? At seventy-two one no longer yields to romantic illusions. Even in his early youth Benjamin Franklin was never so youthful that he would have surrendered his life's work for a woman."

She pouted in protest, but it was evident that his words had made an impression.

When Madame Helvétius was back home again, she walked from room to room inspecting the portraits of her Claude-Adrien, whose joy in life had been no less keen than his philosophic reasoning, as even Jacques-Robert had been compelled to admit. Doctor Franklin—

Benjamin—had much in common with Claude-Adrien. It would be nice to live with him. But she and Claude-Adrien had both been young, and they had not found it difficult to adapt themselves to one another's ways. Doctor Franklin had the reputation of getting his own way in the end, for all his gentle manner. The American Ambassador, she pondered, would have to ask her to do a number of things that she would not want to do. She stood in front of the mirror. She felt young, but was she still young enough, still sufficiently adaptable, not to find restrictions irksome? For many years she had been behaving exactly as she liked. When she had declined the impetuous Jacques-Robert's offer of marriage, it was from fear of losing her independence. Benjamin was less impetuous, but scarcely less stubborn. Madame Helvétius heaved a sigh.

Seating herself at her escritoire, she wrote her Benjamin a good-humoured but serious letter. If any man, she assured him, were capable of shaking her resolve to live alone with the memory of her dear departed Claude-Adrien, that man was Benjamin Franklin. But her resolve stood firm even against this temptation. She wept a little as she folded the note, sealed it, and sent it off.

Franklin, too, had been pondering on the advantages and disadvantages that would accrue from marriage with Marie-Félicité. He pictured to himself her plump and pleasing personality, so much more attractive than the austere, though more scantily clad, females who usually in the honourable engravings came to wreathe his brow with laurel. Then he thought of Marie-Félicité's boisterous ways, and how self-willed she was. He would have even fewer hours for reading and peaceful meditation than at present. Yet he could not help recalling how she had stood before him, blushing so innocently and addressing him by his Christian name; her voice and bearing were almost irresistible even in memory. There was just as much to be said in favour of the marriage as against it, and whatever Madame Helvétius might decide, he would accept the situation philosophically and draw what satisfaction he could from it.

When the letter arrived, he adhered to his determination. He was not sorry that he had made his proposal of marriage, but neither was he sorry that he was to be spared the complications of married life.

Marie-Félicité's letter, in fact, pleased him mightily. He noted the numerous mistakes of grammar and orthography, and reflected that this too was a trait which Madame Helvétius had in common with Deborah.

Taking it all in all, it would be better to continue seeing her two or three days a week than to have her about the house for seven days a week. During the rest of the time he would have to content himself with the allegorical ladies of the engravings.

He proceeded to write his reply:

Your resolve, my dearest Marie-Félicité, to live alone for the rest of your life with the memory of your beloved husband has touched me deeply and kept me awake the greater part of the night. When I eventually fell asleep, I was visited by a strange dream. I dreamt that I was dead and in the Elysian Fields. I was asked whether there were any particular personages whom I wished to see, and I said that I would like to meet some philosophers. "There are two living quite close to here," I was informed. "They are excellent neighbours and on very good terms with one another." "What are their names?" I inquired. "Socrates and Helvétius," was the reply. "I esteem them both," I responded, "but I should like first of all to meet Helvétius; I talk a little French, but no Greek."

Helvétius received me with much courtesy. He asked me a thousand questions relative to the war, the present state of religion, of liberty, and of the government in France. "You do not inquire, then," said I, "after your dear friend, Madame Helvétius; yet she loves you exceedingly. I was in her company not more than an hour ago." "Ah!" said he. "You remind me of my past happiness. For many years I could think of nothing but her, though at last I am consoled. I have taken another wife, the most like her that I could find. She is not, indeed, altogether so handsome, but she has a great fund of wit and good sense, and her whole study is to please me. She is at this moment gone to fetch the best nectar and ambrosia to regale me. Stay here awhile and you will see her." "I perceive," said I, "that your former friend is more faithful to you than you are to her; she has had several good offers, but has refused them all. I will confess to you that I loved her exceedingly." "I pity you sincerely," said he, "for she is an excellent woman, handsome and amiable." Then the new Madame Helvétius came in with the nectar, and I recognized her immediately as my former American friend, Mrs. Franklin. I reclaimed her, but she answered me coldly, "I was a good wife to you for forty-nine years and four months, nearly half a century. Let that content you. I have formed a new connexion here which will last for eternity."

Indignant at this refusal from my Eurydice, I immediately resolved to quit those ungrateful shades and return to this good world again, to behold the sun and you. Here I am. Let us avenge ourselves.

Franklin read through this letter, and chuckled, *"Vive la bagatelle!"* He was glad that he had made his offer of marriage, and very glad that it had been refused.

That evening he was the guest of Madame Brillon. He was in good spirits, and his cheerfulness was enhanced by the reflection that as the husband of Madame Helvétius his visits to his charming tutor in the French language would of necessity have had to be far less frequent.

Madame Brillon had ordered her bath to be prepared for ten o'clock, but when the time came they were deeply immersed in conversation and she declined to let him go. For another two hours or so he sat upon the wooden lid of her bathtub while they continued to talk.

☆   ☆   ☆

Immediately after the performance of *Figaro*, Vaudreuil had set off for Brittany to take over command of the invasion army. He found the troops in a state of demoralization owing to the long wait, and the theme on which the officers continually harped was, "We don't mind dying, we are longing for a fight, we hate being bored."

Vaudreuil was determined to force the Government into giving orders for the attack, and it was not unusual for him to send two couriers to Versailles on the same day, but his efforts met with no more success than had those of his less energetic predecessor, the old Marquis de Castries. Versailles invented a thousand pretexts for postponement, pointed to the necessity of preparing an expeditionary corps for the West, and even referred to a new plan which would involve the dispatch of an army to Senegal. Vaudreuil alternated between entreaties, threats and curses, but it was all no use. There he was, in the midst of this war, but stuck in Brittany, and more bored than he had ever been in Versailles.

Then, during the weeks of this devastating tedium, he received news that a number of French ships on their way to Brest had been surprised by an English squadron and that there had been a heavy engagement. The French ships had succeeded in breaking contact with the superior enemy forces, and their arrival in Brest was expected shortly. The frigate *La Surveillante* had particularly distinguished herself by sinking the man-o'-war *Quebec*.

With the help of his valet Baptiste and an orderly, Vaudreuil hastily put on his full-dress uniform, mounted his charger, and started for the Port of Brest in order to welcome the heroic seamen.

The place was agog with excitement and there were all sorts of rumours flying about concerning the gallant action of the French ships. Everybody, troops and civilians alike, was streaming towards the docks.

Reaching the quai, he pulled up his horse and remained in the saddle, towering above the crowd, with his eyes strained towards the sea. It was a sultry day in September, and both horse and rider were sweating. It was said that the *Surveillante* had blown the *Quebec* out of the water, but that she was herself on fire and her captain, the Chevalier de Couédic, seriously wounded.

Far off on the horizon they espied the *Surveillante,* moving slowly and enveloped in smoke. Tugs made ready to go to her assistance, and Vaudreuil, impatient to greet the victorious squadron that had given fresh nourishment to his hopes, rode up one of the tug-boats which was about to push off. He considered it unsoldierly to receive the victors on foot; he thought of the imposing equestrian statue of his uncle, Marshal Vaudreuil; he thought of Gabrielle who once had whispered in his ear, "When you are in the saddle, you look like Mars himself." So he led his horse up the gangway and onto the boat. Everyone shouted, *"Vive Vaudreuil."*

The air was still and heavy. Slowly the tug made its way towards the *Surveillante,* which, an unwieldy shape in her cloud of smoke, seemed scarcely to be moving. Vaudreuil, sitting on his charger, gazed out to sea. From the distance came a heavy detonation, and the horse, which had been restless from the start, reared. Vaudreuil, keeping a tight hold on the reins, stayed in the saddle, a magnificent, virile figure and in everybody's way. He turned his head and stared towards the north, in the direction of the English coast. After this naval victory the fat fellow would no longer be able to prevent him from setting off on his great enterprise. At the head of his army he would fall upon the shores of England.

Another explosion was heard, and this time it was much nearer. With a sudden leap the charger sprang over the rails and into the sea.

Vaudreuil was a good swimmer, and how he came to be drowned was later the cause of much surmise. He was hampered by his riding-boots and heavy full-dress uniform, and may have received a kick from his horse as it struggled in the water. The sailors who at once jumped in to help him were unable to do anything. For awhile his hat and one of his gloves continued to float on the surface as the burning ship slowly approached.

The news of the Marquis de Vaudreuil's strange end struck like a thunderbolt in Paris and Versailles. Only a short time had elapsed since another distinguished French officer, Major General du Coudray, had died through a similar accident. He had been commissioned by Silas Deane to take up a command in America, and his appointment had been ratified by the Congress when he reported at Philadelphia. While he was crossing the Schuylkill River on his way to General Headquarters his horse, from which he had not dismounted, had leapt from the ferry and he had been drowned.

When old General Castries had been relieved of his command in favour of Vaudreuil, there had been many who hoped that France would now take the war seriously and carry hostilities into the enemy's country. They were disconcerted at the incongruous end of the proud commander and the destruction of their hopes.

Pierre was saddened. Of all the haughty aristocrats whom he numbered among his acquaintances Vaudreuil had been the haughtiest, nevertheless he had liked him. He had found a piquant satisfaction in presenting Count Almaviva as a figure of mockery, but he had invested the character with considerable brilliance and had done so sincerely. Pierre was genuinely grieved at the death of his friend Vaudreuil whom he had loved and hated, whom he had both admired and despised.

He was surprised when Désirée took the occurrence calmly. For a fleeting second, when he first informed her of what had happened, she seemed to feel a pang, but then she commented, "His invasion would have come to nothing in any case," and the epitaph she composed for him could not have been more dispassionate. "For an aristocrat," she said, "he wasn't so bad. He was less stupid than the others, but more conceited. As a lover he was not at all agreeable. He acted as if he were conferring a favour. He died at the right moment, having fulfilled his mission: *Figaro* has been produced, and he lives on as Count Almaviva."

The Lilac Coterie felt orphaned. Prince Charles, who did not normally take things to heart, was deeply depressed. He had lost a friend such as he would never find again. François Vaudreuil had been to him a mirror of fashion, the acme of chivalry, an exemplar of the true way in which an aristocrat should live, a man whose counsel could be blindly followed. Henceforth, brooded Prince Charles, there would devolve upon him the duty of representing the nobility of France and the aristocratic way of life. He would be alone, and there would be no model for him to copy.

The effect upon Gabrielle Polignac was shattering. Lethargic by nature, her emotions were not easily stirred, but François had set her pulse beating faster. His fierce, handsome looks, his elegant figure, his gestures, his manner of speaking, his wit and cultivated virility, his very presence, had cast a spell over her. So long as François Vaudreuil was in the world she had known the meaning of love. She sat quietly in her room and wept without ceasing. Her husband, Jules Polignac, understood and sympathized. "We have lost a great deal," he said, and there was conviction in his words.

There was a pressing problem to solve. How was the dreadful news to be broken to Toinette in her delicate condition? Diane Polignac consulted Doctor Lassone. She was afraid that if Gabrielle, who had herself been so attached to François, were to be the bearer of the news, her grief might only serve to aggravate the effect upon Toinette. Lassone thought it over. How would it be if Mademoiselle Mesnard were entrusted with the task? She was on fairly intimate terms with the illustrious patient, yet not too intimate. It would be better for Toinette to learn of the catastrophe from Mademoiselle Mesnard than from a stranger, or by chance.

Doctor Lassone himself, on behalf of the Queen's friends, begged Désirée to comply with their wishes. She welcomed the suggestion and even looked forward with a certain pleasure to informing Toinette of the death of the man who had been the friend of them both. There was a strange link between Toinette, herself, the Countess Polignac, and the dead man.

As it turned out, Doctor Lassone, too, was linked to them, for he drew very personal inferences from Vaudreuil's death. Believing that Désirée had been deeply attached to Vaudreuil, he assumed that the main obstacle to his ambition had been removed. So, immediately after she had accepted the mission, he proceeded with a mingled air of pomposity, embarrassment, and sarcasm to offer her his hand in marriage.

Désirée was not taken by surprise, for she had realized that the proposal was bound to come, but the fact that he was using Vaudreuil's ludicrous end for making it nearly provoked her into a fit of laughter. She managed to control herself, however, feigned astonishment, and begged him, with an appearance of being deeply touched, to allow her time to think it over.

"How long will you need to think it over?" he inquired.

"If you press me to give you an answer now, my dear Doctor," she replied, with her eyes fixed on his, "you will force me, I am afraid, to say no."

"I do not press you," he hastened to assure her.

When Désirée informed her that Vaudreuil was dead, Toinette turned pale. "How terrible!" she cried. "How perfectly dreadful!" Yet Désirée, accustomed to seeing through the emotions of others, saw at once that Toinette was less deeply affected than her friends had feared. It even seemed that she was experiencing something like a sense of relief.

And so she was. Profoundly grieved though she might be at the heroic demise of her François, without admitting it to herself, she felt grateful to Providence. She had been willing to keep her promise to Vaudreuil, for she had persuaded herself that adulterous betrayal of the weak and pitiful Louis would be less of a sin than failure to keep the word she had pledged to such a noble and brilliant soldier, who might be driven by her refusal into a state of despair and conceivably to suicide. God had rescued her from an ominous conflict

of duties and preserved her, the mother of the Dauphin, from becoming an adulteress. It was a thousand pities, nevertheless. She
thought of the rapturous thrill that had shuddered through her when
François seized her so brutally by the wrist, and tears came into her
eyes.

"How dreadful," she repeated. "What a brave, heroic end. How we
shall all miss him. He was such a great general, such a nobleman, such
an artist. Do you not think so, Désirée?"

"Certainly, Madame," rejoined Désirée dryly.

"He must have a State funeral," decided Toinette. "I shall go and
see Louis at once."

Louis had likewise discerned the finger of God in the matter when
he heard that Vaudreuil was dead.

The humiliating peace that had been imposed upon France in 1763
must be blotted out. Of that there could be no doubt, and the American conflict offered a favourable opportunity. Yet he cherished no
hatred for his cousin at the Court of St. James's, and he considered
it unfair to fall upon him in his own island. It would be more chivalrous to settle the dispute in distant continents. On the other hand,
the King of France could hardly return a blunt *no* when his generals
besieged him with demands to issue orders for a landing in England.
Now Vaudreuil, the most insistent advocate of invasion, had tumbled
into the sea and taken his plans with him. The expeditionary corps
would in due course, but without too much haste, set sail for America,
and the troops massing on the northern coasts would be dispatched to
Africa, to Senegal. The two expeditions together would reduce the
British Empire to its proper proportions, carrying out the task in a
seemly manner.

He had shared the solicitude of Toinette's friends as to how she
would take the news of Vaudreuil's sudden end, and when she came
to see him he was relieved to observe that her grief was not excessive.
She said it was very consoling to know that he had died in such an
heroic manner on his way to invade England, which had always been
his dream. Louis thought to himself, "Nobody told the fellow to go
aboard ship on horseback." But he was careful not to utter his thoughts
aloud. Caressing Toinette's arm, he murmured, "Yes, it really is a
pity about our Vaudreuil."

Toinette suggested that Louis was no doubt intending to invest the
departed hero with the *Cordon Bleu* and to order a State funeral. He
thought this rather overdoing it, in fact ludicrous, but he did not
want to upset her so he replied, "Yes, Madame. An excellent idea,
Madame."

The interment took place with all the pomp and ceremony that Versailles could display on such occasions. The whole court was present,

including all the Ministers and Ambassadors, many of the ladies wept copiously, and even Gabrielle Polignac did less to conceal her sorrow than good manners should have dictated. Prince Charles, contrary to his habit, appeared very much affected, while Jules Polignac allowed the tears to course freely down his cheeks.

☆   ☆   ☆

There had been ten ships travelling in convoy under the escort of the *Orfraye* when the man-o'-war was requisitioned by Admiral d'Estaing, and after continuing on their way without protection the whole ten fell into the hands of the English. It was generally agreed that the firm of Hortalez was entitled to compensation by the Government for the loss it had suffered, but there was by no means general agreement as to the amount due to the firm. A number of the merchantmen had already discharged part of their cargo in the West Indies, and in any case the *Orfraye* would not have been able to escort each individual vessel throughout its voyage. Such were the arguments with which the Ministry of Finance excused its delay in settling Pierre's just claims.

Eventually a commission composed of three *fermiers généraux* was set up to establish the precise nature of the losses suffered by the firm of Hortalez and the exact sum that should be paid in compensation. The members of the commission were in no hurry. They called for documentary evidence which had to be procured from the West Indies, and in some cases from the United States, and when the evidence had been supplied they asked for further information which again necessitated inquiry across the ocean. In these circumstances it was likely that the commission would take months, or even years, to come to a decision. Pierre demanded an instalment in advance, but the Ministry of Finance, like the Congress in Philadelphia, took the position that nothing could be paid out until the total amount due had been ascertained. In the end Vergennes sanctioned an advance to Pierre of a mere 150,000 livres.

There were mysterious enemies of Pierre who saw to it that every detail of his financial difficulties became public property. He was being dunned by his creditors, and in order to save Hortalez and Company, he had to transfer to it new funds from his other enterprises. For the twentieth time Maigron explained that Hortalez was slowly eating into every sound undertaking that Pierre possessed. "It is idealistic folly," he insisted, "to continue supplying arms to these people overseas who have not the slightest intention of paying for them. I beg you to be sensible, Monsieur. Abandon it. Let me announce that the firm of Hortalez is insolvent."

Pierre had already set himself a time limit, the first of September. The first of September had come and gone. The reliable, devoted Maigron was right; it would be madness to try to hold out any further. "Let me announce that the firm is insolvent," demanded Maigron with quiet insistence.

With face averted, Pierre said, "I will think it over and let you know tomorrow."

Maigron was taken aback. He had expected that Pierre would refuse, as he always did, and send him off with a flea in his ear. In all the years they had worked together it was the first time that his brilliant, easy-going employer had lost faith in his star. Maigron's impassive features twitched as he played nervously with his pencil. "Everything will turn out all right, Monsieur," he said with an effort.

But Pierre was not in a mood to accept cheap consolation. "Why don't you be sensible, Maigron?" he cried in a tone of ironic despair that cut the other to the heart. "I am aware that you have offers from many quarters. Go to the *Compagnie des Indes*. Go to Lenormant. Abandon the ship, which is now drifting with neither sails nor mast. You will be better off anywhere else. I thank you, Maigron, but you had better seek a wiser master."

Maigron glared at him angrily. "Do not talk nonsense," he said, and left.

Pierre, alone, sat at his writing-table, drained and weary as never before. He knew that the moment he ceased to be convinced that the world belonged to him he was lost. Catching sight of his face in the mirror, he became conscious for the first time that he was no longer young. "I am sinking," he said, "I am sinking. I have already gone down."

Gudin called and was horrified when he saw his friend. "What has gone wrong, for Heaven's sake?" he cried.

"I am bankrupt," said Pierre.

Gudin had expected more. "But you always have been," he rejoined.

"This time I really am bankrupt," declared Pierre heatedly. "I haven't a sou left. Even the chair on which I am sitting and the ring on my finger do not belong to me."

Gudin did not altogether grasp the situation. A business man was up one day and down the next, that was the nature of his calling. There must be some other reason, some moral reason, for the evident emotion displayed by his normally self-confident friend. Those knavish Americans must have dealt him another treacherous blow. Gudin summoned up a look of sympathy.

"I have done a little to help America," went on Pierre in the same quiet, grim tone. "Or am I mistaken? The *Ferragus*, the *Eugénie*, the *Thérèse*, the *Heureux*, the *Mercure*, these ships carried arms to

America, arms and equipment that cost me six million livres. Or have I been dreaming? I delivered supplies amounting to another three million to the States of Virginia, New Hampshire, and North Carolina. Or is that only my imagination? And the *Orfraye* took part in the Battle of Grenada. Or was that a mere delusion? What is now my reward? They are taking away the roof from over my head."

Despite the compassion he felt for his friend, Gudin was edified at being thus privileged to witness a scene of historical significance which would furnish an admirable page or two for his *Chronicle of the Life and Opinions of Caron de Beaumarchais*. In an access of fervour he cried, "It is due to you, Pierre, that there is still freedom in the world. That is something which nobody can dispute. It is an historical fact. You have in your chest the great letter of thanks sent to you by the Congress. You have been the saviour of liberty, Pierre," he concluded in a ringing voice.

"And my reward is to be thrown to the dogs," commented Pierre.

When Gudin had gone Pierre fetched from his chest the honourable witnesses to his achievements—the judgment of the court by which he had been freed from the "stain" on his character, the letter of thanks from Philadelphia, the manuscripts of his memoranda, of *The Barber* and of *Figaro*. But the sight of them gave him no comfort. He was now in his forty-eighth year, and the greater part of his life had been spent in toil and effort in the interests of others rather than his own, and now he was once more facing complete ruin. There was ample proof that this ruin was attributable solely and simply to the United States, his country's ally, but though that truth might be acknowledged by history, the thought of the honour that would be paid to him by posterity did not sweeten the pill that he now had to swallow. The insolvency of the firm of Hortalez would involve humiliating formalities and he would once more be compelled to undergo the bitter experiences of the past. And Charlot would shake that large head of his and remind him with his usual irritating smile, "Well, I told you so, didn't I?"

Next morning Maigron arrived with the forms announcing the bankruptcy already filled out ready for signature. Pierre took up his pen, but before he could set it to paper Maigron interjected, "I must tell you about a talk I had last night with Monsieur Brunelet. I think you know Brunelet. He sometimes acts as a front for the Marquis d'Aubespine."

Pierre put down his quill. "He is prepared to let you have a loan?" he demanded, his face lighting up.

"He is willing to let you have a mortgage on your house in the rue Saint-Antoine," said Maigron.

Pierre showed his disappointment. He had already tried to raise a

loan on the house, but the only offers he had received were far too low
and the conditions had made it too much of a risk. "That will not help
us a great deal," he responded.

"Monsieur Brunelet would be prepared," went on Maigron reluctantly, "to advance you 600,000 livres."

"600,000 livres!" cried Pierre radiantly. "Tell him we accept."

"Wait," warned Maigron. "The offer smells fishy. Brunelet will require repayment in two months, and he demands as security not only
the house, but the whole of its contents—furniture, works of art,
everything. It is as clear as daylight that Brunelet and the man behind
him are counting on the house falling into their hands."

"In two months," cried Pierre, "I shall have the money three times
over, from America and from the compensation due to me for my
ships. Two months. Sixty days. Sixty-one days. And yet you hesitate.
You are a sluggard, Maigron. True as steel—but a sluggard. I would
accept the mortgage even if it were limited to a single month."

So the mortgage was taken up, and on receipt of his 600,000 livres
Pierre at once sent 25,000 to the sculptor Houdon.

☆   ☆   ☆

Louis went to view the exhibition at the *Salon*. With Greuze and
Duplessis as his guides, and followed by a respectful throng, he inspected the paintings and sculptures. Little as he was interested in art,
he was attracted in a number of cases by the subject matter. There
were genre scenes by his artists at the porcelain factory in Sèvres
which really delighted him. In one picture by Pourrat, for instance,
an old woman was depicted toppling off a cart that was loaded high
with household furniture. "Poor old thing," he commented gleefully,
and his guffaw made the canvas tremble. His attention was also drawn
to a few landscapes, and from the abundance of geographical detail
that he had stored up in his mind he delivered little lectures to his
guides on the population figures of the regions concerned or the
industries which flourished there.

They came to a small gallery which contained nothing but three
busts. "Here," explained Greuze, "we see this year's contribution
from our Praxiteles, Monsieur Houdon." Houdon was hovering
modestly in the background.

Louis stared and knitted his brows. In a semicircle, white and marble
stood the three men he loathed most in all the world—Voltaire, Franklin, and Beaumarchais. They had not the appearance of heretics and
rebels. On the contrary they looked like men of dignity and virtue,
and might almost have been taken for heroes of antiquity. The flashing eyes of Voltaire revealed a roguish kindliness. The head of Frank-

lin bespoke simplicity and wisdom. The features of Beaumarchais reflected a sense of humour and a superior, sympathetic intelligence. Louis breathed hoarsely. To conceal his annoyance he stepped close up to the busts and blinked at them short-sightedly.

The silence grew embarrassing. "Our Monsieur Houdon," ventured Greuze, "is the first sculptor who has ever succeeded in endowing eyes of stone with the semblance of life."

The awkward Duplessis summoned up the courage to say, "Yes, Sire. The greatest artist in your realm has modelled the three greatest writers of your capital."

These remarks augmented Louis's wrath, but he had to control himself; he was expected to say something. "I am aware," he said to Houdon, "that you are an excellent artist. I was very pleased with the bust you made of me. You did not need many sittings either. Very well, then," he concluded. "Very well." He continued his tour.

On his way back to Versailles he brooded angrily. When the greatest artist of the day, the Praxiteles of France, looked for the finest heads to model, he had to pick on these three. "The three greatest writers of your capital," Duplessis had said. His own court painter had dared to praise them with such shameless naïveté in his presence. It was an ominous sign for his dynasty that these three should be regarded as the representative men of his epoch. It meant that all his honest efforts had been in vain.

That same day he received in audience the Duc de Fronsac, director of the *Théâtre français,* who came to report on matters connected with his office. The heir to the Russian throne had not been indulging in empty compliments when he had spoken to Pierre about *Figaro.* He actually intended to present the comedy, *The Crazy Day, or the Marriage of Figaro,* in St. Petersburg and the Russian Ambassador had requested permission to engage some of the actors from the *Théâtre français* for the purpose. Monsieur de Bibikoff, the Intendant of the Imperial Court Theatres, was only waiting the royal consent before setting out on a journey to Paris.

Louis foamed. Of the three rebels whose heads he had been forced to gaze at without being able to smash them to fragments, the worst was that fellow Caron. Voltaire was dead and Franklin was an old man, but Caron was not only alive, he was even comparatively young and Louis always felt driven and tricked by him. The venomous fellow had taken advantage of Toinette's delicate state of health to wheedle him into permitting the performance at Gennevilliers, and though he had expressly stipulated that not another word must ever be uttered in his hearing about the licentious, seditious piece, here was the shameless rascal instigating a fresh intrigue from behind the skirts of Catherine of Russia.

"I don't like it," he grated. "It is really asking too much. What do these Esquimaux think they are doing? Do they expect me to close the *Théâtre français* so that they can amuse themselves with this swinish comedy?"

"What does Your Majesty command me to reply to the Grand Duke?" inquired de Fronsac.

"The Russians can kiss my backside!" growled Louis ungraciously. "Tell them so in polite terms."

"It will not be easy, Sire," sighed de Fronsac.

"I know," conceded Louis. "This is a wretched situation in which we have been plunged by that fellow Caron."

"We could perhaps," suggested de Fronsac, "without incurring any suspicion of discourtesy, decline the request from St. Petersburg if we were to produce the comedy ourselves. The Grand Duke will fully understand that we could in that case hardly spare our actors."

"I will not resort to such a drastic measure merely for the sake of politeness," retorted Louis angrily. "You will please to remember, *Monsieur le Duc,* that I said *never.*"

De Fronsac bowed.

Less than twenty-four hours later the King found Monsieur Caron once more astride his path. This time it was the *Collected Works of Voltaire.* Whereas other forbidden books were tacitly tolerated, this contemplated edition was particularly offensive in the eyes of Louis, and therefore Pierre's *Société Littéraire et Typographique* was being faced with the greatest of difficulties. Not only in Paris, but throughout the country, the police were taking the strictest steps to enforce the ban. Pierre, however, employed more and more agents, to whom he allowed an unusually high commission. In Paris alone, and in the course of a single day, three travelling agents had been arrested while canvassing at the houses of his wealthier subjects for subscriptions to the banned edition of Voltaire's writings.

When Louis read this in the police report, he took the matter into his own hands, and instructed Lenoir to lock up the delinquents not for three days, as was customary, but for five weeks, with one day's fasting in every seven. "I am determined," he declared, "to teach Monsieur Caron and his pack of underlings that the censorship exercised by the Crown is nothing to laugh at. They are not going to play the fool with me. You disappoint me, Monsieur," he admonished his Chief of Police. "You are too slack, Monsieur."

Lenoir pointed out that he had not sufficient funds at his disposal to enforce the censorship regulations.

"Very well," cried Louis in annoyance. "I will allow you another 100,000 livres. I wish this slackness to cease." His voice had risen to a falsetto. "Am I understood, Monsieur?"

Suddenly his mood changed. "My officials have no marrow in their bones," he lamented, and gloomily he predicted to his bewildered Chief of Police: "You will see, Lenoir, in the end this Beaumarchais and his *Figaro* will get the better of both of us."

Within another forty-eight hours the subject of the detestable Monsieur Caron was broached by Vergennes during a routine audience. In view of the precarious situation of the firm of Hortalez, Pierre had made a request for an advance payment of half a million on account of the sum due for compensation. This time, the Minister explained, the firm really was in a bad way, and if it were to be forced into bankruptcy it was very much to be feared that Monsieur Caron would make public the secret association between his firm and the Government before the conclusion of the alliance. Such a revelation would be eagerly welcomed by the English as proof that Versailles had been guilty for years of a breach of neutrality. In any case, there could be no question but that the firm had suffered serious losses in the West Indies. To sum up, Vergennes supported Pierre's request.

Louis, however, was in a bad temper. "I am sick to death of the importunities of your Monsieur Caron," he snapped in a tone that brooked no argument. "A man of affairs who speculates on enormous profits must expect to take a corresponding risk. It would suit Monsieur Caron's book very well to pocket the profits and let me pay his losses. I'm not a fool whose purse can be slit by any footpad. And if the fellow starts any threats, I believe the Crown still possesses ways and means of dealing with its seditious subjects."

☆   ☆   ☆

The fame of Pierre's unproduced play called forth much envy and ill will. Even the Archbishop of Paris poured out the vials of his wrath in a pastoral letter. Its most bitter opponent, however, was the Abbé Suard, a gifted and influential writer with a seat in the Academy. At first he contented himself with addressing the forty immortals on the cheap eroticism of the modern stage, with frequent, unmistakable allusions to *Figaro*. Then he proceeded to attack the play in the *Journal de Paris,* devoting two long, anonymous articles to the subject.

When a third article appeared, also signed *An Abbé,* Pierre could no longer restrain himself. He replied to the anonymous author, whom he suspected to be the Abbé Suard, in an open letter which he sent to the *Mercure.* "What extraordinary creatures there are today calling themselves priests!" he scoffed. "Formerly it was only wise, enlightened men who were considered worthy of that appellation. Today one has to cry out to every ragamuffin and blockhead, *Be quiet, Abbé! Off with you, Abbé! Begone, Abbé!* What is really your object, gentlemen, in allowing your anonymous stupidities to appear in print? Do you wish to force me, who in order that my play might be presented did not shun a struggle with lions and tigers, do you wish to force me to carry out the duties of a serving-maid who slaughters insignificant little bugs with a feather duster?"

When Pierre spoke of "insignificant little bugs" he was thinking of the dwarfish Abbé Suard, but the article against which he was launching his invective, the third and final article, had not been written by the little Abbé. It had come from the pen of a large and corpulent gentleman whose name was Prince Xavier.

Prince Xavier, though he bore little resemblance to his brother in other ways, shared the latter's loathing for the author of *Figaro,* and since he indulged in literary ambitions he had written the third anonymous article against the licentious comedy in the Abbé Suard's *Journal.*

Now this impudent fellow Caron had designated him in the *Mercure* as an "insignificant little bug." He resolved that the insult should be avenged.

Louis and his brothers met nearly every day, gibing at one another, making it up again, and then resuming their mutual taunts. This evening Louis and Xavier were playing the card game which it had recently become the fashion to call *Boston,* but which Louis, for whom the word had disagreeable associations, persisted in calling by its old name, *l'Hombre.* He and Count Gramont were playing against Xavier and the latter's first chamberlain, Monsieur d'Arnoult. Louis was in a very good humour, for the card-table offered him one of the very few opportunities he had of taking money from his brother instead of giving it to him, and though Gramont was not a good player he was, even so, much better than Xavier's partner, d'Arnoult, who was moreover cowardly by nature and did not dare to win money from the King.

"You now owe me one louis, six livres, and three sous, Messieurs," he announced cheerfully.

"It seems to be your lucky evening, Sire," said Xavier.

"Well, I don't think I play badly," responded Louis. Xavier felt that the moment was opportune to mention the disgraceful zoological comparisons that Monsieur Caron had published. Wisely refraining from any allusion to his own article, or even expressing any objection to the insect in question, he gave it as his opinion that the lion was a reference to the King and the tiger a reference to himself, though it was quite possible that the tiger was intended for the Queen.

Louis thought wrathfully of Monsieur Caron's American affairs, of the Voltaire, of Houdon's bust. Now the fellow was even spoiling

his game of *l'Hombre*. However he kept his temper and went on playing calmly and making notes of the score as before.

Now, though, he began to lose. "You owe me only eight livres and
four sous," he said ill-humouredly.

They went on playing, and he lost more. When the last hand was
thrown in, he counted. "You were lucky, Xavier, and you, Monsieur
d'Arnoult, after all," he announced. "I owe you one louis, three livres,
and eight sous."

He was fuming inwardly as he paid. He was more than a match for
the Xavier-d'Arnoult combination, and he had lost only because his
mind had been harping on that fellow Caron.

"Did you hear, what I told you about the article in the *Mercure?*"
asked Xavier.

"I did, Monsieur," replied Louis.

"And do you propose to do anything about it?" inquired Xavier
further.

"I do, Monsieur," answered Louis, fixing his wandering, widely
spaced eyes on his brother with gloomy resolve, thinking now how
that fellow Caron had given him no peace with that shameless impudent play of his. He had even turned the Russians loose on him;
that was almost high treason.

"I am curious to know what you will decide, Sire," Xavier remarked.

"You will not have long to wait, Monsieur," rejoined Louis.

Picking up the card on which he had noted down the score, he looked
at it again. One louis, three livres, and eight sous. "You will be surprised, Monsieur," he observed to Xavier. Turning the card over he
wrote on the back, *To the Chief of Police. Immediately upon receipt
of this document you will please issue orders for the conveyance of
the Sieur de Beaumarchais to the Bastille.* The fellow had dared to
make deprecatory references to the Bastille, to his, the King's Bastille! He was not worthy of a sojourn in the Bastille. Striking through
the words *to the Bastille,* Louis wrote above them, *to Saint-Lazare.*
Saint-Lazare was a house of correction for dissolute priests and
ne'er-do-well youths of the middle classes, and one of the normal
methods of reform was by whipping. A whipping was administered
upon entry into the institution and was laid down as the customary
punishment for every breach of the regulations.

After having triumphantly held the card out for Xavier to see, he
added the formal phrase, *This is Our Royal Will,* signed his name,
folded it, allowed the sealing-wax to drip on it, sealed it with his ring,
and sent it off.

That night he entered in his diary: *Shot 13 hares, 18 Pheasants, 32*

Partridges. Translated Gibbon, Vol. II, pages 118–120. Sanctioned 33,317,436 livres for the Army. Disciplined Our seditious subject Caron.

☆   ☆   ☆

Lenoir gazed in embarrassment at the royal order. It would have created sufficient stir if Beaumarchais had been taken to the Bastille. To send the liberator of America, the most popular author in France, the hero of the Battle of Grenada, to Saint-Lazare was unwise of His Most Christian Majesty. It was going to recoil upon His Majesty's head, to say nothing of that of his Chief of Police. But the command was clear and left no room for interpretation.

So on the following day, at nine o'clock in the evening, one of Lenoir's officers named Chenu called at the house in the rue Saint-Antoine where Pierre was sitting at table. He and Thérèse were entertaining the old Duc de Richelieu, the Prince of Nassau, Doctor Lassone, and Désirée. Chenu requested Pierre to see him for a moment in the anteroom, where he informed him that orders had been issued to take him into custody. Pierre pondered on his possible recent misdeeds, but could not think of anything. He returned to his guests and said that unfortunately he must leave them, since his presence was urgently needed at Versailles. Then rejoining the police officer he announced that he was ready. Chenu inquired courteously whether Monsieur would not like to order his carriage, but Pierre replied with a smile that he had built himself a house near the Place Saint-Antoine so that he should not have a long way to go to the Bastille. Chenu revealed with an air of regret that it was not the Bastille to which they were going, but Saint-Lazare. Pierre turned pale and said, "I had not really expected that."

Meanwhile the others had come out from the dining-room, and Pierre's confusion showed them what was amiss. Old Richelieu asked the police officer, who had sprung stiffly to attention, what was the trouble, and Chenu reluctantly enlightened him. Shaking his head angrily, Richelieu commented, "In all my eighty-nine years I have never known anything like this."

Désirée, pale and trembling, cried bluntly. "It's sheer meanness!" Chenu, seriously, but without raising his voice, observed, "I did not hear your remark, Madame. It's His Majesty's order."

Thérèse embraced her husband. She did not weep. Then he was conveyed in his own splendid carriage to the house of correction at Saint-Lazare. During the journey he was unable to maintain his self-control and was shaken by a fit of nervous sobbing.

"Pull yourself together, Monsieur," urged Chenu in an effort to console him. "Monsieur Lenoir has given instructions that you are to be well treated. I am sure that the worst will be spared you."

That night Gudin described in fiery terms how a fresh persecution of his celebrated friend had begun, and with what dignity he had accepted this further martyrdom.

On the following day, however, Gudin experienced a disappointment. He had expected the whole of Paris to rise in wrath and demonstrate in favour of its greatest son, but the Parisians thought it comical that a man like Beaumarchais, who was on the verge of fifty, should be confined in an institution together with dissolute priests and young ne'er-do-wells. The incalculable Parisians laughed. They laughed uproariously. Innumerable caricatures and lampoons appeared in the streets, one wood-cut depicting Beaumarchais as an urchin being whipped by a lay brother.

☆　　☆　　☆

The mortgage on the house in the rue Saint-Antoine fell due, but there was no money to meet it. It was less feasible than ever to raise credit on the strength of Pierre's claims against his American balances or against the French Crown, since in both cases the firm of Hortalez was dependent upon the King's favour and the royal attitude had been sufficiently manifested by Pierre's arrest.

Since visitors were not allowed at Saint-Lazare, Maigron consulted Thérèse and Gudin. He explained that if they defaulted on the mortgage the house would be put under seal two days from that date and offered at auction in three weeks' time. The distraint upon the house would deal the firm another severe blow, but it could be avoided if the *Société Industrielle de Chinon,* for which he had received an offer far below its real value, were to be disposed of.

Gudin was unable to sit quietly in his chair, but strode up and down the room with flushed face. Perhaps the liquidation of the businesses might have its good side, he burst out. Pierre was being warned by destiny to concentrate for a time on his writing. Socrates had distinguished himself as a soldier, among his other achievements, but it had not been his military exploits which had rendered him immortal. Pierre Beaumarchais would likewise be able to reinforce his claim to immortality by renouncing his business activities for a year or two and communing with his Muse among his books and works of art. As Pierre's friend and biographer he supported the suggestion that the *Société Industrielle* should be abandoned and the house in the rue Saint-Antoine saved.

Thérèse had been sitting silently, her high, arched brows knit in

a frown. She had been deeply stirred by the latest cruel injustice
against Pierre. Unable though she had been to discover the reason
why he had so suddenly been carried off to his humiliating confinement at Saint-Lazare, she was convinced that the ultimate cause was
his zeal for liberty and for the welfare of mankind. But the tyrants
had misjudged their man. Pierre was not the sort to bow his head beneath the yoke and surrender his American enterprise. She must not
allow him to lose the firm of Hortalez simply because he was in prison
and powerless to look after his affairs. "I believe," she said in her
deep, calm voice, "that it would not be in accordance with Pierre's
wishes if the *Société Industrielle* were to be liquidated."

"Then you prefer, Madame," asked the business-like Maigron, "to
have the house put up for auction?"

"Yes," she replied.

Two days later Monsieur Brunelet, who held the mortgage, appeared with a police officer and a couple of bailiffs. Brunelet, a
small, unpretentious-looking man, requested permission to wait upon
Madame de Beaumarchais, produced a bulky inventory of the contents of the house, and invited her respectfully to accompany him on
his tour of inspection since, as he had learned with regret, Monsieur
de Beaumarchais was prevented by unforeseen circumstances from
being present. Thérèse complied with his wish, but sent for Maigron.
Gudin also turned up, with a view to witnessing the final act of humiliation with his own eyes so that his heart might be filled with the holy
wrath necessary for its adequate recording.

The first seals were affixed at the main gateway, the large seal of
the King and the little seal of Monsieur Brunelet. During their tour
of the garden Gudin was unable to refrain from sarcastic comments.
"Do not forget," he would say, "to affix your seal to the Gladiator,
Messieurs." Or, "What about sealing the Voltaire temple? One of
Monsieur de Beaumarchais's millions of admirers might take it into
his head to put it in his pocket and carry it away." Brunelet merely
shrugged his shoulders and protested that it was a very painful duty,
or that it cut him to the heart, but after all he was a business man.

Accompanied by the police officer, the bailiffs, and Pierre's representatives, Brunelet entered the house. Here Julie rushed to meet
them in a blazing fury. "Are you not satisfied," she shrieked, "with
having locked up the best and noblest man in France in your rat-hole?
Must you rob him of his house, of his last refuge when he returns
sick in mind and body from the tortures that have been inflicted
on him?" Her attitude grew so violent that the police officer threatened to intervene, but Gudin eventually managed to lead her away
to her room in a flood of tears.

In the study the bailiffs set about sealing Pierre's chest, with his documents, and the drawers with his other papers. "I should be exceedingly obliged," said Thérèse, "if you would leave these unsealed."

Maigron, in his colourless voice, protested, "I doubt whether your action is legal. The articles of furniture in which manuscripts are stored away are included in the inventory, but not the manuscripts themselves."

"Do you realize," demanded Gudin, "that you are perpetrating the greatest crime any mortal can commit, namely, the desecration of art?"

Maigron continued to protest: "I shall institute a claim for damages if you distrain upon articles which are not to be found in the inventory. In the absence of Monsieur de Beaumarchais I possess his power of attorney to conduct his business affairs. You will render it impossible for me to carry out my task if you prevent me from having access to important documents."

The police officer looked questioningly at Brunelet. "If you will wait," said the latter, "I should like to consult a business friend." He went off, and returned in the company of Lenormant.

Charlot had looked forward eagerly to the day when he would take possession of the chimney-piece, and the portrait of Désirée, saying amiably to Pierre, "Did I not tell you so, *mon cher?*" Perhaps he would merely have taken the few objects on which his heart was set and left Pierre the house. It was the encounter with Pierre in the offices of his bankrupt firm or his bankrupt home which Lenormant had pictured with satisfaction. But this had all been spoiled. So he had stayed away from the act of seizure. But now, since he had been called in expressly, he was unable to resist the temptation at least to witness the distress of Pierre's family. So there he was, accompanying his agent.

With old-fashioned courtesy he assured Thérèse that it was some consolation to him in the midst of all this grief to come to her assistance. Countering both the disdainful observations of the impassive Maigron and the outspoken home-thrusts of the angry Gudin with silent irony, he declared after a while that the contents of the house could not be in better hands than those of Madame, and he kept Monsieur Brunelet and his bailiffs from affixing more seals.

But he felt nothing of the fierce joy which he had expected from this hour. From its gilded frame the portrait of Désirée looked down upon him with a cool, mocking smile, the gilded frame on which shone the seal of his own agent. The painted Désirée now belonged to him, the magnificent canvas of the magnificent painter Quentin de Latour. What a poor, pitiful, triumph, and how senselessly had he paid for it with the loss of the living Désirée.

When Lenormant and the melancholy procession of the minions of the law had gone, Julie came down and joined the others. Her eyes red with weeping, she pointed wrathfully at the painting. "I am convinced," she asserted, "that Pierre's arrest and this black day are to be traced to that woman's door."

To which Maigron replied dryly, "You are mistaken, Mademoiselle. It is America that we have to thank for this."

☆   ☆   ☆

Franklin felt discomfort when he learnt that the owner of the firm of Hortalez had at last reached the end of his tether, and that his private dwelling had been taken possession of by his creditors. It was being noised all over Paris that the tardiness of the Congress was responsible for the misfortune of its most important contractor.

Franklin held a conference with his colleagues. Adams coldly declared that the immediate reason for the collapse had been Beaumarchais's arrest, and even the most embittered enemy of the United States could not honestly maintain that the Congress had a part in it. "At any rate," suggested Franklin, "it cannot be denied that Monsieur Caron would still be in possession of his house if the Congress had been more prompt in its payments. Be that as it may, it would be an effective gesture if we were to place at his disposal sufficient funds to save his house from distraint."

Arthur Lee could hardly conceal his indignation at the ludicrous proposal of the Doctor *honoris causa*. In his opinion, he asserted vigorously, both the arrest and the act of distraint were nothing but a further swindling manœuvre by the notorious charlatan, who had already caused Congress and the envoys sufficient trouble with his falsified invoices. Franklin replied mildly that he could not conceive of anyone arranging for himself to be conveyed to Saint-Lazare as part of a scheme to procure financial advantages, but Lee insisted that on the contrary he could quite well imagine a Frenchman and scribbler, who was so obsessed as was Monsieur Caron by the desire to achieve theatrical effect, promising himself some worth-while reward from voluntary subjection to a theatrical martyrdom. "This much is certain," he declared. "The French Government has also come to realize at last that the man is a swindler, and has branded him as such. In my opinion we now have an added reason to scrutinize his accounts with the utmost care, instead of flinging our money at his feet."

Adams suggested sourly that judging from the experiences which had come his way, the French were an extraordinarily sensitive nation. If the Commissioners were to transmit funds to Monsieur Beaumarchais at the present juncture, it was quite possible that Vergennes, who was wont to take umbrage very easily, might regard their action as an unwarranted intervention in French affairs, and even perhaps as an affront to the King.

Franklin sighed, and since they had no money anyway he let the matter drop.

About the same time Désirée received a communication from Maigron. She might be interested, he said, to know that the mortgage which had caused the seizure of the house in the rue Saint-Antoine amounted to 600,000 livres. If this sum were not found within twenty days the house would be irretrievably lost.

During all this time Désirée had been racking her brains desperately for some means of procuring Pierre's release. The first essential was to discover on what charge he had been incarcerated. Nobody could give her any precise information, not even the Chief of Police, since Gramont and d'Arnoult, the only ones who knew what it was all about, preserved an apprehensive silence. Now that pig of a Charlot was trying to take advantage of Pierre's absence by robbing him of his house. He was going to be disappointed.

Money flowed into Désirée's purse from many sources, but she was very extravagant and it did not stay there long. She did not have 600,000 livres, and it would be no easy task to raise such a huge sum so quickly. She went to Doctor Lassone.

The celebrated physician turned pale. All his pride and all his avarice surged up in revolt. What a naïve, shameless wench she was. Because it amused her to sleep now and then with that wind-bag Caron, she had the audacity to expect him, Josèphe-Marie-François Lassone, to throw the fruits of from ten to fifteen years' hard toil into the gutter. Yet if he refused he knew what would happen. The insolent, cursed, beloved harlot wouldn't say much. She would curtsy prettily and leave. And his proposal of marriage would join the many others in her waste-paper basket. But he did want to marry her, the bitch. It would be damned difficult and expensive to pry such a large amount loose from the investments in which he had put his fortune so as not to spend it. So it would not be 600,000; it would come to 610,000 or even 620,000. 620,000 for this wench and that wind-bag.

"I asked you a question just now, Doctor," Désirée reminded him sweetly, roguishly.

Lassone swallowed. "What is the latest date by which you must have the money?" he asked.

She drew Maigron's letter from her bosom. "Within twenty days, so I am informed," she replied. "But that was two days ago."

"600,000 livres is a lot of money," he protested, "and eighteen days will not give me much time."

Désirée said nothing, contenting herself with looking pretty and smiling mockingly.

Lassone prepared to take the plunge. "The sum will be at your disposal within eighteen days," he said hoarsely.

"I knew you would do it if I asked you, Doctor," said Désirée amiably. "You really are generous, in spite of what people say. Thank you very much indeed." Lassone raised her hand to his lips.

He realized that he was doing the wrong thing, but he could not help himself. With a rather twisted smile he said, "I had the honour, Madame, to ask you for your hand."

"So far as my recollection goes," replied Désirée, "I did not say no. I still do not say no, for you have shown yourself to possess a magnanimous nature." With a coy smile she inclined her head, that he might imprint a kiss upon her neck.

"One thing more," she remarked, looking him in the eyes again. "Please try to find out why our friend was put in prison. If he should be released in time it may save you your 600,000."

☆   ☆   ☆

Meanwhile Pierre was lying in Saint-Lazare.

During the reign of the kind-hearted Louis XVI a reform of the Paris prisons had been set on foot, but the house of correction at Saint-Lazare had so far not been affected. Monsieur Lepin, the warden of the penitentiary, was an old soldier with a wooden leg, a stout heart, and a sense of justice according to his own lights. He did not have an easy time with his young gaolbirds, who had already made three attempts to kill him. On the last occasion he had been able to save himself only by cracking the skull of one of the would-be assassins with his wooden leg.

He was unaccustomed to intercourse with a philosopher and politician such as Monsieur de Beaumarchais. Lenoir had instructed him to treat Pierre well. So he omitted the usual corporal punishment, but in all other things Pierre fared the same as the rest.

He slept on rotten straw, together with fifteen evil-looking, malodorous young louts, in a low and narrow room. There was an abundance of rats and vermin but barely enough to eat.

The tattered crew of ne'er-do-wells was astounded at the arrival in their midst of an elegant, fragrant gentleman of mature years, and they thought he must be an extremely cunning fellow to have helped himself to such a smart gentleman's outfit. "What have you been up to?" they inquired, but he did not deign to reply. Both his eloquence and his humour had deserted him. "Who are you? What is your name?" they demanded again. He still refused to answer. One of his room-mates, an alert-looking youth, remembered having seen a face like this somewhere before. "I know," he cried. "He looks like Beaumarchais, who writes for the papers and whose picture you see every-where." He began to whistle the ballad of Chérubin, and the others joined in. This was too much for Pierre. "I am Pierre Beaumar-chais," he said shortly, with an air of disdain. The louts exchanged glances and nudged one another with their elbows. There was a general titter and finally they burst into uproarious guffaws. The newcomer evidently had humour and promised to be an amusing companion.

Pierre lay through the black, stinking night in despair. This was where he had got to as he approached his fiftieth year, rotting in the company of a horde of criminal youths. He felt more helpless than ever before in his life. Everything he had done had been wrong. Who had asked him to bother about mankind? Who had asked him to save America and liberty? Who had asked him to write memoirs and wrathful plays against injustice? If he had devoted his time to writing erotic farces and swindling on a large scale, leaving America and the rest of humanity to look after themselves, he would now be rolling in money and honours would have fallen upon him thick and fast. He had been a fool, a gigantic ass.

However hard he thought, he could not imagine who it could have been that had denounced him, or why he had been denounced. All he knew was that the warrant which Chenu had allowed him to see was signed by the King. It had been a *lettre de cachet*. What could he have done to infuriate Louis to such a pitch? He reflected on his actions during the past few weeks, but could find no explanation, and no visitors were permitted from whom he might have sought enlighten-ment.

He demanded to see the warden. Lepin inquired courteously, "What can I do for you, Monsieur?" Pierre asked why he was there. "On account of general misbehaviour, Monsieur," replied Lepin. "That, I am afraid, is all I know."

"May I see one of my friends?" Pierre urged. "Either Count Maurepas or the Foreign Minister, or at least my lawyer? Or can I be permitted to write a letter?"

"That is not allowed by the regulations until four weeks have elapsed," Lepin informed him.

The old veteran was not a stickler for cleanliness, and Pierre's ele-gance soon wore off. The splendid suit he had donned for the dinner with his guests became soiled and tattered, his cheeks, lips, and chin were covered with a greyish-brown stubble, and the stink of his own body prevented him from noticing the smell of the others. Thus he lived in his crowded cell, almost suffocated by his sense of help-lessness.

It was about this time that a certain Abbé da Ponte procured a copy of *The Marriage of Figaro* and turned it into an opera libretto, for which the score was composed by a musician called Mozart.

☆ ☆ ☆

Monsieur Lenoir inquired from the warden of Saint-Lazare how the new inmate was getting on and how he was behaving. The old soldier reported that Monsieur de Beaumarchais offered no special cause for complaint. He was conducting himself no differently from the other delinquents who had been entrusted to his care and, like them, was looking a little shabby and ill-groomed. "Hum!" growled Lenoir, and demanded further details.

The Chief of Police communicated what he had learnt to Count Maurepas. "A greyish-brown stubble on lips and cheeks, you say?" The Minister pursed his lips. "I am sure that that is not in accord with His Majesty's intention. Will you please issue instructions that our Pierrot is to be kept neat and tidy."

Henceforth Pierre slept in a room by himself. He was also well fed, almost to the point of luxury. Lepin asked whether he would like to receive a visit from a barber, but he declined.

He was then granted the privilege of being called upon by two gentlemen with whom he could discuss his affairs, and he asked for Gudin and Maigron.

When they saw him they were shocked. Gudin could not withhold his tears. "Let us not speak of it, my friends," said Pierre with a casualness that made Gudin shudder. "Are they making many jokes about me in Paris? Do tell me some."

Maigron proceeded to report on the distraint that had been levied on the house. It was quite evident, he said, that the mortgagee in the background was none other than Lenormant. Gudin touched up the picture of the scene at the sealing of Pierre's possessions with a number of colourful details. Pierre winced, and scolded Maigron for not having disposed of the *Société Industrielle,* thus sparing him this final humiliation. Maigron gazed calmly at the angry, unkempt figure of his employer and remarked, "I have grounds for assuming that you will retain possession of your house even without having to sacrifice the *Société Industrielle.* There is a lady who is prepared to advance the 600,000 livres before the days of grace are up."

Pierre stared at him in bewilderment. "A lady?" he demanded. "Tell me, man! Who is she? The Baroness d'Houdetot? Madame de Clonard?" He mentioned a number of other aristocratic ladies of his acquaintance.

"The lady does not wish her name to be divulged," replied Maigron.

"Who is she, in the devil's name?" Pierre thundered.

"Mademoiselle Mesnard," said Maigron.

"*Morbleu!*" swore Pierre, surprised at his own lack of intuition. He always forgot the woman who was the best of all his friends. "I wonder where she could have raised the money?" he mused aloud.

"These artists!" commented Gudin. "Art is the true softener of hearts."

Pierre was accorded permission to see members of his family and his closest friends. "Madame de Beaumarchais has expressed a desire to visit you, Monsieur," he was informed by Lepin. But he refused to let Thérèse come. He did not want to part from the growth of greyish-brown beard that was the symbol of his humiliation and martyrdom, but neither did he wish Thérèse to see him looking so aged and unprepossessing; for he loved her.

He did, however, wish to see Désirée. She came. Young, very prettily dressed, radiant, she entered the wretched room. She saw Pierre and was shocked. It was only for a moment, and he did not notice it, for he was too busy displaying his misery.

"By the way, Désirée, I have to thank you," Pierre said warmly. "I hear that you have behaved wonderfully again—not that I wouldn't have managed to get out of my difficulties anyway, for if there is one of my feminine friends who remains loyal to me, it is the goddess Fortuna."

They were sitting side by side on his plank bed, her dainty figure contrasting oddly with his tattered garb.

"I am probably going to marry Lassone," she said. "Did I tell you?"

"Old Lassone?" he cried. "You really have no need to do that, Désirée."

"He is very easy-going," she explained, "and he is madly in love with me. Besides, he amuses me."

Pierre pondered. Moving nearer to her, he asked in a flattered tone and with an intimate air, "Is it Lassone who is prepared to lay down the money for me?"

She was silent, but her face said yes.

"I am sure that I shall pay it back soon," Pierre consoled himself and her.

"You don't believe that yourself," she replied, "but this time I think it will even be true. There is something rather strange and, I think, agreeable that I have to tell you. I should never have found it out if it had not been for my Lassone." Thereupon she told him the reason for his arrest. It appeared that Monsieur d'Arnoult, Prince Xavier's partner at the card-table on the fateful night, had fallen sick and, sick men being loquacious, he had told Doctor Lassone what had happened.

This certainly was agreeable news. To a man of Pierre's impulsive nature, the fact that the King had been induced by such a petty cause to inflict upon him such monstrous punishment was sufficient at once to rouse the most extravagant hopes. Désirée, too, was of the opinion that the King's absurd suspicion could easily be refuted. She had already asked for an audience with Toinette and had been told to be present at Versailles on the following day. "I think I can secure your release before many hours have gone by," she said encouragingly.

But Pierre was way ahead of her. "Release!" he scoffed. "Satisfaction is what I want! I shall demand satisfaction. And I shall get it." In his filthy, ragged garments he strode up and down, again young and vigorous. "No!" he cried jubilantly. "Now I shall not need your money. I shall pick up the 600,000 livres without even having to bend."

☆   ☆   ☆

Désirée and her friends saw to it that the whole of Paris became acquainted with the absurd charges which had induced the King to send the author of *Figaro* to Saint-Lazare, and the Parisians' amusement at Pierre's plight changed abruptly to indignation at the behaviour of Louis. If a man of Beaumarchais's rank and merits could be consigned without more ado to the most humiliating form of incarceration, merely because a harmless remark had been stupidly misinterpreted, was anybody safe from being torn out of his bed at night? Paris again re-echoed to shouts of "Despotism!" and "Tyranny!"

Louis learnt of the discontented state of his capital from the secret police reports. He had already begun to question the wisdom of his action, and when Maurepas brought him a copy of the article which had led Pierre to publish his open letter it became quite clear to him that the Sieur Caron's zoological metaphors had not been directed either at him or the Queen; the whole concatenation of circumstances dawned upon his mind. He was both angry and ashamed. That scheming brother of his had once more set a snare for his feet and inveigled him into precipitate action. Though he might have been right in principle, for the Sieur Caron was at bottom nothing but a middle-aged good-for-nothing, a grown-up street arab, on this occasion he had undoubtedly done the man wrong.

Toinette came to his apartments and reinforced his heart-searching with her indignant reproaches. Désirée had done her best to stir the Queen's wrath, and her realistic description of Pierre's neglected condition had had its effect. Toinette was deeply moved and did not fail to let Louis feel the force of her angry scorn. "Nobody with any feeling for literature," she declared, "can have the slightest objection to being compared to a lion or a tiger. There are lots of such animals in our various coats of arms, and to send a great writer to Saint-Lazare for having made such a comparison is hardly worthy of your royal dignity, Sire."

Louis twisted and turned guiltily. "Very well, then," he muttered. "Very well. I was falsely informed, unfortunately. Do not agitate yourself any further, Toinette. I shall set everything to rights."

He ordered that Pierre was to be released at once and reinstated in all the titles, offices, and privileges that had been forfeited with his commitment to Saint-Lazare. *This is Our Royal Will,* he wrote, signed the document, affixed his seal, and sent it off.

The old soldier Lepin donned his full-dress uniform dating from the Seven Years' War, pinned on his medals and decorations, and solemnly clumped along with his wooden leg to inform Pierre of the royal will. Pierre listened frowningly, but said nothing. "You are free to go, Monsieur," announced Lepin uncomfortably. As Pierre still made no reply, he added, "Would you like me to send a barber to your room? Do you wish to order your carriage?"

Pierre shook his head. "I have no intention of being sent away from here in this casual fashion," he said. "They have not even taken the trouble to communicate to me the charge under which I have been immured within these walls. There is, I think some satisfaction due to me."

Lepin was at a loss for an answer that would not either offend this peculiar delinquent or be disloyal to the King. "I have imparted to you, Monsieur," he said, "that which I had to impart. The rest is for you to decide." He withdrew and reported the situation to the Chief of Police.

The unrest among the people of Paris was growing. There were demonstrations in front of Pierre's house and even before Saint-Lazare. Pierre's continued confinement had become a public scandal.

Monsieur Lenoir invited Gudin and Maigron to come and see him, and entreated them to use their influence with Pierre. It was essential, he declared, that Monsieur de Beaumarchais should leave Saint-Lazare forthwith. Such defiance of the King's will constituted a flagrant act of disloyalty. Even if Monsieur de Beaumarchais *had* been the victim of injustice, it might be wiser not to stir the royal wrath any further but to place his trust in the King's clemency.

Gudin and Maigron drove to Saint-Lazare. "I have come," announced Gudin joyfully, "as the envoys of the Roman Senate appeared before Coriolanus, to escort you with humble solemnity back to the Capitol."

"Would you have the goodness to express yourself a little less picturesquely?" demanded Pierre.

"You are to leave this place," said Maigron. "You are to go home."

Gudin added, "The King requests you to quit this house of humiliation. The King urges you not to deny him any further the favour of your tried and trusty services."

"That would no doubt suit his book very well," replied Pierre. Revelling in the ignominy that had been heaped upon him, he went on, "Look at me, my friends! You see the condition to which I have been reduced! After having degraded me to the lowest level to which a man can be degraded, after having compelled me to consort with the scum of humanity, this King comes to me and says cheerfully, 'Right! Now you can go!' No, Sire! I prefer to stay. That is not the way in which Pierre Beaumarchais permits himself to be sent home."

"What do you propose to do?" asked Maigron.

"I shall write to the King," Pierre declared. "I shall tell him what I think. I shall inform him of my demands. I shall insist on satisfaction."

He proceeded to dictate a letter to the King of France and Navarre. In the first place, he refuted the incomprehensible charge that had been laid against him. To impute to him the intention of abusing the King in an open letter, was tantamount to asserting that he was bereft of his senses. Since, however, he had been conveyed to Saint-Lazare, and not to a madhouse, it was incumbent upon him to request the institution of formal proceedings in a court of law in order that he might clear his name and that his honour might be restored. "I am unable, Sire, to accept from your hand the restoration of my offices and titles," he concluded, "since my name has for the time being been erased, through the act of injustice to which I have been exposed, from the list of your subjects who are in enjoyment of their civil rights. If justice cannot be accorded me, Sire, then I must remain an outcast. My honour has been besmirched and my position in society undermined. Until the clouds have been dispersed which at present obscure my person in the eyes of the nation, of Europe, and of America, my credit will continue to be shaken, my fortune diminished and jeopardized, together with that of the fifty associates who are concerned with me in my business undertakings."

"A masterpiece of prose!" cried Gudin gleefully. "In the whole of literature I know of only one counterpart to which this piece of dignified pleading can be compared—the last canto of the *Iliad* in which the aged Priam entreats Achilles to deliver up to him the desecrated body of his dead son Hector."

Even the more sober Maigron was content. "I think," he commented, "that the King will have to eat humble pie and that Monsieur Necker will have to loosen his purse-strings a little."

The way in which Caron made him taste Injustice, pinched and tormented the King. He consulted Maurepas and Vergennes, who advised that it might be discreet to comply with the request of a man who knew so much. He had, in any case, been rather brusquely treated. Louis replied glumly, "I fear, gentlemen, that you are right," and he promised to set the matter right within twenty-four hours.

Once again Gudin and Maigron were selected to bear the tidings and inform Pierre of His Most Christian Majesty's favours. "*Sursum corda,*" announced Gudin. "Lift up your hearts," and he began to enumerate. "As a token of his graciousness, the King has conferred upon you an annuity from his private purse to the amount of twelve hundred livres per annum. He has issued orders to the censorship authorities to the effect that no further ban is to be placed on publication of the work known as *The Marriage of Figaro.*"

At this point he was interrupted by Maigron, who had been listening impatiently to the philosopher's pedantry in dwelling upon such trifling items. "The King is willing," he said, "to acknowledge our claims to compensation and to fix the sum payable to us at 2,150,000 livres."

Pierre gaped at him. "Will you repeat that?" he asked. "How much, did you say? Did you say 1,150,000?"

"No," replied Maigron. "I said 2,150,000. Monsieur Necker will be very annoyed. The King has clearly gone crazy."

☆   ☆   ☆

Thanks to Désirée's efforts, Pierre's departure from Saint-Lazare was staged as a great popular spectacle. Thousands stood before the gates and the police did not dare to intervene.

The door opened. And passing the saluting Monsieur Lepin, escorted by Gudin and Maigron, Pierre stepped out. There he stood, filthy and bearded and blinking in the sun. And the crowd was silent. For surrounding him was a great, invisible convoy: Figaro and Almaviva and Rosina and Chérubin, and countless tars who had manned ships that carried arms for America. There was half a minute of silence, then the throng burst into a wild shout, carried Pierre to his carriage, and brought him home.

The carriage halted at the entrance to the park in the rue Saint-Antoine. Pierre did not allow the gates to be opened at once; he gazed at the seals that had been affixed there by Monsieur Brunelet, the big seal of the King and the small seal of Brunelet himself. Only then he walked towards the house; he felt weak in the knees and was grateful for the support of his friends Gudin and Maigron.

From the house rushed the shrieking Julie. She was laughing and crying at the same time as she flung herself upon his neck. Thérèse stood in the doorway. Pierre looked at her and she looked at him, then they slowly moved towards each other. Now Pierre regretted that he had not tidied his appearance and removed his matted growth of beard. Neither said a word; each knew the other, and both knew that he was ridiculous and magnificent. They embraced almost shyly.

The bitch Caprice dashed out, barking with delight as she leapt up at him and almost knocked him over as she frantically licked his face. Pierre swallowed.

While he was in his bath Emile inquired a little timorously whether he would like his beard removed. "No!" he snapped ill-temperedly. They all sat down to table and he ate with good appetite, but hardly spoke. Many visitors drove up to call upon him, but he would receive no one. He sent word that he still felt soiled and humiliated, and would see nobody but his family and his most intimate friends.

On the following day he wrote a preface to *Figaro* for inclusion in the forthcoming edition. Now and then he would lift his pen from the paper, stride to and fro, catch sight of his altered visage in the mirror, and then return to his writing with redoubled zeal.

In this preface he proudly ranked himself with Racine and Molière, defending his right to set his own characters upon the stage, whether they be scamps or great lords. Was a fable to be deemed immoral because the lion was a savage creature, the wolf a beast of prey, the fox a crafty fellow? Was he to blame because the great lords were what they were? Was it he who had made them so? "My theme," he declared, "is that to be seen in many a fable of which the protagonists are animals, namely, the conquest of brute force by wit and cunning. These lines," concluded the bearded man, still bearing the traces of his incarceration, "these lines are not written for my present readers. But after eighty years authors will compare their lot with mine, and from my description posterity will realize the price that had to be paid by those of their predecessors who wished to amuse their fellow men."

Thus unburdened, he felt lighter, but still continued to sulk.

Then the money arrived which had been allowed to him in settlement of his claim to compensation. It came in the form of gold and treasury bills, flooding his room in an abundance such as he had never set eyes on before: 2,150,000 livres. At this sight, Pierre threw away his mask of martyrdom, and the mirror, which had reflected a thousand Pierres, frivolous, enthusiastic, melodramatic, creative, angry, and despairing, now reflected a crazy Pierre. His amusement at the way in which his greatest misfortune had been transformed into his greatest stroke of luck was almost more overwhelming than his feeling of triumph. In abrupt transition the tragically humiliated man changed into the buffoon he was born, destined to overcome death and the devil with a thousand tricks. The bearded, ageing Pierre danced round the table upon which the money was heaped, stuck out his tongue, and cried to his reflection in the mirror, *"Eh, parbleu, j'y suis—* Well, here I am."

That day he shaved, and an invitation was issued to all the members of his family and his most intimate friends to attend a celebration banquet in the evening. They all came, his sister Tonton and her husband, the old Duc de Richelieu, the Prince of Nassau, and Désirée, who was escorted by Doctor Lassone. Lassone was proud at having been invited and subdued at having been unable to refuse the invitation. Course after course was served, the dining-room was illuminated with hundreds of candles, everyone ate, drank, and made merry. Pierre had a kindly word and a joke for each of his guests, and they all vowed that they had never seen him in such good spirits.

On the following day Maigron wished to repay Monsieur Brunelet the amount of the mortgage, but Pierre replied that he would attend to that himself. With the draft in his pocket he drove out to Etioles. Charlot was not at home. So Pierre handed it to Lenormant's secretary and said, "Please give this to your master. I have no doubt that it will then be in the right hands. And here are a further thousand livres in payment of the meals taken by me at Monsieur Lenormant's house in the past, inclusive of *pourboires*."

★ ❆ ★ ❆ ★ ❆ ★ ❆ ★

Chapter Four

ÇA IRA

❆ ★ ❆

THE American frigate *Alliance* had crammed on full sail and was making good headway. The very thin young gentleman with the red hair and the rather long nose was standing at the rails. There was a chill in the air and he had just got over a serious illness after the hardships to which he had been exposed, but he was on his way home and the shores of France were in sight. He strained his eyes in the direction of the sharp cliff which dominated the entrance to the harbour of Brest, and he could already make out the forts.

It had not been an easy crossing. Even before the ship sailed there had been trouble at Boston in finding a crew. The young gentleman, whose name was Josèphe-Paul-Gilbert, Marquis de Lafayette, had been obliged to sign on a crew of convicts and deserters from the English Army, and later they had run into a howling storm. There had been one black, endless night when it seemed that there was no hope of saving the vessel, and Lafayette, still weak from his illness, had cursed the fate which had torn him from the beautiful, luxurious Palais Noailles and cast him upon this wild sea. During the past few days the rabble of which the greater part of the crew was composed had been hatching a plot to seize the ship, for the English Government, in its efforts to capture rebel vessels, had promised that mutinous crews bringing such vessels into English ports should be allowed to retain possession of their prizes. The sailors of the *Alliance* were counting on a particularly warm welcome when they handed over the celebrated Lafayette, and a plan was brewing to overpower the officers when they were near the English coast, but at the last moment the situation had been saved partly by a stroke of good fortune and partly by the quickness of mind shown by the Marquis. Now the shores of France were in sight and the mutineers lay in irons in the hold.

As the coastline grew clearer Lafayette mused on the reception that was likely to greet him. His position was a little obscure. Having thrown up his commission in the French Army and left the country against the express orders of the King, he was, strictly speaking, a deserter. Meanwhile, however, the policy he had followed in his desertion, had become the official policy of his country; France was at war with England, and he was returning with a halo of glory on account of his military exploits against the enemy.

As they entered the harbour the guns of the fortress thundered a salute. They were greeting the flag with the Stars and Stripes which, when he went out, had not been permitted to fly. He compared the way he had crept out of the Spanish harbour by night in a ship purchased with the money of Monsieur de Beaumarchais, with the way he now returned, greeted by the salute of his King.

He drove swiftly to Paris, to the rue Saint-Honoré, to the Hôtel Noailles. Here his nineteen-year-old wife, Adrienne, welcomed him in a trembling embrace. Old Ségur, the Minister for War, called to see him, offered his leathery cheek to be kissed, patted him on the back, and announced his punishment. It was not unduly severe—a week's arrest, to be spent at the Hôtel Noailles.

Before the week was up the Marquis wrote a humble letter to the King. "Nothing is further from my mind," he wrote, "than an attempt to justify my disobedience, for which I feel deep remorse. Yet the nature of my offence warrants the hope that I shall be afforded the opportunity to make amends. Perhaps Your Majesty will be gracious enough to accord me the happiness of being able to wipe out the memory of my transgression in his service wherever and in whatever manner Your Majesty may be pleased to command."

He was instructed to appear at Versailles on the very next day to receive the King's reprimand. When he was ushered into the library, the corpulent young monarch blinked at his emaciated young officer and said awkwardly, "You know, Monsieur, you ought not to have done what you did!" Then, after Lafayette had stood in silence for half a minute looking guiltily in front of him, Louis demanded in an animated tone, "And now, my dear Marquis, perhaps you can tell me where exactly this Saratoga is. I cannot find it on any of my maps." Soon they were engaged in a lively geographical discussion.

When this topic had been exhausted, Lafayette announced, "I have the honour to transmit to Your Majesty a letter from the Congress of the United States." Louis accepted the letter and read it through. The document began, *To our great, loyal, and beloved Ally and friend, Louis the Sixteenth, King of France and Navarre,* and it went on to praise the noble youth who was its bearer. He had proved himself wise in counsel, courageous on the battlefield, and steadfast in the hardships of war. The leaders of the Congress then once more, and yet a third time, declared themselves to be *the good friends and*

Allies of the King, and they concluded, *We pray to God that He may keep Your Majesty under His holy protection.*

Louis's day was ruined. These shopkeepers, these farmers and provincial lawyers, called him, the King of France, their *beloved friend* and most graciously recommended to his notice an officer belonging to the ancient nobility of France. This was exactly what he had feared. It was the dawn of revolution, the disintegration of the social order. "I gather, *Monsieur le Marquis,*" he·observed a little dryly, "that you have succeeded in gaining the affection of these" —he searched his mind for the proper word—"of these citizens. It was no more than I had expected, that a French officer should have borne himself with distinction among these"—again he hesitated— "among these citizens." With that the audience was at an end.

All of Paris and Versailles, and the women in particular, demonstrated their sympathy and appreciation for Lafayette. He had never been remarkable for good looks, even apart from his shambling gait and awkward manner, and with his fiery red hair and small inflamed eyes he had not enjoyed much success with the opposite sex prior to his departure overseas and subsequent fame. Toinette had once left him standing in the middle of a dance because he was so clumsy. Things were very different now. In covering himself with glory he had acquired a radiant beauty in the eyes of his feminine admirers. He was no longer thin, but slender; his eyes were no longer inflamed, but flashed a look of keen intelligence combined with romantic sentiment; his movements were no longer fidgety but bore witness to an unparalleled energy. All the women loved him.

Two days after he had been received in audience by the King and released from house-arrest, he drove out to call upon the old man in the garden at Passy. On that day Franklin had spent a disagreeable forenoon.

Mr. Digges, who had been sent to London on the warm recommendation of Arthur Lee to look after the American prisoners, had embezzled nearly £400 of the money entrusted to him for that purpose, £388.4.0 to be precise, and that very morning an altercation had taken place between Lee and Franklin.

Lee insisted that they must not come to any hasty judgment. Though appearances, for the time being, might be against Mr. Digges, that gentleman had announced his intention of returning to Paris and clearing the matter up. So Arthur Lee wanted judgment deferred until Mr. Digges should have arrived in Paris.

"I fear," commented Franklin, "that we may have a long time to wait."

Lee flushed and replied, "I am not a rich man, but if it should indeed turn out that the prisoners have suffered loss through the short-

comings of Mr. Digges, I shall be prepared to advance fifty pounds
out of my own pocket towards making up the deficiency." Franklin
said nothing, and Lee went on in a determined tone, "I must ask you
to spare me any further discussion on this matter. And above all, I
protest most emphatically against any inferences you may draw concerning my knowledge of men and affairs."

"There is, however, one thing you will permit me," Franklin answered tranquilly, "and that is, to draw inferences concerning the
character of your Mr. Digges. He that robs a rich man of a guinea
is, as you will readily admit, a villain. But what is he who can break
his sacred trust by robbing a poor prisoner of eighteen pence given
for his relief? And who can repeat that crime as often as there are
weeks in a winter? And who can multiply it by robbing as many
poor men every week as make up the number of near six hundred?
Tell me that, Mr. Lee!"

"We have all allowed ourselves to be deceived at one time or another," retorted Lee haughtily. "I could present you with a lengthy
list of the persons who have betrayed your confidence, Doctor Franklin."

"It appears then," said Franklin, suppressing his anger with difficulty, "that you too can find no word to describe a creature like this
Digges, who was employed by us on your recommendation. I am not
surprised. We have no name in our language for such atrocious
wickedness. If such a fellow is not damned, then it was not worth
while to invent the Devil."

"I observe," replied Lee, "that Mr. Digges has provided you with
a very opportune pretext."

"Be silent, sir!" commanded Franklin, quietly, but in a tone that
caused the other to recoil.

This was the conversation that had preceded Lafayette's visit,
and so the Doctor was not in a good mood to receive him. Furthermore, he was not the man to be dazzled by the aura of heroism that
surrounded the young Marquis, and he had heard from more than
one source that Lafayette was little more than a poseur. He therefore greeted his visitor courteously, but not too warmly.

Lafayette, however, turned out to be an agreeable, intelligent young
man, without any false modesty, but also without pretentiousness.
He addressed Franklin with an air of the greatest respect, yet with
an entire lack of that meaningless charm of manner which the old
man sometimes found so irritating in Frenchmen.

He had heard with regret, he said, that a great deal of mail from
the United States had fallen into the hands of the English. It was
with all the greater pleasure, therefore, that he was able to hand the
Doctor a letter which had been entrusted to him for safe transmission

by the Congress. As he drew the letter from his pocket he added with a blush, and a smile that made his features more attractive, that if it should contain any references to himself he would be glad if the Doctor would read them quickly without paying too much attention to what was said. He had been dreadfully spoilt in America, and the people there had praised him far beyond his merits.

"I am happy," replied Franklin, placing the letter unopened upon the table, "to know that they endeavoured to make amends for the way in which, as I was sorry to hear, they received you when you first arrived in Philadelphia."

The young Frenchman laughed, and when he laughed one forgot his plain looks. "Of course," he said, "I was annoyed at Mr. Lovell's brusqueness, but I learnt later to understand why he had behaved like that. What the Congress was hoping for from France at that time was a large sack of money. Instead of which they got a horde of young French officers who all wanted to be generals."

He began to talk of George Washington who, he said, never lost his calm in the most difficult of situations and retained his equanimity in the midst of the eternal cabals and intrigues which the Congress allowed to be contrived against him. It had been the greatest good fortune of his life, he concluded warmly, to enjoy the fatherly friendship of such a man.

The Doctor found himself beginning to cherish a liking for the young Frenchman. He seemed a little too fond of the sound of his own voice and was pretty free with his opinions, but for his twenty-one years he had a wide knowledge of the world and possessed sound judgment. It may have been an immature ambition and love of adventure that first impelled him to undertake his voyage to America, nevertheless his experiences there, combined with the example of the great and patient Washington, appeared to have taught him much. It was evident that Lafayette had watched with a clear understanding the imperturbable manner in which the General had frustrated the spiteful incapacity and greed of certain members of the Congress who sought to deny his Army its most essential needs.

With a portentous air that might have suited a veteran politician, but seemed a little precocious for him, Lafayette spoke his mind on the discord that prevailed in the United States and which was tending to make Versailles distrustful of its ally. He himself, he declared, was doing his best to smooth matters over and to present the American situation in a more favourable light. Franklin smiled as he listened to the eager young man's attempts to furnish proof of his active good will and grasp of the facts. Such enthusiasm was useful to the cause, but it had to be kept in restraint lest harm be done through excess of zeal.

He had taken up enough of the Doctor's time, Lafayette said at last, and he rose to take his leave. He had already reached the door when he announced with a shyness which was half genuine and half feigned that he had a second letter for Franklin, one which had been given to him by General Washington, but he had left it at home. "Why did you not bring it with you?" asked Franklin in surprise, to which Lafayette replied with his attractive smile, "I have reason to believe that the letter is chiefly about me, so it cannot be very important. In any case, I wanted to have an excuse to come and see you again."

"You need no excuse, *Monsieur le Marquis*," said Franklin amiably. "Come whenever you feel like it, either with or without a letter."

When Franklin was alone again he reflected on the character of his visitor and the experiences that had fallen to his lot. Here was a young aristocrat who had been inspired by the example of George Washington to direct all his energies and ambitions towards the destruction of the pernicious traditions of the past, though his own existence was rooted in those traditions. Goodness was truly an infectious force.

The Doctor's mind turned to the wider philosophical aspects. It was the Tory laws, checking the young country's development, which had been so pernicious. They had been repealed and would remain repealed, but the time would come, and probably in the not very distant future, when the youthful American republic would have grown old and much that it had achieved would have grown old with it and lost its meaning. Just as today a quarter of the population, by dint of sacrifice and self-conquest, had to struggle for the establishment of a new and meaningful world against the sluggish, selfish majority who clung to the meaningless survivals of the past, so in a future generation a more active, wiser, and more humane minority would again have to defend itself against the slow-witted mass, against those who were sluggish both in heart and mind. Just as these sluggish spirits spoke today of the good old traditional English way, so would they in the time to come prattle about the good old traditional American way.

☆　　☆　　☆

He picked up the letter which the Congress had transmitted to him by the hand of Lafayette. As he had expected, it recommended the Marquis to his notice in glowing terms. Lafayette, wrote Mr. Lovell, Chairman of the Committee for Foreign Affairs, had performed exceedingly useful services to the United States, and he begged Franklin not only to aid him in whatever way he could, but also to seek his advice on all important matters that might arise for discussion during his sojourn in Paris. Franklin was further instructed to present the Marquis with a sword of honour.

Then, however, the letter then went on to deal with another topic, and as Franklin read he sat more erect and his eyes glistened. In dry words Lovell told him that the Congress had decided to appoint him sole plenipotentiary at the Court of Versailles. His credentials would follow by the next boat, but Lovell had taken the opportunity afforded by Lafayette's return to send him the news more speedily than he could have otherwise, and offered his congratulations.

With a slow movement of his old hand Franklin put the letter down again upon the table.

He had expected this. It was only right that things should have turned out this way. Yet they might quite well have turned out differently, and he had taken the possibility into account. It was fateful news that the letter contained. A heavy burden had been taken from his shoulders, but he had assumed a no less heavy one in exchange. It had been decided that he was to remain in France, and perhaps he would never see his homeland again. It had been a long way from the meeting with the Queen to this. The alliance was an accomplished fact. It now devolved upon him to secure the loan of which his country stood in such sore need. There would again be a long and arduous path to traverse, and when that goal had been reached it would still be a long way to peace. He would succeed, nevertheless, and he was firmly resolved to live until success was achieved. *Ça ira.*

He would have liked to go at once to Maurepas and remind him of his promise to enter into negotiations for a loan as soon as Messrs. Lee and Adams were out of the way. But he must not be too precipitate. From his knowledge of Maurepas he knew well enough that the Minister would congratulate him cordially on his appointment, and then proceed to explain that until he was officially informed of the new and agreeable turn which matters had taken he could deal only with the three envoys as a whole. It would therefore be advisable to wait.

The normally calm and philosophic Franklin was pricked by impatience. Something must be done to get things moving in preparation for the negotiations, and he needed the advice of someone whom he could trust. There was only one such, Monsieur Le Grand, the experienced and reliable banker of the United States. Le Grand, however, lived at Amsterdam, in neutral territory, so the newly appointed sole plenipotentiary, as his first official action in that capacity, promptly wrote to the banker and requested him to come to Paris without delay.

Only then did he begin to consider the significance to himself of the appointment. He pictured the effect that the news would have on his colleagues, who were now no longer his colleagues. Monsieur Malaprop would doubtless put a good face on his dismissal, but what would dear Arthur Lee have to say? Franklin's wide mouth broadened in a smile, and for a fleeting moment he looked not at all sage, but rather gleeful.

Yet immediately afterwards, it seemed a petty thing to gloat over the disappointment of his former fellow envoys. Now, since he himself was sure, he could afford to wait until the young gentlemen learnt the unwelcome news in their own dispatches from Philadelphia. It would be more dignified and wiser to keep silent, saying nothing even to his secretaries or most intimate friends. There was nothing useful to be done until his credentials arrived. If he preserved his secret he would find it amusing to listen while Adams and Lee tried to impose their advice and domineering arguments upon him during the short time that still remained to them.

A few days later he was resting beneath the beech-tree. There was already a wintry chill in the air, and he was wearing his fur coat and cap, but as the friendly beams of the sun shone through the bare branches he removed his cap so that the top of his head might be exposed to the pleasant warmth. Little Benjamin came and sat beside him, and the old man reflected that his son Franky would have looked very like his grandson Benjamin if he had lived.

All at once the temptation became irresistible. "Now let us see, my boy," he said, "whether you can keep a secret. Do you think you can?"

"I believe so, Grandfather," replied the child eagerly.

"Do you give me your word of honour," asked the Doctor, "that you will not divulge it to a soul if I tell you something very important and very secret? To nobody whatsoever? Not even to William?"

"I promise you I won't tell anybody," declared Benjamin.

"On your word of honour?" insisted Franklin.

"On my word of honour," the lad repeated solemnly.

"Well, listen then," said Franklin. "Your grandfather has been made sole plenipotentiary of the United States."

Little Benjamin looked rather disappointed, but he answered politely, "Congratulations, Grandfather. You can be sure I won't tell a soul."

But Franklin smiled about himself. Friend Dubourg would probably have cited the story of King Midas. Midas, who had been one of the judges at a musical contest between Pan and Apollo, was in favour of awarding the prize to Pan, whereupon Apollo endowed him with asses' ears. Midas hid these carefully under his Phrygian cap, but they were discovered by his barber who, knowing that his life would be forfeit if he revealed the secret, kept it to himself. Eventually, how-

ever, unable to preserve silence any longer, he dug a hole in the ground and whispered into it, "Midas has asses' ears! Midas has asses' ears!" But from the hole reeds sprang up and these announced to all the world, "Midas has asses' ears!"

All the same, Franklin felt no remorse. On the contrary it amused him hugely when later on the lad winked at him with an air of self-importance in the consciousness of the weighty knowledge that he alone shared with his grandfather.

☆   ☆   ☆

Lafayette went about in Paris and enjoyed his glory. The twenty-one-year-old hero was the recipient of ovations such as had been accorded to the eighty-three-year-old Voltaire six months before. The one had sowed the ideas from which had sprung the independence of America. The other had been the first Frenchman to make the alliance a reality. This was not quite accurate, but the people liked to believe it.

One of the first upon whom Lafayette called was Pierre Beaumarchais, for without Monsieur de Beaumarchais's active support he could hardly have succeeded in quitting France, and even on the other side Pierre's agent had generously supplied him with funds. Now he wanted to offer his thanks in person.

It was not without a certain envy that Pierre gazed at the young aristocrat whose achievements had met with such overwhelming recognition. If Lafayette had been a commoner, like himself, his experiences on both sides of the ocean would probably have been very different. It was true, reflected Pierre, that he had himself tasted glory in many forms, yet for all his fame, his dearest ambition was still unrealized; the work which he regarded as his most mature, the *Figaro,* had still not been produced on the public stage. Louis was still obdurate in his dull objections to its performance.

Yet Pierre was genuinely glad at the other's success and expressed his admiration in glowing terms, to which Lafayette replied with equally exuberant assurances of his profound esteem.

Then he proceeded to talk of matters which could not but interest Pierre deeply. He painted a heart-rending picture of Silas Deane's wretched situation at Philadelphia, where he was exposed to the merciless attacks of his enemies while those whom he had once considered his friends hardly troubled to hide their yawns as they listened to his tale of woe. With a wealth of circumstantial detail he told of the machinations of the brothers Lee, assuring Pierre that he had done his utmost to counteract their lies. There could be no doubt that slowly, though surely, Pierre's services would be accorded their due recognition by the Congress.

He went on to tell the story of a literary success which Pierre, without knowing it, had achieved in the United States. Monsieur Quesnay, the young philosopher and son of Madame de Pompadour's celebrated physician, had crossed the Atlantic in order to further an understanding of French philosophy and art in an atmosphere more liberal than that of his native land. He was now living in Philadelphia, where he was instructing the ladies of local society in French, and at a time when stage productions were forbidden there as frivolous entertainments he had managed to produce Pierre's drama *Eugénie* in French. "Please do not ask me," Lafayette added with a smile, "in what kind of French."

Pierre told himself that they would have understood his play nevertheless, and it filled him with a childish delight to think that he had won over the hearts of the people in the Antipodes to the beauties of the French tongue and of French art.

☆   ☆   ☆

The sword of honour which the Congress proposed to present to Lafayette was the first gift of the kind that Franklin had to bestow in his capacity as sole plenipotentiary, and it was his intention that the youthful republic should cut a good figure at the most splendid court in Europe; its gifts should not lag behind those of any other nation, and this time, luckily, he would not have to wrangle with his former colleagues about the cost. He thought out symbols, ornamentation, and scrolls with suitable mottoes that should be both pregnant with allegorical significance and pleasing to the eye. Bassenge, the court jeweller, was commissioned to make the sword, and Pourrat, of the porcelain manufactory at Sèvres, to execute the reliefs and embellishments.

Bassenge, mistakenly assuming that he had been commissioned to carry out the work by all three envoys, consulted Arthur Lee about a certain detail, and the latter at once choked with indignation. The Doctor *honoris causa* had dared to order a horrifyingly expensive gift without consulting his colleagues. Once again he was flinging away Congress funds in a most reprehensible and irresponsible manner.

Driving angrily out to Passy he called the Doctor to account.

"I have reason to believe," remarked Franklin calmly, "that this gift to Lafayette is in accordance with the wishes of the Congress."

"I was unaware," scoffed Lee, "that you possess the power to read thoughts across the ocean."

For a moment Franklin was tempted to inform Arthur Lee that his part was over, but he resisted the temptation. "Would you suggest," he asked in a tranquil tone which only added fuel to Lee's fury, "that Lafayette and the whole of France should be affronted by our withdrawing the order to make the sword?"

"Unfortunately that would hardly be feasible," replied Lee, "though I must admit that I think the services of this adolescent French aristocrat have been vastly overrated and I must protest vigorously your expenditure of five thousand livres on a mere gesture while our country is harassed by the gravest financial embarrassment."

Franklin removed his spectacles and fixed his large eyes on the agitated man. His brows appeared to arch even higher than was their wont, his wide mouth closed more tightly, a sterner look came into his eyes; it was Duplessis's Franklin who looked at Lee. Arthur Lee grew uncomfortable. At last the old man opened his lips. "You are right," he said. "Five thousand livres is a large sum. It would buy a great deal of bread, and possibly a little ham, to feed hungry Americans. Yet I did not think it worthy of our cause, to which this youth had rendered such great service, and for which he has on several occasions risked his life, to offer him a trifling gift. I had considered making a contribution towards the cost out of my own pocket, but then I decided to follow your example and to donate fifty pounds for the benefit of our prisoners in England, who are compelled to go hungry through the knavery of that villain Digges."

Arthur Lee thought Franklin's method of argument unfair. The old man only wanted to humiliate him by referring to a matter that had nothing whatsoever to do with the subject under discussion, namely, the criminal waste of public funds. "The fact that we suffered losses in London in a way that was not to be foreseen," he declared, "furnishes an added reason why we should avoid unnecessary expenditure now." Folding his arms, he stood stiffly erect and thrust his head forward.

Franklin was about to reply sharply, but then he reflected, "Alas, Poor Richard, if you only knew!" He saw the virtuous indignation in the other's face, and he smiled broadly in amusement. Arthur Lee did not know what to make of it. The old man's behaviour was no longer insulting, it was just crazy. Lee shrugged his shoulders and took his departure.

A few days later he learnt the meaning of Franklin's smile. Official news arrived via Amsterdam of the Doctor's appointment as sole plenipotentiary of the United States at the Court of Versailles.

The blood rushed to Arthur Lee's heart, the world grew black before his eyes, he fell to the floor, fainting.

When he came to, still lying on the floor, he slowly thought over what had happened. A boundless fury overwhelmed him, but he threw it back. Not to be carried away by his feelings, to think rationally, logically—that was his strength, that's where he was superior to the Doctor *honoris causa.*

He painfully rose, groaning slightly, and seated himself in an arm-chair. Once more he read the letter from the Congress, this time at-tentively. It also contained instructions to present Lafayette with a sword of honour. In the top right-hand corner appeared the figure 4; so this letter was a fourth copy. Three other copies had therefore gone astray. Clenching his teeth, with lips tightly pressed together, he thought it out. Yet the old man must have known of his appointment as well as of the instructions regarding the sword of honour. Other-wise he would not have treated him with such insolent disdain. Arthur Lee felt more humiliated than he had ever done in his life. What a pitiful picture he must have presented as he stood before Franklin, reprimanding him for his extravagance, and the conceited old man had not even considered it worth while to inform him and crush him. What base treachery! What fathomless malice! The spiteful pride of this Nestor, this patriarch, had only increased with the years. What a mean trick it was to withhold the truth in order that he might gloat over his ignorance! Lee thought of Franklin's smile, his deep, amused, unutterably insolent smile. It was the way one would smile at the entertaining antics of a monkey trying to reach a fruit that was kept beyond its grasp by an iron grating.

He was a devil, this Doctor *honoris causa.* He had tried to put him in the shade from the very outset with his electrical discoveries, his fame as a scholar, and he, Arthur Lee, had meekly given way. Yet he, Arthur Lee, was by far the better statesman, and no amount of envy could suppress the fact. Yet however much he had borne with the old man, the old man had refused to accept the hand of friendship. Frank-lin had tried to get rid of him because he stood firm in his virtuous republicanism, because he remonstrated with him for his corrupt con-duct, his nepotism, his so-called liberal, or in other words dissolute, way of life which brought their country's name into disrepute. He had no use for an honest witness to his own and his friends' underhand dealings. That was why he had sheltered behind the worshippers of idols, behind the minions of tyranny. In the emergency the Congress had been forced to yield to the hereditary enemy, and henceforth the double-dealing Franklin would be sitting at Passy with nobody to supervise his actions, free to exercise his duplicity and work what harm he might to America and the cause of liberty.

The United States must be in a parlous condition if Richard Henry Lee, the creator of American independence, had to stand aside while such humiliation and ingratitude were heaped upon his brother Arthur.

Still feeling very faint, he sat in his arm-chair for an eternity. Then he pulled himself together, stood up, folded his arms across his breast, and thrust out his chin in defiance of the absent enemy, the Doctor *honoris causa*. The latter was very much mistaken if he believed that an Arthur Lee would give up the struggle so soon. He was entitled to remain in Paris, and by no means in an unofficial capacity, for he continued to hold his appointment as American envoy at Madrid. The instructions which his brother William and Ralph Izard had received from the Congress applied consequently to him also. So long as he was not able to take up his post at Madrid, it was his duty to stay in Paris and attend to the interests of his country, in other words, to watch over the old man and prevent him from taking any steps that might lead to the nation's ruin.

On that same day John Adams at Passy learnt that it was not he, but Franklin, who had been selected as sole plenipotentiary. For a moment he knitted his brows and decided gloomily that even in the promised land of America the blockheads were in a vast majority, but it was not long before he overcame his disappointment and realized that since the treaty had been concluded before his arrival in France his sojourn there had been a mistake from the start. It was just as well that the time had come for him to depart and return to his Abigail, and if one looked at the matter objectively, it was the wisest thing to leave only one man in charge of affairs in Paris, even if this one was not particularly suited.

John Adams had a sense of fairness and a flair for gestures. Crossing over to Franklin's rooms he seized the old man's brown, dried-up hand in his own warm, plump one and declared cordially, "I offer my congratulations, Doctor Franklin. I candidly confess that I hoped to continue looking after affairs here myself, but I know that in your hands as sole plenipotentiary the interests of our country will be better safeguarded than if the three of us were to tinker with them as hitherto. Moreover you like living among the French, while I prefer to be at home. So after all perhaps the Congress in its wisdom may have discovered the best solution."

To his wife Abigail he wrote as follows: "When news reached me of the resolution which had been hatched out by fate and certain undiscerning members of the Congress, I was filled with regret at this fresh ordeal to which our country is now to be exposed. On the other hand, it seemed to me only proper that I should offer my congratulations to the Doctor, who has behaved unobjectionably in his private conduct towards me, though of course without concealing my opinion. I found him, by the way, sitting at his writing-table, with one of his feet stripped of shoe and stocking and his hair so unkempt and disorderly that it reminded me of his spiritual condition."

Franklin had received by the same post detailed accounts from trusted friends of the way in which his appointment had come about.

After the resolution had been taken to maintain only one envoy at Versailles, a committee of thirteen members had been set up to put forward names. Five members of the committee had voted for Arthur Lee, four for John Adams, and only two for Franklin, with two members abstaining. Since the supporters of Lee were unable to come to an agreement with those who wanted Adams, it was suggested that all three envoys should be recalled and a new man sent in their place. Meanwhile, however, the French Ambassador let it be known that, in his opinion, no one but Franklin enjoyed sufficient prestige with his Government to negotiate a loan successfully. He made his point emphatically and with insistence, until at last Franklin was nominated by a majority of one vote. At the plenary session his own State of Pennsylvania voted against him unanimously.

Franklin was not very surprised at this information. He possessed many enemies in the United States; he was the son of a tallow-chandler, in Pennsylvania he had led the party of little men against the landed proprietors, and the treachery of his son William provided welcome propaganda. So the decision had gone in his favour by no more than a hair's breadth. He had been lucky, had old Benjamin, the son of the right hand, the son of fortune, for if he wanted to be candid with himself he was bound to confess that his recall would have come as a severe blow. Perhaps the fact that it was he who was staying behind, and not Arthur Lee, was due solely to that supper at The Redoute Chinoise. But all this was idle reverie. There was meaning in history, and it was Providence that the better representative of the American cause remained.

He smiled. This, even the Congress had realized in the end, though only with the help of the French Ambassador.

☆   ☆   ☆

Among Franklin's friends at Passy, at Versailles, and in Paris there was great jubilation. Little Benjamin observed with pride that the secret entrusted to him by his grandfather had been a very important one indeed.

Madame Helvétius gave a dinner-party for him and overcame her feelings sufficiently to include Madame Brillon among the guests. The Doctor ate heartily, doing more than justice to the viands, particularly the whipped cream. Nor did he shun the madeira. He wanted to show his old enemy, the gout, that he was not afraid of it.

The Abbé Morellet composed for the occasion a song in Franklin's honour which mingled profound admiration and harmless gaiety with jolly, imperfect rhymes and meter:

Let history our Franklin's name
Grave on brass with pen and fame;
'Tis to me the task belongs,
Him to sing in drinking songs;
Come, begin,
Drink and sing our Benjamin!

Great in politics is he,
At the table gay and free;
Founding empires, see him quaff
Flowing cups and hear him laugh,
Gay and grave as Capuchin,
Such is our Benjamin.

If you see our heroes brave
Both the English and the wave,
'Tis that our Catholic wine
May, America, be thine,
Clear and fine,
Such as loveth Benjamin.

And so the cheerful nonsense went on for seven stanzas. Franklin was hugely delighted, and he accompanied the song, which was rendered by the daughters of Madame Helvétius, on a musical instrument of his own invention, a kind of harmonica. After this he himself sang a couple of melancholy Scottish airs of which he was particularly fond, one of them a folk-ballad about Mary, Queen of Scots, and the other a mournful tune, beginning "We once were happy."

Next morning he called at Versailles to inform Vergennes and Maurepas officially of his appointment.

The two Ministers were already fully conversant with the circumstances preceding his nomination. Vergennes took no pains to conceal his opinion of the Congress. "You will not misunderstand me," he said, "if I speak frankly to you. What *is* this strange crew that your countrymen have elected to represent them? If we had not fortunately been able to prevent it, your godforsaken Congress would have recalled its best man in the hour when it needs him most."

Nor did Maurepas trouble to hide his pleasure. "I at once commissioned Duplessis to do another portrait of you," he said cheerfully. "It is my intention to present it to the Queen. Her Majesty was afforded the opportunity of making your acquaintance at a very early stage of your residence in Paris, and if she now hangs your portrait where it will be visible to all, it will be a token, so to speak, that the child which arrived too soon has been formally adopted. You will be seeing the King again, of course, when you come to present your credentials.

His Most Christian Majesty will gradually become accustomed to the sight of you."

Neither of the Ministers made any reference to the prospective loan, nor did Franklin consider it advisable to broach such a delicate topic on this first visit in his new capacity.

William and de la Motte were kept busy filling their portfolios with additional evidence of Franklin's popularity among the people of Paris as the apostle of liberty and reason, while there was a constant procession of carriages driving out to Passy with callers who had come to offer their felicitations.

Among these was Pierre Beaumarchais. He had been jubilant when he learnt of the dismissal of the guileful and thoroughly obnoxious Arthur Lee. Now, finally, he was afforded the satisfaction of witnessing the fall of the scoundrel who had all along opposed the payment of the debt due to him from the United States.

The Doctor felt a sense of relief as he listened to Pierre's exuberant congratulations. When this Monsieur Caron was recently in very grave difficulties, not without the fault of the Congress, he had not lifted a finger to help the man. But his visitor did not seem to bear him the slightest ill will. In his buoyant, naïve way, he was saying, "You, too, Doctor Franklin, must be rejoicing that we have at last succeeded in ridding ourselves of this horse-fly, Mr. Lee. I believe that you also had to put up with a great deal from him, did you not?"

Franklin was a little embarrassed by Pierre's remark, for he remembered Dubourg and the *mouche au coche*. Cautiously, and a little stiffly, he replied, "Yes, you have suffered much injustice, Monsieur."

"We both have," Pierre hastened to respond. "We both have. I am honoured, Doctor, at having shared such a fate with you. I am honoured that we should have so much in common. We always manage to extract ourselves from the misfortunes that befall us."

Franklin told himself that his visitor had done more for the American cause than anyone else in France, more than Lafayette who had been lauded to the skies, and that he had been ill rewarded for his efforts. Yet he could not bring himself to regard Monsieur Caron with any less distaste than at their first meeting, and he did not like the suggestion that they had much in common. Sententiously he remarked, "Let us not rejoice too soon. We still have a long way to go."

Pierre failed to see the connexion between this comment and his own observations, but he at once interpreted it in his own way. "Yes," he agreed, "in that respect, too, we are alike. I also look upon every success as merely a beginning, as if I were traversing a pass through a mountain range whose peaks are lost in the clouds."

Franklin, somewhat taken aback by this rejoinder, countered it by heaving a little sigh. "My dear Monsieur de Beaumarchais," he said,

"I do not think there is time enough left to me for scaling mountain peaks. When I walk through the Cimetière des Innocents I have the feeling that I am choosing myself a final abode."

Pierre protested energetically. "Come, come, my dear Doctor," he urged. "Come, come. Don't lose courage. I have as great a faith in your star as in my own. We two will yet see the end of this war. That's what I, Pierre Beaumarchais, tell you."

☆   ☆   ☆

In the meantime Monsieur Le Grand, the banker, had arrived from Amsterdam, and Franklin set to work with him on the drafting of a memorandum which he proposed to submit to the French Government demonstrating that the United States were in urgent need of financial assistance. It was growing more and more evident that the loan of twenty-five million livres for which the Congress asked was a matter of vital necessity, and that the grant must be made quickly.

Yet Franklin hesitated. It was not an opportune moment to demand such a large sum, for with the increasing intercourse between France and America since the conclusion of the alliance the French had become better informed about the wrangles that were going on in the Congress and the situation generally throughout the country. Discontented officers had returned suggesting that no more than a quarter of the people over there had any faith in the cause for which they were fighting. One of these officers, named Laroche, had originated the malicious witticism that there were more friends of the United States in Paris than there were in America, while Captain de Portail, who had been wounded while serving with Admiral d'Estaing, was saying that there was no getting on with the Americans, who were lazy, sat about smoking and drinking tea with rum all day and half the night, shirked whatever hardships they could, and would undoubtedly throw in their hand in the long run. Moreover, they had a strong antipathy to the French and were more likely to go over to the English than to fight side by side with their allies. Monsieur Pellier, an official of the Ministry of Finance, had been travelling in the United States on behalf of Monsieur Necker and copies of his report had been circulated by enemies of the republic. In this report Monsieur Pellier had stated that the agents of the American Government were receiving fabulous commissions from the contractors, and the whole country was dominated by a spirit of calculating selfishness and greed. Nobody thought of condemning this state of things, for the chief characteristic of the American mentality was the desire to make vast profits, particularly in the northern territories.

It seemed inadvisable to Franklin, at a time when the salons and coffee-houses of Paris were echoing with such stories, to ask for the enormous sum demanded by the Congress. The French Ministers had, it was true, assured him that they were only waiting for him to become sole plenipotentiary before proceeding to negotiate a loan, but he knew from experience how little reliance was to be placed on the promises of diplomats. The most unequivocal pledge could be twisted and manipulated until at last it dissolved.

During these weeks he had a number of conversations with Lafayette. General Washington, the Marquis told him, was convinced of the impossibility of fighting a decisive battle and of winning the war without the help of a French army and a French fleet. A French expeditionary corps had been mustered, and it constituted a force that was by no means to be despised. Lafayette himself was under orders to travel to Le Havre as Deputy Quartermaster-General for the purpose of inspecting the troops. Yet the contingent was unable to sail because the Congress stubbornly refused to allow French troops to enter the country. There had been considerable friction with Admiral d'Estaing, and the Americans were afraid of worse to come if a whole French army should be stationed on their soil. "The Congress," complained Lafayette, "does not want troops, it does not want experienced officers, all it wants is money. Please help me, Doctor Franklin," he begged. "Persuade the Congress to accept a French auxiliary corps. Explain to these gentlemen that a French army will also bring in French money. Oh, what shopkeepers they are, these statesmen of yours at Philadelphia. I always thought that we Frenchmen were avaricious, but compared with your countrymen we are veritable spendthrifts."

One thing was certain. The dispatch of the French expeditionary force, without which the war could not be won, depended on the loan. Franklin's logic advised him to wait. His heart demanded that he should act.

And now even General Washington urged him to act. The letter was very brief. The Army and the country generally, he said in his simple, forthright way, were in a grievous state. They must either obtain money from France or sue for peace.

Franklin hesitated no longer. He sent to Count Vergennes the memorandum which he had drafted with the help of Monsieur Le Grand, adding a letter in which he struck a more personal note. Without referring to the promise made him by Maurepas, he wrote: "I am grown old, I feel myself much enfeebled by illness, and it is probable I shall not long have any more concern in these affairs. I therefore take this occasion to express my opinion to Your Excellency that the present conjuncture is critical. There is some danger lest the Congress should lose its influence over the people if it is found unable to procure the aids that are wanted, and that the whole system of the new Government in America may thereby be shaken. If the English are suffered once to recover that country, such an opportunity of effectual separation as the present may not occur again in the course of ages. The possession of those fertile and extensive regions and that vast seacoast will afford them so broad a basis for future greatness, by the rapid growth of their commerce and the breed of seamen and soldiers, as will enable them to become the terror of Europe and to exercise with impunity that insolence which is so natural to their nation, and which will increase enormously with the increase of their power."

☆   ☆   ☆

The sword of honour was ready and Franklin regarded the masterpiece of craftsmanship with a delighted eye. The hilt and embellishments were of solid gold and the whole weapon—hilt, pommel, guard, and scabbard—was covered with decoration. There was Lafayette's coat-of-arms with its bold motto, *Cur non?* A crescent represented the rising glory of America. The British lion lay stretched beneath Lafayette's foot, and America was handing the youthful hero a branch of laurel. The Battles of Gloucester and Monmouth were depicted, as well as the retreats from Barren Hill and Rhode Island. A winged *Fama* flew ahead of the frigate that was carrying Lafayette back to the shores of France, bearing in one of her hands the wreath which America had conferred upon him, and in the other a trumpet with which she was to proclaim his deeds to Europe. It was astonishing what a wealth of allegory Franklin and Pourrat had succeeded in bringing within the compass of the available space.

Lafayette was at Le Havre inspecting the troops destined for service overseas, so that Franklin was unable to present the handsome gift to him personally, but this was not without its advantages, for it gave the Doctor an opportunity to send young William on the journey that he had so long desired to make.

Young William's attachment to Blanchette Caillot was deeper than he had allowed to appear, and it would have been a grievous blow to him if he had been compelled to return to America and leave her behind. He had therefore been overjoyed at his grandfather's appointment, for he now had the prospect of maintaining his association with her for a long time to come.

For many weeks he had been entreating permission to go and see her at Le Havre, but there was a great deal to do and the Doctor thought it best to keep the lad's nose to the grindstone, in order to impress upon him that the most important thing in his life was his work. He would give him leave to visit Le Havre only if the journey could be combined with some official mission. A more fitting occasion than the presentation of the sword of honour could hardly have occurred.

William radiated happiness. The prospect opened up to him was one of pure bliss. He was to be entrusted with a highly honourable mission, that of presenting a splendid gift to a famous soldier, and at the same time he was going to see the girl he loved, the mother of his child.

Before he left, Franklin composed a letter for him to hand to La-fayette. "Upon the sword," he wrote, "are represented some of the principal actions of the war, in which you distinguished yourself by your bravery and conduct. These, with a few emblematic figures, all admirably well executed, make its principal value. By the help of the exquisite artists France affords I find it easy to express everything but the sense we have of your worth and our obligation to you. For this, figures and even words are found insufficient."

After revising the French style with the assistance of Madame Brillon, he read through the final version and chuckled. This was the proper French high-flown way to express your admiration for a French general.

☆　　　☆　　　☆

Count de Maurepas was breakfasting alone for the third day in suc-cession. His Countess had gone off to Paris to supervise in person the last touches that were being put to the restoration of the Hôtel Phélypeau, and he missed her sorely, particularly at breakfast time.

He dipped his croissant into the chocolate, but did not put it in his mouth. His appetite was gone. There was no pleasure in eating alone. *"Par mon âme, si'l en fût en moi,"* he mused. "I am growing old." He felt tired. If only the day were over, so that he could curl up in bed and fall asleep.

Jean-Frédéric Maurepas had enjoyed everything that any man could desire—riches, women, and honours. His wit and intellectual gifts had been matched by audacity and taste. Exciting experiences had fallen to his lot, his ambitions had been fulfilled, every appetite had been quenched, all his dreams had become reality. One goal alone re-mained. He intended to die in harness.

It was an unutterable strain being the progressive Minister of a re-actionary monarch. Was it worth the effort, he wondered. He sat hud-dled up in his chair, a little, dried-up, morose old man wrapped in his scarves and shawls. Vergennes was again worrying him about that stupid loan for Franklin, leaving him no peace until he had promised to obtain the royal signature at the first favourable opportunity. There would be another tough struggle with the reluctant Louis. And what was the object of all this exertion? What did he care about America? With envious ill humour he fixed his eyes on the portrait hanging on the opposite wall. With cool, searching gaze Franklin looked through him and beyond him. The American certainly had the advantage. He represented a youthful country and could carry out his progressive precepts without having to fight and argue all the time.

Gris-gris, the cat, stretched herself, and mewed. Maurepas held out a piece of his croissant, but she merely sniffed at it and turned away. Gris-gris was a little supercilious towards her master. He thought of the last talk he had had with the Countess about the cat. She had been unable to make up her mind whether to take it with her to Paris or to leave it behind. "I am going to miss Gris-gris terribly," she had lamented. "I can't enjoy my breakfast if Gris-gris isn't there to beg for morsels."

"Then why not take her with you, my sweetest?" suggested Maurepas.

"The poor thing won't feel happy in Paris," she had protested. "I tried it two or three times before, and she was very wretched. She will find it more uncomfortable than ever with all these repairs going on. Here at Versailles she feels at home. She has her regular hunting grounds and knows the exact position of every mouse-hole. Cats are attached to houses, not people."

"Well, my love," he had replied, "so at least you will be comforted by the thought that Gris-gris is being well looked after here."

"Yet I do sometimes have the feeling," she had said pensively, "that the dear creature mopes when I am away, and I am not quite certain whether Gaspard always serves her milk at the right temperature."

"If you are worried about it, my love," he had responded, "perhaps it would be better to take her with you after all."

"You are simply intolerable, Jean-Frédéric," she had complained. "You never know what you want. Take her with you. Leave her here. I can never get you to give a clear and unequivocal opinion."

The old man cheered up a little at the recollection of this conversation. It warmed his chilly heart to think how dependent he was on his Countess, while at the same time being intellectually her superior. He stroked the cat, which moved away ungraciously, and then dozed off in his chair.

A slight noise awoke him. The door had closed. Someone had probably looked into the room with the intention of clearing away the breakfast things, but had tip-toed out again so as not to disturb him. Glancing at the clock on the mantelpiece, a work of art by Falconet, he saw that his nap must have lasted more than a quarter of an hour.

Another quarter of an hour had gone by, fifteen minutes, nine hundred seconds. The minutes and hours were passing quickly, bringing ever nearer the moment when he would die in harness.

Ringing the bell, he sent for Sallé. Putting his morning mood into words, he dictated witty, cynical observations on the futility of life. "Read it back to me, Sallé," he ordered. The secretary, in his hollow voice, did as he was bid. "Excellent," commented Maurepas gleefully. "Don't you think it is excellent, Sallé?" In his delight at the exquisiteness of his style he forgot the futility of life. "It is almost as good as *Ecclesiastes*. Don't you think so, my dear Sallé?" he insisted. "Read me a few verses from *Ecclesiastes,* just for comparison."

Sallé brought the Bible and read:

While the evil days come not, nor the years draw nigh, when thou shalt say, I have no pleasure in them:
While the sun, or the light, or the moon, or the stars, be not darkened, nor the clouds return after the rain:
In the day when the keepers of the house shall tremble, and the strong men shall bow themselves, and the grinders cease because they are few, and those that look out of the windows be darkened,
And the doors shall be shut in the streets, when the sound of the grinding is low, and he shall rise up at the voice of the bird, and all the daughters of music shall be brought low.
Also when the almond tree shall flourish, and the grasshopper shall be a burden, and desire shall fail: because man goeth to his long home, and the mourners go about the streets:
Or ever the silver cord be loosed, or the golden bowl be broken, or the pitcher be broken at the fountain, or the wheel broken at the cistern.
Then shall the dust return to the earth as it was.

"All right, Sallé," interrupted Maurepas ill-humouredly, "I do not wish to hear any more. The old Jew was the better writer after all. He expresses himself a little too obscurely for my taste, but he is evidently referring to the frailties of old age and his style is very vivid, though the translation appears to have its weaknesses. Ah well, growing old was probably no different two thousand years ago than it is today. There is nothing new under the sun." Dismissing his secretary, he sank into brooding thought until he dozed off once more.

☆   ☆   ☆

Louis sat in his library, studying the dispatches from Madrid. It was certainly a good thing that Spain had joined in the war at last.

It was comforting to know that his cousin in Aranjuez, a most admirable prince, who was so effectively upholding the divinely ordained social order in his realm, had not been able in the long run to keep aloof from the alliance with the rebels. He, Louis, would no longer be the only one who was forced to send money, ships, and soldiers to the mutinous Americans.

On the other hand, his Ministers were using this welcome turn of events as a lever to extort still more money from him. Now that part of the subsidies could be placed to the charge of Spain, they were urging him to sanction the tremendous loan for which the Americans were pleading. Whatever happened it would be he who would have to fork out by far the larger share. Whether good or ill ensued, it was always he who had to pay. It really was outrageous. It was a mercy that Monsieur Necker, a Swiss and a Protestant, was so stubborn in resisting the demands of the other Ministers.

On the previous day, when Maurepas and Vergennes were bombarding him with their arguments, Necker had mentioned a perfectly startling figure in the course of the discussion. He had declared that expenditure on the war already amounted to over five hundred millions. Louis could hardly believe his ears. He had hoped that the estimate was exaggerated, that Necker had rounded it off to the next hundred million so as to counter the demands of his colleagues. When the others had gone, however, and he had questioned Necker in confidence, the latter had refused to budge an inch. He repeated that expenditure had already exceeded five hundred millions and promised to submit a detailed balance-sheet before the day was out. Louis was waiting for the statement to arrive and had given orders that it was to be brought to him immediately it was received.

Banishing his gloomy premonitions, he bent his thoughts on the great joy to which he was looking forward in the near future. There were only a few weeks to go before Toinette's confinement, which was expected about the middle of December, and he had evolved an idea that would surprise the world. The Dauphin would, of course, be called Louis-Auguste, like himself, but he was going to endow his eldest son, the future Louis the Seventeenth, with another name, a name such as no King of France had ever borne before. He had been forced to ally himself with rebels, and for that very reason he would demonstrate his piety, his trust in the Lord, by the gesture of conferring upon the Dauphin the name of Adeodatus, Dieudonné. It was a good and most pious idea. How his mentor, that secret heretic, would goggle. *Upon my soul, if I possess one.* He had not failed to overhear the wicked remark, and just because he had heard it he was more than ever resolved to give the Dauphin the name of Dieudonné. The old sinner would not dare to utter a word in protest.

The soft-footed Monsieur de Sept-Chênes entered, deposited a document on the table, and withdrew at once. Monsieur Necker's memorandum. Wetting his thick fingers, Louis peered short-sightedly at the sheets as he excitedly turned them over to find the final figures. Here they were. His face turned red, he snorted heavily, he felt constricted round the middle and loosened his belt to give himself room to breathe. *Five hundred and thirty-two million.*

Maurepas and Vergennes had laughed in disbelief when Necker gloomily predicted that the war would cost a thousand million. And while he himself pretended that he took his Finance Minister's estimate seriously, in his soul he had never placed much credence in it. He had rather listened to the comforting assurances of the others that the war would be of only short duration and England would very soon be constrained to sue for peace before she collapsed. Yet Necker had repeated the figure again and again in his severe, pedantic voice that reminded Louis of his former tutor Vauguyon— "A thousand millions! A thousand millions!"

Now the rebels wanted another loan. Another twenty-five million. By a single stroke of the pen the figure would jump to 557,000,000. There was no satisfying the insatiable old Franklin.

He could not bear it to sit idly in his library any longer. Without troubling to change his clothes, he stamped angrily through the corridors and up the stairways until he reached his smithy. He had to work off his rage by hard manual labour. He wanted to bang away at his forge.

The low, heavy door was locked, but he always carried the key. As it swung open an unexpected sound met his ears, a long-drawn-out, mournful and yet relieved miaouwing. Up there, on the top of the tool rack, crouched the source of the noise—a cat. Either Laudry or Gamain must have been so careless that he had allowed an animal to creep into his last place of refuge, in spite of his severe orders. Here in his smithy he wanted to be alone, without the company of either men or animals.

He set about chasing the cat away. As it was sitting high up on the tool rack, he climbed onto a stool, but it leapt over his shoulder and when he clumsily tried to grab it, sprang onto the work-bench. Some tools feel to the floor with a loud clatter and his fury rose. Opening the door wide, he rushed after the cat, but it fled to the opposite corner of the room. Seizing the heavy tongs he hurled them at the animal, which uttered a pitiful howl and limped into the passage. With grim satisfaction, Louis closed the door. At last he was alone.

Taking off his outer garments, he stood there in shirt and breeches blowing up the forge, busying himself with his pieces of iron, swinging his sledge. He banged and swung and banged and swung.

At last Gamain arrived. "Was it you who let the cat in?" shouted Louis, his voice rising to a falsetto.

"What cat, Sire?" asked the locksmith in bewilderment.

"You know quite well what cat," cried Louis furiously.

Gamain stoutly denied having seen any cat. "If there was a cat here," he declared, "it must have slipped in as I left. Or it might have crept in through the window. I opened it for a few minutes because it was so hot in here."

"I will not have any cats in this room," Louis insisted. "Remember that, you bastard, you whoreson! I am not going to let you all trample on me like this."

He continued to swear obscenely for a while and then, still cursing resentfully, he returned to his forge. Cursed, banged, swung. His rage subsided, and when he left his smithy he had reconciled himself to the cost of the war.

☆   ☆   ☆

Gaspard, the footman, and Séraphine, the housekeeper, carried the corpse of Gris-gris, the cat, into their master's presence in a hat-box. Maurepas was more deeply shaken at the sight than he had ever been by any political disaster. He was no coward, but a cold fear penetrated his very bones at the thought of the grief and wrath of his Countess.

He was a man of equable temperament who seldom raised his voice. But now, at the sight of the dead Gris-gris, he shrieked at the two domestics who had been in his service for decades, heaping them with meaningless abuse, and he fell back in a chair gasping for breath.

Circumspectly Gaspard told the story of the cat's demise, the details of which he had learned from Gamain. The King had found Gris-gris sitting alone in his smithy, and later she had been seen by a number of people limping through the corridors of Versailles, half-dead and howling pitifully, until some sympathetic soul had recognized her and brought her back to the apartments where she belonged. Séraphine had sent for Doctor Lassone, but Gaspard had seen at once that there was nothing to be done. The cat was dead before the physician arrived. And here was the corpse, in the box for the big Florentine hat.

The Countess dropped everything she was doing at the Hôtel Phély-peau and returned post-haste to Versailles. Normally a match for any situation, she was beside herself at the death of Gris-gris. It was all the fault of that old fool Jean-Frédéric, who had kept the cat at home and then let her fall into the hands of that savage buffoon of a Louis, King of France by the wrath of God.

Without mincing her words she told Maurepas to his face what she thought of both him and his royal pupil. "I have reached the end of my patience, Monsieur," she declared, her alert black eyes fixed on him in cold menace. "I shall leave you to ruin the evening of your life alone in pursuit of your empty ambition. I am still comparatively young; I'm walking out. It is incomprehensible to me how a man who is still in possession of his senses can continue to wear himself out in the service of this clownish barbarian."

It took the old man's breath away. "But, my love," he stammered at last, "I must most respectfully protest. You are speaking of the King of France and Navarre."

"Certainly, Monsieur," she retorted. "It is of that fool and barbarian that I am speaking, of your pupil, your Télémaque. A fine creature you have made of him, forsooth. A bloodthirsty blockhead who persecutes everything that's lovable and charming. What did my Gris-gris do to your Louis? To hurl glowing tongs at helpless cats, that's what you taught your pupil. You can be proud of his achievements. He has put every obstacle he could in my Franklin's way, he locked up my Toutou and banned the best comedy in France, and he slew my Gris-gris. What can he do further to open your eyes?" Drawing herself up, she cried challengingly, "If you still possess a spark of dignity, Jean-Frédéric, you will resign and quit this Court at once, where they slaughter defenceless animals. Let us move to Paris, where we shall no longer have to live under the same roof as this tyrant. But first let us go to Pontchartrain. I need solitude to recover from all that has happened."

It was at Pontchartrain that Maurepas had passed the long years of his banishment, and the memory only served to heighten his gloom. He slept miserably that night.

"Great tidings, Your Excellency! Great tidings!" announced Vergennes joyfully next morning.

"Have the Spaniards won a victory?" asked Maurepas apathetically.

"Something far more important," cried Vergennes jubilantly. "The Austrians are eating humble pie." Waving a letter that he held in his hand, he went on to report that Monsieur de Breteuil, the French Ambassador at Vienna, had informed him that Maria Theresa and Joseph requested the King to mediate between Austria and Prussia.

This was certainly great news. Louis, who had been deeply depressed by the Austrian conflict, would feel immeasurably relieved; he would be ready to make concessions in other directions and put his signature to the American loan.

"We must go across at once, Your Excellency," urged Vergennes.

But Maurepas replied gloomily, "Please, go alone, *mon ami*. I am not in the mood this morning to face the King."

Vergennes had been so full of his tidings that he had not noticed before how downcast Maurepas was looking. "For Heaven's sake," he cried. "What has happened?"

Maurepas told him the whole story. Vergennes was relieved, but he displayed sympathy and did his best to comfort his colleague.

Vergennes, however, was a subtle diplomat and knew that every cloud had its silver lining. Choosing his words carefully, he hinted that the wrong inflicted upon Maurepas by the Crown afforded a most favourable opportunity for putting pressure upon the Crown.

☆　　☆　　☆

His cheeks reddened with the frost, Louis had just returned in blithe spirits from a hunting expedition when Vergennes called to inform him of the good news. His fat, good-humoured countenance beamed with pleasure. It was indeed a source of great satisfaction that his brother-in-law, the Holy Roman Emperor, should have come to see the light of reason. So he was prepared to reduce his demands to a mere claim upon the Inn region? That was very moderate of him. Very shrewd. The territory was tiny, hardly more than a token conquest, which Frederick of Prussia would certainly not wish to begrudge Joseph. "The Inn region," he explained, proud of his geographical knowledge, "has only one town of any consequence, and even that is quite unimportant, a few hundred inhabitants, certainly less than a thousand, a very small place. Its name is Braunau." He went at once to consult his maps, and was delighted to find that they all confirmed his statement.

Mediating in the interests of peace was just the sort of thing that the sixteenth Louis liked doing. To the astonishment of his Foreign Minister, he began to hum an old song that had been popular at the *halles* some forty years before, when the peace of 1735 had been signed:

> The King said to the Emperor,
> "You must pack your traps, old squirt,
> I regret to be so curt,
> But with peace there's an end to shooting,
> You must quit your pillage and looting,
> We're at peace, my dear King,
> Kiss my backside and sing,
> Diridam, diridum, diridumdum."

Louis could not help gloating a little at the thought of his brother-in-law Joseph, whose plan had come to grief so ingloriously, but any touch of malice was soon absorbed in worthier feelings. Now in particular, when he was looking forward to becoming a father in the near future, he felt deeply grateful to the man whose advice had made this possible, and he was willing to do whatever lay in his power to settle the conflict quickly. "What would you suggest, Your Excellency," he asked his Foreign Minister, "as our immediate course of procedure? And what would my mentor suggest?"

Only now Louis noticed the absence of his Prime Minister. News of such moment was usually communicated to him by his two principal advisers jointly. "What has happened to Maurepas?" he asked in surprise. "Why did he not come with you? What is he doing?"

"The Count is very downcast," replied Vergennes cautiously.

Louis blinked at him in bewilderment. "Downcast?" he repeated stupidly. "Why is he downcast?"

In a low, but significant tone Vergennes replied, "It is on account of the cat, Sire."

Louis was more nonplussed than ever. "The cat?" he demanded. "What cat? What have cats got to do with the Austrian war? I do not understand a word you are saying?"

"I am referring to the cat Gris-gris, Sire," explained Vergennes. "She was the Countess's only joy. Somebody wounded her with a heavy instrument, one such as blacksmiths use, a pair of tongs if I am correctly informed."

A light began to dawn on Louis. "So it was Maurepas's cat," he exclaimed uneasily, "that stole into my smithy. Was she badly hurt?"

"If I am correctly informed, Sire," replied Vergennes, "the cat is dead."

"Well, here's a pretty kettle of fish," lamented Louis, very much upset.

"To be perfectly frank, Sire," said Vergennes, "I have never seen my friend Maurepas so deeply depressed."

"I can well believe it," replied Louis mournfully. "The Countess is a strong-minded lady." He thought of his own feelings when he had done anything that aroused the disapproval of Toinette. "The poor fellow must be having a bad time," he muttered. "It is really dreadful that the cat should have died. All I wanted to do was to chase it out, and now the wretched animal has gone and died. I will tell you what, Vergennes," he went on in a more animated tone. "I must make up for what I have done. I will go across to his apartments at once and offer my condolences."

He went off without more ado to see Maurepas.

Maurepas had meanwhile been considering what penance he should impose upon his pupil. He was not a vengeful man, but he did not see why he should be the only one to suffer the consequences of his Countess's grief. There was no reason why Louis should not take his share. As a politician, moreover, of nearly sixty years' experience, the Devil must be in it if he did not succeed in exploiting the cat's demise to the advantage of human progress.

One thing was certain. Louis must be made to realize in full measure the sorrow he had caused and his remorse turned to immediate profit. The young monarch must agree to sign the American loan.

This, however, would not be adequate requital. The twenty-five millions could be obtained by making use of the favourable turn of events that had been brought about through the approaching end of the Austro-Prussian war. The slaying of Gris-gris demanded sterner retribution. When his Countess had enumerated the sins of the refractory Louis, she had mentioned not only his unfriendly attitude towards Franklin, but the wrongs he had inflicted on their joint protégé, Pierre Beaumarchais. Progressive statesman that he was, his failure to secure the public performance of *Figaro* still rankled in the heart of Maurepas. Louis must give him satisfaction in this respect, too.

When the embarrassed Louis called upon him, therefore, in his apartments, the old Minister had made up his mind both upon the exact demands he proposed to submit and the tactics he intended to pursue. The fact that Louis had come in person, and with such celerity, strengthened his resolve to achieve his twin purposes.

Still enveloped in his wraps, he rose from his arm-chair. "Please remain seated, my dear Maurepas," begged Louis.

But the old man remained on his feet, and with a deep bow replied gloomily, "I thank you, Sire, for the honour you have done me by this visit. I hear that the Holy Roman Emperor has requested you to mediate in his conflict with Prussia. May I be permitted to offer my humble congratulations, Sire."

"Thank you, Your Excellency, thank you," said Louis awkwardly, as if brushing the matter aside. "But now please do be seated. I hear to my regret that you are indisposed. That troublesome rheumatism of yours, I suppose?"

"Partly, Sire, partly," responded Maurepas mournfully. "But it is chiefly the sorrow that has befallen me. The loss of her cat has cut my dear Countess to the heart."

"I am truly grieved," said Louis, "that the cat should have passed away. You see, I found her unexpectedly in my smithy, where she was making a dreadful noise and had knocked everything over."

"I understand, Sire," replied Maurepas. "Gris-gris was well-trained, but she may have behaved in an unseemly manner in a strange apartment. Such chastisement, however, was hardly merited."

"I did not want to hurt her," said Louis unhappily. "You know me well enough to believe that. I only wanted to drive her out of the room. That was all. I am terribly sorry."

"I am grateful for your sympathy, Sire," observed Maurepas. "It will afford some comfort to my Countess."

"I will offer my condolences in person to Madame de Maurepas," declared Louis, "both in person and in writing."

"I am well aware of your generous heart, Sire," rejoined Maurepas.

Louis felt that he had now made sufficient amends and was justified in dropping the uncomfortable subject. "What do you say to the great news from Vienna?" he asked. "Is it not splendid that Joseph has decided to exercise such praiseworthy moderation? You will have to see Count Mercy without delay and discuss the matter with him."

"I shall do what I can," replied Maurepas unenthusiastically, "but I shall probably have to leave most of the work to Vergennes, for I fear that my own contribution cannot amount to much. I am tired and depressed. It is not only that the grief of my dear Countess weighs so heavily upon me, but I am harassed by the thought that the question of the American loan has been kept in abeyance for so long. It is particularly important at the present juncture, when we are anxious that our counsels should prevail at Vienna and Potsdam, for those Courts to be assured of vigorous and purposeful action by the French Crown. Yet our procrastination in the matter of the American loan is scarcely calculated to create such an impression. Our allies are in need of money, and Vergennes has joined with me in making certain promises. This is a matter of common knowledge, and the fact that these pledges are still unredeemed must necessarily offer the appearance of vacillation. The impression that we lack the power of decision is liable to render ineffective any steps we may take in other spheres. Our efforts at mediation cannot but suffer, for Frederick is a student of human nature and Count Mercy a crafty diplomat. The negotiations will be difficult."

Louis remained morosely silent. Quietly, though emphatically, the old Minister continued, "I am no longer young, Sire. I cannot conduct our Austrian policy, or exercise the other duties of my office, as effectively as I could wish when my mind is beset by anxieties with regard to the American situation."

Louis listened in helpless irritation. He could not fail to notice the veiled threat that lay behind the Minister's shrewdly chosen words. The old man was resentful because of what had happened to the cat, and if the loan were not sanctioned he would resign.

Though Louis knew that he would have to give in eventually, every fibre in him resisted this further admission of defeat. A thousand millions. Such a figure was unprecedented, yet it would be attained before many months had passed. On the wall in front of him, in the apartments of his principal Minister, hung challengingly the detested portrait of the American rebel. Wherever he went it hung. Even in the Queen's chamber it hung, for Maurepas, with consummate effrontery, had given her a copy. There he was, gazing down upon him, the insatiable Franklin, looking through him and beyond him, cool, stern, and arrogant, confident of ultimate victory.

The obese young man was suddenly overcome by great weariness and an irresistible longing to relax. If only he no longer had to fight. If only there were not this continual effort to hold his own against the host of those who were striving to beat down his will. "Very well, then," he said. "Very well. I shall have another talk with Necker. Maybe I shall grant the loan. But not until after the Queen's confinement," he added hastily. "And the money must not be paid to the Congress. I want nothing to do with that pack of rascals and profiteers. All drafts must be made out in the name of General Washington personally. Then we can at least be sure that they are used for war needs and not for fishy private enterprises."

"I thank you, Sire," said Maurepas. Without pausing for breath he went on, "And since I find you in such a gracious mood, permit me to speak of the second cause for anxiety to which I owe many sleepless nights."

Louis took little pains to conceal his ill humour. Were not twenty-five million livres sufficient indemnity for a dead cat? The old man was asking too much.

Maurepas was not to be deterred. "The people of Paris," he said, "are in a bad mood. They feel that our war effort is not commensurate with the high war taxes. We ought to do something, Sire, to improve their morale. Since the earliest times there have been only two means to this end—bread and circuses. Since we cannot give them more bread, we should give them more comedies."

Louis realized at once what Maurepas was driving at. It was the mutinous fellow Caron again, and his obscene play. It was his, Louis's, own fault. Once he had the fellow locked up at Saint-Lazare, he should have kept him there. But, at least, he had not agreed to a public performance of the opprobrious work, and that was a decision he was going to stick to. *Never,* he had said, and never would he allow a public performance.

"If you should be contemplating a public performance of that notorious comedy *Figaro,* Your Excellency," he observed stiffly, though his little double chin was trembling, "I must draw your attention to the fact that when the late Marquis de Vaudreuil produced the play, only the ladies and gentlemen of the Court were present. That was a stipulation on which I insisted. From the very outset I made it clear that I should never permit a public performance. I shall not tolerate the poisoning of my subjects' minds by rebellious insolence and boisterous lewdness. God has seen fit to take from us the most ardent advocate of this piece, the late Vaudreuil. I am surprised, Your Excellency, that now you should now assume his role."

These were sharper words than Louis had ever before addressed to his mentor, and he fully expected that Maurepas would beat a hasty retreat. The old Minister thought, however, that if he did not seize the present opportunity to help progress by getting the play performed, he would never do it, and would cut a poor figure in the eyes of posterity. So he refused to yield. He did not argue with the King, yet he sat there, wrapped in his shawls, looking old and feeble, weighed down with grief and anxiety, gazing sadly at the plump, agitated countenance of his sovereign, a living reproach.

Presently Louis's resolution began to break down. He made a last attempt to pull himself together. "Please, Your Excellency," he entreated, "remember that I said *never.*" But this time it was a pathetic *never,* and Maurepas knew that he had won.

"You see, Sire, you should not have said it," he remonstrated gently, "but since you did say it you now must modify its meaning. Circumstances are sometimes stronger even than a royal word. The vetoing of the play is undermining the morale of the people. It is spoiling their mood for the war. Withdraw the veto, Sire. Conquer your reluctance. The war demands sacrifices from us all."

Louis rose, and paced heavily up and down the room. The cynical old man was telling him to his face that having agreed to the war he must also agree to *Figaro.* Unfortunately, the old man was right. Having taken the first step he had to keep on down the slippery path, and the descent was growing steeper. He had to fling twenty-five millions into Doctor Franklin's maw. He had to clear the way for the obscene and mutinous Caron.

Peevishly he said, "I shall insist that a reliable censor be appointed to expunge all offensive passages."

"That is of course understood, Sire," replied Maurepas in a tone of simple sincerity. "You cannot believe that Monsieur Lenoir would permit a single equivocal word to be uttered upon the stage of your theatre."

Louis brightened. "You will see, my dear Count," he said, confidentially, "when the indecent passages have been eliminated everyone will find the comedy so tedious that it will be a failure."

The old Minister's dry lips twisted in a thin smile. "*Figaro* may be a failure, Sire," he replied, "but a failure that will be repeated a hundred times."

Louis gazed at his mentor and shook his head. "It is remarkable," he commented, "how the fellow has bewitched you all. By the way," he added hastily, "if I *do* withdraw my veto, it will not be until after the Queen's confinement."

"An excellent notion, Sire," acknowledged Maurepas respectfully. "The birth of the Dauphin will be an excellent occasion for granting favours. There could be found no better fitting gift for the Parisians than that charming comedy, and for the Americans than that generous loan." He rose, bowed low and said, "On behalf of both the city of Paris and the United States I thank you, Sire."

"And now, my dear and honoured sovereign," he urged. "Let us go to the Countess. You will offer her your hand and your sympathy, permit her to hear from your own illustrious lips of your gracious decisions, and all will be peace and harmony."

☆   ☆   ☆

Pierre applied himself to the production of *Figaro* with all his energy.

The first step was to rescue what he could of the text.

The Chief of Police had entrusted the delicate task of expunging the offensive passages to a certain Monsieur Coquely, who was of a very pedantic turn of mind. His main concern was to delete as many words as possible, adding them up as he went along without paying too much attention to their meaning. Pierre and Gudin would bargain with him, offering longer passages for deletion in return for shorter ones which they were anxious to retain. Gudin was more obdurate than Pierre. "If you expect Monsieur de Beaumarchais to agree to this deletion," he would declare heatedly, "you are asking him to destroy his play with his own hands." On another occasion he hissed, "If Monsieur de Beaumarchais were to permit this obliteration, he would be like Medea who slew her own children." The number of words removed amounted in the end to 2,022. This was a large number of words, and Monsieur Coquely was proud of his achievement, and since very few of them were such as to cause Pierre much regret everybody was satisfied.

Monsieur Lenoir read the script in its final version, as amended by the censor. The cuts had certainly been drastic, it was true, 2,022 words, but the play still smelt of sedition. He read and read and did not dare to permit and did not dare to forbid. He had a complete list made of the expunged passages, plucked up his courage, took both the list and the script to Louis and entreated His Most Christian Majesty to be so gracious as to make the ultimate decision himself.

With wrinkled brow Louis stared at the manuscript and at the list. He was tired. The manuscript was handsomely bound and the

list neatly written out, but he had no wish to soil his eyes and his
hands by touching and reading the repulsive text. He had hoped to
have heard and seen the last of the wretched play. There was nothing
more he could do to stem the rising tide of slime, and he was sick to
death of Monsieur Caron and all his works.

But there was Monsieur Lenoir waiting to receive his orders. "How
many passages have been expunged?" asked Louis.

The Chief of Police picked up his list. "A total of 53 passages,"
he said. "Some are short and some are long. The number of words
eliminated amounts altogether to 2,022."

"Humph," growled Louis, a little mollified. "Your Monsieur
Coquely appears to have done a good job of work."

Lenoir bowed in flattered acknowledgment. "Am I to understand,
Sire," he asked, "that you are pleased to be satisfied with the deletions
that have been made?"

"Very well, then," decided Louis. "Very well." Hastily, and with
some sharpness of tone, he added, "But you will not have forgotten,
Monsieur, that the members of the *Théâtre français* are to have it impressed upon them that no word of the projected performance must
be allowed to leak out until after the confinement of Her Majesty the
Queen."

Pierre was not perturbed by the prospect of a brief delay, but
Désirée was furious. What in Heaven's name had Toinette's confinement to do with *Figaro?* This very last silly attempt, however, to
delay anew the performance helped her to conceive a brilliant notion.
If the King insisted on linking the two events, she would do her
best to assist towards that end.

It was the custom, when the Queen first drove out after the birth
of a royal child, to offer free performances at the theatres to the
people of Paris. Désirée suggested to Pierre that the first public performance of *Figaro* should take place on the day when Toinette
showed herself to the citizens of the capital so that it should be free
to all.

Pierre, used to bold projects, was surprised at the audacious proposal. He realized at once both the advantages and dangers of the
scheme. Would not the King interpret such action as a fresh challenge?
Would they not be offering him a pretext for again vetoing the performance, or at least postponing it once more? But Désirée had a good
answer.

"When the King invites his people to the theatre," she replied,
"only the best will be good enough. And what could be better than
the first performance of a long-awaited play by the best actors of
the best theatrical company in the world?"

Pierre laughed. Tempted by danger, as he always was, he agreed.

And they persuaded the actors of the *Théâtre français* to fall in with the rash plan.

☆   ☆   ☆

When a "child of France" was born, there were many things to be done at the Court of Versailles which were bound up with a complicated ceremonial, and numerous couriers had to go to and from Paris, Vienna, and Madrid before all the various details of political import contingent upon that event were decided and regulated.

Maria Theresa and King Charles of Spain were to be the godparents; the Empress would be represented by Madame Joséphine, the consort of Prince Xavier and the first lady in the land after the Queen herself. Gifts had to be held in readiness for all concerned, and Maria Theresa sent to her Ambassador, Count Mercy, presents of all kinds—rings, bracelets, watches, and snuff-boxes—for distribution to Madame Joséphine, the Princess Rohan, as the governess of the royal children, Doctor Lassone, and many others. She included precise instructions as to who was to be the recipient of each particular gift, but busy as she was over the peace negotiations with Prussia, her first decisions later appeared to her not altogether wise. Would Madame Joséphine not be offended at receiving the same gift as the Princess Rohan—a bracelet adorned with the Empress's portrait? The second courier bringing new instructions from Vienna followed fast upon the heels of the first.

These commands did not cause Count Mercy any special anxiety, but unfortunately a further commission with which he was entrusted by his sovereign proved impossible of execution. Maria Theresa did not wish to have to wait a moment longer for news from Paris than was absolutely necessary, and she requested Mercy to prepare his report on the confinement in advance, leaving only the date and the child's sex to be added. Count Vergennes protested. It was not the Austrian Ambassador in Paris, but the French Ambassador in Vienna, who enjoyed the privilege of informing the Austrian Court of the joyful occurrence. Vergennes therefore demanded that his own courier must be allowed to set off forty-eight hours before Count Mercy dispatched his messenger, and he instructed Monsieur Lenoir to make special arrangements for controlling the departure of couriers from Paris. He feared that the wily Count Mercy might have a card up his sleeve.

Meanwhile the search for a suitable nurse had been successful. A country woman had been found, who, according to the testimony of numerous doctors and priests, was both physically and morally unspoiled. Her name was Madame Poitrine. Count Mercy reported to the Empress that she had made an unusually favourable impression on him, and Toinette wrote to her mother she was already delighting in Madame Poitrine's lullabies.

All this time the professional lampooners were busily engaged in casting doubts upon the child's parentage before it had seen the light of day. Brochures querying the identity of the father were circulating in Paris, and Monsieur Lenoir had his hands full. A small volume of obscene verses was even hurled through the King's window, but the investigation that was immediately set on foot was very soon abandoned, for the clues ended within the precincts of the Palace of Versailles itself, in the apartments of Prince Xavier.

The Church and people throughout the realm manifested their lively interest in Toinette's approaching confinement. The Archbishop of Paris ordered special prayers to be read every other day. From the most distant provinces the King's subjects set out to take part in the celebrations that would be organized both in the capital and at Versailles. Hundreds of noble families, who normally lived on their estates, moved to Versailles so as not to miss the happy day and the royal favours of which they hoped to be the recipients. The little town was already crowded to capacity, and the cost of food began to rise. Monsieur Leboiteux, who held a licence to operate stage-coaches between Versailles and Paris, put extra vehicles into service.

The confinement was expected on the 16th of December. From the 14th onwards Doctor Lassone, together with the Princess Rohan and two of the Queen's ladies-in-waiting, held themselves in readiness, occupying at night the side-rooms which had given rise to so much gossip and were now fulfilling the purpose for which they were intended.

The 16th of December passed, and so did the 17th. Even on the evening of the 18th Toinette retired to bed without any indication of labour-pains.

That night, however, at half-past one, the pains set in and Doctor Lassone announced that the time had come. The Princess Rohan rang the bell in the ante-room. Pages and messengers hurried in all directions, to Paris and Saint-Cloud, to summon the princes of the blood and the members of the Privy Council.

All these, together with the King's lords-in-waiting, the Queen's ladies-in-waiting, the holders of the *Cordon Bleu,* and the ladies who enjoyed the privilege of sitting on a tabouret in the Queen's presence, gathered in Toinette's card-room. The other members of the nobility filled all the apartments of the royal family.

Along the great highway that led from Paris to Versailles there was a constant procession of people throughout the frosty night. By ancient custom every French citizen was entitled to be present at the

Queen's confinement, and to convince himself with his own eyes
that the child who would one day be ruler of the country had in fact
sprung from the Queen's womb. The people had come to see that
no changeling was being foisted upon them.

Those responsible for looking after the Palace of Versailles had
made arrangements for the reception of these visitors. Thousands
were expected; tens of thousands arrived. The lackeys and the Swiss
Guards had a difficult task that night. Chains and strong ropes barred
every entrance until the Queen's physician should have made the
official announcement, *"La reine va accoucher."* Before sixty seconds
had passed the cry, echoing through the corridors, would reach the
courtyards, whereupon the chains and ropes would fall and the people
would be allowed to stream into Toinette's bed-chamber.

In this chamber, around the alcove in which the bed of state had
been set up, there were placed seventeen arm-chairs for the members
of the royal family, nine for the House of Bourbon and eight for
the House of Orleans. Behind these stood fifty-eight smaller chairs
for the nobles of France and the Privy Council. The rest of the room,
where there was space for some two hundred to two hundred and fifty
spectators if they stood pressed closely together, was allotted to the
petty nobility and the common people. Louis had been afraid that the
rods and curtains of the alcove might be torn down by the pressure
of the crowd, injuring Toinette or the child, and he had strengthened
the rods and bars with his own hands.

In this blue and gold alcove, on her low, spacious bed of state,
there was Toinette half-sitting, half-lying. Her back was supported
by numerous cushions and her legs were raised up. At the bedside
were Doctor Lassone, Gabrielle Polignac, and the Princess Rohan.

Lassone appeared cool and collected, confident of his skill and the
dexterity of his hands, but beneath the calm surface he was a prey to
mingled emotions. Much depended on the next few hours. If anything untoward should happen to either mother or child, whether by
his fault or not, that would be the end of his career. If all went well
he could look forward to high rewards. If the child should be a princess, he would receive the customary fee of 12,000 livres. If it were
a prince, he could expect two titles of nobility, together with the
privileges appertaining thereto, and a fee of 50,000 livres. And there
was even more at stake. Lassone knew his Désirée. It had been a
happy inspiration that induced him to place at her disposal the 600,000
for which she had asked, but which he had fortunately not had to
pay. All the same, he had still not been able to persuade her to fix a
date for their marriage. And he knew that, should anything go wrong
with this confinement, the date would never be fixed. On the other
hand, if the sweating, white-skinned woman on the bed should give

birth to the Dauphin the marriage would be consummated within the next two months. "Will you be so good, Madame, as to lie just a little farther back," he instructed. "And please press down, Madame. Press hard."

Toinette did as he bade. The room was hot, all the windows had been sealed with plaster of Paris to exclude draughts, and she lay bathed in perspiration. Every now and then a flush suffused her cheeks. Though she was in great pain she forced herself not to cry out. "I must not lose my poise," she kept urging herself. Her mother had undergone this ordeal thirteen times, and everybody had said how courageous she had always been. If only her mother were with her now. Gabrielle was a very good friend, and it was comforting to see her sympathetic face hovering above her, but the Princess Rohan made her feel uneasy and she wished she were not there. Lassone could not be dispensed with and he was able to relieve the pain to some extent, but the way he kept staring at her made her frightened.

All at once the pains vanished, for a minute, for two. She felt very happy. She was going to give birth to the Dauphin, her figure would return to normal, she would be slim again, able to carry on with her amateur theatricals, and she would have a Dauphin.

The pains set in again and Gabrielle, with infinite compassion, placed her hand tenderly beneath Toinette's back. "How brave you are, my dear," she said.

"Press hard, Madame," said Lassone. "Everything is going very well. It will soon be over." He spoke in an authoritative tone and she tried to believe that what he said was true, but it was not soon over. On the contrary, the pains grew worse.

"God, O God," she prayed. "Don't let me cry out." And she did not cry out. She bit her lip till it bled. "It is a *corvée*," she said to herself. "There is no word in German to describe these pains. It is a *corvée*, it is my duty, my hard task, and I must not cry out."

Prince Xavier and Prince Charles were sitting in the front row. If the child should be a boy, Xavier would lose all hope of the throne and any faint hope that Charles might have cherished would also be gone. The brothers were seated side by side in their arm-chairs gazing at the scene as if they were in a theatre. Xavier was pleased that the spectacle was so long-drawn-out and that Toinette was suffering. Now and then he would pass some spiteful remark to his brother. "At least," he whispered, "the father of the child is spared the sight of the mother's pains. He is lying in his grave, keeping himself warm with his *Cordon Bleu.*"

Diane Polignac's sharp, restless eyes hovered between Toinette and Prince Charles. She was not beautiful. In fact she was decidedly plain with her dark, thin face and pointed nose, but she was Prince Charles's acknowledged mistress. She was the cleverest member of the Lilac Coterie, and he needed her. He liked to make a show of wit, and depended on her to help him. Since the death of Vaudreuil the ambitious Diane had become the leader of the Coterie owing to her influence over the Prince. What was happening in that room could only be of advantage to her; for Toinette's power over Louis would be increased, and so would her own.

Louis himself could not keep still Perspiring profusely and carelessly dressed, he stamped and waddled around, pushing his way through the crowded room with no apparent object in view, muttering abstractedly, "I beg your pardon, my son," or observing to someone whose name was as strange to him as his face, "It is taking a dreadful time, but she is wonderfully brave, isn't she?" When he had said this, he would laugh rather stupidly and add, "Well, what takes long, is good."

Then he went up to his smithy. He had made a secret lock for the Dauphin's money-box and wanted to give it to Toinette straightway. On his way back to the bed-chamber, however, he grew frightened of the many faces staring with such heartless curiosity at his dear wife; so he took refuge in his library which, apart from the smithy, was the only apartment that was not filled with visitors. There he sat alone for a quarter of an hour. Moving his lips silently, he prayed, "Let it turn out well, O Lord, and if I have sinned do not punish her for it." Then pulling himself together he returned to the great bed-chamber. The Swiss Guards and lackeys had difficulty in clearing a way for him.

The spectators were still seated in their chairs staring at Toinette, and the room was fearfully hot and stuffy. Toinette lay with her legs raised and in evident pain, but she did not cry out. Now and then her lips moved, and with anxious sympathy he noted that they were German words she was uttering. "*O Gott,*" she was saying. "*O mein Gott.*"

The thousands who were patiently spending the chilly night in the corridors, on the staircases, in the entrance halls and courtyards, turned the long period of waiting into a popular entertainment. Hawkers provided a constant supply of hot snacks, which were torn from their hands as soon as they appeared. Those who knew their way about the Palace reaped a harvest of tips by passing on their knowledge of the quickest way to reach Toinette's bed-chamber as soon as the barriers should be removed. Others offered, whispering, the forbidden satirical brochures. The pamphlets were not cheap, but the crowd read them to kill time, they were good-humoured, they did not scoff, they laughed.

The late December morning began to dawn, it grew lighter in the corridors and outside in the courtyards, but in Toinette's bed-chamber with its curtained windows it was still night. The candles were burning, having been renewed for the second time, and the air was thicker than ever. When the day had fully dawned the privileged guests waiting in the bed-chamber were served with coffee, chocolate, and rolls. During the morning soup was handed round. The morning passed and it was mid-day. The hands of the clock moved to twelve-thirty, to twelve-forty.

Then Lassone turned towards the waiting throng and announced hoarsely, *"La reine va accoucher."*

The cry was repeated in the ante-room, echoed through the corridors, ran through the courtyards, and the crowd surged forward in a shouting, stampeding mass. Neither servants nor Swiss Guards could halt them. They trampled over one another, swept aside those who were waiting in the various apartments, and in a flash, just as Louis had foreseen, the bed-chamber was crammed to suffocation.

The occupants of the arm-chairs nearest the bed had risen to their feet with their eyes fixed on the woman writhing in labour. How haughty she looked even now, with her aquiline nose and Habsburg under lip. People in the rows behind had climbed onto their chairs, one of which toppled over. A couple of Savoyard chimney-sweeps, who were familiar with the place, had lifted themselves up onto the mantelpiece and were crying triumphantly, "Hooray! We've got the best seats! We can see everything."

The long-awaited moment had arrived. The child gradually emerged from the womb, Lassone assisting with his long, skilled fingers. He saw it was a female, and 38,000 livres faded away.

The nurse, Madame Poitrine, took the infant and carried it into the neighbouring room to bathe it before handing it over to the Princess Rohan. Louis, his mind in a whirl and a look of happy pride mingled with helpless bewilderment on his plump features, followed behind her and the others surged after him. No one bothered about Toinette, except Lassone.

Suddenly the physician cried in his sharp, authoritative voice, "The Queen has fainted. Fresh air! Open the windows! The Queen's in danger." Toinette lay in a deep coma, overcome by her tremendous effort at self-control for so many hours and suffocated by the close, poisoned atmosphere. The cry of the physician snatched Louis from his half blissful, half apprehensive stupor. With unusually swift decision he elbowed his way through the startled throng and smashed a pane of one of the sealed windows with his bare fist, letting in a stream of cold, fresh air. Lassone bled Toinette, and after a while she opened her eyes. Louis breathed again; laughing, embarrassed, a little stupidly, he gazed at his lacerated, bleeding hand.

Meanwhile the lackeys, with the help of the Swiss Guards, were shepherding the crowd from the room and pulling the resisting chimney-sweeps down from their perch.

Court ceremonial demanded that the Princess Rohan, as governess of the "children of France," should present the infant to Toinette and inform her that she had given birth to a girl. Before the Princess had returned to the bed-chamber, however, Gabrielle had already told the Queen.

Toinette was exhausted and happy that her sufferings were over. Therefore she was not too deeply disappointed. "It is well as it is," she said. Next time it will be the Dauphin, she thought, resigned, and: she will be unwelcome to everybody, but to me she is welcome. And aloud she added: "Had it been a boy, he would have belonged to the State. My daughter belongs to me."

Louis was sitting at the bedside. He had carelessly tied a piece of linen round his hand and there was blood smeared over his face. Lassone wanted to put on a proper bandage, but he waved him away. Holding Toinette's white hand in his own gory one, he spoke words of comfort. "I am so happy," he said, "and you were so brave. You are my dear, courageous Toinette, and I thank you. I am so glad it is all over." But in his eyes and in his heart there was dismay. "So that's the end of Dieudonné," he was thinking. "That's the end of Louis the Seventeenth. It is my punishment. It is retribution for my alliance with the rebels."

Count Mercy had been filled with compassion and anxiety as he watched the sufferings endured by the daughter of his friend the Empress. He was a stickler for etiquette and ceremonial, but after a word with Lassone the two of them turned to Louis and suggested that it was imperative that not all those whose rank normally entitled them to the privilege be accorded access to the bed-chamber of the illustrious patient. The Queen must have rest, otherwise her health might be endangered. Louis agreed whole-heartedly, and it was arranged that during the next few days Toinette must have complete peace and quiet. None should be allowed to enter except those whom it was absolutely impossible to exclude, that is to say, the members of the royal family, the ladies in close attendance upon the Queen, the physician, and the Abbé Vermond. In brief, no more than twenty-six persons in all should be permitted to share the rest and seclusion of the illustrious patient.

When it became known in Paris that the expected Dauphin had failed to arrive, the reaction was disappointment and glee. To all outward appearance, however, both the Court and the capital were in a state of joyous excitement. A *Te Deum* was sung in the churches, and on the Place d'Armes in front of the Palace preparations were made for a great fireworks display. The two Presidents of the municipal council of Paris went personally into the prisons to redeem poor debtors.

The little Princess was baptized on the day she was born, the names conferred upon her being Marie-Thérèse-Charlotte. Her official title was Madame Royale.

Though his report could not yet be sent off, Count Mercy wrote to the Empress immediately after the solemn act of christening. "Your granddaughter's tiny face, Madame," he informed her, "possesses agreeable and very regular features, large eyes, and a remarkably pretty mouth. I took the liberty of touching Her Royal Highness's skin, and it is my impression that Her Royal Highness is a thoroughly healthy infant."

That same day, during the first few hours of her existence, Madame Royale held her first audience. All the members of the royal family, as well as the Privy Council and the ambassadors accredited to the Court of Versailles, came to pay their respects. Doctor Franklin, too, was present, bowing before the royal infant.

☆ ☆ ☆

The most brilliant celebrations were reserved for the day when the Queen would drive to Paris for the service of thanksgiving at Notre Dame. Louis was anxious that she should not make the effort too soon and he fixed the 8th of February for the ceremony, fifty-one days after the birth of the child.

Preparations for rejoicing were made on an extensive scale. For a whole night, a whole day, and the night after that, Paris was to be filled with music and dancing. The King invited his people to partake of sausages and cakes at his expense, the fountains were to flow with wine, and a marvellous pyrotechnic spectacle was to take place over the Seine.

All the theatres in Paris advertised gala performances, admission free, the cost being met by the King.

The *Théâtre français* advertised the first public performance of *The Crazy Day, or The Marriage of Figaro* by Monsieur de Beaumarchais. Admission free. The cost would be met by the King.

This announcement was greeted with astonishment, laughter, exultation. That Beaumarchais should produce his famous comedy, which the King had vetoed, on this crazy day and at the King's expense was a master-stroke, and the performance was looked forward to with far greater excitement than was the royal procession through the streets of Paris.

The management of the *Théâtre français* had its hands full. The people of Paris had been invited, the people of Paris would come, the people of Paris were numerous. No more than an infinitesimal proportion of the thousands who would clamour for admission could find accommodation in the theatre, and thousands of others were asking for tickets—aristocrats, courtiers, relatives of the actors, writers and critics. It was decided to reserve a quarter of the seats for these distinguished applicants and to throw the remaining eight hundred places open to the populace.

When the doors were opened at five o'clock there was a wild scramble in which men and women struggled with one another and many were trampled underfoot. The well-schooled police of Paris had the utmost difficulty in preventing women and children from being crushed to death.

At last all had taken their seats, shouting, lamenting, laughing. Then the guests of honour made their entrance. According to an ancient tradition, at these free performances the best seats were reserved for the ladies of the *halles* and the coal-heavers. As guests of honour they arrived, as was only fitting, after all the rest of the audience was assembled. The attendants cleared a path, and the other spectators greeted them with cheers as they were escorted to their seats, the coal-heavers to the King's box, the fishwives to that of the Queen.

Never had the *Théâtre français* seen such a queerly assorted audience for a *première*. Side by side sat ladies of the Court and glove-stitchers, *fermiers généraux* and chair-menders, duchesses and women from the *halles*. Academicians and butchers' assistants, in short, the people of Paris. The actors were in a fever of excitement and most of them were already regretting their rashness. Monsieur de Beaumarchais's comedy had not been written for such an audience. This was not Athens, and it was hardly to be expected that the salted wit of *Figaro* would be appreciated by this motley gathering.

The three thuds were heard and the curtains parted. The audience blew their noses, cleared their throats, and went on chattering for a time. Figaro-Préville had to start three times, until eventually, after cries of "Hush! Hush!" and "Really, Madame, don't you think you might finish your conversation at home?" the spectators settled down to listen in silence. There was some perfunctory clapping after a moment or two, and a voice asked, "What did he say? I didn't understand," while others shouted, "Repeat! Repeat!" but the audience was evidently in a good humour.

Gradually the people began to grasp who these gentlemen and ladies on the stage were and what they wanted and what it was all about, that was to say that this aristocrat wanted to sleep with the bride of this nice fellow who, by the way, was one of their own class. That was nothing unusual and not much to bother about, but the aristocrat was particularly arrogant, and Figaro, who was one of themselves, was particularly engaging and had his good brains, and it was amusing and heartwarming how he told the aristocrat off. It became evident in the first half-hour that Pierre, with his sure sense of the theatre, had written a comedy which could stand the test of any audience.

Especially of this audience. Yes, Désirée's advice had been excellent. The people of Paris did not take long to relish the points of the play. They realized that the elegant, airy words were not so harmless as they sounded, that they were charged with the hatred and scorn they felt themselves, that the struggle for the place in Suzanne's bed was by no means merely an entertaining spectacle. The people laughed and were highly amused, but their laughter was more savage and dangerous than any with which the rafters of the *Théâtre français* had ever rung. This performance which the King was presenting to his subjects was a strange celebration of the birth of a royal infant; without realizing it clearly, they all felt that there was something oddly piquant and provoking about it. The scions of the nobility who were present, and who shared in the general enjoyment, were even more aware than the others of the peculiar savour of the situation.

Désirée, believing that this being a gala performance, a certain latitude was permissible, had suggested that they should boldly speak some of the expunged lines. Most of the actors were shy about such a dangerous proposal, but with so responsive an audience everything seemed possible and Désirée spoke a few of the forbidden lines. Madame Dugazon followed, and eventually the reluctant Préville. The police official who had been detailed to watch the performance grew uneasy. Nothing like this had ever happened in the hundred and twenty-five years of the theatre's history. But it was a special performance for the people of Paris in honour of Madame Royale, the King himself had given it his patronage, and if it were closed down the scandal might have incalculable consequences. So the official did not dare to intervene and the actors became still bolder. More censored lines were spoken, understood, cheered. The audience insisted on some of the dangerous passages being repeated three and four times.

Pierre was sitting in a box with Gudin and his fellow dramatist Sedaine. The success which he had often pictured in his imagination was now a reality, but it was a success of a very different kind. The people of Paris were not as able to appreciate the wit and artistry of his piece as the ladies and gentlemen at Gennevilliers, but they did have a keener understanding of its truths. He was startled when the first of the censored lines struck his ears, and he was deeply and happily moved when he sensed the savage joy of the audience. Gradually he sank into a thoughtful silence, totally absorbed in what was happening on the stage. "Did I do this?" he asked himself. "Is this what I wanted to do?"

When Sedaine spoke to him, he did not hear. He was overwhelmed by the realization that the situations, the characters, the words, he had created, had gone on growing by their own power, which now clutched the people of Paris in a breathless grip.

It was beyond belief. They were not only thoroughly amused, his people of Paris, they were stirred to their depths, incited to think, roused to indignation by his work. He had put into words their latent feelings. This was the best hour he had ever enjoyed, better than financial and political triumph, better than love. In this hour was concentrated the meaning of his life.

"Minerva," whispered Gudin, and Pierre smiled and nodded gratefully. A few days ago Gudin had spoken to him of the two kinds of success, that which was conferred by Mercury, the crafty god who distributed gold and outward honours, and that which was afforded by Minerva, the exalted goddess of wisdom who had sprung from the head of Zeus. Pierre had tasted to the full of the gifts of Mercury. Now for the first time he was experiencing the blissful happiness of the triumphs which Minerva had to bestow.

The further the play proceeded, the more the people of Paris felt themselves part of it. Every situation, every word, every gesture, struck home. The house was filled with wild, rebellious joy.

Among the spectators was Doctor Lassone. He had eyes and ears only for Chérubin. Chérubin and Désirée were fused in one, and the ovations she received caused his heart to swell. He had frequently been tormented by the thought that when she stood upon the stage she belonged to so many others, and once he had even ventured in discreet terms to tell her so, but she had merely laughed at him and he had realized that he must not repeat his protest. Now he understood that the stage, the crowded, concentrated, manifold existence of the actor, was in truth her life.

He himself forgot his daily existence, absorbed by the life of the characters on the stage. Though he was anything but a revolutionary, he could not help falling under the spell of the unseemly, rebellious gaiety that radiated from beyond the footlights. The excitement was alien to his nature and certainly not good for him. He led a strenuous life, and since he was no longer young he was well aware that any excess of excitement such as he was experiencing on the present evening might shorten his days. Yet he was prepared to pay the price, and allowed himself to enjoy his rebellious, erotic excitement to the full. He shared with the others their eager wish to see Figaro's cunning overcome the power of the Count, and rejoiced with them when Almaviva, for all his suppleness, was outwitted in his attempt to seize for himself *le droit du seigneur,* the privilege of the first night. But he alone, Josèphe-Marie Lassone, savoured with heart-bursting anticipation the thought that after the performance he would have Chérubin.

Among the audience was also Mr. John Adams. He had made all his preparations for the homeward journey and would be leaving France the following week, but he wanted to take advantage of every moment left to him to study the corrupt manners of his country's allies and their wretched serfdom. It was on this account that he had come hither this evening, in order that he might witness with his own eyes the way in which the servile city of Paris paid homage to the royal despot because he had just become a father. The spectacle had turned out differently from what he had anticipated. But he did not disapprove any the less of the French public's conduct. True, he was at moments carried away by the general atmosphere, and he felt moved as he had been in 1761 by the speech delivered by James Otis. On that occasion he had compared his emotions with those of the youthful Hannibal when his father, Hamilcar, demanded that he swear a solemn oath of enmity against Rome. As he sat in the hall of justice when the child Independence was being born, he had been ready to take up arms against England, as had all the others who participated in the scene, and there were moments during this performance of *Figaro* when a similar tide of feeling threatened to sweep him away, but each time he called himself back to earth and with a shudder focused his powers of reasoning on the essential difference between the two situations. The emotions which swayed this screeching, hysterical rabble had nothing in common with the love of liberty which inflamed the New World or that passion for independence which he and Jefferson had proclaimed in their great Declaration. What he was witnessing this evening was mere unbridled licence, disobedience to authority, insubordination, lack of discipline. If the worst came to the worst, this mob could hardly be trusted to refrain from attacking honest citizens and burning their houses over their heads. But however he put the matter to himself, it availed him little, and his aversion would vanish again and again in the frenzy of wrath and laughter which swept all before it.

Sitting at the back of his box was Monsieur Charles Lenormant d'Etioles. It was not very seemly for him to be present, and he had hesitated for a long time before coming, in the fear lest the emotions by which he had been dominated at the rehearsals in the Menus Plaisirs and later at the Gennevilliers performance, that almost unbearable commingling of admiration, hatred, and despair, should once again take possession of him. He had been unable to resist the temptation, and his apprehensions were realized.

At first his interest was concentrated solely on Désirée. He loved her madly and his heart was filled with a raging bitterness of frustration. He had cast away his chance of happiness through a colossal error. Jeanne would probably never have stayed with him, but Désirée, even more piquant, more vivacious, lusty child of the people that she was, he *had* had the power to keep. Yet at the crucial moment he had taken a false step, sacrificing the greatest joy of his life for the pleasure of revelling in the helplessness of his friend Pierrot.

But Pierre was not helpless. Pierre was invulnerable.

Lenormant did not lose his composure. He clapped when the others clapped, almost mechanically and because he did not want to appear an exception. Inwardly, however, he was on the verge of collapse. *Vanitatum vanitas.* He had the inscription over the entrance to his house arrogantly chiselled into the stone in the defiant belief that he had, in spite of everything, done the best with his life that he could. But the motto spoke the truth.

Familiar as he was with the play, he too was carried away by the excitement of the audience. Their emotions mingled with his own and with a boundless, blinding hatred of Pierre. It was Pierre who was the enemy, the eternal reproach, the eternal contradiction of everything for which he, Charles Lenormant, stood. Undisturbed by any access of doubt, Pierre flung himself with every last iota of his being into all that came his way, whether it be cause for joy or cause for wrath. Caring not a straw for dignity, he did and said what he wanted to do or say, came out with whatever sprang to his lips, whether noble or base, everything turned eventually in his favour, and from everything he was able to extract enjoyment. Lenormant was consumed with jealousy and impotent greed. What rapture it must be to tell one's enemies exactly what one thought of them, as this fellow Pierre did without scruple. It was worth while even though one's enemies should strike one dead for it, but Pierre's enemies did not strike him dead; they overwhelmed him with adulation.

Hardly able to bear it any longer, he wanted to leave the theatre and go home. Yet he could not tear himself away. He had to stay and listen, filling his heart to overflowing with the irritating poison.

At last there came the monologue, and though Lenormant had already learnt at Gennevilliers that its length was no bar to the audience's enjoyment, he still cherished a faint, baseless hope that this time it would after all cause the play to end in failure.

Pierre had, as a matter of fact, discussed with the actors the advisability of·cutting the monologue to a few lines for this particular performance, since it could hardly be expected that the coal-heavers and fishwives would put up with such a long soliloquy after four or five hours in the theatre.

They not only put up with it, they fired Préville with their enthusiasm, and he lived his lines, speaking them with burning passion.

Lenormant listened in astonished indignation, mixed with tension, as the actor, who was not noted for his courage, grew bolder and bolder. Now he was coming to the line about the prisons, the Bastille. Would he dare to deliver this line?

Préville was aware that it was this reference in particular which had roused the ire of Louis, and it had been his intention to omit the very risky, challenging sentences. He did not even remember the words very clearly. But, carried away, he began to speak, improvising. After a word or two, however, he checked himself in sudden fright, to the surprise of the majority of the audience who did not understand what was the matter; but those who knew what was coming burst out laughing and explained to their neighbours. The laughter grew, and someone called out, "Give us your line, Figaro! This is a holiday." The cry was taken up until the whole theatre was shouting, "Give us your line, Figaro!" And Préville spoke his line, the line about the prison-gates, and the people of Paris cheered like children and cried jubilantly, "The Bastille! He is talking about the Bastille!"

Lenormant was stupefied, but he waited feverishly to see whether the actor would be so audacious as to include the next censored passage, the most dangerous of all. In an agony of confused emotions he wanted him to speak the lines and was apprehensive lest he might do so.

There it was. And lo, Préville strode up to the footlights. Obviously he did not want to speak these lines in the depths of the chestnut grove, he did not want to drop them. Obviously he intended that the audience should hear clearly every syllable. He advanced to the very front, raised his arms and half-clenched his fists and, with an expression rapturous with scorn and desire, he said softly, but so that not a word was lost in the deathly silence, "Oh, if only I held one of these powerful lords within my grasp!" He sighed it, he groaned it, voluptuously. A more direct incitement to revolution could hardly be conceived, and they were incited indeed; they sprang to their feet—all of them—shouting approval, the fishwives in the Queen's box shrieking with savage joy and the coal-heavers clapping thunderously with brawny paws.

Monsieur Charles Lenormant d'Etioles sat elegantly calm. Not even by the slightest distortion of his features did he reveal what was going on in his breast. He felt that if he displayed the faintest sign of disapproval the audience would tear him to pieces. Behind his cool brow, however, he was ravaged by unmeasured panic. There were many other noblemen in the auditorium, and they were laughing, applauding and rejoicing with the rest. Even now they did not see, blind dolts that they were. They believed that they were looking at a sparkling fountain; did they not understand that this was the deluge?

His heart constricted with black despair. Here it was—his downfall and the destruction of all that made life worth living for him and his kind.

There came the final couplets, and at last, much too soon for most of the audience, the curtain fell. The people applauded the actors, and a few shouted "Beaumarchais! Beaumarchais!" and the cry was taken up until the whole theatre reverberated with it, and everyone thronged towards the small box at the side of the auditorium in which Pierre was sitting with his friends.

Sedaine, his envy submerged in his rapture, said, "Such a triumph is more rare than a miracle."

Gudin commented, "The history of the theatre has known but one such instance of unrestrained enthusiasm, and that was the ovation Voltaire received after the production of *Irène*. But that was the end of an epoch, and this is a beginning."

The people continued to shout, "Pierre Beaumarchais! Our Pierre! Long live Pierrot, the liberator of America, the victor of Grenada!" And they shrieked, "Pierre, Figaro, Chérubin!" And, "Pierre, America, Pierre!"

Pierre did not hear, and did not move. He sat as if in a dream. He was seeing with a blinding suddenness the unity of what he had done and what he had written. He had never realized that the same feeling had inspired him to deliver arms to America and to write the monologue of Figaro. The victory at Saratoga and his present victory in Paris were fruits from the same tree. He had not recognized it before, but now it had been brought home to him by the people.

But even not being aware of it, he had striven towards this evening with his whole being. *Through laughter I change the world*. He had twice printed this motto on the title-page of one of his works. Now his destiny was being fulfilled. Now he had reached the greatest height that a man can reach; he was transforming the world by his words. He was Voltaire's heir, and was accepted as such by the people. With Figaro's laughter he had achieved even more than with his arms for America.

Had such happiness ever fallen to the lot of any man? He thought of his father, the Huguenot who had been compelled to deny his faith so that his son should make good. Now his son had made good. *Through laughter I change the world*. Now he was avenging his father.

That evening the actors of the *Théâtre français* resolved to set up the bust of Pierre Beaumarchais besides the busts of their great ones—Corneille, Racine, Molière, Voltaire.

☆　　☆　　☆

Arthur Lee was sitting in the Brown Library waiting to say fare-well to Doctor Franklin. He was about to sail for Philadelphia, where he hoped to receive fresh instructions. There was considerable prospect of his being appointed envoy to the Netherlands, and when this further charge had been entrusted to him he proposed to return with all speed, once more in a dual capacity, to his duties in Europe. No longer hampered by the senile and megalomaniac Franklin, he would show America and the world what an Arthur Lee could do.

He had been sitting in the library for close on five minutes. This last time, too, Franklin was letting him cool his heels. He had many things to do before his departure, and it was merely out of an innate sense of courtesy that he was paying this farewell visit to the Doctor *honoris causa,* but Franklin was riding the crest of the wave and consequently behaving more arrogantly than ever.

Franklin was riding the crest of the wave indeed. Versailles had consented to the loan, and though the agreements had not yet been signed all the preliminaries had been discussed and the King had given his word. It was true that the loan had been granted to the Army in the person of its Commander-in-Chief, General Washington, not to the Congress, and Arthur Lee himself would never have accepted such a humiliating stipulation, but unfortunately he no longer possessed the authority to intervene.

It had taken long enough, in all conscience. Franklin had no doubt dragged out the negotiations so that the loan should not materialize before he and Adams had left Paris. The Doctor wanted to be able to maintain that it was due solely to his own prestige, so that he might be regarded as the only American able to carry anything off in Europe.

Franklin entered and thanked his visitor for having found time, busy as he must be, to drive out to Passy. Lee bowed stiffly. "We have occasionally had our differences of opinion, Doctor Franklin," he said, "but you will, I think, concede that I have always done my best to understand your point of view."

"Yes," replied Franklin, "you have done your best."

"It would have been easier," went on Lee, "to fall in with all your proposals, but the interests of the country we both have the honour to represent demanded that I should express my opinion clearly and without equivocation."

"Yes," replied Franklin, "you have expressed your opinion clearly and without equivocation."

"If you have any dispatches that you would like me to deliver in the United States," said Lee, "I shall be happy to see that they reach their destination."

The Doctor thanked him, but replied that he had no dispatches ready. He preferred—though this, of course, he did not mention—to forward them through other channels.

Arthur Lee rose. "It only remains for me," he concluded, "to offer you and our country my best wishes for your further sojourn in this city."

"Thank you," replied Franklin. "Have a pleasant voyage and a fair wind behind."

Lee bowed once more. "Good-bye," he said. With that the bitter young gentleman stepped out of the Brown Library, and out of Franklin's sight—forever, the Doctor hoped.

On the following morning Franklin listened to his little grandson repeating his homework. The tutor, Monsieur Lefèvre, had compiled a number of maxims from the classical authors concerning friendship and enmity for the boy to learn by heart. Hesitantly, in Latin and French, Benjamin recited the quotations while the Doctor bent an attentive ear. One of them was from Plutarch. "To break one's word in an unjust manner," said King Agesilaus, "is wicked; but to deceive one's enemy is not only good and praiseworthy, but amusing and useful." And after Xerxes had been defeated at the Battle of Salamis, Aristides remarked to Themistocles, "It appears to me unwise to cut off the beaten King in Greece, since that will only drive him to despair and make him resort to extreme measures. He will no longer be content to sit beneath his gilded canopy and watch the battle with a tranquil mind, but fear will cause him to employ his best strategy and to assume every risk. Therefore, instead of destroying the bridges behind him we should, if possible, build an additional one so that he can make his exit from Europe as quickly as possible."

"Yes, my boy," commented Franklin, "there were wise men among the ancient Greeks. But there is something I should like to tell you."

"Is it another important secret, Grandfather?" inquired Benjamin eagerly.

"No," replied Franklin. "It is not a secret. What I wanted to say to you is this. It is an advantage to have an enemy who is keenly on the watch for any false step you may take, so that you are compelled to be continually on your guard."

"I know a lot of boys," little Benjamin assured him, "who can't stand me because I am a foreigner."

"You see," said the Doctor, "you have to be far more careful here than you would have to be in Philadelphia, for instance."

"If any of them gives me away to Doctor Lefèvre," declared Benjamin stoutly, "I beat him black and blue."

The thought of Arthur Lee rankled more deeply in Franklin's heart than he had believed. "At present," he wrote to his friend Joseph

Reed, "I do not know of more than one enemy that I enjoy, viz., Arthur Lee. I owe his enmity to the people of France, who happened to respect me too much and him too little; which I could bear, and he could not."

There came the day when de la Motte announced with a smile, "Monsieur Malaprop is in the Brown Library and would like to bid you farewell."

John Adams was pacing to and fro beneath the painting of General Washington. He would be glad when his official association with Doctor Franklin was at an end and he no longer had to live with him under the same roof. Though they had always been on amiable terms, it had cost him a considerable effort at self-control, for the Doctor's faults were such as to try the patience of any mortal. The old man had spent the greater part of his life during an epoch when morals were lax, and no one could jump over his own shadow. On the other hand, it could not be denied that he possessed certain merits. He had even succeeded in the end in obtaining the twenty-five millions, though somewhat tardily and with humiliating terms attached.

Adams considered it his duty, at this final interview, to draw the Doctor's attention to the dangerous qualities of the French. In eloquent language he described the profound effect produced upon the people by Monsieur Caron's comedy, an effect which was intolerably repugnant to any right-thinking man. The scenes which had taken place at the performance of *Figaro* must provide food for thought to every American patriot. He himself, as Doctor Franklin well knew, had from the outset regarded the alliance with France as an unfortunate but necessary evil. The treatment accorded by the mother-country to its colony had been contrary to Nature, none the less it was painful that the daughter should have to ally herself with the hereditary enemy of the family. His sojourn in France had served to convince him all the more forcibly that the distaste for that country which he shared with the majority of Americans was only too justified. The production of *Figaro* had been merely a further proof. "Believe me, my dear Doctor Franklin," he concluded, "the whole of France, both the Court and the people, is in process of complete dissolution. We have tied ourselves to a corpse. *Iam foetet,* I say. It is already beginning to stink."

"I am an old man," replied Franklin, "and unable altogether to follow your argument. You tell me that the production of a dramatic work, which is remarkable for its progressive ideas, excited the Parisians to an extraordinary pitch, and from this you infer that the whole country is on the verge of downfall. Could you elaborate your views a little?"

"Well then," Adams explained, pleased with the opportunity for delivering a final lecture, "there was the ban on the play; there was the King's famous *never, never* dictum; there were the many other similar events preceding the performance. You are aware of all this, Doctor Franklin. Yet the play was produced. Do you need more than this to convince you of the breakdown of authority in this country? The public's reaction to the performance but reinforces the evidence. We should draw our logical deductions with regard to our policy towards France. On the one hand, we ought to extract whatever profit we can from our association with a State that is about to founder; on the other hand, we must guard against becoming too closely involved with a monarchy whose absolute sovereign has so little to say, whose ruling class is so decadent, and whose common citizens are so eager for revolution."

"You will pardon me," rejoined Franklin, "but I still do not quite understand. If the people here are as great lovers of liberty as we are ourselves, that surely can only be in accordance with our wishes."

"Pray forgive me, Doctor Franklin," said Adams, "but I must protest against your placing the desire of the United States for independence, and the power to determine its own destiny, on a par with the iconoclasm and morbid craving for change which are characteristic of the Paris mob, that seeks to bring about disturbances merely in order that it may fish in troubled waters. What I witnessed at the performance of *Figaro* was not the indignation of a people impelled as we were to rise in wrath against a tyrant who had violated their well-understood interests and repudiated his treaties. The rabble that I saw there will be unbridled in its actions and there is little likelihood that its excesses will be halted at the doors even of liberal-minded men such as we are."

"Well," replied Franklin, "if I am correctly informed, our own countrymen made no bones at times about employing the methods that seemed to them best. We, too, failed sometimes to avoid violence where it could have been avoided, and we sometimes committed injustices where justice could have been done. I fear, Mr. Adams," and here he sat a little more erect and looked like the Duplessis portrait, "that without a modicum of violence and injustice it will never be possible to establish freedom and a better order in the world. You may be right. The French people may one day shake off the reins and, as you predict, the convulsions may be attended with some disagreeable circumstances. But do you not think that the blessings may outweigh the harm that will have been done? I am an old man, and I occasionally permit myself to indulge in dreams. I dream of a time when not only the love of liberty, but a thorough knowledge of the rights of man, may pervade all the nations of the earth, so that men like ourselves may set forth anywhere on its surface and say, 'This is my country.' If such an age could be established only by violence, Mr. Adams, do you think that some shedding of blood would be too high a price?"

Adams listened with respectful attention, but not without uneasiness. He was thinking to himself, "This Franklin is a son of the eighteenth century, incapable of grasping the trend of these, our times. He is dreaming of a world established and governed according to the ideas of the French philosophers. I am already living in the nineteenth century and see an *American* empire expanding until it has conferred liberty and happiness upon the whole world, liberty and happiness as *we* understand them." But he allowed none of these thoughts to escape his lips. It would have been useless, and he wanted to depart in an atmosphere of amity. "That is a problem, Doctor Franklin," he replied courteously, "to which neither of us can provide an answer today."

Drawing forth an album, he continued, "I have promised Mrs. Adams that I would request the distinguished men whom I should meet to record their names and a suitable inscription in the pages of this volume. Would you, too, Doctor Franklin, be so kind?"

"Most willingly," said Franklin, taking the album. He meditated for a moment, and then wrote, *"Dei providentia et hominum confusione Helvetia regitur."*

Adams read the motto and was taken aback. "It is by the providence of God and the confusion among men that Switzerland is enabled to govern itself," he translated incredulously.

"Yes," responded Franklin, "a favourite quotation of our friend Monsieur Necker. It is said to be as familiar in Switzerland as the story of William Tell. Do you not think it is an admirable aphorism?"

Adams found the reference to Monsieur Necker distasteful. "I suppose so," he said vaguely. "The Swiss are a sceptical nation."

"But optimistic," suggested Franklin. "They believe in Providence and have established a republic that has now lasted quite a while."

John Adams had already reached the doorway when Franklin suddenly pointed to the picture of Washington standing beneath a blood-red sun and said, "It is rising."

"What is? How do you mean?" inquired the startled Adams.

"The sun," replied Franklin. "I asked the painter himself, and he ought to know." He smiled. "It is rising," he repeated, "despite the confusion among men."

"Well," said Adams. "My very best wishes." And he hastily closed the door behind him. "The old man is growing senile," he mused. "I must remember all of that drivel word for word, and tell it to Abigail. *The sun is rising.* It's almost idiotic." John Adams resolved that when he reached Philadelphia he would do his utmost to ensure that the

affairs of the United States in France should not continue to be left
in the hands of such an irresponsible and wayward old man.

When his visitor had gone, Franklin ordered Monsieur Prunier's
painting to be removed to the attic. Then he seated himself at his
writing-table and drafted a letter to General Washington, to whom he
felt very close. After referring to the successful conclusion of the
negotiations for a loan and congratulating both the General and himself, he suggested to Washington that upon the cessation of hostilities, which could not now be very far off, he should come to Europe.
"I should be happy," he wrote, "to see Your Excellency in Europe and
to accompany you. You would, on this side of the sea, enjoy the great
reputation you have acquired, pure and free from those little shades
that the jealousy and envy of a man's countrymen and contemporaries are ever endeavouring to cast over living merit. Here you would
know and enjoy what posterity will say of Washington. For a thousand leagues have nearly the same effect as a thousand years. The
feeble voice of those grovelling passions cannot extend so far either
in time or distance. At present I enjoy that pleasure for you; as I
frequently hear the generals of this martial country, who study the
maps of America and mark upon them all your operations, speak with
sincere approbation and great applause of your conduct and join in
giving you the character of one of the greatest captains of the age."

☆   ☆   ☆

Louis was anxious to return to affairs of State, which he had been
compelled to neglect during the celebrations consequent upon Toinette's confinement. He had a partiality for balance-sheets and reports,
and he had requested his Ministers to submit to him a statement on
the condition of France in that month of February, 1779.

He sat in his library, listening to Maurepas and Vergennes presenting their summary of the financial and political situation. France, as
they proved by reference to detailed documents, offered today, at the
end of the fifth year of His Majesty's reign, a picture of a prosperous
and contented nation, the greatest and most powerful in Europe, a
proud fabric indeed. The two Ministers were quoting endless data and
statistics reinforcing this assurance.

Louis allowed his thoughts to wander. He had done his best to
govern his realm to the greater glory of God and the well-being of his
subjects, but Heaven's blessing had not rested upon him. He had involved his country in a fateful alliance with the rebels and permitted
the people of Paris to be carried still further along the path of licence
and upheaval by withdrawing the veto he had placed upon that insolent stage-play. He had been determined to stem the onrush of evil,

but they had all tugged at him until at last he had been forced to yield. He had given way not once, but time after time, and that was why God had punished him and refused to let him have his Dieudonné, the son for whom he had so ardently longed.

He made an effort to disperse his absurd hypochondria. He was only twenty-four and Toinette a year younger. The birth of the princess had proved that they were both capable of bringing healthy offspring into the world, and the hope that by the grace of God they might yet be blessed with a son was more justified than ever.

He forced his attention back to his Ministers. Vergennes was now summarizing the outcome of the war to date. The situation could hardly be more favourable. The formidable English Navy had not a single victory to record. At every encounter with French ships it had been beaten. It could only be a matter of time before Gibraltar was captured. The army destined for America under the command of Rochambeau was ready almost to the last button, and it was a model force unequalled anywhere in the world.

In a low but surly tone Louis interjected, "You defend the alliance, of course, because it was your work. It is all very well for you to talk, Messieurs, but my first intuition was right. This work of ours, this alliance with the rebels, *your* alliance, Messieurs, was and remains a fateful mistake."

He stood up, and with him the Ministers. "Please keep your seats," he demanded testily, but he himself went on pacing heavily up and down. Finally he came to a halt before the large globe which he had set up a few days previously in his crowded library. It had been made by George Adams the elder, cartographer to the King of England, and King George had sent it to him as a present despite the fact that their two countries were at war. It had arrived without any accompanying letter, but it was clearly intended as a friendly gesture on the occasion of the birth of Madame Royale. The gift had been carefully chosen, even with a certain affection, for his cousin in England was aware of his passion for maps.

The great sphere had been executed with admirable forethought. There were many features marked on it which Louis had not been able to discover on any of his charts, such as, for instance, that place of ill-omen, Saratoga. The gift was a silent reminder that it was the duty of Kings to maintain a solid front before God and man, particularly at critical times such as those through which they were now passing. His cousin George could hardly have found a more striking way of impressing upon him the wrong he had committed by entering into the alliance.

Standing in front of the globe he spoke over his shoulder to the silent Ministers. "No, Messieurs, I cannot share your optimism. It does not appear to me that you have been justified by the course of events. I fear that this war is going to last longer than you predict, and that our sacrifices will be greater than you assume. A thousand million livres was the estimate made by Monsieur Necker, if the war should be a short one. And it will not be a short war. The advantages we have derived from our association with the rebels have been meagre, our losses horrifying. France has grown poorer during the five years of my reign. Our indebtedness is continually increasing. In a few months we shall have exceeded the thousand millions, and no country can sustain such a burden."

"Your imagination is carrying you away, Sire," protested Vergennes respectfully, but with determination. "The peace between Austria and Prussia will be signed within the next few days. That signifies a great strengthening of our prestige. The military situation is such that England is ready to lay down her arms at the earliest possible moment. Even now we may claim that the humiliation of 1763 has been wiped out. There is not a single one of your subjects, Sire, there is no one in Europe, who would designate such results as meagre."

Maurepas took up the tale. "The figure which Monsieur Necker flung into our discussions," he said in his dry, cynical voice, "sounds more menacing than it is in reality. A thousand millions." He shrugged his shoulders, and the sum became quite insignificant the way he uttered it. "What we have achieved is worth many times the money." And with animation he spoke of the decline of England and the rise of France, by which the first auspicious lustrum of the young monarch's reign had been characterized. He spoke of the strength of the army, of the increased commercial turn-overs, the swifter circulation of money, the progress of agriculture and industry. Harvests were growing more abundant year by year, the price of corn had been reduced, salaries and wages were continually on the up-grade, the population figures were rising. Again he quoted statistics. "During your reign, Sire," he declared enthusiastically, "no less than 12,387 miles of new roads have been built. The ports of Nantes, Marseilles, Bordeaux, and Rouen have been extended. The city of Lyons has won over three-quarters of the civilized world to French dressmaking and French fashions. Home consumption has improved, the tax on consumers' goods has increased by three millions this year. Your people, Sire, enjoy a better standard of living than they did during the decades before you came to the throne."

These figures lifted Louis's gloom, but only for a moment. "A whited sepulchre!" he brooded. "These gentlemen are praising the proud fabric that France has become under my rule; Monsieur Turgot would doubtless be of a different opinion." He recalled the letter that Turgot had written to him— *People think you are weak, Sire.*

The Ministers had begun to speak of the way in which the arts and sciences were flourishing during the reign of Louis the Sixteenth, citing names, taking the cue from one another: Lavoisier, Monge, Lagrange, Houdon, Clodion, Hubert Robert, Louis David, Marmontel, Sedaine, Beaumarchais.

When the detested name of Beaumarchais sounded in his ears, Louis saw himself once more at the Salon, in the little gallery with the busts of the three heretics who were looked upon as the most illustrious minds of the epoch. There could be no mistake. His trusted advisers, too, had uttered the name of Beaumarchais as one of the great names of the age. And they meant it in earnest; praising the poisonous man, they meant to praise their King.

The arts and sciences were flourishing. Fine fruits they had brought forth, forsooth. He had received a report on what had happened at the *Théâtre français.* The actors who, in the overheated atmosphere of a gala performance, had impudently restored the censored passages had, of course, been sternly reprimanded, and since then the censored passages had no more been spoken. But even so the poison of the comedy was working. Since the times of the late Voltaire the *Théâtre français* had not seen such a success.

He had been glad that Rousseau and Voltaire were dead. But the rebellious heretics in their graves were linking hands with those who were still alive. The chain remained unbroken. The tide of revolution was rising. Once the Americans had won their final victory with the help of his army, his ships and his millions, his soldiers would return as rebels, and then he would be swept away in the flood.

His Ministers were still discoursing upon the glories of the first five years of his reign. Commerce and industry, the arts and sciences, the Army and the Navy, all were in the ascendant. It was blissful to be living in such an age, it was glorious to be a citizen of France under the sixteenth Louis. The young monarch merited his second Christian name of Augustus, for he was truly the augmenter of his realm.

Louis had ceased to listen. He stood in the bay-window abstractedly gazing down into the courtyard.

A sudden bustle on the great outside staircase attracted his attention. He blinked short-sightedly in an attempt to discern what was going on. People were forming up in two rows as was customary when some notable was about to arrive or depart. Louis asked, "Can you tell me, Messieurs, what is happening down there?"

They both stepped to the window. Maurepas, proud that his sight was still so keen, said, "It is Doctor Franklin."

Vergennes added in explanation, "He has probably come from his meeting with Monsieur Necker. If I am not mistaken, it was today that the loan agreements were to be signed."

"I ought to have remembered it," said Louis, annoyed that his bad conscience had caused the unwelcome date to slip his memory.

He wanted to avert his eyes and thoughts from the spectacle on the great staircase, but he could not. On the contrary, his knowledge of what was going on sharpened his sight. He saw Doctor Franklin descending slowly between two rows of respectfully bowing gentlemen and deeply curtsying ladies. Franklin was leaning on someone's shoulder, presumably his grandson's. From the secret police reports Louis knew that a French girl had had a child by young William Franklin. They were scattering their seed all over his realm, the rebels.

The three of them stood at the bay-window and gazed down at the great staircase. It was unseemly to betray such curiosity, childishly undignified both for the youthful King and the elderly Ministers, but they could not turn their eyes from the spectacle.

Louis blinked more rapidly. Tell me, Messieurs," he said. "Can you see whether he has at least taken the trouble to dress himself decently for the ceremony of signing such an important agreement with me?"

"He appears to be wearing his fur coat and cap," replied Vergennes hesitantly.

"He is wearing the costume in which the people like to see him," said Maurepas.

Louis growled. "In return for a present of twenty-five millions," he grumbled, "he might at least have taken the trouble to dress himself decently." He sounded not so much irate as sadly resigned.

He continued to watch as the old man made his way down. His broad back slightly bowed, Franklin slowly descended, step by step, and behind him his vast shadow fell upon the great staircase, carpeted with snow and shining in the sun, of the Palace of Versailles.

☆   ☆   ☆

Here ends the third and last part of the novel *Proud Destiny,* also called *Arms for America.*